BELISARIUS II:
Storm at Noontide

ERIC FLINT
DAVID DRAKE

BAEN

BELISARIUS II:STORM AT NOONTIDE

A Baen Book

Baen Publishing Enterprises
P.O. Box 1403
Riverdale, NY 10471
www.baen.com

ISBN 10:1-4165-9166-4
ISBN 13:978-1-4165-9166-5

Cover art by Kurt Miller

First Baen printing, March 2009

Distributed by Simon & Schuster
1230 Avenue of the Americas
New York, NY 10020

Library of Congress Cataloging-in-Publication Data

Flint, Eric.
  Belisarius II : storm at noontide / Eric Flint, David Drake.
     p. cm.
  ISBN 1-4165-9148-6—ISBN 1-4165-9166-4 (pbk.)
  1. Belisarius, 505 (ca.)-565—Fiction. 2. Malwa (Madhya Pradesh and Rajasthan, India)—History—Fiction. 3. Good and evil—Fiction. 4. Supercomputers—Fiction. I. Drake, David. II. Title. III. Title: Belisarius two.

  PS3556.L548B454 2008
  813'.54—dc22

2008052062

Printed in the United States of America

10 9 8 7 6 5 4 3 2 1

BELISARIUS II:
Storm at Noontide

CONTENTS

Introduction:
THREE OR SIX PASSAGES TO INDIA

When I took up Jim Baen's idea of plotting a series of novels in which the real Byzantine general Belisarius would be aided by a supercomputer, the first thing I needed was a worthy enemy for him (for them) to fight. The obvious choice was the Persian Empire, which by then had for over a thousand years (off and on) been the traditional opponent of whichever power was dominant in the Greco-Roman world.

The Persians were going to be major players in the series, but I decided I didn't want them as the Great Enemy. The major problem was that they were too close. To get the sort of situation I wanted, I had to begin changing recorded history a couple generations before the action of the series began. That would affect the Byzantine Empire immediately if it was going on in an adjacent nation. I wanted instead to start with the major historical players—Belisarius and his wife Antonia, Justinian and his wife Theodora—and the structures of their government pretty much as they were in consensus reality.

That meant I had to look eastward. I've read too much contemporary British/English/Germanic history to believe in any of the western states as a serious threat even if it had a supercomputer of its own. But that wasn't a problem, because I'd had a very good course in Chinese history and I knew that there was lots of information available.

1

Well, that didn't work either: the lifetime of Belisarius corresponded with a long period of extreme fragmentation in China (the Six Dynasties, following the Three Kingdoms). I thought about it for a while—there were ways to make it work—but decided to check India. I didn't know much Indian history.

As it turned out, nobody knows much Indian history. India has unquestionably had a developed culture for a very long time, but unlike many western cultures and particularly unlike the Chinese, the Indians weren't very interested in keeping historical records. You can mine religious texts like the *Rig Veda* and come up with widely varying results, but if you want a connected description of history and institutions you're left with records left by non-Indians. Of these there are two major early examples: a Greek physician in Persian service, and a Chinese monk touring Buddhist kingdoms.

That wasn't all bad, however: if *nobody* knew what had really happened, my imagination had a fair amount of leeway. It isn't the way I like to operate (or Eric likes to operate; we'll get to Eric soon), but you play the hand you're dealt.

I did my research on the assumption that Indian village culture hadn't changed a great deal in the thousand years following the 6th century AD. This is reasonable, because in many ways village culture hasn't changed from then till now. There are quite a number of histories and memoirs written by westerners involved in trade in and with India in the 17th century. I bought a number of such accounts and took copious notes. (Peter Mundy's journals were particularly valuable, in part because he made drawings of things that were hard to describe with words alone.)

I then wrote the three plots. In the General series I had simply adapted real events to a future milieu. I departed from consensus reality very quickly in the Belisarius series, but I had a good deal of plotting experience even in 1996. I was pleased with the result.

That left the question of who was going to turn my plots into novels. I gave Jim Baen *carte blanche* to choose the author, but I explicitly retained the right to take my name off the finished product. Jim and I had gotten into difficulties in the recent past when we'd differed on the capacity of the person he was pushing to write a couple novels from my plots. He won, but I'd been right as he freely admitted when he saw the result. Neither of us wanted that to happen again.

Jim called in delight: he'd found the perfect author, a fellow named Eric Flint with an MA in history from UCLA, whose first novel Jim had just bought. Even better, Flint was a Commie who'd spent the past twenty years as an organizer for a Trotskyite (that should've been "Trotskyist") labor union. (Jim was a libertarian and this appealed to his sense of humor.)

I was . . . cautious. I'd get more money if I allowed David Drake to appear on the cover, but it wasn't enough money to make me put my name on a bad book. (Come to think, there isn't enough money to make me do that. When it's happened, it's happened for reasons that had nothing to do with money.)

Mr. Flint (as he then was in my mind) called me after he read my outlines. He was going to make a number of changes, among them adding at least one novel set in the Balkans. I said he'd have to clear additional novels with Jim; as for changes to my outlines . . . that was fine if they worked.

I didn't say so, but I remained cautious. I didn't think Mr. Flint had any idea of the difficulty of what he proposed to do, but if he could pull it off, more power to him.

I was right that Eric (we quickly became friends) had misjudged the complexity of my plots. What surprised and delighted me was that each time he began cutting and moving things, *he* realized that it wouldn't work before I had to tell him. Pretty soon he stopped and concentrated on writing the books as I'd intended them.

And boy! could he do research. My bad experience with that earlier book had convinced me that I couldn't trust the author developing my outline to do even the most basic research on his own. Therefore I'd created a religion for Great Enemy (the Malwa, Eric's change, because he liked the Gupta dynasty which I'd made the bad guys): a cult based on Mangala, the demigod of the planet Mars. That way I wouldn't offend a billion or so Hindus if the book made a ludicrous botch of their religion.

Eric called. He'd tried desperately to learn the rituals of Mangala worship, but he just couldn't find anything beyond the bare name of the deity. He was embarrassed to ask, but could I direct him to my sources?

After I stopped laughing, I explained what had happened—and why. That cemented our friendship.

Eric did indeed follow my plots, but he made them his own with an enormous amount of richness that wasn't in what I'd sent him. Most of the subordinate characters are his, as are most of the subordinate cultures. For example (one of very many), his Kushans fill the slot I created for the White Huns, also known as the Yellow Huns, Ye-tai, or Epthalites. The Ye-tai were the tribe which brought down the Guptas, and Eric didn't want to show them in a positive light.

A side-effect of Eric's embellishment is that there was a lot more material than could easily fit in three novels. We therefore broke each plot in two.

That worked—but the story works better in three self-standing volumes, as Baen Books is now republishing them. The titles of the combined volumes are those I gave to the plots, so you're reading my original conception for the first time.

But because of Eric, you're reading much, much more than what I imagined. Enjoy!

Dave Drake
david-drake.com

Destiny's Shield

To Donald

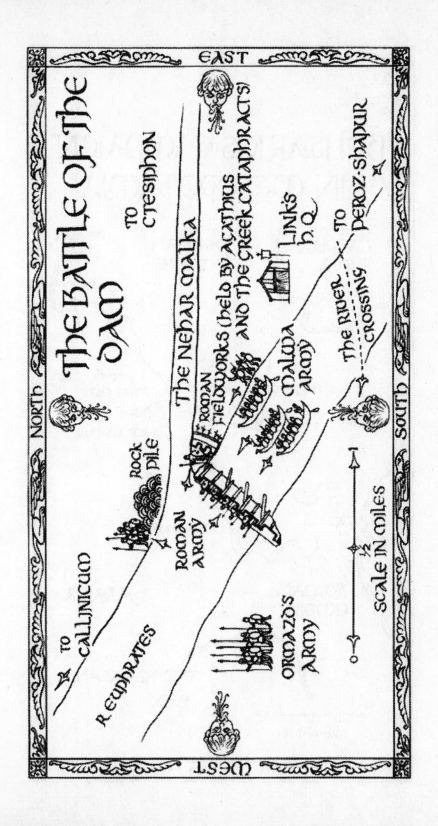

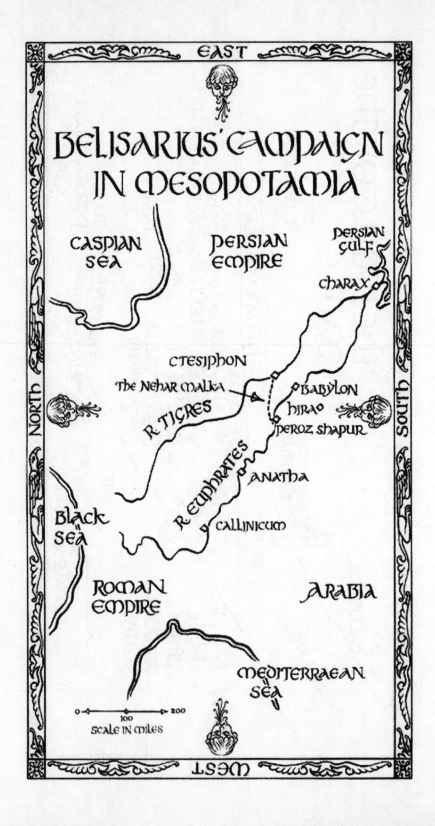

Prologue

It was the Emperor's first public appearance since he had been acclaimed the new sovereign of Rome, and he was nervous. The ambassador from Persia was about to be presented to his court.

"He's going to be mean to me, Mommy," predicted the Emperor.

"Hush," whispered the Empress Regent. "And *don't* call me 'Mommy.' It's undignified."

The Emperor stared up at the tall imposing figure of his new mother, seated on her own throne next to him. Meeting her cold black eyes, he hastily looked away.

His new mother made him nervous, too. Even though his old mother said his new mother was a good friend, the Emperor wasn't fooled. The Empress Regent Theodora was *not* a nice lady.

The Empress Regent leaned over and whispered into his ear:

"Why do you think he'll be mean to you?"

The Emperor frowned.

"Well—because Daddy gave the Persians such a fierce whipping." Then, remembering: "My old daddy, I mean."

The Emperor glanced guiltily at the figure of his new father, standing not far away to his right. Then, meeting the sightless gaze of those empty sockets, he looked away. Very hastily. Not even his real mother tried to claim that *Justinian* was a "nice man."

Theodora, again, hissing:

"And don't call the Empire's *strategos* 'daddy.' It's not dignified, even if he is your stepfather."

The Emperor hunched down on his throne, thoroughly miserable.

It's too confusing. Nobody should have this many mommies and daddies.

He began to turn his head, hoping to catch a reassuring glimpse of his real parents. He knew they would be standing nearby, among the other high notables of the Roman court. But the Empress Regent hissed him still.

"Stop fidgeting! It's not regal."

The Emperor made himself sit motionless. He grew more and more nervous, watching the stately advance of the Persian ambassador down the long aisle leading to the throne.

The Persian ambassador, he saw, was staring at him. Everybody was staring at him. The throne room was packed with Roman officials, every one of whom had their eyes fixed on the Emperor. Most of them, he thought, were not very nice—judging, at least, from sarcastic remarks he had heard his parents make. *All four* of his parents. The scurrilous nature of officialdom was one of the few subjects they did not quarrel about.

The ambassador was now much closer. He was rather tall, and slender of build. His complexion was perhaps a bit darker than that of most Greeks. His face was lean-jawed and aquiline, dominated by a large nose. His beard was cut in the short square style favored by Persians.

The ambassador was wearing the costume of a Persian nobleman. His gray hair was capped by the traditional gold-embroidered headdress, which Persians called a *citaris*. His tunic, though much like a Roman one, had sleeves which reached all the way down to the wrists. His trousers also reached far down, almost covering the red leather of his boots.

Seeing the bright color of the ambassador's boot-tips, the Emperor felt a momentary pang. His old father—his *real* father—had a pair of boots just like those. "Parthian boots," they were called. His father favored them, as did many of his Thracian cataphracts.

The ambassador was now close enough that the Emperor could make out his eyes. Brown eyes, just like his father's. (His old father; his new father had no eyes.)

But the Emperor could detect none of the warmth which was always in his old father's eyes. The Persian's eyes seemed cold to him. The Emperor lifted his gaze. High above, the huge mosaic figures on the walls of the throne room stared down upon him. They were saints, he knew. Very holy folk. But their eyes, too, seemed cold. Darkly, the Emperor suspected they probably hadn't been very nice either. The severe expressions on their faces reminded him of his tutors. Sour old men, whose only pleasure in life was finding fault with their charge.

He felt as if he were being buried alive.

"I'm hot," he complained.

"Of course you're hot," whispered Theodora. "You're wearing imperial robes on a warm day in April. What do you expect?"

Unkindly:

"Get used to it." Then:

"Now, *act properly*. The ambassador is here."

Twenty feet away, the Persian ambassador's retinue came to a halt. The ambassador stepped forward two paces and prostrated himself on the thick, luxurious rug which had been placed for that purpose on the tiled floor of the throne room.

That rug, the Emperor knew, was only brought out from its special storage place for the use of envoys representing the Persian King of Kings, the *Shahanshah*. It was the best rug the Roman Empire owned, he had heard.

Persia was the traditional great rival of the Roman Empire. It wouldn't do to offend its representatives. No, it wouldn't do at all.

The Persian ambassador was rising. Now, he was stepping forward. The ambassador extended his hand, holding the scroll which proclaimed his status to the Roman court. The motion brought a slight wince to the face of the ambassador, and the Roman Emperor's fear multiplied. The wince, he knew, was caused by the great wound which the ambassador had received to his shoulder three years before.

The Emperor's real father had given him that wound, at a famous place called Mindouos.

He's going to be mean to me.

"I bring greetings to the *Basileus* of Rome from my master Khusrau Anushirvan, King of Kings of Iran and non-Iran."

The ambassador spoke loudly, so everyone in the huge throne room could hear. His voice was very deep, as deep as anyone's the Emperor had ever heard except church singers'.

"My name is Baresmanas," continued the ambassador. "Baresmanas, of the Suren."

The Emperor heard a whispering rustle sweep the throne room. He understood the meaning of that rustle, and felt a moment's pride in his understanding. For weeks, now, his tutors had drilled him mercilessly in the history and traditions of Persia. The Emperor had not forgotten his lessons.

Officially, the Suren were one of the *sahrdaran*, the seven greatest noble families of Persia. Unofficially, they were the greatest. Rustam, the legendary hero of the Aryans—their equivalent of Hercules—was purported to have been of that family. And the Persian general who shattered Crassus' Roman army at Carrhae had been a Suren.

Sending a Suren ambassador, the Emperor knew, was the Shahanshah's way of indicating his respect for Rome. But the knowledge did not allay his fear.

He's going to be mean to me.

The stern, haughty, aristocratic face of the Persian ambassador broke into a sudden smile. White teeth flashed in a rich, well-groomed beard.

"It is a great pleasure to meet you, Your Majesty," said the ambassador. Baresmanas bowed toward Theodora. "And your mother, the Regent Theodora."

The Emperor reached out his hand to take the scroll. After unrolling the parchment, he saw with relief that the document was written in Greek. The Emperor could read, now, though still with no great facility. And this document was full of long-winded words that he didn't recognize at all. He began studying it intently until he heard a slight cough.

Out of the corner of his eye, the Emperor saw the Empress Regent nodding graciously. Remembering his instructions, the Emperor hastily rolled up the parchment and followed her example. Then, seeing the hint of a frown on Theodora's brow, he belatedly remembered the rest of her coaching.

"We welcome the representative of our brother," he piped, "the Basileus of Pers—"

The Emperor froze with fear at his blunder.

By long-standing protocol, the Emperor of Rome always called the Emperor of Persia the "Basileus" rather than the "King of Kings." By using the same title as his own, the Roman Emperor thereby indicated the special status of the Persian monarch. No other ruler was ever granted that title by Romans, except, on occasion, the negusa nagast of Ethiopia.

But Persians *never* called themselves Persians. That term was a Greek bastardization of the Persian province of Fars, the homeland of the old Achaemenid dynasty. Persians called their land Iran—land of the Aryans. They were immensely snooty on the matter, too, especially the distinction between Aryans and all lesser breeds. Many non-Aryan nations were ruled by the Shahanshah, but they were not considered part of the land of the Aryans itself. *Those* were simply "non-Iran."

The Emperor's paralysis was broken by the slight, encouraging smile on the ambassador's face.

"—the Basileus *of Iran and non-Iran*," he quickly corrected himself.

The ambassador's smile widened. A very friendly gleam came into his brown eyes. For a moment—a blessed moment—the Roman Emperor was reminded of his father. His old father.

He glanced at the mutilated face of his new father, the former Emperor Justinian. That sightless face was fixed upon him, as if Justinian still had eyes to see. That sightless, harsh, bitter face.

It's not fair, whimpered the Emperor in his mind. *I want my old father back. My real father.*

The ambassador was backing away. The Emperor of Rome began to sigh with relief, until, catching a hint of Theodora's disapproval, he stiffened with imperial dignity.

Maybe he won't be mean to me, after all.

The ambassador was fifteen feet off, now. He still seemed to be smiling.

It's not fair. The Sassanids are from Fars, too, so why can't we call them Persians?

Now, he did sigh, slightly. He felt the Empress Regent's disapproval, but ignored it.

It's too much to remember all at once.

Another sigh. The Empress Consort hissed. Again, he ignored her reproof.

I'm the Emperor. I can do what I want.

That was patently false, and he knew it.

It's not fair.

I'm only eight years old.

The ambassador was thirty feet away, now. Out of hearing range. Theodora leaned over.

The Emperor braced himself for her reproach.

Nasty lady. I want my old mother back.

But all she said was:

"That was very well done, Photius. Your mother will be proud of you." Then, with a slight smile: "Your *real* mother."

"I'm proud of you, Photius," said Antonina. "You did very well." She leaned over the throne's armrest and kissed him on the cheek.

Her son flushed, partly from pleasure and partly from guilt. He didn't think being kissed in public by his mother fit the imperial image he was supposed to project. But, when his eyes quickly scanned the throne room, he saw that few people were watching. After the Empress Regent had left, to hold a private meeting with the Persian ambassador and his father (*both* of his fathers), the reception had dissolved into a far more relaxed affair. Most of the crowd were busy eating, drinking and chattering. They were ignoring, for all practical purposes, the august personage of the Emperor. No-one standing anywhere near to him, of course, committed the gross indiscretion of actually turning their back on the throne's small occupant. But neither was anyone anxious to ingratiate themselves to the new Emperor. Everyone knew that the real power was in the hands of Theodora.

Photius was not disgruntled by the crowd's indifference to him. To the contrary, he was immensely relieved. For the first time since the reception began, he felt he could relax. He even pondered, tentatively, the thought of reaching up and scratching behind his ear.

Then, squaring his shoulders, he did so. Scratched furiously, in fact.

I'm the Emperor of Rome. I can do what I want.

"Stop scratching behind your ear!" hissed his mother. "You're the Emperor of Rome! It's undignified."

The Emperor sighed, but obeyed.

It's not fair. I never asked them to make me Emperor.

Chapter 1
CONSTANTINOPLE
Spring, 531 A.D.

As soon as Antonina put Photius to bed, she hastened to the imperial audience chamber. By the time she arrived, the Persian ambassador was reaching the conclusion of what had apparently been a lengthy speech.

Taking her seat next to Belisarius, Antonina scanned the room quickly. Except for the guards standing against the walls, the huge chamber was almost empty. The usual mob of advisers who sat in on Theodora's audiences was absent. The only Romans present to hear the Persian ambassador were Theodora, Justinian, and Belisarius.

Baresmanas himself was the only Persian present. Antonina knew that the extremely limited participation had been at the request of the Persians. That fact alone made clear the seriousness with which they took this meeting. She focussed her attention on the ambassador's final remarks.

"And so," said Baresmanas sternly, "I must caution you once again. Do not think that Roman meddling in the current internal situation in Persia will go unchallenged. Your spies may have told you that our realm verges on civil war. I, for one, do not believe that is true. But even if it is—all Aryans will unite against Roman intrusion. Do not doubt that for a moment."

15

The ambassador's stern expression relaxed, replaced by a semi-apologetic smile which was, under the circumstances, quite warm. Antonina was struck by Baresmanas' change in demeanor. She suspected that the friendly face which now confronted the Roman Empress and her top advisers was much closer to the man himself than the stiff mask which had delivered the previous words.

"Of course, it is quite possible that all of my teeth-baring is unnecessary. I do not mean to be rude. Rome is known for its wisdom as well as its martial prowess, after all. It is quite possible—likely, I should say—that the thought of intervening in Persia has never once crossed your mind."

Antonina was impressed. Baresmanas had managed to deliver the last sentence with a straight face. The statement, of course, was preposterous. For the last five hundred years, no Roman emperor had spent more than three consecutive days without at least *thinking* about attacking Persia. The reverse, needless to say, was equally true.

She leaned over and whispered into Belisarius' ear:

"What's this about?"

His reply also came in a whisper:

"The usual, whenever the Persians have to find a new emperor. Khusrau's been the leading candidate ever since Kavad died—he's been officially proclaimed, actually—but his half-brother Ormazd is apparently not reconciled to the situation. Baresmanas was sent here by Khusrau to warn us not to muck around in the mess."

Antonina made a little grimace.

"As if we would," she muttered.

Belisarius smiled crookedly. "Now, love, let's not be quite so self-righteous. It *has* happened, you know. Emperor Carus took advantage of the civil war between Bahram II and Hormizd to invade Persia. Even captured their capital of Ctesiphon."

"That was over two hundred years ago," she protested softly.

"So? Persians have long memories. So do we, for that matter. Carus' invasion was retribution for Ardashir's attack on us during our civil war after Alexander Severus was murdered."

Antonina shrugged. "The situation's different. We've got the Malwa to worry about, now."

Belisarius started to make some response, but fell silent. The great double doors to the audience chamber were opening. A moment later, a worn-looking Persian officer was being ushered in by Irene Macrembolitissa, the chief of the Roman Empire's spy network.

"Speaking of which—" he muttered.

Antonina started. "You think—?"

He shrugged. "We'll know soon enough. But we've been expecting the Malwa to invade Mesopotamia, sooner or later. From the look of that Persian officer, I suspect 'sooner' has arrived."

The Persian officer had reached Baresmanas. The ambassador was standing some fifteen feet away from Theodora. Although a chair had been provided for him, Baresmanas apparently felt that his stern message would carry more weight if delivered standing.

The ambassador stooped slightly to hear what the officer had to say. The newly arrived Persian whispered urgently into his ear.

Antonina could see an unmistakable look of surprise and apprehension come to the ambassador's face. But Baresmanas was an experienced diplomat. Within seconds, the ambassador had regained his composure. By the time the Persian officer finished imparting whatever report he had brought with him, Baresmanas' expression was impassive and opaque.

When the officer finished, Baresmanas nodded and whispered a few words of his own. Immediately, the man bowed to the Roman Empress and hastily backed out of the room.

Antonina glanced over at Irene. The spymaster, after ushering the officer into the audience chamber, had discreetly taken position against the wall next to the door.

Antonina's gaze met Irene's. To all outward appearance, the spymaster's own face seemed void of expression. But Antonina knew Irene very well, and could not miss her friend's suppressed excitement.

Behind Baresmanas' back, Irene gave Antonina a quick little gesture. Thumbs up.

Antonina sighed. "You're right," she whispered to her husband. "Irene's like a shark smelling blood."

"The woman does love a challenge," murmured Belisarius. "I think she'd rather be tortured in the Pit for eternity than go for a week without excitement." A chuckle. "Provided, of course, that Satan let her keep her books."

Baresmanas cleared his throat, and addressed Theodora once again.

"Your Majesty, I have just received some important news. With your permission, I would like to leave now. I must discuss these matters with my own entourage."

Theodora nodded graciously. Then:

"Would you like to schedule another meeting?"

Baresmanas' nod was abrupt, almost curt.

"Yes. Tomorrow, if possible."

"Certainly," replied Theodora.

Antonina ignored the rest of the interchange between the Empress and Baresmanas. Diplomatic formalities did not interest her.

What *did* interest her was Irene.

"What do you think?" she whispered to Belisarius. "Is she going to be the first person in history to actually explode?"

Belisarius shook his head. He whispered in return:

"Nonsense. Spontaneous human eruption's impossible. Says so in the most scholarly volumes. Irene knows that perfectly well. She owns every one of those tomes, after all."

"I don't know," mused Antonina, keeping a covert eye on her friend against the wall. "She's starting to tremble, now. Shiver, quiver and quake. Vibrating like a harp string."

"Not possible," repeated Belisarius. "Precluded by all the best philosophers."

Baresmanas was finally ushered out of the room.

Irene exploded.

"It's on! It's on! It's on! It's on! It's on!"

Bouncing like a ball. Spinning like a top.

"The Malwa invaded Mesopotamia! Attacked Persia!"

Quiver, shiver; quake and shake.

"My spies got their hands on the message! Khusrau's instructed Baresmanas to seek Roman help!"

Vibrating like a harp string; beating like a drum.

"See?" demanded Antonina.

Chapter 2

Three nights later, the imperial audience chamber was again the scene of a meeting. After concluding an initial round of discussions with Baresmanas, Theodora had summoned her top advisers and officials.

Theodora had a multitude of advisers, but the ten people in that room constituted the majority of what both she and Belisarius thought of as the "inner circle." Membership in that circle depended not on formal post or official position—although post and position generally accompanied them. Membership in the inner circle depended on two far more important things:

First, the personal trust of Belisarius and what passed for "personal trust" from the perennially suspicious Theodora.

Second, knowledge of the great secret. Knowledge of the messenger from the future, the crystalline quasi-jewel which called itself Aide, who had attached itself to Belisarius and warned the Roman Empire's greatest general that his world had become the battleground for powerful and mysterious forces of the far distant future.

Theodora herself occupied a place in her circle of advisers, sitting below a great mosaic depicting Saint Peter. The seating arrangement was odd, for an imperial conference—the more so in that Theodora was not sitting on a throne, but a simple chair. ("Simple," at least, by imperial standards.) Traditionally, when Roman sovereigns discussed affairs of state with their advisers, the advisers stood on their feet while the monarchs lounged in massive thrones.

But—

"*Of course* we should accept the Persian proposal," came a harsh voice.

The Empress cocked her head and examined the speaker. He returned her gaze, with his scarred and empty eye-sockets.

Justinian was the cause of that peculiar seating arrangement. By custom, the former Emperor could no longer sit by her side. Officially, he was nothing now but one of her advisers. But Theodora had not been able to bear the thought of humiliating her husband further, and so she had gladly accepted Belisarius' suggestion that she solve the problem in the simplest way possible. Henceforth, when she met with her advisers, Theodora would sit with them in a circle.

"Explain, Justinian," said Anthony Cassian. The newly-elevated Patriarch of Constantinople leaned forward in his chair, clasping his pudgy hands.

"Yes, do," added Germanicus forcefully. The commander of the Army of Illyria was scowling.

Germanicus nodded to Theodora. "With all due respect, Your Majesty, I do not view *any* alliance with Persia favorably. Damn the Medes, anyway! They've always been our enemy. Persia and the Malwa Empire can claw each other to pieces, as far as I'm concerned."

A murmur of protest began to rise from several of the people sitting in the room.

"Yes, yes," snapped Germanicus, "I know that Malwa is our ultimate enemy." He glanced at Belisarius' chest, where the "jewel" from the future lay nestled in a pouch under the general's tunic. "But I don't see why—"

Justinian's harsh voice interrupted. "*Damn the Persians.* And the Malwa! It's the dynasty I'm thinking about." Justinian's bony hands clenched the arms of his chair. "Don't fool yourselves," he snarled. "Do you really think the aristocracy is happy with the situation? Do you really?" He cawed a harsh, humorless laugh. "This very night—I guarantee it—half the Greek nobility is plotting our overthrow."

"Let them plot all they want," said Sittas, shrugging. The heavy-set general smiled cheerfully.

"I'm a Greek nobleman, myself, mind you. So I'm not about to dispute Justinian's words. If anything, he's being charitable. By my own estimate, *two-thirds* of the Greek aristocracy is plotting our overthrow. This very night, just as he says."

Sittas yawned. "So are the rats in my cellar, I imagine. I'm more concerned about the rats."

Chrysopolis shook his head vigorously. "You are much too complacent, Sittas," he argued. "I myself share Justinian's concerns."

Chrysopolis had replaced the executed traitor John of Cappadocia as the empire's praetorian prefect. He was the one other member of the inner circle, who, like Germanicus, was not personally well-known to Belisarius. But the general himself had proposed his inclusion. Among the highest Roman officials who survived the purge after the failed coup d'etat which had been suppressed by Belisarius and Antonina a few months before, Chrysopolis had a reputation for ability and—a far rarer characteristic among those circles—scrupulous honesty.

"Do you really think this alliance would have that good an effect?" he asked.

"Of course," stated Justinian. He held up a thumb. "First. The Army will be ecstatic. Persia's the enemy they fear, not Malwa. Anything that prevents another war with Persia will meet their approval. Even after Belisarius' great victory at Mindouos, the Army still has no desire to match Persian lancers on the field of battle."

"The Malwa will be worse," pointed out Antonina. "Their numbers are much larger, and they have the new gunpowder weapons."

Justinian shrugged. "So? Roman soldiers have no experience with the Malwa, so they're not worried about them. Over time, that will probably change. But it's the present I'm concerned with. And, right now, I can think of no better way to cement the Army's allegiance to the dynasty than for Photius to forge a Hundred Years' Peace with Persia."

Justinian held up his forefinger alongside his thumb. "Two. It'll please the populace at large, especially in the borderlands." His head turned, the sightless sockets fixing on Anthony Cassian. "The peasants of the region are already delighted with Cassian's succession to the Patriarchate. They're Monophysite heretics, the lot of them, and they know Cassian will rein in the persecution."

"I have no formal authority over Patriarch Ephraim of Antioch," demurred Anthony. "The border regions fall under his jurisdiction."

"The hell with Ephraim," hissed Justinian. "If the dynasty's hold on the throne stabilizes, we'll crush that bastard soon enough. I know it, you know it, Ephraim knows it—*and so do the peasants of the borderlands.*"

Belisarius saw that Germanicus was still scowling. The Illyrian general, quite obviously, was unmoved by Justinian and Chrysopolis' concerns. Belisarius decided it was time to intervene.

"We can live with Persia, Germanicus," he stated. "We have, after all, for a millennium. *We cannot live with Malwa.* The Malwa seek to rule the world. Their invasion of Persia is simply the first step toward their intended conquest of Rome. I say we fight them now, on Persian soil, with Persia's lancers as our allies. Or else we will fight them later, on Roman soil, with the Persian lancers shackled into the ranks of Malwa's gigantic army alongside their Rajput and Kushan vassals."

Germanicus eyed him skeptically. Belisarius repressed a sigh. He was aggravated by the man's stubbornness, but he could not in good conscience condemn him for it. The commander of the Army of Illyria had only been made privy to the great secret a month before. Germanicus, like Chrysopolis, had no longstanding personal relationship with Belisarius. But he was a close kinsman of Justinian and an excellent general in his own right. Theodora had urged his inclusion in the inner circle—this was the one subject where she never issued commands to Belisarius—and Belisarius had agreed.

Abstractly, he knew, the Illyrian general accepted the truth of Aide's nature, and the crystal's warning of the future. But, like most generals, Germanicus was conservative by temperament. Persia, not India, was the traditional rival of the Roman Empire.

No, he could not condemn Germanicus for his prejudiced blindness. He simply returned the man's glare with a serene, confident gaze.

After a moment, Germanicus stopped glaring.

"Are you so certain, Belisarius?" he asked. The Illyrian general's tone was not hostile, simply—*serious*. Like most Roman soldiers he had the deepest respect for Belisarius.

Belisarius nodded his head firmly. "Trust me in this, Germanicus. If Malwa is not checked, the day will come when the Roman Empire will vanish as if it had never existed."

After a moment, Germanicus sighed. "Very well, then. I will defer to your judgement. I'm not happy about it, but—" He sat up, squaring his shoulders. "Enough. I withdraw my objections."

Theodora saw that all of her advisers had reached the same conclusion.

"So be it," she announced. "We'll tell the Persian ambassador that we accept the offer of alliance. In principle, at least. Let's move on to the specifics of their proposal."

She turned to Irene Macrembolitissa. Officially, Irene was the most junior member of the high bureaucracy, having been elevated only recently to the post of *sacellarius*, the "keeper of the privy purse." Her actual power was immense. She was Theodora's spymaster and the chief of the Empire's unofficial secret police, the *agentes in rebus*. She had also become one of Theodora's few—very, very few—genuine friends.

"Begin by summarizing the situation with the invasion, if you would."

Irene leaned forward, brushing back her thick brown hair. "The Malwa attack on Persia began two months ago," she said. "As Belisarius had predicted, they began with a massive sea-borne invasion of the Tigris-Euphrates delta. Within two days, they captured the great port at Charax and have been turning it into the entrepot for their invasion of Mesopotamia."

"Aren't they attacking in the north as well?" asked Hermogenes.

Irene nodded. "Yes. They have a large army pressing into Persia's eastern provinces. That army, however, seems to be only lightly equipped with gunpowder weapons. For the most part, they're made up of traditional forces—Malwa infantry backed by Ye-tai security battalions, with a very large force of Rajput cavalrymen."

"Second-raters, then," stated Germanicus.

Belisarius shook his head.

"Not at all. The Rajput cavalry are excellent, and they're under the command of Rana Sanga. I know him from my trip to India. Know him rather well, in fact. He's as good a general as you'll find anywhere. And while I don't personally know the top Malwa commander of the northern expedition, Lord Damodara, I do know that Rana Sanga respected him deeply."

Germanicus frowned. "Why—?"

Belisarius chuckled. "There's a method to the Malwa madness. The Rajputs are the heart of Damodara's army, and the Malwa don't trust their Rajput vassals. So they put their best general in charge of the toughest campaign, gave him little in the way of gunpowder weapons, and placed almost all the Rajput cavalry at his disposal. Damodara will have no choice. He'll have to rely on Rana Sanga and the Rajputs for his shock troops, slugging it out for months against Persian cavalry in some of the worst terrain you can imagine. The Malwa are killing two birds with one stone. The Persians can't ignore the threat, so they have to divert much of their army from the main campaign in Mesopotamia. And, at the same time, the Malwa will be—"

Germanicus nodded. "Bleeding the Rajputs white."

"Exactly."

Sittas grunted. "That means the northern expedition isn't something we need to worry about. Not for some time, at least. That'll be up to the Persians to deal with."

He eyed Irene. "How big is the Malwa army in Mesopotamia?"

She hesitated, knowing that her next words would be met with disbelief. "At least two hundred thousand men. Probably more."

"That's nonsense!" exclaimed Germanicus.

Belisarius overrode him. "It is *not* nonsense. Believe it, Germanicus. The Malwa Empire is the one power in the world which can field that big an army. *And keep it supplied*, so long as they hold Charax. When I was in Bharakuccha, India's great western seaport, I saw with my own eyes the huge fleet of supply ships they were constructing."

Germanicus' face was pale. "Two hundred thousand," he whispered.

"*At least*," emphasized Belisarius. "And they'll have the bulk of their gunpowder units, too. About their only weakness will be in cavalry."

Irene shook her head. "Not even that, Belisarius. Not light cavalry, at least. I just got word yesterday that the Lakhmite dynasty has transferred its allegiance from Persia to the Malwa. That gives the Malwa a large force of Arab cavalry—*and* a camel force that can operate in the desert regions on the right bank of the Euphrates. Which, by the way, seems to be the river which the Malwa are using as their invasion route."

"Slow going," commented Hermogenes. "The Euphrates meanders all over the flood plain. The Tigris would be quicker."

Belisarius shrugged. "The Malwa aren't relying on speed and maneuver. They've got a sledgehammer moving up the Euphrates. Once they reach Peroz-Shapur, they can cross over to the Tigris. They'll have the Persian capital at Ctesiphon surrounded."

"What's the Persian response?" asked Germanicus.

"From what Baresmanas told me," responded Irene, "it seems that Emperor Khusrau intends to make a stand at Babylon."

"*Babylon?*" exclaimed Cassian. "There *is* no Babylon! That city's been deserted for centuries!" He shook his head. "It's in ruins."

Irene smiled. "The city, yes. But the *walls* of Babylon are still standing. And, by all accounts, those walls are almost as mighty as they were in the days of Hammurabi and Assurbanipal."

"What are the Persians asking of us?" queried Antonina.

Irene glanced at Chrysopolis. The praetorian prefect had handled that part of the initial discussions with Baresmanas.

"They want an alliance with Rome, and as many troops as we can send to help Khusrau at Babylon." He nodded to Sittas. "The Persians do not expect us to help them against the Malwa thrust into their eastern provinces. But they are—well, *desperate*—to get our help in Mesopotamia."

"How many troops do they want us to send?" asked Justinian.

Chrysopolis took a deep breath. "They're asking for forty thousand. The entire Army of Syria, and the remaining twenty thousand from Anatolia and our European units."

The room exploded.

"That's insane!" cried Sittas. "That's half the Roman army!"

"It'd strip the Danube naked," snarled Germanicus. "Every barbarian tribe in the Balkans would be pouring across within a month!" He turned to Belisarius. "You can't be seriously considering this proposal!"

Belisarius shook his head. "No, I'm not, Germanicus. *Although I would if I thought we could do it.*" Again, Belisarius shrugged. "But, the simple fact is that we can't. We have to maintain a strong force on the Danube, as you said. And, unfortunately, we have to keep Sittas' army in and around Constantinople. As we all know, the dynasty's hold is still shaky. Most of the nobility would back another coup, if they thought it would succeed."

Germanicus tugged on his beard. "At the moment, in other words, we have nothing to send Persia except the existing armies in Syria and Egypt."

"Not even that," said Theodora. "We've got a crisis in Egypt, too."

She looked to her spymaster. "Tell them."

"As you all know," said Irene, "the former Patriarch of Alexandria, Timothy IV, was murdered during the Nika insurrection—at the same time as Anthony's predecessor Epiphanios. The culprits were never found, but I'm quite sure it was the work of Malwa assassins."

"Aided and abetted by ultra-orthodox forces in the Church," said Justinian forcefully.

Irene nodded. "After three months of wrangling, the Greek nobility in Alexandria imposed a new Patriarch. An ultra-orthodox monk by the name of Paul. The very next day he reinstated the persecution. Alexandria's been in turmoil ever since. Riots and street fights almost daily, mostly between ultra-orthodox and ultra-Monophysite monks. We just got the news yesterday."

"What the hell is the Army of Egypt doing?" demanded Germanicus.

"They've sided with the new Patriarch," replied Irene. "According to my reports, in fact, the army's commander was Paul's chief advocate."

"That's General Ambrose, isn't it?" asked Hermogenes.

Irene nodded. Sittas growled:

"I know that bastard. He's not worth a damn on the battlefield. A politician down to his toenails. Ambitious as Satan."

The praetorian prefect sighed. "So much for the Army of Egypt. We won't be able to send them to Persia."

"It's worse than that, Chrysopolis," stated Belisarius. "We're going to have to send a military force to Egypt to set the situation straight."

"You think we should intervene?"

"I most certainly do. Egypt is the largest and richest province of the Empire. In the long run, we're relying on Egypt to be the bastion for our naval campaign in the Erythrean Sea. The last thing we can afford is to have its population riddled with disaffection and rebellion."

Theodora added her voice. "I am in complete agreement with Belisarius on this matter." She nodded toward Cassian. "At Anthony's recommendation, I'm sending a deacon named Theodosius to replace Paul as Alexandria's Patriarch. He's a moderate Monophysite. A member of the Severan school like Timothy."

Chrysopolis frowned. "How are you going to enforce the appointment?"

For the first time since the meeting started, Theodora grinned. But there was not a trace of humor in the expression. "With a combination of the old and the new. You know of the religious order which Michael of Macedonia has founded? He's offered to send several thousand of them to Egypt, to counter the existing monastic orders."

"That's fine against other monks in the streets, armed with cudgels," grunted Hermogenes. "But the Army of Egypt—"

"Will be dealt with by the Theodoran Cohort," stated Belisarius.

The announcement brought dead silence to the room. All eyes turned to Antonina.

The little Egyptian woman shrugged. "I'm all we've got, I'm afraid."

"Not quite," said Belisarius. He looked at Hermogenes. "I think we can spare one of your legions, to give Antonina's grenadiers an infantry bulwark. And I'm going to give her five hundred of my cataphracts for a cavalry force."

Hermogenes nodded. Frowning, Germanicus looked back and forth between Belisarius and Antonina.

"I would have thought you'd want to use the grenadiers in Persia," he commented.

Before Belisarius could reply, Theodora spoke up. "*Absolutely not*. Other than Belisarius' small unit of rocketeers, Antonina's cohort is our only military force equipped with gunpowder weapons. They've never been in a real battle. I'm not going to risk them in Persia. Not this early in the war."

Germanicus' frown deepened. "Then who—?"

"Me," said Belisarius. "Me, and whatever troops we can scrape up." He scratched his chin. "I think we can spare five or six thousand men from the Army of Syria, along with my own bucellarii."

"I can give you two thousand cataphracts," interjected Sittas. He glanced at Germanicus.

The Illyrian army commander winced. "I can probably spare five hundred. No more than that, I'm afraid. There's bound to be trouble with the northern barbarians within the next year. The Malwa will be spreading their gold with a lavish hand."

Hermogenes finished counting on his fingers and looked up.

"That doesn't give you much of an army, Belisarius. You've got, what—a thousand cataphracts, after you give five hundred to Antonina?"

Belisarius nodded.

Hermogenes blew out his cheeks. "Plus two thousand from Sittas and five hundred from Germanicus. That's three and a half thousand heavy cavalry. The Army of Syria can probably give you three or four thousand infantry and a couple of thousand cavalry. But the cavalry will be light horse archers, not cataphract lancers."

"Ten thousand men, at the most," concluded Germanicus. "As he says, that's not much of an army."

Belisarius shrugged. "It's what we've got."

"I'm not happy at the idea of Belisarius personally leading this army," stated Chrysopolis. "He's the Empire's strategos. He should really stay here in the capital."

"Nonsense!" barked Justinian. For the first time since the meeting began, he too broke into a grin. And, like that of his wife's, the expression was utterly humorless.

"You want an alliance with Persia, don't you?" he demanded. "They won't be happy at our counter-offer of ten thousand men. But Belisarius' reputation will make up the difference." Now, a bit of humor crept into that ravaged face. "Stop frowning, Chrysopolis. I can see your sour face as if I still had eyes."

He leaned forward, gripping the armrests of his chair. His head scanned the entire circle of advisers. For just a fleeting moment, everyone would have sworn Justinian could actually see them.

"I made that man a general," said the former emperor. "It's one of the few decisions I made that I've never regretted."

He leaned back in his seat. "The Persians will be delighted. Believe it."

Chapter 3

The next morning, when the Empress Regent gave Baresmanas the Roman response to Persia's proposal, he *was* delighted. He had hoped for a larger army, true. But neither he nor Emperor Khusrau had really expected the Romans to send them forty thousand troops.

The Roman generosity in not demanding territorial concessions in the borderlands also pleased him immensely. That was quite unexpected.

But, best of all—*Belisarius.*

Not every member of the Persian delegation shared his attitude—including his own wife, the Lady Maleka. As soon as Baresmanas returned to the small palace in which the Persians had been housed, right in the middle of the imperial complex, she strode into the main salon, scowling fiercely.

"I do not approve," she told her husband, very forcefully. "We should not be currying favor from these wretched Roman mongrels, as if we were lowborn beggars."

Baresmanas ignored her. He stood before the flames burning in the salon's fireplace, warming his hands from the chill of an April morning.

"I do not approve!" repeated Lady Maleka.

Baresmanas sighed, turned away from the fire. "The Emperor approves," he said mildly.

"Khusrau is but a boy!"

"He most certainly is *not*," replied her husband firmly. "True, he is a young man. But he is in every respect as fine an Emperor as ever sat the Aryan throne. Do not doubt it, wife."

Lady Maleka scowled. "Even so— He is too preoccupied with the Malwa invasion! He forgets our glorious Aryan heritage!"

Her husband bit off a sharp retort. Unlike his wife, Baresmanas was well-educated. A scholar, actually, which was unusual for a sahrdaran. Lady Maleka, on the other hand, was a perfect specimen of their class. Like all Persian high noblewomen, she was literate. But it was a skill which she had never utilized once she reached adulthood. She much preferred to learn her history seated on rich cushions at their palace in Ctesiphon, listening to bards recounting the epics of the Aryans.

Baresmanas studied the angry face of his wife, trying to think of a way to explain reality that would penetrate her prejudiced ignorance.

The truth of history, he knew, was quite different from her fantasy version of it. The Iranians who ruled Persia and Central Asia had originated, like their Scythian brethren, from the steppes of Asia. They, too, had been nomadic barbarians once. Over a millennium ago, the Aryan tribes had marched south from the steppes, in their great epic of conquest. The westward-moving tribes had become known as the Iranians and had created the glory of the ancient Medes and Persians. Their eastward-bound cousins had conquered northern India and created the Vedic culture which eventually permeated the entire sub-continent.

And then, having done so, both branches of the Aryans had invented a new history for themselves. A history full of airy legends and grandiose claims, and precious little in the way of fact.

Myths and fables, grown up in the feudal soil of the east. The real power of the Iranians, now as before, lay on the Persian plateau and the great rich lands of Mesopotamia. But the Aryans—the nobility, at least—chose to remember the legends of the northeastern steppes.

And then, he thought sourly, remember them upside down. They don't remember the military strength of barbarian horsemen. Only the myth of pure blood, and divine ancestry.

Studying his wife, Baresmanas recognized the impossibility of penetrating her prejudices.

So be it. The Aryans had other customs, too.

"Obey your husband, wife," he commanded. "And your Emperor."

She opened her mouth.

"Do it."

Lady Maleka bowed her head. Sullenly, she stalked from the room.

Baresmanas lowered himself onto a couch near the fire. He stared into the flames. The hot glow seemed to lurk within his dark eyes, as if he saw a different conflagration there.

Which, indeed, he did. The memory of a fire called the battle of Mindouos. Where, three years before, a Roman general had shattered the Persian army. Outfoxed them, trapped then, slaughtered them—even captured the Persian camp.

Belisarius.

Baresmanas had been at that battle. So had his children, in the Persian camp.

He looked away from the fire, wincing.

His children would never have been at Mindouos had Baresmanas not brought them there. He, too, for all his scholarship, had lapsed into Aryan haughtiness. It was the long-standing custom of noble Persians to bring their families to the field of battle. Displaying, to the enemy and all the world, their arrogant confidence in Aryan invincibility.

His wife had refused to come, pleading her health. (Not from the enemy, but from the heat of the Syrian desert.) But his children had come, avidly—his daughter as much as his son. Avid to watch their famous father, second-in-command to Firuz, destroy the insolent Romans.

Baresmanas sighed. He reached up with his left hand and caressed his right shoulder. The shoulder ached, as always, and he could feel the ridged scar tissue under the silk of his tunic.

A Roman lance had put that scar there. At Mindouos. Baresmanas, like all the charging noble lancers, had been trapped in the center. Trapped, by the cunning of the Roman commander; and, then, hammered under by the force of his counter-blow.

Belisarius.

Baresmanas could remember little of the battle's final moments. Only the confusion and the choking dust; the growing, horrible knowledge that they had been outwitted and outmaneuvered; the shock and pain, as he lay dazed and bleeding on the trampled ground, his shoulder almost severed.

Most of all, he remembered the terror which had coursed through his heart, as if hot iron instead of blood flowed through his veins. Terror, not for himself, but for his helpless children. The Persian camp was unprotected, then, from the triumphing Romans. Baresmanas had known the Roman soldiers would ravage it like wolves, especially their Hun auxiliaries, raping and murdering.

And so they had; or, at least, had started to do.

Until Belisarius, and his cataphracts, had put a stop to the atrocities. He had been as decisive and ruthless toward his own Huns as he had been toward the Persians.

Weeks later, after he had been ransomed by his family, Baresmanas had heard the tale from his daughter Tahmina. Seeing the oncoming Huns, she and her brother had hidden themselves under the silk cushions in their tent. But the savages had not been fooled. A squad of Huns had found Tahmina soon enough, and dragged her out of the tent. Her brother had tried to come to her rescue, but it had been a futile gesture. The Huns had not killed the boy—alive, he would bring a good price on the slave market. They had simply split his scalp with a blow, casually, while they began stripping off his sister's clothing.

The Roman general had arrived then, accompanied by his cataphracts, and ordered the Huns to cease. Tahmina had described to Baresmanas how the Hun who held her by the hair had taunted Belisarius. And how the general, cold-faced, had simply spoken the name of his cataphract. A cataphract whose face was even colder, and as wicked-looking as a weasel. The cataphract had been as quick and deadly as a weasel, too. His arrows had slaughtered the Huns holding Tahmina like so many chickens.

Belisarius.

Strange, peculiar man. With that odd streak of mercy, lying under the edge of his ruthless and cunning brain.

Baresmanas turned his head, staring back at the fire. And now, for the first time since he learned of the Malwa butchery of Mesopotamia, could see the enemy roasting in the flames.

Belisarius.

Chapter 4

It was the most beautiful cathedral Justinian had ever seen. More beautiful, and more majestic, than he had even dreamed. The capstone to his life. The Hagia Sophia that he had planned to build.

The Mese, the great central thoroughfare of Constantinople, began at the Golden Gate and ended at the base of the cathedral. Down its entire length—here in scatters; there, mounded up in piles like so much offal—were the bodies of the plague victims.

Half the city was dead, or dying. The stench of uncollected rotting bodies mingled with the sickly smell of burning cadavers to produce a thick miasma, hanging over Constantinople like a constant fog. The same miasma that he had seen hanging over Italy, and North Africa, and every province which Belisarius had reconquered for him.

Justinian the Great. Who, in the name of restoring the greatness of the Roman Empire, had bankrupted the eastern half to destroy the western. And left the entire Mediterranean a war-ravaged breeding ground for the worst plague in centuries.

Justinian the Great. Who, more than any other man, caused the final splintering of Greco-Roman civilization.

Justinian jerked erect in his chair.

"No more," he croaked. "I can bear it no longer."

He leaned forward and extended his arm, shakily. In the palm of his hand rested a shimmering, glowing object. A jewel, some might have called it. A magical gem.

Belisarius took the "jewel" from Justinian and replaced it in its pouch. A moment later, the pouch was once again suspended from his neck.

The "jewel" spoke in his mind.

He is not a nice man.

Belisarius smiled crookedly.

No, Aide, he is not. But he can be a great man.

The crystalline being from the future exuded skepticism.

Not sure. Not a nice man, at all.

"Are you satisfied, Justinian?" Belisarius asked.

The former Emperor nodded.

"Yes. It was everything you said. I almost wish, now, that I had never asked for the experience. But I needed—"

He made a vague motion with his hand, as if to summon up unknown words.

Belisarius provided them:

"You needed to know if your suspicions were warranted, or not. You needed to know if the elevation of my stepson to the imperial throne stemmed from motives of personal ambition and aggrandizement, or—as I claimed at the time—from the needs of the war against the Malwa."

Justinian lowered his head. "I am a mistrustful man," he muttered. "It is rooted in my nature." He opened his mouth to speak again. Clamped it shut.

"There is no need, Justinian," said Belisarius. "There is no need."

The general's smile grew more crooked still. He had had this conversation once before, in a nightmare vision. "It would take you hours to say what you are trying to say. It will not come easily to you, if at all."

Justinian shook his head. "No, Belisarius. There *is* a need. For my sake, if not yours." Harshly: "I sometimes think losing my eyes improved my vision." He took a deep breath. Another. Then, like a stone might bleed:

"I apologize."

The third occupant of the room chuckled. "Even in this," he said, "you are still arrogant. Do you think you are the world's only sinner, Justinian? Or simply its greatest?"

Justinian swiveled his head.

"I will ignore that remark," he said, with considerable dignity. "And are *you* certain, Michael of Macedonia? Of this—creature—you call the Talisman of God?"

"Quite certain," replied the stony voice of the monk. "It is a messenger sent by the Lord to warn us all."

"Especially me," muttered Justinian. The blind man rubbed his mangled eye-sockets. "Has Theodora—?"

"No," replied Belisarius. "I offered, once, but she declined. She said she preferred to take the future as it comes, rather than seeing it in a vision."

"Good," stated Justinian. "She does not know about the cancer, then?"

It was Belisarius' turn to jerk erect in his chair, startled. "No. *Good God!* I never thought of that, when I offered to give her the jewel."

"Seventeen years," stated Justinian. His voice was very bleak. "She will die, then, from cancer."

The Macedonian cleared his throat. "If we succeed in defeating the Malwa—"

Justinian waved him off. "That's irrelevant, Michael. Whatever other evils the Malwa will bring, they are not responsible for cancer. And don't forget—the vision which the jewel gave me was of the future that would have been. The future where the Malwa were never elevated to world mastery by this demonic power called Link. The future where I remained Emperor, and we reconquered the western Mediterranean."

He fell silent, head bowed. "I am right, Belisarius, am I not?"

Belisarius hesitated. He cast his thoughts toward Aide.

He is right, came the reply. Aide forestalled the next question: **And there is no cure for cancer. Not, at least, anything that will be within your capability for many, many years. Centuries.**

Belisarius took a deep breath.

"Yes, Justinian. You are right. Regardless of what else happens, Theodora will die of cancer in seventeen years."

The former Emperor sighed. "They burned out my tear ducts, along with my eyes. I damn the traitors for that, sometimes, even more than my lost vision."

Shaking himself, Justinian rose to his feet and began pacing about the room.

The plethora of statuary which had once adorned his room was gone, now. Theodora had ordered them removed, during Justinian's convalescence, worried that her blind husband might stumble and fall.

That fear had been quickly allayed. Watching the former Emperor maneuver through the obstacles littering the floor, Belisarius was struck again by the man's uncanny intelligence. Justinian seemed to know, by sheer memory, where every one of those potential obstructions lay, and he avoided them unerringly.

But the obstacles were no longer statuary. Justinian had no use, any longer, for such visual ornament. Instead, he had filled his room with the objects of his oldest and favorite hobby—gadgets. Half the floor seemed to be covered by odd contrivances and weird contraptions. Justinian even claimed that his blindness was an asset, in this regard, since it forced him to master the inner logic of his devices. Nor could Belisarius deny the claim. The general stared at one of the larger mechanisms in the room, standing in a corner. The device was quiescent, at the moment. But he had seen it work. Justinian had designed the thing based on Belisarius' own description of a vision given to him by Aide.

The first true steam engine ever built in Rome—or anywhere in the world, so far as he knew. He had not seen its like even during his long visit to Malwa India. The thing itself was not much more than a toy, but it was the model for the first locomotive which was already being planned. The day would come when Belisarius would be able to shuttle his troops from one campaign to another in the same way he had seen Aide describe in visions. Visions of a terrible carnage in the future which would be called the American Civil War.

A voice drew him back to the present.

"Seventeen years," mused Justinian sadly. "Whereas I, according to the jewel, will live to a ripe old age." Pain came to his ravaged face. "I had always hoped she might outlive me," he whispered. Justinian squared his shoulders.

"So be it. I will give her seventeen good years. The best I can manage."

"Yes," said Belisarius.

Justinian shook his head. "God, what a waste. Did the jewel ever show it to you, Belisarius? That future that would have been, had the Malwa never risen? The future where I had you ravage the western Mediterranean in the name of reconstituting Roman glory? Only to see half the Empire die from the plague while I used the royal treasury to build one grandiose, useless monument after another?"

"The Hagia Sophia was not useless, Justinian," demurred Belisarius. "It was—would have been—one of the world's genuine glories."

Justinian snorted. "I will allow that one exception. No—two. I also codified Roman law. But the rest? The—" He snapped his fingers. "That secretary of yours. You know, the foul gossip. What's his name?"

"Procopius."

"Yes, him. That fawning toad even wrote a book glorifying those preposterous structures. Did you see that?"

"Yes."

Michael spoke. "I hear you've dispensed with the reptile's services, now that you no longer need him to pass false rumors to the enemy. Good riddance."

Belisarius chuckled. "Yes, I did. I doubt very much that Malwa spies place any more credence in his claims that Antonina was spending all her time at our estate in Syria holding orgies in my absence."

"Not after she showed up at the Hippodrome with her force of Syrian grenadiers and smashed the Nika insurrection!" barked Justinian. The former Emperor rubbed his eye-sockets. "Since he's out of work, Belisarius, send him to me. I'll give him a book to write. Just the kind of fawning propaganda he wrote for me in another future. Only it won't be called *The Buildings*. It'll be called *The Laws*, and it will praise to the skies the Grand Justiciar Justinian's magnificent work providing the Roman Empire with the finest legal system in the world."

Justinian resumed his seat. "Enough of that," he said. "There's something else I want to raise. Belisarius, I am a bit concerned about Antonina's expedition to Egypt."

The general cocked an eyebrow. "So am I!" he exclaimed. "She's my wife, you know. I'm not happy at the idea of sending her into a battle with only—"

"Nonsense!" snapped the former Emperor. "The woman'll do fine, as far as any battles go. Don't underestimate her, Belisarius. Any woman that small who can slaughter half a dozen street thugs in a knife fight can handle that sorry bastard Ambrose. It's the *aftermath* I'm worried about. Once she's crushed this mini-rebellion, she'll be moving on. To the naval side of your campaign. What then?" He leaned forward, fixing Belisarius with his eyeless gaze.

"Who's going to *keep* Egypt under control?"

"You know our plans, Justinian. Hermogenes will assume command of the Army of Egypt and—"

The former Emperor snorted. "He's a soldier, man! Oh, a damned fine one, to be sure. But soldiers aren't much use, when it comes to suppressing the kind of religious fanatics who keep Egypt in a turmoil." He sighed heavily. "Trust me, Belisarius. I speak from experience. If you use a soldier to squash a monk, all you create is a martyr."

Justinian now turned to face Michael. "You're the key here, Michael. We will need your religious authority."

"And Anthony's," qualified the monk.

Justinian waved his hand impatiently. "Yes, yes, and the Patriarch's help, of course. But you are the key."

"Why?" demanded Michael.

Belisarius replied. "Because changing an empire's habits and customs—built through the centuries—will require religious fervor. A popular movement, driven by zeal and conviction. I don't disagree with Justinian, on that point. He's right—soldiers just create martyrs." He cleared his throat. "And, for the other—well, Anthony is as kindly, even saintly, a man as I ever hope to meet. The ideal Patriarch. But—"

A wintry smile came to the monk's gaunt face. "He is not given to smiting the unrighteous," concluded Michael. The Macedonian shifted position in his chair, much like a hawk sets his talons on a tree limb. "I have no such qualms, on the other hand."

"Rather the contrary," murmured Justinian.

The former Emperor smiled grimly. He quite approved of Michael of Macedonia. The Stylite monk was a holy man, which Justinian most certainly was not. Yet they shared a certainly commonality of spirit. A Thracian peasant and a Macedonian shepherd, as youths. Simple men, ultimately. And quite savage, each in their own way.

Belisarius spoke again, shaking his head. "We've already decided to send Michael's monks to Egypt, Justinian. I agree that they'll help. The fact remains, however, that without military force those monks will just wind up another brawling faction in the streets. Our military forces were already stretched—and now, I will be taking what few troops we can spare to combat the Malwa in Persia. We cannot divert those forces, Justinian, and the imperial treasury is too bare to finance the creation of a new army."

Suddenly, images flashed through Belisarius' mind.

Ranks of cavalrymen. Their weapons and armor, though well made, were simple and utilitarian. Over the armor, they wore plain tunics. White tunics, bearing red crosses. Parading through the main thoroughfare of a great city. Behind them marched foot soldiers, also wearing that simple white tunic emblazoned with a huge red cross.

The general burst into laughter.

Thank you, Aide!

He turned to Michael. "Have you chosen a name for your new religious order?"

The Macedonian grimaced. "Please, Belisarius. I did not create that order. It was created by others—"

"Inspired by your teachings," interjected Justinian.

"—and practically foisted upon me." The monk scowled. "I have no idea what to do with them. As much as anything else, I offered to send them with Antonina to Egypt because they were demanding some holy task of me and I couldn't think of anything else to do with them."

The general smiled. For all his incredible—even messianic—force of character, Michael of Macedonia was as ill-suited a man as Belisarius had ever met for the executive task of leading a coherent and disciplined religious movement.

"Someone must have brought them together," he said. "Organized them. It wasn't more than a month after you began your public sermons in the Forum of Constantine that bands of them began to appear in the streets spreading your message."

The Macedonian snorted. "Three of them, in fact. Their names are Mark of Athens, Zeno Symmachus, and Gaiseric. Zeno is an Egyptian, from the Fayum; Gaiseric, a Goth. Mark, of course, is Greek. Mark is orthodox, Zeno is a Monophysite, and Gaiseric is an Arian."

"And they get along?" asked Belisarius lightly.

Michael began to smolder, then relaxed. "Yes, Belisarius. They regard the issue of the Trinity as I do—a decoy of the Devil's, to distract men while Satan does his work." He smiled. "Not, mind you, that any room they jointly inhabit isn't occasionally filled with the sound of disputatious voices. But there is never any anger in it. They are each other's brothers, as they are mine."

"And what position do you advance, in these occasional disputes?" queried Justinian.

"You know perfectly well my position," snapped Michael.

The former emperor smiled. Justinian adored theological discussion. Other than Theodora's care, it had been the company of Michael and Patriarch Cassian which, more than anything, had enabled him to find his way through the darkness of the soul, in the months after his blinding.

"My opinion on the Trinity is orthodox, in the same way as Anthony's," stated Michael. "Though more plainly put." He snorted. "My friend Anthony Cassian is Greek, and is therefore not satisfied with simple truth until he can parse it with clever Greek syllogisms and make it dance to dialectical Greek tunes. But I am not Greek. I am Macedonian. True, we are a related people. But to the Greeks God gave his intellect, and to us he gave his common sense."

Here, a wintry smile. "This, of course, is why the great Philip of my ancestry lost his patience and decided to subdue the whole fractious lot of quarreling southrons. And why his son, the *Macedonian* Alexander, conquered the world."

"So the Greeks could inherit it," quipped Justinian.

"Place them in charge of the order, then," said Belisarius. "And find women with similar talents. There must be some."

Michael stroked his great beard. "Yes," he said, after a moment's thought. "Two, in particular, come immediately to mind. Juliana Syagrius and Helen of Armenia."

"Juliana Syagrius?" demanded Justinian. "The widow of—?"

Michael nodded. "The very same. Not all of my followers are common folk, Justinian. Any number of them are from the nobility—although usually from the equestrian order. Juliana is the only member of the senatorial classes who has responded to my teachings. She has even offered to place her entire fortune at my disposal."

"Good Lord!" exclaimed Justinian. "She's one of the richest people in the empire!"

Michael glared. "I am well aware of that, thank you! And what am I supposed to do with it? I have lived on alms since I was a youth—a habit I have no intention of changing."

The sour look on his face made plain the monk's attitude toward wealth. He began to mutter various phrases concerning camels and the eye of a needle. Unkind phrases. *Very* unkind phrases, in point of fact.

Belisarius interrupted the gathering storm.

"You will use that fortune to buy arms and armor, Michael. And the provisions needed to support your new order."

"They will beg for their support, damn them!" snapped Michael. "Just as I do!"

Belisarius shook his head. "They will be too busy. Much too busy." The general smiled—broadly, not crookedly. "Yours will be a religious order of a new kind, Michael. A *military* order."

A name flashed through the general's mind.

"We will call them the *Knights Hospitaler*," he said, leaning forward in his chair.

Guided by Aide through the labyrinth of future history, Belisarius began to explain.

After Michael was gone, hurrying his way out of the Great Palace, Justinian sighed. "It will not work, Belisarius. Oh, to be sure, at first—" The former emperor, veteran of intrigue and maneuver, shook his head sadly. "Men are sinners. In time, your new monks will simply become another lot of ambitious schemers, grasping for anything in sight."

Image. A magnificent palace. Through its corridors, adorned with expensive statuary and tapestries, moved men in secretive discourse. They wore tunics—still white, with a simple red cross. But the tunics were silk, now, and the hilts of the swords suspended from their scabbards were encrusted with gems.

"True," replied Belisarius. His voice lost none of its good cheer. "But they will not lapse until Malwa is done. After that—" Belisarius shrugged. "I do not know much, Justinian, of the struggle in the far distant future in which we find ourselves ensnared. But I have always known we were on the right side, because our enemies—those who call themselves the 'new gods'—seek human perfection. There is no such thing, and never will be." He rose from his chair.

"You know that as well as I. Do you really think that your new laws and your judgements will bring paradise on earth? An end to all injustice?"

Justinian grunted sarcastically.

"Why do it, then?" demanded Belisarius.

"Because it's worth doing," growled Justinian.

The general nodded. "God judges us by what we seek, not what we find."

Belisarius began to leave. Justinian called him back.

"One other thing, Belisarius. Speaking of visions." The former Emperor's face twisted into a half-smile. It was a skeptical sort of expression—almost sardonic.

"Have you had any further visions about your little protegé in India? Is she making Malwa howl yet?"

Belisarius returned Justinian's smile with a shake of the head. "Shakuntala? I don't *know*—I've certainly had no visions! Aide is not a magician, Justinian. He is no more clairvoyant than you or I." The general smiled himself, now. There was nothing sardonic in that expression, though. And it was not in the least bit crooked. "I imagine she's doing splendidly. She's probably already got a little army collected around her, by now."

"Where is she?"

Belisarius shrugged. "The plan was for her to seek exile in south India. Her grandfather's the King of Kerala. Whether she's there or not, however, I don't know. I've received no word. That's the very reason Irene is accompanying Antonina to Egypt. She'll try to re-establish contact with Shakuntala and Rao through the Ethiopians."

"I can't say I'm happy about that, by the way," grumbled Justinian. "I didn't oppose the idea at the council, since you seemed so set upon it. But—Irene's a fiendishly capable spymaster. I'd be a lot happier if she were here at Theodora's side in the capital, keeping an eye on traitors."

Skeptically:

"Do you *really* think this little rebellion you took so much time—and money—to foster is anything but wishful thinking?"

Belisarius studied the blind man for a moment, before replying. Justinian, for all his brilliance, was ill-equipped by temperament to gauge the power of a popular rebellion. The man thought like an emperor, still. Belisarius suspected that he always had, even when he was a peasant himself.

"I know the girl, Justinian. You don't. For all her youth, she has the potential to be a great ruler. And in Rao she has one of the finest generals in India."

"So?" grunted Justinian. "If the success of your rebellion hinges so completely on two people, the Malwa can take care of that with a couple of assassinations."

Belisarius laughed.

"Assassinate *Rao?* He's the best assassin in India himself! God help the Malwa who tries to slip a knife into that man's back!" He shook his head. "As for Shakuntala—she's quite a proficient killer in her own right. Rao trained her, from the time she was seven. And she has the best bodyguards in the world. An elite Kushan unit, led by a man named Kungas."

The skepticism was still evident on the former emperor's face. Belisarius, watching, decided it was hopeless to shake Justinian's attitude.

He was not there, as I was—to see Shakuntala win the allegiance of the very Kushans who had been assigned by Malwa to be her captors. God, the sheer force in that girl's soul!

He turned away. Then, struck by a memory, turned back.

"Aide *did* give me a vision, once, while I was in India. That vision confirmed me in my determination to set Shakuntala free."

Justinian cocked his head, listening.

"Many centuries from now, in the future—in *a* future, it might be better to say—all of Europe will be under the domination of one of history's greatest generals and conquerors. His name will be Napoleon. He will be defeated, in the end, brought down by his own overweening ambition. That defeat will be caused, as much as anything, by a great bleeding wound in Spain. He will conquer Spain, but never rule it. For years, his soldiers will die fighting the Spanish rebellion. The rebels will be aided by a nation which will arise on the island we call Britannia. The Peninsular War, those islanders will call it. And when Napoleon is finally brought down, they will look back upon that war and see in it one of the chief sources of their victory."

Still nothing. Skepticism.

Belisarius shrugged. Left.

Outside, in the corridor, Aide spoke in his mind.

Not a nice man, at all.

The facets flashed and spun into a new configuration. Like a kaleidoscope, the colors of Aide's emotion shifted. Sour distaste was replaced by a kind of wry humor.

Of course, the Duke of Wellington was not a nice man, either.

In the room, Justinian remained in his chair. He spent some time pondering the general's last words, but not much. He was far more interested in contemplating a different vision. Somewhere, in the midst of the horror which the jewel had shown him, Justinian had caught a glimpse of something which gave him hope.

A statue, he had seen. Carved by a sculptor of the figure, to depict justice.

The figure had been blind.

"In the future," murmured the former emperor, "when men wish to praise the quality of justice, they will say that justice is blind."

The man who had once been perhaps the most capable emperor in the long history of the Roman Empire—and certainly its most intelligent—rubbed his empty eye-sockets. For the first time since his mutilation, the gesture was not simply one of despair and bitterness.

Justinian the Great. So, more than anything, had he wanted to be known for posterity.

Perhaps . . .

Theodora, at Belisarius' urging, had created a position specifically tailored for Justinian. He was now the empire's Grand Justiciar. For the first time in centuries, the law of Rome would be codified, interpreted and enforced by the best man for the task. Whatever had been his faults as an Emperor, there was no one who doubted that Justinian's was the finest legal mind in the empire.

Perhaps . . .

There had been Solomon and Solon, after all, and Hammurabi before them.

So why not add the name Justinian to that list?

It was a shorter list, now that he thought about, than the list of great emperors. Much shorter.

Chapter 5

MUZIRIS

Spring, 531 A.D.

"Any minute now," whispered the assassin at the window. "I can see the first contingents of her cavalrymen coming around the corner."

The leader of the Malwa assassination team came to the window. The lookout stepped aside. Carefully, using only one fingertip, the leader drew the curtain aside a couple of inches. He peered down onto the street below.

"Yes," he murmured. He turned and made a gesturing motion with his right hand. The other two assassins in the room came forward, carrying the bombard between them. They moved slowly and laboriously. The bombard was two feet long and measured eight inches across. It was made of wrought iron bars, square in cross section and an inch thick. The bars were welded together to form a rough barrel about six inches in diameter, which was then further strengthened with four iron hoops. A thick plate was welded to the back of the bars. The bombard was bolted down to a wooden base—teak, reinforced with brass strips—measuring three feet by two feet. The two men strained under the effort of carrying the device.

Part of their careful progress, however, was due to the obstacles in their way. The room was littered with the squalid debris of a poor family's cramped apartment.

As they came forward, they maneuvered around the bodies of the family who had once lived there. A man, his wife, her mother, and their four children. After killing the family, the assassins had piled the corpses in a corner. But the room was so small that the seven bodies still took up a full quarter of the floor space. Most of the floor was covered with blood, dried now, but still sticky. A swarm of flies covered the corpses and the bloodstains.

One of the assassins wrinkled his nose.

"They're already starting to stink," he muttered. "Damn southwest India and its fucking tropical climate—and we're in the hot season. We should have kept them alive until—"

"Shut up," hissed the leader. "What were we going to do? Guard them for almost a full day? The baby would have begun squawling, anyway."

His subordinate lapsed into sullen silence. A few seconds later, he and his companion levered the bombard onto the hastily-improvised firing platform which the assassination squad had erected that morning. It was a rickety contraption—simply a mounded up pile of the pallets and two wicker chairs which had been the murdered family's only furniture. But it would suffice. The bombard was not a full-size cannon. It would fire only one round, a sack full of drop shot. The recoil would send the bombard hurtling into the far wall, out of action.

That would be good enough. When she passed through the street below the window of the apartment, the Empress-in-exile of Andhra would be not more than twenty yards distant. There was nowhere for her to escape, either, even if the alarm was given at the last moment. The narrow street was hemmed in, on both sides, by mud-brick tenement buildings identical to the one in which the assassins lay waiting. At that point blank range, the cannister would sweep a large swath of the street clean of life.

"Here she comes," whispered the lookout. He was peering through a second window, now. Like his leader, he had drawn the curtain aside no more than an inch or two.

"Are you certain it is she?" demanded the leader. The lookout had been assigned to the squad because he was one of the few Malwa assassins who had personally seen the rebel Empress after her capture at the siege of Amaravati. The girl had aged, of course, since then. But not so much that the lookout wouldn't recognize her.

"It must be Shakuntala," he replied. "I can't see her face, because she's wearing a veil. But she's small—dark-skinned—wearing imperial regalia. Who else would it be?"

The leader scowled. He would have preferred a more positive identification, but—

He hissed an unspoken command to the other two assassins in the room. The command was unnecessary. They were already loading the gunpowder and the cannister round into the bombard. The leader scampered back and sighted along its length. He could only estimate the angle, since the curtain hanging in the window obscured his view of the street below. But the estimate would be good enough. It was not a weapon of finesse and pinpoint accuracy.

The leader made a last inspection of the cannon. He could not restrain a grimace. The blast and the recoil, confined in that small room, was almost certain to cause some injuries to the assassins themselves. Hopefully, those injuries would not disable any of them—not enough, at least, to prevent them making their escape in the chaos and confusion after Shakuntala and her immediate entourage were slaughtered.

"I wish they'd perfected those new impact fuses they've been working on," muttered one of the assassins. "Then we could have used a real cannon at long range. This misbegotten—"

"Why not wish she didn't have thousands of Maratha cavalrymen to protect her, while you're at it?" snarled the leader. "And those fucking Kushan cutthroats? Then we could have just slid a knife into her ribs instead of—"

"She's fifty yards away," hissed the lookout. "The first cavalry escorts are already passing below."

He plastered himself against the wall, crouching down as far as he could while still being able to peek through the window. The expression on his face, beneath the professional calm, was grim. He was almost certain to be scorched by the exhaust from the cannon blast. And there was also the possibility that a weak weld could result in the cannon blowing up when it was fired.

"Forty yards."

One of the two bombard handlers retreated to a far corner, curling into a ball. The other drew out a lighting device and ignited the slow match. After handing it to the squad leader, he hurried to join his comrade in the corner. The leader crouched next to the bombard's firehole, ready to set off the charge.

"Thirty-five yards," announced the lookout by the window. "Get ready."

The men in the room took a deep breath. They had already decided to fire the bombard when the Empress was twenty-five yards distant. They knew that Shakuntala's horse would travel less than five yards in the time it took for the slow match to ignite the charge. If all went as planned, the sack full of lead pellets would turn the ruler-in-exile of conquered Andhra into so much mincemeat.

The leader held up the slow match. Brought it close to the firehole.

"Thirty yards."

The door behind them erupted like a volcano. The first man coming through the door cut the squad leader aside before the assassin had time to do more than flinch. It was a brutal sword strike—not fatal, simply enough to hurl the man away from the cannon. Quick, quick. The assassin screeched with pain. His right arm dangled loose, half-severed at the elbow. The slow match fell harmlessly to the floor, hissing in a patch of blood.

The lookout at the window had time to recognize the man who killed him, before that same sword went into his heart. As agile and skilled as he was, the assassin had no more chance of evading that expert thrust than a tethered goat.

In the few seconds that it took him to die, the assassin tried to remember his killer's name. He knew the name, but it would not come. He knew only that he had been slain by the commander of Shakuntala's Kushan bodyguard. The man whom he and his squad simply called *Iron-face*.

One of the assassins huddled in the corner died soon thereafter, hacked into pieces by the three Kushan soldiers who piled into the room after their commander. The commander himself took care of the last Malwa. This one he did not kill outright. He wanted him for questioning. The Kushan lopped off the man's right hand as it came up holding a blade, then struck him senseless with a blow of the sword's pommel on the forehead.

The Kushan commander scanned the room. By now, with another five Kushans crowding in, the room was packed like a meat tin. Three of them had subdued the assassin whose arm the commander had half-severed upon bursting through the door.

"That's enough," he commanded. "See to the Empress."

"No need, Kungas," murmured one of his men. The Kushan soldier had pushed back the curtains in one of the windows. "She's on her way here already."

"Damn the girl!" growled Kungas. "I told her to stay back."

The Kushan commander strode to the window and glared out onto the street below. The Empress—the supposed "Empress" at the head of the column—was sitting on her horse. The girl was beginning to shake, now. A trembling hand came up and removed the veil. She wiped her face, smearing off some of the dye which had darkened her skin.

But Kungas was looking elsewhere, farther back along the column of cavalry escort. At the figure of another small girl, urging her horse forward. Unlike the "Empress," this girl was wearing simple and unadorned clothing: nothing more than a colorfully dyed tunic over pantaloons, the garments of a typical camp-follower—a soldier's common-law wife, perhaps. She, also, was dark-skinned. But her skin-tone was natural, and there was not the slightest trace of trembling in *her* hands.

"You're going to catch an earful," said the Kushan standing next to Kungas. "She looks angrier than a tigress guarding her cubs." He added cheerfully: "Of course, she's a *small* tigress. For what it's worth."

Kungas grunted. For a moment, something that might have been a sigh almost escaped his lips. But only for the briefest instant. Thereafter, the mask closed down.

On the street below, the true Empress halted her horse long enough to see to the well-being of her double. Then she dismounted and charged into the entrance of the tenement building.

She was lost from Kungas' sight, but he could hear her stamping up the narrow wooden stairs leading to the rooms on the upper floor. He could also hear her voice.

"How can such a small girl have such a loud voice?" wondered the other Kushan. "And how can slippers make such a stamping clatter?"

"Shut up, Kanishka," growled Kungas. Kanishka smiled seraphically.

The Empress' voice, coming from below:

"Never again, Kungas! Do you hear me? Never again!"

She burst into the room. Her eyes immediately fixed on those of Kungas. Black, hot eyes.

"Never again! Jijabai might have been killed!"

Kungas' iron face never wavered. Nor did his harsh voice. "So might you, Empress. And you are irreplaceable."

Shakuntala glared at him for a few seconds. Then, recognizing the futility of trying to browbeat the commander of her bodyguard, she glared around the room. When she saw the bodies of the family, she recoiled.

"Malwa beasts," she hissed.

"It's how we spotted them," said Kungas. "Our spies saw that this building seemed lifeless, everyone hiding in their rooms. Then they smelled the bodies."

He glanced at the bombard. Three of his men were already disarming the weapon. "But we only discovered them just in time. It was a well-laid ambush. Their only mistake was killing the family too soon."

"The baby would have squawled all night," com-mented Kan-ishka.

Kungas shrugged. "So? It would hardly be the only shrieking infant in a slum."

Shakuntala grimaced. Kungas, in his way, was the hardest man she had ever met.

She tore her eyes away from the pitiable sight of the dead family and stared at the assassins. "How many did you keep alive?"

"Two," replied Kanishka. "Better than we hoped."

"They'll talk," said Kungas. "Not easily—not Malwa assassins. But they'll talk."

"They won't know much," said Shakuntala.

"Enough. I was right. You will see."

The Empress stared at Kungas. After a moment, she looked away. "That it would come to this. My own grandfather."

"What did you expect?" came a voice from the door.

Shakuntala turned. Dadaji Holkar was standing in the doorway. Her imperial adviser's eyes scanned the room, coming to rest on the piled-up bodies of the dead family.

"Malwa," he said softly. The word was not condemning, nor accusatory. It was simply a term of explanation. Self-evident. His eyes returned to Shakuntala. "What did you expect, girl?" he repeated. "You threaten his kingdom with Malwa's gaze, and Mal-wa's fury. You organize a private army in his largest seaport. You disrupt his streets with riot and tumult."

"I did not! It was Malwa provocateurs who stirred up the Keralan mob against the refugees from Andhra!"

Holkar stroked his beard, smiling. "True. But it was your Maratha cavalrymen who sabred the mob and spit them on their lances."

"As well they should!" came her hot reply. "Many of those refugees were Maratha themselves!"

Holkar chuckled. "I am not arguing the merits of the thing, girl. I am simply pointing out that you have become a major—*embarrassment*—to the King of Kerala. That old man is no doting village grandfather, Shakuntala. He is as cold-blooded as any ruler needs to be. With the Malwa Empire now at war with Persia, he thinks he is safe from their ambitions—as long as he can avoid drawing their attention. The last thing he wants is his granddaughter forging a rebellion in the Deccan from a base in his own kingdom."

Holkar stepped into the room, avoiding the bodies which littered the floor. When he came up to the Empress, he placed a gentle hand on her shoulder. He was the only member of her entourage who ever took that liberty. He was the only one who dared.

"He is my grandfather," whispered Shakuntala. Her voice throbbed with pain. "I can remember sitting on his knee, when I was a little girl." She stared out the window, blinking away tears. "I did not really expect him to help me. But I still didn't think—"

"He may not have given the orders, Your Majesty," said Kungas. "Probably didn't, in fact." The Kushan commander gestured at the dead assassins. "These are Malwa, not Keralan."

Shakuntala's black eyes grew hard.

"So what? You predicted it yourself, Kungas. A Malwa assassination attempt, with the tacit approval of the Keralan authorities." She turned away, shaking her shoulders angrily. "The viceroy would not have done this on his own. He would not dare."

"Why not? He can deny everything." Again, Kungas gestured to the dead assassins. "Malwa, not Keralan."

Shakuntala stalked toward the door.

"He would not *dare*," she repeated. At the door, she cast a final glance at the dead family. "This was my grandfather's work," she hissed. "I will not forget."

A moment later, she was gone. The stamping sounds of her slippered feet going down the stairs came through the door. Dadaji Holkar and Kungas exchanged a glance. The adviser's expression was rueful. That of Kungas' was sympathetic, insofar as a mask of iron can be said to have an expression.

Kanishka had finished tying a tourniquet around the maimed arm of the Malwa assassin leader. He stooped and hauled the man to his feet. The Malwa began to moan. Kanishka silenced him with a savage blow.

"Glad I'm not her imperial adviser," he muttered. "Be like advising a tigress to eat rice." He draped the unconscious assassin over his shoulder and made for the door.

Then he said cheerfully, "A small tigress, true. For all the good that'll do her grandpa."

Within a minute, the Kushans had cleared the bodies from the small apartment—including, at Kungas' command, the bodies of the dead family. They would find a priest to give them the rites. The two dead Malwa assassins would be tossed into a dung-heap. After their interrogation, the two still alive would follow them.

Kungas and Holkar were left alone in the room.

"That *was* very close," commented Holkar. The statement was not a criticism, simply an observation.

"There will be another," replied the Kushan commander. "And another after that. It's obvious that the Keralan authorities will turn a blind eye to Malwa spies and assassins coming after her. We must get the Empress to a place of safety, Dadaji—*and soon*. After today, she will no longer let me use Jijabai as her double."

Kungas' shoulders twitched. Coming from another man, the gesture would have been called a shrug. "I can only protect her for so long, here in Muziris."

Holkar broke into a little smile. "How about Deogiri?" he asked. Then, laughed outright, seeing Kungas' face. For once—just for an instant—there had been an expression on that iron mask. Kungas' eyes had actually widened. In another man, the gesture would have been called a goggle.

"*Deogiri?*" he choked. "*Are you mad?* The place is a Malwa stronghold! It's the largest city in Majarasthra, except for Bharakuccha. The Malwa have a garrison of—"

He broke off. The iron face was back. "You know something," he stated.

Dadaji nodded. "We just got word this morning, from a courier sent by Rao. Rao believes he can seize Deogiri. He has apparently managed to infiltrate thousands of his fighters into the city. The garrison is big, but—so he says, and he is a man who knows—sloppy and unprepared."

Kungas paced to the window. Stared out, as if he were gauging the Maratha cavalrymen in the street below.

Which, as a matter of fact, he was.

"Over three thousand of them, we've got now," he mused, "with more coming in every day as the word spreads."

"You've got more Kushans, too," pointed out Holkar.

"Six hundred," agreed Kungas. "Most of them are my own kinfolk, who deserted the Malwa once they heard the news of my change of allegiance. But a good third of them are from other clans. Odd, that."

From behind, unobserved by Kungas' sharp eyes, Holkar studied the stocky figure standing at the window. His face softened.

He had come to love Kungas, as he had few other men in his life.

Belisarius, of course, who had freed him from slavery and breathed new life into his soul. His son, still laboring in captivity somewhere in India along with the rest of Holkar's shattered family. Rao, the national hero of the Maratha people, whom he had idolized all his life. A brother, killed long ago, in battle against the Malwa. A few others.

But Kungas occupied a special place on that short list. He and Holkar were comrades-in-arms, united in a purpose and welded to a young Empress' destiny. Close friends, they had become—two men who would otherwise have been like total strangers, each to the other.

Dadaji Holkar, the former slave; low-caste by birth, and a scribe and scholar by profession. A man whose approach to the world was intrinsically philosophical, but whose soft and kindly soul had a rod of iron at its center.

Kungas, the former Malwa mercenary; a Kushan vassal by birth, a soldier by trade. A man whose view of the world was as pragmatic as a tiger's, and whose hard soul was much like his iron-masked face.

The one was now an imperial adviser—no, more. Shakuntala had named Holkar the *peshwa* of Andhra-in-exile, the premier of a people laboring in Malwa chains. The other, Kungas, was her chief bodyguard as well as one of her central military leaders.

The girl's own soul was like a lodestone for such men. Others had been drawn by that magnet in the months since she set herself up in exile at Muziris. Men like Shahji and Kondev, cavalry commanders—and those who followed them, Maratha horsemen burning to strike a blow at the Malwa.

Most were Maratha, of course, like Holkar himself. But not all. By no means. Men had come from all over the subcontinent, as soon as they heard that India's most ancient dynasty still lived, and roared defiance at the Malwa behemoth. Fighters, in the main—or simply men who wanted to be—from many Malwa subject nations. There were Bengali peasants in her small little army taking shape in the refugee camps at Muziris; not many, but a few. And Biharis, and Orissans, and Gujaratis.

Nor were all of them warriors. Hindu priests had come, too. Sadhus like Bindusara, who would hurl their own defiance at the Mahaveda abomination to their faith. And Buddhist monks, and Jains, seeking refuge in the shelter which the Satavahana dynasty had always given their own creeds.

In the few months since she had arrived in Muziris, Shakuntala's court-in-exile had become something of a small splendor. Modest, measured by formal standards; luminous, measured by its quality.

But of all those men who had come, Holkar treasured one sort above all others.

Malwa power rested on four pillars:

First and foremost, their monopoly of gunpowder and their Ye-tai barbarians.

Holkar intended to steal the first, or get it from the Romans. The other—*death to the Ye-tai.*

Then, there were the two other pillars—the soldiers who formed the Malwa army's true elite: the Rajputs and the Kushans.

No Rajputs had come. Holkar would have been astonished if they had. The Rajputs had sworn allegiance to the Malwa empire, and they were a people who held their honor sacred.

Still, he had hopes. Perhaps someday—what man can know?

But the Kushans—ah, that was a different matter. A steadfast folk, the Kushans. But they had none of Rajputana's exaggerated concept of honor and loyalty. The Kushans had been a great people themselves, in their day, conquerors and rulers of Central Asia and Northern India. But that day was long gone. Persia had conquered half their empire, and the other half had been overrun by the Ye-tai. For centuries, now, the Kushans had been mere vassals under the thumb of others, valued for their military skills, but otherwise treated with disdain. Their loyalty to Malwa, Dadaji had often thought, was much like Kungas' face. To the outer world, iron; but still a mask, when all was said and done.

Kungas' voice interrupted his little reverie.

"Odd," he repeated. He turned away from the window. "We started with only thirty. The men in my immediate command. I expected I would draw some of my own kinfolk, since I am high-ranked in the clan. But the others—"

Holkar shook his head. "I do not think it strange at all, my friend."

He reached out his hand and tapped his finger on Kungas' chest. It was like tapping a cuirass. "The Buddha's teachings still lurk there, somewhere inside your skeptical soul."

Kungas' lips quirked, just a bit. "I doubt that, Dadaji. What good did the Buddha do us, when the Ye-tai ravaged Peshawar? Where was he, when Malwa fit us with the yoke?"

"Still there," repeated the peshwa. "You disbelieve? Think more about those Kushans who have come, from other clans. What brought them here, Kungas?"

The Kushan looked away. Holkar drove on. "I will tell you, skeptic. Memory brought them here. The memory of Peshawar—and Begram, and Dalverzin and Khalchayan, and all the other great cities of the Kushan realm. The memory of Emperor Vima, and his gigantic irrigation works, which turned the desert green. The memory of Kanishka the Great, who spread Buddhism through half of Asia."

Kungas shook his head. "Ah! Gone, all gone. It is the nature of things. They come, they go."

Dadaji took Kungas by the arm, and began leading him out of the blood-soaked, fly-infested room. "Yes, they do. And then they come back. Or, at least, their children, inspired by ancient memory."

Irritably, Kungas twitched off Holkar's hand. They were in the narrow corridor now, heading for the rickety stairs leading to the street below.

"Enough of this foolishness," he commanded. "I am a man who lives in the present, and as much of the future as I can hope to see—which is not much. Tell me more of Rao's plan for Deogiri. If he takes the city, he cannot hold it alone for more than a year. Not even Deogiri is that great a fortress—not against the siege cannons which Venandakatra will bring to bear. He will need reinforcement. And then, we will need—somehow!—to maintain a supply route. *How?* And we will need to get cannons of our own. *How?* From the Romans?"

He stopped, from one step to the next, and gave Holkar a sharp glance. "Ha! They have their own problems to deal with. Belisarius will be marching into Persia, soon. You know that as well as I do. That will help, of course—help greatly. The Malwa will not be able to release forces from their Persian campaign—not with Belisarius at their front—but Venandakatra still has a powerful army of his own, in the Deccan."

He strode on, almost stamping down the stairs. Over his shoulder:

"So—tell me, philosopher! How will we get the cannons?"

Dadaji did not reply until both men were out on the street. He took a deep breath, cleansing the stench of death out of his nostrils. Then said, still smiling:

"Some of them, we will steal from the Malwa. As for the rest—Belisarius will provide."

Kungas' brow lowered, slightly. On another man, that would have been a fierce scowl. "He is thousands of miles away, Dadaji!"

Holkar's smile was positively serene, now. For an instant, Kungas was reminded of a statue of the Buddha. "He will provide, skeptic. Trust me in this. Belisarius set this rebellion of ours in motion in the first place. He has not forgotten us. Be sure of it."

Kungas made his little version of a shrug, and strode off behind the diminishing figure of his Empress. Holkar remained behind, staring after him.

"Trust me in this, my friend," he whispered. "Of five things in this world I am certain. Malwa will fall. My Empress will restore Andhra. Peshawar will rise again. Belisarius will not fail us. And I—"

His eyes teared. He could not speak the words.

I will find my wife and children. Wherever the Malwa beasts have scattered them, I will find them.

Chapter 6

"I will not take Maurice with me to Egypt, Belisarius. *Absolutely not*. So stop pestering me about it. And stop pestering me about Valentinian and Anastasius. I refuse to take them either."

Belisarius stared at his wife for a moment, before blowing out his cheeks. He leaned back in his chair and glared at Antonina. "You do not understand the danger, woman! You need the best military adviser in the world. *And* the best bodyguards."

Seeing the set and stubborn expression on his wife's face, and the way she clasped her hands firmly on the table between them, Belisarius cast a furious glare about the salon. His hot eyes scanned the mosaics which decorated the walls of their small palace within the imperial complex, without really seeing them. The gaze did, however, linger for a moment on a small statue perched on a corner stand.

"Damn cherub," he growled. "What's that naked little wretch smirking about?"

Antonina tried to fight down a smile. Her struggle was unsuccessful, however, and the sight of her quirking lips only added to her husband's outrage.

Belisarius grit his teeth and twisted in his chair, swiveling his head to the right. "Sit down, Maurice!" he commanded. "Damn you and your stiff ways! I promoted you, remember? You're a general yourself, now. A chiliarch, no less!" Belisarius made a curt motion with his hand, as if to sweep Maurice forward. "So sit down!"

The commander of Belisarius' personal retinue of bucellarii shrugged, stepped forward, and pulled up a chair. As soon as he took his seat at the table, Belisarius leaned toward him and said:

"Explain it to her, Maurice. She won't listen to me, because she thinks I'm just being a fretful husband. But she'll listen to you."

Maurice shook his head. "No."

Belisarius' eyes widened. "No?" His eyes bulged. "*No?*" His next words were not, entirely, coherent.

Maurice grinned at Antonina.

"Never actually seen him gobble before. Have you?"

Antonina matched his grin. "Oh, any number of times." The grin began a demure smirk. "Intimate circumstances, you understand?"

Maurice nodded sagely. "Of course. Dancing naked on his chest, that sort of thing."

"Not to mention the whip and the iced—"

"*Enough!*" roared Belisarius. He slammed his fist on the table.

Antonina and Maurice peered at him with identical, quizzical expressions. Much like two owls might study a bellowing mouse.

"He usually does that much better, I seem to recall," mused Antonina.

"*Much* better," agreed Maurice. "The key is under-statement. The sense of steel under the soft voice."

Belisarius began to roar again; but, seeing the widening grins, managed to bring himself under control.

"*Why not?*" he demanded, through clenched teeth.

Maurice's grin faded. The grizzled veteran stroked his stiff, curly gray beard. "I won't do it," he replied, "because she's right and you're wrong. You *are* thinking like a fretful husband—instead of a general."

He waved down Belisarius' protest. "She doesn't need me because she's not going to be fighting pitched battles on the open field against vastly superior forces. *You are.*"

Antonina nodded.

Again, Belisarius began to protest; again, Maurice drove him down.

"Besides, she'll have Ashot. That stubby little Armenian may not have quite as much battlefield experience as I do, but he's not far short of the mark. You know that as well as I do. He's certainly got the experience to handle whatever Antonina will run up against in Alexandria."

"But—"

"Oh—*be quiet*, young man," snapped Maurice. For just an instant, the chiliarch's stony face reverted to an expression he had not worn in years. Not since the days he had taken under his wing a precocious teenage officer, fresh from his father's little estate in Thrace, and taught him the trade of war.

"Have you *already* forgotten your own battle plan?"

Belisarius sat back. Maurice snorted.

"Thought so. Since when do you subordinate strategy to tactics, young man? Alexandria's just a step on the road. Your whole strategy against the Malwa pivots on seapower. While you distract them in Persia, Antonina will lead a flanking attack against the enemy's logistics, in alliance—we hope—with the Kingdom of Axum. The Ethiopians, with their naval power, are critical to that plan. For that matter, the Axumite navy will be essential for providing support to the rebellion in Majarashtra which you did everything in your power to foment, while you were in India. They'll need cannons, gunpowder—everything you've talked about supplying them. That's why you've always insisted on building our armaments industry in Alexandria. So we can provide logistical support for the Ethiopians and the Indian rebellion."

The chiliarch took a deep breath. "For all those reasons, Ashot is far better suited to serve as her adviser than I am. The man's a former seaman. What I know about boats—" He snapped his fingers. "Not to mention the Ethiopians," he rolled on. "Ashot's familiar with them—even speaks the language. I know exactly two words in Ge'ez. Beer, and the future subjunctive tense of the verb 'to copulate.' That'll be useful, coordinating an allied naval campaign and a transoceanic logistics route!"

Belisarius slumped into his chair.

"All right," he said sourly. "But I still insist that she take Valentinian and Anastasius! They're the best fighters we've got. She'll need the protection they can—"

"For what?" demanded Maurice. He planted his thick hands on his knees and leaned forward. For a moment, he and Belisarius matched glares. Then Maurice's lips quirked. He cocked an eye at the little Egyptian woman sitting across the table.

"Are you planning to lead any cavalry charges, girl?"

Antonina giggled.

"Furious boarding parties, storming across the decks of ships?"
Giggle, giggle.

"Leading the troops scaling the walls of a town under siege?"
Giggle, giggle, giggle.

"Cut and thrust? Hack and hew?"

The giggles erupted into outright laughter.

"Actually," choked Antonina, "I was thinking more along the
lines of guiding from the rear. You know. Ladylike."

She leaned back, arching her neck haughtily, and began pointing
with an imperious finger. "You there! That way. And you—over
there. Move smartly, d'you hear?"

Belisarius rubbed his face. "It's not that simple, Maurice—and
you know it, even if Antonina doesn't."

For a moment, the old crooked smile came back. A feeble trav-
esty of it, rather.

"Aren't you the one who taught me the law of battle? 'Everything gets fucked up as soon as the enemy arrives. That's why—' "

"—he's called the enemy," concluded Maurice. The veteran
shook his head. "That's not the point, Belisarius. It may well happen, despite all our plans, that Antonina finds herself swept up in
the fray. So be it. She'll still have hundreds of Thracian bucellarii
protecting her, each and every one of whom—as you damn well
know—will lay down his life for her, if need be. None of them may
be quite as murderous as Valentinian or Anastasius, but they're still
the best soldiers in the world. In my humble opinion. If they can't
protect her, Valentinian and Anastasius won't make the difference.

"*Whereas*," he snarled, "the two of them might very well make
the difference for *you*. Because unlike Antonina, you *will* be leading cavalry charges and hacking and hewing way more than any
respectable general has any business doing."

Glare.

"As you well know."

Maurice stared at Belisarius in silence. The general slouched
further down in his chair. Further. Further.

"Never actually seen him pout before," mused the chiliarch.
Again, he cocked his eye at Antonina. "Have you?"

"Oh, certainly!" piped the little woman. "Any number of times.
Intimate circumstances, of course. When I have a headache and
refuse to smear olive oil all over his—"

"Enough," whined Belisarius.

Antonina and Maurice peered at him with identical, quizzical expressions. Much like two mice might study a whimpering piece of cheese.

Several hours later, Belisarius was in a more philosophical mood.

"I suppose it'll work out all right, in the end," he said, almost complacently.

Antonina levered herself up on her elbow and smiled down at her husband.

"Feeling less anxiety-ridden, are we?"

Belisarius stretched out his legs and clasped his hands behind his head.

"Now that I've had more time to think about it," he allowed graciously, "I've decided that perhaps Maurice was—"

"Liar!" laughed Antonina, slapping his arm. "You haven't been doing any thinking at all since we came to bed! Other than figuring out new and bizarre positions from which to stick your—"

"Don't be coarse, woman," grunted Belisarius. "Besides, I didn't hear you complaining. Rather the opposite, judging from the noises you were making."

"You didn't hear me claim that I was enjoying the metaphysics of the enterprise, either."

She sprawled flat on the bed, aping her husband's pose. Hands clasped behind her head, legs stretched out.

"I say," she pontificated, "now that I've had a bit of time to ponder the question—in between getting fucked silly—I have come to the conclusion that perhaps that uncouth Maurice fellow may have raised the odd valid point, here and there."

Belisarius eyed his wife's naked body, glistening with sweat. Antonina smiled seraphically. She took a deep breath, swelling her heavy breasts, then languidly spread her legs.

"Ontologically speaking, of course," she continued, "the man's daft. But the past several hours of epistemological discourse have led me to the tentative conclusion that perhaps—"

She spread her legs wider. Took another deep breath.

"—some of the fellow's more Socratic excogitations may have elucidated aspects of the purely phenomenological ramifications of—"

Belisarius discarded all complacency. Antonina stopped talking then, though she was by no means silent.

Some time later, she murmured, "Yes, all anxieties seem to be gone."

"That's because my brains are gone," came her husband's sleepy reply. "Fucked right out of my head."

In the morning, Photius made an entrance into his parents' sleeping chamber and perched himself upon their bed. Despite the many other changes in his life, the boy insisted on maintaining this precious daily ritual. A pox on imperial protocol and decorum.

The gaggle of servants and bodyguards who now followed the young Emperor everywhere remained outside in the corridor. The servants thought the entire situation was grotesque—and quite demeaning to their august status as imperial valets and maids. But they maintained a discreet silence. The bodyguards were members of the general's Thracian bucellarii, led by a young cataphract named Julian. Julian had been assigned the task of serving as Photius' chief bodyguard for two reasons. First, he was married to Hypatia, the young woman who had been Photius' nanny for years. (And still was, though she now bore the resplendent title of "imperial governess.") Second, for all his youth and cheerful temperament, Julian was a very tough soldier. Julian and the men under his command had made quite clear upon assuming their new duties that they were not even remotely interested in listening to the complaints of menials. So, while Photius enjoyed his private moment with his parents, his bodyguards chatted amiably in the corridor outside and his servants nursed their injured pride.

Photius' stay in his parents' bedroom was longer than usual. His stepfather was leaving that day, to begin his new campaign in Mesopotamia. Photius no longer felt the same dread of that prospective absence that he once had. The boy's confidence in Belisarius' ability to overcome all obstacles and perils was now positively sublime. But he would miss him, deeply. More deeply now, perhaps, than ever before.

Eventually, however, he emerged. A new sense of duty had fallen on the boy's little shoulders, and he knew that his stepfather had many responsibilities of his own that day.

"All right," he sighed, after closing the door behind him. "Let's go. What's first?"

Julian grinned down at him. "Your tutor in rhetoric insists—*insists*—that you must see him at once. Something to do with tropes, I believe. He says your slackness in mastering synecdoche has become a public scandal."

Glumly, Photius began trudging down the corridor. "That's great," he muttered. "Just great." The boy craned his neck, looking up at Julian's homely, ruddy-hued face. "Do you have any idea how *boring* that man is?"

"Look at it this way, Emperor. Someday you'll be able to have him executed for high tedium."

Photius scowled. "No I won't. I think he's already dead."

Trudge, trudge.

"Life was a lot more fun, before they made me Emperor."

Trudge, trudge.

Before mounting his horse, Belisarius gave Antonina a last, lingering embrace.

"How long, do you think?" she whispered.

Her husband shrugged. "Impossible to tell, love. If things go as we've planned—and that's a big if—we won't see each other for a year and a half, thereabouts. You'll have to wait until July of next year for the monsoon to be blowing the way we need it."

She grimaced. "What a way to meet."

Belisarius smiled. "That's *if* things go as planned. If they don't—who knows? We may meet sooner."

Staring up at him, Antonina found it impossible to match his smile. She knew the unspoken—and far more likely—corollary.

If our plans fail, one or both of us will probably be dead.

She buried her face into his shoulder. "Such a long time," she murmured. "You've only been back for a few months since your trip to India. And that lasted a year and a half."

Belisarius stroked her long black hair. "I know. But it can't be helped."

"*Damn Theodora*," hissed Antonina. "If it weren't for her obsession with keeping the gunpowder weapons under female control, I wouldn't have to—"

"That's nonsense!" snapped Belisarius. He took his wife by the shoulders and held her away from him. Then, with none of his usual whimsy, said:

"Even if Theodora didn't have her foibles, *I'd* insist that you command the Theodoran Cohort. You're the best person for the job. It's that simple."

Antonina stared back at him for a moment, before lowering her eyes. "So *long*," she whispered. "A year and a half." Suddenly, unexpectedly, she smiled. "But at least we'll be able to stay in touch. I almost forgot—a present came from John of Rhodes yesterday."

She turned and summoned a servant standing nearby in the courtyard. The man advanced, bearing a package wrapped in heavy layers of wool.

Antonina took the package from him and unfolded the cloth. Within, carefully nestled, were two identical objects.

She held one of them out to her husband.

"Here they are. John's first telescopes. One for you and one for me."

Grinning delightedly, Belisarius immediately began looking through the telescope. He became so entranced with the marvelous contrivance that he momentarily forgot everything else, until Antonina's little cough brought him back.

"Wonderful," he said, wrapping the telescope back into the woolen cloths. "With these, and the new semaphore stations, we'll be able to communicate within days."

Antonina chuckled. "Once the stations are built, that is. And assuming John can produce enough of the telescopes."

"They will and he will," said her husband confidently. He stroked her cheek. "Count on it, love. Within a few months, you'll get your first message from me."

There was nothing more to be said. For a moment, husband and wife gazed at each other. Then, a last embrace; a last kiss. Belisarius mounted his horse and rode out of the courtyard, Maurice at his side. His two personal bodyguards, Anastasius and Valentinian, followed just behind.

At the gate, Belisarius turned in his saddle and waved. Antonina did not wave back. She simply held up the telescope.

"I'll be waiting for your message!" she shouted.

An hour later, Irene arrived, bearing her own cloth-wrapped gifts.

"Don't drop them!" she warned Antonina, as she passed the bundle over. "I stole them from Theodora's own wine cellar. Best vintage in the Roman Empire."

Antonina staggered a bit, from the weight.

"Mother of God, how many bottles did you bring?"

Irene propelled her little friend down the corridor. "As many as we need to get you through the day. Tradition, girl, tradition. The last time Belisarius went off on one of these quests, you and I got blind drunk. Well, you did. I was simply there to lend a comforting shoulder."

"Lying wench!" squawked Antonina. "You passed out before I did."

"A fable," stated Irene firmly. "I fell asleep, that's all."

Antonina snorted. "Sure. On the floor, flat on your belly."

"I've only got your word for that," came the dignified response. "Hearsay, pure hearsay."

Once in the salon, Antonina lined up the bottles on a side table. "Like so many soldiers," she murmured admiringly.

Irene seized the first bottle. "It'll be a massacre. Get the goblets."

Two hours later, well into the carnage, Antonina hiccuped.

" 'Nough o' this maudlinnininess!" Another hiccup. "Le'ss look t'the future! Be leaving soon, we will. For Egypt. 'S'my homeland, y'know?" Hiccup. "Land o' my birt. *Birth*."

Studiously, she poured more wine into her goblet. "I'm still s'prised Theodora agreed t'let you go," she said. "Never thought she let her chief spy"—giggle—"spy-*ess*, should say, out of her zight. Sight."

Irene's shrug was a marvel—a simple gesture turned into a profound, philosophical statement.

"What else c'ld she do? *Somebody* has to go to India. *Somebody* 'as to rish—re-ish—" Deep breath; concentration. "*Re-es-ta-blish* contact with Shakuntala."

Irene levered herself up on the couch, assuming a proud and erect stance. The dignity of the moment, alas, was undermined by flatulence.

"How gross," she pronounced, as if she were discussing someone else's gaucherie. Then, breezed straight on to the matter at hand. Again, a pronouncement:

"I am the obvious person for the job. My qualifications are immense. Legion, I dare say."

"Ha!" barked Antonina. "You're a woman, that's it. Who else would Theodora trust for that kind of—of—of—" She groped for the words.

"Subtle statecraft," offered Irene. "Deft diplomacy."

Antonina sneered. "I was thinking more along the lines of—of—"

"Sophisticated stratagems. Sagacious subterfuges."

"—of—of—"

"Dirty rotten sneaky—"

" 'At's it! 'At's it!"

Both women dissolved into uproarious laughter. This went on for a bit. Quite a bit. A sober observer might have drawn unkind conclusions.

Eventually, however, they settled down. Another bottle was immediately brought to the execution block. Half the bottle gone, Antonina peered at Irene solemnly.

"Hermogenes'll be staying wit' me, you know. In Egypt. After we part comp'ny and you head off t'India. You'll be having your own heartbreak then. But we prob'ly won' be able to com-mimmi—*commiserate*—properly. Then. Be too busy. Ressaponza-bilities. So we better do it now."

Irene sprawled back on her couch. "Too late. 'S'already done." She shook her head sadly. "Hermo-genes and I are *hic*—" Hiccup. "Are *hic*— Dammit! Hist—*hic*story. Dammit! *History.*"

Antonina's eyes widened.

"What? But I heard—rumor flies—he asked you to marry him."

Irene winced. "Yes, he did. I'd been dreading it for months. That was the death-knell, of course."

Seeing her friend's puzzled frown, Irene laughed. Half-gaily; half-sadly.

"Sweet woman," she murmured. "You forget Hermogenes's not Belisarius." She spread her hands ruefully. Then, remembering too late that one hand held a full wine goblet, stared even more ruefully at the floor.

"Sorry about that," she muttered.

Antonina shrugged. "We've got servants to clean it up. Lots of 'em."

"Don't care about th'floor! Best wine in the Roman Empire." She tore her eyes from the gruesome sight. Tried to focus on Antonina.

"Something about Hermogenes not being Belisarius," prompted the little Egyptian. "But I don't see the point. *You* don't have a disreputable past to live down, like I did." Giggle. "Still do, actually. That's the thing about the past, you know? Since it's over it never goes away and you're always stuck with the damned thing." Her eyes almost crossed with deep thought. "Hey, that's philosophical. I bet even Plato never said it so well."

Irene smiled. "It's not the past that's the problem. With me and Hermogenes. It's the *future*. Hermogenes—" She waved her hand again, but managed to restrain the gesture before adding further insult to the best vintage in the Roman Empire. "—Hergomenes," she continued. "He's a sweet man, no doubt about it. But—conventional, y'know? Outside of military tactics, anyway. He wants a proper Greek wife. Matron. Not—" She sighed, slumping back into the couch. "Not a spymaster who's out and about doing God knows what at any hour of the day and night."

Irene stared sadly at her half-filled wine goblet. Then, drained away her sorrows.

Antonina peered at her owlishly.

"You sure?" she asked. Irene lurched up and tottered over to the wine-bearing side-table. Another soldier fell to the fray.

"Oh, yes," she murmured. She turned and stared down at Antonina, maintaining a careful balance. "Do I really seem like the matron-type to you?"

Antonina giggled; then, guffawed.

Irene smiled. "No, not hardly." She shrugged fatalistically. "Fact is, I don't think I'll ever marry. I'm jus—I don' know. Too—I don' know. Something. Can't imagine a man who'd live wit' it."

She staggered back to her couch and collapsed upon it.

Antonina examined her. "Does that bother you?" she asked, very slowly and carefully.

Irene stared at the far wall. "Yes," she replied softly. Sadly.

But a moment later, with great vehemence, she shook her head.

" 'Nough o' this maudilinitity!" she cried, raising her goblet high. " 'Ere's to adaventureness!"

Two hours later, Antonina gazed down at Irene in triumph. "Belly down, onna floor, jus' like I said."

She lurched to her feet, holding the last wine bottle aloft like a battle standard. "Vittorous again!" she cried. Then, proving the point, collapsed on top of her friend.

The servants who carried the two women into Antonina's bedroom a short time later neither clucked with scandal nor muttered
with disrespect. Not with Julian and three other grinning bucellarii
following close behind, ready to enforce Thracian protocol.

"Let 'em sleep it off together," commanded Julian.

He turned to his comrades.

"Tradition."

Thracian heads nodded solemnly.

The next morning, after he entered the bedchamber, Photius
was seized with dismay.

"Where's my mother?" he demanded.

Irene's eyes popped open. Closed with instant pain.

"Where's my mother?" he cried.

Irene stared at him through slitted eyelids.

"Who're you?" she croaked.

"I'm the Emperor of Rome!"

Irene hissed. "Fool boy. Do you know how many Roman emperors have been assassinated?"

"Where's my mother?"

Her eyelids crunched with agony. "Yell one more time and I'll
add another emperor to the list."

She dragged a pillow over her head. From beneath the silk-
covered cushion her voice faintly emerged:

"Go away. If you want your stupid mother—the drunken
sot—go look for her somewhere else."

"Where's my mother?"

"Find the nearest horse. Crazy woman'll be staring at it."

After the boy charged out of the room, heading for the stables,
Irene gingerly lifted the pillow. The blinding sight of sunrise filter-
ing through the heavy drapes immediately sent her scurrying back
for cover. Only her voice remained at large in the room.

"Stupid fucking tradition."

Moan.

"Why can't that woman just commit suicide like any reasonable
abandoned wife?"

Moan.

Chapter 7

MESOPOTAMIA
Summer, 531 A.D.

When he encountered the first units from the Army of Syria, just outside Callinicum, Belisarius heaved a small sigh of relief.

Baresmanas, riding next to him at the head of the column, said nothing. But the very stillness of his face gave him away.

"Go ahead and laugh," grumbled Belisarius.

Baresmanas did not take Belisarius up on the offer. Diplomatic tact was far too ingrained in his habits. He simply nodded his head, and murmured in return:

"There are certain disadvantages to elite troops from the capital, accustomed to imperial style. It cannot be denied."

The sahrdaran twisted in his saddle and looked back at the long column. The cavalrymen were riding along a road near the right bank of the Euphrates. The road was not paved, but it was quite wide and well-maintained. The road ran from Callinicum to the Cilician Gates, passing through the river towns of Barbalissus and Zeugma. It was the principal route bearing trade goods between the Roman Empire and Persia.

Belisarius' own bucellarii rode at the head of the column—a thousand cataphracts, three abreast, maintaining good order. Behind them came the small contingent of artillery wagons and ambulances, along with the ten rocket-bearing chariots which the general had dubbed *katyushas*. These vehicles were also maintaining a good order.

Then—

Straggling and straying, drifting and disjointed, came the remaining twenty-five hundred heavy cavalry in Belisarius' little army.

The majority of these—two thousand men—were from the Constantinople garrison. The remainder were from Germanicus' Army of Illyria. The Illyrians had maintained a semblance of good order for the first few hundred miles of their forced march. Unlike the troops from the capital, they had some recent experience on campaign. But even they, by the time the army passed through the Cilician Gates into the northern desert of Syria, had become as disorganized as the Greek cataphracts.

Disorganized—and exceedingly disgruntled.

The troops were much too far back for Baresmanas to hear their conversations, but he had no difficulty imagining them. He had been listening to their grousing for days, even weeks. The troops from Constantinople, in particular, had not been hesitant in making their sentiments known, each and every night, as they slumped about their campfires.

Crazy fucking Thracian.

How did this lunatic ever get to be a general, anyway?

By the time we get there, a litter of kittens could whip us, we'll be so worn out.

Crazy fucking Thracian.

How did this lunatic ever get to be a general, anyway?

"You *have* been pushing them rather hard," said Baresmanas.

Belisarius snorted. "You think so?" He turned in his own saddle, scowling. "In point of fact, Baresmanas, the pace we've been maintaining since we left Constantinople is considerably *less* than my own troops are accustomed to. For my bucellarii, this has been a pleasant promenade."

His scowl deepened. "*Two months*—to cover six hundred miles. Twenty miles a day, no better. For a large infantry army, that would be good. But for a small force of cavalrymen—on decent roads, most of the time—it's disgraceful."

Now, Barasmanas did laugh. More of a dry chuckle, perhaps. He pointed to the small group, led by two officers, trotting toward them from the direction of Callinicum.

"I take it you think these Syrian lads will be a good influence."

Belisarius examined the approaching Roman soldiers. "Not exactly. Those damned garritroopers are too full of themselves to take a bunch of scruffy border troops as an *example*. But I do believe I can use them to shame the bastards."

The oncoming officers were now close enough to discern their individual features.

"If I'm not mistaken," commented Baresmanas, "the two in front are Bouzes and Coutzes. The same brothers whom we captured just a few days before the battle at Mindouos. While they were—ah—"

"Leading a reconnaisance in force," said Belisarius firmly.

"Ah. Is that what it was?"

The sahrdaran's eyebrows lifted.

"At the time, I had the impression the headstrong fellows were charging about trying to capture a mysterious pay caravan which, oddly enough, was never found by anyone."

Belisarius shook his head sadly. "Isn't it just terrible? The way vicious rumors get started?"

Very firmly:

"Reconnaissance in force."

Less than a minute later, the oncoming Romans reached Belisarius. The general reined in his horse. Behind him, the long column came to a halt. A moment later, Maurice drew up alongside.

Bouzes and Coutzes sat in their saddles stiff-backed and erect. Their young faces were reasonably expressionless, but it took no great perspicacity to deduce that they were more than a bit apprehensive. Their last encounter with Belisarius had been unfortunate, to say the least.

But Belisarius had known that the brothers would be leading the troops from the Army of Syria, and he had already decided on his course of action. Whatever hotheaded folly the two had been guilty of in the past, both Sittas and Hermogenes had been favorably impressed by the brothers in the three years which had elapsed since the battle of Mindouos.

So he greeted them with a wide smile and an outstretched hand, and made an elaborate show of introducing them to Baresmanas. He was a bit concerned, for a moment, that the brothers might behave rudely toward the sahrdaran. Bouzes and Coutzes, during the time he had worked with them leading up to the battle of

Mindouos, had been quite vociferous regarding their dislike for Persians. But the brothers allayed that concern immediately.

As soon as the introductions were made, Coutzes said to Baresmanas:

"Your nephew Kurush has already arrived at Callinicum. Along with seven hundred of your cavalrymen. They've set up camp just next to our own."

"We would have brought him with us to meet you," added Bouzes, "but the commander of the Roman garrison in Callinicum wouldn't allow it."

"The stupid jackass is buried up to his ass in regulations," snapped Coutzes. "Said it was forbidden to allow Persian military personnel beyond the trading emporium."

Belisarius laughed. Romans and Persians had been trading for as long as they had been fighting each other. In truth, trade was the basic relationship. For all that the two empires had clashed many times on the field of battle, peace was the more common state of affairs. And, during wartime or peacetime, the trade never stopped. Year after year, decade after decade, century after century, caravans had been passing along that very road.

But—empires being empires—the trade was heavily regulated. (Officially. The border populations, Roman and Persian alike, were the world's most notorious smugglers.) For decades, Callinicum had been established as the official entrepot for Persians seeking to trade with Rome—just as Nisibis was, on the other side of the border, for Romans desiring to enter Persia.

"Leave it to a garrison commander," growled Maurice. "He *does* know we're at war with the Malwa, doesn't he? In alliance with Persia?"

Bouzes nodded. Coutzes snarled:

"He says that doesn't change regulations. Gave us quite a lecture, he did, on the unrelenting struggle against the mortal sin of smuggling."

Now, Baresmanas laughed. "My nephew wouldn't know how to smuggle if his life depended on it! He's much too rich."

Belisarius spurred his horse into motion. "Let's get to Callinicum. I'll have a word or two with this garrison commander."

"Just one or two?" asked Coutzes. He seemed a bit aggrieved.

Belisarius smiled. "Five, actually. *You are relieved of command.*"

"Oh."

" 'Deadly with a blade, is Belisarius,' " murmured Maurice.

They entered Callinicum two hours later, in mid-afternoon.

The general's first order of business was to ensure that the last group of builders and artisans still with him were adequately housed. When he left Constantinople, Belisarius had brought no less than eight hundred such men with his army. Small groups of them had been dropped off, at appropriate intervals, to begin the construction of the semaphore stations which would soon become the Roman Empire's new communication network. Callinicum would be the final leg of the Constantinople-Mesopotamia branch of that web.

That business done, Belisarius went off to speak his five words to the garrison commander.

Five words, in the event, grew into several hundred. The garrison commander's replacement had to be relieved, himself. After the general took a few dozen words to inform the new commander that Belisarius would be taking half the town's garrison with him into Mesopotamia, the man sputtered at length on the imperative demands of the war against illicit trade.

Belisarius spoke five more words.

His replacement, in turn, had to be relieved. After Belisarius used perhaps two hundred words, more or less thinking aloud, to reach the decision that it made more sense to take the entire garrison except for a token force, the third commander in as many hours shrieked on the danger of brigand raids.

Belisarius spoke five more words.

In the end, command of the Roman forces in Callinicum fell on the shoulders of a grizzled, gap-toothed hecatontarch.

"Hundred men'll be dandy," that worthy informed the general. "Just enough to keep reasonable order in the town. Nothing else for them to do. Callinicum's a fortress, for the sake of Christ—the walls are forty feet high and as wide to match. The sorry-ass brigands in these parts'd die of nosebleed if they climbed that high."

Cheerfully: "As for smuggling, fuck it. You couldn't stop it with the whole Roman army. Soon as the sun goes down, you throw a rock off these walls in any direction you'll bounce it off three smugglers before it hits the ground. At least one of them'll be a relative of mine."

Very cheerfully: "Any given Tuesday, prob'ly be my wife."

At sunset, Belisarius led his army out of Callinicum toward the military camp a few miles away where the forces from the Army of Syria were awaiting them. The freshly-conscripted soldiers from the town's garrison—seven hundred *very* unhappy infantrymen—were marched out between units of the general's bucellarii. The Thracians encouraged the new recruits with tales of glory in the past, booty in the future, and drawn bows in the present. Cataphract bows, with hundred-pound pulls and arrowheads you could shave with.

Baresmanas, riding at the head of the column, was out of earshot of the Callinicum garrison. But he had no difficulty imagining their muttered conversation.

Crazy fucking Thracian.

How did this lunatic ever get to be a general, anyway?

Chapter 8

Kurush's pavilion was far smaller than the gigantic construct which the Emperor of Malwa had erected at the siege of Ranapur. But, thought Belisarius, it was possibly even more richly adorned and accoutered. And with much better taste.

As he reclined on a pile of plump, silk-covered cushions placed at one end of a low table, Kurush himself placed a goblet of wine before him. Belisarius eyed the thing uneasily. It was not the wine which caused that trepidation. The general had no doubt that it was the finest vintage produced by Persia. No, it was the goblet itself. The drinking vessel was easily the most elaborate and expensive such object Belisarius had ever seen. For all the goblet's massive size, the design was thin and delicate, especially the flower-shaped stem—and, worst of all, made entirely of glass. Embedded throughout the bowl was gold leaf, highlighting the intricate facets cut in the form of overlapping, slightly concave disks. The finishing touch was the four medallions inset around the side of the bowl, standing out in high relief. About an inch in diameter, each carried a marvelous etching of a winged horse.

Gold medallions, naturally. Except for the silver wings, and the tiny little garnet eyes.

Belisarius glanced around the table. Bouzes, Coutzes and Maurice were all staring at their own identical goblets. The brothers with astonishment, Maurice with deep gloom.

"Afraid to touch the damned thing," he heard Maurice mutter.

Fortunately, Baresmanas intervened.

"Have no fear, comrades," he said, smiling. "My nephew has two chests full of these things."

He gestured gaily. "Besides, even if you should happen to drop one, it would hardly break on *this* floor."

The four Romans eyed the carpet. In truth, the pile was so thick that the cushions on which they sat were entirely redundant.

Kurush, taking his place at the other end of the table from Belisarius, frowned. Not with irritation, but simply from puzzlement. "Is there a problem?" he asked. His Greek, like that of most Persian noblemen, was accented but fluent.

Baresmanas chuckled. "Not everyone, nephew, is accustomed to drinking wine out of a king's ransom."

The young Persian stared at the goblet in his hand. "This thing?" He looked up at his uncle. "It is valuable?"

All four of the Romans joined Baresmanas in the ensuing laughter. Their reaction was not diplomatic, perhaps, but they found it impossible to resist.

Fortunately, Kurush proved to be the affable type. He seemed to possess little of the prickly hauteur of most Persian noblemen. After a moment, he even joined in the laughter himself.

"I'm afraid I don't pay any attention to these matters," he confessed. Shrugging: "My retainers take care of that." He made a sweeping gesture. "But—please, please! Drink up! You must all be dying of thirst, after that miserable desert."

Kurush's words swept hesitation aside. All four Romans drank deeply from their goblets. And found, not to their surprise, that the vintage was marvelous.

Belisarius took advantage of the distraction to give Kurush a careful study. He had already learned, from Baresmanas, that Kurush had been charged by Emperor Khusrau to be the Persians' principal military liaison with Belisarius and his Roman forces.

The nobleman was in his mid-twenties, he estimated. The young officer was tall and slender, with a narrow face and rather delicate features.

At first glance, he reminded Belisarius of certain hyper-cultured Athenian aesthetes whom the general had occasionally encountered. The sort of soulful young men who could not complete a sentence without two or three allusions to the classics, and whose view of the world was, to put it mildly, impractical.

The likeness was emphasized by the way in which Kurush wore his clothing. The garments themselves were expensive and well-made. (As were those of Athenian aesthetes—all of whom were aristocrats, not shepherds.) But they seemed to have been tossed on with little care for precision of fit and none at all for color coordination.

Closer examination, however, undermined the initial impression. Kurush's hands, though slim-fingered, were strong-looking. And Belisarius did not miss the significance of the worn indentation on Kurush's right thumb. Unlike Romans, who favored the three-fingered draw, Persians drew their bows with thumb-rings.

Then, there was the way he moved. Kurush's stride, his gestures—even his facial expressions—all had a nervous quickness about them. Almost eager, like a spirited thoroughbred before a race. They bore no resemblance whatever to the affected languor of aesthetes.

Finally, there were the eyes. Like most Medes—and most Athenian aesthetes, for that matter—Kurush's eyes were brown. But there was nothing vague and unfocussed in their gaze. Despite his youth, the Persian was already beginning to develop faint wrinkles around the sockets. Those wrinkles did not come from studying poetry in Athens by candlelight. They came from studying terrain under the scorching desert sun.

Kurush's first words, after setting down his goblet, were to Maurice. "I understand that you were in command of the Roman forces on the hill, at Mindouos."

Maurice nodded. Kurush shook his head.

"You must have laughed at us, trying to drive our horses up that demon-created slope."

Maurice hesitated, gauging the Persian. Then, with a little shrug: "You'd have done better to dismount."

Kurush smiled. Quite cheerfully. "So I discovered! My horse was shot out from under me right at the start. I cursed my bad luck, at the time. But I think it was all that saved my life. On foot, I could duck behind boulders. Not even *your* arrows could penetrate rock!"

Again, he shook his head. "I'd been warned—" He nodded toward Baresmanas. "—by my uncle, in fact, that no one in the world uses more powerful bows than Roman cataphracts. I didn't shrug off his warning—not *that* voice of experience—but I still hadn't expected to see an arrow drive right through my mount's armor."

Then, with a frown:

"You've got a very slow rate of fire, though. Do you really think the trade-off is worth it?"

Belisarius had to fight down a laugh. The young Persian's frown was not hostile. Not in the least. For all the world, it reminded the general of nothing so much as a young aesthete's frown, contemplating the relative merits of two styles of lyric poetry.

Maurice shrugged. "I don't think the question can be answered in purely military terms. There's the matter of national temperament, too. You Persians have a flair for mounted archery that I don't think Romans could ever match. So why make the attempt? Better to concentrate on what we do well, rather than become second-rate Persian imitations."

Kurush nodded. "Well said." The young officer sighed. "It's probably all a moot point, anyway. These infernal new Malwa devices have changed everything."

"Have you seen them in action?" asked Belisarius.

Kurush winced. "Oh, yes. Three times, in fact. I've been at all the pitched battles we fought against the invaders on the open field, until we finally decided to withdraw and take a defensive stance at Babylon."

"Describe the invasion for me, if you would," requested Belisarius. He gestured politely toward Baresmanas. "Your uncle has given me an excellent overall picture, but he was not a direct eyewitness. I would appreciate more detail."

"Certainly." Kurush drained his goblet and reached for one of the small amphorae on the table. He began speaking while in the process of pouring himself more wine.

"There were hundreds of ships in the Malwa invasion fleet. Gigantic vessels, many of them. I'm no seaman, but those of my staff with maritime experience tell me that their big sailing ships have a carrying capacity of at least a thousand tons."

"More like two thousand," interjected Belisarius, "if they're the same ships I saw being built at Bharakuccha."

Kurush eyed him with respectful surprise. "I did not realize you had experience with naval matters."

Belisarius chuckled. "I don't. Or very little, at least. But one of my companions in Bharakuccha was Garmat, the chief adviser for

the King of Axum. That was his estimate, after seeing the ships. I
think that estimate can be trusted. In my experience, all high-
ranking Ethiopians are most definitely naval experts."

"That's my experience as well," commented Baresmanas. He
grimaced. "Two thousand tons. I don't think any Persian ship has
that big a carrying capacity."

"Nor any of ours," added Bouzes. "Except for a handful of the
grain ships which sail out of Egypt."

Belasarius nodded toward Kurush. "Please continue."

"The fleet arrived with no warning—well—" He scowled. "No
warning which was heeded. A few merchants gave the alarm, but
they were ignored by the imperial authorities." The scowl deepened. "Arrogant bastards."

Belisarius was amused to see the stiff, diplomatically expressionless faces of Bouzes, Coutzes, and Maurice. It was the commonly
held opinion of most Romans that *all* Persian officials were "arrogant bastards." Belisarius did not share that opinion—Baresmanas
and Kurush were not the first Persian nobles he had found likeable,
even charming—but there was no denying that the charge had
some basis in fact. Roman officials also, of course, could often be
accused of "arrogant bastardom." But there was nothing in the
world quite like a Persian aristocrat—especially one who also occupied a post in the imperial hierarchy—when it came to sheer,
unadulterated, icy haughtiness. Compared to such, Rajput nobility
could almost be described as casual and warm-hearted. Even the
Malwa dynastic clan, for all their unparalleled brutality and mega-
lomania, did not—quite—exhibit that sense of unthinking superiority over all other men.

Apparently, Roman tact was insufficient. Either that, or Kurush
was more perceptive than Belisarius had realized. The young Persian glanced around the table at the distant, polite expressions of
the Romans. Then, with a little smile, added, "But perhaps no
more so than others of their ilk."

He quaffed some wine. Then continued:

"The fleet entered the confluence of the Tigris-Euphrates Rivers
and landed a huge army. The ships carried horses and even a score
of elephants, in addition to their terrible new weapons. Within two
days, they overwhelmed the garrison at Charax."

The scowl returned in full force. "The murderous swine massacred the garrison and enslaved the entire population. The women-
folk were treated horridly, especially by those stinking Ye-tai

barbarians whom the Malwa seem to dote on. The nobility were singled out for particular persecution. The Malwa were not in the least interested in obtaining ransom. Instead, they slaughtered all the male azadan—even babies—and all noblewomen except those who were young and pretty. Such girls were taken by the Malwa officers as concubines."

He ran his long fingers through his thick hair. The scowl faded a bit, pushed aside by an expression of scholarly thoughtfulness. "In all the centuries that we Persians and you Romans have fought each other, there have been many atrocities committed." He waved his hand. "By both sides, by both sides. Still—I cannot think of a single instance of such gross and unvarnished cruelty. Not one."

"There *is* no such instance," stated Baresmanas firmly. "Nothing on such a scale, at least. And let us also note that, for all the savageries which both our people have been guilty of in our dealings with each other, there have also been many—*many*—instances of generosity and chivalry."

He bestowed an appreciative look on Belisarius. "Your mercy at Mindouos being one of the most outstanding examples."

"Well said!" exclaimed his nephew. Kurush drained his wine. When he set the goblet back on the table, his expression combined good cheer and ruefulness.

"I *know*," he chuckled. "For a time, there, I was quite certain my throat was going to be slit." He shuddered, slightly. "Three of your damned Isaurians had me down—talk about mean, tough bastards!—grinning like wolves. They sounded like wolves, too, quarreling over which one was going to get the first bite."

He grinned at Maurice. "Then one of you Thracian lads rode up and reasoned with them. Partly with a drawn bow, and partly with talk of my money."

Maurice grinned back. "And how much was your ransom?"

Kurush snorted. "Enough to set those three Isaurians up for life! Would you believe, the damned barbarians demanded—"

He broke off. "But I'm straying. That was three years ago. The Malwa are here today—and, as my learned uncle so cogently remarks, I think we will see no such instances of mercy and forbearance coming from the Malwa."

"It is not their method," agreed Belisarius. "The Malwa aristocracy is already rich. They are not even slightly interested in ransom.

And the troops, who might be, are completely subjugated to their rule."

He drained his own cup. "The Malwa seek to conquer the world. Nothing less. And they intend to rule it with a hand of iron. Charax was only the first atrocity of the many they will commit in Persia—and Rome, later, if Persia falls. But it was by no means their first. By no means." The general's face grew bleak. "I was at Ranapur, when the Malwa broke the rebellion. Two hundred thousand people were still alive in that great city, when the Malwa finally breached the walls. Five days later, after unspeakable atrocities, there were not more than fifty survivors. A few young noblewomen tough enough to survive their ordeal, and then sold into slavery."

For a moment, the pavilion was filled with a grim silence. Then Maurice muttered:

"Continue, please."

Kurush shook off the mood. "After the Malwa finished their conquest of Charax, the bulk of their army proceeded upriver, accompanied by over a hundred of their smaller ships. The remainder of the fleet waited in Charax, while the Malwa began expanding and strengthening the port. We assume that those ships will return to India for further provisions, once the monsoon changes." He glanced toward the entrance of the pavilion, as if to gauge the season. "We're in the beginning of June, now. Within a month, the winds will be right for them."

Belisarius nodded. "Their fleet will sail for Bharakuccha in July. Then, after reprovisioning, they'll begin their return journey toward the end of October. Early November, at the latest."

"What are their actual military forces?" asked Coutzes.

Kurush spread his hands on the table and leaned back. "You'll find this hard to believe, but—"

"No, we won't," said Belisarius, quite forcefully, with a warning glance at Bouzes and Coutzes.

"—based on my own personal observation, I estimate the total number of their troops—*not counting the large garrison they left in Charax*—at two hundred thousand men."

When the expected Roman reaction did not emerge, Kurush's eyes widened slightly.

Maurice cleared his throat. "Break that down a bit, if you would."

Kurush paused, thinking.

"I don't think they have more than forty thousand cavalry. The great mass of their troops are infantry, and most of them seem of mediocre quality. The Ye-tai, of course, are quite ferocious in combat. But the Malwa seem to use them principally as a stiffener for their common troops."

"They're primarily security battalions," interjected Belisarius. "That's how I saw the Malwa using them, when I was in India. In battle, their main job is to make sure that the common soldiers obey their officers. They're utterly ruthless toward deserters or even stragglers."

Kurush nodded. "Most of the infantry are simply armed with traditional weapons. Spears, swords, axes. And their armor is flimsy, for the most part. As I said, mediocre-quality troops." He shrugged. "But with those huge numbers, they simply overwhelm their opposition. *After* they've ravaged the opponent with their demon weapons."

"Describe the weapons," said Belisarius.

Kurush spread his hands apologetically. "I will do so as best I can, Belisarius. But keep in mind that I only saw the damned things at a distance, and I was never sure exactly what I was watching."

"Let's do it the other way around, then. Let *me* tell you what I think the Malwa are using, and you can correct me based on your direct experience."

The Persian nodded. Belisarius took a sip of his wine, thinking, and then said, "I think—I *hope*, actually—their weapons fall into three main categories. Siege cannons, rockets, and grenades." After describing these three types of gunpowder weapons, based on his observations in India, Belisarius continued, "The rockets will be used in much the same manner that we Romans have traditionally used field artillery in a battle. The disadvantage of the rockets is their extreme inaccuracy—"

He hesitated for a moment, fighting temptation. His *own* rockets—the katyusha rockets—had proven to be fairly accurate, in tests. Not as accurate as catapults, but much less erratic than the Malwa rockets he had observed. Guided by Aide, Belisarius had had real venturi made for his rockets, using all the skills of Greek metalsmiths. He had even insisted on machining the bronze exhaust nozzles. But he hoped their accuracy would come as a surprise to the enemy. He had no reason to distrust Baresmanas and Kurush, or to suspect they were loose-mouthed. Still—

He glided over the problem, for the moment.

"—but they compensate by their destructiveness and their relative ease of operation. You don't have to lug around a heavy onager or scorpion to fire a rocket. Just a trough and a simple firing device. Then, too, the things tend to panic the opponent's cavalry horses."

Kurush nodded gloomily. "It's impossible to control horses under a rocket barrage."

Again, Belisarius hesitated, torn between the need for secrecy and distaste at hiding secrets from his own allies. This time, distaste won the struggle.

"That's not actually true, Kurush." Seeing the look of surprise in the young sahrdaran's face, Belisarius smiled crookedly.

"I thought the same, once, when I first encountered rockets. My subsequent experience, however, taught me that horses can become accustomed to the sound and fury of gunpowder weapons. The secret is to expose them to the noise at an early age. A full-grown warhorse, as a rule, will usually remain skittish. But a horse trained as a foal will manage well enough."

He gestured toward the open flap of the pavilion. "The horses which pull my katyushas, for instance, have been specially selected for their steadiness under fire. And most of my bucellarii have been equipped with mounts trained to stand up under gunpowder fire."

The two Persians at the table were stroking their beards thoughtfully. To Belisarius, their thoughts were obvious. *Awkwardly* obvious.

Great news. But we Persians have no gunpowder weapons with which to train our horses. How to steal them from the enemy? Or—better yet—convince the Romans to supply us with the infernal things?

For a moment, Belisarius and Baresmanas stared at each other. Then, seeing the Roman general's faint nod, Baresmanas looked away.

We will discuss the matter later was the meaning of the nod. That, and:

I have my opinion, but—

That was enough. An experienced diplomat, Baresmanas was well aware of the controversies which were undoubtedly raging among the Romans over this very delicate problem. An alliance with Persia was one thing. Arming the ancient Medean foe with gunpowder weapons was a different proposition altogether.

There was no point in pressing the matter at the moment, so Baresmanas changed the subject.

"And the grenades?" He pointed to Kurush. "According to my nephew, the things are solely used in close order assaults."

"He's quite right. That is their function. I never observed them used any other way in India."

He decided to pass on a secret, now. The enemy almost certainly knew it anyway. Some of their spies must have escaped the slaughter at the Hippodrome where Belisarius and Antonina crushed the Malwa-engineered Nika rebellion. If nothing else, the bodies of the traitor Narses and his companion Ajatasutra had never been found. Both Belisarius and Theodora were certain that the former Grand Chamberlain, with his legendary wiliness, had managed to make his escape.

So:

"My wife—she commands our only force of grenadiers, the Theodoran Cohort—*has* introduced a more long-range capability to grenade warfare."

He described, briefly, the sling and sling-staff methods of Antonina's grenadiers, before concluding: "—but, even so, we are still talking about bow-range, no more."

Baresmanas and Kurush nodded understandingly. Slings were not a weapon which Persian nobility favored personally, but they were quite familiar with the ancient devices.

Belisarius poured himself some more wine and, then, after glancing inquiringly about the table, refilled the goblets of Bouzes and Baresmanas as well.

As he set the wine down, the general reflected upon the absence of servants in the pavilion. That simple fact told him a great deal about his host, all of which met his complete approval.

Kurush seemed otherwordly and absent-minded, in some ways. More precisely, he seemed absent-minded in the way that very rich people often are—so accustomed to personal service that they treat it as a routine fact of life. But when it came to military matters, Kurush had obviously been able to discard his class attitudes. The battle-tested officer had not made the nobleman's mistake of forgetting that lowly menials have ears, and minds, and tongues. So he and his distinguished guests would pour their own wine, and serve each other as comrades.

Belisarius, after taking a sip of that excellent vintage, continued:

"You will probably not have experienced the siege cannons, as yet. The devices are huge, heavy, and ungainly. Useless in a field battle. But you will encounter then soon enough, at Babylon. The Malwa will surely bring them up to reduce the walls."

"How powerful are they?" asked Baresmanas.

"Think of the largest catapult you've ever seen, and then multiply the force of the projectile by a factor of three. No, four or five." He shrugged. "The Malwa do not use the things particularly well, in my opinion. Based, at least, on my observations at Ranapur. But they hardly need to. Ranapur was a great city, with the tallest and thickest brick walls I've ever seen. By the time the siege cannons were done—which still took months, mind you—those great walls were so much rubble."

Kurush grimaced. "The walls of Babylon are not brick, more's the pity. At least, not kiln-brick. The outer walls were, at one time, but the city's been deserted for centuries. Over the years, the peasants of the region have used that good brick to build their own huts. All that's left of the outer walls is the rubble core. The inner walls are still standing, but they're made entirely of sun-dried bricks. After all these centuries, the walls aren't much stronger than packed earth."

"Thick walls, though, aren't they?" asked Maurice.

Kurush nodded. "Oh, yes. Very thick! The outer walls are still over fifty yards wide, with a hundred yard moat in front of them. The inner walls are a double wall, with a military road in the middle. Counting that road—say, seven yards in width—the inner walls probably measure some twenty yards in thickness."

Maurice's eyes widened. Coutzes whistled softly, shaking his head. "God in heaven," he muttered. "I had no idea the ancients could build on such a scale."

Bouzes snorted. "Why not, brother? You've seen the pyramids in Egypt. I know you have. I was standing right next to you when you whistled softly, shook your head, and said: 'God in Heaven. I had no idea the ancients could build on such a scale.'"

The room erupted in laughter. Even Coutzes, after a momentary glare at his brother, started chuckling ruefully.

The moment of humor was brief, however. Soon enough, grim reality returned.

Again, Belisarius was torn by warring impulses. The need for secrecy, on the one hand, especially with regard to Aide's existence; the need—certainly the personal desire—for frankness with his new allies, on the other.

He decided to steer a tricky middle course.

"Actually," he said, clearing his throat, "I think the nature of Babylon's walls will work entirely to your—I should say, *our*—advantage. Cannon fire—delivered by gigantic siege cannon, at any rate—is too powerful to be resisted by hard walls, whether brick or even stone. You're actually much better off using thick, soft walls. Such walls simply absorb the cannon shot, rather than trying to deflect it."

All the other men at the table, except Maurice, stared at Belisarius with wide-eyed surprise. Maurice simply tightened his lips and gazed down at his goblet.

Maurice was the only one in the pavilion who knew Belisarius' secret. The general had finally divulged it to him, months earlier, after his return from India. Belisarius had always felt guilty, during the long months he had kept that secret from Maurice. So, when he finally did reveal Aide's existence, he compensated by sharing Aide's insights with Maurice to a greater extent than he ever had with anyone else, even Antonina.

Yet, if he had initially done so from guilt, his reasons had changed soon enough. In truth, he had found Maurice to be his most useful confidant—when it came, at least, to Aide's military advice. Not to Belisarius' surprise, the phlegmatic and practical Thracian peasant-turned-cataphract had been more receptive to Aide's often-bizarre advice than anyone else.

"You saw this in India?" queried Kurush. "Such fortifications?"

Maurice gave Belisarius a quick, warning glance. The chiliarch knew full well where Belisarius had seen "such fortifications." Not in India, but in visions. Visions which Aide had put in his mind, of the siege warfare of the future. Especially the theories and the practice of a great student of fortifications over a millennium in the future. A man named Vauban, who would live in a country which would be called France.

"Not directly, no, Kurush. But I did notice, toward the end of the siege of Ranapur, that the crumbled walls actually resisted the siege cannons better than they had while the brickwork was still intact."

He mentally patted himself on the back. It was not entirely a lie, after all. He consoled himself with the thought that the rubbled walls of Ranapur *had*, in retrospect, resisted the cannon shot quite well. Even if he hadn't noticed at the time.

Fortunately, the lie passed muster. Kurush and Baresmanas seemed so relieved by the information that they showed no inclination to press Belisarius on the point.

The conversation now began to turn toward the Malwa's relative weakness in cavalry, especially heavy cavalry, and how the allied forces might best take advantage of it. But before the discussion had gotten very far, they were interrupted.

A Persian officer bearing the insignia of an imperial courier entered the tent, somewhat apologetically, and approached the table. As he leaned over and whispered something to Baresmanas, Belisarius politely looked away and diverted the Romans' attention with an anecdote from the siege of Ranapur. The anecdote, involving his assessment of the relative merits of Rajput and Ye-tai cavalry, was interesting enough to capture the full attention of Bouzes and Coutzes and, to all appearances, Maurice. But he noted that Kurush was paying hardly any attention at all. The young sahrdaran's face was stiff. Whatever news was being whispered into Baresmanas' ear, Belisarius was certain, his nephew suspected its content. And was not happy in his suspicion.

When the courier left, Baresmanas gave Belisarius a quick look which, subtly, conveyed both apology and request.

Understanding, Belisarius rose and said: "It's late, and we're all tired. I think it would be best to continue this discussion later. We'll have plenty of opportunity to talk during our march south."

The other Romans immediately followed his example. Within two minutes, they were mounting their horses outside the pavilion and riding toward the Roman encampment nearby.

"Something's up," said Coutzes.

"Politics," announced his brother. "Got to be."

Belisarius was a bit startled. Abstractly, he knew Bouzes and Coutzes were not stupid. But the brothers had behaved with such thoroughgoing foolishness, during his previous encounter with them three years earlier, that he had not expected such quick perspicacity.

He said nothing in reply, however. Not until he and Maurice parted company with the brothers at their tent, and began riding toward the Thracian part of the encampment.

"He's right, you know," commented Maurice.

Belisarius nodded. "They've got a succession crisis. Khusrau's new to the throne and he's got lots of half-brothers. Ormazd, in particular, was not happy with the situation. Civil war probably would have broken out, if the Malwa hadn't invaded. Persians can sneer at us crude adoption-happy Romans all they want, but they've got their own sorry history of instability whenever the throne's up for grabs. Often enough in the past, when a Persian Emperor died, a civil war erupted. One claimant from the Sassanid dynasty fighting another. Three or four of them at once, sometimes."

They rode on a little further in silence. Then, Maurice smiled and remarked:

"I thought you did quite well, by the way. Lying through your teeth, I mean. The little touch about the crumbling brick walls of Ranapur was especially nice. Had such a ring of authenticity about it. Completely avoided the—uh, *awkwardness*—of explaining to a couple of Persian sahrdaran that your experience with fortifications in the new age of gunpowder comes from the advice of a fucking barbarian—a *Gaul*, no less—who won't even be born for twelve hundred years."

Belisarius grimaced. Maurice plowed on cheerfully.

"You did let one thing slip, though. When you mentioned that you *hoped* the only weapons the Malwa had were siege guns, rockets and grenades."

Belisarius winced. But Maurice seemed determined to till the entire field.

"Bad slip, that. Fortunately, the Persians didn't catch it. Or they might have asked: 'what particular weapons do you *fear* seeing?'"

The chiliarch glanced at his general slyly. "Then what would you have said?"

Belisarius stared ahead, stiff-faced, silent.

"Oh, yes," chuckled Maurice. "Difficult, that would have been."

He mimicked Belisarius' distinctive baritone: "I hope we don't see mobile artillery. Or, even worse, handcannons. You know—the stuff we Romans have been trying to develop through our secret weapons project, guided by visions of the future from a magical jewel some of us call the Talisman of God. Not, mind you, with any instant success."

They were at the tent which they shared. Belisarius dismounted. On the ground, he stared up at Maurice's grinning countenance. Then said, firmly, even severely, "I have the utmost confidence in John of Rhodes."

Maurice shook his head. "That's because you've never worked with him."

The chiliarch dismounted from his own horse, and followed Belisarius into the tent. "I *have*, on the other hand," he grumbled. "Quite the exciting experience, that is."

Chapter 9
RHODES
Summer, 531 A.D.

"Get down, you idiot!"

Antonina ducked behind the barricade. Just in time. There was a sharp, nasty-sounding, explosive crack. An instant later, an object went whizzing overhead somewhere in her vicinity.

John's head popped up behind his own barricade. When Antonina gingerly looked up, she found the naval officer's blue eyes glaring at her fiercely.

"How many times do I have to tell you?" he demanded. "This stuff is dangerous!"

The other observers of the test, five Roman officers, were beginning to rise from behind the heavy wooden barricades which surrounded, on three sides, the cannon which had been tested.

The late, lamented cannon. Lying on its side, off the heavy wooden cradle, with one of the wrought iron bars which made up its barrel missing. Seeing that gaping, scorched split running down the entire length of the barrel, Antonina winced. The missing iron bar was the object which had whizzed past—and it could have easily taken off her head.

John stumped out from behind his barricade.

"That's it! That's it!" he cried. He transferred his glare to the little cluster of Roman officers and pointed a imperious finger at

Antonina. "This woman is henceforth banned for all time from the testing area!" he pronounced. "You are encharged with enforcing that order!"

Hermogenes cleared his throat. "Can't do that, John. Antonina's in command, you know. Of you and me both. Direct imperial mandate. If you want to inform the Empress Theodora that you're over-riding her authority, you go right ahead and do it. Not me."

" 'Druther piss on a dragon, myself," muttered one of the other officers, the young Syrian named Euphronius who served as Antonina's chief executive officer for the Theodoran Cohort.

The regular infantry officer standing next to him, who served Hermogenes in the same capacity, nodded sagely.

"So would I," agreed Callixtos. "A big, angry, wide-awake, *hungry* dragon—"

"—guarding its hoard," concluded another officer. This man, Ashot, was the commander of the Thracian bucellarii whom Belisarius had assigned to accompany his wife to Egypt.

The last of the officers said nothing. His name was Menander, and he was new to his post. A hecatontarch, he was now—theoretically, the commander of a hundred men. A lad of twenty, who had never before commanded anyone. But Menander's title was a mere formality. His real position was that of Antonina's "special adviser."

Menander was the third of the three cataphracts who had accompanied Belisarius in his expedition to India. The other two, Valentinian and Anastasius, had remained with the general as his personal bodyguards. Menander, who had little of their frightening expertise in slaughter, had been assigned a different task. Belisarius thought Menander had gained an excellent grasp of gunpowder weapons and tactics during the course of their adventures in India, and so he had presented him to his wife with praise so fulsome the fair-skinned youth turned beet-red.

So, unsure of himself, Menander said nothing. But, quite sure of his loyalties, he squared his shoulders and stepped to Antonina's side.

John, seeing the united opposition of the entire military command of the expedition, threw up his hands in despair.

"I'm not responsible then!" The blue-eyed glare focussed again on Antonina. "You are doomed, woman. Doomed, I say! Destined for an early grave!"

John began stumping about, arms akimbo. "Dismembered," he predicted. "Disemboweled," he forecast. "Decapitated."

With a serene air of augury: "Shredded into a bloody, corpuscular mass of mutilated and mangled flesh."

Antonina, from long experience, waited until John had stumped about for a minute or so before she spoke.

"Exactly what happened, John?" she asked.

As always, once his irascibility was properly exercised, the naval officer's quick mind moved back to the forefront.

John gave the splintered cannon a cursory glance. "Same thing that usually happens with these damned wrought-iron cannons," he growled. "If there's any flaw at all in the welding, one of the staves will burst."

He stepped over to the cannon and squatted next to it.

"Come here," he commanded. "I'll show you the problem."

Antonina came around the barricade and stooped next to him. A moment later, the five officers were also gathered around.

John pointed to one of the iron bars which ran down the length of the barrel. The barrel was made up of twelve such bars—eleven, now, on this ruptured one. The bars were an inch square in cross-section and about three feet long. The corners of each bar joined its mates on the inside of the barrel, forming a dodecagonal tube about three inches in diameter. On the outside diameter of the barrel, the gaps between the bars had been filled up with weld.

John pointed to the broken welds which had once held the missing bar in place. "That's where they always rupture," he said. "And they do it about a third of the time."

He scowled, more thoughtfully than angrily. "I wouldn't even mind if the things were predictable. Then I could just test each one of them, and discard the failures. Won't work. I've seen one of these things blow up after it had fired successfully at least twenty times."

Hesitantly, Euphronius spoke up. "I notice you don't have the same hoops welded around the barrel that you have on the hand-cannons. Wouldn't that strengthen the barrel, if you added them?"

Antonina watched John struggle with his temper. The struggle was very brief, however. When the naval officer spoke his voice was mild, and his tone simply that of patient explanation. It was one of the many things she liked about the Rhodian. For all of John's legendary irritability, Antonina had long ago realized that

John was one of those rare hot-tempered people who is rude to superiors yet, as a rule, courteous to social inferiors.

"Yes, it would, Euphronius," he said. "But here's the problem. The handcannons are small, and reasonably light—even with the addition of a few reinforcing hoops. Furthermore, the powder charge isn't really all that big. But to accomplish the same purpose with these three-inchers, I'd have to surround the barrel with hoops down its entire length. That adds a lot of weight—"

He hesitated, calculating.

"Right now, these things weigh about one hundred and fifty pounds. If you add the hoops—as I said, we'd have to run the hoops all the way down the length, not just occasional reinforcement like the handcannons—you'd wind up with a barrel weighing another fifty pounds or so. Say two hundred pounds—and that's just the weight of the barrel. Doesn't include the cradle."

"That's not so bad," commented Ashot. "Especially if you use it on a warship."

"Yes and no," replied John. "It's true that the weight wouldn't matter on a ship. The problem is with the integrity of the iron."

He glanced at Antonina.

"One of the things Belisarius told me—and I've verified it with my own tests—is that these welded wrought-iron cannons have to be properly maintained. The damned things have to be cleaned in boiling water after each period of use, or else the powder residues build up and start corroding the metal." He grimaced. So did Ashot.

Hermogenes, staring back and forth at the two men, frowned with puzzlement. "I don't see the problem," he said. "Sure, that'd be a real nuisance for a land army, having to boil water and wash out the cannons. Especially in the desert. But on a ship—"

John's eyes bugged out. Before the naval officer could give vent to his outrage, Ashot intervened.

"Don't forget, John. He's never served at sea."

John clenched his jaws. "Obviously not," he growled.

Ashot, smiling, said to Hermogenes, "The one thing you do *not* want to do on a ship is build a big fire in order to boil a huge kettle of water. Believe me, Hermogenes, you don't. There's nothing in the world that'll burn like a ship. All that oil-soaked wood—pitch—rigging—"

"Damned ships are like so much kindling, just waiting to go up," concurred John. "Besides, what water would you use? *Sea-water?* That'd corrode the barrels even faster!"

Antonina straightened. "That's it, then. We'll go with cast bronze guns for the warships. And the field artillery. We'll restrict the wrought-iron weapons for the infantry's handguns."

"They'll still blow up, now and then," warned John.

Euphronius smiled, with surprising good cheer. "Yes, John, they will. I've seen it happen—had it happen to me, once—and it's a bit scary. But my grenadiers can handle it. The one nice thing about these wrought-iron guns, when they do go, is that they blow sideways, not back. Startling as hell, but it's not really that dangerous."

"Except to the man standing next to you," muttered Callixtos.

"Not really. Don't forget—the handcannons have those hoop reinforcements. So far, every time one of the guns has blown—which, by the way, doesn't happen all that often—the hoops have kept the staves from flying off like so many spears. What you get is ruptured pieces. Those can hurt you, sure—even kill you, maybe—but the odds aren't bad." Euphronius shrugged. "That's life. We're farmers and shepherds, Callixtos. Farming's dangerous too, believe it or not. Especially dealing with livestock. My cousin was crippled just last year, when—"

He broke off, waving aside the incident. All who watched the Syrian peasant-turned-grenadier were struck by the calm fatalism of the gesture.

"We'll manage," he repeated. The cheerful smile returned. "Though I will emphasize the importance of keeping the guns clean, to my grenadiers. Even if that means having to haul a bunch of heavy kettles around."

Now, chuckling:

"The wives'll scream bloody murder, of course, since they'll wind up doing most of the hauling."

John was still not satisfied. "Bronze is expensive," he complained. "Iron cannons are a *lot* cheaper."

Antonina shook her head.

"We'll just have to live with the cost. I won't subject my soldiers and sailors to that kind of gamble. Let the treasury officials wail all they want."

Grimly: "If they wail too much, I'll refer them to Theodora."

Her usual good humor returned. "Besides, John, we can make the giant fortress cannons out of wrought iron. Once we get to Alexandria. It won't matter what they weigh, since they'll never be moved once they're erected to defend the city. And there'll be no problem keeping them clean. The garrison gunners won't have anything else to do anyway. Hopefully, the guns'll never be used."

John scowled. "Are you *sure* about this?" he demanded.

He was not talking about the cannons, now. He was raising—again—the argument he had been having with Antonina since she arrived at Rhodes. The very first instruction Antonina had given John, almost the minute she set foot on the island, was to organize the transfer of the armaments complex he had so painstakingly built up, in its entirety, to Alexandria.

Antonina sighed.

"John, we've been over this a hundred times. Rhodes is just too isolated. The war with the Malwa will be won in the south. Egypt's the key. And besides—"

She hesitated. Like most Rhodians of her acquaintance, John had a fierce attachment to his native island. But—

"Face the truth, John. Rhodes isn't just isolated—it's too damn small."

She waved her hand toward the cluster of workshops some fifty yards away from the testing range. The workshops, like the testing area, were perched on a small bluff overlooking the sea. Behind them rose a steep and rocky ridge.

"This is a war like no other ever fought. We need to build a gigantic arms complex to fight it. That means Alexandria, John, not this little island. Alexandria's the second largest city in the Empire, after Constantinople, and it has by far the greatest concentration of manufactories, artisans, and skilled craftsmen. There's nowhere else we can put together the materials—and, most importantly, the workforce—quickly enough."

"Egypt's the richest agricultural province of the Empire, too," added Hermogenes. "So we won't have any problems keeping that workforce fed. Whereas here on Rhodes—"

He left off, gesturing at the rugged terrain surrounding them. Rhodes was famous, throughout the Mediterranean world, for the skill of its seamen and the savvy of its merchants. Both of which talents had developed, over the centuries, to compensate for the island's hardscrabble agriculture.

John stood up slowly. "All right," he sighed. Then, with a suspicious glance at Antonina:

"You sure this isn't just an elaborate scheme to justify a triumphant return to your native city?"

Antonina laughed. There was no humor in that sound. None at all. "When I left Alexandria, John, I swore I'd never set foot in that place again." For a moment, her beautiful face twisted into a harsh, cold mask. *"Fuck Alexandria.* All I remember is poverty, scraping, and—"

She paused, shrugged. All of the men standing around knew her history. All of them except Euphronius had long known.

The Syrian peasant had only learned that history three months earlier, when Antonina selected him as her executive officer and invited him and his wife to her villa for dinner. She had told them, then, over the wine after the meal. Watching carefully for their reaction. Euphronius had been shocked, a bit, but his admiration for Antonina had enabled him to overcome the moment.

His wife Mary had not been shocked at all. She, too, admired Antonina. But, unlike her husband, she understood the choices facing girls born into poverty. Mary had chosen a different path than Antonina—for a moment, her hand had caressed her husband's, remembering the tenderness of a sixteen-year-old shepherd boy—but she did not condemn the alternative. She had thought about it herself, more than once, before deciding to marry Euphronius and accept the life of a peasant's wife.

Antonina turned away. "Fuck Alexandria," she repeated.

Chapter 10
MESOPOTAMIA
Summer, 531 A.D.

An hour into the march from Callinicum, Baresmanas passed on the bad news.

"It seems we may face a civil war, after all, on top of the Malwa invasion," he said grimly.

The Persian nobleman stared out over the arid landscape of northern Mesopotamia. Other than the occasional oasis, the only relief from the bleak desolation was the Euphrates, half a mile east of the road the army was taking.

Belisarius cocked an eyebrow toward the sahrdaran, but said nothing. After a moment, Baresmanas sighed.

"I had hoped it would not come to this. But Ormazd was always a fool. Khusrau's half-brother has a great deal of support among some of the sahrdaran families, especially the Varazes and the Andigans. A large part of the Karen are favorable to him, also. And he is quite popular among the imperial *vur-zurgan*. All of that has apparently gone to his head.

"*Stupid!*" he snorted. "The great mass of the dehgans have made clear that their loyalty is to Khusrau. Without them—" Baresmanas shrugged.

Belisarius nodded thoughtfully, reviewing his knowledge of the power structure in Persia.

Persian society was rigidly divided into classes, and class position usually translated directly into political power. The seven sahrd-aran families provided the satraps of major provinces and, often enough, the royalty of subordinate kingdoms. Below the great sahrdaran houses came the class of "grandees," whom the Persians called *vurzurgan*. The vuzurgan ruled small provinces, and filled the higher ranks of the imperial officialdom.

Finally, at the base of the Persian aristocracy, came the *azadan*—"men of noble birth." Most of these consisted of small landed gentry, that class which the Persians called the *dehgans*. It was the dehgans who provided the feared armored lancers which were the heart of the mighty Persian army.

So—Khusrau's rival Ormazd, for all that he had gained the support of many high-ranked noblemen, had failed to win the allegiance of the men who provided Persia's rulers with their mailed fist.

Belisarius smiled his crooked smile. "Even Aryan principles," he murmured, "have to take crude reality into account."

Baresmanas matched the sly smile with one of his own, saying: "It's your fault, actually."

Belisarius' eyes widened. "*My* fault? How in the world—"

"Ormazd's most powerful and influential supporter is Firuz. Who is a Karen, as you may know."

Belisarius shook his head. "No, I did not know. We *are* speaking of the same Firuz who—"

"Yes, indeed. The same Firuz—the same illustrious champion—who led the Aryan army at Mindouos. Led it to its most ignominious defeat in well over a century—at your hands, my friend."

Belisarius frowned. "I knew he had survived the battle. I even visited, while we held him captive, to pay my respects. He was quite rude, so my visit was very brief. But I did not know he was Karen, and I had no idea he held such sway in dynastic affairs."

Baresmanas chuckled scornfully. "Oh, yes. He is quite the favorite of imperial grandees, and the Mazda priesthood thinks well of him also. That favoritism, in fact, is what led to him being given the command of the army at Nisibis. Despite his obvious"—all humor vanished—"military incompetence."

Belisarius was distracted for a moment. A serpent slithering off the road had unsettled his mount. After calming the horse, he turned back to Baresmanas and said: "That would explain, I imagine, the hostility of the dehgans to his candidate Ormazd."

The sahrdaran tightened his lips. "They have not forgotten that insane charge he led at Mindouos, which trapped us against your field fortifications." He shuddered. "What a hideous slaughter!"

For a moment, the sahrdaran's face was drawn, almost haggard. Belisarius looked away, controlling his own grimace. It *had* been pure butchery in the center at Mindouos. Just as he had planned—trapping the Persian lancers against his infantry while he hammered them from the flank with his own heavy cavalry.

He sighed. Over the past months, he had become quite fond of Baresmanas. Yet he knew he would do it all again, if the necessity arose.

Something of his sentiments must have been clear to the Persian. Baresmanas leaned over and said, almost in a whisper:

"Such is war, my friend. In this, if nothing else, we are much alike—neither of us gives any credence to myths of glory and martial grandeur."

"As my chiliarch Maurice taught me," Belisarius replied harshly, "war is murder. Organized, systematic murder—nothing more and nothing less. It was the first thing he said to me on the day I assumed command as an officer. Seventeen, I was, at the time. But I had enough sense to ask my chief subordinate—he was a decarch, then—his opinion."

Baresmanas twisted in his saddle, looking back at the long column which followed them.

"Where is Maurice, by the way? I did not see him when we set out this morning." He studied the column more closely. "For that matter, where are your two bodyguards?"

Now, Belisarius did grimace. "There's been a problem. I asked Maurice to deal with it. I sent Valentinian and Anastasius with him, along with a regiment of my bucellarii."

Baresmanas eyed him shrewdly. "Looting?"

The general's grimace deepened. "Worse. In Callinicum last night, some of the Constantinople garrison got drunk in a tavern and raped the girl who was serving them. The tavernkeeper's own daughter, as it happened. When the tavernkeeper and his two sons tried to intervene, the soldiers murdered all three of them."

Baresmanas shook his head. "It happens. Especially with troops—"

"*Not in my army it doesn't.*" The general's jaws were tight. "Not more than once, anyway."

"You have punished the culprits."

"I had all eight of them beheaded."

Baresmanas was silent for a moment. An experienced officer, he understood full well the implications. Armies, like empires, have their own internal divisions.

"You are expecting trouble from the Constantinople garrison troops," he stated. "They will resent the execution of their comrades by your Thracian retinue."

"They can resent it all they want," snarled Belisarius. "Just so long as they've learned to fear my bucellarii."

He twisted in his saddle, looking back.

"The reason Maurice and his men aren't at the front of the army this morning is because they're riding on the flanks of the Constantinople troops. Dragging eight bodies behind them on ropes. And a sack full of eight heads."

He turned back, his face set in a cold glare. "We've got enough problems to deal with. If those garrison soldiers get the idea they can run wild in a *Roman* town, just imagine what they'd do once we reach Persian territory."

Baresmanas pursed his lips. "That *would* be difficult. Especially with Ormazd stirring up trouble against what he's calling Khusrau's 'capitulation' to the Roman Empire."

Belisarius chuckled. "The Malwa Empire is ravaging Persia and Ormazd is denouncing his half-brother for finding an *ally*?"

The sahrdaran shrugged. "If it weren't that, it would be something else. The man's ambitions are unchecked. We had hoped he would accept his status, but—"

Belisarius looked at him directly. "What exactly is the news that was brought by your courier?"

"It is not news, Belisarius, so much as an assessment. After the Malwa invaded, Ormazd formally acquiesced to Khusrau's assumption of the throne. In return, Khusrau named him satrap of northern Mesopotamia—the rich province we call Asuristan and you call by its ancient name of Assyria. Ormazd pledged to bring thirty thousand troops to the Emperor's aid at Babylon. We have learned that he has in fact gathered those troops, but is remaining encamped near the capital at Ctesiphon. At your ancient Greek city of Seleucia, in fact, just across the Tigris."

The sahrdaran bestowed his own cold glare on the landscape. "Well positioned, in short, to seize *our* capital. And serving no use in the war against Malwa. We suspect the worst."

"You think Ormazd is in collusion with the Malwa?"

Baresmanas heaved a sigh.

"Who is to know? For myself, I do not believe so—not at the moment, at least. I think Ormazd is simply waiting on the side, ready to strike if Khusrau is driven out of Babylon." He rubbed his face wearily. "I must also tell you, Belisarius, that the courier brought instructions for me. Once we reach Peroz-Shapur, I will have to part company with your army. I am instructed by the Emperor to take Kurush and my soldiers—and the remainder of my household troops, who await me at Peroz-Shapur—to Ormazd's camp."

"And do what?" asked Belisarius.

Baresmanas shrugged. "Whatever I can. 'Encourage' Ormazd, you might say, to join the battle against the invaders."

Belisarius eyed him for a moment. "How many household troops will there be at Peroz-Shapur?"

"Two thousand, possibly three."

Belisarius looked over his shoulder, as if to gauge Baresmanas' forces. The seven hundred Persian cavalrymen who escorted the sahrdaran were barely visible further back in the long column.

"Less than four thousand men," he murmured. "That's not going to be much of an encouragement."

Again, Baresmanas shrugged.

Belisarius broke into a grin. "Such a diplomat! Do you mean to tell me that Emperor Khusrau made no suggestion that you might request a bit of help from his Roman allies?"

Baresmanas glanced at him. "Well . . . The courier *did* mention, as a matter of fact, that the Emperor had idly mused that if the Roman commander were to be suddenly taken by a desire to see the ancient ruins of the glorious former capital of the Greek Seleucids—that he would have no objections." Baresmanas nodded. "None whatsoever."

Belisarius scratched his chin. "Seleucia. Yes, yes. I feel a sudden hankering to see the place. Been a life-long dream, in fact."

They rode on for a bit, in companionable silence, until Belisarius remarked: "Seleucia wasn't actually founded by Greeks, by the way. Macedonians."

Baresmanas waved his hand. "Please, Belisarius! You can hardly expect a pureblood Aryan to understand these petty distinctions. As far as we are concerned, you mongrels from the west come in only two varieties. Bad Greeks and worse Greeks."

Chapter 11

Two days later, the long-simmering discontent of the Constantinople troops came to a boil. After the midday break, when the order was given to resume the march, the garrison soldiers remained squatting by their campfires, refusing to mount up.

Their action had obviously been coordinated in advance. Several of his Thracian bucellarii, including Maurice, reported to Belisarius that the garrison troopers' sub-officers had been seen circulating through the route camp during the break. The top officers of the Constantinople soldiers, the chiliarch and the tribunes, were apparently not involved directly. But they were just as apparently making no effort to restore discipline to their troops.

"It's an organized mutiny," concluded Maurice angrily. "This is not just some spontaneous outburst."

Belisarius made a calming gesture with his hand. For a moment, he stared at the Euphrates, as if seeking inspiration from its placidly moving waters. As usual, whenever possible, the army had taken its midday break at a place where the road ran next to the river.

He wiped his face with a cloth. The heat was oppressive, even in the shade provided by the canopy which his men had erected for him at the break. The shelter was not a tent—simply a canvas stretched across six poles. Enough to provide some relief from the sun, while not blocking the slight breeze.

"Let's not use that term," the general stated firmly. He met Maurice's glare with a calm gaze. " 'Mutiny' isn't just a curse word, Maurice. It's also a legal definition. If I call this a mutiny, I am required by imperial edict to deal with it in specific ways. Ways which, at the moment, I am not convinced are necessary. Or wise."

Belisarius scanned the faces of the other men crowded into the shelter of the lean-to. All of the top commanders of the army were there, except for the officers in charge of the Constantinople troops. Their absence made their own shaky allegiance quite clear.

Baresmanas and Kurush were also standing there. Belisarius decided to deal with that problem first.

"I would appreciate it, Kurush, if you would resume the march with your own troops. Move as slowly as you can, without obviously dawdling, so that we Romans can catch up to you as soon as this problem is settled. But, for the moment, I think it would be best if—"

Kurush nodded. "There's no need to explain, Belisarius. You don't need Aryan soldiers mixed into this brew. We'd just become another source of tension."

He turned away, moving with his usual nervous energy, and began giving quick orders to his subordinates. Baresmanas followed, after giving Belisarius a supportive smile.

With none but Romans now present, the atmosphere eased a bit. Or, it might be better to say, Roman inhibitions relaxed.

"Call it what you want," snarled Coutzes. "I think you ought to give those fucking garrison commanders the same treatment you gave those eight fucking—"

"*I* think we ought to hear what the general thinks," interjected Bouzes. He laid a restraining hand on his brother's arm. "He *is* noted for his cunning, you know. Or have you forgotten?"

Coutzes made a sour face, but fell silent. Bouzes grinned at Belisarius. "Perhaps we might announce the suddenly-discovered presence of a Malwa pay caravan?" he suggested cheerfully. "Send the garritroopers off on a 'reconnaissance-in-force'?"

All the officers standing around erupted in laughter, except Belisarius. But even he, in the humor of the moment, could not help returning Bouzes' grin.

In the few days since Bouzes and Coutzes had joined his forces, Belisarius had come to share Sittas and Hermogenes' assessment of the two brothers. Neither one, it was true—especially

Coutzes—had entirely shed their youthful tendencies toward hot-headedness. But those tendencies, in the three years since Min-douos, had clearly been tempered by experience.

Belisarius' grin faded, but a smile remained. Yes, he had already decided that he approved of the Thracian brothers. Not all men have the temperament to learn from experience. Belisarius himself did, and he prized that ability in others.

Humor, he thought, was the key—especially the ability to laugh at oneself. When he heard Bouzes and Coutzes, in Callinicum, invite Maurice to join them in a "reconnaissance-in-force" to the nearest tavern, he knew the brothers would work out just fine.

He shook off the humor. His problem remained, and it was not comical in the least. "I want to settle this without bloodshed," he announced. "And I don't think it's needed, anyway. Maurice, I'm not quibbling with you over legal definitions. I simply think that you're misreading the situation."

Maurice tugged his beard. "Maybe," he said, grudgingly. "But—"

Again, Belisarius held up a hand. Maurice shrugged, slightly, and fell silent.

The general now turned toward Timasius, the commander of the five hundred Illyrian cavalrymen given to him by Germanicus.

"Your men are the key to the situation," he announced. "Key, at least, to the way I handle it. Where do they stand?"

Timasius frowned. "Stand? Exactly how do you mean that, general?"

Timasius' thick accent—like most Illyrians from Dacia, his native language was Latin rather than Greek—always made him seem a bit dull-witted. At first, Belisarius had dismissed the impression, until further acquaintance with the man had led him to the conclu-sion that Timasius was, in fact, a bit on the dim side. He seemed a competent enough officer, true, when dealing with routine mat-ters. But—

Belisarius decided he had no time to be anything other than blunt and direct.

"What I mean, Timasius, is that you Illyrians have also been complaining loudly since we began the march two months ago." He waved down the officer's gathering sputter of protest. "I am not accusing you of anything! I am simply stating a fact."

Timasius lapsed into mulish, resentful silence. Belisarius tightened his jaws, prepared to drive the matter through. But it proved unnecessary. Timasius' chief subordinate, a hecatontarch by the name of Liberius, spoke up.

"It's not the same, general. It's true, our men have been grousing a lot—but that's just due to the unaccustomed exertions of this forced march."

The man scowled. On his heavy-set, low-browed face, the expression made him seem like an absolute dullard. But his ensuing words contradicted the impression.

"You've got to distinguish between that and what's eating the Constantinople men. *They're* a lot of pampered garrison troops. True, they're not nobility, except the officers—not *that* unit—but they've picked up the attitude. They're used to lording it over everybody, friend and foe alike." The scowl deepened. The man's brow disappeared almost completely. "*Especially* over their own, the snotty bastards. That girl in Callinicum wasn't the first tavern maid they've been free with, you can be sure of that. Probably been quite a few in Constantinople itself given that same treatment—and had it hushed up afterward, by the capital's authorities."

A little growl from several of the other officers under the canopy indicated their concurrence.

"Illyrian soldiers aren't exactly famous for their gentle manners, either," commented Belisarius mildly.

Liberius winced. In point of fact, Illyrian troops had the reputation of being the most atrocity-prone of any Roman army, other than outright mercenaries.

"It's still not the same," he stated—forcefully, but not sullenly. Belisarius was impressed by the man's dispassionate composure.

Liberius gestured toward Bouzes and Coutzes, and the other officers from the Syrian army. "These lads are used to dealing with Persians. Civilized, the Medes are. Sure, when war breaks out both sides have been known to act badly. But, even then, it's a matter between empires. And in between the wars—which is most of the time—the borderlands are quiet and peaceful."

Several of the Syrian officers nodded. Liberius continued: "What you *don't* get is what we have in Illyricum—constant, unending skirmishes with a lot of barbarian savages. Border villages ravaged by some band of Goths or Avars who are just engaging in casual plunder. Their own kings—if you can call them that—don't even know about it, most of the time." He shrugged. "So we repay the favor on the nearest barbarian village."

The scowl returned in full force. "That is *not* the same thing as raping a girl in your own town—and then murdering half her family in the bargain!"

Again, the growl of agreement swept the room. Louder, this time. Much louder.

Belisarius glanced at Timasius. Liberius' slow-thinking commander had finally caught up with his subordinate's thoughts. He too, now, was nodding vehemently.

Belisarius was satisfied. For the moment, at least. But he made a note to speak to the Illyrian commanders in the near future. To remind them that they would soon be operating in Persia, and that the treatment which Illyrians were accustomed to handing out to barbarians in the trans-Danube would *not* be tolerated in Mesopotamia.

He moved out of the shade, toward his horse. "All right, then."

His officers made to follow. Belisarius waved them back. "No," he announced. "I'll handle this myself."

"*What*?" demanded Coutzes. "You're not taking anyone with you?"

Belisarius smiled crookedly, holding up two fingers.

"Two." He pointed toward Valentinian and Anastasius, who had been waiting just outside the canopy throughout the conference. As soon as they saw his gesture, the two cataphracts began mounting their horses.

Once he was on his own horse, Belisarius smiled down at his officers—all of whom, except Maurice, were staring at him as if he were insane.

"Two should be enough," he announced placidly, and spurred his horse into motion.

As the three men began riding off, Valentinian muttered something under his breath.

"What did he say?" wondered Bouzes. "I didn't catch it."

Maurice smiled, thinly. "I think he said 'piss on crazy strategoi.' "

He turned back toward the shade of the shelter. "But maybe not. Be terribly disrespectful of the high command! Maybe he just said 'wish on daisies, attaboy.' Encouraging his horse, you know. Poor beast's probably as sick of this desert as we are."

◇   ◇   ◇

As they headed down the road, Belisarius waved Valentinian and Anastasius forward. Once the two men were riding on either side, he said:

"Don't touch your weapons unless the muti—ah, dispirited troops—take up theirs."

He gave both men a hard glance. Anastasius' heavy face held no expression. Valentinian scowled, but made no open protest.

A thin smile came to the general's face. "Mainly, what I want you to do after we arrive at the Greeks' camp is to disagree with me."

Anastasius' eyes widened. "*Disagree*, sir?"

Belisarius nodded. "Yes. Disagree. Not *too* openly, mind. I *am* your commanding officer, after all. But I want you to make clear, in no uncertain terms, that you think I'm an idiot."

Anastasius frowned. Valentinian muttered.

"What was that last, Valentinian?" queried Belisarius. "I'm not sure I caught it."

Silence. Anastasius rumbled: "He said: '*That* won't be hard.' "

"That's what I thought he said," mused Belisarius. He grinned. "Well! You won't have any difficulty with the assignment, then. It'll come naturally to you."

Valentinian muttered again, at some length. Anastasius, not waiting for a cue, interpreted. "He said—I'm summarizing—that clever fellows usually wind up outsmarting themselves. Words to that effect."

Belisarius frowned. "That's all? It seemed to me he muttered quite a few more words than that. Entire sentences, even."

Anastasius shook his head sadly. "Most of the other words were just useless adjectives. Very redundant." The giant bestowed a reproving glance on his comrade. "He's given to profanity."

They were nearing the encampment of the Constantinople garrison troops. Belisarius spurred his horse into a trot. After Valentinian and Anastasius dropped back to their usual position as his bodyguards, Belisarius cocked his head and said:

"Remember. *Disagree. Disapprove.* If I say something reasonable, scowl. Pleasant, snarl. Calm and soothing—spit on the ground."

Mutter, mutter, mutter.

Belisarius repressed his smile. He did not ask for a translation. He was quite sure the words had been pure profanity.

They began encountering the first outposts of the Constantinople garrison. Within a minute, trotting forward, they passed several
hundred soldiers, huddled in small groups at the outer perimeter
of the route camp. As Belisarius had expected, a large number of
the troops were holding back from the body of men milling around
in the center. These would be the faint-hearts and the fence-
sitters—or the "semi-loyalists," if you preferred.

He made it a point to bestow a very cordial smile upon all
those men. Even a verbal greeting, here and there. Valentinian
and Anastasius immediately responded with their own glowers,
which Valentinian accompanied by a nonstop muttering. The garrison troops responded to the general's smile, in the main, with
expressions of uncertainty. But Belisarius noted that a number of
them managed their own smiles in return. Timid smiles; sickly
smiles—but smiles nonetheless.

I knew it, he thought, with considerable self-satisfaction.

Aide's voice came into his mind. **Knew what? And what is
going on? I am confused**.

Belisarius hesitated, before responding. To his—"its," technically, but the general had long since come to think of Aide as
"he"—consciousness, insubordination and rebellion were bizarre
conceptions. Aide had been produced by a race of intelligent crystals in the far distant future and sent back in time, to save them
from enslavement (and possibly outright destruction) by those they
called the "new gods." The intelligence of those crystals was utterly
inhuman, in many ways. One of those ways was their lack of indi-
viduality. Each crystal, though distinct, was a part of their collective
mentality—just as each crystal, in its turn, was the composite being
created by the ever-moving facets which generated that strange
intelligence. To those crystals, and to Aide, the type of internal
discord and dispute which humans took for granted was almost
unfathomable.

We are having what we call a "mutiny," Aide. Or a "rebellion."

From long experience, Belisarius had learned how to project his
own visions into the consciousness of Aide. He had found that
such visions often served as a better means of communication
than words.

He did so now, summoning up images of various mutinies and
rebellions of the past, culminating with the revolt of Spartacus and
its gruesome finale.

He could sense the facets flashing around the visions, trying to absorb their essence.

While they did so, and Aide ruminated, Belisarius and his bodyguards reached the center of the camp. At least four hundred soldiers from the Constantinople garrison were clustered there, most of them in small groups centered around the older soldiers.

Belisarius was not surprised. The men, he gauged, were leaning heavily on the judgements and opinions of their squad leaders and immediate superiors. This was an army led by pentarchs, decarchs, and hecatontarchs, now, not officers.

Good. I can deal with those veterans. They'll be sullen and angry, but they'll also be thinking about their pensions. Unlike the officers, they don't have rich estates to retire to.

Silence fell over the mob. Belisarius slowly rode his horse into the very center of the crowd. After drawing up his mount, he scanned the soldiers staring up at him with a long, calm gaze.

A thought came from Aide.

This is stupid. Your plan is ridiculous.

The facets had reached their conclusion, firmly and surely, from their assessment of the general's vision. Especially the last vision, the suppression of the Spartacus rebellion.

Preposterous. Absurd. Irrational. You cannot possibly crucify all these men. There is not that much wood in the area.

Belisarius struggled mightily with sudden laughter. He managed, barely, to transform the hilarity into good cheer.

So it was, to their astonishment, that the mutinous soldiers of the Constantinople garrison witnessed their commanding general, whom they assumed had come to thunder threats and condemnation, bestow upon them a smile of sheer goodwill.

They barely noticed the savage snarls on the faces of his two companions. Only two or three even took umbrage at Valentinian's loud expectoration.

An officer scurried forward, after pushing his way through the first line of the crowd standing around the general. Four other officers followed.

Belisarius recognized them immediately. The officer in front was Sunicas, the chiliarch who commanded the Constantinople troops. The men following him were the tribunes who served as his chief subordinates. He knew only one of them by name—Boraides.

When the five men drew up alongside his horse, Belisarius simply looked down upon them, cocking an eyebrow, but saying nothing.

"We have a problem here, general," stated Sunicas. "As you can see, the men—"

"We certainly do!" boomed Belisarius. His voice was startlingly loud, enough so that an instant silence fell over the entire mob of soldiers. The general was so soft-spoken, as a rule, that men tended to forget that his powerful baritone had been trained to pierce the din of battles.

Belisarius, again, scanned the immediate circle of soldiers. This time, however, there was nothing benign in that gaze. His scrutiny was intent and purposeful.

He pointed to one of the soldiers in the inner ring. A hecatontarch, young for his rank. The man was bigger than average, and very burly. He was also quite a handsome man, in a large-nosed and strong-featured way. But beneath the outward appearance of a muscular bruiser, Belisarius did not miss the intelligence in the man's brown eyes. Nor the steadiness of his gaze. "What is your name?" he asked.

"Agathius." The hecatontarch's expression was grim and tightly-held, and his answer had been given in a curt growl which bordered on disrespect. But the general was much more impressed by the man's instant willingness to identify himself.

Belisarius waved his hand in a casual little gesture which encompassed the entire encampment. "You are in command of these men." The statement was firm, but matter-of-fact. Much like a man might announce that the sun rises in the east.

Agathius frowned.

"*You* are in command of these men," repeated Belisarius. "*Now. Today.*"

Agathius' frown deepened. For a moment, he began to look toward the men at his side. But then—to Belisarius' delight—he squared his broad shoulders and lifted his head. The frown vanished, replaced by a look of stony determination. "You may say so, yes."

"What do *you* say?" came the general's immediate response.

Agathius hesitated, for the briefest instant. Then, shrugging: "Yes."

Belisarius waited, staring at him. After a moment, grudgingly, Agathius added: "General. Sir."

Belisarius waited, staring at him. Agathius stared back. A little look of surprise flitted across his face, then. The young hecatont-arch blew out his cheeks and stood very erect. "I am in command here, sir. Today. Now."

Belisarius nodded. "Tomorrow, also," he said. Very pleasantly, as if announcing good weather. "And, I hope, for many days to come."

From the corner of his eye, Belisarius caught a glimpse of Anastasius' bug-eyed glare of disapproval. He heard Valentinian mutter something. The words were too soft to understand, but the sullen tone was not.

The general shifted his gaze to the chiliarch and the tribunes standing by his stirrup. The calm, mild expression on his face vanished—replaced by pitiless condemnation.

"You are relieved of command, Sunicas. Your tribunes also. I want you on the road to Constantinople within the hour. You may take your personal gear with you. And your servants, of course. Nothing else."

Sunicas goggled. The tribune Boraides exclaimed: "You can't do that! *On what grounds?"*

Belisarius heard Valentinian immediately growl: "Quite right!" Then: loud muttering, in which the words "outrageous" and "unjust" figured prominently. Anastasius, for his part, simply glowered at the newly-promoted mutineer Agathius. But, oh, such a wondrous glower it was! Worthy of a Titan!

The hecatontarch's returning glare was a more modest affair. Merely Herculean. The sub-officers of the Constantinople troops in the circle began closing ranks with Agathius. In seconds, three other hecatontarchs and perhaps a dozen decarchs were standing shoulder-to-shoulder, matching hard stares with the Thracian cataphracts.

Belisarius immediately sided with the Greek soldiers.

Twisting sharply in his saddle, he bestowed his own very respectable glower on Valentinian and Anastasius.

"I'll stand for no insubordination!" he snapped. "Do you understand?" He almost added "from knaves and varlets," but decided that would be a bit overmuch.

Valentinian and Anastasius lowered their heads submissively. But not *too* submissively, Belisarius was pleased to see. Their stance exuded that of the chastened but still stubborn underlings, resentful of their commander's grotesque violation of military norms and protocol.

Belisarius whipped his harsh gaze back to Boraides.

"On what grounds?" he demanded. *"On what grounds?"*

The general's own glower now ascended into the mythic heights. Worthy of Theseus, perhaps, confronting the minotaur. *"On the grounds of gross incompetence!"* he roared.

Again, he swept his hand in a circle. The gesture, this time, was neither little nor casual. He stood erect in his stirrups, moving his arm as if to command the tides. "The first duty of any commander is to *command*," he bellowed. "You have obviously failed in that duty. These men are not under your command. You have admitted as much yourself." He sat back in the saddle. "Therefore I have replaced you with a man who is capable of command." He pointed to Agathius. *"Him.* He is the new chiliarch of this unit."

Now looking at Agathius, Belisarius gestured toward Sunicas and the tribunes. "See to it, Agathius. I want these—these fellows—on the road. Within the hour."

Agathius stared at the general. Belisarius met his gaze with calm assurance. After a few seconds, the new chiliarch cocked his head toward one of the men standing next to him, without taking his eyes from Belisarius, and murmured:

"Take care of it, Cyril. You heard the general. Within the hour."

Cyril, a scarred veteran perhaps ten years older than Agathius, gave his newly-promoted superior a sly little grin. "As you wish, *sir!*" he boomed.

Cyril strode toward Sunicas and the tribunes. His grin widened, widened. Became rather evil, in fact. "You've got your orders. *Move.*"

The former commanding officers ogled him. Cyril made a little gesture. Four decarchs closed ranks with him, fingering their swords.

Anastasius' eyes bugged out. His expression verged on apoplexy.

Valentinian muttered. The words "outrageous" and "unjust" were, again, distinct. Belisarius thought he also heard the phrase "oh, heavens, what shall we do?" But, maybe not.

He glared at Anastasius and Valentinian. The cataphracts avoided his gaze, but, still, held their stubborn pose. Several more sub-officers from the garrison troops sidled forward. Two of them went to assist Cyril and his decarchs—who were now, almost physically, driving the former commanders off—but most of them edged toward Belisarius. Prepared, it was clear, to defend the general against his own bodyguards. If necessary.

"Well, that's that," announced Belisarius.

He began climbing down from his horse. A pentarch hastened forward to assist him.

Once on the ground, Belisarius strode over to Agathius and said: "It's a miserably hot day. Would you have some wine, by any chance?"

This time, Agathius did not hesitate for more than a second. "Yes, sir. We do. May we offer you some?"

"I would be delighted. And let us take the opportunity to become acquainted. I should like to be introduced to your subordinates, also. You'll need to appoint new tribunes, of course." He shrugged. "I leave it to your judgement to select them. You know your men better than I do."

Agathius eyed him wonderingly, but said nothing. He led the way to a canvas shelter nearby. Most of the sub-officers in the circle followed, in a little mob. Only a handful remained behind, faithfully at their new post, keeping a vigilant eye on the general's sullen and untrustworthy bodyguards.

Within seconds, amphorae began appearing and wine was poured. Within two minutes, Belisarius was squatting in the shelter of the canopy, with no fewer than three dozen of the Constantinople troopers' chief sub-officers forming an audience. The men were very tightly packed, trying to crowd their way into the shade.

For all the world, the impromptu gathering had the flavor of a mid-afternoon chat.

"All right," said Belisarius pleasantly, after finishing his cup. "I'll tell you what I want. Then you'll tell me what you want. Then we'll see if we can reach a settlement."

He scanned the small crowd briefly, before settling his gaze on Agathius.

"I want an end to the slackness of your marching order. The men can grouse and grumble all they want, but I want them to do it in formation. Some reasonable approximation of it, at least." He held out his cup. A decarch refilled it.

"I realize that you're unaccustomed to the conditions, here in the desert—and that it's been a long time since you've had to undertake a forced march like this. But enough's enough. You're not weaklings, for the sake of Christ. You've had two months to get into shape! The truth is, I don't think the march is that hard on you, anymore. You've just gotten into the habit of resentfulness."

He stopped to sip at his wine, gazing at Agathius. The new chiliarch took a deep breath. For a moment, his eyes wandered, staring out at the harsh-lit desert.

One of the sub-officers behind him started to say something—a protest, by the tone—but Agathius waved him down. "Shut up, Paul," he growled. "Tell the truth, I'm sick of it myself."

His eyes returned to Belisarius. He nodded. "All right, general. I'll see to it. What else?"

"I want you to accept some detachments from the Army of Syria. Light cavalry." A crooked smile. "Call them advisers. Part of the problem is that you've no experience in the desert, and you've been too arrogant to listen to anyone."

He pointed to the canvas stretched over his head. "You didn't figure this out, for instance, until a week ago. Till then you set up regular tents, every night, and sweltered without a breeze."

Agathius grimaced. Belisarius plowed on.

"There's been a hundred little things like that. Your cocksure capital city attitude has done nothing but make your life harder, and caused resentment in the other units. I want it to stop. I'll have the Syrian units send you some light auxiliaries. They'll be Arabs, the most of them—know the desert better than anyone. If you treat them properly, they'll be a big help to you."

Agathius rubbed the back of his neck. "Agreed. What else?"

Belisarius shrugged. "What I expect from all my other units. Henceforth, Agathius, you will attend the command conferences. Bring your tribunes. A few hecatontarchs, if you want. But don't bring many—I like my conferences to be small enough that we can have a real discussion and get some work done. I'm not given to speeches."

Agathius eyed him skeptically.

"And what else?"

"Nothing." Belisarius drained the cup, held it out. Again, it was refilled.

"Your turn," he said mildly.

Agathius twitched his shoulders irritably.

"Ah—!" he exclaimed. He was silent, for a moment, frowning. Then:

"It's like this, general. The real problem isn't the march, and it isn't the desert. As you said, we've gotten used to it by now. It's—" He gestured vaguely. "It's the way we got hauled out of the barracks, without a day's notice, and sent off on this damned expedition. Off to Mesopotamia, for the sake of Christ, while—"

He lapsed into a bitter silence. One of the decarchs behind him piped up.

"While all the fucking *noble* units got to stay behind, cozy in the capital. Living like lords."

Belisarius lifted his head, laughing. "Well, of course!" he exclaimed. "The last thing I wanted on this expedition was a bunch of aristocrats."

He shook his head ruefully. "God, think of it! Every cataphract in those units can't move without twelve servants and his own personal baggage train. I'd be lucky to make five miles a day."

He bestowed a very approving smile on the soldiers squatting around him.

"I told Sittas I wanted his best *fighting* unit. Had quite a set-to with him, I did. Naturally, he tried to fob off his most useless parade ground troops on me, but I wouldn't have it. 'Fighters,' I said. Fighters, Sittas. I've got no use for anything else."

The Greeks' chests swelled a bit. Their heads lifted.

Belisarius drained his cup. Held it out for another refill.

"Stop worrying about those lordly troops, lounging in their barracks in Constantinople. Within a year, you'll have enough booty to sneer at them. Not to mention a glorious name and the gratitude of Rome."

The soldiers' gaze became eager. "Booty, sir?" asked one. "Do you think so? We'd heard—"

He fell silent. Another spoke: "We'd heard you frown on booty, sir."

Belisarius' eyes widened. "From whom did you hear *that*? Not the Syrian soldiers! Each one of those lads came away from Mindouos with more treasure than they knew what to do with. And you certainly didn't hear it from my Thracian cataphracts!"

The Greeks exchanged glances with each other. Suddenly, Cyril laughed.

"We heard it from the other garrison units. In Constantinople. They said Belisarius was a delicate sort, who wouldn't let his men enjoy the gleanings of a campaign."

Belisarius' good humor vanished. "That's not booty. That's *looting*. And they're damn well right about that!"

He brought a full Homeric scowl to bear.

"*I won't tolerate looting and indiscipline.* I never have, and I never will. Have no doubt about that, any of you. The penalty for looting in my army is fifty lashes. And I'll execute a man who murders and rapes. On the second offense, in the same unit, the officer in command'll be strapped to the whipping post himself. Or hung."

He drained his cup. Held it out. Immediately drained the refill. Held it out again. The soldiers eyed the cup, then him. To all appearances, the general seemed not in the slightest affected by the wine he had drunk.

"Make no mistake about it," he said. Softly, but very firmly. "If you can't abide by those rules—"

He tossed his head dismissively. "—then follow those five bums back to your cozy barracks in Constantinople."

He drained the cup. Held it out. As it was being refilled, he remarked casually: "The reason those noble fellows in Constantinople are confused on this point is because those fine aristocratic champions don't know what a campaign looks like in the first place. When's the last time they went to war?"

A chuckle swept through the little crowd.

"A *campaign*, men, is when you set out to thrash the enemy senseless and *do it*. Once that job's done—we call it *winning the war*—booty's no problem at all. But we're not talking about 'gleanings' here."

Scornfully: " 'Gleanings' means stealing silver plate from a peasant's hut. His *only* silver plate, if he has one in the first place. Or his chickens. *Booty* means the wealth of empires, disgorged to their conquerors."

He lifted his cup, waved it in the general direction of the east.

"There's no empire in the world richer than the Malwa. And they travel in style, too, let me tell you. When I was at Ranapur, the Malwa Emperor erected a pavilion damned near as big as the Great Palace. And you wouldn't believe what he filled it with!

His throne alone—his 'traveling chair,' he called it—was made of solid—"

Belisarius continued in this happy vein for another ten minutes. Half that time he spent regaling his audience with tales of Malwa treasure, spoken in a tone of awe and wonder. The other half, with tales of Malwa fecklessness and cowardice, in tones of scorn and derision.

None of it was, quite, outright lies. None of it was, quite, cold sober truth.

By the time he finished, he had emptied another amphora of wine. His audience had emptied their fair share, also.

He glanced up at the sun. Yawned.

"Ah, hell. It's too late to start a proper march now, anyway."

He rose to his feet.

"Give me a minute, boys, to give the order. Then we can get down to some serious drinking."

The soldiers ogled him. The general was not only standing erect, with perfect ease, he wasn't even swaying. Belisarius strode toward Valentinian and Anastasius. His two cataphracts had remained on their horses, sweating rivers in the hot sun. Glaring resentfully at the Constantinople troops.

In a loud voice, he called out to them: "Pass the word to Maurice! We'll take a break for the rest of the day. Resume the march tomorrow morning."

He began to turn away, waving his hand in a gesture of dismissal. Then, as if taken by a sudden happy thought, added: "And tell my servants to bring some wine! Plenty of it—enough for all of us. Good vintage, too—d'ye hear? I'll have no swill for these men!"

By the time the servants appeared, leading a small mule train carrying many large amphorae, the encampment of the Constantinople troops had turned into a cheerful celebration. The audience surrounding the general had grown much, much larger. Dozens of common soldiers—hundreds, counting those milling on the edges—had crowded around the sub-officers in the inner circle.

When the sun fell, Belisarius ordered the canopy dismantled, so that all of his soldiers could hear him better. That done, he continued his tales.

Tales of Malwa treasure and Malwa military incompetence, of course. But, woven among those tunes, were other melodies as well. He spoke of the huge numbers of the Malwa, which could only be thwarted by disciplined and spirited troops. Of the valor of their Persian allies, and the imperative necessity of not offending them with misconduct. Of his own nature as a general—good-hearted but, when necessary, *firm.*

But most of all, as the evening progressed, he spoke of Rome. Rome, and its thousand years of glory. Rome, often defeated in battle—rarely in war. Rome, savage when it needed to be—but, in the end, an empire of laws. Whose very emperor—and here his troops suddenly remembered, with not a little awe, that the genial man sharing their cups was the Emperor's own father—only ruled with the consent of the governed. *Especially* the consent of those valiant men whose blood and courage had forged Rome and kept it safe through the centuries.

The very men who shared his wine.

He drained his last cup. "I believe I've had enough," he announced. He rose to his feet—slowly, carefully, but without staggering—and eyed his horse. "Fuck it," he muttered. "Too far to ride."

He turned toward Agathius. "With your permission, chiliarch, I'd like to make my bed here tonight."

Agathius' eyes widened. He rose himself, rather shakily, and stared about. He seemed both startled and a bit embarassed. "We don't have much in the way of—"

Belisarius casually waved his hand.

"A blanket'll do. Often enough I've used my saddle for a pillow, on campaign."

Two decarchs hastily scrambled about, digging up the best blanket they could find.

As they saw to that task, Belisarius straightened and said, very loudly:

"If there is any request that you have, make it now. It will be granted, if it is within my power to do so."

There was a moment's hesitation. Then, a hecatontarch cleared his throat and said: "It's about the men you've—your Thracians have been dragging alongside us."

A little mutter of agreement swept the crowd. There was resentment in that mutter, even some anger, but nothing in the way of hot fury.

Agathius spoke, very firmly: "Those boys were a bad lot, sir. We all knew it. Wasn't the first time they mistreated folk. Still—"

"Shouldn't be *dragged*," someone complained.

A different voice spoke: "Fuck that! A stinking *filthy* bunch they were—and you all know it!"

The man who had spoken rose.

"Drag them all you want, sir. Just don't do it next to us. It's—it's not right."

The mutter which swept the crowd was more in the nature of a growl, now.

Belisarius nodded. "Fair enough. I'll have them buried first thing in the morning. A Christian burial, if I can find a priest to do the rites."

A soldier nearby snorted. "Fat lot of good that'll do 'em, once Satan gives 'em the eye."

A ripple of laughter swept the encampment.

Belisarius smiled himself, but said: "That's for the Lord to decide, not us. They'll have a Christian burial."

He paused, then spoke again. His powerful voice was low-pitched, but carried very well. Very well.

"There will be no more of this business."

He made no threats. The hundreds of soldiers who heard him noted the absence of threats, and appreciated it. They also understood and appreciated, now, that their general was not a man who issued threats. But that, came to it, he would have half an army drag the corpses of the other half, if that was what it took to make it *his* army.

"Yes, sir," came from many throats.

"My name is Belisarius. I am your general."

"Yes, sir," came from all throats.

The next morning, shortly after the army resumed its march, a courier arrived from the Persian forces who had gone ahead. The courier had been sent back by Kurush to inquire—delicately, delicately—as to the current state of the Roman army.

Belisarius was not there to meet the courier. He was spending the day marching in the company of his Constantinople troops. But Maurice apprised the Persian of the recent developments.

After the courier returned to Kurush's tent, that evening, and related the tale, the young Persian commander managed to restrain himself until the courier was gone.

Then, with only his uncle for an audience, he exploded.

"I can't believe it!" he hissed. "The man is utterly mad! He deals with a mutiny by dismissing the *officers*?—and then promotes the *mutineers*? And then spends the whole night carousing with them as if—"

"Remind me again, nephew," interrupted Baresmanas, coldly. "I seem to have forgotten. Which one of us was it—who won the battle at Mindouos?"

Kurush's mouth snapped shut.

That same evening, in the Roman encampment, the new chiliarch of the Constantinople troops arrived for his first command meeting. He brought with him the newly appointed tribunes—Cyril was one of them—and two hecatontarchs. Throughout the ensuing conference, the seven Greek soldiers sat uneasily to one side. They did not participate, that night, in the discussion. But they listened closely, and were struck by four things.

One. The discussion was lively, free-wheeling, and relaxed. Belisarius clearly did not object to his subordinates expressing their opinions openly—quite unlike most Roman generals in their experience.

Two. That said, it was always the general who made the final decisions. Clear decisions, clearly stated, leading to clear lines of action. Quite unlike the murky orders which were often issued by commanders, which left their subordinates in the unenviable position of being blamed in the event of miscommunication.

Three. No one was in the least hostile toward them. Not even the general's Thracian cataphracts.

Indeed, the commander of his bucellarii, Maurice, singled them out following the meeting, and invited them to join him in a cup of wine. And both commanders of the Syrian troops, the brothers Bouzes and Coutzes, were quick to add their company.

Many cups later in the evening, Agathius shook his head ruefully.

"I can't figure it out," he muttered, "but somehow I think I've been swindled."

"You'll get no sympathy from us," belched Coutzes.

"Certainly not!" agreed his brother cheerfully. Bouzes leaned over and refilled Agathius' cup. "At least you got swindled *into* an army," he murmured.

Agathius stared at him, a bit bleary-eyed. "What's *that* supposed to mean?"

"Never mind," stated Maurice. The burly veteran held out his own cup. "I believe I'll make my own reconnaissance-in-force on that amphora, Bouzes. If you would be so kind."

And that produced the fourth, and final, impression in the minds of the Constantinople men that night.

A peculiar sense of humor, those Thracians and Syrians seemed to have. The quip was witty, to be sure—but to produce such a howling gale of knee-slapping laughter?

Chapter 12
MUZIRIS
Summer, 531 A.D.

"Under no circumstances, Empress," stated the viceroy of Muziris firmly. "Your grandfather will neither see you, nor will he rescind the ban on your travel to the capital at Vanji."

The viceroy turned in his plush, heavily-upholstered chair and gestured to a man sitting to his right. Like the viceroy, this man was dressed in the expensive finery of a high Keralan official. But instead of wearing the ruby-encrusted sword of a viceroy, he carried the emerald-topped staff of office which identified him as one of Kerala's *Matisachiva*. The title meant "privy councillor," and he was one of the half-dozen most powerful men in the South Indian kingdom.

The Matisachiva was slender; the viceroy, corpulent. Otherwise, their appearance was similar and quite typical of Keralans. Kerala was a Dravidian land. Its people were small and very dark-skinned—almost as dark as Africans. Shakuntala's own size and skin color, along with her lustrous black eyes, were inherited from her Keralan mother.

The Matisachiva's name was Ganapati. The moment Shakuntala had seen him, sitting next to the viceroy in his audience chamber, she understood the significance of his presence. She remembered Ganapati. Ten years before, at the age of nine, she had spent a pleasant six months in Vanji, the capital city in the interior. At the time, she had been the daughter of the great Emperor of Andhra, visiting her mother's family. She had been well-received then, even doted upon—and by none more so than her grandfather. But, even then, there had been times that a head-strong girl had to be held in check. Whenever such times came, it had always been Ganapati who was sent to do the deed.

Andhra was gone now, crushed under the Malwa heel. But she was quite sure that Ganapati retained his old special post—saying *no* for the King of Kerala.

Ganapati cleared his throat.

"The King—your grandfather—is in a difficult situation. Very difficult. The Malwa Empire is not directly threatening us. Nor are they likely to, in the foreseeable future. Malwa's ambitions in the Deccan seem to have been satisfied by their"—he grimaced apologetically—"conquest of your father's realm. And now their attention is focussed to the northwest. Their recent invasion of Persia, from our point of view, was a blessing. The great bulk of their army is tied up there, unavailable for use against the independent south Indian monarchies. Persia will not fall easily, not even to the Malwa."

The viceroy leaned forward, interjecting earnestly: "That's especially true in light of the newest development. According to the most recent reports, it seems that the Roman Empire will throw its weight on the side of the Aryans. Their most prestigious general, in fact, is apparently leading an army into Persia. A man by the name of Belisarius. As Ganapati says, the Malwa Empire is now embroiled in a war which will last for years. Decades, even."

Ganapati cleared his throat.

"Under these circumstances, the obvious course of action for Kerala is to do nothing that might aggravate the Malwa. They are oriented northwest, not south. Let us keep it that way."

Dadaji Holkar interrupted. "That is only true for the immediate period, Matisachiva. The time will come when Malwa will resume its march to the south. They will not rest until they have conquered all of India."

Ganapati gave Shakuntala's adviser a cold stare. For all of Holkar's decorum and obvious erudition, the Keralan councillor suspected that the headstrong Empress-in-exile had chosen a most unsuitable man to be her adviser. The impetuous child had even named the man as her *peshwa*! As if her ridiculous "government-in-exile" needed a premier.

The Matisachiva sniffed. No doubt Holkar was brahmin, as Maratha counted such things. But Maratha blood claims were threadbare, at best. Like all Maratha, Holkar was a deeply polluted individual.

Still—Ganapati was a diplomat. So he responded politely.

"That is perhaps true," he said. "Although I think it is unwise to believe we can read the future. Who really knows Malwa's ultimate aims?"

He held up a hand, forestalling Shakuntala's angry outburst.

"Please, Your Majesty! Let us not quarrel over the point. Even if your adviser's assessment is accurate, it changes nothing. Malwa intentions are one thing. Their capabilities are another. Let us suppose, for a moment, that the Malwa succeed in their conquest of Persia. They will be exhausted by the effort—*and* preoccupied with the task of administering vast and newly-subjugated territories."

He leaned back in his chair, exuding self-satisfaction.

"Either way, you see, Malwa poses no danger to Kerala—*so long as we do not provoke them.*"

The Matisachiva frowned, casting a stony glance at Holkar.

"Unfortunately, the recent actions of the Maratha rebels are stirring up the—"

"They are not *rebels*," snapped Shakuntala. "They are Andhra *loyalists*, fighting to restore the legitimate power to the Deccan. Which is *me*. I am the rightful ruler of Andhra, not the Malwa invaders."

For a moment, Ganapati was nonplussed.

"Well—yes. Perhaps. In the best of all worlds. But we do not live in that world, Empress." The frown returned. "The fact is that Malwa *has* conquered Andhra. In *that* world—the *real* world—Raghunath Rao and his little band of outlaws—"

"Not so little," interjected Holkar. "And hardly outlaws! Speaking of new developments—we just received word yesterday that Rao has seized the city of Deogiri after overwhelming the large Malwa garrison."

Ganapati and the viceroy jerked erect in their chairs.

"*What?*" demanded the viceroy. "*Deogiri?*"

"Madness," muttered the Matisachiva. "Utter madness."

Ganapati rose to his feet and began pacing. For all the councillor's practiced diplomacy, he was obviously very agitated.

"Deogiri?"

Holkar nodded.

"Yes, Matisachiva—*Deogiri*. Which, as you know, is both the largest and the best fortified city in southern Majarashtra."

The Matisachiva pressed both hands against his beard.

"This is a catastrophe!" he exclaimed. He turned toward Holkar and Shakuntala, waving his hands in midair.

"Do you know what this means? The Malwa will be sending a large army to subdue the rebels! And Deogiri is not far from Kerala's northern frontier!"

Holkar smiled icily.

"What 'large' army?" he demanded. "You just got through pointing out that most of the Malwa Empire's forces are tied up in Persia."

Shakuntala's adviser overrode the Matisachiva's splutter of protest.

"You can't have it both ways, Councillor Ganapati! The fact is that Rao's stroke was masterful. The fact is that he does *not* lead a 'small band of outlaws.' The fact is that he seized Deogiri with a large force, and has every chance of holding it for some time. The Malwa satrap Venandakatra has nothing at his disposal beyond provincial troops and what small portions of the regular Malwa army can be spared from the war in Persia. Personally, I doubt if they will be able to release *any* of those forces. As it happens, I know the Roman general Belisarius personally. His military reputation is quite deserved."

Ganapati's hand-waving now resembled the flapping of an outraged hen. "This in intolerable! The whole situation is intolerable!" He glared furiously at Shakuntala and her peshwa. "Enough!" he cried. "We have tried to be diplomatic—*but enough*! You and your Marathas have practically taken possession of Muziris! At least two thousand of your brigand horsemen—"

Shakuntala shot to her feet. "They are not brigand horsemen! They are Maratha cavalrymen who escaped from Andhra after the Malwa conquest and have been reconstituted as my regular army under properly appointed officers!"

"And there are quite a bit more than 'at least two thousand,'" growled Holkar. "By last count, the Empress of Andhra's Maratha cavalry force in Muziris numbers over four thousand. In addition, we have two thousand or so infantrymen, being trained by eight hundred Kushans who have spurned Malwa and given their loyalty to Shakuntala. Elite soldiers, those Kushans—each and every one of them—as you well know.

"In short," he concluded coldly, "the Empress has a considerably larger force than the Keralan garrison residing in the city." Very coldly: "And a much better force, as well."

Ganapati ogled the peshwa. "Are you threatening us?" he cried. *"You would dare?"*

Holkar rose to his own feet. It was not an angry, lunging gesture; simply the firm stance of a serious man who has reached the limit of his patience. "That's enough," he said, quietly but firmly. He placed a hand on Shakuntala's shoulder, restraining her anger.

"There is no point in pursuing this further," he continued. "The situation is clear. The King of Kerala has abandoned his duty to his own kin, and acquiesces in the Malwa subjugation of Andhra. *So be it.* In the meantime, refugees from the Malwa tyranny have poured into Kerala. Most of these refugees have concentrated in Muziris. Among them are thousands of superb Maratha cavalry loyal to Empress Shakuntala. All of which means that, at the moment, she constitutes the real power in the city."

Ganapati and the viceroy were staring wide-eyed at Holkar. The peshwa was speaking the simple, unadorned truth—which was the last thing they had been expecting.

Holkar spread his hands in a sharp, forceful gesture. "As you say, Ganapati, the situation is intolerable. For us as much as for you."

"You threaten us?" gobbled the Matisachiva. "You would dare? You would—"

"Be silent!" commanded Shakuntala.

Ganapati's gobbling ceased instantly. Holkar fought down a grin. The Keralan dignitary had never encountered Shakuntala in full imperial fury. When she threw herself into it, Shakuntala could be quite overpowering, for all her tender years.

"We do not intend to occupy Muziris," she stated, coldly—almost contemptuously. "Since my grandfather has demonstrated for all the world his unmanliness and disrespect for kin, I cast him from my sight. I will leave Kerala—and take all my people with me."

She glared at the two Keralan officials. "*All of them*. Not just the cavalrymen, but all of the other refugees, as well."

The viceroy shook his head, frowning. "There are at least forty thousand of them," he muttered. "Where will—"

"We will go to Tamraparni. The ruler of that great island has offered one of his sons in marriage to me. He has also said he would welcome Andhra's refugees and will assist me in my struggle to regain my rightful place. In light of my grandfather's treachery, I have decided to accept the offer."

She fell silent. After a moment, Ganapati and the viceroy exchanged stares.

At first, their expressions registered astonishment. Then, delight. Then, once the obvious obstacle occured to them, puzzlement.

Gauging the moment, Shakuntala spoke again. "Yes. I will require a fleet of transport ships. At least a hundred and fifty. Preferably two hundred. You will provide them for me, along with the funds needed to carry through this great migration."

Again, the squawks of official outrage filled the room. But Holkar, watching, sensed the victory. When it came, even sooner than he had expected, he was gratified but not surprised. Following his sovereign through the corridors of the viceregal palace, back to their waiting escort, he took the time to admire the small figure of the girl striding before him.

She is listening to me. Finally.

As they rode back toward the refugee camps, Shakuntala leaned over her saddle and smiled at Holkar.

"That went quite well."

"I told you it would work."

"Yes, yes," she murmured. "I see now that I really must listen more closely to my adviser."

Holkar did not miss the sly smile.

"Impudent child," he grumbled.

"Impudent?" she demanded. "This—coming from you? Wait till the ruler of Tamraparni discovers that he has promised to aid me in my war against Malwa! And his son's hand in marriage!"

"He has a son," replied Holkar, with dignity. "Several of them, in fact. And I have no doubt that he *would* have made the offer, if he listened carefully to his advisers."

Shakuntala laughed. "You are an incorrigible schemer, Dadaji!"

"*Me?* You are no slouch yourself, Your Majesty."

Holkar gave her a wry smile. "Although there are times you petrify me with your boldness. I thought you were mad, to order Rao—"

"I *told* you Rome would enter the Persian war immediately," the Empress stated. The satisfaction on the girl's face was obvious. It was not often that the nineteen-year-old Empress had been proven right in a disagreement with her canny, middle-aged peshwa. "And I *told* you Belisarius would be leading their army."

"Yes, you did," agreed Holkar. "That was why you overrode my protest at the insane idea of having Rao seize Deogiri immediately. I had thought to wait, until we were certain that Belisarius and the Romans had entered the war."

The humor left Shakuntala's face. "I had no choice, Dadaji," she whispered. "You were there when Rao's courier told us of Venandakatra's atrocities in the Majarashtra countryside. The beast was murdering ten villagers for every one of his soldiers lost to Rao's raiders."

Holkar's own face was drawn. "He will butcher even more, in retaliation for Deogiri."

The Empress shook her head.

"I think you are wrong, Dadaji. With southern Majarashtra's largest city in our hands, Venandakatra will have no choice. His own status with the Malwa Emperor will depend on retaking Deogiri. He does not have so great an army that he can besiege Deogiri—you know how strong it is; the place is a fortress—and still send his cavalry on punitive rampages throughout the Deccan. Nor can he call for assistance from Emperor Skandagupta. You know as well as I do that the Malwa have been pressing him to release troops for the Persian campaign. With Rome—and Belisarius—now in the war, they will most certainly not send him reinforcements."

Again, she shook her head. "No, I am right here also—I am sure of it. The pressure on the Maratha country folk will ease, while the Vile One concentrates on Deogiri."

"And what if he takes Deogiri?" demanded Holkar. "What then? And what if the Malwa defeat the Persians and Romans quickly?"

Shakuntala laughed. "*Quickly?* With *Belisarius* leading the Romans?"

Holkar smiled. "I admit, the likelihood is not great." He cocked an eye at her. "You're counting on that, aren't you?"

She nodded—firmly, seriously. "I never would have ordered Rao to take Deogiri, otherwise."

The look she now gave her adviser was not that of an impetuous child. It was almost ancient in its cold calculation.

"He is using us, you know—Belisarius, I mean. That was why he freed me from captivity, and gave me most of the treasure he stole from the Malwa. To start a rebellion in their rear, draining forces which would otherwise be sent against him."

Dadaji nodded. "It is his way of thinking." He studied her face. "You do not seem indignant about the matter," he commented.

The Empress shrugged. "Why should I be? Belisarius was never dishonest about it. He *told* me what he was doing. And he also promised me that he would do what was in his power to aid us. Which"—she chuckled—"he is certainly doing."

She urged her horse into a faster pace. "You know the man well, Dadaji—better than I do, when it comes down to it. He is the most cunning man in the world, yes—unpredictable, in his tactics. But there is one thing about Belisarius which is as predictable as the sunrise."

"His honor."

She nodded. "He *promised* me. And he has not failed to keep that promise. He will batter the Malwa beasts in Persia, while we bleed them in the Deccan."

She urged her mount into a trot. There was no reason for that, really, other than her irrepressible energy.

"I was right to order Rao to seize Deogiri," she pronounced. "Now, we must see to it that he can keep the city."

Chapter 13

THE EASTERN MEDITERRANEAN
Summer, 531 A.D.

The expedition which set sail from Rhodes toward the end of summer was an impressive armada.

Antonina had brought a sizable fleet with her from Constantinople, to begin with. She had enough transport ships to carry her grenadiers, the five hundred bucellari under Ashot's command, and the infantrymen from the Army of Syria who would embark later at Seleuceia. The transports, all of them merchant sailing vessels, were escorted by two dromons, the oared warships favored by the Roman navy.

She had even requisitioned three of the great grain ships. The merchant combines which financed those ships had complained bitterly, despite Antonina's generous compensation, but the Empress Theodora had cowed them into submission. Quite easily. A simple frown, a purse of the lips, a glance at the Grand Justiciar. The merchants had suddenly discovered their compensation was quite ample, thank you.

The huge grain haulers slowed her fleet considerably, but Antonina had had no choice. At a great ceremony in the Forum of Constantine, five days before her departure from Constantinople, Michael of Macedonia had presented her with the Knights Hospitaler who had volunteered for the Egyptian expedition. Antonina had been expecting the monks from the new religious order—but not *three thousand* of them, proudly drawn up in their simple white tunics, marked by the distinctive red cross.

What she had conceived of, initially, as a lean military expedition, had grown by leaps and bounds. No sooner had she obtained the grain ships for the Knights Hospitaler than a small horde of officials and bureaucrats showed up at the docks. These were staffs—the typically bloated staffs—for the newly-appointed civil and canonical authorities of Egypt, clerks, and scribes, in the main, to serve the new Praetorian Prefect of Egypt and the Patriarch of Alexandria. Each and every one of whom, naturally, luxuriated in the grandiose titles with which those mundane occupations were invariably annointed by Roman official custom: *tabularii, scrinarii, cornicularii, commentarienses, magister libellorum, magister studiorum, speculatores, beneficiarii . . .*

And so on and so forth.

They, too, wailed like lost sheep when presented with their crude shipboard accommodations—tents, for the most part, pitched on the decks of the small sailing ships which Antonina hastily rounded up, naturally over the wails of *their* owners. But they, too, like the disgruntled grain traders, reconciled themselves to their fate. Theodora's frown had almost magical capabilities, when it came to quelling indignant merchants and bureaucrats.

Then, the very day before departure, Michael had shown up to inform her, quite casually—*insufferable saint! damnable prophet!*—that many more Knights Hospitaler would be waiting in Seleuceia and Tyre and possibly other ports along the Levant, eager to join the crusade in Egypt.

Three more grain ships were seized—one of them overhauled by her dromons as it tried to flee the Golden Horn—emptied hurriedly of their cargoes and pressed into imperial service. Again, Theodora put her frown to work.

Finally, departure came. For a few days, Antonina luxuriated in the relative quiet of a sea voyage, until her arrival at Rhodes placed new demands upon her. John had been forewarned, by courier, of the imperial plan to transfer his armaments complex to Egypt. But, with his stubborn, mulish nature, he had made only half-hearted and lackadaisical efforts to organize the transfer. So, once again, the task had fallen on Antonina. She scrambled about, requisitioning ships on Rhodes itself—and then, coming up short, sending

Ashot with the dromons to commandeer some of the vessels at Seleuceia—until the expedition was finally ready to sail.

But, in the end, sail it did. With the newest addition to the fleet proudly in the fore—John's new warship.

John took immense pride in the craft. It was the first warship in the history of the world, he announced, which was designed exclusively for gunpowder tactics. Menander demurred, at first, on hearing that claim, pointing out that the Malwa had already developed rocket ships. But John had convinced the young cataphract otherwise. The Malwa rocket ships, he pointed out, were a bastard breed. Clumsy merchant ships, at bottom, with a few portable rocket troughs added on. Jury-rigged artillery platforms, nothing more.

Menander, after seeing the ship for himself, had quickly changed his mind. Indeed, this was something new in the world.

John's pride and joy was not completely new, of course. In the press of time, the Rhodian had not been able to build a ship from scratch. So he had started with the existing hull of an *epaktrokeles*—a larger version of the Roman Empire's courier vessels. He had then added gunwales and strengthened the ship's deck with bulwarks, so that the recoil of the cannons would not cave in the planking.

In the end, he had a swift sailing craft armed with ten cast-bronze guns, arranged five on a side. The cannons were short-barreled, with five-inch bores which had been scraped and polished to near-uniform size. For solid shot, which they could fire with reasonable accuracy up to three hundred yards, John had selected marble cannon balls. The balls had been smoothed and polished to fit the bores properly. For cannister, the cannons were provided with lead drop-shot.

"What did you decide to call her?" asked Menander.

"The Theodora."

"Good choice," said Menander, nodding his head vigorously.

John grinned. "I am mulish, stubborn, contrary, pig-headed and irascible, Menander. I am *not* stupid."

Had her fleet consisted purely of warships, Antonina could have made the voyage to Alexandria in less than a week; with favorable winds, three or four days.

The winds, in fact, *were* favorable. Antonina learned, from John and Ashot, that the winds in the eastern Mediterranean were almost always favorable for southward travel during the summer months. Eight days out of ten, they could count on a steady breeze from the northwest.

The slow grain ships, of course, set the pace for the armada. But even those ships, with favorable winds, could have made the passage in a week.

Yet, she estimated the voyage would take at least a month, probably two. The reason was not nautical, but political and military.

The immediate goal of her expedition was to stabilize the Empire's hold over Egypt and Alexandria. But Irene and Cassian had counseled—and Theodora had agreed—that Antonina should kill two birds with one stone. Or, to use a more apt metaphor, should intimidate the cubs on her way to bearding the lion.

The religious turmoil had not spread—yet—to the Levant. But the same forces which were undermining the Empire in Egypt were equally at work in Syria and Palestine, and, in the person of Patriarch Ephraim, had an authoritative figure around which to coalesce.

So Theodora had instructed her, as she sailed along the eastern shore of the Mediterranean, to "show the standard."

Antonina had been quite taken by that expression. When she mentioned it to Belisarius, her husband had smiled crookedly and said:

"Catchy, isn't it? She got it from me, you know. From Aide, I should say—although the proper expression is 'show the flag.' "

Antonina frowned, puzzled.

"What's a 'flag'?"

After Belisarius explained, Antonina shook her head.

"Some of what they do in the future is just plain stupid. Why would anyone in their right mind replace a perfectly good imperial gold standard with a raggedy piece of cloth?"

"Oh, I don't know. As a soldier, I have to say I approve. A flag's light. *You* try hauling around a great heavy gold standard in a battle someday. In Syria, in the summertime."

Antonina brushed the problem aside, with great dignity.

"Nonsense. *I'm* not a lowly foot soldier. *I'm* an admiral. *My* ships will damn well 'show the standard.' "

◊   ◊   ◊

And show it they did.

At Seleuceia, first. They stayed in that great port for a full week. Two of those days were required to embark the hundreds of new Knights Hospitaler who came aboard. But most of the time was spent bearding Patriarch Ephraim in his den.

Seleuceia was Antioch's outlet to the sea. Antioch was the Empire's third greatest city, after Constantinople and Alexandria. Antonina did not take her troops into Antioch itself, but she spent the week parading about the streets of Antioch's harbor. By the third day, most of the population—especially the Syrian commoners—were cheering her madly. Those who weren't were huddling in their villas and monasteries. Thinking dark thoughts, but saying nothing above the level of a mutter.

On her seventh and last day in Seleuceia, a large contingent from the Army of Syria arrived from their fortress in Daras. Most of those soldiers boarded her ships. The rest—

With great ceremony, Antonina turned over to their safe-keeping the large band of artisans who would erect the semaphore stations between Antioch and Seleuceia. Those stations would serve as the link between the coastal network she would create and the Anatolian-Mesopotamian leg which Belisarius was constructing.

While Antonina engaged in public browbeating, Irene occupied herself with subterfuge. She traveled secretly to Antioch, and, by end of the week, had solidified the previously-shaky imperial spy network in Ephraim's domain.

South, now, to Tyre. Stopping, if only for a few hours, at every port of any size along the way.

Showing the standard.

Tyre was a celebration. And a great, subtle victory.

The population of the city was out in force, packed into the harbor, awaiting her arrival. She and her soldiers could hear the cheering from a mile away. Standing on the docks, proudly drawn up, were another thousand Knights Hospitaler.

And, standing among them, the Bishop of Jerusalem.

Theodosius, the newly-designated Patriarch of Alexandria whom Antonina was taking to Egypt, pointed him out to her as soon as her flagship drew near the docks. He began to whisper urgently into her ear, explaining the significance of the Bishop's presence. On her other side, Irene was doing the same.

Antonina stilled them both with a gesture. "I know quite well what it means, Theodosius—Irene. The Bishop of Jerusalem has decided to break from Patriarch Ephraim's authority and submit to that of the imperium's church."

She chuckled drily. "Of course, he has his own fish to fry. The See of Jerusalem has been trying to get official recognition as a Patriarchate for—what is it, now? Three centuries?"

Theodosius nodded.

Antonina's chuckle turn into a little laugh. "Well, and why not? Isn't Jerusalem the holiest city in Christendom, when you come right down to it?"

Theodosius stroked his beard furiously. "Well, yes, I suppose. But the Church councils have always ruled against Jerusalem's claim, on the grounds—"

"—that it's a dinky little border town. Filled—or rather, not so filled—by a bunch of sleepy provincials."

Theodosius winced. "That's putting it rather crudely. But—yes. In essence."

"And what's wrong with sleepy provincials? You won't see *them* ruining a perfectly good afternoon nap by wrangling over the relationship between the *prosopon* and the *hypostasis* of Christ."

She turned away from the rail, still smiling. "*Patriarch* of Jerusalem," she murmured. "Yes, yes. Has a nice sound to it."

In the end, she actually *went* to Jerusalem. Suspending her voyage for a full month, while she and her Theodoran Cohort—and all of the Knights Hospitaler from Constantinople, eager to finally see the Holy Land for themselves—marched inland.

A great, grand escort for the Bishop of Jerusalem in his triumphant return. Antonina found the bishop to be, in his person, a thoroughly obnoxious creature. Petty in his concerns, and petulant in his manner. But she took great delight in his *persona*. By the time she left Jerusalem, the Bishop—who was already calling himself the Patriarch—had given his complete and public blessing to her enterprise.

By tradition and church rulings, the Patriarch of Antioch had always held authority over that great area of Syria and the Levant which Romans called *Oriens*. No longer. In a week at Seleuceia, Antonina had undermined Ephraim's prestige. Now, in a month in Palestine, she had cut his ecclesiastical territory in half.

A new council would have to be called, of course, to confirm—or, again, deny—Jerusalem's claim. Antonina did not begin to have the authority to do so. Not even the Emperor, without the approval of a council, could establish a new Patriarchate. But any such council was far in the future. Theodora would stall, stall, stall. For years to come, the Bishop of Jerusalem would defy Ephraim and cling as closely as possible to the Empress Regent's imperial robes.

Show the standard, indeed. As her flagship sailed away from Tyre, Antonina gazed up admiringly at the great, gold imperial standard affixed to the mainmast.

"A 'flag'!" she snorted. "How in the name of Christ could you intimidate anybody with a stupid rag?"

But the best—the very best—came at a fishing village. Antonina was pleased, of course, by the welcome given to her by the small but enthusiastic population, who greeted her armada from their boats. But she was absolutely delighted by the welcome given by the men aboard the much bigger ship which sailed among those humble fishermen.

A warship from Axum. Carrying Prince Eon and his dawazz, who bore official salutations from the negusa nagast to the new Roman Emperor. Along with a proposal for an alliance against Malwa.

Her first words to Eon were: "How in the world did you get a warship into the Mediterranean from the Red Sea?"

His, to her with a grimace. "We portaged. Don't ask me how. I can't remember."

"Fool boy!" Ousanos said. "He can't remember because it's impossible. I told him so."

Irene to Ousanas, grinning: "You must have slapped his head a thousand times."

Ousanas groaned: "Couldn't. Was much too weary. Idiot Prince made me carry the stern. All by myself."

Eon, proudly: "Ousanas is the strongest man in the world."

Ousanas slapped the Prince atop his head. "Suckling babe! Strongest man in the world is resting somewhere in his bed. Conserving his strength for sane endeavors!"

Chapter 14

MESOPOTAMIA
Summer, 531 A.D.

The first sign of trouble came just a few hours after the army bypassed Anatha. The town, located directly on the Euphrates, was one of the chain of fortified strongholds which the Sassanid emperors had erected, over the centuries, to guard Persia from Roman invasion.

Baresmanas and Kurush had offered to billet the Roman troops in the town itself, along with their own soldiers, but Belisarius had declined.

There was always the risk of incidents with the local inhabitants, whenever a passing army was billeted in a town. That was especially true with an army of foreigners. Had Belisarius' forces consisted of nothing but his Thracians and the Syrian units, he would not have been concerned. His bucellarii were long accustomed to his discipline, and the soldiers from the Army of Syria were only technically foreigners.

The Syrians were closely akin, racially and linguistically, with the people of western Mesopotamia. And the Arabs who constituted a large portion of the Syrian army were identical. Arabs—on both sides of the border—tended to view the political boundaries between Rome and Persia as figments of imperial imagination. Those soldiers were familiar with Persian ways and customs, and

most of them spoke at least passable Pahlavi. Many of those men
had relatives scattered all across the western provinces of the Persian empire.

The same was not true—most definitely not true—with his
Greek and Illyrian troops.

The problem was that Anatha was not large enough to hold his
entire army. He would not trust the Greek and Illyrian soldiers,
without his Thracian and Syrian troops to help keep order. On the
other hand, if he allowed the Syrians and Thracians to enjoy the
comforts of the town, while the Constantinople and Illyrian troops
camped outside—

He would rekindle the resentments which he had finally managed, for the most part, to overcome.

So he ordered the army to bypass the town altogether.

The command, of course, caused hard feelings among his
troops—all of it aimed at him. But the general was not concerned.
To the contrary—he accepted the collective glare of his soldiers
quite cheerfully. The animosity expressed in those glowering eyes
would cement his army, not undermine it. Not so long as *all* of
his soldiers were equally resentful and could enjoy the mutual
bond of grumbling at the lunacies of high command: Sour Thracian
grousing to disgruntled Illyrian, sullen Greek cataphract to surly
Arab cavalryman.

Fucking jackass.

Whoever made this clown a general, anyway?

*By the time we get wherever we're going—the moon, seems
like—we'll be too worn out to spank a brat.*

Fucking jackass.

Whoever made this clown a general, anyway?

Three hours after the walls of Anatha fell below the horizon,
Belisarius saw a contigent of the Arab light cavalry he was using
as scouts come galloping up.

Maurice trotted his horse forward to meet them, while Belisarius
ordered a halt in the march. After a brief consultation with the
scouts, the chiliarch hastened back to Belisarius. By the time he
arrived, Baresmanas and Kurush were already at the general's side,
along with Bouzes and Coutzes.

"There's a mob of refugees pouring up the road from the east,"
reported Maurice. "The scouts interviewed some of them. They

say that a large Malwa cavalry force—" He shrugged. "You know how it is—according to the refugees, there's probably a million Malwa. But it's a large enough force, apparently, to have sacked a town called Thilutha."

"*Thilutha?*" exclaimed Kurush. The young sahrdaran stared to the east.

"Thilutha's not as big as Anatha," he announced, "but it's still a fortified garrison town. There's no way a pure cavalry force should have been able to capture it."

"They've got gunpowder," Belisarius pointed out.

Maurice nodded. "The refugees are babbling tales about witch-craft used to shatter the town's gates."

Belisarius squinted into the distance. "What's your guess, Maurice? And how far away are they?"

The chiliarch stroked his beard thoughtfully. "It's a big force, general. Even allowing for refugee exaggeration, the Arab scouts think there must be at least ten thousand soldiers. Probably more."

"A raiding party," stated Bouzes. His snub-nosed face twisted into a rueful grimace. "A reconnaissance-in-force, probably."

Belisarius nodded. "It's good news, actually. It means Emperor Khusrau is still holding them at Babylon. So the Malwa have sent a large cavalry force around him, to ravage his rear and disrupt his supplies and communications."

He paused for a moment, thinking. "I'm not sure Khusrau can hold Babylon forever, but the longer he does the better it is. We need to buy time. Time for Persia, time for Rome. Best way to do that, right now, is to teach the Malwa they can't raid Mesopotamia with impunity."

His tone hardened. "I want to destroy that force. Hammer them into splinters." He stood in his stirrups, scanning the area around them. "We need a place to trap them."

Kurush frowned. "Anatha is only a few hours behind us. We could return and—"

Belisarius shook his head. "Anatha's much too strong, with us there to aid in the defense. The Malwa will take one look and go elsewhere. Then we'll have to chase *them*, and fight a battle on ground of *their* choosing."

A little smile came to Baresmanas' face. "You want something feeble," he announced. "Some pathetic little fortification that looks like nothing much, but has places to conceal your troops." The smile widened. "Something like that wretched infantry camp you built at Mindouos."

Belisarius' lips twisted. "Yes, Baresmanas. That's exactly what I want."

Comprehension came to Kurush. The young Persian nobleman's face grew pinched, for an instant. Then, suddenly, he laughed.

"You are a cold-blooded man, Belisarius!" he exclaimed. With a sad shake of his head:

"You'd never make a proper Aryan, I'm afraid. Rustam, dehgan of dehgans, would not approve."

Belisarius shrugged. "With all due respect to the legendary national hero of the Aryans, and the fearsome power of his bull-headed mace—Rustam died, in the end."

"Trapped in a pit by his enemies, while hunting," agreed Kurush cheerfully. "Speaking of which—"

The sahrdaran looked to his uncle. "Isn't there an imperial hunting park somewhere in this vicinity?"

Baresmanas pointed across the river, toward a large patch of greenery a few miles away.

"There," he announced.

All the officers in the little group followed his pointing finger. At that moment, Agathius rode up, along with his chief tribune Cyril. Seconds later, the Illyrian commanders arrived also. The top leadership of the Allied army was now assembled. Quickly, the newcomers were informed of the situation and Belisarius' plan.

"We'll need to cross the Euphrates," remarked Coutzes. "Is there a ford nearby?"

"Has to be," replied Maurice. "The refugees are on that side of the river. Since the scouts talked to them, they must have found a way across."

The chiliarch gestured toward the Arab cavalrymen, who had been waiting a short distance away. They trotted up to him and he began a quick consultation.

"It makes sense," commented Kurush. "Thilutha is on the left bank. At this time of year, the river can be forded any number of places. The Malwa have probably been crossing back and forth, ravaging both sides."

Maurice returned.

"The fork's not far, according to the scouts." He gauged the sun. "We can have the whole army across the river by nightfall, if we press the matter."

"Press it," commanded the general.

Belisarius scanned his group of officers. The gaze was not cold, but it was stern. His eyes lingered for a moment on Agathius.

The commander of the garrison troops broke into a grin. "Don't worry, general. My boys won't drag their feet. Not with the prospect of something besides another fucking day's march to look forward to."

His eyes grew a bit unfocussed. "Imperial hunting park," he mused. "Be a royal villa and everything there, I imagine."

He took up his reins, shaking his head. "Terrible, terrible," he murmured, spurring his horse. "Such damage the wondrous thing'll suffer, in a battle and all."

After Agathius was gone, along with all the other subordinate officers except Maurice, Kurush gave Belisarius a cold stare.

"There is *always* a villa in an imperial hunting park," he stated. "Accoutered in a manner fit for the King of Kings. Filled with precious objects."

The general returned the gaze unflinchingly. "He's right, Kurush. I'm afraid the Emperor's possessions are going to take a terrible beating."

"Especially with gunpowder weapons," added Maurice. The Thracian chiliarch did not seem particularly distressed at the thought.

"I'm not concerned about the destruction caused by the *enemy*," snapped the young Persian nobleman.

"Be silent, nephew!" commanded Baresmanas. The sahrdaran's tone was harsh, and his own icy gaze was directed entirely at Kurush.

"I know the Emperor much better than you," he growled. "I have known him since he was a child. Khusrau Anushirvan, he is called—Khusrau 'of the immortal soul.' It is the proper name for that man, believe me. No finer soul has sat the Aryan throne since Cyrus. Do you think such an emperor would begrudge a few tokens to the brave men who come to his aid, when his people are ravaged by demons?"

Kurush shrank back in his saddle. Then, sighing, he reined his horse around and trotted toward his troops. A moment later, Maurice left, heading toward his own soldiers.

Once they were alone, Baresmanas smiled rue-fully. "Quite a few tokens, of course. And such tokens they are!"

Belisarius felt a sudden, deep friendship for the man beside him. And then, an instant later, was seized by a powerful impulse.

"You are quite right, you know."

Baresmanas eyed him.

"About Khusrau, I mean. He will rule the Aryans for fifty years, and will be remembered for as long as Iran exists. 'Khusrau the Just,' they will call him, over the centuries."

Baresmanas' face seemed to pale, a bit, under the desert-darkened complexion.

"I had heard—" he whispered. He took a breath, shakily. "There are rumors that you can foretell the future, Belisarius. Is it true?"

Belisarius could sense Aide's agitation, swirling in his mind. He sent a quick thought toward the flashing facets.

No, Aide. There are times when secrecy defeats its purpose.

He returned the sahrdaran's piercing stare with his own steady gaze.

"No, Baresmanas. Not in the sense that you mean the term."

The army was beginning to resume the march. Belisarius clucked his own horse into forward motion, as did Baresmanas.

The general leaned toward the sahrdaran. "The future is not fixed, Baresmanas. This much I know. Though, it is true, I have received visions of the possible ways that future river might flow."

He paused. Then said, "We worship different gods, my friend. Or, perhaps, it is the same God seen in different ways. But neither of us believes that darkness rules."

He gestured ahead, as if to indicate the still-unseen enemy.

"The Malwa are guided by a demon. That demon brought them the secret of gunpowder, and filled them with their foul ambition. Do you really think such a demon could come into the world—unanswered by divinity?"

Baresmanas thought upon his words, for a time, as they rode along. Then, he said softly, "So. As always, God gives us the choice."

Belisarius nodded. The sahrdaran's pallor faded. He smiled, then, rather slyly.

"Tell me one more thing, Belisarius. I will ask nothing else on this matter, I promise. Did a divine spirit guide you at Mindouos?"

The general shook his head. "No. At least— *No.* I believe such a spirit kept me from harm in the battle. Personally, I mean. But the tactics were mine."

The sahrdaran's sly smile broadened, became a cheerful grin. "For some reason, that makes me feel better. Odd, really. You'd think it would be the opposite—that I would take comfort from knowing we were defeated by a superhuman force."

Belisarius shook his head. "I don't think it's strange at all, Baresmanas. There is—"

He fell silent. There was no way to explain, simply, the titanic struggle in the far distant future of which their own battles were a product. Belisarius himself understood that struggle only dimly, from glimpses. But—

"It is what we are fighting about, I think, in the end. Whether the course of human history is to be shaped by those who make it, or be imposed upon them by others."

He spoke no further words on the subject.

Nor did Baresmanas—then, or ever. In this, the sahrdaran was true to his Aryan myths and legends. He had given his word; he would keep it.

The skeptical scholar in him, of course, found his own stiff honor amusing. Just as he found it amusing that the cunning, low-born Roman would never have revealed his secret, had he not understood that Aryan rigor.

Most amusing, of course, was another thought.

To have picked such a man for an enemy! Demons, when all is said and done, are stupid.

Aide, however, was not amused at all. In the hours that followed, while the army found the ford scouted by the Arab cavalrymen and crossed to the left bank of the Euphrates, and then encamped for the night, Belisarius could sense the facets shimmering in their thoughts. The thoughts themselves he could not grasp, but he knew that Aide was pondering something of great importance to him.

The crystal did not speak to him directly until the camp had settled down, the soldiers all asleep except for the posted sentinels. And a general, who had patiently stayed awake himself, waiting in the darkness for his friend to speak.

Do you really think that is what it is about? Our struggle with the new gods?

Yes.

Pause. Then, plaintively:

And what of us? Do we play no role? Or is it only humans that matter?

Belisarius smiled.

Of course not. You are part of us. You, too, are human.

We are not! shrieked the crystal. **We are different! That is why you created us, because—because—**

Aide was in a frenzy such as Belisarius had not seen since the earliest days of his encounter with the jewel. Despair—frustration—loneliness—confusion—most of all, a frantic need to *communicate*.

But it was *not* the early days. The differences between two mentalities had eased, over the years. Eased far more than either had known.

Finally, finally, the barrier was ruptured completely. A shattering vision swept Belisarius away, as if he were cast into the heavens by a tidal wave.

Chapter 15

Worlds upon worlds upon worlds, circling an incomprehensible number of suns. People on those worlds, everywhere—but people changed and transformed. Misshapen and distorted, most of them. So, at least, most men would say, flinching.

Death comes, striking many of those worlds. The very Earth itself, scoured clean by a plague which spared no form of life. Nothing left—except, slowly, here and there, an advancing network of crystals.

Aide's folk, Belisarius realized, come to replace those who had destroyed their own worlds. Created, by those who had slain themselves, to be their heirs.

Belisarius hung in the darkness. Around him, below him, above him—in all directions—spun great whirling spirals of light and beauty.

Galaxies.

He sensed a new presence, and immediately understood its meaning. A great sigh of relief swept through him.

Finally, finally—

He saw a point of light in the void. A point, nothing more, which seemed infinitely distant. But he knew, even in the seeing, that the distance was one of time not space.

Time opened, and the future came.

The point of light erupted, surged forward. A moment later, floating before Belisarius, was one of the Great Ones.

147

The general had seen glimpses of them, before. Now, for the first time, he saw a Great One clearly.

As clearly, at least, as he ever could. He understood, now, that he would never see them fully. Too much of their structure lay in mysterious forces which would never be seen by earthly eyes.

A new voice came to him. Like Aide's, in a way, but different.

force fields. energy matrices. there is little in us left of our earthly origins. and no flesh at all.

Like a winged whale, vaguely, in its broad appearance. If ever a whale could swim the heavens, glowing from an inner light. But much, much larger. The Great One dwarfed any animal that had ever lived.

OUR DIMENSIONS MEASURE EIGHT BY THREE BY TWO, APPROXIMATELY, IN THE VISIBLE SPECTRUM. WHAT YOU CALL MILES. OUR MASS IS—DIFFICULT TO CALCULATE. IT DEPENDS ON VELOCITY. WE CAN ATTAIN 93% LIGHT SPEED, AT OUR UTMOST—CALL IT EXERTION. WE MUST BE VERY CAREFUL, APPROACHING A SOLAR SYSTEM. SHOULD ONE OF US IMPACT A PLANET, AT THAT VELOCITY, WE WOULD DESTROY IT. AND POSSIBLY OURSELVES AS WELL.

The being had no eyes, no mouth, no apparent sense organs of any kind. Yet the general knew that the Great One could detect everything that any human could, and much else besides.

He saw into the being, now. Saw the glittering network of crystals which formed the Great One's—heart? Soul?

THEY ARE OUR HERITAGE NOW. OUR CREATORS, AS MUCH AS OUR CREATIONS. THEY DO FOR US WHAT SOMETHING CALLED DNA ONCE DID FOR OUR ANCIENT ANCESTORS. ALLOW THE FUTURE TO EXIST.

Belisarius studied the crystalline network more closely. The crystals, he thought, seemed much like Aide. Yet, somehow different.

AIDE IS MUCH DIFFERENT. IT—NO, FOR YOU IT WILL ALWAYS BE "HE"—BEARS THE SAME RELATIONSHIP TO THESE AS YOU DO TO A BACTERIUM. AKIN, BUT GREATER.

The Great One sensed the general's incomprehension. *What is a "bacterium"?*

AS YOU DO TO AN EARTHWORM. OR, BETTER, A MUSHROOM. WE DESIGNED THESE CRYSTALS FOR OUR OWN SURVIVAL. BUT THEN DISCOVERED WE COULD NOT MAKE THEM, OR USE THEM, UNLESS WE CREATED A CRYSTAL INTELLIGENCE TO GUIDE AND ASSIST US. THOSE BECAME AIDE'S PEOPLE.

They were your slaves, then. As I have heard the "new gods" say.

NEVER.

There came a sense of mirth; vast, yet whimsical. And the general knew, then—finally—that these almost inconceivable beings were truly his own folk. He had but to look in a mirror, to see the crooked smile that would, someday, become that universe-encompassing irony—and that delight in irony.

THE PEASANT WHO TILLS THE FIELD BRINGS CHILDREN INTO THE WORLD—TO HELP IN THE LABOR, AMONG OTHER THINGS. ARE THOSE CHILDREN SLAVES?

They can be, replied the general. I have seen it, more often than I like to remember.

The sense of wry humor never faded.

NOT IN YOUR HOUSE. NOT IN YOUR FIELD. NOT IN YOUR SMITHY.

No, but—

The Great One swelled, swirled. Looped the heavens, prancing on wings of light and shadow.

AND WHOSE CHILD AM I—CRAFTSMAN?

There was a soundless peal, that might be called joyful laughter. The Great One swept off, dwindling.

Wait! called out Belisarius.

NO. YOU HAVE ENOUGH. I MUST BE OFF TO JOIN MY BRETHREN AND SEE THE UNIVERSE. OUR FAMILY—YOUR DESCENDANTS—HAVE FILLED THAT UNIVERSE. FILLED IT WITH WONDER THAT WE WOULD SHARE AND BUILD UPON. WE DO NOT HAVE MUCH TIME, IN OUR SHORT LIVES, TO DELVE THAT SPLENDOR. A MILLION YEARS, PERHAPS—NOT COUNTING TIME DILATION.

Nothing but a tiny dot of light, now.

Wait! cried Belisarius again. There is so much I need to know!

The faint dot paused; then, swirled back. A moment later, Belisarius was staring awe-struck at a towering wall of blazing glory.

THERE IS NOTHING YOU NEED TO KNOW, THAT YOU DO NOT ALREADY. WE ARE YOUR CREATION, AS AIDE'S FOLK ARE OURS. AND NOW YOUR GRANDCHILDREN HAVE COME TO YOU FOR HELP, IN THEIR TIME OF TROUBLE.

SO WHAT DO YOU NEED TO KNOW—*OLD MAN*? YOU ARE THE ELDER OF THAT VILLAGE WHICH NOW SPANS GALAXIES. YOU ARE THE BLACKSMITH WHO FORGED HUMANITY ON ITS OWN ANVIL.

Belisarius laughed himself then, and it seemed that the galaxies shivered with his mirth. The Great One before him rippled; waves of humor matching his own.

IT IS OUR MOST ANCIENT RELIGION, GRANDFATHER. AND WITH GOOD REASON.

Swoop—away, away. Gone now, almost. A faint dot, no more.

A faint voice; laughing voice:

CALL IT—ANCESTOR WORSHIP.

When Belisarius returned to the world, he simply stared for a time. Looking beyond the hanging canopy to the great band of stars girdling the night sky. The outposts of that great village of the future.

Then, as he had not done in weeks, he withdrew Aide from his pouch.

There was no need, really. He had long since learned to communicate with the "jewel" without holding it. But he needed to see Aide with his own eyes. Much as he often needed to hold Photius with his own hands. To rejoice in love; and to find comfort in eternity.

Aide spoke.

You did not answer me.

Belisarius:

Weren't you there—when I met the Great One?

Uncertainly:

Yes, but—I do not think I understood. I am not sure.

Plaintively, like a child complaining of the difficulty of its lessons:

We are not like you. We are not like the Great Ones. We are not human. We are not—

Be quiet, Aide. And stop whining. How do you expect to grow up if you whimper at every task?

Silence. Then: **We will grow up?**

Of course. I am your ancestor. One of them, at least. How do you think you got into the world in the first place?

Everything that is made of us grows up. Certainly my offspring!

A long, long silence. Then: We never dreamed. That we, too, could grow.

Aide spoke no more. Belisarius could sense the facets withdrawing into themselves, flashing internal dialogue.

After a time, he replaced the "jewel" in the pouch and lay down on his pallet. He needed to sleep. A battle would erupt soon, possibly even the next day.

But, just as he was drifting into slumber, he was awakened by Aide's voice.

Very faint; very indistinct.

What are you saying? he mumbled sleepily. I can't hear you.

That's because I'm muttering.

Proudly:

It's good you can't hear me. That means I'm doing it right, even though I'm just starting.

Very proudly:

I'll get better, I know I will. Practice makes perfect. Valentinian always says that.

The general's eyes popped open. "Sweet Jesus," he whispered.

I thought I'd start with Valentinian. Growing up, I mean. He's pretty easy. Not the swordplay, of course. But the muttering's not so hard. And—

A string of profanity followed.

Belisarius bolted upright.

"Don't use that sort of language!" he commanded. Much as he had often instructed his son Photius. And with approximately the same result.

Mutter, mutter, mutter.

Chapter 16

By the time Belisarius arrived at the hunting park, the Arab scouts had already had one brief skirmish with the advance units of the oncoming Malwa army. When they returned, the scouts reported that the Malwa main force was less than ten miles away. They had been able to get close enough to examine that force before the Malwa drove them off.

There was good news and bad news.

The good news, as the scout leader put it:

"Shit-pot soldiers. Keep no decent skirmishers. Didn't even see us until we were pissing on their heads. Good thing they didn't bring women. We seduce all of them. Have three bastards each, probably, before shit-pot Malwa notice their new children too smart and good-looking."

The bad news:

"Shit-pot lot of them. *Big* shit-pot."

Belisarius looked to the west. There was only an hour of daylight left, he estimated.

He turned to Maurice. "Take all the bucellarii and the katyushas. When the Persians arrive, I'll have them join you." He pondered, a moment. "And take the Illyrians, too."

A quick look at Timasius, the Illyrian commander. "You'll be under Maurice's command. Any problem with that?"

Timasius shook his head—without hesitation, to Belisarius' relief. His opinion of the Illyrian rose. Smart, the man might not be. But at least he was well-disciplined and cooperative.

The general studied the woods to the northeast.

"Judging from what I saw as we rode in, I think there'll be plenty of good cover over there. I want all the men well hidden, Maurice. No fires, tonight, when you make camp. You'll be my surprise, when I need it, and I don't want the Malwa alerted."

Belisarius did not elaborate any further. With Maurice, there was no need. "You've got signal rockets?"

The Thracian chiliarch nodded.

"Remember, green means—"

"Green means we attack the enemy directly. Red means start the attack with a rocket volley. Yellow—come to your assistance. White—run for our lives."

Maurice glared at Belisarius. "Any instructions on how to lace up my boots?" He glanced at the horizon. "If you're going to tell me which direction the sun goes down, you'd better make it quick. It's already setting. North, I think."

Belisarius chuckled. "Be off, Maurice."

Once the chiliarch trotted off—still glowering—Belisarius spoke to Bouzes and Coutzes.

"One of you—either one, I don't care—take the Syrian infantrymen and start fortifying the royal villa. Take the Callinicum garrison also. The men will probably have to work through the night."

The brothers grimaced. Belisarius smiled.

"Tell them to look on the bright side. They'll have to dismantle the interior of the villa. Be all sorts of loose odds and ends lying around. Have to be picked up, of course, so nobody gets hurt falling all over them."

Bouzes and Coutzes cheered up immediately. Belisarius continued.

"Don't make the fortifications look *too* solid, but make sure you have the grenade screens ready to be erected at a moment's notice. And make sure there's plenty of portals for a quick sally."

The brothers nodded, then looked at each other. After a moment's unspoken discussion—using facial gestures that meant nothing to anyone else—Bouzes reined his horse around and trotted off.

"All right, then," said Belisarius. "Coutzes, I want you to take the Syrian cavalry—and all of the Arab skirmishers except the few we need for scouts—and get them ready for a sally first thing tomorrow morning. It'll be a Hunnish sort of sally, you understand?"

Coutzes nodded. A moment later, he too was trotting away. Only Agathius was left, of the command group, along with his chief tribune Cyril.

Belisarius studied them for a moment.

"I want you and your Constantinople unit to get well rested, tonight. Set a regular camp, not far from the villa. Make sure it's on the eastern grounds of the park, where the terrain is open. I want you between the Malwa and the villa itself. You understand?"

Agathius nodded. Belisarius continued:

"Build campfires—big ones. Allow the men a double ration of wine, and let them enjoy themselves loudly. Encourage them to sing, if they've a taste for it. Just don't let them get drunk."

Cyril frowned. "You're not worried the enemy will see—"

"I'm *hoping* the enemy will scout you out."

Agathius chuckled. "So they *won't* go snooping through the woods on the north, where they might stumble on the Thracians and Illyrians. Or sniff around the villa itself, where they could see how the Syrians are fortifying it."

The burly officer stroked his beard.

"It'll probably work," he mused. "If their skirmishers are as bad as Abbu says, they'll be satisfied with spotting us. Easy, that'll be. They can get back to their army without spending all night creeping through a forest that might have God knows what lurking in it."

Belisarius nodded. Agathius eyed him. His gaze was shrewd—and a bit cold.

"You're going to hammer the shit out of us, aren't you?"

Again, Belisarius nodded.

"Yes, Agathius. Your men are probably going to have the worst of it. In the beginning, at least. I'm hoping the Syrian cavalrymen can draw them into a running battle, lead them back here. If they do—"

"You want us to sally. A big, straight-up, heavy cavalry lance charge. Kind of thing minstrels like to sing about."

"Yes. But you've got to be disciplined about it. That charge has to be solid, but I want you to disengage before you get cut to pieces. Can you do that? I want an honest answer. In my experience, cataphracts tend to think they're invincible. They get so caught up in the—"

Agathius barked a harsh laugh. "For the sake of Christ, general! Do we look like a bunch of aristocrats to you?"

"Right good at disengaging, we are," added Cyril, chuckling. "If you'll forgive me saying so, sir."

Belisarius grinned. "If it'll make you feel any better, I'll be joining you in the charge. I'm rather good at disengaging myself. If you'll forgive me saying so."

The two Greeks laughed—and gaily now. But when their humor died away, there was still a residue of coldness lurking in the back of their eyes.

Belisarius understood immediately. "You've had no experience under my command," he said softly. "I ask you to trust me in this matter. Don't worry about the booty. Tell your men they'll get their fair share—after the battle's won."

Cyril glanced toward the villa. The Syrian infantrymen were already pouring into the lavish structure. Even at the distance—a hundred yards—the glee in their voices was evident.

Agathius' eyes remained on the general. The suspicion in those eyes was open, now.

Belisarius smiled crookedly. "Those Syrians *do* have experience under my command. They know the penalty for private looting. Don't forget, Agathius, my bucellarii won't be anywhere near that villa, either. You didn't see Maurice complain, did you? That's because he's not worried about it. Anybody holds out on my Thracians, there'll be hell to pay."

Agathius couldn't help wincing.

All whimsy left Belisarius' face. When he spoke, his tone was low and earnest.

"In my army, we all share in the spoils. Fairly apportioned *after* the battle. Except for what we set aside to care for the disabled and the families of the men who died, each soldier will get his share. Regardless of where he was or what he was doing."

Agathius and Cyril stared at him. Then Agathius nodded his head. It was not a gesture of assent. It was more in the nature of a bow of fealty. A moment later, Cyril copied him.

When their heads lifted, the familiar crooked smile was back on the general's face.

"And now, if you don't mind, I'd like to discuss the tactics of this—what'd you call it, Agathius—*minstrel charge*?" He chuckled.

"I like the sound of that! Especially if the minstrel can sing a cheerful tune—every hero survived, after all."

Agathius grinned. "I've always preferred cheerful tunes, myself."

"Me too," added Cyril. "Loathe dirges. Detest the damn things."

An hour after sunset, the Persian cavalry showed up at the hunting park. Belisarius met them a mile away from the villa, and explained his plans for the coming battle.

To his relief, Kurush immediately agreed. The young nobleman did cast a sour glance in the direction of the villa, but he made no inquiry as to its condition.

Belisarius himself, with the aid of several Thracian cataphracts sent by Maurice, guided the Persians to the spot in the northeast woods where his bucellarii and the Illyrians had made their camp.

Their progress was slow. The woods were dense—no local woodcutter would dare hew down an imperial tree—and the only illumination came from the last glimmer of twilight. Belisarius took advantage of the time to explain his plans in great detail. He was particularly concerned with impressing upon Kurush the need to let his katyushas open the attack. The rocket chariots had never been used in a battle before. Belisarius wanted to find out how effective they would be.

In the course of their conversation, Kurush filled in some further information on the enemy. The Persians had spent the day scouting the left flank of the approaching Malwa army. Like his own scouts, they had found the enemy's skirmish line to be ragged and ineffective. But—unlike his small group of lightly-armed Arabs—the heavy Persian cavalrymen had been willing to hammer the advance guards and press very close to the Malwa main army before disengaging.

They had seen more of that army, thus, and Kurush was able to add further specifics to the information Belisarius had already obtained.

The Malwa army *was* large—very large, for what was in essence a cavalry raid. Kurush estimated the main body of regular troops numbered twelve thousand. They were not as heavily armed as Persian lancers or Roman cataphracts, but they were not light cavalry either. There *was* a force of light cavalry serving the Malwa—about five hundred Arabs wearing the colors of the Lakhmid dynasty.

Interspersed among the regular troops were battalions of Ye-tai horsemen. Their exact numbers had been difficult to determine, but Kurush thought there were two thousand of the barbarians. Possibly more.

In addition, riding at the center of the Malwa army, the Persians had seen hundreds of Malwa kshatriya and several dozen Mahaveda priests. The priests, unlike the kshatriya, were not on horseback. They were riding in large wagons drawn by mules. The contents of those wagons were hidden under canvas, but Kurush assumed that the wagons contained their gunpowder weapons and devices.

None of this information caused the Roman general any particular distress. The force structure was about what he had guessed, and he was not disturbed by the size of the Malwa army. True, the odds were at least 3–to-2 against him, so far as the numbers were concerned. Still, he would be fighting the battle on the tactical defensive, on ground of his choosing.

But the last item of information which Kurush imparted made him wince.

"Describe them again," he commanded.

"They number perhaps two thousand, Belisarius. They form the Malwa rear guard—which is quite odd, in my opinion. If *I* were leading that army, I would have those troops in the vanguard. They keep formation as well as any parade ground troops I've ever seen, but I don't think—"

Belisarius shook his head. "They are most definitely not parade troops, Kurush."

He sighed. "And the reason they're bringing up the rear is because the Malwa don't trust them much. The problem, however, is not military. It's political."

"Damn," he grumbled. "There were two things I didn't want to run into. One of them are Rajputs, and the other—you're sure about the topknots?"

Kurush nodded. "It's quite a distinctive hairstyle. Their helmets are even designed for it."

"Yes, I know. I've seen them. Kushan helmets."

The Persian winced himself, now. "*Kushans?* You're sure?"

"Yes. No other enemy troops look like that. To the best of my knowledge, anyway—and remember, I spent over a year in India. I got a very close look at the Malwa army."

Kurush started to say something, but broke off in order to dodge a low-hanging branch in the trail. When he straightened, he muttered: "We *did* defeat them, you know. We Aryans. Centuries ago. Conquered half the Kushan empire, in fact."

Belisarius smiled. "No doubt your minstrels sing about it to this day."

"They sing about it, all right," replied Kurush glumly. "Dirges, mostly, about glorious victories with maybe three survivors. The casualties were *very* heavy."

At midnight, after his return, Belisarius took a tour of the villa. Baresmanas came with him. The Persian ambassador had been a warrior, in his day—a renowned one, in fact—but the combination of his advancing years and the terrible injury he had suffered at Mindouos made it impossible for him to participate in thundering lance charges. So he had cheerfully offered his services to the infantry who would be standing on the defensive at the villa.

Bouzes and three of his officers guided Belisarius and Baresmanas through the villa, holding torches aloft, proudly pointing out the cunning of the fortifications. They were especially swell-chested with regard to the grenade screens. The screens were doubled linen, strengthened by slender iron rods sewn lengthwise into the sheets. The design allowed for easy transportation, since the screens could be folded up into pleats and carried on mule back. The screens were now mounted onto bronze frameworks. These had been hastily brazed together out of the multitude of railings which had once adorned the balconies surrounding the villa's interior gardens. The frameworks had then been attached to every entryway or opening in the villa's outer walls with rawhide strips, looped through regularly spaced holes in the former railings.

"We didn't make the holes," admitted Bouzes. "They'd already been drilled, as fittings for the uprights. But we realized they'd allow for leather hinges. You see? Each one of the screens can be moved into place just like a door. Takes less than five seconds. Until then, there's no way to see them from outside the villa."

Belisarius was not surprised, actually, by the shrewdness of the design. He already knew that his Syrian infantrymen, with the jack-of-all-trades attitude of typical borderers, were past masters at the art of jury-rigging fortifications out of whatever materials were available. But he complimented them, nonetheless, quite lavishly.

Baresmanas was even more effusive in his praise. And he made no mention of the pearls which had once adorned the Emperor's railings, nestled in each one of the holes which now held simple rawhide lashings.

Nor did the sahrdaran comment on the peculiar appearance of the great bronze plaques which the Roman infantry had used to bulwark some of the flimsier portions of the outer wall. Those plaques had once hung suspended in the Emperor's huge dining hall, where his noble guests, feasting after a day's hunting, could gaze up at the marvelously etched figures. The etchwork was still there. But the hunting scenes they depicted seemed pallid. The lions wan, without their emerald eyes; the antelopes plebeian, without their silver antlers; the panthers drab, without their jade and ruby spots; and the elephants positively absurd—like big-nosed sheep!—without their ivory tusks.

Baresmanas said nothing in the dining room itself, either, when he and Belisarius joined the infantrymen in a late meal, other than to exchange pleasantries with the troops on the subject of the excellence of the food. Fine fare it was, the Syrians allowed—marvelous, marvelous. Truly fit for an Emperor! And if Baresmanas thought it odd that the splendid meal was served on wooden platters and eaten with peasant daggers, he held his tongue. He did not inquire as to the whereabouts of the gold plates and utensils which would, by all reasonable standards, have made much more sensible dining ware for such a regal feast.

Only once, in that entire tour, did Baresmanas momentarily lose his composure. Hearing Bouzes laud the metalworking skills of his troops, which could finally be put to full use by virtue of the extraordinarily well-equipped smithy located in the rear of the imperial compound, Baresmanas expressed a desire to observe the soldiers at their work.

Bouzes coughed. "Uh, well—it's very hot back there, lord. Terrible! And dirty? You wouldn't believe it! Oh, no, you wouldn't—with those fine clothes? No, you wouldn't—"

"I insist," said Baresmanas. Politely, but firmly. He brushed the silk sleeve of his tunic in a gesture which combined whimsy and unconcern.

"There's going to be a battle tomorrow. I doubt these garments will be usable afterward, anyway. And I am fascinated by the skills of your soldiers. There's nothing comparable in the Persian army.

Our dehgan lancers and their mounted retainers wouldn't stoop to this kind of work. And our peasant levees don't know how to do anything beside till the soil."

Bouzes swallowed. "But—"

Belisarius intervened.

"Do as the sahrdaran asks, Bouzes. I'd like to see the workshop myself. I've always loved watching skilled smiths at their trade."

Bouzes sighed. With a little shrug, he turned and led the way toward the rear of the compound. Out of the royal chambers, through the servant quarters, and into the cluster of adjoining buildings where the practical needs of Persia's emperors were met, far from the fastidious eyes of Aryan royalty.

When they entered the smithy, all work ceased immediately. The dozen or so Syrian infantrymen in the workshop froze at their labors, staring goggle-eyed at the newcomers.

Baresmanas stared himself. Goggle-eyed.

The center of the shop was occupied by a gigantic cauldron, designed to smelt metal. The cauldron was being put to use. It was almost brim-full with molten substance. At that very moment, two infantrymen were standing paralyzed, staring at the sahrdaran, stooped from the effort of carrying a large two-handled ladle over to the ingot-molds ranged against a far wall.

The mystery of the imperial diningware was solved at once. Only a small number of the gold plates—and not more than a basket's worth, perhaps, of gold utensils—still remained on a shelf next to the cauldron. That small number immediately shrank, as a handful of gold plate slipped out of the loose fingers of the Roman soldier gaping at Baresmanas. Plop, plop, plop, into the brew.

But it was not the plates which held the Persian nobleman trans-fixed. It was the sight of the much larger objects which were slowly joining the melt.

Baresmanas' gaze settled on a winged horse which perched atop a heavy post. The post was softening rapidly. Within a few seconds, the horse sank below the cauldron's rim.

"That was the Emperor's bed," he choked. "It's made out of solid gold."

The soldiers in the smithy paled. Bouzes glanced appealingly at Belisarius.

The general cleared his throat. "Excellent work, men!" he boomed. "I'm delighted to see how well you've carried out my instructions." He placed a firm hand on Baresmanas' shoulder. "It's terrible, what military necessity drives us to."

The sahrdaran tore his eyes away from the cauldron and stared at Belisarius.

"I believe I mentioned, Baresmanas, that I hope to capture Malwa cannons in the course of the campaign. The problem, of course, is with the shot." The general scowled fiercely. "You wouldn't believe the crap the Malwa use! Stone balls, for siege work. And the same—broken stones, for the sake of God!—do for their cannister." He pursed his lips, as if to spit. Restrained himself. "I won't have it! Proper cannister can make all the difference, breaking a charge. But for that, you need good lead."

He fixed the soldiers with an eagle eye. "You found no lead, I take it?"

The soldiers stared at him, for a moment. Then one of them squeaked: "No, sir! No, sir!"

Another, bobbing his head: "We looked, sir. Indeed we did. Scoured the place! But—"

A third: "Only lead's in the water pipes." His face grew lugubrious. "Have to tear the walls apart to get at 'em."

A fourth, shaking his head solemnly: "Didn't want to do that, of course. A royal palace, and all."

Every infantryman's face assumed a grave expression. Well-nigh funereal. Heads bobbed in unison.

"Be a terrible desecration," muttered one.

" 'Orrible," groaned another.

Belisarius stepped forward and looked down into the cauldron, hands clasped behind his back. The general's gaze was stern, fastidious, determined—much like that of a farmer examining night-soil.

"Gold!" he snorted. Then, shrugging heavily: "Well, I suppose it'll have to do."

He turned away, took Baresmanas by the arm—the sahrdaran was still standing stiff and rigid—and began leading him toward the entrance.

"A cruel business, war," he muttered.

Baresmanas moved with him, but the Persian's head swiveled, staring back over his shoulder. His eyes never left the cauldron until they were out of the smithy altogether.

Then, suddenly, he burst into laughter. No light-hearted chuckling, either. No, this was shoulder-shaking, belly-heaving, convulsive laughter. He leaned weakly against a nearby wall.

"This was Emperor Kavad's favorite hunting park," he choked. "Spent half his time here, before age overcame him."

Another round of uproarious laughter. Then:

"He told me once—ho! ho!—that he was quite sure his son Khusrau was conceived on that bed! Ho! Ho! So proud he was! He had slain a lion, that day, and thought it was an omen for his son's future."

Belisarius grinned at him. "Poetic justice, then! A thing for legend! Even at his conception, Khusrau Anushirvan was destined to rend the Malwa!"

Baresmanas pushed himself away from the wall. Now it was he who took Belisarius by the arm, and began leading the way back to the central villa.

Still laughing, he murmured: "Perhaps we should keep that legend to ourselves, my friend. Myths are so easy to misinterpret."

They walked a few steps. The sahrdaran gave Belisarius a sly glance. "What will you tell Emperor Khusrau about his hunting villa—if there's no battle, I mean?"

Belisarius smiled crookedly.

"I was just wondering that myself."

He blew out his cheeks.

"Pray for an earthquake, I suppose."

Chapter 17

"It's a good thing you sent the Persian troops to us last night," remarked Maurice, after dismounting from his horse. "We're not the only ones who figured out that those woods are the best hiding place in the area. All the servants fled the villa when they saw the Syrians coming and they wound up with us. If it hadn't been for Kurush and his men, who settled them down, they'd be scampering all over the landscape squawking like chickens. The Malwa would have been bound to capture a few."

Belisarius winced.

"I hadn't thought of that," he muttered. The general glanced back at the villa behind him. "When we arrived, the place was empty. I should have realized there must have been a little army of servants living here, even when the Emperor's not in residence."

"*Little* army? You should see that mob!"

Belisarius cocked an eye. "Will it be a problem?"

Maurice shook his head. "I don't imagine. The Persians quieted them down and then moved them farther back into the woods. They instructed the servants to remain there, but Kurush told me he made sure to explain which direction was what. He thinks at least half the servants will start running as soon as the Persians take their battle positions, but at least they'll be running deeper into the woods, *away* from the Malwa. If the enemy catches any of them, it'll be too late for the information to do them any good."

Maurice looked toward the villa.

"What's the situation here?" he asked. The chiliarch examined the villa and the area surrounding it.

The imperial villa was not a single structure, but an interconnected series of buildings. The buildings formed an oblong whose long axis was oriented north-to-south. The center of the oblong was open, forming an interior garden. The buildings were enclosed within a brick wall which formed the outer grounds of the villa. The outer wall was low, and not massive. The buildings were nestled near the northeast corner of the wall. To the west, the wall extended outward for hundreds of yards before looping back around. The western grounds of the villa were well-tended and open, except for small copses of trees scattered about.

North and west of the villa, just beyond the wall, began the small forest which formed the actual hunting park. Those woods were dense, and covered many square miles of territory. Maurice's troops were hidden away in a part of that forest, about two miles northeast of the villa. To the south, the villa was separated from the Euphrates by a much thinner stretch of woods. The river was less than a mile away.

Examining the scene, Maurice could see that the forest and the river would act as a funnel, channeling the Malwa directly toward the villa. The area to the east of the villa was the only terrain on which a large army could move. No general would even consider trying to maneuver through the forest. Maurice had been able to get his cataphracts into those woods, true. But he was just setting an ambush, hiding his troops behind the first screen of trees. Even then, the task had been difficult.

He studied the open terrain east of the villa more closely. That would be the battleground. Units of the Constantinople garrison were visible, here and there, eating their morning meal. To the southwest, nestled on the edge of the woods lining the river, Maurice could see portions of the barns, horsepens, and corrals where the imperial livestock were fed and sheltered.

Then, more carefully, Maurice examined the wall which enclosed the compound itself—the villa proper, with its adjoining buildings and the gardens. Finally, very closely, he studied the gateway in which he and Belisarius were standing.

He did not seem exactly thrilled by what he saw.

"A lame mule could kick that wall apart," he grumbled. "And as for this ridiculous so-called gate—I'd pit a half-grown puppy against it. Give three-to-one odds on the mutt."

Belisarius glanced at the objects of Maurice's disfavor. The general smiled. "Pretty though, aren't they?"

He patted Maurice on the shoulder.

"Relax, you morose old bastard. This is a hunting villa, not a fortress. The outer wall's purely decorative, I admit. But the villa itself was built for an Emperor. It's solid enough, even where the separate buildings connect with each other. Besides, Bouzes' boys did wonders last night, beefing it up. They'll hold—long enough, at least."

Maurice said nothing, but the sour expression on his face never faded.

The general's smile broadened. "Like I said—morose old bastard."

"I'm not morose," countered Maurice. "I'm a pessimist. What if your trap doesn't work?"

Belisarius shrugged. "If it doesn't work, we'll just have to fight it out, that's all." He waved at the villa. "Sure, it isn't much—but it's better than anything the Malwa have."

Before Maurice could reply, a cheery hail cut him off. Turning, he and Belisarius saw that Coutzes had arrived. The commander of the Syrian light cavalry was trotting up the road leading to the villa. With him were all three of the cavalry's tribunes as well as Abbu, his chief scout.

Maurice glanced up at the sky. The sun was just beginning to peek over the eastern horizon. "If he's got news already, they either did a hell of a good job themselves, last night—or the enemy's breathing down our necks."

Belisarius chuckled. "Like I said—morose." He gestured with his head. "Look at those insouciant fellows, Maurice! Do those smiling faces look like men running for their lives?"

Maurice scowled. "Don't call soldiers 'insouciant.' It's ridiculous. Especially when it comes to Abbu."

The chiliarch studied the approaching figure of the scout leader. His somber mien lightened, somewhat. Maurice approved of Abbu. The Arab had a world-view which closely approximated his own. Every silver lining has a cloud; into each life a deluge must fall.

Abbu's first words, upon reining in his horse: "The enemy is laying a terrible trap for us, general. I foresee disaster."

Coutzes laughed. "The old grouch is just pissed because he had to work so hard last night."

"No enemy is that stupid!" Abbu snarled. "We practically had to lead them by the hand!" The Arab's close-set eyes were almost crossed with outrage. Belisarius had to restrain his own laugh.

Abbu's face was long and lean, dominated by heavy brows and a sheer hook of a nose. His hair was salt and pepper, but his beard was pure white. There was no air of the benign grandfather about him, however—the scar running from his temple down into the lush beard gave the man a purely piratical appearance.

Yet, at the moment, the fierce old desert warrior reminded the general of nothing so much as a rustic matron, her proprieties offended beyond measure by the latest escapade of the village idiot.

"No army has skirmishers so incompetent!" Abbu insisted. "It is not possible. They would have drowned by now, marching all of them into a well."

With gloomy assurance:

"The only explanation—obvious, obvious!—is that the enemy is perpetrating a cunning ruse upon our trusting, babe-innocent selves. You have finally met your match, general Belisarius. The fox, trapped by the wilier wolf."

Maurice grunted sourly, much as the Cassandra of legend, seeing all her forebodings realized.

Belisarius, on the other hand, did not seem noticeably chagrined. Rather the contrary, in fact. The general was practically beaming.

"I take it you had to chivvy the Malwa vanguard, to get them to follow you to our camps?"

Abbu snorted. "For a while, we thought we were going to have to dismount and explain it to them. 'See this, Malwa so-called scout? This is a campfire. That—over there—is known as a tent. These fellows you see lounging about are called Roman troops. Can you say: *Ro-man*? Can you find your way back in the dark? Do you need us to make the report to your commanders? Or have you already mastered speech?' "

His lips pursed, as if he had eaten a lemon. "No enemy is so—"

"Yes, they are," interrupted Belisarius. The humor was still apparent on the general's face, but when he spoke, his tone was utterly serious. He addressed his words not to Abbu alone, but to all the commanders.

"Understand *this* enemy. They are immensely powerful, because of their weapons and the great weight of forces they can bring to bear on the field of war. But the same methods which created that gigantic empire are also their Achilles heel. *They trust no-one but Malwa.* Not even the Ye-tai. And with good reason! All other peoples are nothing but their beasts."

He scanned the faces staring at him, ending with Abbu's.

"They have scouts as good as any in the world, Abbu. The Kushans, for instance, are excellent. And the Pathan trackers who serve the Rajputs are even better. But where are the Kushans? *At the rear.* Where are the Rajputs?" He gestured to the northeast. "Being bled dry in the mountains, that's where. Here, in Mesopotamia, they are using common cavalrymen for skirmishers." He shrugged. "Without Ye-tai to shepherd them, those soldiers will shirk their duty at every opportunity."

"They're arrogant bastards, all right," chimed in Coutzes. "It's not just that their vanguard elements are sloppy—they've got almost no flankers at all."

Belisarius glanced at the rising sun. "How soon?" he asked.

Coutzes' reply was immediate. "An hour and a half, general. Two, at the most." The young Thracian gave Abbu an approving look.

"Despite all his grumbling, Abbu and his men did a beautiful job last night. The Malwa are headed directly for us, and they've assumed a new marching order. A battle formation, it looks like to me—although it's like none I've ever seen."

"Describe it," commanded Belisarius.

"They've got their regular cavalry massed along the front. It's a deep formation. They're still in columns, but the columns are so wide they might as well be advancing in a line."

"Slower than honey, they're moving," chipped in one of Coutzes' tribunes. Coutzes nodded. "Then, most of their barbarians—Ye-tai—are on the flanks. But they're not moving out like flankers should be. Instead, they're pressed right against—"

"They're not flankers," interrupted Belisarius, shaking his head. "The Ye-tai are used mainly as security battalions. The Malwa commander has them on the flanks in order to make sure that his regular troops don't break and run when the battle starts."

Coutzes snorted. "I can believe that. They're some tough-looking bastards, that's for sure."

"Yes, they are," agreed Belisarius. "That's their other function. The Malwa commander will be counting on them to beat off any flank attack."

One of the other tribunes sneered. "They're not *that* tough. Not against Thracian and Illyrian cataphracts, when the hammer comes down."

Belisarius grinned. "My opinion—exactly." To Coutzes:

"The Kushans are still in the rear? Pressed up close, I imagine, against the formation in the center—the war wagons with the priests and the kshatriya?"

Coutzes nodded. Belisarius copied the gesture.

"It all makes sense," he stated. "The key to that formation—the reason it looks odd to you, Coutzes—is that the Malwa approach battle like a blacksmith approaches an anvil. Their only thought is to use a hammer, which, in this case, is a mass of cavalry backed up by rocket platforms. If the hammer doesn't work"—he shrugged—"get a bigger hammer."

"What about the Lakhmids?" asked Maurice.

Coutzes and the tribunes burst into laughter. Even Abbu, for the first time, allowed a smile to creep into his face.

"*They're* no fools," chuckled the scout leader. Approvingly: "Proper good Arabs, even if they are a lot of stinking Lakhmites. They're—"

Coutzes interrupted, still laughing.

"They *are* assuming a true flank position—*way* out on the flank. The left flank, of course, as near to the desert as they can get without fighting an actual pitched battle with the Ye-tai."

"Who are *not* happy with the Lakhmids," added one of the tribunes. Another chimed in, "They'll break in a minute, general. It's as obvious as udders on a cow. You know how those Arabs think."

Abbu snorted. "Like any sane man thinks! What's the point of riding a horse if you're not going to run the damn beast? Especially with an idiot commander who maneuvers his troops like—" the scout nodded at Belisarius "—just like the general says. Like a musclebound, pot-bellied blacksmith, waddling up to his anvil."

Belisarius clapped his hands, once.

"Enough," he said. "Coutzes, start the attack as soon as you can. By now, the Constantinople men will be up and ready. I'll be with them, when the time comes."

Coutzes peered at him. The look combined hesitation and concern. "Are you sure about that, general? The casualties are going to be—"

"I'll be with them," repeated Belisarius.

Coutzes made a little motion with his shoulders, like an abandoned shrug. He turned his horse and trotted off. His tribunes and Abbu immediately followed.

Once they were gone, Maurice glanced at Belisarius.

"Odd," he remarked. "Hearing you make such sarcastic remarks about blacksmiths, I mean. I always thought you admired the fellows."

"I do," came the vigorous response. "Spent half my time, as a kid, hanging around the smithy. Wanted to be a blacksmith myself, when I grew up."

The general turned and began walking through the gate back to the villa, Maurice at his side.

"I wasn't poking fun at *blacksmiths*, Maurice. I was ridiculing generals who think *they're* blacksmiths."

He shook his head. "Smithing's a craft. And, like any craft, it has its own special rules. Fine rules—as long as you don't confuse them with the rules of another trade. The thing about an anvil, you see, is that it's just a big lump of metal. Anvils don't fight back."

A half hour later, after parting company with Maurice, Belisarius rode his horse into the Constantinople encampment. Valentinian and Anastasius accompanied him, as always, trailing just a few yards behind.

The Greek troops were already up and about. Fed, watered, fully armed and armored—and champing at the bit. The soldiers greeted him enthusiastically when he rode up. Belisarius listened to their cheers carefully. There was nothing feigned in those salutations, he decided. Word had already spread, obviously, that Belisarius would be fighting with them in the upcoming battle. As he had estimated, the news that their general would be sharing the risks of a cavalry charge had completed the work of cementing the cataphracts' allegiance.

I've got an army, finally, he thought with relief. Then, a bit sardonically: Now, I've only got to worry about surviving the charge.

Aide spoke in his mind:

I think you should not do this. It is very dangerous. They will have rockets.

Belisarius scratched his chin before making his reply.

I don't think that will be a problem, Aide. The Syrians should have the enemy cavalry confused and disorganized by the time we charge. If we move in fast they'll have no clear targets for their rockets.

Aide was not mollified.

It is very dangerous. You should not do this. You are irreplaceable.

Belisarius sighed. Aide's fears, he realized, had nothing to do with his estimation of the tactical odds. They were far more deeply rooted.

No man is irreplaceable, Aide.

That is not true. You are. Without you, the Malwa will win. Link will win. We will be lost.

The general spoke, very firmly. If I am irreplaceable, Aide, it is because of my ability as a general. True?

Silence.

Belisarius demanded: *True?*

Yes, came Aide's grudging reply.

Then you must accept this. The risk is part of the generalship.

He could sense the uncertainty of the facets. He pressed home the lesson.

I have a small army. The enemy is huge. If I am to win—the war, not just this battle—I must have an army which is supple and quick to act. Only a united, welded army can do that.

He paused, thinking how best to explain. Aide's knowledge and understanding of humanity was vast, in many ways—much greater than his own. But the crystalline being's own nature made some aspects of human reality obscure to him, even opaque. Aide often astonished Belisarius with his uncanny understanding of the great forces which moved the human race. And then, astonished him as much with his ignorance of the people who made up that race.

Humanity, as a tapestry, Aide understood. But he groped, dimly, at the human threads themselves.

We are much like Malwa, we Romans. We, too, have built a great empire out of many different peoples and nations. They organize their empire by rigid hierarchical rules—purity separated from pollution, by carefully delineated stages. We do it otherwise. Their methods give them great power, but little flexibility. And, most important, nothing in the way of genuine loyalty.

We will only defeat them with cunning—and loyalty.

He closed in on his point, almost ruthlessly. He could feel Aide resisting the logic.

It is true, Aide. I am the premier general of Rome because of my victories over Persians and barbarians. I won those victories with border troops—Thracians, of course, but also Syrians and Illyrians. The Greek soldiers who form the heart of the Roman army know little of me beyond my reputation.

That is too abstract. For the war against Malwa, those men are key. I must have their unswerving loyalty and trust. Not just these men, today, but all the others who will follow.

Firmly, finally:

There is no other way. A general can only gain the loyalty of troops who know he is loyal to them, also. I have already shown the garrison troops that I cannot be trifled with. Now I must show them that I will not trifle with them. Their charge is the key to the battle. If it is pressed home savagely, it will fix the enemy's attention on the Greeks. They will not dream that there might be others—even more dangerous—hidden in the woods.

Silence. Then, plaintively:

It will be very dangerous. You might be killed.

Belisarius made no answer. By now, he was approaching the center of the Constantinople encampment. He could see Agathius astride his armored charger, fifty yards away, surrounded by his tribunes and hecatontarchs. The young chiliarch was issuing last-minute instructions. He was not bellowing or roaring those commands histrionically, however, as Belisarius had seen many Roman officers do on the morning of a battle. Even at a distance, the relaxed camaraderie of the Constantinople command group was obvious.

Aide's voice cut through the general's satisfaction.

I would miss you. Very much.

Belisarius focussed all his attention on the facets. He was dazzled, as so many times before, by the kaleidoscopic beauty of that strangest of God's creations. That wondrous soul which called itself Aide.

I would miss you, also. Very much.

A small part of his mind heard Agathius' welcoming hail. A small part of his mind raised a hand in acknowledgement. For the rest—

Whimsy returned.

Let's try to avoid the problem, shall we?

The facets flashed and spun, assuming a new configuration. A shape—a form—Belisarius had never sensed in them, before, began to crystallize.

I will help, came the thought. Firm, solid—lean and sinewy. Almost weaselish.

Those sorry bastards are fucked. Fucked!

Belisarius started with surprise. Aide's next words caused him to twist in his saddle, to make sure that he had not heard Valentinian himself.

Mutter, mutter, mutter.

"I didn't say a thing," protested Valentinian, seeing the general's accusing eyes. With an air of aggrieved injury, he pointed a thumb at the huge cataphract riding next to him. "Ask him."

"Man's been as silent as a tomb, general," averred Anastasius. "Although I doubt he's been thinking philosophical thoughts, as I have. I always contemplate before a battle, you know. I find the words of Marcus Aurelius particularly—"

Valentinian muttered. Anastasius cocked an eye.

"What was that? I didn't catch it."

Belisarius grinned.

"I think he said 'sodomize philosophy.' But, maybe not. Maybe he said 'sod of my patrimony.' Praying to the ancestral spirits of Thrace, you understand, for their protection in the coming fray."

Mutter, mutter, mutter.

Mutter, mutter, mutter.

Chapter 18

Belisarius ordered the charge as soon as he saw the first units of the Syrian light cavalry pouring back from the battlefield.

The battlefield itself, directly to the east, was too distant to make out clearly. From a mile away, it was just a cloud of dust on a level plain—fertile fields, once—further obscured by the little copses of trees which were the outposts of the imperial hunting park. But the general, from experience, had been able to gauge the tempo of the battle by sound alone.

Based on what he had heard, he thought the situation was progressing very nicely. He was particularly pleased—if he had interpreted the sounds correctly—by the situation on his right. There, Abbu and his men had concentrated their attentions on their Arab counterparts.

Abbu's scouts were bedouin tribesmen, pledged to the service of the Ghassanid dynasty. The Ghassanids were Rome's traditional allies in northwest Arabia. More in the way of vassals, actually, but Rome had always been careful to tread lightly on their prickly Arab sensibilities. The Lakhmids had served Persia in the same capacity, in northeast Arabia, until switching their allegiance to the Malwa.

The Malwa were a new enemy, for Rome and its Ghassanid allies. But their Arab skirmishers were the same Lakhmids that Abbu and his men—and their ancestors—had been fighting for centuries. That conflict had ancient, bitter roots.

Both sides in that fray ululated in the Arab manner, but there were subtleties which were quite distinct to the general's educated ear. For a time, the ululations had swelled and swayed, back and forth. Now, there was a different pattern to the chanting rhythm of that battle.

Unless Belisarius missed his guess badly, Abbu and his men had fairly routed the Lakhmids—and with them, the only competent scouts in the enemy's army besides the Kushans.

He was pleased—no, delighted. Many things Maurice had taught him until the general, finally, outstripped his tutor, but one of the earliest lessons had been simple and brutal:

First thing you do, you blind the bastards.

The "charge" which Belisarius ordered was more in the nature of a vigorous trot. The enemy was still almost a mile away, even if, as he expected, they were advancing toward him. A mile, especially in the heat of a Syrian summer, was much too far to race a warhorse carrying its own armor and an armored man.

So he simply trotted forward. At first, he kept a vigilant eye on the garrison troopers, making sure that the hotheads among them didn't spur the rest into a faster pace. His vigilance eased, after a bit, once it became obvious that Agathius' sub-officers were a steady and capable lot. Veterans all, they did an excellent job of restraining the overeager.

Even in a trot, two thousand cataphracts—along with Persian dehgans, the heaviest cavalry in the world—sounded like distant thunder. The Syrian light horsemen, scampering away from the enemy they had goaded into a furious charge, heard that sound and knew its meaning. Knew that their mightier brothers were coming to their aid. Knew, most of all, that their general—once again—had not failed them.

The first Syrians who galloped through the gaps left for them by the oncoming cataphracts were whooping and grinning ear to ear. Shouting their cheerful cries.

Belisarius! Belisarius!

Some—then more and more, as the battlecry gained favor: *Constantinople! Constantinople!*

Throughout, as the retreating Syrians poured through their ranks, chanting and hollering, the capital troopers maintained a dignified silence. But Belisarius could sense the hidden satisfaction lurking beneath those helmeted faces. All memories of town brawls and executed comrades vanished; all resentments of sharp-tongued borderers fled; all bitterness at aristocratic units lounging in Constantinople while they sweated in the desert were forgotten.

There was nothing, now, but the fierce pride of the toughest fighters the world had ever known.

Greeks.

Latin armies had outfought them, centuries before, with superior organization and tactics. Beaten them so thoroughly, in fact, that they had even adopted the name of their conquerors. The Empire was Greek, now, at its core. But they called it the Roman Empire, still, and took pride in the name.

Persian armies, in modern cavalry battles, had outmaneuvered and outshot them, time after time. Until the proud Greeks, who called themselves Romans, had finally imitated their ancient Medean foe. The cataphracts were nothing but a copy of the Persian dehgans, at bottom.

In war, others had been better than the Greeks, many times. But no-one had ever been better in a fight. The Greek hoplite had been the most terrible of foes, on the ancient battlefield. They had introduced into warfare a style of bloody, smashing, in-your-face combat that had shocked all their opponents.

Achilles come to life; Ajax reborn. The same blood flowed in the veins of the grim men riding alongside Belisarius that day. The armor was different. The weapons had changed. They rode forward on horseback rather than striding on phalanx feet. But they were still the same tough, tough, tough Greeks.

A half mile, now. Syrian cavalrymen were still swirling in the ground between Belisarius and the oncoming Malwa. "A Hunnish kind of sally," the general had asked for—and Huns couldn't have done it better. Advance. Volley. Retreat—but with the "Parthian shot," firing arrows over the shoulder. Counter-attack. Volley. Retreat. Swirl forward; swirl away. Kill; cripple; wound—and evade retaliation.

Belisarius could finally see a few of the advancing Malwa. He could sense their frenzied rage at the Syrian tactics. Full of their own arrogance, the Malwa thought only of closing with this infuriating army of skirmishers. Their lead units were pushing ahead, maintaining no battle order. The Ye-tai "enforcers" scattered among them were not driving the troopers forward. There was no need. The Ye-tai themselves were seized up in that same heedless fury.

The Malwa troops knew little of Mesopotamia, and the Ye-tai even less. Knew nothing of the crumbled bones which littered that soil—the bones of Roman soldiers, often enough, who had made their same mistake. Crassus and his legions had been slaughtered by the Parthians, half a millennium before, not so very far away.

Belisarius' main concern had been that the Malwa might precede their troops with rocket volleys. He had not been particularly worried about casualties, as such. The Malwa rockets were much too erratic and inaccurate to fire genuine barrages. But he had been worried that the noise might panic some of his garrison troopers' horses. The mounts which his Constantinople soldiers rode were the steadiest available, true. But they had little of the training with gunpowder weapons which his Syrian and Thracian cavalry had enjoyed.

It was obvious, however, that there would be no barrages. As he had hoped, the Syrians' light cavalry tactics had been too agile and confusing to give the Malwa kshatriya a clear target. Now, it was too late. The dust thrown up by thousands of horsemen—friend and foe alike—had completely obscured the front of the battlefield from the Malwa commanders in the center. They would not even be able to see the charge of his Constantinople heavy cavalry. They would *hear* it, certainly. Even in the din of battle, a full charge by two thousand cataphracts would shake the very earth. But the sound of thunder is not a suitable target for rockets, and the sound would be short-lived in any event. Once the cataphracts closed, rockets would kill more Malwa troops than Roman.

Belisarius spurred his horse forward. No gallop, simply an easy canter. To either side, the garrison troopers matched the pace. There was no need, any longer, for the hecatontarchs and decarchs to maintain a steady formation. The cataphracts' lines were as steady as if they had been drawn in ink. Battle was very near, and these were the same Greeks whose forefathers had marched in step at Marathon.

Five hundred yards. Though they were closer, the enemy had disappeared completely—swallowed by the dust which hovered over the battlefield, unstirred by even a gentle breeze.

Four hundred yards.

Out of the dust galloped a small body of Arab cavalrymen. They headed straight for the oncoming Greeks. As they approached, Belisarius recognized the figure of Abbu.

The scout leader swept past the general, ululating fiercely. Blood dripped from a small gash on his cheek, but the old warrior seemed otherwise unharmed.

A moment later, Abbu drew his horse alongside Belisarius. His mount's flanks were heaving and sheened with sweat, but the horse seemed not in the least exhausted.

Abbu certainly wasn't.

"The Lakhmids are done!" he cried gaily. "Beaten like dogs! We whipped the curs into the river!"

Belisarius met that savage grin with his own smile.

"All of them?"

Abbu sneered.

"*Lakhmids*. Stinking Lakhmids are not bedouin, general Belisarius. River-rats. Oasis-huddlers. Die of fright in the good desert. I'm sure most of them are scurrying down this bank of the Euphrates. Doesn't matter. You won't see them again. Not for days, if ever. Nothing else, they'll get lost."

An exquisite sneer.

"Camel-fuckers, the lot. Don't even have the excuse of being perverts. Lakhmids are just too stupid to know the difference between a woman and a camel."

A *royal* sneer.

"Hard to blame them, of course. Lakhmid women are uglier than camels. Meaner, too."

Three hundred yards. There was a sudden rush of Syrians—the last die-hards, finally breaking off with the enemy. Then, a second or two later, the first ranks of the Malwa cavalry appeared in the dust. Galloping forward in a full and furious charge.

Belisarius caught a glimpse of Abbu's gleaming eyes. At that moment, the old man truly seemed a pirate, ogling a chest of gold.

The general laughed. "Let them be, Abbu. Our job, now." He jerked his head backward. "Be off. Regroup your men. Rejoin Coutzes and the Syrians. I want to be sure you're there to cover us—especially on the left—when we make our own retreat. I don't want any Malwa—*not one*—to get into those woods and find my surprise."

Abbu snorted.

"Worry about something else, general. Worry about *anything* else. No Malwa will get into those woods."

He began reining his horse around, taking a last glance at the Malwa. Two hundred and fifty yards away.

"God be with you, General Belisarius."

Hundreds of Malwa cavalry were visible now. Perhaps a thousand. It was hard to gauge, since they were so disorganized.

The enemy troopers finally caught sight of the heavily armored cataphracts approaching them. Some, apparently, began to have second thoughts about the reckless advance—judging from their attempts to rein in their mounts. But those doubters were instantly quelled by the Ye-tai. The Malwa army—more of a mob, really—continued its headlong charge.

Two hundred yards. The cataphracts drew their bows; notched their arrows.

Time.

Belisarius gave the order. The cornicens blew wild and loud.

The Roman cataphracts brought their mounts to a halt. As soon as the horses had steadied, all two thousand cavalrymen raised up in their stirrups. With the full power of their chests and shoulders, they drew back their bows and fired in unison.

The cataphracts were four ranks deep. The ranks were staggered in a checkerboard pattern to allow each rank a clear line of fire. With the gaps between the regiments, which provided escape routes for the retreating Syrians, the Constantinople mounted archers covered well over a mile of battlefront. Firing in a coordinated volley, at that short range, their arrows swept the front ranks of the oncoming Malwa like a giant scythe.

At least half of the arrows missed, burying their cruel warheads in the soft soil. But hundreds didn't, and most of those hundreds brought death and horrible injury. No bows in the world were as powerful as cataphract bows, few arrowheads as sharp, and none as heavy.

The Malwa staggered. Many shouted and screamed—some with shock and agony, others with fear and disbelief. Their light armor had been like so much tissue against those incredible arrows.

Belisarius motioned. Again, the cornicens blew.

The cataphracts sheathed their bows, reached back and drew their lances. Within seconds, they sent their horses back into motion. Not more than a hundred yards separated the two armies when the Romans began their charge. Those yards shrank like magic.

Ironically, it was the Malwa—the bleeding, battered, mangled Malwa—who closed most of that distance. Those Malwa in the front ranks who had survived the volley were driving their horses forward at a furious gallop, desperate to close before more arrows could be brought to bear on them.

It was a natural reaction—an inevitable reaction, actually, as Belisarius had known it would be—but it was disastrous nonetheless. A man on a galloping horse must concentrate most of his attention on staying in the saddle. That is especially true for men like the Malwa cavalry, who did not possess the stirrups of their Roman enemies. Men in that position, for all the dramatic furor of their charge, are simply not in position to wield their weapons effectively.

For their part, the Roman cataphracts did not advance at a gallop. They spurred their horses forward in a canter—a pace easy to ride, while they concentrated on their murderous work. They set their feet in the stirrups, leaned into the charge, positioned their heavy lances securely, and aimed the spearpoints.

When the two cavalry forces met, seconds later, the result was sheer slaughter.

Malwa horsemen were better armed and armored than Malwa infantry. But, by Roman or Persian standards, they were not much more than light cavalry. Their armor was mail—flimsy at that—and simply covered their torsos; the cataphract armor was heavy scale, covering not only the torso but the left arm and the body down to mid-thigh. Malwa helmets were leather caps, reinforced with scale; the cataphracts wore German-style Spangenhelm, their heads protected by segmented steel plate. The Malwa lances—in the tradition of stirrupless cavalry—were simply long and slender spears; the Greeks were wielding lances twice as heavy and half again as long.

The Ye-tai were better equipped than the common Malwa cavalrymen. Yet they, also, were hopelessly outclassed as lancers—and would have been, even had Belisarius not refitted his cavalry with the stirrups which Aide had shown him in a vision.

The Romans shattered the Malwa charge, across the entire line. Some Malwa in the first ranks, on both edges of the battlefront, were able to veer aside. The majority were simply hammered under. Over five hundred Malwa cavalrymen died or were seriously injured in that brutal collision. Half of them were spitted on lances. The other half, within seconds, were being butchered by cataphract swords and axes. And here, too, history showed—Malwa hand weapons had none of the weight of Roman swords and axes. The Malwa had only months of experience fighting Persian dehgans; the Romans, centuries.

There were perhaps six thousand Malwa cavalrymen directly involved in this first major clash of the two armies. In less than two minutes, between the volley and the lance charge, they had suffered casualties in excess of fifteen percent—a horrendous rate, measured by the standards of any human army in history.

Then, the bloodletting worsened. The front ranks of the Malwa had been brought to a complete halt. Many of them, along with their horses, were spilled to the ground. Those still in the saddle were off-balance, bewildered, shocked.

The Malwa charging from behind had seen little of the battle due to the dust and the noise. Still driving their horses, they slammed into the immobilized mass at the front. Thousands of Malwa horsemen were now hopelessly tangled up and being driven willy-nilly against the Roman line.

Belisarius had been planning to call the retreat as soon as the initial clash was done. But now, seeing the confusion in the Malwa ranks, he ordered a standing fight. The cornicens blew again. The rear ranks of the cataphracts moved up, filling out the front line. The gaps were closed; the horsemen were almost shoulder to shoulder.

Flanked by Valentinian and Anastasius, Belisarius took a place in the center of the line. His lance had already been discarded. The Ye-tai that lance had spitted in the first clash had taken it with him, as he fell to the ground. The general drew his sword—not the spatha he generally favored, but the long Persian-style cavalry sword which he carried in a baldric. He rose in the stirrups and struck down a Malwa before him. The heavy sword cut through the man's helmet and split his skull.

Belisarius jerked loose the sword, struck another foe. Another. Another.

As before in battle, Aide was assisting him, giving the general almost superhuman reflexes and an uncanny ability to perceive everything sharply and clearly. But the assistance was almost moot. This battle—this brawl—called for strength and endurance, not speed and agility.

No matter. Belisarius was a big man, and a powerful one. His endurance had been shaped by the teachings and training of Maurice—who considered stamina the soldier's best friend—and his skill with a sword, by Valentinian. At no time in the ensuing fray did he fail to cut down his opponent, and at no time was he in danger of being struck down himself. That would have been true even if Valentinian had not been there to protect him on the left, just as the giant Anastasius did on his right.

That battle was as savage as any Belisarius had ever seen—on that scale, at least—and he was no stranger to mayhem. It was more like butchers chopping meat than anything else. The Malwa at the front could barely wield their weapons, so great was the press. The Romans hammered them down; hammered the ones who were pushed atop the corpses; hammered the ones who came after them.

At many places along the line, after a few minutes, the battle effectively ended. The Greeks could no longer reach live enemies, due to the obstruction of the dead ones.

The Malwa at the front began to recoil. The ones pressing from the rear had finally sensed the tide and eased away, allowing the men before them to stagger back. Belisarius, sensing the break in the battle, left off his merciless swordwork. Quickly, he scanned the front. He was in the very middle of the Roman ranks, and could no longer see either end of the battle line. But he knew the danger. For all their losses, the Malwa greatly outnumbered his Constantinople troops. Whether from conscious direction by their commanders, or the simple flow of individuals, they would soon be curling around his flanks.

He gave two quick orders. The cornicens blew, then blew again.

The first order was for the retrieval of casualties. The cataphracts, hearing that call, shouted their fury and contempt at the Malwa. It was as if the entire Constantinople unit was sneering, as one man.

We whipped your fucking worthless butts. Now, we'll take the time to gather up our own, before we amble on our way. Fuck you. You don't like it? Try and do something about it!

For all their braggadocio, the Greeks did not linger at the task. They were veterans, and knew as well as their general the danger of being outflanked before they could make their retreat. So, one cataphract aiding another, they quickly gathered up their casualties and draped them across their horses.

It did not take long, even though the Greeks took the time to collect the dead as well as the wounded. Their casualties had been incredibly light—much lighter than they had expected. *Much* lighter. They were almost shocked, once they realized how few bodies there were to retrieve.

The retreat started. Belisarius had been concerned about that retreat, before the battle. It is always difficult to keep soldiers, even the best of soldiers, under control at such times. There is an powerful tendency for men to speed up, anxious to gain distance from a pursuing enemy. Whether quickly, or almost imperceptibly, a retreat can easily turn into a chaotic rout.

Not this time. Within seconds, Belisarius knew he had nothing to fear. The Constantinople men, it was obvious, did not even consider themselves to be retreating. They were simply leaving, because there was nothing more to be done at the moment.

An easy canter, no more. The ranks reformed, even dressed their lines.

Belisarius took his place at the rear, during that retreat, just as he had taken a place at the front during the charge. The Greeks noticed—again—and a great cheer surged through their ranks. *Belisarius! Belisarius!*

He smiled—he even waved—but he took no other notice of the acclaim. He spent most of the time, during that almost-leisurely retreat, staring over his shoulder. Watching the enemy. Gauging. Assessing.

He caught sight of Syrian and Arab units charging forward, ready to provide covering fire for the cataphracts. He waved them off. There was no need. The Malwa were pursuing, true. But it was not a furious, frenzied charge led by eager warriors. It was a sodden, leaden, sullen movement, driven forward by screaming Ye-tai.

The Malwa cavalrymen had had enough of Romans, for the moment.

Belisarius turned back, satisfied, and glanced at the sun. It was not yet noontime. He thought the Malwa commanders would not be able to drive their army back into battle for at least two hours. Possibly three.

Plenty of time. He had taken no pleasure in the killing. He never had, in any battle he had ever fought. But he did take satisfaction in a job well done, and he intended to do the same again. In two hours. Possibly three.

Plenty of time, for a craftsman at his trade.

Chapter 19

Two and a half hours later, the enemy began taking positions for the assault on the villa. The Malwa forces lined up on the open ground east of the royal compound, at a distance of half a mile. The front lines were composed of cavalry regulars, backed by Ye-tai. The rocket wagons, guarded by the Kushans, were brought to a halt fifty yards behind the front ranks. The kshatriya, overseen by Mahaveda priests, removed the tarpaulins covering the wagons and began unloading rockets and firing troughs. Within a few minutes, they had the artillery devices set up. There were eighteen of the rocket troughs, erected in a single line, spaced thirty feet apart.

From a room on the second floor of the villa, Belisarius studied the Malwa formation with his telescope. Standing just behind him were the top officers of the Syrian and Constantinople troops forted up in the imperial compound—Bouzes and Coutzes, Agathius and Cyril. They were listening intently as Belisarius passed on his assessment of the situation.

The general began by examining the rockets, but spent little time on that problem. Once the first two or three had been erected, he was satisfied that he understood them perfectly. The rockets were the same type he had seen—at much closer range—during the sea battle he had fought against pirates while traveling to India on a Malwa embassy ship. In that battle, the rockets had wreaked havoc on the Arab ships. But, he told his officers, he did not think they would have that effect here.

"Most of the damage done by the rockets in the pirate battle," he explained, lowering the telescope for a moment, "was incendiary. The pirate galleys, like all wooden boats, were bonfires waiting to happen."

Seeing the puzzlement on the faces of Bouzes and Coutzes, the two Constantinople officers chuckled.

"Farm boys!" snorted Cyril. "You think 'cause a boat's floating on water that she won't burn? *Shit*. The planks are made of the driest wood anyone can find, and what's worse—"

"—they're caulked with pitch," concluded Agathius. Like his fellow Greek, the chiliarch was smirking—that particular, unmistakable, insufferable smirk which seafarers the world over bestow upon landlubbers.

"Not to mention the cordage and the sails," added Cyril.

Bouzes and Coutzes, Thracian leaders of a Syrian army, took no offense at the Greeks' sarcasm. On some other day, they might. But not on the day when those same Greeks had given the enemy such a thorough pounding. They simply grinned, shrugged at their ignorance, and studied the interior of the villa with new and enlightened eyes.

"A different matter altogether, isn't it?" commented Belisarius.

Under the fancy trappings and elaborate decorations, the royal compound was about as fireproof as a granite tor. The walls were made of kiln-fired brick, and the sloping roof was covered with tiles. Neither would burn—those bricks and tiles had been *made* in ovens—and he was quite sure the thick walls could withstand the explosive power of the rockets' relatively small warheads.

True, the roof tiles would probably shatter under a direct hit by a rocket. Belisarius did not think there would be many such hits, if any. He knew from experience that the Malwa rockets were not only erratic in their trajectories, but erratic in their destruction as well. They had no contact fuses. They simply exploded whenever the burning fuel reached the warhead. In order to shatter the roof, a rocket would have to hit directly—not at a glancing angle—*and* explode at just the right time.

The likelihood of that happening, in his estimation, was not much greater than being hit by lightning. And if, against all odds, a rocket should score a direct hit—

"Might break in the roof tiles," commented Bouzes.

Belisarius shrugged. "The tiles are supported by heavy beams. Wooden beams, yes. But these beams aren't anything like the thin planks of pirate galleys. They're much thicker, and, what's more important, *not* saturated with inflammable pitch."

He began studying the positions of the Malwa cavalry, now. Again, passing on his conclusions.

"They'll start with a rocket barrage, and then follow it up with a direct assault." A moment's silence, then:

"I thought so. They're dismounting, now. It'll be an infantry attack."

"Those are cavalry!" protested Coutzes.

Belisarius pressed his lips together to keep from smiling. He remembered, from three years before, that Coutzes and Bouzes had been trained in the cavalry tradition. The young Thracian commander, it was obvious, had still not quite abandoned his contempt for foot-fighting.

His brother, however, had.

"Don't be stupid. We've been training our own men to be dragoons. Why shouldn't the Malwa?"

"Well said," murmured Belisarius. For a moment, he took his eye from the telescope and glanced at Coutzes.

"You're about to see why I insisted on training our cavalry to fight on foot. I know you think that was a waste of time—"

He drove over Coutzes' little protest. "—but the reason I did so was because I knew the time would come when we'd be able to arm those dragoons with grenades. And handcannons, I'm hoping."

He nodded toward the enemy, visible through the window.

"They already have grenades. The kshatriya are starting to pass them out to the regulars."

He took up the telescope again, and continued his scrutiny.

"They'll come in waves. Probably be one grenadier for every ten soldiers. The Ye-tai will be scattered through the lines in small squads, driving the regulars forward and pressing the assault. Some of the kshatriya will be in those lines, too, but most of them will stay at the center with the priests, manning the rockets. They'll also help the Kushans guard the wagons. They might—*damn!*"

He stiffened, staring through the telescope intently.

"*Damn,*" he repeated. "They're bringing up the Kushans. All two thousand of them."

"On foot?" asked Agathius.

Belisarius lowered the telescope, nodded. Then, with a bit of a rueful smile:

"Kushans, in my experience, don't have any fetishes when it comes to fighting. On foot, on horse, on boats—it doesn't matter to them. Whatever, they'll do it well. Very well."

He turned away from the window. It was obvious from his stance and expression that he had reached a decision. His officers gathered closer.

"This changes things," Belisarius announced. "As you know, I'd wanted to wait until tomorrow before bringing in Maurice and his boys."

He tapped the palm of his hand with the telescope, emphasizing his words.

"We're going to beat these bastards, one way or the other. But I want more than that—I want to *pulverize* them. The best way to do that is to rout them early in the morning, so we've got a full day for pursuit."

The officers nodded. All of them—even the two young brothers—were experienced combatants. They knew that a battle won at the end of day was a battle half-won. The kind of relentless, driving pursuit which could utterly destroy a retreating enemy was simply impossible once daylight was gone.

Agathius glanced out the window. "It's still before noon," he mused. "If the battle starts soon enough—"

Belisarius shook his head. "I'd wanted to let the Malwa spend all day hammering their heads against us here. Bleed them dry, exhaust them—then hit them at dawn with a massive flank attack by Maurice and Kurush. The attack would break their army, and then we'd sally out of the villa and drive over them."

He saw that his officers still didn't understand. He didn't blame them. Their brief experience with Malwa soldiers had not prepared them for the Kushans.

"The Kushans are a different breed. They *won't* come at us in a mass, chivvied by Ye-tai, depending on their grenades to do the work. They'll come at us like the best kind of Roman infantry would attack this place."

Of the officers standing around him, Bouzes was the most familiar with Belisarius' infantry tactics. The general saw dawning comprehension in his face.

"Shit," muttered the young Thracian. He glanced around the room. "The villa's not a fortress, when you come down to it. The fortifications we jury-rigged were designed to fend off grenades, not—"

Belisarius finished the thought.

"Not two thousand of the finest foot soldiers anywhere in the world, charging in squads, aiming to push into every door and portal so they can use their swords and spears."

Cyril scowled. "Let 'em! I don't care how good they are. We're not lambs ourselves, general. Our cataphracts can fight on foot—just watch! With us to back up the Syrians, we'll chop those—"

Belisarius waved his hand.

"That's not the point, Cyril. I don't doubt that we'll beat back the Kushans. But I can guarantee that we won't be doing it without suffering lots of casualties *and* without being exhausted ourselves, when the day's over. I don't think we'll be in any shape to be pursuing anybody, tomorrow."

He rubbed his jaw thoughtfully. "I wonder . . . "

Belisarius stepped back to the window and looked through the telescope again. For a minute, he studied the Kushans taking up their position. Then, pressing himself against the wall to the left of the window, he aimed the telescope at a sharp angle, studying something to the southwest.

"We've got no troops stationed at the corrals." He cast a quick, inquisitive glance at Bouzes. The young Thracian shook his head.

"No, sir." His tone grew a bit defensive: "I thought about it, but it's at least half a mile away. There didn't seem any point to—"

Belisarius smiled crookedly.

"No, there wasn't. I'm not criticizing your decision, Bouzes. I just wanted to make sure."

Again, Bouzes shook his head. "We've got nobody there, general."

"Good," stated Belisarius. He stared through the telescope for another minute, before turning away from the window.

"We're going to turn everything inside out. Instead of waiting until tomorrow, I'll have Maurice start the counterattack at the beginning of the battle."

He hesitated. "Well, not quite. I don't think the Kushans will lead the first assault. Unless that Malwa commander's dumber than a chicken, he won't want to use his best troops until he's softened this place up a bit. He'll let regulars and Ye-tai hammer us with grenades. See what happens. If that doesn't work, then he'll send in the Kushans. They'll head up the second attack. And *that's* when I'll order Maurice to make his charge."

The look of incomprehension was back on the faces of the general's subordinates. Belisarius' own face broke into a cheerful grin. "The trick to dealing with Kushans, I've learned, is to exploit their talents."

"Begging your pardon, sir," spoke up Cyril, "but I don't understand what you're getting at. If Maurice attacks when the Kushans are still fresh—"

"What will the Kushans do?" demanded Belisarius. "*Think*, Cyril. And remember—they'll be excellent troops, with good commanders, *on foot*, suddenly finding themselves caught between a fortified villa and a heavy cavalry charge on their right flank."

Cyril was still frowning. Belisarius drove on.

"The rest of the Malwa army will be shattering, under that charge. Not to mention—"

He turned to Agathius. "Are your boys up for another bit of lance work? A sally, straight out of the villa?"

Agathius grinned. "After that promenade this morning? Hell, yes. It'll be a bitch, mind you, getting the horses through all those little gates."

Belisarius waved the matter off. "I don't care if the sally's ragged. It doesn't matter. All that matters is that while Maurice and Kurush are breaking the Malwa in half from the flank, the front lines of their army see a new threat coming at them straight ahead. The Ye-tai'll go berserk, trying to force the regulars to stand and fight. But the Kushans—"

"Sweet Jesus, *yes*," whispered Bouzes. He strode to the window and stared through it at a sharp angle. "They'll break for the corrals, and the barns and horse pens. Only place around where infantry could fort up and have a chance against heavy cavalry."

He stared back at Belisarius. "They'll have to react instantly, general. Are they really that good?"

"I'm counting on it," came the firm reply. "It's a gamble, I know. If they don't—if they stand their ground—then we'll be in one bloody mess of a brawl. It'll last all day."

He shrugged. "We'll still win, but half the Malwa army will make their escape."

Cyril and Agathius looked at each other. Then, at Belisarius.

"Glad I'm not a general," muttered Cyril. "I'd die from headache."

Agathius tugged at his beard. "If I understand correctly, general, you're planning to wreck the Malwa by isolating their best troops while we concentrate on chewing the rest of them to pieces."

Belisarius nodded. Agathius' beard-tugging grew intense.

"What's to stop the Kushans from sallying themselves? Coming to the aid of—"

Bouzes grinned. "Of what? The same stupid fucking Malwa jackasses who got them treed in the first place?"

Belisarius shook his head. "They won't, Agathius. The Malwa don't trust the Kushans for the good and simple reason that they can't. The Kushans will fight, in a battle. But they've got no love for their overlords. When the hammer falls, the Kushans will look out for themselves."

He turned to Bouzes. "After the initial sally—after we break them—move your Syrian troops to cover the Kushans. The infantry can't play any useful role, anyway, in a pursuit. But don't attack the Kushans—be a bloodbath if you do—just hold them there."

He grinned himself, now.

"Until tomorrow morning."

"We'll finish the Kushans then?" asked Coutzes.

Belisarius' grin faded to a crooked smile. He made a little fluttering motion with his hands.

"We'll see," he said. "Maybe. Maybe not. They're tough, Kushans. But I saw a girl work wonders with them, once, using the right words."

Half an hour later, the attack began. With a rocket barrage, as Belisarius had predicted.

As he watched the rockets soaring all over the sky, exploding haphazardly and landing hither and yon, Belisarius realized that the Malwa were actually doing him a large favor. Although his troops had always maintained a soldierly sangfroid on the subject, he knew that they had been quite apprehensive about the enemy's mysterious gunpowder weapons. Except for Valentinian and Anastasius, who had accompanied him to India, none of Belisarius' men had any real experience with gunpowder weapons. True, most of the soldiers had seen grenades used—some of them had even practiced with the devices. But even his katyusha rocket-men had never seen gunpowder weapons used in the fury and chaos of an actual battle.

Now, the men were getting their first taste of Malwa gunpowder weapons. And the main result, after the first five minutes of that barrage, was—

"They'd do better to use scorpions and onagers," commented a Syrian infantryman, crouched behind a plaque-strengthened window not far from the general.

A Greek cataphract pressed against a nearby wall barked a laugh. "They'd do better to build an assault tower and piss on us," he sneered.

The Syrian watched a skittering rocket sail overhead and burst in midair. The man, Belisarius noted, did not even flinch. In the first moments of the barrage, the Roman soldiers had been shaken by the sound and fury which the rockets produced. But now, with experience, they were taking the matter in stride.

The same Syrian, catching a glimpse of Belisarius, cocked his head and asked:

"What's the point of this, sir, if you don't mind my asking?" The infantryman made a little gesture toward the window. "I don't think more than a dozen of these things have exploded anywhere in the compound. And only a few of them's done any real damage—the ones that blew up over the gardens."

"Don't get too overconfident, men," said Belisarius. He spoke loudly, knowing that all the soldiers crammed into the large room were listening.

"In the proper circumstances, these rockets can be effective. But you're right, in this situation they'd do a lot better to use old-style catapults. Rockets are an area-effect weapon—especially *their* rockets, which aren't anywhere near as accurate as ours."

He paused, allowing the happy thought of Roman rockets to boost morale, before continuing:

"They're almost useless used against a protected fixed position like this one. The reason the Malwa are using them"—he grinned—"is because the arrogant bastards are so sure of themselves that they didn't bother to bring any catapults. Like we did."

The general's grin was answered by a little cheer. When the cheer died down, the Syrian who had spoken up earlier asked another question.

"How would they be doing if they had those siege guns you've talked about?"

Belisarius grimaced. It was more of a whimsical expression than a rueful one, however.

"If they'd had siege guns, I never would have forted us up here in the first place." He waved his hand, casually. "Big siege guns would flatten a place like this inside of five minutes. In ten minutes, there'd be nothing but rubble."

Carefully—gauging—he watched the cheer fade from his soldiers' faces. Then, just before solemnity turned grim, he boomed:

"*On the other hand*, siege guns are so big and awkward that they're sitting ducks on a battleground."

Again, he waved his hand. The gesture, this time, was not casual in the least. It was the motion of a master craftsman, demonstrating an aspect of his skill.

"If they'd brought siege guns, we'd have ripped them with open-field maneuvers."

The grin returned.

"Either way, either way—it doesn't matter, men. We'll thrash the Malwa any way it takes!"

Outside, two rockets burst in unison. But the sound, loud as it was, completely failed to drown the cheers which erupted through the crowded room.

Belisarius! Belisarius!

One soldier only, in that festive outburst, did not participate in the acclaim—the same Syrian, still crouched by the window, still watching everything outside with a keen and vigilant gaze.

"I think that's it, general," he remarked. "I'm pretty sure they're getting ready to charge."

Belisarius moved to the window, and crouched down next to the soldier. He drew out his telescope and peered through it. For a few seconds, no longer.

"You're right," he announced. The general leaned over and placed a hand on the Syrian's shoulder.

"What's your name?" he asked softly.

The man looked a bit startled. "Felix, sir. Felix Chalcenterus."

Belisarius nodded, rose, and strode out of the room. In the hallway beyond, he turned right and headed toward the villa's central gardens. The Greek cataphracts massed in the hallway squeezed to the sides, allowing him a narrow passageway through which to move. A *very* narrow passageway—crooked, cramped, and lined with scale armor.

By the time he emerged into the gardens—a bit the way a seed bursts out of a crushed grape—he felt like he had been through a grape-press himself. For all its imperial size, the villa was far too small a structure to hold thousands of troops packed within its walls. Still, Belisarius had insisted on crowding as many men as possible into the buildings. The villa was not a fortress. But its solidly-built walls and roofs provided far more protection from rockets and arrows than the leather screens and canopies which provided the only missile shelter for the troops resting in the villa's open grounds.

When he finally emerged into the central gardens, he saw that even here the casualties from the barrage had been very light. This, despite the fact that the area was packed as tightly as the buildings were.

The horticultural splendor which had once reigned here was nothing but a memory, now. Every plant and shrub had been obliterated by the heavily-armored men who were jammed into every nook and cranny of the gardens. But few of those men seemed the slightest bit injured.

Belisarius was relieved, even though he was not surprised. Belisarius had been almost certain that the rockets' trajectories would be too flat to plunge into the gardens.

Obviously, his estimate had been correct. What few injuries had occured had resulted from the handful of rockets which, by bad luck, had exploded directly overhead. And even those had done little damage, due to the leather shrapnel screens stretched across much of the garden areas.

Again, Belisarius forced his way forward. Once he was through the gardens, he plunged into the jam-packed hallways of the buildings on the opposite side. Squeeze, squeeze, squeeze. By the time he finally staggered into the open grounds in the rear of the villa, he felt almost as if he had been through another lance charge.

The expedition had taken much longer than he had expected. No sooner did he emerge into the open than he heard a cacophony of distant shouting behind him. Malwa battle cries. The enemy had launched their ground assault.

Belisarius did not even think of turning back. The thought of undergoing that gauntlet again almost made him shudder. There would be no point, anyway. Bouzes was in command of the three thousand infantrymen manning the villa, with five hundred Constantinople cataphracts to back him up. Belisarius was quite confident of their ability to fight off the first attack.

Coutzes and Agathius, seeing the general emerge, hurried to meet him. Their own pace was not quick. The area to the rear of the villa held the rest of the Greek cataphracts and the Syrian cavalry—over four thousand men, along with their horses. But the population density was not as extreme as it had been in the villa itself. The imperial compound's wall-enclosed western grounds were many acres in extent. Open areas, for the most part, interspersed with bridle paths, hedges, patios and scattered trees.

Within a few seconds, Belisarius was consulting with his cavalry commanders. All three of them spoke loudly, due to the rapidly escalating noise coming from the other side of the villa. Malwa and Roman battle cries were mingled with the sound of grenade explosions.

Belisarius' first words were, "How many casualties?"

"They'd have done better to use catapults," snorted Agathius. He looked at Coutzes. "What would you say? Twenty, maybe—overall?"

Coutzes shrugged. "If that many. Only three fatalities, that I know of."

"What about the horses?" asked the general.

Agathius rocked his head back and forth. "They're a little skittish, general. But we were able to keep them pretty much under control. Don't think we lost more than a dozen. Most of those'll be back, in a few hours, except a couple who broke their fool necks jumping the rear wall."

Coutzes laughed. "I don't think Abbu's precious horse will be coming back! I swear, general, the fucking thing almost jumped over the trees as well as the wall!"

Agathius grinned. Belisarius' eyes widened.

"*Abbu's*—you mean that gelding he dotes on?"

" 'Dotes on'?" demanded Coutzes. "That gelding's the apple of the old brigand's eye! He practically sleeps with the damn beast."

"Not any more," chuckled Agathius. "He's fit to be tied, he is. Last I saw he was standing on the wall shooting arrows at the creature. Didn't come close, of course—the gelding was already halfway to Antioch."

Belisarius shook his head. He was smiling, but the smile was overlaid with concern. "Did he manage—"

Coutzes cut him off.

"Don't worry, general. Abbu sent the Arab couriers off as soon as we gave him the word. Half an hour ago, at least. Maurice'll have plenty of warning that the plans have changed."

Belisarius' smile grew very crooked. "I'm glad I won't be there to hear him, cursing me for a fussbudget." He did a fair imitation of Maurice's rasping voice: "What am I? A babe in swaddling clothes—*a toddler*—has to be told to pay attention because plans are changing? Of course the plan's changing! Aren't I the one who taught that—that—*that general*—that plans always change when the enemy arrives?"

Coutzes grinned. Agathius' expression was serious.

"You think he'll be ready, then?" he asked. "I'll admit, I'm a bit worried about it. They weren't expecting to be called on this soon."

Belisarius clapped a hand on Agathius' heavy shoulder.

"Don't," he said softly. "If there's one thing in this world you can be sure of, it's that Maurice won't ever be caught napping in a battle. The only reason I sent the couriers was to make sure he'd move out the second we fired the signal rockets, instead of fifteen seconds later."

He turned to Coutzes. "Speaking of which . . ."

Coutzes pointed to a small copse of trees fifty yards distant.

"In there, general. Aimed and ready to fire as soon as you give the word. One red; followed by a green. And we've got three back-up rockets of each color in case one of them misfires."

Belisarius nodded. He turned his head back toward the villa, listening to the sound of the battle. Even buffered by the villa, the noise was intense. Intense, and growing more so by the second. The grenade explosions were almost continuous, now.

The general and his two officers listened for perhaps a minute, without speaking. Then Coutzes stated, very firmly, "Not a chance."

Agathius immediately nodded. So did Belisarius. All three men had reached the same assessment, just from the sound of the battle.

For all the evident fury with which the Malwa were pressing the attack, their efforts would be futile. There had been not a trace of the unmistakable sounds of defenders losing heart. Not one cry of despair, not one desperate shriek—only a steady roar of Roman battle cries and shouts of confident triumph.

The assault would break, recoil; the Malwa stagger away, trailing small rivers of blood.

Belisarius turned away from the villa and quickly scanned the area.

"You're ready." It was a statement, not a question. Agathius and Bouzes didn't even bother to speak their affirmation.

The general sighed.

"Nothing for it, then." He looked back at the villa, wincing.

"Back into the vise, for me." He began walking toward the buildings, saying, over his shoulder: "I'll have the message relayed. Watch for it. Fire off the rockets at once."

To his relief, the crowd had thinned out a bit—in the rear buildings, at least. All of the soldiers who could had forced themselves into the buildings directly facing the Malwa, fired with determination to help beat off the attack. It only took Belisarius a couple of minutes to thread his way back to the central gardens.

There, however, he was stopped cold. Cursed himself for a fool.

He had forgotten that he had given orders, the day before, to use the gardens as a field hospital. The grounds were completely impassable, now. The casualties were not particularly severe, given the situation. But wounded men, along with their attendants, take up more space than men standing.

As he scrutinized the scene, a part of Belisarius was grimly pleased with what he saw. Outside of the terrible losses suffered by a routed army being pursued, there was no kind of battle which produced casualties as quickly as a close assault on fieldworks. Most of those casualties, of course, would be inflicted on the attackers. But the defenders would take their share also.

Yet, what he now saw in the gardens were light casualties, given the circumstances. And—even better—a much higher proportion of men wounded rather than killed, compared to the usual.

The screens worked, by God!

He had thought they would. Malwa grenades, like Roman ones, were ignited by hand-lit fuses. It was almost inevitable that the man lighting that fuse would cut it a bit too long, from fear of having the bomb blow up in his hand. The Malwa would have concentrated their grenades on the many doors and portals which lined the villa's walls and buildings. With the screens in place—put up almost instantly, without warning—the Malwa grenades would have bounced off and exploded too far away to do any concussive damage. True, shrapnel would pierce the leather—would eventually shred the screens entirely. But the screens had served to blunt the fury of the first assault, and almost all the Roman casualties had been the relatively minor wounds caused by leather-deflected shrapnel.

Pleased as he was, however, Belisarius did not spend much time examining the scene. He was too preoccupied with the unexpected problem of getting himself to a position where he could assess the next Malwa attack—the attack he was certain would be spear-headed by the Kushans. Timing would be all important, then, and he could not possibly order Maurice's attack when he had no idea what was happening.

For a moment, he considered working his way to the front by circumnavigating the interconnected buildings which made up the compound. But he dismissed the idea almost immediately. Every one of those buildings would be so jampacked with soldiers as to make forward progress all but impossible.

He had just about come to the grotesque but inescapable conclusion that he was going to have to make his way through the gardens by walking on the bodies of wounded men, when he heard his name called.

"General Belisarius! General Belisarius! Over here!"

He looked across the gardens. Standing in a doorway on the opposite side was the same infantryman he had spoken with earlier. Felix—Felix Chalcenterus.

"You won't be able to get across, sir!" shouted the Syrian soldier. "The chiliarch sent me back here to watch for you! Wait a minute! Just a minute!"

The man disappeared. He returned about a minute later, preceded by Bouzes. As soon as he stepped into the doorway, Bouzes cupped his hands around his mouth, forming an impromptu megaphone, and hollered:

"Let's set up a relay! With your permission, sir!"

Belisarius thought the problem over. For a second or two, no more. He nodded, and waved his hand. Then, copying Bouzes' handcupping, shouted back:

"Good idea! Leave Felix in the door! If the Kushans lead the next charge, let me know!" He paused, taking a deep breath, before continuing:

"If they do—tell me the moment they start their charge!"

Bouzes waved back, acknowledging. The chiliarch spoke a few words to Felix and disappeared. The Syrian soldier remained in the doorway. His stance was erect and alert. Even from the distance, Belisarius could see the stern expression on the man's face. A young face, it was—almost a boy's face. But it was also the face of a man determined to do his duty, come what may.

Belisarius smiled. "You're in for a promotion, lad," he whispered. "As soon as the battle's over, I think."

The general now concentrated on listening. The sounds of battle had died away, in the last few minutes. Clearly enough, the Malwa had been beaten back and were regrouping.

He decided he had enough time to make his own preparations.

Again, he made his way back through the rear building and onto the western grounds. Agathius was waiting, not twenty feet from the doorway. The Constantinople cataphract was already mounted on his horse.

Quickly, Belisarius explained the signal relay. Then:

"It'll be a few minutes. Get me a horse, will you? I won't be relaying the message. I'll just come straight back and join you."

He pointed to the doorway.

"As soon as you see me coming through that door, have the cornicens order the sally. That'll give me just enough time to mount up."

Agathius nodded. Then, with a frown:

"Where are your bodyguards?"

Belisarius shrugged, smiling whimsically.

"We got separated, it seems. They must be lost in the crowd."

The Greek chiliarch's frown deepened.

"I'm not sure I like that, general. The idea of you leading a sally without your bodyguards, I mean."

Belisarius scowled.

"I assure you, Agathius, I was taking care of myself long before—"

"*Still—*"

"Enough."

Agathius opened his mouth, closed it. "Yes, sir. It'll be as you say."

Belisarius nodded and strode back toward the gardens. This time, as he made his way through the building, he ordered the men inside to clear a lane for him.

"I'll be coming through here, soon enough, running as fast as I can. I warn you, boys—I'll trample right over the man standing in my way. And I'm wearing spurs, I hope you notice."

The soldiers grinned, pressed aside, cheered.

Belisarius! Belisarius!

His only acknowledgement:

That sorry bastard will be fucked.

Ten minutes later, Felix called out the news across the gardens. *"The Kushans are lining up! They'll be leading the attack!"*

Five minutes after he shouted, *"They're coming!"*

Then:

"Now! Now! Now!"

For a man wearing full cataphract armor, Belisarius thought he did quite well, racing—so to speak—through the building. The men who formed the flesh-and-steel walls on both sides certainly thought so, judging from their encouragement.

Belisarius! Belisarius!

Go, general! Go! Go!

And, one enthusiast:

"Goddamn, that man can waddle!"

As soon as he burst out of the doorway onto the grounds, the cornicens started blowing. From the corner of his eye, Belisarius caught the red and green bursts of the signal rockets. But the sole focus of his eyes was the saddled and readied horse ahead of him.

Belisarius almost stumbled, then, from sheer surprise. Standing by the horse, ready to hoist the general aboard, was Anastasius. The giant's own charger was not far away, with a mounting stool at its side.

"How'd you get here?" demanded the general.

"Don't ask," grunted Anastasius, heaving Belisarius onto the horse by sheer brute strength. The huge cataphract headed for his own horse.

Belisarius gathered up the reins. He could see the mass of Greek cataphracts and Syrian light cavalry starting their sally. The horsemen were already dividing into columns, splitting around the villa, heading for the portals in the opposite walls.

A part of his mind noticed that their formations were good—reasonably orderly, and, best of all, well organized. The rest of his mind, briefly, wrestled with a mystery.

"How did you get here?" he asked again. This time, to the man already mounted and ready at his side.

"Don't ask," hissed Valentinian. The cataphract gave Anastasius a weasel glare. "*His* doing. 'Impossible,' I told him. 'Even Moses couldn't part that mob.' "

Anastasius, trotting up on his horse, caught the last words. A grin split his rock-hewn face.

"Moses wasn't as big as I am," he said. He extended his enormous hand, like an usher.

"After you, sir. Victory is waiting."

"So it is!" cried Belisarius. "So it is!"

He spurred his mount into a gallop. He was not worried about exhausting his horse, now. They didn't have far to go. He was only concerned with getting to the front of the charge, and leading it to victory.

By the time he pounded around the villa, and saw the nearest portal, he had achieved that immediate goal. The Syrian infantrymen who were hastily opening the gates—tossing aside the splintered wreckage of the gates, more precisely—barely had time to dodge aside before Belisarius drove past. Valentinian and Anastasius came right behind, followed by droves of cataphracts.

The infantrymen were cheering wildly; the cataphracts were bellowing their battle cries. But Belisarius only had ears for an expected mutter.

It never came. He glanced over his shoulder, cocking a quizzical eye.

A weasel's glare met his gaze. A weasel's hiss:

"Ah, what's the fucking use?"

Chapter 20

The general's first thought, as he came around the villa onto its eastern grounds, was to make a quick assessment of the tactical situation. He had seen nothing of the battle directly, since his return to the villa after the first cavalry charge.

That urgent purpose almost led him to an immediate and humiliating downfall.

Downfall, in the literal sense. Dead, dying and badly wounded Malwa soldiers were scattered all across the grounds in front of the villa. In places, the bodies were piled two and three deep. Belisarius was concentrating so intently on the live Malwa troops that he was oblivious to the obstacles posed by the dead ones. His mount stumbled on a corpse and almost spilled his rider. Only the superhuman reflexes which Aide gave him enabled Belisarius to keep himself in the saddle and his horse on its feet.

First things first! he snarled at himself. For the next few seconds, until he was through the carnage on the villa's eastern grounds, he ignored everything but leading his horse forward. Only a cold, distant, and detached part of his mind took note of the terrible losses the enemy had suffered in their first assault. Arrow wounds, in the main, although a number of the Malwa casualties had apparently been caused by their own grenades, bouncing off the screens.

Finally, he was through the mounded bodies and could concentrate on the active enemy.

His first concern was with the katyushas. He could already hear the hissing shriek of the rockets—unmistakably different from the sound produced by Malwa rockets. The Roman missiles, following Belisarius' instructions, had been fitted with machined bronze venturi. The evenly-distributed thrust provided by those exhaust nozzles made his katyusha rockets far more accurate than their Malwa counterparts. They also made a distinctively different noise.

He could not see the rocket-chariots themselves. The katyushas would be charging at the Malwa from their hiding place in the northeast woods, followed by the Thracian and Illyrian cataphracts. A screen of trees blocked Belisarius' view in that direction. But he could see the rockets themselves. The first volley was even now impacting on the enemy. He watched a line of explosions stitching its way across the Malwa army's right flank, knocking cavalrymen out of saddles and their horses to the ground.

He held his breath. That first volley had come perilously close to landing in the very center of the enemy formation, where the Mahaveda priests were perched atop the gunpowder wagons. It was no part of his plan to have that ammunition—

His held-in breath exploded. The second and third volleys *did* land in the center of the enemy—several of them right among the wagons. Many of the priests standing on those wagons were swept off as if by a broom. One of the wagons was tipped over by a rocket exploding almost directly beneath it. The ammunition cart teetered on two wheels. Teetered, teetered, before finally slamming back down. One of the wheels collapsed under the shock.

Belisarius hunched low, waiting for the whole ammunition supply to blow up. He turned his head and began yelling at the men behind him to brace themselves for the eruption.

Then, abruptly, stopped. There had been no explosion.

Astonished, he turned his head back and saw that, for all the destruction strewn by the katyushas, the Malwa ammunition had not caught fire.

An arrow sailing past his head reminded him that there were other dangers. The first ranks of dismounted Malwa regulars were less than a hundred and fifty yards away. The enemy soldiers were obviously confused by the sudden and unexpected attack on their flank. But many of them still had enough presence of mind to fire arrows at the Romans sallying from the villa.

Their arrows were neither well-aimed nor fired in coordination, however. Belisarius was about to congratulate himself for surprising his enemy—again—when another flight of arrows erased all sense of self-satisfaction.

Those arrows were well-aimed, and had been fired in a coordinated volley from a hundred yards away. The volley looked like a flight of homing pigeons, coming toward him unerringly from his right front. The general raised his shield, crouching in the saddle as best he could.

No less than three glanced off his shield; another, off the armor guarding his mount's withers; and a fifth, painfully, on his heavily armored right arm. Fortunately, the bow which had launched that arrow lacked the power of a cataphract bow. The arrowhead failed to penetrate the scale armor, although Belisarius was quite sure he would be sporting a bad bruise by morning.

The rest of the volley landed amidst the cataphracts following him. From the cries of pain and surprise, he knew that many had hit their targets.

When the general peeked over the rim of his shield, looking forward and to his right, he saw what he expected to see. The Kushans were already forming a square—shields interlocked, spears bristling, with a line of archers standing right behind the shield wall. The Kushan commander had instantly assessed the new situation and was doing the best thing he could under the circumstances—hunker down, snarl, and bristle like a porcupine surrounded by wolves.

Smart wolves hunt easier prey. So did Belisarius. He angled his horse to the left, guiding his men away from the Kushan formation. He would ride in a shallow arc around the Kushans and fall on the disorganized mass of Malwa regulars who had been following the Kushan vanguard.

His cataphracts—no fools, themselves—immediately followed his lead. None of them, in Belisarius' column, even fired back at the Kushans. The general had led the sally erupting from the northern portals and gates of the villa. The Kushans, therefore, were to their right as they galloped past—the worst location for a mounted archer to fire at without exposing his whole body.

So Belisarius and his men simply grit their teeth, sheltered as best they could behind angled shields, and endured the Kushans' raking fire.

The *other* Roman sally, on the other hand—the one which Agathius was leading from the southern portals—was in the ideal position for mounted archers. As they came charging out, the Kushans were on their left front. Every one of those thousand cataphracts who pounded past the Kushan hedgehog, fired at least one arrow into the enemy mass. At a range of fifty yards, full-drawn cataphract bows could send arrows through any kind of armor—even through iron-reinforced laminated wood shields, unless the shields were properly angled.

The Kushan shield wall crumpled under that withering missile fire. Belisarius and his men on the opposite side were the immediate beneficiaries. The Kushans on the north left off their raking fire and hastened to shore up their bleeding ranks on the south.

Now, the Kushan vanguard was behind the Roman cavalry sally. Belisarius and his cataphracts were within fifty yards of the Malwa regulars who had been advancing behind the Kushans.

Those troops—thousands of dismounted cavalrymen—suddenly broke into headlong flight. Caught between a completely unexpected flank attack and the mass sally of the Romans in the villa, their nerve collapsed. The still-mounted Ye-tai security squads tried to rally the fleeing soldiers—viciously sabring dozens of them as they ran past—but to no avail.

Belisarius gave a quick glance over his shoulder. The Syrian cavalry, following the heavily-armored Greeks, were already spreading wide and beginning to pull ahead of the slower cataphracts. They were staying well away from the Kushans. Their purpose was to ravage the flanks of the rapidly-disintegrating main force of the enemy. Behind them, trotting out of the villa and taking up positions, came the Syrian infantry. They were concentrating in front of the villa itself and to the north—leaving the now-isolated Kushans with a clear line of retreat toward the corrals.

Satisfied, the general turned back. The Malwa soldier nearest to him, racing away, stumbled and fell. Belisarius did not waste a lance thrust. He simply trampled the man under and kept going.

A Ye-tai horsemen came charging, his own lance held high. Belisarius braced in the stirrups and swept the Ye-tai off his saddle with a lance thrust which spilled open his intestines.

Another Malwa regular ran away, his feet flashing like an antelope's. The general's lance took him between the shoulder blades.

Belisarius killed three more soldiers in the same manner before he lost his lance, stuck in a Malwa spine. He drew his long cavalry sword and continued the slaughter.

The front ranks of the enemy were completely routed, now. Even the Ye-tai had given up their efforts to rally the troops. The barbarians, still mounted, were outpacing all others in the retreat.

The Malwa regulars had no thought in their minds but to outrun the Roman cavalry. They were not the first men, in a battle, to be seized by that panicky, hopeless notion. And they were not the first to suffer the penalty.

The general never ceased from his ruthless work, leaving a trail of slashed corpses behind him. But the inner man almost flinched away from the horror, until he found refuge—as he had so often before—in the cold workings of his intellect.

It's the worst mistake infantry ever makes, he thought. If they stood their ground against a cavalry charge, like the Kushans did, they'd have a chance. Now—nothing. Nothing.

A sudden line of explosions nearby—almost directly to his left—broke through his grim thoughts. He saw, out of the corner of an eye, one of his cataphracts clutch his face with both hands and fall off his saddle. Another cataphract's horse tumbled, spilling his rider.

Those were katyusha rockets! God damn it, hold your fire!

No luck. Belisarius could see another volley of rockets sailing toward them.

The rockets, of course, had been intended for the Malwa—part of the plan to cave in the enemy's right flank. That was little comfort, when several of those rockets overshot the enemy and wreaked havoc in his own ranks. Loudly and profanely, the general cursed Maurice for a fool—and Basil, the katyusha commander, for a moron sired by an imbecile.

But—

Belisarius himself had instructed Maurice to lead the charge with katyushas. Knowing full well that even Roman rockets were not very accurate, the general had given the orders nonetheless. He had simply not expected the Malwa to cave in so quickly. He had assumed that the rocket volleys would be over and done with by the time the cataphracts arrived.

So he cursed himself, for an idiot.

Rockets are an area-effect weapon, you fucking jackass! Don't ever do this again!

He pushed self-recrimination aside. He had almost reached the center of the Malwa army. Ahead of him, he could see kshatriya and priests frantically trying to turn the wagons around. The mules hauling those wagons, true to their stubborn nature, were obeying their masters' shrieking commands with mute recalcitrance.

The sight almost made him laugh. What did the priests hope to accomplish? Mule-drawn wagons had no more chance of escaping a cavalry pursuit than did men on foot.

One of the Mahaveda standing atop the nearest wagon apparently reached the same conclusion. Belisarius was only twenty yards away when he saw the priest's face stiffen with resolve. The man stooped, seized a small barrel of gunpowder, and spilled its contents over the barrel-stacks.

The priest was just drawing a lighting device out of his tunic when Belisarius' saber cut the legs out from under him. The priest sprawled across the barrels, still holding the striker. Belisarius' next slash removed that hand; his next, the Mahaveda's head.

The general reined in his horse and clambered onto the wagon. From that perch, he began bellowing orders in his thunderous battlefield voice.

The orders were pungent, profane, simple—and quite unnecessary. Anastasius and Valentinian had already secured the two closest wagons. The Greek cataphracts, within ten seconds, had done the same with the rest.

All of the kshatriya still on the wagons—perhaps fifty—tried to surrender, along with the remaining two dozen priests. The cataphracts would have none of it. Many of those men had seen the first priest's suicidal attempt to blow up the ammunition cart. The Greeks slaughtered any Malwa among the wagons without mercy.

Belisarius left off his bellowing. The deed was done. The Malwa wagons, with their great load of gunpowder, were safely in Roman hands.

He clambered onto the highest-placed barrel. From that precarious perch, he strained to see what he could of the battle.

Battle, no longer. The rout was complete.

Maurice's hammer blow had completely shattered the Malwa right. The Ye-tai who had guarded that flank had taken frightful casualties before breaking. Whatever their other characteristics, no one had ever accused Ye-tai of cowardice. So they had stood their ground—almost to a man, Belisarius judged, estimating the mound of corpses.

Their courage had been useless, of course. Not even the best troops, in Belisarius' experience, could put up an effective defense against a surprise mass attack coming on their flank. Not on an open field of battle, at any rate, with no place to shelter and regroup. Such troops could fight—fight bravely—but they would fight as confused individuals against a well-organized, steady and determined attacker. The conclusion was foregone.

It was equally obvious that the Malwa regulars had not come to the assistance of the barbarians. The Malwa regulars clustered with the main force had still been mounted, unlike their luckless comrades who had been advancing on foot behind the Kushan attack. They had seen no reason to abandon that good fortune, and had immediately taken flight away from the Roman flank attack.

Good fortune—fleeting fortune. In their natural desire to make the quickest escape from that frightening mass of oncoming Thracians, Illyrians and Persians—heavy cavalry, all of them, shaking the very earth in their charge out of the northeast woods—the Malwa regulars had broken to the south.

A mass rout, thousands of horsemen galloping frantically around the edge of the forest—into the Euphrates. As soon as they realized their error, of course, the fleeing Malwa began racing east down the riverbank, toward the far-distant refuge of the Malwa forces besieging Babylon.

Few of those men would ever find that refuge, two hundred miles away. Very few.

The men pursuing them were veterans, led by experienced and capable commanders. Maurice and Kurush, seeing the direction of the Malwa retreat, had sent their cataphracts and dehgans angling southeast. They would cut off the Malwa escape, trap them against the river.

Belisarius watched his katyusha rocket-chariots wheel into a line, some three hundred yards away. A small figure—their commander Basil, he assumed, although he could not recognize any faces at the distance—was prancing back and forth on his horse issuing commands. A moment later, a volley of hissing rockets sailed toward the Euphrates.

Belisarius watched their flight. It was his first opportunity to observe the rockets without the distraction of immediate battle. The missiles flew in a shallow trajectory, with little of the erratic serpentine motion of Malwa rockets. Seconds later, the general saw the warheads erupt, scattering shrapnel through the milling mob of Malwa packed on the riverbank.

The carnage was impressive. Belisarius had seen to it that Roman rockets carried well-designed shrapnel in their warheads. Lead drop-shot, rather than the pebbles and other odds-and-ends which Malwa rockets used.

Belisarius now looked toward the villa. Here too, he saw, the situation was progressing nicely. Those Malwa infantrymen who had managed to escape the sally were also pouring toward the river. The Syrian cavalry had peeled off from the captured powder wagons and were driving the Malwa toward the north bank of the Euphrates.

Behind them, the Syrian infantry had taken formations opposite the Kushans. The Kushans were already withdrawing toward the corrals. The Syrians followed, at a respectful distance, content to let them go.

He heard Agathius' voice, raised in a cheerful hail. Turning, Belisarius saw Agathius and several of his cataphracts trotting toward him. "I sent most of my men to help the Syrians," he announced, "after I saw you doing the same."

Belisarius had not actually given that order. There had been no need, since Cyril had done so without any prompting, and the general had wanted to concentrate his attention on watching Maurice's half of the battle. But now, looking around, he saw that there were only a hundred or so cataphracts left, guarding the wagons.

Belisarius was immensely pleased. *Immensely*. There were few things the general treasured more than quick-thinking and self-reliant subordinates. He was firmly convinced that at least half his success as a commander was due to his ability to gather such men around him. Men like Maurice, Ashot, Hermogenes, John of Rhodes—even Bouzes and Coutzes, once he'd knocked the crap out of them.

And now, men like Agathius and Cyril.

Something of his delight must have shown. A moment later, he and his two new Greek officers were beaming at each other. There was nothing at all crooked in the general's grin, now; and not a trace of veteran sardonicism, in those of Agathius and Cyril.

"Jesus, general," exclaimed Agathius, "this is the sweetest damn battle I ever saw!"

"Beautiful, beautiful," agreed Cyril. "Only fuck-up was that one rocket volley."

Belisarius grimaced. "My fault, that. I should have remembered the damn things still aren't that accurate. And I wasn't expecting we'd get so close this quickly."

Cyril did not seem in the slightest aggrieved, even though it was his men who had suffered from that friendly fire. The Greek cataphract simply shrugged and pronounced the oldest of all veteran wisdom:

"Shit happens."

Agathius nodded his agreement. "Live and learn, that's all you can do. Besides—" He twisted in his saddle, studying the effect of the current rocket volleys on the Malwa massed by the river.

"—they're doing fine work now. Save a lot of Roman boys, the katyushas will, by the time they're done. Those Malwa shits'll be like stunned sheep."

Belisarius heard another hail. Turning, he saw that Maurice was approaching from the north. The chiliarch was accompanied by one of his hecatontarchs, Gregory, and a half-dozen cataphracts.

When Maurice drew up alongside the wagon, his first words were to Cyril and Agathius.

"Sorry about the rockets," he stated. His voice was firm and level. Very courteous in tone, although the expression on his face seemed more one of embarassment than remorse.

Maurice now looked to Belisarius.

"Don't even bother asking," he growled. "The answer's no. My boys'd probably be willing enough, even if those raggedy-ass Malwa fucks couldn't come up with two solidus ransom amongst them. But the Persians are completely berserk and there's no way to stop them without—"

Belisarius shook his head. "I know. I can hear their battle cries."

He cocked his ear, listening. Even at the distance, the Persian voices were quite distinct.

Charax! Charax!
Death to Malwa!
No quarter!

Seeing the look of confusion on the faces of Agathius and Cyril, Maurice chuckled.

"The young general here"—he pointed a thumb at Belisarius—"has a soft and tender heart. Likes to avoid atrocities, when he can."

The two Greek officers eyed the general uncertainly, much as men gaze upon someone pronounced to be a living saint. Possible, possible—but, more likely, just a babbling madman.

Then, remembering his savage punishment of the eight cataphracts at Callinicum, uncertainty fled.

Agathius winced. "Mother of God, general, Maurice is right. There's no way—"

Again, Belisarius shook his head, smiling crookedly. "I'm not asking, Agathius. The Persians won't be stopped, not after Charax. I'm quite aware of that."

The smile faded, replaced by a look of scrutiny. "But I'll ask you to remember this day, in the future. The very near future, in fact. When the Persians demand the heads of two thousand Kushans, and I refuse."

He pointed toward the river.

"Atrocities produce this kind of massacre. That's one of the reasons I try to avoid them. You might be on the other end, the next time. Pleading for mercy, and not getting it, because you showed none yourself."

"Wouldn't get it from the Malwa, anyway," pointed out Maurice. He spoke mildly—as usual, when he was contradicting Belisarius in public—but firmly.

"From Malwa, no," replied the general. "But what *is* Malwa, Maurice?"

He nodded toward the river. "You think those men are all Malwa? Or Ye-tai? Precious few of them, in truth. The priests and kshatriyas, most of the officers. Perhaps a thousand of the regulars. The rest? Biharis, Bengalis, Orissans—every subject nation of India is spilling its life blood into that river."

He transferred his scrutiny to Agathius and Cyril. "In the end," Belisarius told them, his voice as hard as steel, "we will not defeat Malwa on a great field of battle, somewhere here in Persia. Or in Anatolia, or Bactria, or the Indus plain. We will shatter them in the heart of India itself, when their subjects finally throw off the yoke."

Uncertainty returned to the faces of the two Greeks. Now, however, it was not the bemused skepticism of men regarding a proclaimed saint. It was the simple doubt—the veteran questioning—of fighting men who were beginning to wonder if their commander might, after all, be that rarest of generals. A supreme strategist, as well as a wizard on the battlefield.

"I would spare all of them who tried to surrender, if I could," mused Belisarius. "All, at least, except the Mahaveda priests. For the sake of the future, if nothing else."

He shrugged heavily. "But—I can't risk an idiot brawl with the Persians. Not today, when their blood's a-boil."

He clambered off the barrel. A moment later, he was back astride his horse. "Today, I can only deal with the Kushans."

He pointed to the river. "Agathius—Cyril—I want you to give full support to the Persians. Back them to the hilt. As maddened as they are, they won't be thinking clearly. There are still thousands of live and armed enemy troops packed against the river. They'll fight like cornered rats, once they realize surrender's not being offered. The Persians are likely to wade into them without thinking, get surrounded."

Agathius and Cyril nodded.

"Take all your men," Belisarius added, "except a hundred or so to guard over the wagons. Have those men bring the wagons back to the villa. But be careful—in fact, better wait until you have some of the katyusha men to help. They're more familiar with handling gunpowder."

The two Greek officers nodded again. They turned their horses and trotted off, shouting commands. Within a few seconds, two thousand Constantinople cataphracts were thundering toward the river, preparing to throw their weight into the butchery on the Euphrates.

Belisarius turned to Maurice and Gregory.

"You do the same, Maurice, with the Thracians and the Illyrians. Gregory, I want you to find Coutzes—and Abbu," he added, chuckling—"if he managed to find a new horse. Get the Arab skirmishers and half the light cavalry across the river. Leave me the other half, to keep the Kushans cornered."

"They'll have to use the ford we found a few miles upstream," remarked Gregory. "That'll lose us several hours."

"Yes, I know. It doesn't matter. They'll still be in time to harry whatever Malwa make their way across the Euphrates."

His face and voice were cold, grim, ruthless.

"Harry them, Gregory. I want them pursued without mercy. For days, if that's what it takes. *I want this Malwa army destroyed.* Not more than a handful of survivors, trickling back to their lines in Babylon. Let the enemy know he can't hope to go around Emperor Khusrau."

Gregory's face twisted into his own crooked smile. "Might not even be a handful, general. Those few that get away from us will still have two hundred miles to go. With the desert on one side, and on the other—every peasant in the flood plain ready to hack them down. Whole villages will turn out, to join the pursuit. They've heard about Charax, too, you can bet on it."

Belisarius nodded. Gregory spurred his horse, heading south. A moment later, going in the opposite direction, Maurice did the same.

Only Valentinian and Anastasius were left, in the immediate vicinity.

"What now, general?" asked Anastasius.

Belisarius clucked his horse into motion, trotting back toward the villa. "We'll make sure the Kushans are completely boxed in. After that—" He looked up, gauging the sun. "That'll probably take the rest of the day. Till late afternoon, for sure. The Kushans may try to break out. We've probably still got some fighting ahead of us."

"Not much," rumbled Anastasius. "The Kushans are no fools. They won't waste much effort trying to find an escape route. Not on foot, knowing we've got cavalry." The giant sighed. "Not Kushans. They'll be working like beavers, instead, doing what they can to turn the barns and corrals into a fortress. Ready to bleed us when we come in after them tomorrow."

"I hope to avoid that problem," said Belisarius.

"You think you can talk them into surrendering?" asked Valentinian skeptically. "After they'll have spent half a day listening to the rest of their army being massacred?"

"That's my plan." Oddly, the general's voice lost none of its confident good cheer.

Neither did Valentinian's its skepticism. "Be like walking into a lion's den, trying to talk them out of their meat."

"Not so hard, that," replied Belisarius. "Not, at least, if you can speak lion."

He eyed Valentinian. Smiled crookedly. "I speak Kushan fluently, you know."

The smile grew *very* crooked. Anastasius scowled. Valentinian hissed.

"Now that I think about it, both of you speak Kushan too. Not as well as I do, perhaps. But—well enough. Well enough."

He cocked his ear toward Valentinian.

"What? No muttering?"

The cataphract eyed Belisarius with a weasel's glare.

"Words fail me," he muttered.

That evening, just as the sun was setting on the horizon, Belisarius approached the forted Kushans for a parley. He was unarmed, accompanied only by Valentinian and Anastasius.

Anastasius, also, was unarmed.

Valentinian—well, he swore the same. Swore it on all the saints and his mother's grave. Belisarius didn't believe him, not for a minute, but he didn't push the matter. Whatever weapons Valentinian carried would be well-hidden. And besides—

He'd rather try to talk lions into surrendering than talk a weasel out of its teeth. An entirely safer proposition.

In the end, talking the Kushan lions out of their determination to fight to the last man proved to be one of the easiest things the general had ever done. And the doing of it brought him great satisfaction.

Once again, a reputation proved worth its weight in gold.

Not a reputation for mercy, this time. Kushans had seen precious little of mercy, in their harsh lives, and would have disbelieved any such tales of a foreign general.

But, as it turned out, they were quite familiar with the name of Belisarius. It was a name of honor, their commander had been told, by one of the few men not of Kushan blood that he trusted.

"Rana Sanga told me himself," the man stated. He drew himself up proudly. "I visited Rajputana's greatest king in his palace, at his own invitation, before he left with Lord Damodara for the Hindu Kush."

The man leaned over, pouring a small libation into Belisarius' drinking cup before doing the same in the one before him. The vessels were plain, utilitarian pieces of pottery, like the bottle from which the wine was poured. After Belisarius had taken his seat, sitting cross-legged like his Kushan counterpart on a thin layer of straw spread in a corner of the stable, the Kushan soldiers gathered around had produced the jug and two cups out of a field kit.

Belisarius took advantage of the momentary pause to study the Kushan commander more closely. The man's name, he had already learned, was Vasudeva.

In appearance, Vasudeva was much like any other Kushan soldier. Short, stocky, thick-chested. Sturdy legs and shoulders. His complexion had a yellowish Asiatic cast, as did his flat nose and narrow eyes. Like most Kushans, the man's hair was drawn up into a topknot. His beard was more in the way of a goatee than the thicker cut favored by Romans or Persians.

And, like most Kushans, his face seemed carved from stone. His expression, almost impossible to read. The Kushan Belisarius knew best—the former Malwa vassal named Kungas, who was now commander of Empress Shakuntala's personal bodyguard—had had a face so hard it had been like a mask.

An iron mask—but a mask, nonetheless, disguising a very different soul.

Remembering Kungas, Belisarius felt his confidence growing.

"And how was Rana Sanga, when you saw him?" he asked politely.

The Kushan shrugged. "Who is to know what that man feels? His wife, perhaps his children. No others."

"Do you know why he asked you to visit him?"

Vasudeva gave Belisarius a long, lingering look. A cold look, at first. Then—

The look did not warm, so much as it grew merry. In a wintry sort of way.

"Yes. We had met before, during the war against Andhra. Worked well together. When he heard that I had been selected one of the Kushan commanders for the Mesopotamian campaign, he called me to visit before his own departure." The Kushan barked a laugh. "He wanted to warn me about a Roman general named Belisarius!"

Vasudeva's eyes lost their focus for a moment, as he remembered the conversation.

" 'Persians you know, of course,' Lord Sanga told me. 'But you have never encountered Romans. Certainly not such a Roman as Belisarius.' "

The Kushan commander's eyes refocussed, fixed on Belisarius.

"He told me you were as tricky and quick as a mongoose." Another barking laugh. " 'Expect only the unexpected, from that man,' he said. 'He adores feints and traps. If he makes an obvious threat, look for the blow to come from elsewhere. If he seems weak, be sure he is strong. Most of all—remember the fate of the arrogant cobra, faced with a mongoose.' "

He laughed again. All the Kushan soldiers standing around shared in that bitter laugh.

"I tried to tell Lord Kumara, when I realized we were facing Roman troops. I was almost sure you would be in command. Lord Kumara is—*was*—the commander of this expedition."

"Lord Fishbait, now," snarled one of the other Kushans. "And good riddance."

Vasudeva scowled. "Of course, he refused to listen. Fell right into the trap."

Belisarius took a sip from his cup. "And what else did Rana Sanga say about me?"

Again, Vasudeva gave Belisarius that long, lingering look. Still cold. Gauging, assessing. "He said that one thing only is predictable about the man Belisarius. He will be a man of honor. He, too, knows the meaning of vows."

Belisarius waited. Vasudeva tugged the point of his goatee with his fingers. Looked away.

"It's difficult, difficult," he murmured.

Belisarius waited.

Vasudeva sighed. "We will not be broken up, sold as slaves to whichever bidder. We must be kept together."

Belisarius nodded. "Agreed."

"Any labor will be acceptable, except the work of menials. Kushan soldiers are not domestic dogs."

Belisarius nodded. "Agreed."

"No whippings. No beatings of any kind. Execution will be acceptable, in cases of disobedience. But it must be by the sword, or the ax. We are not criminals, to be hung or impaled."

Belisarius nodded. "Agreed."

"Decent food. A bit of wine, now and again."

Belisarius shook his head. "That I cannot promise. I am on campaign, myself, and will be using you for a labor force. My own men may eat poorly, at times, and go without wine. I can only promise that you will eat no worse than they do. And enjoy some wine, if there is any to spare."

From the little murmur which came from the surrounding soldiers, the general knew that his forthright answer had pleased them. He suspected, although he was not sure, that the last question had been Vasudeva's own little trap. The Kushan commander was obviously a seasoned veteran. He would have known, full well, that any other answer would be either a lie or the words of a cocksure and foolhardy man.

"Agreed," said Vasudeva.

Belisarius waited.

Finally, the word came: "Swear."

Belisarius gave his oath. Gave it twice, in fact. Once in the name of his own Christian god. And then, to the Kushans' great surprise, on the name of the Buddha to whom they swore in private, when there were no Mahaveda priests to hear the heresy.

That evening, late at night, Belisarius began his negotiations with the Persians—seated, now, amidst the splendid wreckage of what had once been an emperor's favorite hunting villa.

Here, too, he found the task much easier than anticipated.

Kurush, in the event, was not baying for Kushan blood. After the young sahrdaran heard what Belisarius had to say, he simply poured himself some wine. A noble vintage, this, poured from a sahrdaran's jug into a sahrdaran's gorgeous goblet.

He drank half the goblet in one gulp. Then said, "All right."

Belisarius eyed him. Kurush scowled.

"I'm not saying I like it," he grumbled, "but you gave your word. We Aryans, you know, understand the meaning of vows."

He emptied the goblet in another single gulp. Then, he gestured toward his blood-soaked garments and armor. "Charax has been well enough avenged, for one day."

Growl: "I suppose."

Belisarius let it be. He saw no reason to press Kurush for anything beyond his grudging acceptance.

He did cast a questioning glance at Baresmanas. The older sahrdaran had said nothing, thus far, and it was obvious that he intended to maintain his silence. He simply returned Belisarius' gaze with his own fair imitation of a mask.

No, Baresmanas would say nothing. But Belisarius suspected that the Persian nobleman had already had his say—earlier, to his young and vigorous nephew. Reminding him of a Roman general's mercy at a place called Mindouos. And teaching him—or trying, at least—that mercy can have its own sharp point. Keener than any lance or blade, and even deadlier to the foe.

Chapter 21

THE MALABAR COAST
Summer, 531 A.D.

The refugee camps in Muziris swarmed like anthills. Families gathered up their few belongings and awaited the voyage to the island of Tamraparni. Maratha cavalrymen and Kushan soldiers readied their gear. The great fleet of ships assembling in the harbor cleared their holds. Keralan officials presented chests full of gold and silver, to fund the migration. An empress and her advisers schemed.

And old friends arrived.

In midafternoon of a sunny day—a rarity, that, in southwest India during the monsoon season—five Axumite warships entered the harbor at Muziris.

They were not hailed by Keralan guard vessels. There was no pretense, any longer, that the port of Muziris was under anyone's control but Shakuntala's. The Ethiopian vessels were met by a warship "requisitioned" from Kerala but manned by Maratha sailors.

Once their identity was established, the Ethiopians were immediately escorted into the presence of the Empress. There were four hundred of the Axumite soldiers, along with four other men. Shakuntala, forewarned, greeted them with a full imperial ceremony before the great mansion she had taken for her palace.

The three Ethiopians who led that march were deeply impressed by what they saw—as were the four men walking with them who were not African. The seven men at the front were familiar with India, and with Shakuntala's situation. They had been expecting something patchwork and ragged. A rebel empress—a hunted young girl—hiding in a precarious refuge, with nothing but the handful of Kushan soldiers who had spirited her out of the Malwa empire.

Instead—

The street down which they were escorted, by hundreds of Maratha cavalrymen, was lined with thousands of cheering people. Most were refugees, from Andhra and other Malwa-conquered lands of India. But there were many dark-skinned Keralans among that crowd, as well. Her own grandfather might have disowned her, and Malwa provocateurs might have stirred up much animosity toward the refugees who had poured into the kingdom, but many of her mother's people had not forgotten that Shakuntala was a daughter of Kerala herself. So they too cheered, and loudly, at this further evidence that the Empress-in-exile of Andhra was a force to be reckoned with. Allies—from far off Africa! And such splendid-looking soldiers!

Which, indeed, they were. The sarwen rose to the occasion, abandoning their usual Axumite informality. In stiff lines they marched, their great spears held high, ostrich-plume headdresses bobbing proudly.

As they approached the Empress' palace, kettledrums began beating. At the steps leading up to the palace doors, the march halted. The doors swung wide, and dozens—then hundreds—of Kushan soldiers trotted out and took positions on the palace steps. The last Kushans to emerge were Shakuntala's personal bodyguard, the small band of men who had been with her since she inherited her throne. Since the very day, in fact. For these were the men who had taken her out of her father's palace in Amaravati, on the day her family was slaughtered, as a Malwa captive. And then, months later, had spit in Malwa's face and taken her to freedom.

Finally, Shakuntala herself emerged, with Dadaji Holkar at her side. Four imperial ladies-in-waiting came behind them.

She stepped—say better, pranced—down the stairs to greet her visitors.

For all the pomp and splendor, the dignity of the occasion was threadbare. Genuine joy has a way of undermining formality.

Among the Ethiopians who stood before the palace were four Kushans—the squad, led by Kujulo, who had assisted Prince Eon in his escape from India the year before. As soon as Shakuntala's bodyguard spotted their long-lost brethren, their discipline frayed considerably. They did not break formation, of course. But the grins on their faces went poorly with the solemnity of the occasion.

It hardly mattered, since their own Empress was grinning just as widely. Partly, at the sight of Kujulo and his men. Mostly, at the familiar faces of the three Ethiopians at the front.

Garmat, Ezana and Wahsi. Three of that small band of men who had rescued her from Malwa captivity.

Seeing an absent face, her grin faded.

Garmat shook his head.

"No, Shakuntala, he did not come with us. The negusa nagast sent Eon on a different mission. But the Prince asked me to convey his greetings and his best wishes."

Shakuntala nodded. "We will speak of it later. For the moment, let me thank you for returning my Kushan bodyguards."

Smiling, she turned and beckoned one of her ladies-in-waiting forward.

"And I have no doubt you will want to take Tarabai back with you. As I promised Eon."

The Maratha woman stepped forward. Although she was trying to maintain her composure, Tarabai's expression was a jumbled combination of happiness and anxiety. Happiness, at the prospect of being reunited with her Prince. Anxiety, that he might have lost interest in her after their long separation. During the course of Prince Eon's adventures in India the year before, he and Tarabai had become almost inseparable. Before they went their separate ways in escaping the Malwa, Eon had asked her to become his concubine, and she had accepted. But—that was then, and princes are notoriously fickle and short of memory.

Garmat immediately allayed her anxiety.

"Eon may not be in Axum upon your arrival, Tarabai. He is occupied elsewhere, at the moment. But he hopes you have not changed your mind."

The old half-Arab smiled.

"Actually, he does more than hope. He is already adding a wing to his palace. Your quarters, when you arrive—as well as those of your children, when *they* arrive. As I'm sure they will, soon enough."

Tarabai blushed. Beamed.

That business done, Garmat's gaze returned to the Empress. His smile faded. "So much is pleasure, Your Majesty. Now, for the rest—"

He straightened. Then, in a loud voice:

"I bring you an official offer of alliance from the negusa nagast of Axum. A full alliance against the Malwa."

A buzz of whispered conversation filled the air at this announcement.

"We heard, upon our arrival, that you plan to transport your people to the island of Ceylon. Let me make clear that, if you desire, you and your people may seek refuge in Ethiopia instead."

Shakuntala would have sworn that her expression never changed. But she had forgotten Garmat's uncanny shrewdness.

"Ah," he murmured. His voice was soft, and pitched low. So low that only she and Dadaji could now hear him. "I had wondered. Exile to a distant land did not really seem in your nature. So. I have five ships, Your Majesty. On board those ships came half of the Dakuen sarwe—four hundred soldiers, under the command of Ezana and Wahsi. One of those ships must convey Tarabai and myself back to Ethiopia. The rest—including all of the sarwen—are at your disposal."

Shakuntala nodded. She, too, spoke softly. "Warships, I believe?"

Garmat's smile returned. "*Axumite* warships, Empress." He coughed modestly. "Rather superior, don't you know, to those Malwa tubs? And I dare say our sarwen could handle three times their number of Malwa's so-called marines."

"Yes, I know," she replied. "As it happens, I can use them. The ships and the sarwen both. Have you heard the news of Deogiri?"

Garmat nodded. His smile widened.

She leaned forward.

"As it happens—"

Three days later, in a pouring rain, the fleet left Muziris. The Matisachiva Ganapati and the city's viceroy stood watching from the docks. All day they remained there, sheltered from the down-pour under a small pavilion, until they were certain that every single one of the cursed "Empress-in-exile's" followers had quit Keralan soil.

Not until the last ship disappeared into the rain did they sum-mon their howdah.

"Thank the gods," muttered the viceroy.

Ganapati's expression was sour.

"For what?" he demanded. "The damage may already have been done. A courier arrived this morning from Vanji. The Malwa have been issuing the most pointed and severe threats. They are demanding that the King arrest Shakuntala and return her to cap-tivity."

The viceroy shook his head.

"They can hardly expect the King to do that. She *is* his grand-daughter, after all."

"Probably not," agreed Ganapati. He shrugged. "Hopefully, they will be satisfied with the fact that we have expelled her—and her followers—from Keralan soil. I will immediately dispatch a courier with the news."

The elephant bearing their howdah loomed up in the rain. Hur-riedly, the two Keralan officials scrambled aboard the great beast. Despite their haste, they were soaked through by the time they reached the shelter of the howdah.

Ganapati's expression was still sour.

"Cursed monsoon," he muttered.

A sudden, freakish gust blew aside a curtain and drenched his companion.

"Cursed monsoon!" cried the viceroy.

"Blessed monsoon," stated Kungas cheerfully. The commander of Shakuntala's bodyguard leaned over the rail of the ship and admired the view. He did not seem in the slightest aggrieved by the fact that he was soaking wet. Or that there was no view to be admired.

Neither did the man standing next to him.

"Blessed monsoon," agreed Dadaji Holkar. "No-one will be able to see which direction we take. Let's just hope that the rain keeps up."

"This time of year?" demanded Kungas, chuckling. "Be serious, Dadaji! Look!"

He pointed eastward. Their ship was not more than two miles from the shore, but the coast of Malabar was completely invisible.

"Can't see a thing," he pronounced. "It'll be that way nine days out of ten, for at least another month. More than long enough for us to reach Suppara, even with this slow fleet."

Dadaji began to stroke his beard, but quickly left off the familiar gesture. It was a bit too much like wringing a sponge.

"True," he murmured. "And there is this additional advantage, as well—the refugees won't know where we're going either. Most of them will continue to think we're heading for Tamraparni until the very day we sail into Suppara."

Kungas cast him a sidelong glance.

"Might be a bit of trouble, then."

Dadaji shook his head.

"I don't think so. I had many spies in the camps, and they all reported that the great majority of the refugees are devoted to the Empress. I believe they will accept her decision. Besides, she intends to offer those who don't want to return to Majarashtra the alternative of Tamraparni. Whichever so choose, she will provide them with the necessary ships to make the voyage. After we've seized Suppara, of course."

A thin smile cracked Kungas' face.

"Not much of an alternative, that. The King of Tamraparni is not going to be pleased when he hears how Shakuntala used his name in vain. His own son in marriage, no less!"

Holkar made no reply. For a few minutes, the two men simply stared out at nothing. Nothing but beautiful, blinding, concealing, sheets of rain.

Eventually, Kungas cleared his throat.

"Speaking of marriage," he stated.

Holkar grimaced. "She refuses to even discuss it," he said softly. "Believe me, my friend, I have tried to broach the subject on many occasions. Each time, she says the question is premature."

Kungas twitched his shoulders. "That's not the point. For her to marry anyone now *would* be premature. She has nothing to offer, at the moment, in exchange for an alliance with real forces. But *after* we take Suppara—*after* we demonstrate to India, and all the world, that Andhra intends to hold southern Majarashtra—*then* the question of a dynastic marriage will pose itself. She must start thinking about it, Dadaji. Or else she will be paralyzed when the time comes."

The Empress' adviser sighed. "You know the problem, my friend."

Kungas stared out to sea. Nodded once, twice. "She is in love with Rao."

Holkar blew out his cheeks. "Please," he growled. "It is the infatuation of a young girl with a man she knew only as a child. She has not seen him—hardly at all—in two years."

"She has seen him for a few hours only, during that time," agreed Kungas. His voice rumbled like stones: "After he gutted the Vile One's palace in order to rescue her. Quite a reunion, that must have been."

Holkar said nothing. Kungas turned his head away, as if something had caught his eye.

In truth, he simply didn't want Holkar to see his face. Not even Kungas, at that moment, could keep from smiling.

Excellent. The thought was full of satisfaction. Excellent—"child"! Poor Holkar. Even he—even he—is blind on this point.

For a moment, as he had many times before, Kungas found himself bemused by that peculiarly Indian obsession with purity and pollution. Even his friend Dadaji could not entirely escape its clutches.

So blind, these Indians. When the truth is so obvious.

He turned away from the rail.

"Enough rain," he announced. "I'm going below. The action's going to start soon, anyway. I have to get ready, in case I'm needed."

As he walked across the deck toward the hatch, Kungas' face was invisible to anyone. Now, finally, he allowed his grin to emerge.

Stay stubborn, Shakuntala. Dig in your heels, girl, refuse to discuss it. When the question of marriage is finally posed, you will know what to do. Then, you will know.

He shook his head, slightly.

So obvious!

An hour later, the fleet changed its course. The change was slow—erratic, confused, haphazard. Part of that fumbling was due to the simple fact that the troop commanders on every ship had a different estimate of the right moment to give the command. The only time-keeping devices available to them were hour-glasses and sundials. Sundials were useless in the pouring monsoon. Hour-glasses, under these circumstances, just as much so. It would have been impossible to provide each commander with an identical hourglass, much less have them turned over simultaneously.

So, each commander simply gave the order when he thought the time was right.

Most of the confusion, however, was due to the fact that the crews and captains of the merchant ships were bitterly opposed to the change of course. They had been hired to transport the Empress and her people to Tamraparni. They were not, to put it mildly, pleased to hear that the destination had been changed—*especially* when they discovered the new one.

Suppara? Are you mad? The Malwa hold Suppara!

But the captains of the ships were not the *commanders*. The commanders were a very different breed altogether. Kushans and Maratha cavalrymen, in the main, who cheerfully accepted the berating abuse of the Keralan ship captains.

For about one minute. Then the steel was drawn.

Thereafter, Keralan captains and seamen scurried about their new-found task. Grumbling, to be sure. But they had no illusions that they could overpower the squads of soldiers placed on each ship. Not *those* soldiers.

One crew tried. Led by a particularly belligerent captain, the Keralan seamen dug out their own weapons and launched a mutiny. They outnumbered the soldiers two-to-one, after all. Perhaps they thought their numbers would make the difference.

They were sadly mistaken. Within two minutes, the four surviving seamen were huddled in the bow, nursing their wounds and casting fearful glances at the Kushan soldiers standing guard over them. Not one of those Kushans had even been scratched in the "melee."

Then, to add to their misery, they saw the prow of a ship looming out of the downpour. Within seconds, the ship had drawn alongside. The Keralan seamen recognized the craft. One of those swift, fearsome Ethiopian warships.

An Axumite officer leaned over the rail.

"Is problem?" he called out. "We hear noise of—of—" He faltered, having reached the limit of his skill with Hindi.

The Kushan commander glared.

"Yes, there's a problem!" he grated, pointing an accusing finger at the four captives. The Keralan seamen hunched lower.

"There's only four of the bastards left. Not enough to run the ship."

Another Ethiopian came to the rail. The Kushan commander immediately recognized him—Ezana, one of the Axumite soldiers' top leaders.

Ezana gave the situation a quick scrutiny. He was familiar with Kushans, and knew that they were not a sea-going folk. No hope they could run the ship themselves.

He turned his head and barked out a quick string of names. Within a minute, six Ethiopian soldiers were standing next to him. While they were mustering, Ezana took the opportunity to close with the merchant vessel. It was the work of but seconds for the Ethiopians to tie up alongside.

Lightly, Ezana sprang across onto the Keralan ship. He strode toward the bow where the Kushan commander was waiting, along with his men and the captives.

Once there, Ezana made a little gesture at the six Axumites who were making their own way across.

"These men will stay with you for the duration of the trip," he explained, speaking in heavily accented but quite good Hindi. "Along with the four surviving mutineers, that should be enough."

He gave the ship a quick examination. Judging from his expression, he was not pleased with what he saw.

"Indian tub," he sneered. "Can run a good Axumite trader with six men. Five—even four—in an emergency."

He transferred the sarcastic expression onto the four Keralan survivors. The seamen hunched lower still, dropping their heads. Doing everything in their power to fade out of sight.

No use. Ezana squatted down next to them.

"Look at me," he commanded. Reluctantly, they raised their heads.

Ezana grinned.

"Don't look so unhappy, lads. Consider your good fortune! My men hate running crappy ships like this. I'd have my own mutiny if I pitched you overboard and appointed four replacements."

Hearing this happy news, the expression on the faces of the Keralans brightened.

A bit, no more—and that little bit immediately vanished under Ezana's ensuing scowl.

"But they don't hate it as much as they hate mutineers," he rumbled. "I'd be on my best behavior from now on, if I were you."

Four Keralan heads bobbed frantic agreement.

Ezana's scowl deepened. "You're seamen. So I assume you're familiar with the Ethiopian treatment for mutineers?"

Four Keralan heads bobbed horrified agreement.

"Good," he grunted.

He rose and turned to the Kushan commander.

"You won't have any more trouble," he pronounced. As he made his way back to the rail, the Kushan accompanied him.

"What *is* the Ethiopian way with mutineers?" he asked.

Ezana climbed onto the rail. Just before making his leap, he bestowed a cheerful grin onto the Kushan commander.

"It involves fishing."

He sprang across. Turned and called back.

"We're partial to shark meat!"

Two days later, Ezana came aboard the Empress' flagship. A council had been called for all the central leaders of the expedition. He, along with Wahsi and Garmat, were to be the Ethiopian representatives at the meeting.

Garmat was already aboard, waiting for him. As the two men fought their way across the deck in the face of a rain so heavy it seemed almost like a waterfall, Ezana grumbled. "This has *got* to be the worst climate in the world."

Garmat smiled. "Oh, I don't know. At least it's not hot. The temperature's rather pleasant, actually. Whereas the Empty Quarter—"

Ezana shook his head firmly. "No contest. At least you can breathe, in Arabia."

He cast a fierce glower at the heavy sky. "How much *does* it rain here, anyway?"

They were at the small shed which provided an entryway into the large cabin amidships. Both men made an effort to wring out their clothes—mere kilts, fortunately—before entering.

Garmat frowned in thought. "I'm not sure, actually. I think I heard somewhere that southwest India during the monsoon season gets—"

He gave a figure in the Ethiopian way of measuring such things. Ezana's eyes widened. The figure was the equivalent of thirteen feet of water in five months.

"Mother of God!"

Garmat nodded toward the east, toward the invisible coast of India.

"Cheer up. If all goes well, soon enough we'll be crossing the mountains into Majarashtra. It's dry, I hear, on that side of the Western Ghats."

"Can't be soon enough," grumbled Ezana. He led the way into the cabin.

The cabin which served as Shakuntala's "imperial quarters" was a bit grotesque, to Ezana's eyes. He was an Ethiopian, brought up in the Axumite traditions of royal regalia. Those traditions leaned toward a style of ornamentation which was massive, but austere. And always practical. When traveling by sea, an Ethiopian royal—even the negusa nagast himself—would enjoy nothing more than a simple cabin decorated with, at most, a lion skin or ostrich feathers.

The Indian tradition was otherwise. Massive also, at times—Ezana had seen, and been impressed by, the size of the Malwa Emperor's palaces and pavilions. But not austere. Not practical.

Never seen so many gewgaws in my life, he thought sourly.

His eye fell on a ivory carving perched atop a slender table by the entrance. The carving, incredibly ornate and intricate, depicted a half-naked couple entwined in a passionate embrace. Ezana almost winced. It was not the eroticism of the carving which offended him—Axumites were not prudes—but the simple absurdity of the thing.

On a warship?

First storm, that thing's so much ballast.

Garmat pushed him forward into the cabin.

"We're diplomats," he whispered. "Be polite."

Shakuntala was perched on a pile of cushions against the far wall of the cabin. Dadaji Holkar sat to her left, in the position of her chief adviser. Next to him sat the religious leader, Bindusara.

Shakuntala's military commanders were clustered to her right. Kungas was there, along with his two chief Kushan subordinates, Kanishka and Kujulo. The Maratha cavalry leaders Shahji and Kondev were accompanied by three of their own top aides.

Wahsi, also, was there. He had arrived earlier. He was perched on a little wooden stool. Two other stools rested nearby. The Empress had provided them, knowing the Ethiopian preference in seating. All of the Indians were squatting on cushions, in the lotus position.

Once Garmat and Ezana took their seats, Shakuntala spoke.

"The first stage of our strategy has been a resounding success. We have broken free from Kerala and eluded the Malwa. It is well-nigh certain that our enemy believes we are headed for exile in Tamraparni."

She paused, scanning the room for any sign of dissent or disagreement. Seeing none, she continued.

"I believe we can assume that our arrival at Suppara will come as a complete surprise for the enemy. That being so, it is now possible for us to concentrate our attention on the more distant future. We will surprise the Malwa at Suppara, and we will take the city. The question is—then what?"

Kondev stirred. Shakuntala turned toward him, cocking her head inquiringly. The gesture was an invitation to speak.

For a moment, the Maratha officer hesitated. He was a relatively new member of the Empress' inner circle. Accustomed to Indian traditions—he had been a top officer of Shakuntala's father, whose haughty imperial manner had been legendary—he was still nonplussed by her relaxed and easy manner with her advisers.

Recognizing his uncertainty, Shakuntala prompted him.

"Please, Kondev. Speak up, if you have some doubt."

The cavalry officer tugged at his beard nervously. "I do not have doubts, Your Majesty. Not precisely. But I thought our course of action after seizing Suppara was simply to march on to Deogiri. Join our forces with Rao's." He ducked his head in a quick, apologetic manner. "Perhaps I misunderstood."

"You did not misunderstand, Kondev," replied Shakuntala. "That *was* our plan. But the unexpected arrival of the Axumites, and their offer of an alliance, has led me to reconsider. Or, at least, to think in more ambitious terms."

She turned toward the Ethiopians.

"If we held Suppara—permanently, I mean—could your navy hold off the Malwa fleet?"

The three Ethiopians exchanged quick glances. Wahsi was the first to speak.

"No, Empress," he said firmly. "If the Malwa did not possess their gunpowder weapons, it might be possible. Their navy is much larger than ours, in men and ships, but ours is better. Besides, most of their fleet is tied up in the Persian invasion."

He shrugged.

"The fact is, however, that they *do* possess the demon weapons. That nullifies our advantage of superior skill. We cannot close with them to board. Their rockets are erratic, at long range, but they are fearsome weapons against a nearby enemy."

Shakuntala nodded. She did not seem particularly chagrined, or surprised, by Wahsi's reply. "You could not break a Malwa blockade of Suppara, then?"

Wahsi shook his head. Shakuntala leaned forward.

"Tell me this, Wahsi. If we were able to hold Suppara—keep the Malwa from recapturing the city—could you *run* the blockade?"

All three Axumites burst into laughter.

"Be like stealing chickens from a cripple!" chuckled Ezana.

"A very *strong* cripple," qualified Garmat. "Have to be a *bit* careful. Still—"

Wahsi had stopped laughing.

"Yes, Empress," he stated firmly. "We could run the blockade. Penetrate it like water through a fish net, in fact. Not one or two ships, now and then. We could run a Malwa blockade almost at our pleasure."

He made a little gesture of qualification.

"You understand, I am speaking of a blockade of the entire coast. If they amass enough ships, the Malwa could close off Suppara itself. But I assume there must be other nearby places where we could land a vessel and offload cargo."

"A multitude of them!" exclaimed Bindusara. All eyes turned toward the *sadhu.*

"I am familiar with the Malabar coast," he explained. "With the entire western coast of India, in fact, from Kerala to the Kathiawar."

Bindusara turned his head eastward, as if studying the nearby shore through the walls of the cabin.

"The Western Ghats run parallel to the coast, from the southernmost tip of India all the way north to the Narmada River. They form the western boundary of the Deccan." He fluttered his hands. "The Ghats are not tall mountains. Nothing like the Himalayas! Their average height is less than a thousand yards. Even the greatest of them, Anai Mudi in Kerala, is not three thousand yards high. But they are quite rugged. The combination of their ruggedness and low altitude means that the western shore of India boasts a huge number of small rivers, instead of a few mighty ones like the Ganges and the Brahmaputra, as does the east coast."

"Smugglers' terrain," grunted Ezana.

Bindusara smiled. " 'Terrain'? Say better—smugglers' *paradise*. Don't forget the climate, Ezana. India's west coast is the wettest part of our land. Each one of those rivers enters the sea through forests of teak and palms. There are any number of hidden and secluded coves in which a cargo could be unloaded. And the local population would be quite happy to assist in the process. Poor farmers and fishermen they are, mostly, with a great need for extra money and no love for the Malwa."

Shakuntala, seeing Wahsi nod, stated:

"You could do it, then?"

"Without question, Empress." The Ethiopian officer ran fingers through his mass of thick, kinky hair, eyeing Shakuntala all the while.

"You want to break the siege of Deogiri by controlling all of southern Majarashtra," he speculated. "Using Suppara as your logistics base."

The Empress nodded. "Exactly. I wouldn't think of trying it if the enemy's main army wasn't tied up in Persia. But with only Venandakatra to face, I think it can be done—*provided we get access to gunpowder weapons.*"

"There are cannons in Suppara," said the Maratha officer Shahji. "If we take the city, we will take them also."

"Not enough," grunted Kungas. "Not by themselves."

He looked at Holkar. "You have spies in Suppara. If I'm not mistaken, those cannons are fixed siege guns."

Holkar nodded. "They're huge bombards. Three of them, positioned to defend the city against seaborne attack." He grimaced. "I suppose they *could* be moved, but—"

"Forget it," interrupted Kungas. "We can use those cannons to defend Suppara against the Malwa fleet, but they'll be no use to us in a land war against Venandakatra's army. For that, we need help from the Romans. By now, I'm quite sure Belisarius has developed a Roman capacity to produce gunpowder weapons. If we can establish contact with him, the Ethiopians could smuggle the weapons to us. And keep us supplied with gunpowder."

Everyone in the cabin exchanged glances.

"We need to send a mission to Rome, then," said Bindusara.

"Not to Rome," demurred Dadaji. "To *Belisarius*. To the Roman government, we are simply bizarre outlanders. Only Belisarius knows us well."

The peshwa straightened his posture.

"I will go," he announced. "Our delegation must be led by someone who is both highly placed in the Empress' government and personally known to Belisarius. I am the obvious choice."

"Nonsense!" exclaimed Shakuntala. "The idea is utterly mad. You are my peshwa, Dadaji. I need you to remain here."

Holkar frowned. "But I am the only one who—"

He broke off, casting a startled glance at Kungas.

The Kushan commander huffed. Coming from someone else, the noise would have been interpreted as humor. Coming from Kungas, it was hard to tell.

"He is the commander of your bodyguard!" protested Dadaji.

Shakuntala waved her hand. "He is not needed in that capacity, anymore. Kanishka is more than capable of taking his place. Actually, his talents are being wasted there."

Everyone in the room was staring at Kungas. The expression on the faces of most of the Indians was a mixture of skepticism and hesitation.

Shahji cleared his throat.

"If you will forgive me, Your Majesty, it seems to me that sending Kungas might be a bad idea. He is not of noble blood—neither brahmin nor kshatriya—and I fear the Roman general Belisarius might be offended if your ambassador were of such a low—"

The rest of the sentence was lost, buried beneath an eruption of laughter. Coming from the Ethiopians, mainly, but the Empress herself was participating and even Kungas emitted a chuckle or two.

Dadaji simply smiled. Then said, shaking his head, "You do not understand, Shahji. Romans in general—and Belisarius in particular—do not look at these things the way we Indians do. They are punctilious about the forms of nobility, but, as to its real content—" He shrugged. "So long as Kungas is the official envoy of the Empress, and carries with him a sufficiently resounding title, the Romans will be quite satisfied. Certainly Belisarius will."

"Excellent point, Dadaji," stated Shakuntala. She bestowed an imperial nod upon Kungas.

"I hereby appoint you my ambassador to Rome, and give you the titles of *Mahadandanayaka* and *Bhatasvapati.*"

Kungas' incipient smile surfaced. Barely.

" 'Great commandant' and 'lord of army and cavalry,' " he murmured. "My, how I've risen in the world!"

Catching a glimpse of Garmat's face, Shakuntala turned toward him. The Ethiopian adviser's gaiety had quite vanished, replaced by a frown.

"You disagree," she stated. There was no accusation in the words, simply a question.

The old half-Arab stroked his beard.

"Yes, Empress, I do." He made a dismissive gesture with his hand. "Not, of course, for the reasons advanced earlier. Kungas would be quite acceptable as an ambassador, from the Roman point of view. More than acceptable, as far as Belisarius is concerned. The general trusts and admires the man, deeply. I know—he told me so himself."

The Indian officers in the cabin moved their eyes to Kungas. As ever, the Kushan commander's face was impassive, like a mask. But they were reminded, again, that the unprepossessing Kushan—whom they tended, unconsciously, to regard as a lowborn half-barbarian—enjoyed a reputation among the greatest folk of their world which was far beyond their own.

"What is the problem, then?" asked Shakuntala.

Garmat pursed his lips. "The problem, Empress, is three-fold." He held up a thumb.

"First. You will be sending off your—*one* of your—most capable military commanders on the very eve of a decisive battle. Suppara can be taken, I believe, despite its guns. But doing so, as we've discussed before, will depend on the Kushans seizing the cannons by a surprise assault. Until they do so, you cannot think to land in Suppara itself with your Maratha cavalry. The ships would be destroyed before they reached the docks."

He pointed at Kungas. "If I were you, that is the man I would want leading that attack. No other."

Shakuntala was shaking her head. Garmat held up a hand, forestalling her words. "No, Empress. You cannot wait until *after* the battle to send Kungas away. There is no time to lose, if you want to get Roman help. I myself must leave this expedition tomorrow, to report back to the negusa nagast. Your ambassador—whoever it is—should accompany me on that ship."

Shakuntala bowed her head, thinking. As always, the young Empress was quick to decide.

"I agree. We *are* pressed for time."

She raised her eyes. "The other reasons?"

Garmat held up a finger alongside his thumb.

"Second. I think Kungas' mission would be futile. *How will he find Belisarius?* In that chaos in Persia?"

The Ethiopian chuckled dryly. "It would be hard enough to find anyone, much less Belisarius. The general told me once that he considered the chaos of war to be his best friend. There is always an advantage to be found, he told me, if you seize it in a willing embrace. Do you understand what that means?"

Shakuntala's Maratha officers were frowning, as was the Empress herself. All of them, it was clear, found the notion of *treasuring* war's confusion bizarre.

But Kungas, understanding, nodded his head.

"Belisarius will be riding the whirlwind," he said. "He will do everything in his power to create chaos, and then take advantage of it."

The Kushan rubbed the topknot on his head. "He not only *could* be anywhere, he will be doing everything he can to make it seem as if he were one place while he is going somewhere else." He grunted, partly with admiration, partly with chagrin. "The intention, of course, is to confuse the enemy. But it will have the same effect on allies trying to find him."

The top-knot rubbing grew vigorous. "It will be difficult. Difficult."

"It will be impossible," countered Garmat. "And, finally, *quite unnecessary.*"

He waited for those last words to register, before raising another finger.

"My third reason, Empress, is simple. There is no need to send Kungas as an ambassador to Rome, for the simple reason that I am quite sure Rome—and Belisarius—are sending an ambassador to *you*. That ambassador, I am certain, will be bringing what you need."

Everyone stared at Garmat. The surprise was obvious on all faces—except those of the other Ethiopians.

"You know something," stated Holkar.

"Nothing specific," said Ezana. "Only—"

Garmat cleared his throat.

"The Kingdom of Axum has maintained a small but quite effective espionage service in the Roman Empire. For well over a century, now." He made a small, half-apologetic grimace. "There has been no trouble between us and Rome, mind you. Ever since the Roman Emperor Diocletian set Elephantine as the southern limit of Roman territory in Africa, the border has been quite tranquil. Still—"

He shrugged.

"Rome is a great empire, ours is much smaller. It always behooves a less powerful kingdom to keep an eye on its more powerful neighbor. Regardless of their current intentions or attitudes. You never know. Things might change."

The Indians in the room all nodded. Common sense, that. And they had their own memories of the long and turbulent history of India.

"Most of our attention, naturally, is given to their province of Egypt. There, we have the advantage that most of the population is Monophysite. Our own creed is very similar, and many of the Egyptian Monophysites look upon us as their religious brethren. Any number of Monophysite religious leaders have taken refuge in Ethiopia, over the years, when-ever the orthodox persecution became—"

He broke off, seeing the incomprehension in the faces of the Indians. Only Dadaji Holkar, he realized, understood anything of what he was saying.

Garmat had to restrain himself from muttering *"Damned arrogant Indians!"*

"Never mind," he sighed. For all that he genuinely liked and admired many Indians, Garmat was struck again by their peculiar insularity. Even the most broad-minded Indians—with a few exceptions like Holkar—tended to look on the whole vast world beyond their own culture as an undifferentiated mass of semi-barbarians. The divisions within Christianity were quite beyond their ken—or interest.

"The point is this," he drove on. "We discovered some time ago that the Roman Empress is sending a military and political expedition to Egypt. The official purpose of that expedition is to quell an incipient rebellion and reestablish tight imperial control over their richest province. But who did they send to command this force? *Belisarius' own wife, Antonina.*"

He shrugged. "We are speculating, of course. But, knowing Belisarius, I think the speculation is quite sound. Antonina's expedition is real enough on its own terms, of course—the Romans *do* need to keep a firm hand on Egypt. But we are quite sure that there is another purpose hidden within that public objective. We think Belisarius is sending his own wife in order to open a second front against the Malwa. It would be astonishing to us if that strategy did not include providing support for Andhra."

He gave Shakuntala and Holkar a quick, knowing glance. The young Empress and her peshwa, understanding, nodded in reply. In order to maintain her prestige, Shakuntala had never publicly explained where she obtained the large fortune which served as her imperial war chest. Her Maratha officers, who rallied to her after her escape from Malwa, had never even thought to ask. Empresses are rich. Everyone knows that. It's a law of nature.

In reality, the hunted young girl had been given that treasure by Belisarius himself, on the eve of her escape. The vast treasure with which Emperor Skandagupta had tried to bribe Belisarius into treason, the Roman general had turned over to Shakuntala in order to finance a rebellion in Malwa's rear.

"Would *that* man have forgotten you?" asked Garmat quietly. "Would *that* man not have continued to develop his plans?"

Shakuntala's eyes widened, slightly.

"You're right," she whispered. "He is sending someone to us. Belisarius has thought of it already."

Her shoulders slumped, just a bit. From relief, it was obvious. It suddenly dawned on everyone how hard a decision it had been for her, to send Kungas away.

"You will stay, Kungas," she announced. "You will stay here, with me."

The Kushan commander nodded. Then, with a sly little smile, murmured, "How quickly fortune passes."

Shakuntala frowned, fiercely.

"Nonsense! I did not remove your titles—except that of ambassador to Rome. You are still Mahadandanayaka. Still, my Bhatasvapati."

Her eyes softened, gazing on the man who had once been her captor, and always her protector.

"As you have been since Amaravati," she whispered. "When you saved me from the Ye-tai beasts."

Later, as they filed out of the cabin, the Maratha commander Shahji remarked to Garmat:

"I wonder who the Romans are sending to us? A general of renown, no doubt."

Fighting down a smile, Garmat made no reply. He glanced at Ezana and Wahsi, and saw that his two Ethiopian compatriots were fighting the same battle.

Shahji moved on.

"Poor fellow," murmured Wahsi.

"What a shock, when he discovers," agreed Ezana.

Now, Garmat found himself fighting down an outright laugh. Ezana and Wahsi had accompanied him, three years earlier, in his mission to Rome. *They* knew the realities of the Roman court. *They* knew the Empress Theodora's foibles.

But he said nothing. Not until after the three Ethiopians had clambered into their small skiff and begun the trip back to their own ship. Only then did he burst into laughter. Ezana and Wahsi joined him in that gaiety.

"It's bound to be a woman!" choked out Ezana.

"Theodora wouldn't trust anyone else," gasped Wahsi. "Shahji'll die of horror!"

Garmat shook his head. "That's not fair, actually. He's Maratha, don't forget. They recognize the legitimacy of female rulers. They even have a tradition of women leading armies. Still—"

He fell silent. He was not sure, of course—it was pure speculation. But he thought he could guess who Theodora and Belisarius would send.

Not Antonina. Garmat was quite sure that Belisarius had bigger plans for her. Of the Empress Theodora's inner circle of advisers—*female* advisers—that left only—

Ezana completed the thought aloud.

"They may have those traditions, Garmat," he chuckled. "But not even the Maratha have a tradition of sarcastic, quick-tongued, rapier-witted women who've read more books than they even knew existed."

"Poor Shahji," concluded Wahsi. "He's such a stiff and proper sort. I foresee chagrin in his future. Great discomfiture."

Chapter 22

THE EASTERN MEDITERRANEAN
Summer, 531 A.D.

"Be careful!" hissed Antonina.

"I *am* being careful," growled Irene. "It's the stupid boat that's being careless!"

Hesitantly, gingerly, the spymaster stuck out her foot again, groping for the rail of the little skiff bobbing alongside Antonina's flagship. The sea was not particularly rough, but Irene's experience with climbing down a large ship into a smaller one was exactly nil.

Her foot touched the rail, pressed down, skidded aside. Frantically, she clutched the rope ladder. A stream of vulgar curses ensued. Coarse phrases; unrefined terms. Aimed at the world in general and boats in particular.

Above, Ousanas grinned down.

"Witness, everyone! A miracle! There *is* a book which Irene has never read, after all! I refer, of course, to *On the Transfer of Personnel From Craft to Craft At Sea,* by the famous author Profanites of Dispepsia."

A stream of *really* vulgar curses ensued. Utterly obscene phrases; incredibly gross terms. Aimed exclusively at one particular African.

The African in question grinned even wider.

"May I lend you a hand?" he asked pleasantly.

Irene glared up at him furiously. "Yes!" she snarled. "Get me into this stupid fucking boat!"

"No problem, noble Greek lady," said Ousanas cheerfully. The dawazz leapt onto the rail of Antonina's flagship, gauged the matter for perhaps a micro-second, and sprang directly down into the boat below. He landed lightly on his feet, easily finding his balance. Then, turned to face Irene. The spymaster was swinging against the hull of the larger ship above him. Her face was pale; the knuckles of her hands, clutching the rope ladder, were white as snow.

"Jump," he said.

Irene's eyes widened. She stared down at him, as if ogling a dangerous lunatic.

"Jump," repeated Ousanas. "I will catch you."

"You are completely insane!" she shrieked.

Ousanas glanced up at the flagship above. Antonina and Eon were both leaning over the rail. Antonina's face was filled with deep concern. Eon's, with a struggle to contain his laughter.

"Eon!" shouted Ousanas. "Cut the ladder!"

"Good idea!" boomed Eon. The Prince drew his blade from its baldric. It was a typical Axumite sword, other than being more finely made than most. Which is to say, it was short, square-tipped, and very heavy—more like a huge cleaver than a Roman spatha.

Irene's terrified eyes stared up at the thing. The sword would obviously cut through the thin ropes of the ladder like an axe.

Eon, muscled like a Hercules, raised the blade high.

"*Oooo!*" she screamed. And then, convulsively, let go of the ladder.

She fell no more than four feet. Ousanas caught her easily, easily; then, neatly, set up her upright on the deck of the skiff. An instant later, she collapsed onto a pile of cordage coiled in the bilge.

"You are a foul creature," she hissed, "from a foul land." Gasp, gasp. "Now I know where Homer got the inspiration for the Cyclops."

Ousanas clucked his tongue. "So cruel," he complained. "So vicious!"

From above came Antonina's voice.

"All you all right, Irene?"

The spymaster took a deep shuddering breath. Then, suddenly, burst into a smile.

"I'm quite fine, actually. The first mission is accomplished!"

She transferred the smile onto Ousanas.

"I apologize for my insulting and intemperate remark."

Ousanas winced, awaiting the inevitable.

Hiss.

"I did not mean to slander the memory of an honorable monster of legend."

Above, Antonina and Eon turned to face each other.

"You are certain, Antonina?" asked the Prince. "You have your own difficult task ahead of you. My sarwen would be of help. I have the authority to use them any way I wish. As I told you, my father's offer is for a full alliance."

Antonina shook her head.

"No, Eon. The negusa nagast's offer we accept, certainly. Theodora gave me the authority to seek out that alliance myself, in fact. But if I can't establish my authority in Egypt with the Roman troops at my disposal, another four hundred Axumite soldiers won't make the difference."

She cast a quick glance toward the Ethiopian warship. The craft was rolling gently in the waves just a hundred yards away. The rail was lined with soldiers of the Dakuen sarwe. There were, she estimated, about fifty of them. The rest of Eon's troops were waiting for him at the small port of Pelusium, at the far eastern end of the Nile Delta.

"Besides," she added, "the presence of Axumite sarwen would create political problems. I want to quell the ultra-Chalcedonian fanatics in Egypt without alienating the majority of orthodox Greeks. You know they'll look on Ethiopians as allies of the Monophysites. Foreign heretics, used by the empire against them."

Thoughtfully, Eon nodded. Antonina laid a friendly hand on his arm.

"So, I must decline your offer. Though I *do* thank you for it. Please pass those thanks on to your father."

"I will."

"Pass on to him also Rome's agreement to the proposed alliance. When she gets to Axum, Irene can negotiate the details with the negusa nagast. She is fully authorized to do so, and you may tell your father that she carries Empress Theodora's complete confidence. Providing an escort for her is the best use of your sarwen, at the moment."

She broke into her own smile.

"And I'm happier this way. I hate sending Irene into that maelstrom in India. But at least I'll have the comfort of knowing she has you, and Ousanas, and four hundred Dakuen to protect her."

Her shoulders shuddered, just slightly. "For that matter, I'll be happier knowing she doesn't have to face Red Sea pirates without—"

"*Pirates*," growled Eon. He barked a laugh.

Behind him stood three officers of the Dakuen sarwe. Leaders of the Prince's own royal regiment, they considered themselves—quite rightly—as elite soldiers. And seamen, for that matter. They matched the Prince's growl with their own glares, Eon's barking laugh with their own sneers of derision.

"*Pirates*," they murmured. So might a pride of lions, if they could, mutter the word, *hyenas*. Or, for that matter, *elands*. *Impalas*.

Meat.

Antonina grinned. She gave the Prince a warm embrace. He returned it, somewhat gingerly, in the way that a courteous and well-bred young royal returns the embrace of a respected, admired—and very voluptuous—older woman.

"Be off," she whispered. "Take care of Irene for me, and for Theodora. And take care of yourself."

A moment later, Eon and his officers made their own easy and effortless descent into the skiff. Once they were aboard, the line was cast off and the boat began pulling away. The officers did their own rowing. In the Axumite tradition, they had all risen from the ranks. They were accustomed to the task, and did it with familiar expertise. Quickly, the skiff pulled toward the waiting Ethiopian warship.

Antonina and Irene stared at each other, for a time, during that short voyage. Close friends—best friends—they had become, during the past three years of joint work and struggle against the Malwa menace. Each of them, now, was taking her own route into the maw of the beast. In all likelihood, they would never see each other again.

Antonina fought back her tears.

"God, I'll miss you," she whispered. "So much."

Thirty yards away, she saw Irene turn her head aside. She did not miss the slight sheen in those distant eyes. Irene, she knew, was fighting back her own tears.

Antonina tore her gaze from the figure of her friend and stared at Eon. The Prince was sitting in the stern-sheet of the skiff. Antonina could see his head slowly turning, as he scanned the surface of the waves.

Already, she realized, Eon was fulfilling his promise to protect Irene from any danger.

Then, seeing the arrogant ferocity lurking in Eon's huge shoulders, she could not help smiling. She found great comfort in those shoulders.

Sharks, of course, do not have shoulders. But if they did, so might a great shark confront the monsters of the sea.

Tuna. Squid. Devil-rays.

Meat.

By the time the skiff bearing Irene reached its destination, other skiffs were making their own way to the Axumite warship from other Roman craft, bearing their own cargoes.

Three of those skiffs carried barrels of gunpowder. Two hauled cannons—brass three-pounders, one in each skiff. And two more carried the small band of Syrian grenadiers, and their wives and children, who had volunteered to accompany Irene to India. Trainers, if all went well, for whatever forces the Empress Shakuntala might have succeeded in gathering around her. Trainers, and their gear, for the future gunpowder-armed rebellion of south India.

Antonina's little hands gripped the rail. Her husband Belisarius, while he was in India, had done everything in his power to help create that rebellion. He was not a man to forget or abandon those he had sent in harm's way.

Not my husband, she thought, proudly, possessively.

She did not know the future. But Antonina would not have been surprised to learn that in humanity's future—*any* of those possible futures—the name of Belisarius would always be remembered for two things, if nothing else.

Military brilliance.

Loyalty.

She cast a last glance at the small and distant figure of her friend Irene and turned away from the rail. Then, walked—marched, rather—to the bow of her own ship and stared across the waters of the Mediterranean.

Stared to the southwest, now. Toward Alexandria.

She gripped the rail again, and even more tightly.

Silently, she made her vows. If Irene reached India safely, she would not be stranded. If Belisarius' determination to support the Andhra rebellion was thwarted, it would not be because Antonina failed her share of that task.

She would take Alexandria, and Egypt, and reestablish the Empire's rule. She would harness the skills and resources of that great province and turn it into the armory of Rome's war against Malwa.

That armory, among other things, would be used to support Shakuntala and her rebels. Many of those guns would go south. Guns, cannons, rockets, gunpowder—and the men and women needed to use them and train others in their use.

South, to Axum. Then, across the Erythrean Sea to Majarashtra. Somehow, someway, those weapons would find their way into the hands of the young Empress whom Belisarius had freed from captivity.

She clutched the rail, glaring at the still-unseen people who would resist her will. The same people—the same type of people, at least—who had sneered at her all her life.

Had a shark, in that moment, caught sight of the small woman at the prow of the Roman warship, it would have recognized her. It would not have recognized the body, of course—Antonina's shapely form did not evenly remotely resemble that of a fish—nor would its primitive brain have understood her intellect.

But it would have known. Oh, yes. Its own instincts would have recognized a kindred spirit.

Hungry. Want meat.

Chapter 23
MESOPOTAMIA
Summer, 531 A.D.

At Peroz-Shapur, Belisarius ordered the first real break in the march since they had left Constantinople, three months earlier. The army would rest in Peroz-Shapur for seven days, he announced. All the soldiers were given leave to enjoy the pleasures of the city, save only those assigned—by all units, on a rotating basis—to serve as a military police force.

After announcing this happy news, before the assembled ranks of the army, Belisarius departed for his tent as quickly as possible. (Ten minutes, in the event, which was the time the troops spent cheering his name.) He left it to Maurice to make the savage, bloodcurdling and grisly warnings regarding the fate of any miscreant who transgressed the proper bounds of Persian hospitality.

The army was not taken aback by Maurice's slavering. His sadistic little monologue was even cheered. Though not, admittedly, for ten minutes. The grinning soldiers had no doubt that the threats would be made good. It was simply that the warnings were quite superfluous.

Those soldiers were in a *very* good mood. As well they should be.

First, there was the prospect of a week with no marching.

Second, there was the prospect of spending that week in a large and well-populated city. The Persians had already arranged billeting. *Beds*—well, pallets at least.

Finally—O rapturous joy!—there was the *delightful* prospect of
spending those days in a large and well-populated city when every
single man in the army had money to burn.

More money that most of them had ever seen in their lives, in
fact. Between the Persian Emperor's involuntary largesse—there
might have been three ounces of gold left in the villa when the
army departed; probably not—and the considerable booty of the
destroyed Malwa army, Belisarius' little army was as flush as any
army in history.

They knew it—and the Persians in Peroz-Shapur knew it too.
The Roman soldiers would have been popular, anyway, even if
they had been penniless. Belisarius and his men had just scored
the only great defeat for the Malwa since they began their invasion
of Persia. And while Kurush and his seven hundred lancers
received their fair share of the glory, most of it went to the arms
of Rome.

The citizens of Peroz-Shapur had just been relieved of any
immediate prospect of a siege, and the men who had eliminated
that threat were also in position—literally overnight—to produce
a massive infusion of cash into the city's coffers.

Hail the conquering heroes!

As the Romans marched into Peroz-Shapur, the streets were
lined with cheering Persians. Many of those were simply there to
applaud.   Others—merchants,   tavern-keepers,   prostitutes,
jewelers—had additional motives. Simple, uncomplicated motives,
which suited the simple and uncomplicated Roman troops to perfection.

So, as he retired to his tent, Belisarius was not concerned that
there would be any unfortunate incidents during the army's stay
in Peroz-Shapur. Which was good, because the general needed
some time for himself, free of distraction.

He wanted to think. And examine a possibility.

Baresmanas visited him in his tent, in midafternoon of the
third day.

"Why are you not staying in the city?" he asked, after being
invited within. The sahrdaran glanced around at the austere living
quarters which Belisarius always maintained on campaign. Other
than an amphora of wine, and the cooling breeze which blew in

through the opened flaps, the general's tent showed no signs of a man enjoying a well-deserved rest.

Belisarius looked up from the pallet where he was sitting, half-reclined against a cushion propped next to the chest which contained his personal goods. Smiling, he closed the book in his hand and gestured toward the chair at his little writing desk. The chair and the desk were the only items of furniture in the tent.

"Have a seat, Baresmanas. You looked exhausted."

The Persian nobleman, half-collapsing on the chair, heaved a sigh.

"I *am* exhausted. The city is a madhouse! People are carousing at every hour of the day and night!"

"Shamelessly and with wild abandon, I should imagine." The general grinned. "You can't get any sleep. You can't hear yourself think. To your astonishment, you find yourself remembering your tent with fond memories."

Baresmanas chuckled. "You anticipated this, I see."

"I have no experience with Persian troops enjoying a celebration. Perhaps they're a subdued lot—"

"Ha!"

"No?" Belisarius grinned. "But I *do* know what Roman soldiers are like. They'd drive the demons of the Pit to mad distraction, just from the noise alone."

The general cocked his head. "There have been no serious problems, I trust?"

Baresmanas shook his head.

"No, no. A slew of complaints from indignant matrons, of course, outraged at the conduct of their wanton daughters. But even they seem more concerned with the unfortunate consequences nine months from now than with the impropriety of the moment. We Aryans frown on bastardy, you know."

Belisarius smiled. "Every folk I know frowns on bastardy—and then, somehow, manages to cope with it."

He scratched his chin. "A donation from the army, do you think? Discreet sort of thing, left in the proper hands after we depart. City notables, perhaps?"

Baresmanas considered the question.

"Better the priesthood, I think." Then, shrugging:

"The problem may not be a major one, in any event. The matrons are more confused than angry. It seems any number of marriage proposals have been advanced—within a day of the army's arrival, in some cases!—and they don't know how to deal with them. As you may be aware, our customs in that respect are more involved than yours."

As it happened, Belisarius was quite familiar with Persian marital traditions. Unlike the simple monogamy of Roman Christians, Persians recognized several different forms of marriage. The fundamental type—what they called *patixsayih*—corresponded quite closely to the Christian marriage, except that polygamy was permissible. But other marriages were also given legal status in Persia, including one which was "for a definite period only."

Belisarius smiled. He was quite certain that his Syrian troops, with their long acquaintance with Medes, had passed on this happy knowledge to the other soldiers.

His smile, after a moment, faded to a more thoughtful expression.

"It occurs to me, Baresmanas—"

The sarhdaran interrupted. His own face bore a pensive little smile.

"Roman troops will be campaigning in Mesopotamia for quite some time. Years, possibly. Peroz-Shapur, because of its location, will be a central base—*the* central base, in all likelihood—for that military presence. Soldiers are men, not beasts. They will suffer from loneliness, many of them—a want in the heart, as much as a lust in the body."

Belisarius was struck again, as he had been many times before, by the uncanny similarity between the workings of his mind and that of the man sitting across from him in the tent. He was reminded of the odd friendship which had developed between him and Rana Sanga, while he had been in India. There, also, differences in birth and breeding had been no barrier—even though Sanga was his sworn enemy.

For a moment, he wondered how the Rajput King was faring in his campaign in Bactria.

All too well, I suspect, came the rueful thought. *Yet I cannot help wishing the man good fortune—in his life, at least, if not his purpose.*

He brought his thoughts back to the matter at hand.

"I think we can make a suitable arrangement, Baresmanas. Talk to your priesthood, would you? If they are willing to be cooperative, I will encourage my soldiers to approach their romantic liaisons with a more—ah, what shall I call it . . . ?"

The sahrdaran grinned.

"Long-term approach," he suggested. "Or, for those who are incorrigibly low-minded, guaranteed recreation."

Baresmanas stroked his beard. The gesture positively exuded satisfaction. A well-groomed man by temperament, he had taken advantage of the stay in Peroz-Shapur to have the beard properly trimmed and shaped. But some of his pleasure, obviously, stemmed from the prospective solution of a problem. A minor problem, now—but small tensions, uncorrected, have a way of festering.

"Yes, yes," he mused. "I foresee no problems from the Mazda priests. Even less from the matrons! It is in every Persian's interest to avoid the shame of illegitimacy, after all. The absence of a legal father is a small thing to explain—especially if there is a subsidy for the child."

He eyed the general, a bit skeptically.

Understanding the look, Belisarius shrugged.

"The subsidy is not a problem. The army is rich. Well over half of that booty is in my personal possession. Much of it is my personal share. The rest is in my trust as a fund for the disabled, along with widows and orphans. Between the two, there's plenty to go around."

"And your soldiers?"

"I can't promise you that all of them will act responsibly, Baresmanas. I do not share the commonly-held opinion that soldiers have the morals of street cats, mind you. But I'm hardly about to hold them up as models of rectitude, either. Many of my troops won't care in the slightest what bastards they leave behind them—even leaving aside the ones who like to boast about it. But I will spread the word. If my commanders support me—which they will—"

He paused for an instant, savoring the words.

Which they will. Oh, yes, I have my army now.

"—then the soldiers will begin to develop their own customs. Armies tend to be conservative. If taking a Persian wife while on campaign in Mesopotamia—a wife of convenience, perhaps, but a

wife nonetheless—becomes ingrained in their habits, they'll frown
on their less reputable comrades. Bad thing, being frowned on by
your mates."

He gave Baresmanas his own skeptical eye.

"You understand, of course, that many of those soldiers will
already have a wife back home. And that any Persian wife will not
be recognized under Roman law?"

Baresmanas laughed. "Please, Belisarius!" He waved his hand
in a grand gesture of dismissal. "What do we pure-blood Aryans
care about the superstitious rituals of foreign barbarians, practiced
in their far-off and distant lands?"

A thought came from Aide.

"Thou hast committed fornication!"

"But that was in another country, and besides, the wench is
not *patixsayih*."

It's from a future poet. A bit hesitantly: **It's appropriate,
though, isn't it?**

Belisarius was astonished. He had never seen Aide exhibit such
a subtle grasp of the intricacies of human relationships.

The "jewel" exuded quiet pride. Belisarius began to send a con-
gratulatory thought, when his attention was drawn away by Baresmanas' next words:

"What are you reading?"

Belisarius glanced down at the book in his lap. For a moment
he was confused, caught between his interrupted dialogue with
Aide and Baresmanas' idle query. But his attention, almost immediately, focussed on the question. To Baresmanas, the matter had
been simply one of polite curiosity. To Belisarius, it was not.

"As a matter of fact, I was meaning to speak to you about it." He
held up the volume. "It's by a Roman historian named Ammianus
Marcellinus. This volume contains books XX through XXV of his
Rerum Gestarum."

"I am not familiar with the man. One of the ancients? A contemporary of Livy or Polybius?"

Belisarius shook his head. "Much more recent than that. Ammianus was a soldier, actually. He accompanied Emperor Julian on
his expedition into Persia, two centuries ago." He tapped the book
on his lap. "This volume contains his memoirs of the episode."

"Ah." The sahrdaran's face exhibited an odd combination of
emotions—shame, satisfaction.

"The thing began badly for us, true," he murmured. "Most of the towns we just marched through—Anatha, for instance—were destroyed by Julian. So was Peroz-Shapur, now that I think about it. Burnt to a shell. In the end, however—"

Satisfaction reigned supreme. Belisarius chuckled.

"In the end, that damned fool Julian burned his boats in one of those histrionic gestures you'll never see *me* doing."

He snorted. A professional deriding the flamboyant excesses of an—admittedly talented—amateur.

"The man won practically every battle he fought, and every siege he undertook. And then—God save us from theatrical commanders!—stranded his army without a supply line. Marched them to surrender from starvation, after losing his own life."

He shook his head. "Talk about snatching defeat from the jaws of victory. Yes, it ended well for you Persians. You got Nisibis and five other provinces in ransom, for allowing the Romans to march out of Mesopotamia."

The satisfaction on Baresmanas' face ebbed.

"Not so well as all that, my friend. The towns were still destroyed, and the countryside ravaged." He rubbed his scarred shoulder, pensively. "In the end, it was just another of the endless wars which Aryans and Greeks seem obsessed with fighting. How many times has Nisibis changed hands, over the centuries? You have sacked Ctesiphon, and we, Antioch. Is either Empire the better for it?"

Belisarius shook his head. "No, Baresmanas. I, for one, would like to see an end to the thing." A crooked smile. "Mind you, I suppose I could be accused of unworthy motives. Ending a millennium-long conflict with a victory at Mindouos, I mean."

Still rubbing his shoulder, Baresmanas smiled.

"I will allow you that personal triumph, Belisarius. Quite cheerfully. I hope never to meet Romans on a field of battle again."

Belisarius laughed. "I, too! You Persians are just too damned tough."

He eyed the sahrdaran slyly. "That was Justinian's main argument for accepting your proposals, you know. He said that making a hundred years' peace would cement the Roman army's allegiance to the dynasty. Anything to avoid another clash with those damned Persian dehgans!"

Baresmanas, for all his scholarly nature, was too much of a deh-gan himself not to be pleased. But he did not linger over the gratification. He pointed at the book.

"Why are you reading it, then?"

Belisarius scratched his chin.

"I brought it with me—borrowed it from a bibliophile friend named Irene—just on speculation. I thought it might contain some useful material. As it happens, I think it does. Quite useful, in fact."

He gave Baresmanas an amused look.

"Have you had enough rest and relaxation in Peroz-Shapur? Does the thought of two days' travel in the countryside appeal to you? It'll be scorching hot, of course. On the other hand, there will be certain subtle pleasures. You know, things like quiet, soli-tude, serenity—"

"Enough!" laughed Baresmanas. "Anything to get away from this insane revelry! The bleakest desert in the world sounds like paradise to me, at the moment."

"It won't be all that bad, actually. I just want to retrace our route. Go back up the river to the old canal we passed by on our way here."

Baresmanas frowned. "The Nehar Malka? The Royal Canal?"

Belisarius nodded. The sahrdaran's puzzlement deepened.

"Whatever for? That canal's as dry as a bone. It hasn't been used since—" He stopped. Belisarius completed the thought:

"Since you Persians blocked it off, two centuries ago. After the Roman Emperor Julian used it to float his ships from the Euphra-tes to the Tigris, in order to besiege Ctesiphon."

Baresmanas blew out his cheeks. "Yes, yes. That little episode—*not* so little, actually. Julian failed to take Ctesiphon, but it was a close thing. Anyway, after that we decided the irrigation and trading value of the canal was not worth the risk of providing Romans with a perfect logistics route to attack our capital."

He cocked his head quizzically. "But still—I ask again? Why are you interested in a canal which is empty of water?"

"That's precisely the reason I *am* interested in it, Baresmanas."

He held up his hand, forestalling further questions.

"Please! At the moment, I am simply engaged in idle speculation brought on by reading an old book. Before I say anything else, I need to look at the thing. I was not able to examine it closely on our way into Peroz-Shapur."

Baresmanas rose. "As you will. When do you wish to depart?"

"Tomorrow morning, as early as possible." A little frown appeared on his brow. "I hate to drag any of my troops away from their celebration, but we'll need an escort. Some of my bucellarii will just have to—"

"No, Belisarius! Leave the lads to their pleasures. My household troops have been awaiting me here for almost a month. We can take our escort from among their ranks. I insist!"

To Belisarius' surprise, the expedition which set out the next morning turned out to be quite a major affair. A full two thousand of Baresmanas' household troops showed up outside his tent, at the crack of dawn. Even if he hadn't already been awake, the sound of those horses would have tumbled him from his pallet. Half-expecting a surprise cavalry raid, the general emerged from his tent with sword in hand.

After dismounting, Baresmanas grinned at the Roman general's wide-eyed stare.

"It seems I am not the only one who seeks a bit of peace and quiet," he remarked. "Almost all of my household troops clamored to join the expedition, once the word got out. But I didn't think we needed six thousand men."

"*Six* thousand?" asked Belisarius.

The sahrdaran's cheerful grin widened.

"Amazing, isn't it? I was expecting three thousand, at the most. It seems the news of our great victory at the battle of Anatha has caused dehgans to spring up from the very soil, desperately seeking to share in the glory. Truth is, I think it was the faint hope that we might encounter another party of Malwa raiders that inspired this great outpouring of enthusiasm for our little expedition."

One of the general's servants approached, leading his horse. As he took the reins, Belisarius remarked:

"They are not all troops from your household, then?"

The sahrdaran gave his shoulders a little inscouciant shake.

"Who is to say? The majority are from my province of Garamig. The rest? Who knows? Most of them, I suspect, are from Ormazd's own province of Arbayistan."

Belisarius nodded, and mounted his horse. As they began to ride off, he mulled over Baresmanas' last words.

For all their similarities, there were some important differences in the way the Roman and Persian Empires were organized. One of those differences—a key difference—was in their military structure. The Roman army was a professional army supplemented by mercenary auxiliaries, usually (though not always) drawn from barbarian tribes. The Persian army, on the other hand, was a much more complicated phenomenon.

Feudalism is always complicated, came Aide's interjection. **Most convoluted system you—*we* humans have ever come up with. And we're a convoluted folk. Especially you protoplasmic types.**

"So it is," murmured Belisarius. He did not inquire as to the meaning of "protoplasmic." He suspected he didn't want to know.

Each nobleman of sahrdaran and vurzurgan rank maintained a private army, made up of soldiers from their province or district. Some of those—the "household troops"—were financially supported by their lord. The rest were dehgans, whose obligation to provide military service was a more nebulous affair.

The dehgans were village and small town knights, essentially. The lowest rank in the aristocracy, but still part of what Aryans called the azadan. Though they were officially under the command of the higher nobility, the dehgans were economically independent and not, as a class, given to subservience. When it came to rallying the support of "his" dehgans, a high lord's prestige counted for more than formal obligation.

For their part, each dehgan maintained a small body of retainers who would accompany him on campaign. Not more than a handful, usually. Well-respected men of their village or town—prosperous farmers and blacksmiths, in the main—who had not only the strength, fitness and skill to serve as armored archers but could afford the horse and gear as well.

The Persian Emperor himself, beyond his own household troops, directly commanded nothing but his personal bodyguard—a regiment of men who still bore the ancient title of the Immortals. For the rest, the Shahanshah depended on the support of the great nobility. Who, in turn, depended on the support of the dehgans.

In theory, it was all very neatly pyramidal. In practice—

Aide summed it up nicely: **Victory has a multitude of fathers. Defeat is an orphan. Or, in this case: victory has a multitude of would-be sons.**

Belisarius smiled.

And defeat is childless.

He twisted in his saddle, passing the smile onto Baresmanas.

"You think Ormazd's joints are aching, then?"

The sahrdaran chuckled.

"I suspect that Ormazd, right now, is feeling very much like a victim of arthritis. Each morning, when he wakes up, he finds his army has shrunk a bit more. While faithless dehgans disappear, seeking fame and fortune in more likely quarters."

Belisarius studied the huge "escort" which surrounded them. The Persians were marching in good order, although, to a Roman general's eye, the formation seemed a bit odd. After a moment, he realized that the peculiar "lumpiness" was due to the formation's social order. Rather than marching in Roman ranks and files, the Persians tended to cluster in small groups. Retainers accompanying their dehgans, he realized. Where the basic unit of the Roman army was a squad, that of the Persian force was a village band. Men who had grown up together, and known each other all their lives.

After a minute or so, Belisarius found himself deep in a rumination over the most effective way to combine Roman and Persian forces, given each people's habits and characteristics. He shook off the thoughts, for now. He had something more immediate to attend to.

"We need to make a stop at the prisoners' camp," he announced.

Baresmanas raised a questioning eyebrow, but made no protest. He simply called out a name.

Immediately, one of the Persians riding nearby trotted his horse over to the sahrdaran and the Roman general. As soon as he arrived, Baresmanas made a little sweeping gesture with his hand.

"I would like to introduce the commander of my household troops, General Belisarius. Merena is his name, from a fine azadan family affiliated to the Suren."

Belisarius nodded politely. The Persian commander returned the nod, very stiffly. Examining him, Belisarius was not sure if the stiffness was inherent in the man himself, or was due to the specific circumstances.

A bit of both, he decided. As a rule, in his experience, Persians tended toward a certain athletic slenderness. Merena, on the other hand, was a large man, almost as heavyset as Belisarius' friend

Sittas. But where Sittas handled his weight and girth with a certain sprawling ease, Merena seemed to prefer a far more immobile method. For all the man's obvious horsemanship, he sat his saddle almost like a statue.

Baresmanas passed on the command to visit the prisoners' camp on the way north. Merena nodded—again, very stiffly—and trotted away to give the orders.

"Not the most informal sort of fellow," remarked Belisarius.

Baresmanas' lips twisted.

"Normally, he is not so rigid and proper. But I think he is unsure of how to manage the current situation. This is not, actually, the first time you and he were introduced. In a manner of speaking."

Belisarius pursed his lips.

"He, too, was at Mindouos." It was a statement more than a question.

"Oh, yes. Right by my side, during Firuz' mad charge. He tried to come to my aid, after a lance spilled me from my horse. But he was disabled himself, by a plumbata right through the thigh."

Belasarius winced. The plumbata was the weapon which modern Roman infantrymen used in place of the pilum, the javelin favored in the earlier days of the Empire. The plumbata was a much shorter weapon—more like a dart than a throwing spear. But what it lost in range it gained in penetrating power, due to the heavy lead weight fitted to the shaft below the spearpoint. At close range, hurled with the underarm motion of an expert, it could penetrate even the armor of cataphracts or dehgans. The wounds it produced were notoriously brutal.

"Pinned him right to the saddle," continued Baresmanas. "Then, when his horse was hamstrung and gutted, the beast rolled over on top of him. Almost took off his leg. Would have, I'm sure, if he were a smaller man. He still walks with a terrible limp."

The general's wince turned into a grimace. Seeing the expression, Baresmanas shrugged.

"He does not bear you any ill-will, Belisarius. Ill-will over that battle, of course, he has in plenty—but all of it is directed toward Firuz. Still, he does not exactly count you among his bosom companions."

"I imagine not!" The general hesitated, for a moment. Then, deciding that politeness was overridden by necessity:

"I must know, however—please do not take offense—if he will be able to serve properly. Being forced in such close—"

"Have no fear on that score," interrupted Baresmanas. "Whatever his attitude may be toward you, there is not the slightest doubt of his feelings for me, and my family."

Belisarius' face must have exhibited a certain skepticism, for the sahrdaran immediately added:

"It is not simply a matter of duty and tradition. Merena's family is noted—even famed—for its military accomplishments. But they are not rich. He would still be in captivity had I not paid his ransom out of my own funds."

Belisarius nodded. He and Baresmanas rode together in silence, for a minute. Then the sahrdaran remarked, almost idly:

"I have noted that you yourself are quite generous to your bucellarii. I was told that you dispense a full half of your battle-gained treasure to them, in fact. Most munificent, indeed."

Belisarius smiled crookedly. "That's quite true. My retainers are sworn to my service anyway, of course. But I'm a practical man. Men are not tools, mind you. Still, a blacksmith takes good care of the implements of his trade. Keeps them clean, sharp—and well-oiled."

Silence fell upon them again, as they neared the prisoners' camp. A very companionable silence, between two men who understood each other quite well.

It was Belisarius' first visit to the camp, since the army had reached Peroz-Shapur. He was pleased to see that his bucellarii had carried out his instructions to the letter.

Merena was riding alongside Baresmanas as they entered. His eyebrows lifted.

"This is a *prisoners'* camp?" he asked.

To all outward appearances, the place looked like any other Roman field encampment. The tents—the multitude of tents; no crowding men like hogs in a pen here—were arranged in neat rows and files. Latrines had been dug to the proper depth and at the proper distance from the tents themselves. The campfires were large and well-supplied, both with fuel and with cooking implements.

By the time they arrived, all two thousand Kushans were standing in the open ground between the tents. They had heard the horses coming, naturally. And while the sound of those hooves hadn't been those of an attacking force, still—

Why two thousand cavalrymen?

Seeing the alert and ready stance of those unarmed men, Merena grunted his approval.

"Good, good! Staunch fellows. Be a massacre, of course, but at least they wouldn't die from back wounds."

At the entrance to the camp, they were greeted by a small contingent of Roman soldiers. A mixed unit, this, made up of men from all the forces under Belisarius' command, serving their assigned rotation in the duty of guarding the prisoners. The very unwanted duty, needless to say, while their comrades were cavorting in Peroz-Shapur. But Belisarius could detect no signs of resentment or bitterness. The men knew that the rotation would be faithfully followed. In a day or so, they too would be enjoying the fleshpots while others took their appointed turn.

Fairly apportioned, in Belisarius' army—the duties as well as the rewards. Of that, his men were by now quite satisfied.

To the general's surprise—and sheer delight—the commander of that detachment proved to be Basil, the man who led his contingent of katyusha rocket chariots. Before leaving on the expedition, Belisarius had toyed with the idea of summoning Basil to go along. But he had dropped the notion, assuming that the man would be well-nigh impossible to find in the saturnalia at Peroz-Shapur.

Yet here he was. One of the two men—three or four, perhaps—that he most wanted to accompany him.

"You'll be going with me, Basil," he announced. "We're taking a little surveying party to that old canal we passed on our way in."

He glanced over his shoulder at the huge mass of Persian cavalrymen waiting outside the camp.

"Well, not all that little. But I need your expertise. You've had more practical experience handling gunpowder than I have."

Basil did not seem sulky at the news, even though it would mean that the hecatontarch would have to forego his own turn at the pleasures of Peroz-Shapur.

Belisarius was not surprised. He had personally selected Basil for his new post, after going over every possibility with Maurice at great length. Both of them had settled on Basil. Partly, for the man's apparent comfort around gunpowder—which was not typical of most of the Thracian cataphracts. Even more, however, for his reliability.

"Yes, sir. When do we leave?"

"Within minutes, I hope. As soon as I can collect a Kushan or two. Where's Vasu—never mind. I see him."

The commander of the Kushans was trotting toward them, accompanied by a handful of his top subordinates. Once he reached the general, Vasudeva gazed up at the man on horseback. There was no expression on his face at all.

"Is there a problem, General?"

Belisarius smiled cordially, shaking his head.

"Not in the least, Vasudeva. I am simply on my way to investigate a nearby ruin. Less than a day's ride away, as it happens. I came here because I would like one or two Kushans to come along."

No expression.

"Me, I assume."

Still, no expression.

Belisarius, on the other hand, grinned from ear to ear.

"Of course not, Vasudeva! That would look terrible, I think—taking the prisoners' commander off on a mysterious trip. From which—judging from all too many sad histories—he might never return. No, no. What I want is the Kushan soldier—or soldiers, if there's more than one—who is most familiar with—"

He groped for the word. There was no equivalent in Kushan, so far as he knew, for the Roman term "engineering."

He settled on an awkward makeshift.

"Field architecture. Watermoving works. Ah—"

Vasudeva nodded. "You want an expert in siegecraft."

"Yes! Well put."

For the first time, Vasudeva's mask slipped a bit. A hint of bitterness came into his face.

"For that, general, you could pick almost any Kushan at random. We are all experts. The Malwa are fond of using us for siegework. Up until the victory, of course. Then we are allowed to bind our wounds, while the Ye-tai and the kshatriyas enjoy the plunder."

The mask returned. "However—" Vasudeva turned his head, looking toward one of the men by his side.

"Vima, you go. You're probably the best."

The Kushan named Vima nodded. He began to move toward one of the saddled but riderless horses which Belisarius had brought with him into the camp. Then, apparently struck by a thought, he paused.

"A question, General Belisarius. You said 'water-moving works.' Is this—whatever we are going to see—is it connected with irrigation?"

Belisarius nodded. Vima glanced at the three extra horses.

"Two more all right?" he asked. Again, Belisarius nodded.

Vima scanned the large crowd of Kushans who, by now, were gathered about.

"Kadphises!" he called out. "You come. And where's Huvishka?"

A man shouldered his way to the front.

"Here," he announced.

Vima gestured. "You also."

Once Belisarius and his party emerged from the prisoners' camp and began heading up the road north from Peroz-Shapur, Vima issued a little sigh.

"Nice to ride a horse again," he commented. Then, eyeing Belisarius:

"I don't suppose this is an omen of things to come?"

Belisarius shook his head, a bit apologetically.

"No, Vima. If we find what I hope to find, I'm afraid you Kushans are in for a long stint of very hard labor in one of the hottest places in the world."

Vima grunted. So did the two Kushans riding beside him.

"Could be worse," mused the one called Huvishka.

"Much worse," agreed Kadphises.

Vima grunted. Curious, Belisarius inquired:

"You are not displeased at the prospect?"

All three Kushans grunted in unison. The sound, oddly, was one of amusement.

"We Kushans tend to approach things from the bottom up, general," remarked Vima. "A *long* stint—of whatever kind of labor—sounds distinctly better than many alternative prospects."

Kadphises grunted. Huvishka interpreted:

"Being executed, for instance, can be viewed as a very short stint of very easy labor. Bow your head, that's about it—*chop!*—it's over. Executioner's the only one working up a sweat."

When Belisarius interpreted the exchange, Baresmanas immediately broke into laughter.

Merena did not. He simply grunted himself.

"Good, good. Staunch fellows, as I said."

Chapter 24

Within an hour of their arrival at the Nehar Malka, Belisarius had settled on his plan. The next two hours he spent with Basil and—separately—the Kushans, making sure that the project was technically feasible.

The rest of the day, that evening, and the entire day following, he spent with Baresmanas. Just the two of them, alone in a tent, discussing the real heart of the plan—which was not technical, but moral.

"You are asking a great deal of us, Belisarius."

"We will do all of the work, and provide most of the material resources needed—"

Baresmanas waved those issues aside.

"That's not the problem, and you know it perfectly well." He gave the Roman general a fish-eyed look.

"An *Aryan*, examining your plan, cannot help but notice that you propose to recreate the very conditions which enabled Emperor Julian to strike so deeply into Mesopotamia, two centuries ago."

The little smile which followed took some of the sting out of the statement. Some.

Belisarius shrugged. "Not exactly, Baresmanas. If my scheme works as I hope, the situation will revert back—"

Again, Baresmanas waved his words aside. "Yes, yes—*if* it works as you hope. Not to mention the fact that a *skeptical and untrusting*

261

Aryan cannot help but notice that you Romans will be in control of that part of the plan which would, as you put it, 'revert back' the situation. What if you decide otherwise?"

Belisarius returned the hard stare calmly. "And *are* you a 'skeptical and untrusting Persian,' Baresmanas?"

The sahrdaran looked away, tugging his beard thoughtfully.

"No," came the reply. "I am not, myself. But others will be, especially once they realize that no Aryan commander will have authority over the final implementation of the complete plan."

Belisarius began to shrug, but stopped the gesture before it started. This matter could not be shrugged off. It had to be faced squarely.

"There is no other way, sahrdaran. In order for it to work, my plan requires complete security—*especially* the final part. You know as well as I do that Persian forces, by now, will have been penetrated by Malwa agents."

"And yours haven't?" snapped Baresmanas.

"It is not likely. Not the troops who will be playing the key role, at least. Keep in mind that the Malwa spy network has been active in Persia longer than it was in Rome—*and* that we smashed the center of that network half a year ago."

Baresmanas scowled. "That's another thing I don't like! Your scheme *presupposes* treachery on the part of Aryans!"

Belisarius said nothing. He simply gave the sahrdaran his own fish-eyed look.

After a moment, Baresmanas sighed. He even chuckled.

"I admit, I think your assessment is accurate. Much as I hate to admit it."

Belisarius chuckled himself. "Don't be so downcast about it. Treachery is probably more of a Roman than an Aryan vice. It's not as if we didn't find our own highest circles riddled with traitors, after all. At least Emperor Khusrau still has his eyes, which is more than Justinian can say."

"Very good eyes," grunted Baresmanas. The sahrdaran straightened in his chair.

"The matter must be put before the Emperor himself, Belisarius. Only he can make this decision. I cannot possibly make it in his stead."

"I do not expect you to," came the immediate response. "I know full well that only Khusrau Anushirvan has that authority. But he will ask you what you think. And the question boils down to this: *Can we trust this man Belisarius?*"

The two men in the tent stared at each other.

"I will give my oath, of course," added Belisarius.

For the last time that day, Baresmanas waved the matter aside.

"An oath is only as good as the man who gives it. Your oath will not be necessary."

Suddenly, Baresmanas laughed. "It occurs to me that Valentinian will be most gratified! His job just got much easier!"

Belisarius' brows knit with puzzlement.

"But it's obvious! Khusrau will only agree if he decides that *the man Belisarius* can be trusted. He will certainly not put his trust in *any* Roman general."

Still frowning. Again, the sahdaran laughed.

"So blind! It's so obvious! You will have to promise the Emperor that you will be *alive*—when the time comes to give the final order."

Belisarius' eyes widened.

"Oh, yes," murmured Baresmanas. "Your days of leading cavalry charges are over, my friend. For quite some time."

"I hadn't thought of that," admitted the general.

Aide spoke in his mind:

I did. Then, with great satisfaction:

And Valentinian isn't the only one who will be most gratified. So will I.

So will I. Very much.

Upon his return to Peroz-Shapur, Belisarius sent couriers into the city, summoning his top commanders to a conference. It took several hours for all of those men to be tracked down. Many—most—were found in the obvious locales. Dens of iniquity, so to speak. Two or three were nabbed in more reputable spots. And one—the last to be found—in a very odd sort of place. For a man of his type.

"Sorry I'm late," said Agathius, as he came into the command tent. Looking around, he winced a bit. He was the last one to enter.

"No matter, chiliarch," said Belisarius pleasantly. "I realize this meeting was called with no warning. Please—take a chair."

As he waited for the commander of the Constantinople troopers to settle in, Belisarius found himself a bit puzzled by the man's behavior—and by those of his subordinates, for that matter. Agathius seemed distracted, as if his mind were elsewhere. That was quite unlike the man. Agathius was only twenty-eight years old, which was quite young for a soldier risen from the ranks to have become a hecatontarch, much less a chiliarch. Yet, despite the man's youth and his outward appearance as a muscular bruiser, Belisarius had found Agathius to be not only intelligent but possessed of an almost ferocious capacity for concentration.

Odd, that air of distraction, mused Belisarius. And why are his subordinates giving him such peculiar sidelong glances? You'd almost think they were smirking.

He pushed the matter out of his mind. To business.

In the three hours which followed, Belisarius presented his commanders with two matters for their consideration.

The first—which took up two of those hours—was an outline of the stratagem he was developing for using the Nehar Malka in their next campaign against the Malwa. Many aspects of his plans he left unspoken—partly, for security reasons, partly, because they were still half-formed. But he said enough to allow the commanders to join in a discussion of the allotment of Roman troops to the different tasks involved.

Interestingly enough, he noted, Agathius' distraction seemed to vanish during that discussion. Indeed, the Greek chiliarch played a leading role in it.

"It's essential that Abbu remain behind," insisted Agathius, "—*with* most of his skirmishers—"

The Constantinople man beat down the protests coming from other commanders.

"Quit whining!" he snapped. "The rest of us are just going on a march to Babylon, by way of Ctesiphon. Right in the heart of Persian territory, for the sake of God! We already crushed the only Malwa raiding force anybody knows of—so what do we need scouts for?"

He jabbed a thumb at Basil, then nodded toward the Syrian infantry leaders.

"Whereas these boys are going to be left alone up here. With two thousand Kushans to keep an eye on, and the desert not ten miles away. They'll be sitting ducks, if the Lakhmids come on them unawares."

Belisarius sat back, more than satisfied to let the Greek handle the problem.

Having squelched that little protest, Agathius rolled over the next.

"And as for this crap about the Callinicum garrison"—here he glowered at his own Constantinople subordinates, who had been the most vocal in their protests—"I don't want to hear it! They did well enough—*damn well*, all things considered—in the fight at the villa. Sure, they're not up to the standards of the Syrian lads—not yet, anyway—but that's all the more reason not to leave them behind. The katyusha-men and the Syrians have got enough on their plate already, without having to train inexperienced men in the kind of heavy engineering work they'll be doing."

Another glare. "So they're coming with us, just as the general proposed. *And* there'll be no grousing about it."

The other Greeks in the tent—who had been doing most of the grousing about "Callinicum crybabies"—lowered their heads. It was all Belisarius could do to keep from grinning. He already knew that Agathius had the easy, relaxed confidence of his subordinates. Now, when needed, the man had shown that he could also break them to his will.

So much met with Belisarius' silent approval. The next, with his admiration.

Agathius' hard eyes left the Greeks, and settled on Celsus, the commander of the Callinicum garrison troops. Celsus was sitting, hunched, on a stool in a corner of the tent. He was a small man, rather elderly for a soldier, and diffident by nature. As usual during command conferences, he had been silent throughout the entire discussion. A silence which had grown purely abject as the qualities of his men had been subjected to the beratement of other, younger, more assertive, more confident—and certainly louder—officers.

Agathius gave the man a little nod, lingering over the gesture just long enough to make his approval clear to everyone. Celsus nodded back, his eyes shining with thanks. For a moment, his skinny shoulders even lost their habitual stoop.

As Agathius resumed his seat, Belisarius sent a quick thought to Aide.

Absolutely marvelous! Did you see that, Aide?—and do you understand why it is so important?

Hesitantly: **I am not sure. I think—**

Hesitation faded. **Yes. It is how humans—your kind of humans—facet each other. Strength grows from building other strength, not from trampling on weakness.**

Exactly.

The officers in the tent were, once again, focussed on Belisarius. The general rose, preparing to speak on another subject. But, before he did so, he took the time for a private moment.

I am so proud of you—grandchild.

You are my old man.

In the next hour, Belisarius broached with his officers the delicate matter which he had discussed with Baresmanas.

"So," he concluded, "I'm not telling anyone what to do. But I repeat: *this war is not going to be settled in one battle*. Not even in one campaign. We're going to be locked against the Malwa for years, probably. Hopefully—eventually—we'll be fighting the Malwa on their own soil. But for now, and probably for quite some time, we'll be fighting here in Persia. Better that, when it comes down to it, than fighting on Roman territory."

He took a little breath.

"I've said this before, many times, but I'll say it again. *We have to stay on good terms with the Persians*. If they start feeling that their Roman allies aren't much better than the Malwa, there'll be the risk that they'll try to back out of the way. Get out of Mesopotamia, retreat to the plateau, and let the Romans fight it out alone."

He gave the gathered men a stern gaze.

"As I said, I'm not telling anyone what to do. But I ask you to try and set an example, at least, for your men. I don't care what any Roman soldier does in taverns and whorehouses, as long as there's no roughhousing. But if you or your men want to cast your net a little wider, so to speak—" he waited for the little chuckle to die down "—keep in mind that Persians have their own customs."

He stopped speaking. Studied his officers, as they sat there staring at him.

Silent themselves, as he had expected. Though he noted, carefully—and with considerable amusement—their differing reactions.

The Syrian officers (as well as Celsus, the Callinicum commander) had little smiles on their faces. Long familiar with Persian customs—*sharing* many of those customs—the Syrians and Arabs obviously found the confusion elsewhere in the room quite entertaining.

His own Thracian bucellarii were also smiling, just a bit—even the dour Maurice. Not with quite the same smirk as the Syrians, true. The Thracians were familiar with Persians, but it could hardly be said that they shared any particular empathy for the haughty Aryans. No, their amusement came from elsewhere. They were *very* familiar with Belisarius. And so they found it entertaining to see neophytes scrambling to catch up with their general's often odd way of looking at the world.

The Illyrian officers were examining Belisarius as if he were one of the fabled two-headed creatures reputed to live somewhere south of Nubia. Illyrians were even more rustic than Thracians, and their experience with "other folks" was restricted almost entirely to barbarians. They understood those barbarians, true. Barbarian blood flowed in their own veins, come down to it. But the idea of *catering* to the so-called "customs" of—of—of—

Belisarius looked away, to keep from laughing. His eyes settled on the Greeks.

They were the key, he knew. The Roman Empire was a Greek Empire, in all but name. A Thracian-Egyptian dynasty might sit on the throne, Egypt might be the richest and most populous province, and Thracians and Syrians might play a disproportionate role in the leadership of the army, but it was the Greeks who were the Empire's heart and soul. Their language was the common language. Their nobility was the axis of the imperial elite. Their traders and merchants commanded the sinews of commerce.

And their soldiers, and officers, were the core of Roman strength.

Here, for the first time, Belisarius found a reaction he had not expected. Agathius' distraction was back, with a vengeance. For all that Belisarius could determine, the man seemed lost in another world. The attitude of his subordinates was equally puzzling. Belisarius had expected the Greeks to react much as the Illyrians. With more sophistication, of course—but, still, he had expected them to be staring at him as if he were at least half-crazed.

Greeks—worry about what a bunch of sorry Persians think?

Instead, they weren't looking at Belisarius at all. They were casting quick, veiled glances at their own commander, with their lips pressed tightly together. As if fighting—very hard—to keep from smirking themselves.

Odd. Very odd.

Belisarius left off his study of the Greeks and glanced at the rest of his subordinates. It was obvious that none of the officers in the tent were prepared to speak on this rather unusual subject. He had expected as much. So, after another minute's silence, he thanked them politely for attending the conference and gave them leave to depart.

Which they did. Agathius led the way, at first, almost charging for the entrance. Then, stopping suddenly, he formed a broad-shouldered stumbling block for the officers who squeezed past him. The man seemed to dance back and forth on his feet, as if torn between two directions. At one point, he began to turn around, as if to re-enter the command tent. Stopped, turned back; turned back again; stopped. Danced back and forth.

Except for Belisarius and Maurice, Agathius was the only one left in the tent. For just a moment, the Constantinople commander's eyes met those of the general. A strange look he had, in his face. Half-pleading; half—angry?

No, decided Belisarius. It was not anger, so much as a deeply buried resentment.

Of what? he wondered.

Suddenly, Agathius was gone. Belisarius cocked an eye at Maurice.

"Do you know something I don't?"

Maurice snorted.

"What do you want? I'm Thracian, for the love of God. Bad enough you want to tax my simple mind with outlandish Persian ways. Am I supposed to understand Greeks, too?"

Two nights later, early in the evening, Agathius showed up at Belisarius' tent.

After being invited within, the man stood rigidly before the general.

"I need to ask you a question, sir," he said. His voice seemed a bit harsh.

Belisarius nodded. Agathius cleared his throat.

"Well. It's this way, sir. I know it's often done—well."

Again, he cleared his throat. The harshness vanished, replaced by a sort of youthful uncertainty. Embarassment, perhaps.

The words came out in a rush.

"I know it's often done that troop commanders—of chiliarch rank, I mean—after a successful campaign—or even sometimes a single battle, if it was a big victory—well—they get taken into the aristocracy. Official rank, I mean."

His mouth clamped shut.

Belisarius scratched his chin.

"Yes," he said, nodding. "It's happened. More than once. Myself, for instance. I was born into the *clarissimate*—as low as it gets in the nobility, outside of equestrians. After Justinian promoted me into his bodyguard, he—Never mind. It's a long story. Today, of course—since my stepson was acclaimed Emperor—I'm ranked at the very top of the senatorial *illustres*." He smiled crookedly. "A *gloriosissimi* I am now, no less."

Agathius did not return the smile. Belisarius realized that he was treading on very sensitive soil. "And yourself, Agathius? I've never asked." A little, dismissive gesture. "I don't care about such things, mind you, in my officers. Only their ability. But tell me—what is your own class origin?"

Agathius stared at the general.

"My father was a baker," he replied. His voice was very soft; but his tone, hard as a rock.

Belisarius nodded, understanding.

In the eastern Roman Empire, unlike the western, men had never been forced by law to remain in their father's trades. Still, the trades tended to be hereditary. All tradesmen were organized into guilds, and were considered freemen. Yet, while some of those trades carried genuine prestige—metalworkers, for instance—none of them were acceptable occupations for members of the nobility.

And *certainly* not bakers, who were considered among the lowest of men, outside of those in outright slavery or servitude.

So. Agathius, like many before him, had sought escape from his father's wretched status through the principal avenue in the Roman Empire which was, relatively speaking, democratic and open to talent: the army.

Yet—Belisarius was still puzzled. He had encountered men—any number of them—who were obsessed with their official class ranking. But Agathius had never seemed to care, one way or another.

The general thrust speculation aside. Whatever might be the man's motives or past state of mind, the question seemed to be of importance to him now.

"This matters to you?" he asked.

Agathius nodded. "Yes, sir. It does. It didn't used to, but—" His lips tightened. "It does now," he finished, softly. Almost through clenched teeth.

Belisarius abandoned his relaxed stance. He sat up straight in his chair.

"You understand that any rank I give you must be confirmed by the Emperor? And by the Senate, in the case of a senatorial rank?"

Agathius nodded. Finally, his rigid countenance seemed to break, just a bit.

"I don't need to be in any senatorial class, sir. Just—something." Belisarius nodded.

"In that case, I see no problem." His crooked smile appeared. "Certainly not with the Emperor!"

Agathius managed a little smile himself, now.

Belisarius scratched his chin. "Let's keep it military, then, if the Senate doesn't matter to you. It is well within my authority to give you the rank of *comes*. How is that—Count Agathius?"

Agathius bowed his head stiffly.

"Thank you, sir." Then, after a moment's hesitation, he asked, "How does that compare to a Persian dehgan?"

"Depends how you look at it. Formally speaking, a Roman count is actually a higher rank than a dehgan. Equivalent"—he wobbled his hand back and forth—"to one of the lower grades of their vurzurgan class, more or less."

Belisarius shrugged.

"But that's the way we Romans look at it. *Officially*, the Persians will accept the equivalence. In practice—in private—?" Again, he shrugged.

"They view our habit of connecting rank in the nobility with official position rather dimly. Bloodlines are far more important, to their way of thinking."

Suddenly, to the general's surprise, Agathius' stiffness disappeared. The burly officer actually grinned.

"Not a problem, that. Not with—"

He fell silent. The grin faded. Agathius squared his shoulders.

"I thank you again, sir. It means much to me. But I would like to impose on you again, if I might."

"Yes?"

"Would you do me the honor of joining me tomorrow afternoon? On a social occasion?"

Belisarius' eyes widened, just a bit. To the best of his knowledge, Agathius' idea of a "social occasion" was a cheerful drinking session at a tavern. But he did not think—

Agathius rushed on.

"Lord Baresmanas will escort you, sir. I've already spoken to him and he agreed. The occasion is taking place at the governor's palace in the city."

By now, Belisarius was quite bewildered. What in the world did Baresmanas have to do with—?

Enough, he told himself firmly. This is important to the man, whatever it is.

"I will be there, Agathius."

The Greek officer nodded again, thanked him again, and left.

Odd. Very odd.

Baresmanas arrived early in the afternoon of the next day. Kurush was with him, as were all of the top commanders of his household troops with the exception of Merena.

None of the men wore armor, and only two were even carrying swords. Seeing the finery of their raiment, Belisarius congratulated himself for having decided to wear his own best clothing. Like the Persians, he was unarmored, carrying no weapon beyond a dagger.

On the ride into the city, the general tried to pry information out of Baresmanas regarding the mysterious "social occasion." But the sahrdaran gave no response beyond an enigmatic little smile.

When they arrived at the governor's palace, Belisarius took a moment to admire the structure. The outer walls were massive, due to the ancient Mesopotamian tradition of using rubble and gypsum mortar for heavy construction. The intrinsic crudity of the material was concealed by an outer layer of stucco painted in a variety of vivid designs. Most of the motifs, ironically, were borrowed from Graeco-Roman civilization—dentils, acanthus, leaf scrolls, even the Greek key. Still, the effect was quite distinct, as

Persians had their own approach to color, in which brilliant black, red and yellow hues predominated.

The edifice was forty yards wide and approximately twice that in length. A complex pattern of recesses and projected mouldings added to the intricacy of the palace's outer walls. The palace was three stories tall, judging from its height. But Belisarius was familiar enough with Persian architecture to realize that most of the palace's interior would be made up of very tall one-story rooms. Only in the rear portions of the palace, given over to the governor's private residence, would there actually be chambers on the upper stories.

The front of the palace was dominated by a great *aivan*—the combined entrance hall/audience chamber which was unique to Persian architecture. In the case of this palace, the aivan was located on the narrower southern wall. Almost half of the wall's forty yards were taken up by a huge arch, which led into the barrel-vaulted aivan itself. The aivan was open to the elements, a feature which, in the Mesopotamian climate, was not only practical but pleasant. It was forty feet high, measuring from the marbled floor to the top of the arch, and its walls were decorated both with Roman-style mosaics as well as the traditional Mesopotamian stucco bas-reliefs.

Belisarius had assumed that, whatever the nature of the social occasion, it would be held in the aivan itself. But, after dismounting and following Baresmanas within, he discovered that the aivan was almost empty. The only people present were Agathius and a small group of his subordinates—Cyril, as well as the other three tribunes of the Constantinople unit.

The five Greek officers were standing in the much smaller arch at the rear of the aivan. Past that arch, Belisarius could see a short hallway—also barrel-vaulted—which opened into a room beyond. That room, from what little he could see of it, seemed to be packed with people.

As they walked through the aivan, Belisarius leaned over to Baresmanas. "I thought—"

Baresmanas shook his head. The enigmatic smile was still on his face, but it was no longer quite so little. "Ridiculous!" he proclaimed. "The aivan is for public gatherings. Given the nature of this event, the governor naturally saw fit to offer the use of his own quarters. His private audience chamber, that is to say."

The sahrdaran gestured ahead. "As you can see, it is just beyond."

Agathius stepped forward to meet them. His expression was very stiff and formal, but Belisarius thought he detected a sense of relief in the man's eyes.

"Thank you for coming, sir," he said softly. He turned on his heel and led the way through the arched corridor.

The room beyond was a large chamber, approximately sixty feet in width and length. The walls rose up thirty feet, decorated with frescoes depicting heroic deeds from the various epics of the Aryans. A great dome surmounted the chamber, rising another twenty feet or so.

There were a multitude of people already present, all of them Persians. Belisarius recognized the district governor, standing against the north wall, surrounded by a little coterie of his high officials. The larger body of men—perhaps a dozen—who stood behind them were obviously scribes.

In the western side of the chamber stood an even larger group of men. Mazda priests, Belisarius realized. He was interested to note, judging from their distinctive garb, that both branches of the Zoroastrian clergy were present. The Persians called their priests either *mobads* or *herbads*. When Belisarius first encountered that distinction, years earlier, he had thought it to be roughly parallel to the distinction which Christians made between priests and monks. Further acquaintance with Persian society had undermined that neat assumption. The differences between mobads and herbads were of a subtler nature, which he had never been able to pinpoint precisely—other than observing that mobads seemed to embody the juridical power of the clergy, where the herbads functioned more like teachers or "wise men."

What was significant, however, was that both were represented. That was a bit unusual. There was considerable, if subdued, rivalry between the two branches of the clergy. As a rule, Belisarius had found, mobads and herbads avoided each other's company.

Now he examined the final, and largest, group of Persians in the room. These men were clustered toward the eastern wall, and they seemed to be made up almost entirely of dehgans. Merena, the commander of Baresmanas' household troops, was standing in the midst of them. As he studied the dehgans, Belisarius suddenly realized that many of them bore a certain resemblance to each other.

Baresmanas' whisper confirmed his guess.

"That's Merena's clan—those of them who were present in the city, at least."

The sahrdaran's enigmatic smile was now almost a grin. He shook his head.

"You still don't understand? Odd, really, for a man who is normally so acutely perceptive. I would have thought—"

A small commotion was taking place. The little mob of dehgans along the eastern wall was stepping aside, clearing a space for a small party advancing into the chamber through an archway in the eastern wall.

Four women appeared—the first women Belisarius had seen since he entered the palace.

Aide's voice—smug, smug:

I figured it out yesterday.

The woman in front was middle-aged. The three walking behind her were quite young. Her daughters, obviously.

Belisarius felt his jaw sag.

What a dummy.

The girl in the center, the oldest, was perhaps sixteen years of age.

It's the first signs of senility, that's what it is.

She was dressed in an elaborate costume. Her sisters, flanking her, wore clothing which was generically similar but not quite as ostentatious.

Don't worry, grandpa.

Her face was covered with a veil, except for her eyes. Dark brown eyes, they were. Gleaming with excitement. Beautiful eyes. Belisarius had no doubt that the rest of the girl was just as beautiful.

I'll take care of you.

Belisarius was not able to follow most of the ritual—the long ritual—which followed. Just the obvious highlights. Partly, because he was caught off-guard. Partly, because it was the ceremony of a foreign religion. Mostly, though, because Aide kept interrupting his train of thought.

The lighting of the sacred fire—

You'll have to stick with porridge from now on.

The presentation by the chief scribe of the intricate property rights and obligations which were a central feature of *patixsayih* marriages—

Can't risk you eating meat. Cut yourself, for sure, forgetting which end of the dagger to use.

The stiff presentations, by Agathius and Merena, of their respective noble rankings—

We'll get rid of your horse, of course.

The learned counsel of the herbads, added to the judgement of the mobads, weighed by the district governor and his assembled advisers—

Find you a donkey to ride.

—who agreed, after lengthy consultation, that the marriage maintained the necessary purity of the Aryan nobility.

A small donkey. So you won't get hurt, all the times you'll fall off.

After the ceremony was over, during the feast which followed, Merena approached Belisarius.

"I have a question," he asked. Stiff as ever.

Politely, Belisarius inclined his head in invitation.

"Was Agathius at Mindouos? I did not wish to ask him, before. And now that he is my son-in-law, I cannot."

"No, Merena. He wasn't."

The dehgan grunted. "Good, good." Merena rubbed his thigh. "That would have been—difficult," he murmured. Then, moved away, limping very badly.

Walking out of the palace, Belisarius glanced at Baresmanas. The smile was still there. Not enigmatic, however. Simply smug.

"And how did you find out about it?" growled the general.

"I didn't 'find out about it,' my friend. I am the one who—ah, what is that word you Romans are so fond of? Yes, yes—I *engineered* the whole thing."

Belisarius' eyes widened. Baresmanas chuckled.

"Oh, yes. *I* am the one who introduced the gallant young officer to Merena and his family—*after* conspiring with his wife to make sure that Sudaba would be present, looking her very—beautiful! beautiful!—best. *I* am the one—"

"Stop bragging," grumbled Belisarius. "I will fully admit that it was a masterstroke, insofar as the problem we discussed—"

"You think I did it because of *that*?" The sahrdaran snorted. "I had a much more immediate problem to solve, my friend. As I told you, Merena is a famous warrior and an absolute paragon of Aryan propriety. He is also, by dehgan standards, poor. So—the man had a daughter of marriageable age and no respectable dowry to give her. Think of the shame! The disgrace! No suitable Persian nobleman would accept a bride with no dowry."

Belisarius smiled crookedly.

"Whereas a vigorous, ambitious young Roman officer risen from the ranks—and newly rich from the booty of Anatha—would be far more concerned with increasing his status than his wealth."

"Precisely."

Belisarius shook his head sadly. "I am a lamb among wolves. An innocent babe surrounded by schemers."

Don't worry, old man. I'll take care of you.

Oh—be careful! There's a step coming up!

Chapter 25

BABYLON
Autumn, 531 A.D.

Khusrau Anushirvan sprang lightly onto the low wall which surmounted the highest level of Esagila, the ancient ruin which had
once been the great temple of the god Marduk. From that vantage
point, the Emperor of Persia could gaze south at the huge Malwa
army encamped before Babylon.

An instant later, Belisarius joined him. The general took a
moment to make sure his footing was good. The wall—almost a
battlement—was at least a yard wide, but there was nothing to
stop someone who overbalanced from plunging to their death on
the stone rubble sixty feet below.

Khusrau smiled.

"Does altitude bother you?" he asked. The question was polite,
not scornful.

The Roman general shook his head. "Not particularly. Still, I
wouldn't want to dance up here."

"Lucky man! I myself am petrified by heights. Anything above
the level of horseback."

Belisarius glanced at the Persian Emperor. In truth, Khusrau's
face seemed a bit pinched, as if he were controlling himself by
sheer force of will.

He was impressed, again, by the Emperor's self-discipline. Since his arrival in Babylon three days before, Belisarius had been struck by the way Khusrau kept his obviously exuberant and dynamic personality under a tight rein. That same self-control was being manifested now, in the Persian ruler's ability to remain standing on a perch which would have sent most men to their knees seeking safety.

For ten minutes or so, the two men said nothing. They simply stood side by side, studying the battle being waged below them.

Belisarius' attention was immediately drawn by the roar of siege guns. A cloud of gunsmoke, well over a mile distant, indicated the presence of a battery of the huge cannons. After the wind blew the cloud away, he could spot the actual guns themselves. Eight of them, sheltered behind a berm. He recognized the pattern from his previous experience at the siege of Ranapur. His eyes ranged north and south, quickly spotting two more batteries. Another roar, another cloud of gunsmoke, and one of those batteries was also hidden from view.

Belisarius shifted his gaze to the walls of the besieged city. His eyes widened.

The defenses of Babylon were gigantic. The outer ring was so massive that it was impossible, almost, to think of it as anything other than a low ridge. The fortifications were not particularly tall—perhaps twenty feet, no more—but they spanned perhaps forty yards in thickness.

Studying it more closely, Belisarius saw that the outer defenses were actually a triple wall—or, at least, had been so once. The inner wall, some twenty feet wide, was constructed of sun-dried mud brick. Squat towers spaced at regular intervals projected another twenty feet above the wall itself, topped with sheltered platforms for Persian soldiers manning scorpions and other artillery engines. A rubble-strewn space fifty feet wide separated this inner wall from the middle wall. The middle wall was a bit thicker than the inner wall, with no towers. Unlike the inner wall, this wall was made of harder and more durable oven-baked brick.

That same type of brick was used in the third, outermost wall. No space separated this outermost wall from the midwall. The third wall, originally ten feet in thickness, served both as a bulwark for the midwall as well as the escarpment for the huge moat beyond it.

There was not much left of that third wall, however. Over the centuries, peasants had plucked away the good bricks for their own use. Today, the moat which lapped at the crumbled edge of the wall seemed more like a natural river than a man-made artifact. The size of the moat, of course, was partly responsible for producing that impression—Belisarius estimated that it was at least a hundred yards wide.

Belisarius watched a cannonball slam into the outer wall. A little avalanche of broken bricks slid into the moat, leaving a ripple in their wake. Other than that, the siege gun seemed to have made no impact whatsoever.

"At that rate," he mused, "they'll fill the moat with rubble and cannonballs before they ever finish breaking down the wall."

Khusrau snorted.

"We were terrified—myself also, I will admit it—when they first began firing with those incredible machines. 'Siege guns,' as you call them. But after a few days—then weeks, and now months—we have little fear of them. It's ironic, actually. Most of my advisers urged me to make a stand at Ctesiphon, taking advantage of its tall, stone walls. But I think if I had done so—"

"You would have been defeated by now," concluded Belisarius. "I have seen these guns in use before, and I have seen the walls of Ctesiphon. Those walls would have been brought down within two months."

He pointed to Babylon's outer fortifications. "Whereas this wall—this wide, soft, low wall—is actually more of a berm. Exactly the best kind of defenses against siege guns."

Both men watched as another cannonball struck the wall—the inner wall, this time. The cannonball buried itself in the crumbly mudbrick, without so much as shaking the tower thirty yards away from the impact.

"The wall just got stronger, I think," chuckled Khusrau.

"How many assaults have they mounted?" asked Belisarius.

"Seven. The last one was a month ago. No—almost six weeks now."

The Persian Emperor turned and pointed to his right, toward the Euphrates.

"That one they attempted with barges, loaded with soldiers. It was a massacre. As you can see, the western walls of the city are still standing, almost as they were built by Nebuchadrezzar a thousand years ago. Stonework. Very tall. We poured burning naphtha on them, and sank many of the barges with catapults."

He elevated his finger, still pointing to the west.

"If they could position their siege guns to the west, they could probably break down those stone walls. But I ordered the dikes and levees broken."

Belisarius gazed toward the river. It was now late in the afternoon, and the sun's rays were reflected off a vast spread of water. Khusrau, following a Mesopotamian military tradition which went back to the ancient Sumerians, had ordered the flooding of the low ground. Unchecked by manmade obstructions, the Euphrates had turned the entire area west of Babylon into a swamp. Impossible terrain even for an infantry assault, much less the positioning of artillery.

The area east of Babylon had been protected in the same manner. The ancient city was almost an island now, surrounded by water and marshes to the west, east and northeast. The Malwa army held the southern ground. Persian forces still retained control of the narrow causeway which led from the Ishtar Gate on Babylon's northwest side to the northern regions of Mesopotamia. Even after all these months, the Malwa had not been able to surround and isolate the besieged city.

Khusrau looked back to the south.

"The first six assaults were made here. The Malwa suffered great losses in all of them, with no success at all except, temporarily, during the third assault. In that attack, some of their troops—those excellent ones with the strange hair style—"

"Kushans."

"Yes. About a thousand of them got past the outer fortifications, in three different places. But—"

He shrugged. Belisarius, gazing down, could not help wincing.

"Must have been a slaughter."

"Yes," agreed Khusrau. The Emperor pointed at the inner fortifications, which consisted of a second ring of walls positioned about two hundred yards inside the outer ring.

"That is a double wall. The outer wall is twenty feet thick; the inner, fifteen. These fortifications were also built by Nebuchadrezzar. Very clever, he was—or his engineers and architects, at least. You can see that the two walls are separated by a space of twenty feet. The area between is a built-up road, perfect for military traffic. Then, beyond the outer wall, is a low berm. You can't see it from here. But you can see the moat which butts up against that berm. It's fifty yards wide."

Belisarius shook his head. "A pure killing ground. If the enemy manages to cross the first moat and fight their way over the outer defenses, they find themselves trapped in the open—with another moat to cross, and still more fortifications to be scaled."

"That, too, was slaughter. I had the road packed with dehgans and their retainers. It is quite solid and wide enough for horsemen. They were able to fire their bows from the saddle, sheltered by the outer wall, and rush to whatever spot looked most in danger. I don't think we lost more than two hundred men. And that's about how many of the Kushans finally made it back across the outer fortifications alive."

He began to add something else, but his attention was distracted by the sight of a rocket arching up from the Malwa lines. Khusrau and Belisarius followed the rocket's erratic trajectory, until it plunged harmlessly into the open area between Babylon's two rings of defenses.

"The rockets actually have been more of a problem," commented the Emperor. "They do almost no damage to the walls, and many of them miss the city entirely. But those which do fly straight have a longer range than the siege guns, and they have caused casualties. It is the unpredictability of the cursed things which bothers my soldiers the most."

Belisarius nodded, but said nothing in reply. He was now preoccupied with studying the enemy's field fortifications.

That study was brief. He had seen their equivalent at Ranapur and, again, was not overly impressed. A Roman army, this many months into a siege, would have constructed much better and more solid field-works.

Now his eyes were drawn to a further distance, and toward the river. Several miles away, he could see the crude piers which the Malwa had constructed on the left bank of the Euphrates. Crudely made, but very capacious. He estimated that there were at least forty ships tied up to those docks, each of which had a capacity of several hundred tons. Another half dozen or so could be seen coming up the river, their oar banks flashing in the sun as they fought their way against the sluggish current.

Remembering Ranapur, he scanned the river more closely. As he expected, the Malwa were providing security for their supply fleet with a small armada of swift war galleys.

"It's incredible, isn't it?" asked Khusrau. "Not even the ancient legends speak of a logistics effort on this scale."

He fell silent, tight-lipped.

Belisarius eyed the Emperor covertly. Khusrau's face was expressionless, but the general realized that the man's fear of heights was taking a toll on him.

"I've seen enough," he announced. He made a little motion, as if to depart.

Still, no expression crossed Khusrau's face.

"You are certain?" he asked.

Belisarius nodded. Now—possibly—a little look of relief came to the Emperor. Quickly, he turned away and leapt down to the temple roof four feet below.

Belisarius copied that leap, although he landed more heavily than the Persian.

Partly that was because Belisarius was a much bigger man. Khusrau was young and athletic, but his was the build of a gymnast—on the short side, and wiry. Mostly, however, Belisarius' thudding arrival on the roof was due to the half-armor he was wearing. The Emperor, in contrast, was clothed in nothing but the simple tunic and trousers of a Persian nobleman taking his ease.

As he landed, the general staggered slightly. Khusrau steadied him with a helping hand.

"It must be dreadful," he remarked with a smile, "to have to wear that stuff all the time."

Belisarius grimaced. "Especially in this heat! But—there it is. Can't have a general prancing around a siege, while all of the soldiers are sweating rivers."

Khusrau shook his head in sympathy. "Wouldn't do at all," he agreed. His smile became an outright grin.

"Whereas an Emperor—"

Belisarius laughed. "I heard all about it, even before we arrived, from your admiring troops. How the fearless Khusrau Anushirvan faces the Malwa with a bared breast."

The Emperor glanced down at his tunic. A simple tunic, in its design. But, of course, not the garment of a simple man.

"Hardly that," he murmured. He fingered the sleeve.

"It's cotton, you know, not linen. Very valuable. Almost as valuable as silk—"

He broke off. Belisarius chuckled.

"More valuable, now. Cotton only comes from India. There won't be more of it for some time."

The two men stared at each other.

Enemies, once. Khusrau had not been at Mindouos, three years earlier. He had been in the capital at Ctesiphon, like all his brothers and half-brothers, plotting to seize the throne after the death of the ailing Emperor Kavad. But it had been his father's army which Belisarius shattered there.

Allies, now.

"Better this way," murmured the Emperor. He took Belisarius by the arm and began leading him toward the small ziggurat at the center of the roof. There was an entrance there, leading to the stairs which descended into Esagila's immense interior.

"Much better," agreed Belisarius.

Much better, chimed in Aide. **The greatest Persian Emperor in a millennium makes for a bad enemy.**

Idly, Belisarius wondered how things might have turned out, had the Malwa never been raised to power by the creature called Link. The thing—half-human, half-computer—which Aide called a cyborg. A cybernetic organism, sent back in time by the "new gods" of the future.

Aide answered. **In that future, you will also defeat the Persians. At a battle near Daras, not far from Mindouos.**

And then?

And then, ten years later, Khusrau will sack Antioch.

They were at the entrance to the ziggurat. Khusrau led the way into the interior. It was much cooler. Belisarius heaved a little sigh of relief.

Much better this way.

Khusrau leaned back in his chair and spread his arms in a gesture which encompassed their entire surroundings.

"I forget, Belisarius—you are a Christian. This must be a marvel for you!"

A little crease of puzzlement came to the general's brow. He paused from raising his wine goblet.

Khusrau laughed.

"Don't tell me you don't know! You're sitting right on top of the Tower of Babel!"

Belisarius' eyes widened. He stared down between his feet. Then, gazed all around him.

He and Khusrau were sitting under a canopy which had been erected at the summit of a large hill right in the middle of what had once been Babylon. The Persian Emperor's great pavilion was located not far to the north, just over the crest of the hill. The two men were alone, except for a handful of servants standing ten yards off.

The hill was the highest point in Babylon, and provided a magnificent view of the entire city. But there was not much left of that city, now, other than its outer fortifications.

Esagila, Marduk's temple, was still largely intact. That huge structure was just to their south. To the west, separated from the foot of the hill by a tall stone wall, the Euphrates carved its way through the soft soil of Mesopotamia. To the north, Belisarius could see the ruins of the ancient royal palaces. Next to them—still standing, almost intact—was the famous Ishtar Gate.

Other than that—

The huge eastern portion of Babylon—almost three-quarters of its entire area—was now farmland, dotted here and there with orchards and livestock pens. And the hill which they sat upon had been the site of a thriving village. On their way up its slopes, they had passed the huts where peasants had succeeded, centuries later, to the former thrones of ancient monarchs.

The peasants were gone from the village, now. The huts had been sequestered for their use by Khusrau's bodyguard. But the farmland was still in use. Belisarius could see men and women at work in those fields, surrounded by Babylon's walls. He noted, with some interest, that none of those people even bothered to look up at the sound of the Malwa cannons. The siege had gone on for months now, and they had grown accustomed to it.

His attention came back to the hill itself. Perhaps half a mile in circumference, several hundred feet high—it was the most elevated spot in Babylon, which was why Khusrau had chosen to pitch his pavilion here—it seemed, to all outward appearances, a hill like many others.

Except—

"It's quite regular, now that I think about it," he mused. "The circumference is almost a perfect circle."

"Not quite," demurred Khusrau. The Emperor leaned forward and pointed quickly to the southwestern and southeastern portions of the hill base.

"If you study it very closely, you can still find traces of the original four corners. The same is true on the northeast and northwest side." Here he gestured with his head, flicking it back over his shoulders in either direction. "I had my architects examine the hill at great length. They even dug a tunnel deep into it from the north. Thirty yards in, they began encountering the baked brick walls of what seems to have been a gigantic ziggurat."

He leaned back, exuding satisfaction. "It's the Tower of Babel of ancient legend. I'm quite sure of it. Crumbling slowly, century after century. Covered with wind-blown soil, century after century. Until it is as you see today. This is not uncommon, by the way. There are many hills like this in Mesopotamia, which are all that's left of ancient ruins."

Belisarius eyed the Emperor with respect. "That must have been a lot of work."

Khusrau laughed.

"Not for me!"

The gaiety vanished. "I was curious, true. But I also needed projects to keep my men occupied. Once it became clear that the Malwa could not break the walls without long effort, and that we would not face starvation, tedium became our worst enemy. You know from experience, I'm sure, how dangerous it can be to have a garrison fretting away their time in idleness."

Belisarius nodded.

"Besides, I was making plans for the future. We are digging out great tunnels and rooms inside this hill. For food storage, and, I hope, ammunition. The food will not spoil quickly—the interior of the hill is much cooler than it is outside. And even if the Malwa eventually breach the outer fortifications, and can move their guns close enough to bombard Babylon's interior, a direct hit on the hill would pose no danger to gunpowder stored deep within its depths."

The Persian Emperor fell silent here, fixing Belisarius with his intense, intelligent eyes.

The Roman general met that gaze squarely. The moment had come, and it could be postponed no further.

"I have already argued in favor of giving gunpowder weapons to the Aryans, Emperor Khusrau. I have gone further, in fact. I have argued that we should give Persians the secret of their manufacture. But—"

"The Empress does not agree," finished Khusrau.

Belisarius fluttered his right hand, indicating that the matter was not quite so simple. "Yes—and no. She agrees that it would aid the war against Malwa. Aid it immensely, in fact. But she fears the repercussions in the future."

Khusrau nodded, calmly. The Emperor of Persia had no difficulty understanding the quandary which faced Rome's ruler. Someday, hopefully, Malwa would be gone. Rome and Persia, on the other hand—those two great Empires had clashed for centuries.

Aide's voice spoke. Belisarius could sense the agitation of the facets.

Stupid woman! She is so unreasonable about this!

The general had to physically restrain himself from making an actual calming gesture. Fortunately, from long experience, he had learned to keep his interchanges with Aide unnoticeable to the people around him. Still, it was distracting, and—

This is not the time for that, Aide!

The facets subsided, grudgingly. Belisarius brought his attention back to the Emperor. Khusrau was speaking.

"I understand her suspicions," he mused. "And, unfortunately, there is nothing I can say or do that would alleviate them. We can swear to a Hundred Years' Peace—we can swear to a *Thousand Years'* Peace, for that matter. But Rome and Persia will still be there, long after Theodora and I are gone. Who is to know if that peace would be kept? Or if Persian and Roman armies would not clash again, on the field of battle, armed this time with cannons and rockets?"

Aide could not control his frustration.

So what? The problem is now—with Malwa! If that problem is not solved, Rome and Persia *won't* be there a century from now to be worrying about this. And besides—

Be quiet! commanded Belisarius. It was one of the few times he had ever been abrupt with Aide. The facets immediately skittered in retreat.

Belisarius could sense the hurt feelings emanating from Aide. He was not concerned. They weren't hurt much. Aide reminded him, in that moment, of a child obeying an adult's command. Sulking, pouting; thinking dark thoughts about cosmic injustice.

But he needed to concentrate on the problem before him. And he already knew Aide's opinion. During the days at Constantinople when this very question had been thrashed out by Theodora and her advisers, Aide had practically overwhelmed him with visions drawn from the human future.

A thousand visions, it had seemed. The ones he remembered best had been the portraits of the British Raj's conquest of India. "Conquest" was not, even, the right term. The establishment of British rule would be a long and complex process which, in the end, would not primarily be decided by military factors. True, the British would have guns. But so, soon enough, would the Indian rajahs who opposed them. Yet those Indian monarchs would never match the superior political, social and economic organization of the British.

For the same reason, Aide had argued, giving the secret of gunpowder to Persia posed no long term threat to Rome. It was not weapons technology, by itself, which ever determined the balance of power between empires and nations. It was the entirety of the societies themselves.

Rome was a cosmopolitan empire, rich in traders, merchants and manufacturers. And, for all the elaborate pomp of its official aristocracy, it was a society open to talent. To a degree, at least.

Persia was none of those things. The Empire of the Aryans was a thoroughly feudal society. It had nothing like the population of Rome, and was positively dwarfed in terms of industry and manufacture. The military equality which Persia had been able to maintain vis-a-vis its western rival was entirely due to the ferocious skill of its heavy cavalry.

Introduce gunpowder into that mix, and the result would be the exact opposite of Theodora's worst fears. Within half a century, Aide had predicted, Persia would be no match for Rome at all.

Belisarius had agreed with Aide, then, and had argued that very case. Along with the more pressing point that the defeat of Malwa overrode all other concerns.

But Theodora—

He shook his head. "She is a suspicious woman, I'm afraid."

Khusrau chuckled. "Nonsense, Belisarius. *All* emperors are suspicious. Trust me on this point. I speak from experience. Even
your own brothers—"

He bit off the sentence. "We will discuss that problem later.
For now, I must officially request that the Roman Empire provide
us with a gunpowder capability."

The Emperor gestured to the south. "As you can see, we have
been able to hold them off so far with traditional weapons. But I
must do more, Belisarius." He clenched his fist. "I must *break*
this siege."

He sighed. "We made one attempt at a sally, early on. It was a
foolish gesture. I cursed myself for it, then, and damn myself for
it to this day. Our soldiers were butchered. As soon as they came
within range, the Malwa fired on us with those great siege guns.
Loaded, this time, not with great stone balls but a multitude of
pebbles and pieces of iron."

"Cannister," said Belisarius.

"They stood no chance at all. The slaughter was horrible, even
in the short time before I ordered the retreat."

He wiped his face, in a gesture combining sorrow with self-
reproach. But Khusrau was not deflected from his purpose.

"I *must* break the siege—within a year, no more. And for that
I need my own cannons. The Malwa siegeworks are not as strong
as the walls of Babylon, of course, but they are still strong enough
to repel a sally. Only cannons in the hands of my own troops could
shatter them enough for a successful counter-attack."

Belisarius frowned.

"Why are you so certain that you *must* break the siege—within
a year?"

He turned a bit in his chair, staring to the south.

"I do not think the Malwa will break into Babylon. Not unless
they bring twice the force to bear. And as powerful as they are,
the Malwa are not *that* powerful."

His eyes now scanned the flooded lowlands to the west. "It's
true that you will begin suffering from disease, soon enough, especially with the marshes. But disease usually strikes the besieger
worse than the besieged."

He turned back, glancing to the east—to the enormous spread
of agricultural land within the walls of Babylon—before adding,
"They will have to starve you out. And I think that would take

many years. Even if you can't grow everything you need right here in Babylon, you can import the rest. The city is not surrounded, after all. We marched in from the north with no opposition. I'm quite sure you can bring barges down the river."

Khusrau waved his hand.

"I'm not worried about *Babylon*, general. I will hold Babylon, of that I have no doubt. But what good will that do me if I lose the rest of Persia?"

Again, he sighed. "They have me penned here, along with most of my army. While they send out raiding parties to ravage Mesopotamia—"

He broke off, for a moment, barking a laugh.

"One less, now—thanks to you! But, still, there are others, destroying everything they can. And what is worse—" He half-rose from his throne, stretching his arm and pointing to the northeast. "They have that damned army marching into eastern Persia. Defeating every force I send against them!"

Belisarius cocked his eyebrow. Khusrau fell back in his throne, nodding bitterly.

"Oh, yes. They win every battle we fight."

For a moment, he scowled. The expression was more one of puzzlement than anger.

"Odd, really. I can't say I've been very impressed by the *quality* of the Malwa army. Not here in Mesopotamia, that's for sure. Immense numbers and gunpowder are what make them powerful. It's certainly not the skill of their commanders. But in the east, where they have little in the way of gunpowder weapons, their forces fight supremely well."

"I'm not surprised, Emperor. Those forces are mainly Rajput, under the command of Rana Sanga. I know him personally. The Rajputs are among the world's finest cavalry—Rana Sanga is certainly among the world's finest generals. And the Malwa who is in overall command of that army, Lord Damodara, is also said to be their best."

"Said? By whom?"

Belisarius smiled crookedly.

"By Rana Sanga, as it happens."

"Ah." The Persian Emperor gripped the armrests tightly. He took a deep breath.

"That explains much. It also illustrates my quandary. I can hold the Malwa here at Babylon, but only at the expense of giving up my freedom to maneuver. If I retreat from Babylon, there is nowhere else I can make a stand to prevent the Malwa from seizing all of Mesopotamia. But if I stay—"

"The Malwa will gut everything around you. And, eventually, take Fars and the entire plateau from the east."

Khusrau nodded. Then, noticing that the goblet which Belisarius was toying with in his hands was empty, began to gesture toward the servants standing a few yards away. But Belisarius waved down the offer.

"No more, please." He set the goblet down firmly on the small table next to his chair.

"I will send instructions to Rome, ordering that cannons be brought to Babylon. Along with a large supply of gunpowder. That much is in my authority. I will also—" here he blew out his cheeks "—strongly urge the Empress to give me permission to train your soldiers in their use."

Khusrau stroked his beard.

"Do you think she will agree?"

"Possibly. She will insist, of course, that the cannons and gunpowder remain under the control of Roman troops. Still, they will be here. And then—"

Khusrau's lips curled into a faint smile. "Under the control of Roman troops," he murmured. "Yes, yes. That has a nice—ah, *secure*—sound to it."

For a moment, a Persian Emperor and a Roman general stared at each other, in silent conspiracy.

Belisarius broke the silence with a little laugh. "She is not naive, Emperor. Far from it! She will understand the inevitable results, once lonely young Roman troops—" He broke off, gazing into the distance. "It's amazing," he mused, "how many beautiful women you Aryans seem to produce."

Khusrau grinned. "We are a comely folk. It cannot be denied." The grin faded. "But you think the Empress Regent will still agree?"

Belisarius nodded. "It will be enough, I think, if Theodora can tell her suspicions that she didn't actually *give* the secrets outright. At least the damned Persians had to sweat for them."

"In a manner of speaking," chuckled Khusrau. He planted his hands on his knees and rose to his feet. As always, the movement was quick and energetic.

"Speaking of beautiful Persian girls," he said, "I have ordered a reception tonight in my pavilion. In honor of Merena's daughter, now married to one of your top commanders. She accompanied him here, I understand."

Belisarius rose, nodding. "Yes, she did. She insisted on it, apparently, much to Agathius' surprise."

The Persian Emperor began leading the way toward the pavilion. He cocked his head.

"Was he angry? Did he really believe all those tales about obedient Persian wives?"

Belisarius laughed. "Actually, he was quite pleased. He's very taken by the girl, I think. It was not simply a marriage of ambition."

Khusrau smiled. "Good. That bodes well for the future. Most auspicious, that wedding—I would like to see more of them."

"So would I," agreed Belisarius.

As they walked slowly toward the pavilion, Khusrau's smile turned a bit sly. "That's part of the reason, of course—well, actually, it is *the* reason—that I commanded this little reception. Once my haughty nobles see the favor which their Emperor bestows on such marriages, they'll find a daughter or two to marry off to some promising Roman officer. Oh, be sure of it—be sure of it! We Aryans like to talk about the purity of our bloodlines, but we are by no means immune to ambition ourselves."

He paused for a moment, struck by the sunset. Belisarius joined him in that admiration.

"It is a beautiful world, in truth, for all the evil in it. Let us never lose sight of that, Belisarius, however dark the future may seem."

The Emperor shook his head, glancing at the pavilion. "Speaking of dark futures—and a near one, at that—my brother Ormazd will be at the reception." He scowled fiercely. "I will have to be polite to him, of course. In the end, he did not—quite!—disobey me."

Belisarius snorted. "It was amazing, actually, how quickly he made his decision. Once Baresmanas and I showed up at his camp outside Ctesiphon, with almost twenty thousand troops *and* the aura of our victory at Anatha. He did not even dawdle, during the march here."

"I should think not," snarled the Emperor. "He had a lot of face-saving to do."

The Roman general's smile faded. Belisarius turned to face Khusrau, his gaze intent. He said nothing. There was no need to explain—not with *this* emperor.

Khusrau sighed.

"Yes, Belisarius. I agree. You have my permission to implement your plan."

Belisarius hesitated. "Do you understand—did Baresmanas explain it to you *fully?* At the end—"

Khusrau made a short, chopping gesture with his hand. "Yes, I understand. I will have to trust you."

"I will give you my oath, if you so desire."

The Emperor laughed, now, quite cheerfully. "Nonsense! I don't want *your* oath. I want—those two bodyguards of yours? That is their permanent duty?"

Belisarius nodded.

Khusrau took the general by the arm and resumed their progress toward the pavilion. His stride was no longer the leisurely amble of a man enjoying the sunset. It was the determined pace of a decisive man, who had made up his mind.

"Good," he announced. "They will be at the reception, then. I will want to meet with them privately."

Belisarius' eyes widened.

"Privately? With Valentinian and Anastasius? Whatever for?"

"I want *their* oath. To keep you safe and alive, at all costs."

He eyed the general. "Even if that means binding you with ropes and hitting you over the head, to keep you from any more of the cavalry charges for which you have become quite famous. Among my dehgans, no less!"

The Emperor shook his head. "Any general who can impress *dehgans* with his heroism and disregard for personal safety needs close supervision. *Strict* supervision."

They were almost at the pavilion, now.

"That Anastasius fellow? Is he the gigantic one?"

Belisarius nodded. Khusrau stopped at the pavilion's entrance, eyeing the general up and down, much like a man estimating livestock.

"Yes, yes," he murmured. "He should have no difficulty. Even if it comes to shackling you."

He turned and strode within. And called over his shoulder: "I will have *his* oath on it!"

Anastasius kept a straight face. Valentinian didn't even try. "—in the name of God and his son Jesus Christ," they concluded simultaneously.

The solemnity of the occasion was undermined, of course, by the fact that Valentinian was grinning from ear to ear. But Khusrau did not seem dissatisfied with the result, judging from his own smiling face.

"Excellent," he pronounced.

Anastasius and Valentinian took that as their cue. A moment later, bowing respectfully, they backed through the silk curtains which separated Khusrau's private quarters from the main area of the imperial pavilion.

A little frown came to the Emperor's brow. He cocked his head toward Belisarius. "What did he say? The smaller one—he muttered something on the way out."

Belisarius smiled. "I think he said: 'God bless wise emperors.' But, perhaps I misunderstood. Perhaps he said—"

"Nonsense!" exclaimed Khusrau. "I'm quite sure that's what he said."

He took Belisarius by the arm and began leading him out. "Excellent fellow! Marvelous, marvelous! Even if he does look like a vicious weasel."

Belisarius kept his own counsel. Aide did not.

I agree. Excellent fellow. And Anastasius!

Try to be philosophical about the whole thing, Belisarius. Perhaps you could ask Anastasius to quote some appropriate words from Marcus Aurelius, or—

What was that? You muttered something in your mind.

Chapter 26

THE EUPHRATES

"And the charges are laid?" asked Belisarius. "*All* of them?"

Seeing the hesitation on Basil's face, the general sighed.

"Don't tell me. You laid as many as you could, using the captured Malwa gunpowder. *But you didn't use any of our own.*"

Basil nodded. His eyes avoided the general's.

Belisarius restrained his angry outburst. He reminded himself, firmly, that he had chosen Basil to command the katyusha rocket force because the man was one of the few Thracian cataphracts who had a liking and affinity for the new weapons. It was hardly surprising, therefore, that he would be unwilling to dismantle them.

"Finish the job, Basil," he rasped. "I don't care if you have to use every single pound of gunpowder in our supply train—even if that includes emptying the katyusha rockets themselves. *Finish the job.*"

Basil opened his mouth; closed it.

"Yes, sir," he said glumly.

Belisarius resumed his study of the work which Basil had overseen in his absence. After a minute or so, he found that his ill-temper with the man had quite vanished. In truth—except for his understandable reluctance to disarm his cherished rockets—Basil had done an excellent job.

There was not much left, now, of the great dam which had formerly sealed off the Nehar Malka from the Euphrates. With the exception of a thin wall barely strong enough to withstand the river's pressure, the vast pile of stones had been removed and mounded up on the north bank of the canal. Already, a thin trickle of water was seeping through, creating a small creek in what had been the dry bed of the former Royal Canal.

Back-breaking work, that must have been, he thought. Most of it, of course, was done by the Kushan captives.

He cocked his head at Basil.

"Did they complain? The Kushans, I mean."

Basil shook his head. "Never the once. They didn't even try to shirk the work. Not much, anyway—no more than our own boys did."

Belisarius grunted with satisfaction. Here, at least, Basil had apparently followed his instructions to the letter.

"What rotation did you use? Three and one?"

"For the first week," was Basil's reply. "After that I went to one and one."

Belisarius' eyes widened.

"Wasn't that a bit—"

"Risky? I don't think so, general."

The katyusha commander glanced at Belisarius, gauging his temper, before adding:

"I thought about the way you handled their surrender, sir. Then, after the first week, I talked to Vasudeva. He gave me his oath that the Kushans would not try an uprising." The cataphract smiled. "Actually, it was he who insisted that we maintain half our troops on guard duty while the other half pitched into the work. After he gave me his oath, I was going to just keep a token force on patrol. But Vasudeva—"

Belisarius laughed, and clapped his hands. "He said it would be too insulting!"

Basil nodded.

Belisarius' usual good humor had completely returned. He placed an approving hand on the cataphract's shoulder. "Nice work, Basil."

Again, Basil eyed the general, gauging his mood. He opened his mouth to speak, but Belisarius cut him off with a shake of the head. Not an angry headshake; but a firm one, nonetheless.

"No, Basil. I won't reconsider. It may well be that the Malwa gunpowder alone would do the trick, but I'm not going to take the chance. I want that dam to rupture instantly—and completely."

He turned to face his subordinate squarely.

"Think it through, Basil. If the charges are insufficient, and we wind up with a half-demolished dam—what then? You know as well as I do that it would be a nightmare to set new charges, with half the river pouring through. Take days, probably—not to mention the lives it would cost. In the meantime, the Malwa down at Babylon would have those same days to try and salvage their fleet. If the Euphrates drops slowly, they could probably get most of their ships downriver to safety before they ground. They could certainly get the ships far enough from Babylon that Khusrau couldn't strike at them."

He didn't raise his voice, not in the least, but his tone was like iron:

"*I want that fleet grounded instantly, Basil.* I want the Euphrates to drop so fast that the Malwa are caught completely off-guard."

Basil took a deep breath. Nodded.

Again, Belisarius clapped him on the shoulder.

"Besides, man—cheer up. We should be getting a new supply of gunpowder and rockets from Callinicum. Good Roman powder and rockets, too, not that Malwa crap. A *big* supply. I sent orders calling for every pound of gunpowder available. We've got more demolition work ahead of us. Lots more."

Basil grimaced.

Belisarius, understanding that grimace, made a little mental wince of his own.

I hope. If the usual screw-ups with logistics aren't worse than normal.

But there was no point in brooding on that matter, so he changed the subject.

"What's your opinion on security?" he asked.

Basil's face cleared up instantly.

"It's beautiful, sir. Between Abbu and our scouts, and Kurush and his Persians, I don't think a lizard could get within ten miles of here without being spotted."

From their vantage point on top of what remained of the ancient dam, the cataphract pointed down at the Nehar Malka. "The Malwa have no idea what we're doing here. I'm sure of it. The one thing I was worried about was that the Kushans might try to sneak out a few of their men to warn the Malwa down at Babylon. No way to do that in the daytime, of course, but I had Abbu maintain full patrols at night and he swears—*swears*—that no Kushan ever tried to—"

"No," interrupted Belisarius, shaking his head firmly. "That wouldn't—how can I say it?—that wouldn't be something the Kushans would do."

Basil's brow creased in a frown. "Why not? Vasudeva's oath was that they wouldn't try a *rebellion*—or a mass breakout. He never swore that he wouldn't send a few men to report back."

Belisarius looked away. It was his turn to hesitate, now. He was as certain of his understanding of the Kushans as he was of anything in the world, but to explain it to Basil would require—

Aide broke through the quandary.

Tell him.

Belisarius almost started.

You are sure of this, Aide?

Tell him. As much, at least, as you need to. It will not matter, Belisarius. Even if he talks, so what? By now, Link will have deduced my presence in this world. At the very least, it will do so very soon. Much sooner than any loose talk among Roman troops could ever find its way to the ears of Malwa spies. Secrecy about me is not so important, anymore. Not as important, certainly, as the trust of your subordinate officers.

Belisarius sighed—with immense relief. He had always believed that his success as a general, as much as anything, rested on his ability to build a team around him. The need to keep Aide's presence a secret had cut across his most basic nature and instincts as a leader.

He was glad to be done with it.

Of course, came the firm thought, **that doesn't mean you have to turn into a babbling babe.**

Belisarius, smiling, turned back to the cataphract standing next to him. "I am—sometimes—blessed with visions of the future, Basil."

The Thracian soldier's eyes widened. But not much, Belisarius noted.

"You are not surprised?"

Basil shrugged. "No, sir. Not really. Nobody talks, mind you. But I'm not stupid. I've noticed how Maurice—and Valentinian and Anastasius, for that matter—get very close-mouthed about certain things. Like exactly how you got the secret of gunpowder from the Malwa—and somehow managed to get it to Antonina in time for her to build a whole secret little army in Syria before you even got back. And exactly what happened—or didn't happen—in India. And exactly how it was that you were so sure that the Malwa would be our enemy, when nobody else ever gave India more than two thoughts. And why did Michael of Macedonia—*Michael of Macedonia?*—wind up such a close friend of a general? And just exactly—"

Belisarius held up his hand, laughing. "Enough!"

He glanced around. He and Basil were quite alone on top of the dam. The nearest Roman soldiers were the small cavalry escort waiting patiently at its base. No Persians could be seen in the vicinity—and there was nowhere to hide, anyway, except in the reeds which lined the Euphrates. The nearest clump of such reeds was thirty yards away. Much too distant for any eyes to see the small thing which Belisarius drew out of a pouch handing from his neck.

He cupped Aide in his hands, sheltered from sight. Basil leaned over, awestruck.

"Michael of Macedonia brought this to me," said Belisarius softly. "Over three years ago, now. He calls it the Talisman of God."

"It is so beautiful," whispered Basil. "I've never seen anything so wondrous."

"It is a marvel. It is a messenger from the future, who came to warn us of the Malwa danger. It did so by giving me a vision of the future which Malwa would bring to the world."

He paused, letting Basil absorb the shimmering glory of the facets. "Later, I will tell you all of what I saw, in that future. Indeed—"

He hesitated. Aide spoke.

Yes. It is time.

"I will tell all of you. All of the army commanders. It is time, now. But, for the moment—"

He spoke gently, then, for a few minutes. Telling the cataphract Basil of the vision he had received, once, of a princess held in captivity by the Malwa. Held for them, by a Kushan vassal named Kungas. And he told how, in that future, the Kushan named Kungas had held his tongue when a Malwa lord had entered his chamber to take possession of his new concubine. Had not warned the great lord that his new concubine was an assassin. And how that lord had died, in that future, because a Kushan had his own harsh concept of honor.

And then he told of how, in the future which Belisarius had created, that same Kushan had held his tongue, once again. Held it, and said nothing to his Malwa masters, when he realized that the Romans were smuggling the girl out of captivity.

"And where is he today, this Kungas?" asked Basil.

Belisarius slipped Aide back into his pouch.

"Today, the Kushan named Kungas—along with all of his men—are the personal bodyguard of the *Empress* Shakuntala. The heir of Satavahana. Rightful ruler of great Andhra."

Basil looked up, startled. His eyes flashed south, looking toward the distant encampment of the Kushan captives.

"You think—?"

Belisarius shrugged.

"Who knows? Kungas is an unusual man. But in some things, I believe all Kushans are much alike. They have their own notions of loyalty, and duty. They are Malwa vassals, and have served them faithfully. But I do not think they bear any great love for their masters. None at all, in fact."

He turned away, and began climbing down the dam.

"Most of all," he added, over his shoulder, "they have their own peculiar sense of humor. Very wry. Rather on the grim side, too. But they cherish it quite deeply."

At the bottom of the slope, he waited for Basil to join him. Once he had done so, Belisarius grinned.

"I'm counting on that sense of humor, you see. The Kushans wouldn't warn the Malwa of what we're doing. God, no—it would spoil a great joke."

That night, in the gloom of his little tent, Vasudeva leaned over and filled Belisarius' cup.

"Good wine," he said. "Not enough, of course. The Persians are stingy. But—good. Good."

He and Belisarius drained their cups. Vasudeva smiled.

"We like to gamble, you know. So we have a great bet going. All the Kushans have taken sides." He shrugged modestly. "We have not much to wager, of course, being war captives. But it is always the spirit of a wager which is exciting, not the stakes."

He refilled Belisarius' cup. Again, he and the general drained their wine. When they lowered their cups, Belisarius stated:

"You are wagering over whether I will succeed. In my plan to drain the Euphrates dry and leave the Malwa stranded at Babylon without supplies."

Vasudeva sneered. Waved his hand in a curt, dismissive little gesture. "Bah! What Kushan would be so stupid as to bet on *that*?"

He refilled the cups, again. Brought his own to his lips; but, before, drinking, added with a little smile: "No, no, Belisarius. We are betting on what you will do *afterward*."

Belisarius managed to drain his cup without choking. Vasudeva's smile became a grin.

"Oh, yes," murmured the Kushan commander. "*That's* the real question."

He drained his own cup.

Vasudeva held up the amphora, in a questioning gesture. Belisarius shook his head, placing his hand over his cup.

"No, thank you. I've had enough. Tomorrow will be a busy day."

As he stoppered the wine jug, Vasudeva grimaced. "Please! We will be doing most of the busy-ness. And in that miserable sun!"

Belisarius rose, stooping in the low shelter provided by the simple tent. Vasudeva rose with him. Much shorter, he did not need to stoop.

The Kushan's little smile returned. "Still—that's the way it is. Really good jokes always take a lot of work."

Outside the tent, in the quiet air of the Kushan encampment, Valentinian and Anastasius were waiting with the horses. Quickly, Belisarius mounted.

Vasudeva had come out of his tent to see the Roman general off. From other tents nearby, Belisarius could see other Kushans watching. For a moment, he and the Kushan commander stared at each other.

"Why did you come tonight, Belisarius?" asked Vasudeva suddenly. "You asked me nothing."

The general smiled, very crookedly. "There was no need, Vasudeva. I simply wanted to know if Kushans still had their sense of humor."

Vasudeva did not match that smile with one of his own. In the moonlit darkness, his hard face grew harder still.

"It is all that is left to us, Roman. When men have little, they keep what they have in a tight fist."

Belisarius nodded. He clucked his horse into motion. Valentinian and Anastasius followed on their own mounts, trailing a few yards behind.

"Yes, they do," he murmured softly to himself. "Yes, they do. Until finally, when they have nothing left, they realize—" His words trailed into a mutter.

"What did he say?" whispered Anastasius, leaning over his saddle.

Valentinian's face was sour. "He said that damned stupid business about only the soul mattering, in the end."

"Quite right," said Anastasius approvingly. Then, spotting Valentinian's expression, the giant added:

"You know, if you ever get tired of being a soldier, I'm sure you could make a good living as a miracle worker. Turning wine into vinegar."

Valentinian began muttering, now, but Anastasius ignored him blithely.

"I thought it was a good joke," he said.

Mutter, mutter, mutter.

"A sense of humor's very important, Valentinian."

Mutter, mutter, mutter.

"Wine into vinegar. Yes, yes. And then—! The possibilities are endless! Turn fresh milk sour. Make puppies grim. Kittens, indolent. Oh, yes! Valentinian of Thrace, they'll be calling you. The miracle worker! Everybody'll avoid you like the plague, of course. Probably be entire villages chasing you with stones, even. But you'll be famous! I'll be able to say: 'I knew him when he was just a simple nasty ill-tempered disgruntled soldier.' Oh, yes! I'll be able—"

Mutter, mutter, mutter.

Early the next morning, construction began on the second phase of Belisarius' plan. The Roman soldiers played more of a role, now, than they had earlier. Undermining the old canal, except for the work of laying the charges, had been simple and uncomplicated work. Brutal work, of course—hauling an enormous quantity of stones out of a canal bed. But simple.

This new project was not.

Belisarius oversaw the work from a tower which his troops erected on the left bank of the Euphrates, just below the place where the Nehar Malka branched off to the east. The tower was sturdy, but otherwise crude—nothing more than a twenty-foot-high wooden framework, which supported a small platform at the top. The platform was six feet square, surrounded by a low railing, and sheltered from the sun by a canopy. Access to it was by means of a ladder built directly onto the framework.

There was only room on that platform to fit three or four men comfortably. Belisarius and Baresmanas, who occupied the platform alone that first day, had ample room.

The Roman general drew the sahrdaran's attention to the work below.

"They're about to place the first pontoon."

Baresmanas leaned over the rail. Below, he could see Roman soldiers guiding a small barge down the Euphrates. The barge was the standard type of rivercraft used in Mesopotamia and throughout the region—what Egyptians called a *skaphe*. It was fifty feet long by sixteen feet wide, with a prow so blunt it was almost shaped like the stern. The craft could be either rowed or sailed. The only thing unusual about this barge was that the mast had been braced and the sails were made of wicker—useless for catching the wind, but excellent for securing the baskets of stones which would eventually be laid against them.

A squad of soldiers were on the barge itself, shouting orders to the mass of soldiers who were doing the actual work of placing the barge. Many of those soldiers were on the riverbank, holding onto the barge by means of long ropes. Others were on the two barges which were serving as tugs—one directly behind, helping to hold the barge against the sluggish current; the other in mid-river, counteracting with its own ropes the pull of the soldiers on land.

Surprisingly quickly, the barge was brought into location about thirty yards from the riverbank. The barge was facing upstream, its bow heading into the current. The craft was riding very low in the water. From their vantage point, Belisarius and Baresmanas could see the stones in the hull which weighted down the craft to the point where it was almost already submerged.

The soldier in charge looked up at Belisarius. The general waved his hand, indicating that he was satisfied with the positioning. Immediately, two of the soldiers on the barge clambered down into the hull. Belisarius and Baresmanas could hear the hammering sounds as the soldiers knocked loose the scuttling pins.

A minute or so later the soldiers reappeared. The entire squad, except for their commander, clambered aboard a small boat tied alongside the barge. They attached the boat to a rope from the tub directly astern, and then released the rest of the ropes coming from that tug. The barge was now settling below the river's surface.

The squad commander quickly climbed up a ladder to the top of the barge's mast. There he remained, watching carefully as the barge sank into the river, ready to issue commands if the current moved it out of location. Not until the water was lapping at his feet did the squad commander climb into the small boat alongside. A moment later, the only thing visible was the upper three feet of the mast. The barge was securely grounded on the riverbed.

"That's the first one," announced Belisarius. "Well done, that was."

Already, another barge was being jockeyed into position next to the first. Baresmanas, watching, was struck by the speed with which the Romans scuttled that craft next to the first, further into the river's main course. And the next. And the next.

The sahrdaran said nothing, but he was deeply impressed. Persians had often matched Roman armies on the battlefield—outmatched them, as often as not. But no people on the face of the earth had that uncanny Roman skill with field fortifications and combat engineering.

"Will you have enough barges?" he asked, toward the end of the day. By then, eleven pontoons had been sunk.

Belisarius shrugged.

"I think so. The supplies are coming from Callinicum steadily now. Since there's nothing to send back on those barges, I can use almost all of them for pontoons."

He smiled, remembering the look of relief on Basil's face when the supply barges which had arrived the day before proved to be carrying an ample supply of gunpowder to refurbish his rocket force. Refurbish it—and more. New stocks of rockets had also arrived, along with three more katyushas and the crews to man them.

Belisarius glanced toward the west. The sun was almost touching the horizon. He decided there wouldn't be enough daylight to position another pontoon, and he didn't want to risk his men's lives in a night operation unless it was critical. For all the relaxed ease with which his soldiers went about their task, it was dangerous work.

So he leaned over the rail and shouted the order to quit for the day. His squad commanders, familiar with their general's attitudes, were obviously anticipating the order. The oncoming barge was gently grounded on the riverbank, where it could be easily pushed off the next morning.

On the third day, Belisarius shifted his operations to the other side of the river, where a similar command tower had been erected. While Maurice oversaw the work on the left bank, Belisarius started the process of extending a line of pontoons from the west.

By the fifth day, the operation was in full swing. The Euphrates, at that point, was a shallow but very broad river—almost a mile wide. Sinking twenty to twenty-five pontoons a day, the Roman engineers were building their dam at the rate which would, theoretically, bridge the river within a fortnight.

Of course, the rate at which the pontoons were sunk began slowing. As the dam took shape, the current became faster. And, what was worse, turbulent.

Two men were killed on the eighth day. After knocking loose the scuttling pins, they failed to emerge from the hold quickly enough. What happened? No-one knew, or ever would. Probably one of them had slipped, and the other had gone to his aid. But there was no time, now, for anything but haste. The river which poured into the settling hull was not the sluggish stream it had been. The water hammered into the barge and drove it down like a pile driver. Days later, one of the bodies floated loose and was salvaged downstream.

By the end of the second week, the Euphrates was a snarling beast. As the Roman engineers extended the two lines of pontoons closer and closer to each other, the center of the river became a thundering torrent of water. The rest was not much better. As the water level rose behind the dam, the entire Euphrates became a cataract, pouring over the line of pontoons all across its width.

Casualties were now occurring daily—a matter of broken limbs and crushed fingers, for the most part, but there were fatalities also. On the twelfth day, the entire crew of a pontoon perished when they lost control of the barge just at the point when they were preparing to scuttle it. The heavily weighted craft was swept into the narrow channel in the center of the river. Before it was halfway through, the barge disintegrated, spilling its men into the torrent. Most of them were dead by the time their bodies were recovered. One man survived for half a day, his skull shattered and pulpy, before he finally expired.

The Roman troops had the worst of it, since they were doing the most dangerous part of the job, but those were not happy days for the Kushans either. Behind the Roman engineers extending the pontoons, the Kushans were set to work building the dam higher. Using their own barges, the captives hauled baskets full of stones and dropped them onto the submerged pontoons. The current piled the heavy baskets up against the wicker "sails." The strain on those sunken masts and spars would probably have broken some of them, except that the Romans had lashed the masts together as they extended the line of pontoons.

Most of the Kushans, however, were engaged elsewhere. The stones used to bolster the dam had to be hauled out of the surrounding landscape. Fortunately, there were many stones to be found within a mile of the river. Mesopotamia had been farmed for millennia, but the topsoil was constantly being blown away and annual plowing brought up another layer of stones. These stones, as the centuries passed, were piled at the center or edges of fields. So there was no lack of stones, and none of them had to be dug up out of the soil. But it was still hard work for the Kushans, loading sledges and dragging them to the river.

At first, the Kushans were disgruntled.

Crazy Roman!

Why doesn't the stupid bastard use the stones we already dug out of the Nehar Malka? Look! There's a giant pile of the things—not three hundred yards away!

Whoever made this idiot a general, anyway?

As the days passed, however, the Kushans began to realize that the cretin Roman general apparently had other plans for those stones. What those plans were, the Kushans did not know. They were no longer permitted in the vicinity of the Nehar Malka. But, from a distance, they could catch glimpses of Roman engineers working around the enormous mound of rocks which the Kushans had piled on the north bank of the Nehar Malka. Digging tunnels, so it appeared. And they noted that the men involved in that work were the same Romans who manned the rocket chariots. Gunpowder experts.

The betting among the Kushan captives intensified.

Kurush and his Persian soldiers were not involved in any of this work. Theirs was the task of ensuring the work-site's security. Every day, Kurush and his ten thousand Persian cavalrymen patrolled the region, extending their skirmishers to a distance of thirty miles in every direction. Abbu and the Arab scouts accompanied them in this work, as did a small number of the Roman troops. On a rotating basis, two battalions of Belisarius' soldiers—one cavalry, one infantry—were assigned each day to assist the Persians. In truth, the assignment was more in the way of a relief than anything else. After the back-breaking and risky work of building the dam, every Roman soldier looked forward to a day spent in a leisurely march.

Finally, on the nineteenth day, the last pontoon was maneuvered into place and scuttled. The Romans took four days well-deserved rest, while the Kushans finished the job of bolstering the pontoons with baskets of stones.

It was done. Twenty-three days' work had turned that strip of the Euphrates into a waterfall. A low waterfall, to be sure. But it was impressive, nonetheless.

The Roman troops and the Kushan captives spent the twenty-fourth day in a cheerful celebration, lining the banks and getting drunk while they admired the raging cataract which they had built. At Belisarius' order, the wine ration was very generous—as much for the Kushans as the Romans. A Malwa officer, had there been one present to notice, would have been outraged at the free and easy fraternization between captives and captors.

Belisarius and his top officers, however, did not join in the revelry. They spent that entire day in the general's command tent. The first two hours of that day were taken up with Belisarius' immediate plans.

The rest was given to awe, and mystery, and wonder.

As he had promised Basil, Belisarius brought his entire command into the secret. He told them the secret, first, using his own words. Then, when he was done, brought forth the Talisman of God.

Aide was prepared. The coruscating colors which filled the command tent were so dazzling that they caused the leather walls to glow.

Roman soldiers who saw, from outside the tent, whispered among themselves. *Witchcraft*, muttered a few. But most simply shrugged the thing off. Belisarius was—unique. A blessed man. Hadn't Michael of Macedonia himself said so?

So why shouldn't his tent glow in daylight?

Kushans also noticed, and discussed the matter. Here, the opinion was unanimous.

Sorcery. The Roman general was a witch. It was obvious. Obvious.

The wagering became feverish.

When evening fell, Belisarius' officers filed quietly out of his tent. None of them said a word, except Agathias. As the commander of the Greek cataphracts passed by Belisarius, he whispered: "We will not fail you, general. This I swear."

Belisarius inclined his head. A moment later, only Maurice was left in the tent.

"When?" asked the Thracian chiliarch.

"How soon can you reach Babylon? A week?"

"Be serious," growled Maurice. "Do I look like a pewling babe?" Belisarius smiled.

"Four days," grunted Maurice. "Three to get there, and a day for Khusrau to make ready."

"Five days," countered Belisarius. "Khusrau should be ready, but an extra day may help. Besides, you never know—you might fall off your horse."

Maurice disdained any reply.

Early the next morning, Maurice left. He was accompanied by a hundred of his Thracian cataphracts as well as a squad of Arab scouts.

At the same time, one of Kurush's top officers—Merena himself, in fact—led a similar expedition to Ctesiphon. Their purpose was to bring warning to the residents of the capital.

The next four days, Belisarius spent overseeing the final preparations at the Nehar Malka. None of the Roman troops except Basil and his men were engaged in this work, however, so they spent those days resting.

By late afternoon of the fifth day, the entire allied force was thronging the banks of the Euphrates. Over twenty thousand men—Romans, Persians, Kushan captives—were jostling each other for a vantage point. Belisarius had to use his bucellarii to keep the onlookers from piling too close to the Nehar Malka.

The general himself was standing atop the command tower. He was joined there by Baresmanas and Kurush.

"You should not have made the announcement," fretted Kurush. "It was impossible to keep the security patrols out beyond noon."

Belisarius shrugged.

"And so? By the time a spy reaches the Malwa with the news, they will know already."

He leaned over the rail. Below him, standing at the base of the tower, Basil looked up. The katyusha commander held a burning slowmatch in his hand.

Belisarius began to give the order to light the fuse. Then, hesitated.

"New times," he murmured. "New times need new traditions. 'Light the fuse' just won't do."

He sent a thought inward.

Aide?

The reply came instantly.

Fire in the hole.

Belisarius grinned. Leaned over.

"Fire in the hole!"

Basil needed no translation. A moment later, the fuse was burning. As it hissed its furious way toward the last barrier across the Nehar Malka, Basil began capering like a child.

"I like that! I like that!" he cried. *"Fire in the hole!"*

The cry was taken up by others. Within three minutes, the entire army was chanting the words. Even the Kushans, in their newly-learned and broken Greek.

"FIRE IN THE HOLE! FIRE IN THE HOLE!"

The fuse reached its destination.

There was fire in the hole.

Chapter 27

The demolition had been well-planned. So much was immediately obvious. Guided by Aide, Belisarius and Basil had emplaced the charges in the optimum locations to do the job.

Across most of its width, the lower bank of the dam blew sidewise, clearing an instant path for the pent-up energy of the Euphrates. The great river, now released, literally burst into the new channel opened for it. Raging like a bull, the torrent charged down the long-dry Nehar Malka, scouring it deeper and wider as it went.

But Belisarius was unable to appreciate the sight. As so often happens in life, practice subverted theory. The charges had been perfectly placed, true. And then, doubled beyond Aide's instructions; and then, doubled again.

Aide had complained, of course. Had warned, cautioned, chastened, chastised; been driven, in fact, into its own crystalline version of a gibbering fit.

To no avail. With the simple logic of men whose familiarity with gunpowder was still primitive, Belisarius and Basil had both insisted that more was vastly preferable than enough. Better to make sure the job was done, after all, than to risk a feeble half-result through cringing niggardliness.

Applied to the task of splitting a log with an axe, such logic simply results in unnecessary exertion. Applied to the task of demolishing a dam with gunpowder, however—

I told you so, groused Aide, as Belisarius watched the *top* layers of the dam sailing into the sky. Hundreds upon hundreds of rocks and boulders—tons and tons of stony projectiles—soaring every which way.

Not all of those missiles, of course, were heading for the tower where Belisarius stood. It just seemed that way.

Baresmanas and Kurush scrambled down the ladder first. The Roman general was halfway down—

Stupid humans.

—when the first rocks began pelting into the tower. By the time he was three-fourths down—

Protoplasmic idiots.

—covered, now, with wood splinters—

Glorified monkeys.

—the tower collapsed completely.

That probably saved his life, as well as those of Baresmanas and Kurush—and Basil, who had also instinctively sought shelter beneath the tower. The half-shattered platform hammered Belisarius and the other three men into the ground, battering them almost senseless. Thereafter, however, it acted as a sort of huge shield, sheltering them—in a manner of speaking—from the hail of rocks which would otherwise have turned two Roman officers and two Persian noblemen into so much undifferentiated pulp.

At the time, Belisarius found little comfort in the fact. The platform lying on him did not deflect the blows, in the manner of a true shield, so much as it simply spread the shock across his entire body. He was not pulped, therefore. Amazingly, none of his bones were even broken. But he did undergo a version of being pounded into flatcake, except that flatcakes do not suffer the added indignity of being lectured throughout the experience.

Crazy fucking Thracian.

Whoever made you a general, anyway?

It's amazing you even made it out of the womb, as stupid as you are. I'm surprised you didn't insist on finding your own way out. God forbid you should listen to your mother.

Crazy fucking Thracian.

Whoever—

And so on, and so forth.

It took his soldiers an hour to dig Belisarius and the others out, after the rocks stopped falling. The digging itself, actually, took

only a few minutes. The delay was caused by the fact that his men
had fled a full half mile away after the barrage started.

His first, semiconscious, croaking words:

"Did it work? I couldn't see."

His ensuing croaks, after being assured of full success in the
project:

"Next time. Smaller charges."

"Much smaller," croaked Basil.

"Crazy fucking Romans," croaked Baresmanas.

"Whoever put him in charge?" croaked Kurush.

Others, also, failed to heed warnings. When Merena arrived at
Ctesiphon to warn the governor of the oncoming tidal wave, the
man responded with derision. Partly, that was due to his personality. Arrogant by nature, his recent naming to the post of *shahrab*
of the Persian Empire's capital city had swelled his head even
further. In the main, however, his attitude was determined by
politics. The shahrab of Ctesiphon—Shiroe was his name—was
allied with Ormazd's faction. The appearance before him of an
officer of Emperor Khusrau's most ferociously-loyal follower, Baresmanas, seemed to him a perfect opportunity to score a political
point. So, Shiroe responded to Merena's warning with jocular
remarks on lunacy, embellished with denunciations of Romans and
those Persians besotted with them, and concluding with a not-so-
veiled thrust on the subject of miscegenation.

Merena's men had to restrain him.

After the unfortunate session, once Merena had calmed down
enough to think clearly, he ordered his men to take informal and
unofficial warnings to the boatmen plying their trade on the Tigris.
As best they could, given their relatively small numbers, his soldiers
tried to warn the city's fishermen and boat captains.

Approximately half of the men they were able to speak to heeded
their warnings. The other half—as well as all the men they were
unable to reach in time—did not.

When the tidal wave arrived, two days later, the destruction of
property was immense. Few lives were lost, however. By the time
the newly-released waters of the Euphrates reached Ctesiphon,
they took the form of a sudden five-foot high surge in elevation
rather than an actual wall of water. Most of the men caught in the
river had time to scramble or swim to safety. But their boats,

as well as a multitude of shore-lining structures, were pounded into splinters.

Shiroe's prestige plummeted, and, with it, the allegiance of most of his military retainers. The huge mob of enraged and impoverished boatmen whom Merena and his soldiers led to the shahrab's palace poured over the few guards still willing to defend their lord. Shiroe was dragged out, weighted down with chains, and pitched into the newly-risen Tigris. In those changed and raging waters, he vanished without a trace.

In Babylon, on the other hand, everything went smoothly and according to plan. Khusrau had been preparing for this moment for weeks. The two days' warning which Maurice gave him were almost unnecessary.

Belisarius had deliberately blown the dam in the late afternoon, calculating that the effects of the river's diversion would thereby strike Babylon the following morning. That would give Emperor Khus-rau a full day in which to take advantage of the new situation.

His calculations, of course, were extremely crude—simply an estimate of the river's current divided into an estimate of the distance between the Nehar Malka and Babylon. In the event, Belisarius' guess was off by several hours. He had failed to make sufficient allowance for the fact that the current would ebb once the built-up pressure of the backwater dropped. So it was not until noon of the next day that the effects of his work made themselves felt.

The difference was moot. The Persian Emperor's confidence in the Roman general was so great that he had decided to launch the attack at daybreak, whether or not the river level had dropped. It was a wise decision. As always, getting a major assault underway took more time than planned. Much more time, in this instance. The Persian troops, lacking the Roman expertise in engineering fieldcraft, required several hours to bring into position and ready the improvised pontoons which they would use to cross the Euphrates.

By then, alerted by the slowly-unfolding work of Khusrau's engineers, the Malwa had realized that the Persians were planning a sally across the Euphrates. But the foreknowledge did them no good at all.

Quite the contrary. Lord Jivita, the Malwa high commander, thought the Persian project was absurd.

"What is the point of this?" he demanded, watching the Persian preparations from his own command tower.

None of the half-dozen officers standing there with him made any reply. The question was clearly rhetorical—as were most of Jivita's queries. The high commander's aides had long since learned that Jivita did not look kindly upon subordinates who provided their own answers to his questions.

Jivita pointed to the Persian troops massing on the left bank of the river, just below the great western wall of Babylon.

"Madness," he decreed. "Even if they succeed in crossing, what is there for them to do? On the *western* side of the Euphrates?"

He swept his arm. The gesture was simultaneously grandiose and dismissive.

"There is nothing on that side, except marshes and desert."

He slapped his hands together.

"No matter! They will not cross in any event. I see the opportunity here for a great victory."

He turned to one of his officers, the subordinate encharged with the Malwa's fleet of war galleys.

"Jayanaga! Send the entire flotilla forward! We will butcher the Persians as they try to cross!"

With a fierce glower: "Make sure your galleys do not fire their rockets until the enemy's lead elements are almost across. I want to make sure we catch as many of them as possible on their pitiful pontoons. Do you understand?"

Jayanaga nodded, and immediately left.

Lord Jivita turned back to his examination of the enemy. Again, he clapped his hands with satisfaction.

"We will butcher them! Butcher them!"

The Malwa flotilla—forty-two galleys, in all—was almost within rocket range of the pontoon bridge when the captain of the lead ship realized that something was wrong.

His first assumption, however, was far off the mark. He turned to the oarmaster.

"Why have you slowed the tempo?" he demanded.

The oarmaster immediately shook his head, pointing to the two men pounding on kettledrums.

"I didn't! Listen! They're beating the right tempo!"

The captain's scowl deepened. Before the oarmaster had even finished speaking, the captain realized that he was right. Still—

The ship was slowing.

No! It was going backward!

"Look!" cried one of the other officers, pointing to the near bank. "The river's dropping!"

"*What?* Impossible! Not that fast!"

The captain leaned over the railing, studying the shore. Within seconds, his face paled.

"They've diverted the river upstream," he whispered. "It must be. Nothing else could—"

He broke off, his attention drawn by the sound of hooves pounding on wooden planks. *Lots* of hooves. Upstream, he could see Persian cavalry racing across the pontoon bridge. Dozens—hundreds—*thousands*—of Persian lancers and armored archers were streaming over to the west bank of the Euphrates.

Like his commander, Lord Jivita, the galley captain had been puzzled by the Persian sally. There had seemed no purpose for the enemy to cross the Euphrates, especially when the crossing itself would expose the Persians to withering rocket fire from the Malwa galleys. Who was there to fight, on that side of the river? The great mass of the Malwa army was concentrated on the east bank, south of Babylon's fortifications.

Now he understood. The captain was a quick-thinking man.

"They knew about it ahead of time," he hissed. "They're going to burn the supply ships."

He twisted, staring back at the huge mass of supply barges some half mile south. Already, he could see the unwieldy craft yawing out of control, driven by the rapidly ebbing waters of the river. Within a minute, he knew, they would start grounding. Helpless targets.

Especially helpless when there would be no war galleys to protect them. His own flotilla would be grounded also—not as quickly, for they had a much shallower draft—unless—

"Row toward the center of the river!" he roared. "Signal the other ships to do likewise!"

Immediately, the drums began beating a new rhythm. The Malwa had no sophisticated signaling system for controlling their fleet. But the captain of the lead galley also served as the commodore of the flotilla. The message of the drums was simple:

Do as I do.

But it was already too late. The drums had barely begun beating when the flotilla commander saw the first of his warships ground. There was no dramatic splintering of wood—the bed of the Euphrates was mud, not rock—just the sudden halting of the galley's motion, a slight tilt as it adjusted to the angle of the riverbed.

Nothing dramatic, nothing spectacular. But the result was still deadly.

Helpless targets.

The captain felt his own galley lurch, heard the slight hissing of mud and sand against the wooden hull. His craft jerked loose. Another hiss, another lurch. Jerked loose. *Stopped.*

A quick-thinking man. He wasted no time trying to pry the vessel out. The muddy soil of the riverbed would hold the hull like glue. Instead, he turned his attention to preparing his defenses.

"Move the rocket troughs around!" he bellowed. "Set them to repel boarders!"

His rocket handlers scurried to obey. One of them cried out, clutching his arm. An arrow was suddenly protruding from his elbow. The cry was cut short by another arrow penetrating his throat.

The captain spun around. To his despair, he saw that the enemy charging down the west bank had drawn parallel to his craft. Already, the first Persian lancers were guiding their mounts into the riverbed. Their pace was slow, due to the thick mud and reeds, but the powerful Persian warhorses were still driving forward relentlessly. They would cover the distance quickly enough.

There would be no time to bring the rockets to bear, he knew. And there was no chance—*no chance*—that his lightly armored sailors could withstand Persian dehgans in hand-to-hand combat.

A quick-thinking man. He began to shout his surrender. But fell instantly silent, hearing the warcry of the oncoming Persians.

Charax! Charax! Charax!

He understood at once that there would be no surrender. *No chance.*

He died eight seconds later, struck down by an arrow which tore through his heart. He made no attempt to evade the missile. There would have been no point. The enemy arrows were like a flock of geese. Instead, he simply stood there, silent, unmoving, presenting his chest to the enemy.

When all was said and done, the quick-thinking man was kshatriya. He would die so.

The Persians who saw were impressed. Hours later, they retrieved his body—the charred remnants of it—from the burned hulk of his galley. They carried the corpse back into Babylon, and gave it an honored resting place along with their own dead. Perched, in the Aryan way, atop a stone tower called a *dakhma*. There, exposed to carrion eaters, the unclean flesh would be stripped away, leaving the soul pure and intact.

But that act of grace was yet to come. For now, the Persian cavalrymen thought only of slaughter and destruction. The dehgans and their archers rampaged down the west bank of the river for miles, destroying every ship within their reach. The huge Malwa army on the opposite shore could only watch in helpless fury.

Malwa officers drove many of their soldiers into the riverbed in an attempt to rescue the stranded ships. But the mud and reeds impeded those troops at least as much as they had the Persian lancers on the west bank—and the Malwa were far more distant. By the time the soldiers struggling through the muck could reach them, the ships would be nothing but burning wreckage.

The Persians were not able to destroy the entire fleet, of course. Many of the Malwa galleys and supply ships—whether through their own effort, or good luck, or both—wound up stranded on the east bank of the river. Those ships, protected by the nearby Malwa troops, were quite safe. They did not even suffer much damage from the grounding itself, due to the soft nature of the riverbed.

But all of the ships which grounded within bow range of the Persians were doomed. Those close enough for the Persians to storm were burned by hand, after their crews were massacred. Those too far into the center of the river to be stormed were simply burned with fire-arrows. Those sailors who could swim survived. Those who could not, died.

At sunset, the Persians broke off their sally and retreated back into Babylon. By the time the last dehgan trotted back across the pontoon bridge, almost a third of the Malwa fleet had been destroyed, along with most of the sailors who had manned those ships.

Those sailors were only the least of the casualties which the Malwa suffered, that day. An hour into the Persian sally, Lord Jivita ordered a mass assault against the walls of Babylon. The assault began almost immediately—his officers were terrified by his temper—and was carried on throughout the rest of the afternoon.

It is possible that Lord Jivita ordered the assault because he thought the Persian sally had emptied Babylon of most of its defenders. Possible, but unlikely. The Malwa espionage service had kept Jivita well-informed of the enemy's strength throughout the siege. A simple count of the Persians across the river should have led the Malwa commander to the conclusion that Emperor Khusrau had kept the big majority of his troops behind the city's walls.

No, Lord Jivita's action was almost certainly the product of nothing more sophisticated than blind fury. The petulant, squawling rage of a thwarted child. A very spoiled child.

The price was paid by his troops. Khusrau had read his opponent's mentality quite accurately. The Emperor had expected just such a mindless attack, and had prepared his defenses accordingly. The Malwa soldiers crossing the no-man's land were ravaged by his catapults and his archers, stymied by the moats and walls, butchered at the walls themselves by heavily armored dehgans for whom they were no match in close-quarter combat. The casualties were horrendous, especially among the Kushans who spearheaded most of the assaults. By the end of day, when the attack was finally called off, six thousand Malwa soldiers lay dead or dying on the field of battle. Thirteen thousand had suffered injuries—from which, within a week, another five thousand would die.

In all, in that one day, the Malwa suffered over twenty thousand casualties. Any other army in the world would have been broken by such losses. And even the Malwa army reeled.

Lord Jivita himself did not reel. His fury grew and grew as the hours passed. By sundown, his despairing officers realized, Jivita was still determined to press the attack through the night.

The abyss of total disaster yawned before them. They were pulled back from that pit by an old woman.

◇   ◇   ◇

When Great Lady Holi clambered painfully up the ladder onto the command tower, silence immediately fell over the small crowd of top officers packed there. Even Lord Jivita broke off his bellowing.

The Great Lady cast only a glance at Jivita.

"You are relieved," she announced. Her empty eyes moved to a figure standing next to Jivita.

"Lord Achyuta, you are now in command of the army."

Jivita's eyes bulged. "You can't do that!" he screeched. "Only the Emperor has the authority—"

"Kill him," said Great Lady Holi.

The two guards stationed on the platform stiffened. Hesitated, their eyes flashing back and forth between Holi and Jivita. *He* was their commander, after all. She was—*officially*—nothing but—

Nothing—*but*. They had heard tales. All Malwa soldiers had heard tales.

The Great Lady's eyes were now utterly barren. When she spoke again, her voice was inhuman. Empty of all life.

"KILL HIM."

The guards had only heard tales. But the officers on that platform were all members of the Malwa dynastic clan. They knew the truth behind the tales.

Lord Achyuta's sword was the first to slice into Jivita's belly, but only because he was standing the closest. Before Jivita slumped to the ground, five other swords had cut and sliced the life from his body.

The two guards were still standing stiff and rigid. Great Lady Holi's vacant eyes fell upon them. If she hesitated at all, it was for less than a second.

"KILL THEM ALSO. THERE MUST BE NO TALES."

Pudgy, middle-aged generals fell upon vigorous young soldiers. If the two guards had not been mentally paralyzed, they would undoubtedly have held their own against those unathletic officers. As it was, they were butchered within seconds.

Great Lady Holi lowered herself into Jivita's chair. She ignored the three bodies and the pools of blood spreading across the platform.

"CALL OFF THIS INSANE ATTACK," she commanded.

"At once, Great Lady Holi!" cried Achyuta. He glanced at one of his subordinates. An instant later, the man was scrambling down the ladder.

Reluctantly, Achyuta came to stand before the old woman. Reluctantly, for he knew that the aged figure hunched on that chair was only an old woman in form. Within that crone's body dwelt the spirit called *Link*. He feared that spirit as much as he was awed by it.

"DESCRIBE THE DAMAGE."

Achyuta did not even try to calculate the casualty figures. Link, he knew, would be utterly indifferent. Instead, he went straight to the heart of the problem.

"Without the supply fleet, we cannot take Babylon."

He glanced toward the Euphrates. The sunset was almost gone, but the river was still well-illuminated by the multitude of burning ships.

"Under the best of circumstances, we have been set back—"

He hesitated, quailing, before summoning his courage. Link, he knew, would punish dishonesty faster than anything. In this, at least, the divine spirit was utterly unlike Jivita. Mindless rages were not Link's way. Simply—cold, cold, cold.

He cleared his throat.

"Until next year," he concluded.

A human would have cocked an eye, or—something. Link simply stared at Achyuta through those empty, old woman's eyes.

"SO LONG?"

Again, he cleared his throat.

"Yes, Great Lady Holi. Until we can replace the destroyed ships, we will only have sufficient supplies to maintain the siege. There will be no chance of pressing home any attacks. And we have—"

He waved his hand helplessly, gesturing toward the invisible barrenness of the region.

"—we have no way to build ships here. They will have to be built in India, and brought here during the monsoon next year."

Great Lady Holi—*Link*—was silent. The old woman's eyes were still empty, but Achyuta could sense the lightning-quick calculations behind those orbs.

"YES. YOU ARE CORRECT. BUT THAT IS NOT THE WORST OF IT."

The last sentence had something of the sense of a question about it. Achyuta nodded vigorously.

"No, Great Lady Holi, it isn't. There will be no point in bringing a new fleet of supply ships if the river—"

Again, that helpless gesture. Great Lady Holi filled the silence.

"WE MUST RESTORE THE RIVER. THEY HAVE DAMMED IT UPSTREAM. AN EXPEDITION MUST BE SENT—AT ONCE—TO DESTROY THE DAM AND THE FORCE WHICH BUILT IT."

"At once!" agreed Achyuta. "I will assemble the force tomorrow! I will lead it myself!"

Great Lady Holi levered herself upright.

"NO, LORD ACHYUTA, YOU WILL NOT LEAD IT. YOU WILL REMAIN HERE, IN CHARGE OF THE SIEGE. APPOINT ONE OF YOUR SUBORDINATES TO COMMAND THE EXPEDITION."

Achyuta did not even think to argue the matter. He nodded his head vigorously. Asked, in a tone which was almost fawning:

"Which one, Great Lady Holi? Do you have a preference?"

The divine spirit glanced around the platform, estimating the officers standing there rigidly. It was a quick, quick glance.

"IT DOES NOT MATTER. I WILL ACCOMPANY THE EXPEDITION PERSONALLY. WHOEVER IT IS WILL OBEY ME."

Achyuta's eyes widened.

"You? You yourself? But—"

He fell silent under the inhuman stare.

"I CAN TRUST NO ONE ELSE, ACHYUTA. THIS WAS BELISARIUS' WORK. HIS—AND THE ONE WHO GOES WITH HIM."

She turned away.

"I KNOW MY ENEMY NOW. I WILL DESTROY IT MYSELF."

Moments later, assisted by the hands of several officers, the figure of the old woman disappeared down the ladder. Achyuta was relieved to see her go. So relieved, in fact, that he did not wonder for more than an instant why Great Lady Holi had referred to the man Belisarius as "it."

Personal peeve, he assumed. Not thinking that the divine spirit named Link was never motivated by such petty concerns.

◇   ◇   ◇

The next morning, from his perch atop the hill which had once been the Tower of Babel, Emperor Khusrau watched the Malwa expeditionary force begin their march to Peroz-Shapur and the Nehar Malka.

The sight was impressive. There were at least sixty thousand soldiers in that army across the Euphrates. At the moment, from what he could see, Khusrau thought the enemy force was infantry-heavy. But he had no doubt that they would be joined along the march by the mounted raiding parties which the Malwa had kept in the field, ravaging Mesopotamia. By the time that army reached its destination, he estimated, its numbers would have swelled by at least another ten thousand.

Most of the Malwa army's supplies were being carried on camel-back, but the expedition was also accompanied by small oared warships which were being laboriously portaged past Babylon. Those vessels would have a shallow enough draft to negotiate the Euphrates upstream. The water level of the river had dropped drastically, but it was still a respectable stream.

He could see no siege guns. He would have been surprised to have done so. Weeks earlier, Belisarius had explained to him that heavy guns, even sectioned, require carts—or better, barges—for transport. Barges would be too heavy for the shrunken river, and, as for carts—how to haul them? Camels make poor draft animals, and horses could not manage a long and heavy-loaded march through the desert. There was no way to haul carts alongside the river itself, of course. The terrain directly adjoining the Euphrates was much too marshy—even more so now that the water level had dropped.

No, he thought with satisfaction, it is just as Belisarius predicted. They will be restricted to rockets and grenades—weapons which they can carry on camelback.

Without taking his eyes from the Malwa army, the Persian Emperor cocked his head toward the man standing at his side.

"You are certain, Maurice? It is still not too late. I can order a sally against that force."

Maurice shook his head.

"That would be unwise, Your Majesty." With only the slightest trace of apology: "If you forgive me saying so."

Maurice pointed to the south. Even at the distance, it was obvious that the main force of the enemy was mobilized and ready.

"They're hoping for that. They'll be prepared, today. They've erected their own pontoon bridges across the river. If you make another sally, they'll overwhelm you."

Khusrau did not pursue the matter further. In truth, he agreed with Maurice. He had made the offer simply out of a sense of obligation. He owed much to the Romans, and he was a man who detested being in debt.

Inwardly, he sighed. He would not be able to repay that debt for some time. If ever. Once again, circumstances forced him to allow his allies to fight for him. The great Malwa expeditionary force would have no Persians to contend with, other than Kurush's ten thousand men. And those troops would be needed to defend Peroz-Shapur, which the Malwa expedition would bypass on its way to the Nehar Malka. Kurush and his men would tie up at least their own number of enemy troops, true. But they would be unavailable to help in the defense of the dam itself.

Once again, Belisarius would fight for him. Almost unaided.

A sour thought came.

Except, of course, for the aid of a traitor.

Khusrau squared his shoulders. The foul deed needed to be done. He would not postpone it.

He turned to one of his aides. "Send for Ormazd," he commanded.

As the officer trotted away, Khusrau grimaced. Then, seeing the slight smile on Maurice's face, he grimaced even more.

"And *this*, Maurice? Are you also certain of *this?*"

The Roman chiliarch shrugged. "If you want my personal opinion, Your Majesty—no. I am not certain. I suspect that Belisarius is being too clever for his own good." Scowl. "*As usual.*"

The scowl faded.

"But—I have thought so before. And, though I'd never admit it to his face, been proven wrong before." Again, he shrugged. "So—best to stick to his plan. Maybe he'll be right again."

Khusrau nodded. For the next few minutes, as they waited for Ormazd to make his appearance, the Persian Emperor and the Roman officer stood together in silence.

Maurice spent the time in a careful study of the enemy's expeditionary army. He would be leaving himself, the next day, to rejoin the Roman army awaiting the Malwa onslaught at the Nehar Malka. Belisarius would want a full and detailed description of his opponent's forces.

Khusrau, on the other hand, spent the time in a careful study—of Maurice.

Not of the man, so much as what he represented. It might be better to say, what the man Maurice told him of the general he followed. Told the Persian Emperor, not by any words he spoke, but by his very nature.

Belisarius.

Khusrau had spent many hours thinking about Belisarius, in the past weeks.

Belisarius, the ally of the present.

Belisarius, the possible enemy of the future.

Khusrau was himself a great leader. He knew that already, despite his youth. Part of that greatness was due to his capacity to examine reality objectively, unswayed by self-esteem and personal grandiosity. No small feat, that, for an Emperor of Iran and non-Iran. And so Khusrau knew that one of the qualities of a great leader was his ability to gather around him other men of talent.

He had never seen such a collection of capable men as Belisarius had cemented together in his army's leadership. He admired that team, envied Belisarius for it, and feared it at the same time.

Crude men, true. Low born, almost to a man. Men like Maurice himself, for instance, whom Khusrau knew had been born a peasant.

But the Persian Emperor was a great emperor, and so he was not blinded by his own class prejudices. Pure-blood empires had been brought down before, by lowborn men. The day could come, in the future, when the peasant-bred Maurice might stand again on that very hilltop. Not as an ally, but a conqueror. On that hill in Babylon; on the walls of Ctesiphon; on the horse-pastures of the heartland plateau.

So, while they waited for Ormazd, and Maurice gave thought to the near future, the Emperor of Iran and non-Iran gave thought to the more distant future. By the time his treacherous half-brother finally made his appearance, Khusrau had decided on a course of action.

He would outrage Aryan opinion. But he shrugged that problem off. With Ormazd removed, Khusrau did not fear the squawks of

Aryan nobility. He trusted Belisarius to remove Ormazd for him, and he would entrust the future of his empire to an alliance with that same man.

Ormazd's progress up the slope of the hill was stately—as much due to his horde of sycophants as to his own majestic pace. So Khusrau had time to lean over and whisper to Maurice, "Tonight. I wish to see you in my pavilion."

Maurice nodded.

When Ormazd was finally standing before the Emperor, Khusrau pointed to the Malwa expedition making its own slow way across the river.

"Tomorrow, brother, you will take your army and join the allied forces at the Nehar Malka. You will give Baresmanas and Belisarius all the assistance you can provide, in their coming battle against that enemy force."

Ormazd scowled.

"I will not take orders from a Roman!" he snapped. "Nor from Baresmanas, for that matter. I am higher-born than—"

Khusrau waved him down.

"Of course not, brother. But it is *I*, not they, who is commanding you in this. I leave it to your judgement how best to assist Belisarius, once you arrive. You will be in full command of your own troops. But you *will* assist them."

His half-brother's scowl deepened. Khusrau's own expression grew fierce.

"You *will* obey your Emperor," he hissed.

Ormazd said nothing. Put *that* way, there was nothing he could say unless he was prepared to rise in open rebellion that very moment. Which he most certainly wasn't—not in the middle of Khusrau's main army. Not after his own prestige had suffered such a battering during the past two months.

After a moment, grudgingly, Ormazd nodded. He muttered a few phrases which, charitably, could be taken for words of obedience, and quickly made his exit.

Later that night, when Maurice arrived at the Emperor's pavilion, he was ushered into Khusrau's private chamber. As he entered, Khusrau was sitting at a small table, occupied with writing a letter.

The Emperor glanced up, smiled, and gestured toward a nearby cushion.

"Please sit, Maurice. I'm almost finished."

After Maurice took his seat, a servant appeared through a curtain and presented him with a goblet of wine. Before Maurice could even take a sip, Khusrau rose from the table and embossed the letter with the seal ring which was one of the Persian Emperor's insignia of office. With no apparent signal being given, a man immediately appeared in the chamber and took the missive from the Emperor. A moment later, he was gone.

Maurice, watching, was impressed but not surprised. Persia had always been famous for the efficiency of its royal postal system. The man who took the letter to its destination was known as a *parvanak*, and it was one of the most prestigious positions in the imperial Persian hierarchy. In contrast, the Roman equivalent—the *agentes in rebus*—were more in the way of spies than postal officials.

Which might be good for imperial control, thought Maurice sourly, but it makes for piss-poor delivery of the mail.

As soon as they were alone in the room, Khusrau took a seat on his own resplendent cushion.

"Tell me about the Emperor Photius," he commanded. "Belisarius' son."

Maurice was puzzled by the question, but he let no sign of it show. "He's not really his son, Your Majesty. His stepson."

Khusrau smiled. "His *son*, I think."

Maurice stared at the Emperor for a moment, then nodded. It was a deep nod. Almost a bow, in fact.

"Yes, Your Majesty. His *son*."

"Tell me about him."

Maurice studied the Persian, still puzzled. Understanding, Khusrau smiled again.

"Perhaps I should give my question more of a focus."

He rose and strode over to one side of his chamber. Drawing aside the curtain, he called out a name. A moment later, moving with stiff and shy uncertainty, a young girl entered the chamber.

Maurice estimated her age at thirteen, perhaps fourteen. The daughter of a high Persian nobleman, obviously. And very beautiful.

"This is Tahmina," said Khusrau. "She is the oldest daughter of Baresmanas, the noblest man of the noble Suren."

With a gesture, Khusrau invited the girl to sit on a nearby cushion. Tahmina did so, quickly and with a surprising grace for one so young.

"My own children are very young," said Khusrau. Then, with a little laugh: "Besides, they are all boys."

The Emperor turned and bestowed an odd look on Maurice. Maurice, at least, thought the look was odd. He was now utterly bewildered as to the Emperor's purpose.

"Baresmanas cherishes his daughter," said Khusrau sternly. Then, even more sternly: "As do I myself, for that matter. Baresmanas placed her in my care when he left for Constantinople with his wife. She is an absolutely delightful child, and I have enjoyed her company immensely. It has made me look forward to having daughters of my own, some day."

The Emperor began pacing back and forth.

"She is of good temper, and intelligent. She is also, as you can see for yourself, very beautiful."

He stopped abruptly. "So. Tell me about the Roman Emperor Photius."

Maurice's eyes widened. His jaw almost dropped. "He's only eight years old," he choked.

The gesture which Khusrau made in response to that statement could only have been made by an emperor: *August dismissal of an utterly trivial matter.*

"He will age," pronounced the Emperor. "Soon enough, he will need a wife."

Again, the stern look. "*So.* Tell me about the Emperor Photius. I do not ask for anything but your personal opinion of the boy himself, Maurice. You will say he is a child. And I will respond that the child is father to the man. Tell me about the *man* Photius."

For just a moment, Khusrau's imperial manner faltered. "The girl is very dear to me, you see. I would not wish to see her abused."

Maurice groped for words. Hesitated; vacillated; jittered back and forth in his mind. He was floundering in waters much too deep for him. *Imperial* waters, for the sake of Christ!

Then, as his eyes roamed about, they happened to meet those of Tahmina. Shy eyes. Uncertain eyes.

Fearful eyes.

That, Maurice understood.

He took a deep breath. When he spoke, his voice had more in it than usual of the Thracian accent of his peasant upbringing. "A good lad, he is, Your Majesty. A sweet-tempered boy. Not nasty-spirited in the least. Bright, too, I think. It's a bit early to tell yet, of course. Precocious lads—which he is—sometimes fritter it all away as they get too sure of themselves. But Photius—no, I think not." He stopped, bringing himself up short. "I really shouldn't say anything more," he announced. "It's not my place."

Khusrau's eyes bore into him. "Damn all that!" he snapped. "I only want the answer to a simple question. Would you marry *your* daughter to him?"

Maurice started to protest that he *had* no daughter—not that he knew of, at least—but the sight of Tahmina's eyes stilled the words.

That, he understood. *That*, he could answer.

"Oh, yes," he whispered. "Oh, yes."

Chapter 28

ALEXANDRIA

Autumn, 531 A.D.

As her ships approached the Great Harbor of Alexandria, Antonina began to worry that her entire fleet might capsize. It seemed to her, at a glance, that the soldiers on every one of her ships were crowding the starboard rails, eager for a look at the world-famous Pharos.

The great lighthouse was perched on a small island, also called Pharos, which was connected to the mainland by an artificial causeway known as the Heptastadium. The causeway, in addition to providing access to the lighthouse, also served to divide the Great Harbor from the Eunostus Harbor on the west.

Built in three huge "stories," the Pharos towered almost four hundred feet high. The lowest section was square in design, the second octagonal, and the third cylindrical. At the very top of the cylindrical structure was a room in which a great fire was kept burning at all hours of the day and night. The light produced by that fire was magnified and projected to seaward by a reflecting device. At night, the light could be seen for a tremendous distance.

She and her troops had seen that light only a few hours earlier, as her fleet approached Alexandria in the early hours of the morning. Now, two hours after dawn, the beam seemed pallid. But in the darkness, the light of the Pharos had truly lived up to its reputation. And now that they could see it clearly, so did the lighthouse itself.

Her soldiers were absolutely *packing* the starboard rails. Antonina was on the verge of issuing orders—futile ones, probably—when a cry from the lookout in the bow drew her attention.

"Ships approaching!" he bellowed. "Dromons! Eight dromons!"

She scrambled down the ladder from the poop deck and hurried along the starboard catwalk to the bow. Within a minute, she was standing alongside the lookout, peering at the small fleet which was emerging from the Great Harbor.

Eight dromons, just as he had said. Five of them were full-size, the other three somewhat smaller. In all, she estimated that there were at least one and a half thousand soldiers manning those dromons. Most of them were oarsmen, but, after a quick count, she decided there were well over four hundred marines aboard as well.

Armed and armored. And the oarsmen would also have weapons ready to hand, in the event of a boarding action.

As she watched, seven of the dromons spread out, forming a barrier across the entrance to the Great Harbor. The eighth, one of the smaller ones, began rowing toward her.

She felt someone at her elbow. Turning her head, she saw that Hermogenes had joined her, along with two of his tribunes and the captain of her flagship.

"What are your orders?" asked the captain.

"Stop the ship," she said. "And signal the rest of the fleet to do likewise."

A pained look came on the captain's face, but he obeyed instantly.

"What did I say wrong *this* time?" grumbled Antonina.

Hermogenes chuckled. "Don't know. I'm not a seaman either. But I'm sure you don't just 'stop' a ship. Much less a whole fleet! That's way too logical and straightforward. Probably something like: 'belay all forward progress' and 'relay the signal for all ships to emulate execution.'"

Smiling, Antonina resumed her study of the approaching dromon. The warship was two hundred yards away, now.

"I assume that dromon is bearing envoys."

"From whom?" he asked. Antonina shrugged.

"We'll find out soon enough."

She pushed herself away from the rail. "When they arrive, usher them into my cabin. I'll wait for them there."

Hermogenes nodded. "Good idea. It'll make you seem more imperial than if you met them on deck."

"The hell with that," muttered Antonina. "It'll make me seem *taller*. I had that chair in my cabin specially designed for it." Ruefully, she looked down at her body. "As short as I am, I can't intimidate anybody standing up."

As she hurried down the catwalk toward her cabin, Antonina noted that the appearance of the eight dromons had at least had the salutory effect of eliminating the danger of capsizing her ships. The soldiers of her fleet had left off their sight-seeing and were taking up battle positions.

She stopped for a moment, steadying herself against a stay. Now that Antonina's fleet had come to a halt, the flagship was wallowing in the waves, drifting slowly before the wind. The sea was calm that morning, however, and the wind not much more than a light breeze. The ship's motion was gentle.

Searching the sea for John's gunship, Antonina spotted the *Theodora* within seconds. To her satisfaction, she saw that John was already tacking to the northwest. In the event of a conflict, the gunship would be in perfect position to sail downwind toward the dromons blocking the harbor.

Ashot came to meet her.

"There'll be several envoys from that ship"—she pointed to the dromon—"coming aboard. Hermogenes will usher them into my cabin. I want you and—" She broke off, studying the officers in the oncoming warship. Taking a count, to be precise. "—And four of your cataphracts to be there with me," she concluded.

Ashot smiled, rather grimly. "Any in particular?"

Antonina's returning smile was just as grim. "Yes. The four biggest, meanest, toughest ones you've got."

Ashot nodded. Before Antonina had taken three paces toward her cabin, the Armenian officer was already bellowing his commands.

"*Synesius! Matthew! Leo! Zenophilus! Front and center!*"

The first thing the visiting officers did, after Hermogenes ushered them in, was to study the four cataphracts standing in each

corner of Antonina's large cabin. A careful study, lasting for at
least half a minute.

Antonina fought down a grin. The visiting officers reminded her
of nothing so much as four sinners in the antechamber of Hell,
examining the denizens of the Pit.

Four devils, one in each corner. Counting arms and armor,
Antonina estimated their collective gross weight at twelve hundred
pounds. Two of the cataphracts were so tall their helmets were
almost brushing the ceiling of the cabin. One of them was so
wide he looked positively deformed. And the last one, Leo, was
considered by all of Belisarius' bucellarii to be the ugliest man
alive.

Not "cute" ugly. Not pug-nosed bulldog "ugly."

Ugly ugly. Rabid vicious slavering monster ugly. Ogre ugly; troll
ugly—even when Leo wasn't scowling, which, at the moment, he
most certainly was. A gut-wrenching, spine-freezing, bowel-loosen-
ing *Moloch* kind of scowl.

Antonina cleared her throat. Demurely. Ladylike.

"What can I do for you, gentlemen?" she asked.

The officer in the forefront tore his eyes away from Leo and
stared at her. He was a middle-aged man, with greying hair and a
beard streaked with white. He was actually a bit on the tall side,
Antonina thought, but he looked like a midget in the same room
with Ashot's four cataphracts.

For a moment, the man's stare was simply blank. Then, as recognition came to him, his eyes narrowed.

"You are the woman Antonina?" he demanded. "The wife of
Belisarius?"

She nodded. The officer's lips tightened.

"We have been told—that is to say, it is our understanding that
you have been appointed in charge of this—uh—fleet."

She nodded. The officer's lips grew thinner still, as if he had
just tasted the world's sourest lemon.

"The situation here in Alexandria is very complicated," the officer stated forcefully. "You must understand that. It will do no one
any good if you simply charge into—"

"The situation in Egypt is *not* complicated," interrupted Antonina. "The situation is very simple. The *former* civil, ecclesiastical
and military authorities have lost the confidence of the Emperor
and the Empress Regent. For that reason, I have been sent here

to oversee their replacement by people who enjoy the imperial trust. On board this fleet are the newly-designated Praetorian Prefect, Patriarch, *and* the merarch of the Army of Egypt."

She pointed a finger at Hermogenes. The young merarch was leaning his shoulder into a nearby wall, the very figure of casual relaxation.

"Him, as it happens. May I introduce you?"

The four naval officers were goggling at her. Antonina smiled sweetly and added:

"I will also be glad to introduce you to the new Praetorian Prefect and Patriarch, as soon as possible. But I'm afraid they are not on this ship."

One of the younger officers in the rear suddenly exploded.

"This is absurd! You can't—"

"I most certainly can. I most certainly will."

The same officer began to speak again, but the older officer in the forefront hushed him with an urgent wave of the hand.

"We agreed that I would do the talking!" he hissed, turning his head a bit.

When he looked back at Antonina, his lips had disappeared entirely. The lemon had been swallowed whole.

"I can see you are not open to reason," he snapped. "So I will speak plainly. The naval authorities in Alexandria—of which we are the representatives—will take no sides in the disputes which are roiling the city. But we must insist that those disputes be settled by the city itself. We cannot agree—we *will* not agree—to the imposition of a forcible solution by outsiders. Therefore—"

"Arrest them," said Antonina. "All four." She spoke softly, calmly, easily.

The officers gaped. One of them reached for his sword. But before he could begin to draw the blade from its scabbard, a hand clamped around his wrist like a vise. Zenophilus' hand, that was about the size of a bear's paw. The other huge hand seized the officer by the back of the neck. The officer began to shout.

Zenophilus *squeezed*. The man stopped shouting instantly. Began to turn blue, in fact.

The other three officers were likewise pinioned, wrist and neck, by the rest of Ashot's cataphracts.

"You can't do this!" shrieked the one in Matthew's grip.

Matthew was one of the cataphracts who almost had to stoop to clear the cabin's ceiling. He grinned cheerfully and *squeezed*.

Silence.

"Why not?" asked Antonina, smiling like a seraph. She made a little gesture at Matthew. The cataphract eased up the pressure on his captive's throat.

The man coughed explosively. Then, gasping: "Those dromons have orders! If we don't return within an hour, they're to assume that hostilities have commenced!"

" 'Hostilities have commenced,' " mused Hermo-genes. "My, that sounds ominous."

He glanced at Ashot, leaning against the opposite wall in an identical pose.

" 'Hostilities have commenced,' " echoed the Armenian cata-phract. "Dire words."

With a little thrust of his shoulder, Ashot stood erect. He and Hermogenes exchanged a smile.

"Dreadful words," said Ashot. "I believe I may defecate."

The officer who had issued the threat snarled.

"Make light of it if you will! But I remind you that those are eight *warships*. What do you have, besides those grain ships and that horde of corbitas? Two dromons—that's it!"

"Not quite," murmured Ashot. He swiveled his head, looking at Antonina.

She nodded. Ashot walked out of the cabin. Seconds later, his voice was heard:

"Send a signal to the Theodora! The blue-and-white flag! Fol-lowed by the red!"

A moment later, he ambled back inside the cabin.

"That means 'hostilities have commenced,' " he explained to the four arrested officers. Then, grinning:

"In a manner of speaking."

The captives were so busy staring at Ashot that they never heard Antonina's little murmur:

" 'Cross the T,' to be precise. And 'fire broadside.' "

Aboard the *Theodora*, John of Rhodes and Eusebius were stand-ing on the poop deck. Seeing the blue-and-white pennant, followed by the red, John whooped.

"Yes! *At last!* Now we'll see what this beautiful bitch can do!"

"Wouldn't let the Empress hear you say that, if I were you," muttered Eusebius. The artificer was standing next to John, clutching the rail. His face was drawn and pale. The *Theodora*'s tacking against the wind had awakened Eusebius' always-latent seasickness.

"Why not?" demanded John cheerfully. "The ship's named after her, isn't it? Isn't the Empress a beauty? And isn't she just the world's meanest bitch?" Gaily, he slapped Eusebius on the shoulder. "But she's *our* bitch, boy! *Ours!*"

John pointed to the ladder leading to the deck below. "Get on down, now, Eusebius. I want you keeping a close eye on those overenthusiastic gunners."

Making his way gingerly down the ladder, Eusebius heard John bellowing to his sailors and steersman:

"Head for that fleet of dromons across the harbor! I want to sail right across their bows!"

When Eusebius reached the gundeck, he headed to the starboard side of the ship. On the *Theodora*'s new heading, northwest to southeast, she would be bringing the five cannons on that side to bear on the enemy.

Soon enough, Eusebius forgot his seasickness. He was utterly preoccupied with the task of preparing the cannons for a broadside. He scampered up and down the gundeck, fretting over every detail of the work.

For once, the Syrian gunners and their wives did not curse him for a fussbudget and mock him for an impractical philosopher. This was not an exercise. This was the real thing. They would not be firing at empty barrels tossed overboard. They would be firing at front-line warships—which would be attacking *them*.

True, those warships had no cannons. But the word *dromon* meant "racer," and the sleek naval craft positioned at the entrance to the Great Harbour lived up to the term. Beautifully designed—elegant, in fact, as no tubby sailing ship ever was—they reminded the Syrian gunners of so many gigantic wasps, ready to strike in an instant.

Long, narrow—deadly.

By the time the *Theodora* was halfway to the dromons, the gunners had the cannons loaded and ready to fire. They were very familiar with the process, now, due to the relentless training exercises which Eusebius had insisted upon during the weeks of their voyage.

They had resented those exercises, at the time. The *Theodora's* gunners were all volunteers from the Theodoran Cohort. When the posts had been opened, the bidding had been fierce. Most of the Syrian grenadiers had wanted those prestigious jobs. Prestigious and, they had all assumed, *easy*—certainly compared to the work of toting grenades and handcannons under the hot sun of Egypt. Lounging about on a ship, never walking more than a few steps—what could be better?

They had soon learned otherwise. Within a week of setting sail from Rhodes, they had become the butt of the Cohort's jokes. The rest of the grenadiers had lolled against the rails of their transports, watching while the gunners were put through their drills. Watching and grinning, day after day, as the gunners sweated under the Mediterranean sun. Not as hot as Egypt's, that sun, but it was hot enough. Especially for men and women who practiced hauling brass cannons to the gunports, lugging ammunition and shot forward from the hold, loading the guns, firing them—and, then, doing it all over again. Time after time, hour after hour, day after day. All of it under the watchful eye of a man who, by temperament, would have made an excellent monk. The kind of monk who vigilantly oversees the work of other monks, copying page after page of manuscript, alert for every misstroke of the quill, every errant drop of ink.

A fussy man. A prim man, for all his youth. A nag, a scold, a worrywart. Just the sort of man to drive peasant borderers half-insane.

Now, as they stood by their guns, the Syrian gunners gave silent thanks for Eusebius. And took comfort from his presence. The young twit was a pain in the ass, sure—but he was *their* pain in the ass.

"Knows his shit, Eusebius does," announced one.

"Best cannon-man alive," agreed another.

Suddenly, one of the wives laughed and cried out, "Let's hear it for Eusebius! Come on! Let's hear it!"

Her call was taken up. An instant later, the entire contingent of gunners was shouting: "EUSEBIUS! EUSEBIUS! EUSEBIUS!"

Startled by the cheers, Eusebius stiffened. He knew that a commanding officer was supposed to give a speech on such occasions. A ringing peroration.

Eusebius was no more capable of ringing perorations than a mouse was of flying. So, after a moment, he simply waved his hand and smiled. Quite shyly, like the awkward young misfit he had been all his life.

The smile was answered by grins on the faces of the Syrians. They were not disappointed by his silence. They knew the man well.

Their overseer. *Their* pain in the ass.

Above, on the poop deck, John of Rhodes smiled also.

Not a shy, awkward smile, this. No, not at all. John of Rhodes was neither shy nor awkward nor a misfit. True, his former naval career had been shipwrecked by his incorrigible womanizing. But he had been universally recognized by his fellow officers—except, perhaps, those whose wives he had seduced—as the Roman navy's finest ship captain.

He knew a fighting crew when he saw one. And now, understanding that Eusebius would give no ringing peroration—*could* give none—John made good the lack.

In his own way, of course. Pericles would have been aghast.

"Gunners! Valiant men and women of the Theodoran Cohort!"

He leaned over the rail, pointing dramatically at the seven dromons some three hundred yards distant.

"Those sorry bastards are fucked! Fucked!"

A loud and boisterous cheer went up from the gunners and their wives. Then, coming from far off, John heard a faint echo. Puzzled, he turned and stared at the causeway leading to the Pharos.

The causeway was now lined with people. He could see more and more running down the Heptastadium, coming from Alexandria. Residents of the city, he realized. The news had spread, and Alexandria's people were pouring out to watch the show.

Alexandria's *poor* people, to be precise. Even at the distance, John could see that the men, women and children on the causeway were dressed in simple clothing. Alexandria's busy harbor area was surrounded by slums. It was the occupants of those tenement buildings who had first gotten the word and were packing the Heptastadium and, he could now see, every other vantage point overlooking the Great Harbor and the sea.

He grinned. *"Our* people, those."

◇   ◇   ◇

Aboard her flagship, Antonina came to the same conclusion. She had come out of her cabin as soon as the four captured officers had been securely bound and gagged. Hearing the distant cheers, she studied the crowd lining the Heptastadium. Then, walked over to the starboard rail and stared at the dromon rolling in the waves not far from her ship. After disembarking the four envoys, the dromon had withdrawn some thirty yards and positioned itself facing her flagship. The oar banks were poised and ready for action. At the moment, they were simply being used to keep the dromon in position. But it was obvious to Antonina that the dromon would be able to ram her on an instant's notice.

She would not give them that instant.

She turned her head and called out for Euphronius. The commander of the Theodoran Cohort immediately trotted over.

Antonina gestured toward the nearby dromon with her head. "I want that ship obliterated. Can you do it?"

The young Syrian officer eyed the dromon. A quick glance, no more. "At that range? Easily. Won't even need to use slings."

"Do it," she commanded. As Euphronius began to turn away, she restrained him with a hand.

"I want a hammer blow, Euphronius. Not just a few grenades. If that dromon can get up to ramming speed, it'll punch a hole right through the side of this ship."

Euphronius nodded. A moment later, using gestures and a hissing whisper, he was assembling his grenadiers amidships. The grenadiers, Antonina saw, would be invisible to the seamen manning the low-lying dromon until they appeared at the rail itself, tossing their grenades.

Hermogenes came out of the cabin. Seeing the activity amidships, he hurried to her side.

"You're not going to give them any warning?" he asked. "Call on them to surrender?"

Antonina shook her head.

"I don't dare. That dromon's too close. If they have a warning, they might be able to ram us before the grenades do their work. And if they get close enough, the grenades'll pose a danger to *us*."

Thoughtfully, Hermogenes nodded. "Good point." He stared out at the nearby warship. He could see several officers standing in the bow of the dromon. They were close enough for their expressions to be quite visible.

Frowns. They were worried. Wondering what had happened to their envoys. Beginning to get suspicious.

"Fuck 'em, then," growled Hermogenes.

Antonina heard a low hiss. Turning, she saw that Euphronius had his grenadiers ready. At least three dozen of them were poised, grenades in hand. Their wives stood immediately behind them, ready to light the fuses. The fuses had been cut *very* short.

Casually, she gestured with her hand held waist-high, waving the grenadiers forward.

Do it.

The wives lit the fuses. The Syrians charged for the rail, shouting their battle slogan.

"For the Empire! The Empire!"

The officers on the dromon stiffened, hearing the sudden outcry. One of them opened his mouth. To shout an order, presumably. But his jaw simply dropped when he saw the mob of grenadiers appearing at the rail of the taller ship.

He never said a word. Simply watched, agape, while the volley of grenades soared into the air. Then, along with all his fellow officers, crouched down and ducked.

He must have thought the objects coming his way were stones. He never learned the truth. The six grenades which landed in the bow blew him into fragments, along with the bow itself.

Grenade explosions savaged the dromon down its entire length. The warship's orientation—faced toward Antonina's flagship, with its ram forward—was the worst possible position in which to avoid a grenade volley. Some of the grenades missed the ship entirely, falling into the water on either side. But in most cases the grenadiers' aim was true. And if one grenadier threw farther than another, it simply spread the havoc. The dromon stretched almost a hundred feet from bow to stern. Most of the grenadiers were easily capable of throwing a grenade across the hundred feet of water which separated Antonina's ship from the target. Many of them could reach halfway down the length of the craft, and some could heave their grenades all the way into the dromon's stern.

The grenades landed almost simultaneously, and exploded within three seconds of each other. Dozens of bodies were hurled overboard. Precious few of the men who remained in the ship survived, and they, primarily in the stern. The middle of the warship, where at least a dozen grenades had landed in the midst of two hundred men, was a mass of blood and shredded pieces of flesh.

The warship's hull had been breached, badly—outright holes, or simply planks driven apart. The sea poured in, pulling the dromon under the waves. Some of the surviving sailors began diving off the stern. Others, not knowing how to swim, simply watched their death approach, too stunned to even cry out in despair.

Without turning her head, Antonina spoke to Hermogenes.

"Rescue the ones you can," she commanded. "Put them under guard in the hold."

Antonina's eyes searched for the other dromons in the mouth of the harbor. The warships were stirring into motion. Already she could see the oar banks begin to flash. But, after a moment, she realized that only four of the dromons were heading toward her. The other three were moving to intercept the *Theodora*, bearing down on them from the northwest.

Trying to intercept the *Theodora*, that is to say. Even to Antonina's inexperienced eye, it was obvious that the gunship would pass across their bows with at least a hundred yards of searoom.

"I'm counting on you, John," she murmured. "Smash up some of those dromons for me."

On the *Theodora*, John was issuing new orders.

"Ignore those three heading for us, Eusebius!" he bellowed. "Concentrate your fire on the ones heading for Antonina!"

Eusebius did not bother to look up. Preoccupied with helping a guncrew lay their cannon, he simply waved a hand in acknowledgement.

Finally, satisfied with the work, he looked up at the enemy. Already they were crossing the bows of the three warships who had peeled off to intercept them. The nearest of those ships was two hundred yards away—much too far to be able to get into ramming position, even given the greater speed of the dromons.

Eusebius turned his attention to the other four ships. The nearest of those was still three hundred yards distant. Estimating the combined speed, Eusebius decided they would be within firing range in less than two minutes.

"Fire on my command!" As always, Eusebius tried to copy John of Rhodes' commanding bellow. As always, the result was more of a screech. But he had been heard by all the gunners, nonetheless.

Again, he screeched:

"No broadside! Fire each cannon as it bears! On my command!"

He scurried forward to the lead cannon. For a moment, he almost pushed the chief gunner aside. Then, restraining himself, he took a position looking over his shoulder. Sighting, with the chief gunner, down the barrel of the cannon.

Two hundred and fifty yards, now.

Two hundred.

They would cross the nearest dromon's bow with a hundred yards to spare. Good range.

Eusebius blocked everything from his mind but the dromon looming ahead. As near-sighted as he was, the ship was not much more than a blur. But it didn't matter. His decision would be based on relative motion, not acute perception.

He and the chief gunner moved aside, so as not to get caught by the cannon's recoil. The effort did not distract Eusebius' attention in the least.

The moment came. He tapped the chief gunner lightly on top of his leather helmet.

"Fire," he said, quite softly.

The cannon roared. Bucked; recoiled. A cloud of gunsmoke hid the target.

But Eusebius wasn't looking at the target, anyway. He was scampering down the line to the next cannon. By the time he got there, the chief gunner had already stepped aside, clearing a space for the cannon's recoil.

He gave a quick, myopic look. Again, all he saw was a blur. Relative motion, relative motion—all that mattered.

He tapped the chief gunner's helmet. "Fire."

Down the line; next cannon.

Blur. Relative motion; relative motion. Tap. *Fire.*

Down the line; next cannon.

Blur. Relative motion; relative motion. Tap. *Fire.*

Down the line; next cannon.

Blur.

Blur.

No motion.

He looked up, squinting. Suddenly, the noise around him registered. Cheers. Syrian gunners cheering. Syrian wives shrieking triumph. And then, above it all, John of Rhodes' powerful bellow.

"Oh, beautiful! Great work, Eusebius! She's nothing but a pile of kindling!"

The chief gunner of the last cannon in line was grinning up at him. "That dromon is still floating," he said. "You want I should smash it up?"

Eusebius shook his head. "No, save it. There's more of them."

He squinted. Everything was a blur. He thought he could make out two ships clustered together, but—

Years later, the young artificer would look back on that moment and decide that was when he finally grew up. All his life he had been sensitive about his terrible eyesight. Yet, too proud—too shy, also—to ask for help.

Finally, he did.

"I can't see very well, chief gunner," he admitted. "Am I right? Are the next two ships lying alongside each other?"

The Syrian's grin widened. "That they are, sir. Bastards almost collided, shying away from the gunfire. They *did* get their oars tangled."

Eusebius nodded. Then, straightened up and screeched: "Gunners! Are the cannons re-loaded?"

Within seconds, a chorus of affirmative answers came.

Screech: "Prepare for a broadside! Aim for those two ships! *Fire on my command!*"

He leaned over, whispering, "Help me out, chief gunner. Tell me when you think—"

"Be just a bit, sir. Captain John's bringing the ship around to bear. Just a bit, just a bit."

The Syrian studied the enemy. Two dromons, a hundred yards away, just now getting their oars untangled. A fat, juicy target.

He tapped Eusebius on the knee. "Do it now, sir," he murmured.

Immediately Eusebius screeched:

"Fire! All cannons fire! All cannons—"

The rest was lost in the broadside's roar.

When the smoke cleared away, a new round of cheers went up. True, the broadside had not inflicted as much damage as the earlier single-gun fire had done to the first dromon. It hardly mattered.

The rams of war galleys were braced and buttressed, but the hulls of the ships themselves were made of thin planking for the sake of speed. Those hulls had never been designed to resist the impact of five-inch diameter marble cannonballs.

One of the warships had been holed in the bow. Not enough to sink it, but more than enough to send it scuttling painfully back to shore.

As for the other—

The bow was badly battered, though not holed. But one cannonball, by sheer good luck, must have caught the portside bank of oars just as they were lifting from the water. Many of those oars were shattered. What was worse, the impact had sent the oarbutts flailing about in the interior of the galley, hammering dozens of rowers like so many giant mallets. Objectively speaking, the warship was still combat-capable. But its crew had had more than enough of these terrible weird weapons. That dromon, too, began heading for the Great Harbor, yawing badly with only half a bank of oars on one side.

On the poop deck, John was bellowing new commands. The four ships which had been heading for Antonina's flagship were effectively destroyed—one sinking, two fleeing, and the last floundering about with indecision. Antonina could handle that one on her own. John had his own problem, now.

The Rhodian brought the ship around to face the three dromons which had tried to intercept him earlier. The war galleys had chased after him and, with their superior speed, were rapidly approaching.

Not rapidly enough. By the time they got within range, John had brought the ship's port side to bear—with its five unfired cannons and fresh guncrews.

Eusebius was already there, prepared. John was a bit puzzled to see that the artificer had brought one of the chief gunners from the starboard battery along with him. He saw Eusebius and the man confer, briefly. Then, Eusebius' unmistakable screech:

"Broadside! On my command!"

John smiled. As he often had before, he found the young artificer's boyish voice comical. But, this time, there was not a trace of condescension in that smile.

Comical, yes. Pathetic, no.

Again, he saw Eusebius and the chief gunner's heads bobbing in urgent discourse. The three dromons were two hundred yards away, their oarbanks flashing, their deadly rams aimed directly at the *Theodora*.

Again, the screech: "Fire! All cannons fire! All—"

Lost in the roar. A cloud of smoke, obscuring the enemy.

Screech: "Reload! Reload! Quick! Quick!"

John watched the guncrews racing through the drill. He gave silent thanks for the endless hours of practice that Eusebius had forced through over the Syrians' bitter complaints.

They weren't complaining, now. Oh, no, not at all. Just racing through the drill. Shouting their slogan:

"For the Empire! The Empire!"

The smoke cleared enough for John to see the enemy. The three dromons were only fifty yards away, now. He flinched. No way to stop them from ramming.

Except—

Their forward motion had stopped, he realized. None of the ships were sinking, true. Only one of them, judging from appearance, had even suffered significant hull damage. Still, the shock had been enough to throw the rowers off their stroke. The men on those galleys were completely unprepared for the sound and fury of a cannon broadside. Instead of driving forward in the terrifying concentration of a war galley's ramming maneuver, the dromons were simply drifting.

Again, the screech: *"Fire! All cannons—"*

Lost in the roar. Cloud of smoke. Enemy invisible.

John leaned over the rail, ready to order—

No need. Eusebius was already doing it.

Screech: "Cannister! Cannister! Load with cannister!"

The smoke cleared. Enough, at least, for John to see.

One dromon was sinking. Another had been battered badly. It was still afloat, but totally out of control. Yawing aside, now, its deadly ram aiming at nothing but the empty Mediterranean.

But the third ship was still coming in. Not driving for a ram, however, so much as clawing forward with broken oars and wounded rowers. Desperately seeking to grapple. Anything to get away from that horrible hail of destruction.

No use. John could see Eusebius at the middle cannon, fussing over the guncrew. The dromon was only ten yards away—close enough for the artificer's myopic eyes.

John saw Eusebius tap the gunner on his helmet. He saw his lips move, but couldn't hear the words.

An instant later, the cannon belched smoke. Cannister swept the length of the dromon like a scythe.

John of Rhodes was, in no sense, a squeamish man. But he could not help flinching at the sheer brutality which that round of cannister inflicted on the dromon's crew. Firing at point-blank range at a mass of men seated side-by-side on oarbanks—one oarbank lined up after another—

He shuddered. Saw Eusebius scamper down to the next cannon in line. Aim. Tap the gunner's helmet.

Another roar. Another round of cannister savaged the dromon. Blood everywhere.

Eusebius scampering. Aim. Tap. *Fire.*

It was sheer murder, now. Pure slaughter.

Eusebius scampering.

John leaned over, bellowing: *"Enough, Eusebius! Enough!"*

The artificer, his hand raised just above the next gunner's helmet, ready to tap, looked up. Squinted near-sightedly at the poop deck.

"Enough!" bellowed John.

Slowly, Eusebius straightened. Slowly, he walked to the rail and leaned over. Looked down into the hull of the dromon, which was now bumping gently against the *Theodora*'s side. Studying—for the first time, really—his handiwork.

Under other circumstances, at another time, the artificer's Syrian gunners—country rubes, the lot of them, coarse fellows—would have derided him then. Mocked and jeered, ridiculed and sneered, at the sight of their commander Eusebius puking his guts into the sea.

But not that day. Not then. Instead, Syrian gunners and their wives slowly gathered around him, the gunners patting him awkwardly on the shoulder as he vomited. And then, after he straightened, a plump Syrian wife held the sobbing young man in a warm embrace, ignoring the tears which soaked her homespun country garments.

Above, on the poop deck, John sighed.

"Welcome to the club, lad. Murderers' row."

He raised his head, scanning the sea.

Victory. Total. Four ships and their crews destroyed. Three battered into a pulp. The only unscathed dromon racing away.

He looked toward Antonina's flagship.

"She's all yours, girl. Alexandria's yours for the taking."

Aboard her flagship, Antonina studied the situation. Studied the pulverized enemy fleet, first, with satisfaction. Studied the wildly cheering mob on the Heptastadium, next, with equal satisfaction.

Then, all satisfaction gone, she studied the city itself. Beyond the harbor, looming in the distance above the tenements and warehouses, she could see Pompey's Pillar. And, not far away, the enormous Church of St. Michael. The Caesareum, that edifice had been called, once—the temple of Caesar. Its two great obelisks still stood before it. But the huge pagan structure, with its famous girdle of silver-and-gold pictures and statues, was now given over to the worship of Christ.

And, of course, to the power of Christ's official spokesmen. The Patriarchs of Alexandria resided there, as they had for two hundred years. A hundred years after they took up residence, in the very street before the Church, a brilliant female teacher of philosophy named Hypatia had been stripped naked and beaten to death by a mob of religious fanatics.

"Fuck Alexandria," she hissed.

Chapter 29

SUPPARA

Autumn, 531 A.D.

By the end of the first hour, Kujulo was complaining.

"What a muck! Gives me fond memories of Venandakatra's palace. Dry. Clean."

Ahead of him, picking his way through the dense, water-soaked forest, Kungas snorted.

"We were there for six months. As I recall, you started complaining the first day. Too dull, you said. Boring. You didn't quit until we got pitched out of the palace to make room for the Empress' new guards."

Another Kushan, forcing his own way forward nearby, sneered:

"Then he started complaining about the new quarters. Too cramped, he said. Too drafty."

Kujulo grinned. "I'm just more discriminating than you peasants, that's all. Cattle, cattle. Munch their lives away, swiping flies with their tails. What—"

He broke off, muttering a curse, swiping at his own fly.

Ahead, Kungas saw the small party of guides come to a halt at a fork in the trail. The three young Maratha woodcutters conferred with each other quickly. Then one of them trotted back toward the column of Kushan soldiers slogging through the forest.

Watching, Kungas was impressed by the light and easy manner in which the woodcutter moved through the dense growth. The "trail" they had been following was nothing more than a convoluted, serpentine series of relatively-clear patches in the forest. The soil was soggy from weeks of heavy rain. The Kushans, encumbered with armor and gear, had made heavy going of the march.

When the woodcutter reached Kungas, he pointed back up the trail and said, "That is it. Just the other side of that line of trees begins the hill leading to the fortress. You can go either right or left. There are trails."

He stopped, staring at the strange-looking soldier standing in front of him. It was obvious that the woodcutter was more than a little afraid of Kungas.

Some of that fear was due to Kungas' appearance. The Maratha fishermen and woodcutters who inhabited the dense forest along the coast were isolated, for the most part, from the rest of India. Kushans, with their topknots and flat, steppe-harsh features, were quite unknown to them.

But most of the young man's apprehension was due to more rational considerations. The woodcutter had good reason to be wary. Poor people in India—poor people in most lands, for that matter—had long memories of the way soldiers generally treated such folk as they.

The woodcutters had agreed to guide the Kushans to the fortress for two reasons only.

First, money. *Lots* of money. A small fortune, by their standards.

Second, the magic name of the Empress Shakuntala. Even here, in the remote coastal forest, the word had spread.

Andhra lived, still. Still, the Satavahana dynasty survived.

For the woodcutter, Andhra was a misty, even semi-mythical notion. The Satavahanas, a name of legend rather than real life. Like most of India's poor, the woodcutter did not consider politics part of his daily existence. Certainly not imperial politics.

Yet—

The new Malwa rulers were beasts. Cruel and rapacious. Everyone knew it.

In truth, the woodcutter himself had no experience with the Malwa. Preoccupied with subjugating the Deccan, the Malwa had not bothered to send forces to the coast, except for seizing the port of Suppara. Isolated by the Western Ghats, the sea-lying forests were of little interest to the Malwa.

But the coast-dwellers were Maratha, and the tales had spread. Tales of Malwa savagery. Tales of Malwa greed and plunder. And, growing ever more legendary with the passing of time, tales of the serene and kindly rule of the Satavahanas.

In actual fact, the woodcutter—for that matter, the oldest great-grandfather of his village—had no personal memory of the methods of Satavahana sovereignty. The Satavahana dynasty had left the poor folk of the coast to their own devices. Which was exactly the way those fishermen and woodcutters liked their rulers. Far off, and absent-minded. Heard of, but never seen.

So, after much hesitation and haggling, the young woodcutters had agreed to guide Kungas and his men to the fortress. They had not inquired as to Kungas' purpose in seeking that fearsome place.

Their work was done. Now, the woodcutter waited apprehensively. Would he be paid the amount still owing, or—

Kungas was a hard, hard man. Hard as stone, in most ways. But he was in no sense cruel. So he was not even tempted to cheat the woodcutter, or toy with the man's fears. He simply dipped into his purse and handed over three small coins.

A huge smile lit up the woodcutter's face. He turned and waved at his two fellows, showing them the money.

Kungas almost smiled himself, then. The other two woodcutters, still waiting twenty yards up the trail, had obviously been ready to bolt into the forest at the first sign of treachery. Now, they trotted eagerly forward.

"And that's another thing," grumbled Kujulo. "I miss the trusting atmosphere of the Vile One's palace."

The Kushans who were close enough to hear him burst into laughter. Even Kungas grinned.

The noise startled the woodcutters. But then, seeing that the jest was not aimed at them, they relaxed.

Not much, of course. Within seconds, they were scampering down the trail toward their village ten miles away. Being very careful to skirt the five hundred Kushan soldiers coming up that trail.

Kungas strode forward.

"Let's take a look at this mighty fortress, shall we?"

◇   ◇   ◇

Twenty minutes later, Kujulo was complaining again.

"I don't believe this shit. *Those* are guards? *That's* a fortress?"

Kungas and the five other Kushan troop leaders who were gathered alongside him, examining the fortress from a screen of trees, grunted their own contempt.

They were situated southeast of the fortress. The structure was perched on top of a small hill just before them. Two hundred feet tall, that hill, no more. On the other side of the hill, still invisible to the Kushans concealed within the trees, stretched the huge reaches of the ocean.

The forest which blanketed the coast was thinner on the hill. But not much. Some trees—mature, full-grown ones—were growing at the base of the fortress' walls. The branches of one particularly large tree even spread over part of the battlements.

"What kind of idiots don't clear the trees around a fortress?" demanded Kujulo.

"My *favorite* kind of idiots," replied Kungas softly. "Really, really, really idiotic idiots."

Kungas turned to face his subordinates. For once, he was actually smiling. A real, genuine smile, too. Not the crack in his iron face that usually passed for such.

"What do you think? Can we do it?"

Five sarcastic grunts came in reply. Kujulo pointed a finger at the fortress' entrance. The heavy wooden gates on the fortress' south side were wide open. In front of them, in the shelter provided by a makeshift canopy, eight Malwa soldiers lounged at their ease. Only one of them was even bothering to stand. The rest were sprawled on the ground. Two were apparently sleeping. The other five seemed to be engaged in a game of chance.

"Fuck the scaling equipment," growled Kujulo. "Don't need it. I can get my men within ten yards of those pigs without being seen. A quick rush and we've got the gate."

"How long could you hold it, do you think?" asked Kungas. The Kushan commander studied the trees growing on the hill. "You can get your men up there without being seen. But I don't think I can get more than three other squads close before they're spotted. The rest of us will have to wait here until you start the attack."

He glanced up, gauging the weather. The sky was overcast, but Kungas did not think it would rain anytime soon. Not for several hours, at least. He lowered his gaze and examined the hill itself. Estimating the distance and the condition of the terrain.

"Five hundred feet. Muddy. Steep climb. It'll take us two minutes."

Kujulo sneered.

"Two minutes? You think I can't hold a big gate like that against *those* sorry shits? With the help of three other squads? *For a lousy two minutes?*"

Kungas was amused. Kujulo's complaint, this time, was filled with genuine aggrievement.

"Do it, then. Pick whichever other squads you want for immediate support. While you're working your way up the hill, I'll get the rest of the men ready for the main charge."

Kujulo began to rise. Kungas stayed him with a hand on the shoulder.

"Remember, Kujulo. *Prisoners.* As many as we can get—especially the ones who're manning the cannons. We'll need them later."

Kujulo nodded. An instant later, he was gone.

The other troop leaders did not wait for Kungas' orders to start organizing the small army for an assault. Kungas did not bother to oversee their work. He had hand-picked the officers for this expedition and had complete confidence in them. He simply spent the time studying the fortress. Trying to determine, as best he could, the most likely internal lay-out of the structure.

Despite the slackness of its guards, the fortress itself was impressive. A simple square in design, the walls were thick, well-cut stone, rising thirty feet from the hilltop. The corners were protected by round towers rising another ten feet above the battlements. Two similar round towers anchored the gatehouse guarding the entrance. Along with the usual merlons and embrasures, the battlements also sported machicolations—enclosed stone shelves jutting a few feet out from the walls, with slots through which projectiles or boiling water could be dropped on besiegers below. The open embrasures were further strengthened by the addition of wooden shutters, which could be closed to shield against missiles.

Those battlements would have posed a tremendous challenge—if the walls had been manned by alert guards. As it was, during the minutes that he watched, Kungas saw only four soldiers appear atop the fortress. From their position, it was obvious that they were moving along an allure, or rampart walk, which served as the fighting platform for the battlements. But the Malwa were simply ambling along, preoccupied with their own business. Not one of those soldiers cast so much as a glance at the surrounding forest.

He tried to spot the location of the three siege guns, but couldn't see them. He knew they were there. Days earlier, from fishermen brought aboard Shakuntala's flagship, Kungas had heard good descriptions of the fortress' seaward appearance. There was some kind of heavy stone platform on the fortress' northwest corner. Atop that platform rested the siege guns. From that vantage point, the huge cannons could cover the harbor of Suppara less than half a mile to the north.

But they were on the opposite side of the fortress from where Kungas lay waiting in the trees.

Inwardly, he shrugged. He was not concerned about the cannons, for the moment. The Maratha fishermen had no idea how those cannons worked, or were positioned. Kungas himself, for that matter, had only a vague notion. Despite the many years he had served the Malwa, he had never gotten a close look at their siege guns. The Malwa were always careful to keep their Kushan and Rajput vassals from knowing too much about the "Veda weapons." But he knew enough, both from his own knowledge and the information imparted by the Ethiopians, to know that such enormous cannons could only be moved with great difficulty. There would be absolutely no way the Malwa in the fortress could reposition them in time to repel the coming assault.

Speaking of which—

He thought that Kujulo was probably in position, by now. No way to tell for sure, of course. Kungas had selected Kujulo to lead the attack because of the man's uncanny stealth. Not even Kungas, knowing what to look for, had caught more than a glimpse or two of Kujulo's men as they worked their way carefully up the hill. He was quite sure the Malwa guards had seen nothing.

He swiveled his head slowly, scanning right and left. He was pleased, though not surprised, to see that his entire army was in position, waiting for the signal.

Satisfied, Kungas turned his eyes back to the fortress. As if that little head motion had been the signal, Kujulo launched his attack.

Kungas could not see all the details of that sudden assault. Partly, because of the distance. Mostly, because of Kujulo.

That was the other reason Kungas had picked the man. Quick, quick, he was. He and the men whom he had trained. Quick, quick. Merciless.

He saw Kujulo's ten men lunging out of the trees. They had gotten within ten yards of the guard canopy without being spotted.

Three seconds later, the killing began. Eight seconds later, the killing ended. Most of that time had been spent spearing the five Malwa gamblers, whose squawling, writhing, squirming huddle had presented a peculiar obstacle to the Kushan soldiers. Almost like spearing a school of fish.

Kungas watched none of it, however. As soon as he saw Kujulo's men lunge out of the trees, he gave the order for the general assault. Five hundred Kushans—less the forty already charging the gate—began storming up the hill.

It was a veteran kind of "storm." The Kushans paced themselves carefully. There was no point in arriving at the fortress too exhausted to fight. Kujulo and his men would just have to hold on as best they could.

That task proved much less difficult than it should have been. Before the alarm was sounded within the fortress, Kujulo and his squad had not only killed the eight guards outside the gates, but had managed to penetrate the gatehouse itself. The tunnel through the gatehouse was occupied by two other men, neither of whom was any more alert than the eight soldiers lounging outside the gate.

Kujulo himself killed the two Malwa soldiers in the gatehouse. That done, he immediately tried to find the murder holes. But, searching the ceiling which arched over the entryway, he could see none.

One of his soldiers trotted up to him. Like Kujulo, the man's eyes were examining the stonework above, looking for the holes through which enemies could thrust spears or drop stones and boiling water.

"Don't see 'em," he muttered.

Kujulo shook his head.

"Aren't any." He spit on the stone floor, then made for the far entrance. His squad followed. Five seconds later, soldiers from the three squads serving as their immediate backup began pouring into the entryway.

The entryway—in effect, a stone tunnel running straight through the gatehouse—was thirty feet long and about half as wide. The arched ceiling, at its summit, was not more than twelve feet high. The inner gate, opening into the fortress' main ground, was standing wide open. When Kujulo reached it, he saw that there were no Malwa troops standing guard.

"Fucking idiots," he sneered. He could hear shouts coming from somewhere inside the fortress. The alarm had finally been given. Either someone had heard the sound of fighting or a guard standing atop the battlements had seen the attack.

After passing through the inner gate, Kujulo took three steps forward before stopping to study the situation. The inside of the fortress was designed like a hollow square. The walls on the north, east and south of the structure were simply fortifications. Outside of the horse pens and corrals nestled up against the northeast corner, there were no rooms built into the walls themselves.

The western end of the fortress was a different proposition altogether. There, massive brick buildings abutted directly against the outer wall. Above those buildings, resting on a stone platform reinforced with heavy timbers, Kujulo could see the fortress' three great cannons.

Those buildings would be the quarters for the garrison. Already, Kujulo could see Malwa soldiers spilling out from the many doors set into the brickwork. The soldiers fumbled with spears and swords. Many of them were still putting on their armor. Flimsy, leather armor. Kujulo almost laughed, seeing one of the Malwa stumble and flop on his belly.

But Kujulo could see no grenades, and, what was better—

"Look at that, will you!" exclaimed one of his men. "They can't have more than two hundred men guarding this place!"

Kujulo nodded. His squad member had immediately spotted the most important thing about the fortress. The first thing Kujulo himself had noticed.

No tents.

The flat, empty ground which formed most of the fortress' interior should have been *covered* with tents. There was not enough room in the brick buildings for more than a small garrison. Kujulo thought his squad member's estimate of two hundred was overgenerous. The garrison's officers, for one thing, would have undoubtedly taken the largest rooms for themselves. For another, Kujulo could see no sign of any cookfires on the open ground. That meant a kitchen, taking up even more of the brick buildings' space.

"A hundred and fifty, tops," he pronounced. He studied the Malwa soldiers advancing toward them from the west—if the term "advancing" can be used to describe a mode of progress that was as skittish as a kitten's. Studied the soldiers, and, more closely, their leather armor.

"Shit." He spit on the ground. "Those aren't soldiers. Not proper ones. Those are nothing but fucking *gunners*. Cannon handlers."

His squad was now ranged on both sides of him. Behind, he could hear the thirty men from the next three squads moving up.

All of his men grinned. Like wolves eyeing a herd of caribou.

"I do believe you're right," said one.

Another laughed. "Think we can hold this gate against them? For the minute it'll take Kungas to get here."

Again, Kujulo spit on the ground.

"Fuck that," he snarled. "I intend to *defeat* those bastards. *Follow me*."

He stalked toward the Malwa gunners. By now, all four squads had taken position in a line stretching a third of the way across the inner grounds. Forty Kushans, wearing good scale armor, hefting their swords and spears with practiced ease, began marching on the Malwa.

The gunners stopped. Stared.

Kujulo broke into an easy trot. Forty Kushans matched his pace.

The gunners stared. Edged back.

Kujulo raised his sword and bellowed the order to charge. Shrieking like madmen, forty Kushans charged the hundred or so Malwa some thirty yards away.

The gunners turned and raced for the brick buildings. Half of them dropped their weapons along the way.

By the time Kungas arrived, a minute or so later, Kujulo was already organizing a siege. And complaining, bitterly, that he would have to go into the fucking forest and cut down a fucking tree since the fucking Malwa didn't have any fucking timber big enough to ram through the fucking doors.

◇   ◇   ◇

Cutting down a tree proved unnecessary. The "siege" was perhaps the shortest in history. As soon as the Malwa gunners forted up in the brick buildings saw Kungas' five hundred men storming into the fortress, they immediately began negotiating a surrender.

The biggest obstacle in those negotiations were the five Mahaveda priests holed up with the gunners. The priests, bound by holy oaths to safeguard the secret of the Veda weapons, demanded a fight to the death. They denounced all talk of surrender as impious treason.

Kungas, hearing the priests' shouting voices, called out his own offer to the Malwa gunners.

Cut the priests' throats. Pitch their bodies out. You'll be given good treatment.

The first corpse sailed through one of the doors not fifteen seconds later. Within a minute, the lifeless bodies of all five priests were sprawled in the dirt of the fortress grounds.

Kungas cocked his head at Kujulo. "What's your opinion? Think those gunners'll spill their secrets?"

Kujulo spit on the ground. "Imagine so. Especially after I reason with them."

"We're family men," complained the garrison commander. He was squatting in the middle of the fortress' gun platform, where Kungas had chosen to interrogate him. Kungas himself was standing by one of the great siege guns, five feet away. Near him, Kujulo sat on a pile of stone cannonballs.

"They told us this was just garrison work," whined the captured officer. "A formality, sort of."

Kungas studied the man quivering with fear in front of him. It was obvious that the garrison was not one of the Malwa's elite kshatriya units. Technically, true, many of the gunners were kshatriya. But, just as there are dogs and dogs—poodles and pit bulls—so also are there kshatriya and kshatriya.

Kungas realized that Rao's savage guerrilla war had stretched Venandakatra's resources badly. The Goptri of the Deccan didn't have enough front-line troops to detail for every task. So he had assigned one of his sorriest units to garrison Suppara's fortress.

And why not? he mused. Suppara's on the coast side of the Western Ghats. Too far away for Venandakatra to worry about. Too far away for Rao to strike at, even if he wanted to.

But none of his good cheer showed on his face. Kungas eyed the captive stonily.

The garrison commander flinched from that pitiless gaze.

"We're fathers and husbands," he wailed. "Way too old for this kind of thing. You won't hurt our families, will you? We brought them with us to Suppara."

Kujulo sat erect, his eyes widening. With a little sideways lurch, he slid off the pile of cannonballs and strode over to the Malwa commander. Then, leaning over the frightened officer, he barked, "Brought your families, did you? *Women, too? Wives and daughters?*"

The garrison commander stared up at Kujulo's leering countenance. The Kushan's expression was venery and lust personified. Gleaming eyes, loose lips—even a hint of slobber.

Now completely terrified, the officer looked appealingly toward the Kushan commander.

"Depends," growled Kungas. Face like an iron mask.

"On what?" squeaked the officer.

Kungas made a little gesture, ordering the man to rise. The Malwa sprang to his feet.

Another gesture. *Follow me.*

Kungas walked over to the edge of the gun platform. A low stone wall, two feet high, was all that stood between him and a vertical drop of about a hundred feet. The western wall of the fortress, atop which the gun platform was situated, rose straight up from a stone escarpment. To the northwest, the town and harbor of Suppara were completely within view. View—and cannon range.

Gingerly, the Malwa officer joined Kungas at the wall. Kungas pointed at the harbor below. To the three war galleys moored in that harbor, more precisely.

"It depends on whether—"

He broke off, seeing that the Malwa officer was not listening to him. Instead, the garrison commander was staring to the southwest.

Kungas followed his eyes. On the horizon, barely visible, were the sails of a fleet. A vast fleet, judging from their number.

"Ah," he grunted. "Just in time."

He bestowed his crack-in-the-iron version of a smile on the Malwa officer. "Such a pleasure, you know, when things happen when they're supposed to. Don't you think?"

The garrison commander transferred his stare from the distant fleet to Kungas. Again, Kungas pointed to the three galleys in the harbor below.

"*Depends*," he growled. The Malwa's eyes bulged.

"You can't be serious!" he exclaimed.

Kungas flicked his eyes toward Kujulo. The Malwa's eyes followed. Kujulo, standing fifteen feet away, grinned savagely and grabbed his crotch.

The Malwa recoiled, pallid-faced.

"*Depends*," growled Kungas. "*Depends*—on whether you and your men destroy those three ships for us. *Depends*—also—on whether you show us how to use the cannons."

Silence followed, for a minute. The garrison commander stared at the galleys below. At Kujulo.

Listened, again, to the growl:

"Depends."

The first cannon fired when Shakuntala's flagship, in the van of the fleet, was not more than three miles from the entrance to the harbor. The Empress and her peshwa, standing in the bow, saw the cloud of gunsmoke; moments later, heard the roar.

Another cannon fired. Then, a third.

"Are they firing at us?" queried Holkar. Ruefully: "I'm afraid my eyes aren't as good as they used to be."

The Empress of Andhra had young eyes, and good ones.

"No, Dadaji. They are firing at something in the harbor. Malwa warships, I assume."

Holkar sighed. "Kungas has done it, then. He has taken the fortress."

Young eyes, good eyes, suddenly filled with tears.

"My Mahadandanayaka," she whispered. "Bhatasvapati."

She clutched Holkar's arm, and pressed her face against his shoulder. For all the world, like a girl seeking shelter and security from her father.

"And you, my peshwa."

As the huge fleet sailed toward the harbor of Suppara, Dadaji Holkar held his small Empress in his arms. Thin arms, they were, attached to the slender shoulders of a middle-aged scholar. But, in that moment, they held all the comfort which the girl needed.

If an Empress found shelter there, the man himself found a greater comfort in the sheltering. His own family was lost to him, perhaps forever, but he had found another to give him comfort in his search. A child, here. A brother, there on the fortress above.

A bigger, tougher kind of brother. The kind every bookish man wishes he had.

"Mine, too," he murmured, staring at the clouds of gunsmoke wafting over the distant harbor. "My *Mahadandanayaka*. My *Bhatasvapati*."

Chapter 30

THE EUPHRATES
Autumn, 531 A.D.

"Tell me again," said Belisarius.

Standing next to the general on top of the giant pile of rocks which the Kushans had hauled out of the Nehar Malka, Maurice decided to misunderstand the question.

"Fifteen thousand cavalry they've got now," he gruffed. He pointed a stubby, thick finger at the cloud of dust rising out of the desert some ten miles to the southeast. "Five thousand of them, by my estimate, are Lakhmid Arabs. They're riding camels, the most, and—"

Belisarius smiled crookedly.

"Tell me again, Maurice."

The chiliarch puffed out his cheeks. Sighed. "This is not my province, general. I don't have any business mucking around in—"

"I'm not asking you to *muck around*," growled Belisarius. "And spare me the protestations of humble modesty. Just tell me what you *think*."

Again, Maurice puffed out his cheeks. Then, exhaled noisily.

"What I think, general, is that the Emperor of Persia is offering the Roman Empire a dynastic marriage. Between Photius and the eldest daughter of his noblest sahrdaran."

Maurice glanced down at Baresmanas. The father of the daughter in question was perched sixty feet away on a large boulder further down the man-made hill. Out of hearing range. Maurice continued:

"He'd offer one of his own daughters in marriage—Khusrau made that clear enough—but he doesn't have any. So Baresmanas' daughter is the best alternative, other than choosing from one of his brothers' or half-brothers' various girls."

Belisarius shook his head. "That's the last thing he'd do. Khusrau's trying to bridle that crowd of ambitious brothers. And, if I'm reading him right, trying to cement the most trustworthy layers of the nobility to his rule."

The general scratched his chin, idly staring at the cloud of dust in the desert. His eyes were not really focussed on the sight, however. From experience, he knew that the Malwa army advancing on him would not be in position to attack until the following day. In the meantime—

"Khusrau's canny," he said. "Part of our conversations in Babylon consisted of his questions regarding the Roman methods of organizing our Empire. I think he's planning—groping, is maybe a better way to put it—to break Persia from its inveterate—"

He paused. The word "feudalism" would mean nothing to Maurice. It had meant nothing to Belisarius, either, until Aide explained it to him.

"—traditions," he concluded, waving his hand vaguely.

"Think he can do it?" asked Maurice. "Persians are set in their ways."

Belisarius pondered the question. Aide had given him, once, a vision of the Persia which Khusrau Anushirvan had created, in the future which would have been if the "new gods" hadn't intervened in human history. The greatest Emperor of the Sassanid dynasty had tried to impose centralized, imperial authority over the unruly Aryan nobility, inspired by Rome's example, to some degree; guided by his own keen intelligence, for the rest.

In many ways, Khusrau would succeed. He would break the military power of the great aristocracy. He would win the allegiance of the dehgans, transform them into the social base for a professional army paid and equipped by the Emperor, and place them under the authority of his own generals—*spahbads*, he would call them. Never again would ambitious sahrdarans or vurzurgans pose a threat to the throne.

Khusrau would succeed elsewhere, too. His greatest reform—the one for which history would call him "Khusrau the Just"—would be his drastic overhaul of taxation. Khusrau would institute a system of taxation which was not only far less burdensome to the common folk but which also stabilized the imperial treasury.

Yet—

If there was one thing which Aide had shown Belisarius, it was that human history never moved in simple, clear channels. Khusrau's dynasty—the Sassanid dynasty—would vanish into history, as all dynasties did. But his tax system would remain. The Arab conquerors of Persia would be so impressed by it that they would use it as the model for the tax system of the great Moslem Caliphates.

Belisarius' mind was now wandering very far from the moment. He knew of the Moslem Caliphates of the future that would have been. Aide had shown him. Just as Aide had shown him the fall of the Roman Empire, almost a thousand years in the future. The sack of Constantinople at the hands of the so-called Fourth Crusade. The final conquest of Byzantium, a quarter of a millennium later, by a new people called the Turks.

Belisarius wondered, now, as he often had before, what he thought of all that Aide had shown him. He was a general in the service of the Roman Empire. Indeed, one of the greatest generals which Rome ever produced. He knew that for a simple fact. And knew, also, that he was the only general in the long history of that great Empire who fought for it while understanding, all along, that the Empire was doomed.

He hoped to saved Rome, and the world, from the Malwa tyranny. But he would not save Rome itself. Rome would fall—someday, somehow. If not by the hand of Sultan Mehmet and his Janissaries, by the hand of someone else. All human creations fell, or collapsed, or simply decayed. Someday, somehow, somewhere.

Mentally, Belisarius shrugged. His was not the task of creating a perfect human future. His was the task of making sure that people had a future they could create. Create badly, perhaps—but *create*. Not be forced into a mold created for them.

Maurice was still waiting patiently for an answer. Belisarius smiled, and gave him the simple one.

"Yes, he can do it. He *will* do it."

Maurice grunted. The grunt carried a great deal of satisfaction—which was odd, really, for a Roman soldier. But Maurice had met Khusrau Anushirvan, and, like many people, even that crusty veteran had come under the spell of the Persian Emperor's powerful personality.

"What do *you* think?" he now asked. "About the proposal for a dynastic marriage, I mean?"

Belisarius smiled again. "I think it's a great idea. Theodora'll be twitchy about it, of course. But Justinian will seize on it with both hands."

Maurice frowned. "Why?"

"Because Justinian always has his—'mind's eye,' let's call it—on the position of the dynasty. *His* dynasty, for all that Photius isn't his own son. And he knows that there'd be nothing that would cement the army's allegiance more than a dynastic marriage with a Persian Princess."

Maurice tugged his beard thoughtfully. "True enough," he agreed. "Anything that would prevent another bloody brawl with those tough fucking dehgans. Bad for your retirement prospects, that is."

A thought came to him. His eyes widened, slightly. "Now that I think about it—When was the last time a Roman Emperor married a Persian noblewoman?"

Belisarius chuckled. "It's *never* happened, Maurice. The Persians consider us Roman mongrels unfit for their blood."

"That's what I thought," mused Maurice. "God, the army'll be tickled pink. They already think of Photius as one of their own, you know. If he marries a Persian sahrdaran's daughter—"

The chiliarch broke off, eyeing the figure of Baresmanas below. "Does *he* know about it, d'you think? It's his daughter we're talking about, after all. Maybe *he* won't like the idea."

Belisarius laughed, clapping the chiliarch on the shoulder.

"Unless I'm badly mistaken, Maurice, the whole thing was Baresmanas' idea in the first place."

As if he had been cued, Baresmanas chose that moment to turn his head and look up at the two Roman officers standing on the very top of the rock-pile. For a moment, he and Belisarius stared at each other. Then, Baresmanas hopped off the rock—his shoulder might be half-crippled, but he was still quite spry for a middle-aged man—and began climbing toward them.

As soon as he reached the hill-top, Baresmanas asked, "So—what do you think?"

For a moment, the Roman general was startled. How could Baresmanas have overheard—?

Then, realizing that the sahrdaran was talking about their military situation, Belisarius grimaced.

"We're not going to be able to surprise them with another flank attack, that's for sure."

Baresmanas nodded. Neither he nor Belisarius had really thought that option would be available. Having been shattered at Anatha, the Malwa would not make the mistake of overconfidence again. The army approaching them from the southeast was much larger than the force they had faced at the hunting park. Still, the commander of those oncoming Malwa was keeping a massive guard on his flanks. *Well* out on his flanks, using his best troops for the job. On his left, in the desert, the Malwa commander was using Lakhmids on camelback. On his right, in the fertile terrain on the other side of the almost-dry Euphrates, he was using Kushan cavalry. Four thousand of them, according to Kurush's scouts, maintaining an excellent marching order, with a large contingent of skirmishers guarding their own flank.

There would be no way to surprise the Malwa with any clever maneuver with concealed troops. Not this time.

"We will have to rely on your main plan, then," said Baresmanas. The sahrdaran heaved a sigh. "Casualties will be high."

Belisarius tightened his lips. "Yes, they will. But I don't see any other option."

Baresmanas turned his head, staring to the west. Across the river, he could see the huge camp where Ormazd's twenty thousand lancers and archers had taken position, after arriving the week before. Even at the distance, he could see Ormazd's own pavilion, towering over the much-less-elaborate tents of his soldiers.

"If he does not—"

"He will," said Belisarius confidently. His crooked smile came, in full force.

"You will have noticed, I'm sure, that Ormazd pitched his camp *there*—instead of further down the river."

Baresmanas nodded, scowling. "The swine," he growled. "Upstream of the dam, where he pitched his camp, there is no way he can cross the Euphrates in time to give you help, should you need it. He should have taken position several miles further down, where the riverbed is almost empty."

Belisarius shook his head.

"Not a chance, Baresmanas. His troops would take the brunt of the assault, then. Whereas now—"

"They are obviously out of the action," concluded the sahrdaran. "The Malwa will recognize that immediately, and concentrate most of their forces here. They will only need to keep a screen against the chance of Ormazd attacking their left."

Belisarius chuckled, making clear his opinion on the likelihood of Ormazd ordering any massive sally. The Persian Emperor's half-brother, it was clear, intended to sit on his hands while the Romans and the Malwa army slugged it out on the other side of the Euphrates.

"How did he explain it?" demanded Baresmanas angrily.

Belisarius shrugged. "In all truth, he didn't have much explaining to do. I didn't press him on the matter, Baresmanas. I *want* him where he is."

Baresmanas' scowl deepened. Intellectually, the sahrdaran understood Belisarius' stratagem. Emotionally, however, the Aryan nobleman still choked at the idea of actually *using* another Aryan's expected treachery. A *Sassanid*, no less.

Baresmanas eyed the Roman general. "I forget, sometimes, just how incredibly cold-blooded you can be," he muttered. "I cannot think of another man who would develop a battle plan based on his expectation that an ally would betray him. Take such a possibility into account, certainly—any sane commander does that, when fighting with foreign allies. But to *plan* on it—No, more! To actually engineer it, to maneuver for it!—"

Baresmanas fell silent, shaking his head. Belisarius, for his part, said nothing. There was nothing to say, really. Despite the many ways in which he and Baresmanas were much alike, there were other ways in which they were as different as two men could be.

For all his sophistication and scholarship, Baresmanas was still, at bottom, the same man who had spent his boyhood admiring Persian lancers and archers. Spent hours of that boyhood watching dehgans on the training fields of his father's vast estate, demonstrating their superb skill as mounted archers.

Whereas Belisarius, for all his own sophistication and subtleties, was still—at bottom—the same man who had spent his boyhood admiring Thracian blacksmiths. Spent hours of that boyhood watching the blacksmiths on his father's modest estate, demonstrating their own more humble but—when all is said and done—much more powerful craft. Men die by the dehgan's steel. People *live* by the blacksmith's iron.

Even as a boy, however, Belisarius had had a subtle mind. So, where other boys admired the strength of the blacksmith, and gasped with awe at the mighty strokes of hammer on anvil, Belisarius had seen the truth. A blacksmith was a strong man, of necessity. But a *good* blacksmith did everything he could to husband that strength. Time after time, watching, the boy Belisarius had seen how cunningly the blacksmith positioned the glowing metal, and with what a precise angle he wielded the hammer.

So, he said nothing to Baresmanas. There was nothing to say.

A few minutes later, called down by one of his tribunes with a problem, Maurice left the artificial hilltop. Belisarius and Baresmanas remained there alone, studying the huge Malwa force advancing toward them.

They did not speak, other than to exchange an occasional professional assessment of the enemy's disposition of its forces. On that subject, not surprisingly, they were always in agreement. If Baresmanas did not have his Roman ally's sheer military genius, he was still an experienced and competent general in his own right.

Underlying that agreement, however, and for all their genuine friendship, two very different souls readied for the coming battle.

The one, an Aryan sahrdaran—noblest man of the noblest line of the world's noblest race—sought strength and courage from that very nobility. Sought for it, found it, and awaited the battle with a calm certitude in his own valor and honor.

The other, a Thracian born into the lower ranks of Rome's parvenu aristocracy, never even thought of nobility. Thought, not once, of honor or of valor. He simply waited for the oncoming enemy, patiently, like a blacksmith waits for iron to heat in the furnace.

A craftsman at his trade. Nothing more.

And nothing less.

Chapter 31
ALEXANDRIA
Autumn, 531 A.D.

"This is madness!" shouted one of the gymnasiarchs. The portly notable was standing in the forefront of a small crowd packed into the audi-ence chamber. All of them were men, all of them were finely dressed, and most were as fat as he was.

Alexandria's city council.

"Madness!" echoed another member of the council.

"Lunacy!" cried a third.

Antonina was not certain which particular titles those men enjoyed. Gymnasiarchs also, perhaps, or possibly *exegetai*.

She did not care. The specific titles were meaningless—hoary traditions from the early centuries of the Empire, when the city council actually exercised power. In modern Alexandria, member-ship in the council was purely a matter of social prestige. The real authority was in the hands of the Praetorian Prefect, the com-mander of the Army of Egypt, and—above all—the Patriarch.

After disembarking her troops, Antonina had immediately seized a palace in the vicinity of the Great Harbor. She was not even sure whose palace it was. The owner had fled before she and her sol-diers occupied the building, along with most of his servants.

Each of the many monarchs who had ruled Egypt in the eight hundred and sixty-two years since the founding of Alexandria had built their own palaces. The city was dotted with the splendiferous things. Over the centuries, most of those royal palaces had become the private residences of the city's high Greek nobility.

No sooner had she established her temporary headquarters than the entire city council appeared outside the palace, demanding the right to present their petitions and their grievances. She had invited them in—well over a hundred of the self-important folk—simply in order to gauge the attitude of Alexandria's upper crust.

Within ten minutes after they surged into the audience chamber, they had made their sentiments clear. As follows:

One. The Empire was ruled by a madwoman.

Two. The mad Empress had sent another madwoman to spread the madness to Alexandria.

Three. They, on the other hand, were not mad.

Four. Nor would they tolerate madness.

Five. Not that they themselves, of course, would think of raising their hands in violence against the Empress and her representative—perish the thought, perish the thought—even if they *were* nothing but a couple of deranged females. But—

Six. The dreaded mob of Alexandria, always prone to erupt at the slightest provocation, was even now coming to a furious boil. Any moment now, madness would be unleashed in the streets. Which—

Seven. Was the inevitable fate for madwomen.

Eight. Who were, they reiterated, utterly mad. Insanity personified. Completely out of their wits. Bereft of all sense and reason. Raving—

Antonina had had enough. "Arrest them," she said. Demurely. Ladylike. "The whole lot."

A little flip of the hand. "Stow them in the hold of one of the grain ships, for now. We'll figure out what to do with them later."

As Ashot and his cataphracts carried out her order, Antonina ignored the squawls of outrage issued by the city's notables as they were hog-tied and frog-marched out of the palace. She had other problems to deal with.

Some of those problems were simple and straightforward.

Representatives from the very large Jewish population of the city inquired as to their likely welfare. Antonina assured them that the Jews would be unmolested, both in their civil and religious affairs, so long as they accepted her authority. Five minutes later, the Jewish representatives were ushered out. On their way, Antonina heard one of them mutter to another, "Let the damned Christians fight it out, then. No business of ours."

Good enough.

Next problem:

Representatives of the city's powerful guilds demanded to know what the Empire's attitude would be toward their ancient prerogatives.

Complicated, but not difficult.

Antonina assured them that neither she, nor Emperor Photius, nor the Empress Regent, had any desire to trample on the guilds' legitimate interests. Other than, in the case of the shipbuilding and metalworking guilds, providing them with a lot of work. Oh, yes, and work for the huge linenmakers guild also. Sails would be needed for all the new ships they'd be building. And no doubt there'd be some imperial money tossed at the glassworkers guild. The Empress Regent—as everyone knew—was exceedingly fond of fine glasswork.

The papyrus-makers, of course, were sitting pretty. The influx of imperial officials would naturally increase the demand for paper. As for the jewelers, well, what with the enormous booty that'd soon be rolling in from the Malwa, writhing in defeat and humiliation, all of the soldiers—the many, many, many soldiers—who would be arriving to strengthen Egypt's garrison would naturally want to convert their bulky loot into items which were both portable and readily liquifiable, of which—O happy coincidence—fine jewelry took pride of place, especially the jewelry produced in Alexandria, which city was famed throughout the Empire—O happy coincidence—for the unexcelled craft of its gold—and silversmiths.

Now, as to the matter of grain-shipping guilds, well, soldiers are strapping lads. Need to eat a lot. So—

Two hours later, the representatives of the city's commercial and manufacturing guilds tottered out of the palace, reeling dizzily at the thought of their newfound wealth.

Other problems, of course, were hard as nails. But those, at least, Antonina did not have to spend hour after hour sitting on a chair to deal with. Those problems could only be dealt with in the streets.

Hermogenes stalked into the audience chamber just as the last guild representatives were leaving. He strode directly to Antonina's chair, leaned over, and whispered, "It's starting. Paul just finished a sermon at the Church of St. Michael, calling on the city's faithful to reject the Whore of Babylon."

"Which one?" asked Antonina whimsically. "Me? Or Theodora?"

Hermogenes shrugged. "From what our spies report, the Patriarch wasn't specific. The former Patriarch, I should say."

Antonina shook her head. "He's *still* the Patriarch, Hermogenes. In fact, if not in name. Theodosius may have the title, but it means nothing until we can install him in the Church of St. Michael and keep him there."

She cast a glance at the man in question. Theodosius was standing twenty feet away, conferring with two of the deacons who served as his ecclesiastical aides. Zeno, the commander of the Knights Hospitaler, was standing next to him, along with two of his own subordinates.

Antonina was pleased to note that Theodosius seemed neither agitated nor apprehensive.

I don't know about his theology, but the man's got good nerves. He'll need them.

She looked back at Hermogenes. "What about Ambrose?"

Hermogenes scowled. "The bastard's holed up at the army camp in Nicopolis. *With* all of his troops."

Ashot and Euphronius arrived just in time to hear the last words.

"Only thing he can do, for the moment," said Ashot. "He's a general in the army, subject to the Empire's stringent rules governing mutiny. Whereas"—the Armenian cataphract sneered—"the Patriarch can give sermons, and claim afterward that he was just preaching to his flock. No fault of his if he was misunderstood when he denounced the Whore of Babylon. *He* was just cautioning men against sin. *He* certainly didn't intend for a huge mob to assault the Empress' representative. He is shocked and distressed to learn that the unfortunate woman was torn limb from limb."

By this time, Theodosius and Zeno had joined the little circle around Antonina. "It's happened before," commented the Knights Hospitaler. "The prefect Petronius was stoned by the mob, during Augustus' reign. And one of the Ptolemies was dragged out into the streets and assassinated. Alexander II, I think it was."

Antonina pursed her lips. "How long do you think Ambrose will sit on the sidelines, Ashot?"

The commander of her Thracian bucellarii shrugged. "Depends on his troops, mostly. Ambrose only has three options." He held up his thumb. "One—accept his dismissal."

"Not a chance," interjected Hermogenes. "I know the man. Sittas was being polite when he called him a stinking bastard. Ambitious, he is."

Ashot nodded. "Rule out that option, then. That only leaves him two." He held up his other thumb. "Mutiny. But—"

Hermogenes started shaking his head.

"—that'd be insane," continued Ashot. "Every one of his soldiers knows the penalty for mutiny in the Roman army. The risk isn't worth it unless—" He held up his forefinger alongside his thumb.

"Option two. Ambrose declares himself the new Emperor. His soldiers hail him, start a civil war, and hope to enjoy the bounty if they win."

Hermogenes nodded vigorously. "He's right. A Patriarch can play games with street violence. A general can't. For him, it's all or nothing."

Antonina looked back and forth between the two officers. "You still haven't told me how long I've got before he decides."

"A day, at the very least," said Ashot immediately. "He's *got* to have the support of his soldiers. Most of them, anyway. That'll take time."

"Speeches," amplified Hermogenes. "Perorations to the assembled troops. Negotiations with his top officers. Promises to make to everybody."

"For sure he'll promise a huge *annona* if he takes the throne," added Ashot immediately. All the officers nodded, their faces grim. The annona was the pay bonus which Roman emperors traditionally granted their troops upon assuming the throne. During the chaotic civil wars three centuries earlier, when Rome often had two or three simultaneous emperors—few of whom survived more than a year or two—the claimants for the throne had bid for the loyalty of the armies by promising absurd bonuses.

"Pay increases," elaborated Hermogenes, "after he's been made Emperor. Better retirement pensions. Anything else he can think of."

"He'll be talking nonstop for hours," concluded Ashot. "All through the day and halfway through the night."

Antonina rose. "Right. The gist of it is that I've got a day to deal with the Patriarch's mob, without interference from the Army of Egypt."

Ashot and Hermogenes nodded.

"Let's get to it, then. How big is that mob?"

Ashot spread his hands. "Hard to know, exactly. Thousands from the crowd packing St. Michael's. Most will be his fanatic adherents, but there'll be a lot of orthodox sympathizers mixed in with them. Then—"

He turned to Theodosius.

"How many hardcore Chalcedonian monks are there, residing in the city?"

The Patriarch grimaced. "At least two thousand."

"Five thousand," added Zeno, "if you include the ones living in monasteries within a day's march of Alexandria."

Ashot turned back to Antonina. "Every last one of those monks will be in with the mob, stirring them up."

"Leading the charge, more like," snarled Hermogenes.

Ashot barked an angry little laugh. "*And* you can bet that the Hippodrome factions will join the fray. The Blues, for sure. They'll be interested in looting, for the most part. But they'll throw their weight in on Paul's side, if for no other reason than to get his blessing for their crimes."

"They'll head for Delta quarter, right off," added Zeno.

Antonina nodded thoughtfully. Alexandria was divided into five quarters, designated by the first five letters of the Greek alphabet. Delta quarter, for centuries, had been the city's Jewish area.

She moved her eyes to Euphronius. Throughout the preceding discussion—as was usual in these command meetings—the commander of the Theodoran Cohort had said nothing. The young Syrian grenadier was too shy to do more than listen.

"How do you feel about Jews?" she asked him abruptly.

Euphronius was startled by the question.

"Jews?" He frowned. "Never thought much about it, to be honest. Can't say I like them, but—"

He fell silent, groping for words.

Antonina was satisfied. Anti-Jewish sentiment was endemic throughout the Roman Empire, but only in Alexandria did it reach rabid proportions. That had been true for centuries. Syrians, on the other hand, had managed to co-exist with Jews without much in the way of trouble.

"I want you and the Cohort to march to the Jewish quarter. It'll be your job to defend it against the Hippodrome thugs. Take one of Hermogenes' infantry cohorts for support."

It was Ashot and Hermogenes' turn to be start-led, now.

"What for, Antonina?" asked Hermogenes. "The Jews can take care of themselves. Won't be the first time they've fought it out with Blues and Greens."

Antonina shook her head. "That's exactly what I'm afraid of. I intend to"—she clenched her fist—"*suppress* this street violence. The last thing I want is for it to spread."

"I agree with Antonina," interjected Theodosius. "If the Jews get involved in street fighting, Paul will use that to further incite the mob."

"*Whereas*," said Antonina, "if the mob is stopped before it can even start the pogrom—*by the Empress' own Cohort*—it'll send a very different signal."

She straightened, back stiff. "I promised their representatives that Alexandria's Jews would be unmolested if they remained loyal to the Empire. I intend to keep that promise."

She began moving toward the great set of double doors leading out of the audience chamber, issuing commands as she went.

"Hermogenes, detail one of your cohorts to back up the grenadiers in the Delta Quarter. Find one with officers who are familiar with Alexandria. The Syrians'll get lost in this city without guides."

"Take Triphiodoros and his boys, Euphronius," said Hermogenes. "He's from Alexandria."

"He's a damned good tribune, too," agreed the Syrian grenadier, nodding with approval.

Antonina stopped abruptly. She turned to face the commander of the Theodoran Cohort. Her expression was stern, almost fierce.

"Good tribune or not, Euphronius—*you're in charge*. The infantry's there to back you up, nothing more."

Euphronius started to make some protest, but Antonina drove over it.

"You've always been subordinate to someone else. Not today. Today, you're leading an independent command. You're ready for it—and so are the grenadiers. *I expect you to shine.*"

The young Syrian commander straightened. "We will, Antonina. We will not fail."

Antonina turned to Ashot and Hermogenes.

"Get your troops ready. I want all of them in full armor. That includes the cataphracts' horses. *Full armor*—nothing less. Make sure of it. In this heat, a lot of the men will try to slide through with half-armor."

"Full armor?" Ashot winced. "Be like an oven. Antonina, we're not dealing with Persian dehgans here, for the sake of Christ. Just a pack of scruffy—"

Antonina shook her head firmly. "That's overkill, I know, against a street mob. But your troops won't be in the middle of the action, anyway, and I want them to look as intimidating as possible."

Ashot's eyes widened. So did Hermogenes'.

"Not in the middle of it?" asked the Armenian cataphract.

Antonina smiled. Then, turned to face Zeno.

"I believe it's time for the Knights Hospitaler to take center stage."

Zeno nodded solemnly. "So do I, Antonina. And this is the perfect opportunity."

"I'm not so sure about that," muttered Hermogenes. He gave Zeno a half-apologetic, half-skeptical glance. "Meaning no offense, but your monks have only had a small amount of training. This is one hell of a messy situation to throw them into."

Antonina started to intervene. But then, seeing the confident expression on Zeno's face, decided to let the Knight Hospitaler handle the matter.

"We have trained much more than you realize, Hermogenes," said Zeno. "Not"—he waved his hand—"with your kind of full armor and weapons in a field battle situation, of course. But we took advantage of the very long voyage here to train on board the grain ships. With quarterstaffs."

Hermogenes stared at the Knights Hospitaler as if the man had just announced that he was armed with bread sticks. Ashot was positively goggling.

"*Quarterstaffs?*" choked the Armenian cataphract.

Now, Antonina did intervene. "That was my husband's idea," she stated. "He said it was the perfect weapon for riot duty."

Hearing the authority of Belisarius invoked, Ashot and Hermogenes reined in their disdain. A bit.

Zeno spoke up again. "I do not think you fully understand the situation here, Hermogenes. Ashot." He cleared his throat. "I am Egyptian myself, you know. I wasn't born in Alexandria—I come from Naucratis, in the Delta—but I am familiar with the place. And its religious politics."

He pointed through the open doors. "We must be very careful. We do not want to create martyrs. And—especially—we don't want to infuriate the great masses of orthodox Greeks who make up a third of Alexandria's populace."

He nodded approvingly at Antonina. "You saw how well Antonina handled the guilds, earlier. But you musn't forget that almost all of those men are Greeks, and orthodox. They completely dominate the city's commerce and manufacture. They are the same men we will be relying on—tomorrow, and for years to come—to forge the Roman arsenal against the Malwa. For doctrinal reasons, most of those people are inclined to support Paul and his diehards. But they are also uneasy about their fanaticism, and their thuggery. Bad for business, if nothing else."

Antonina pitched in. "It's essential that we drive a wedge between Paul's fanatics and the majority of the orthodox population. If we have a massacre, the city's Greeks will be driven into open opposition. And you know as well as I do—*better* than I do—how the cataphracts and the regular infantry will hammer into that mob if they're in the forefront."

She stared at Ashot and Hermogenes. The two officers looked away.

"You know!" she snapped. "Those men are trained to do one thing, and one thing only. *Slaughter people.* Do you really want to unleash a volley of cataphract arrows against a crowd? This is not the Nika revolt, God damn it! There, we were dealing with Malwa kshatriya and thousands of professional thugs armed to the teeth. Here—"

She blew out her breath. "Christ! Half of that crowd will be there more out of excitement and curiosity than anything else. Many of them will be women and children. You may be crazy, but I'm not. Theodora sent me here to stabilize imperial rule in Egypt. To *stop* a civil war, not start one."

Ashot and Hermogenes were looking hangdog, now. But Antonina was relentless.

"That's the way it's going to be. *I* have complete confidence that the Knights Hospitaler can handle the situation. I simply want you there—*in the background, but fully armed and armored*—to add a little spice to the meal. Just to let the crowd know, after Paul's goons have been beaten into a pulp and routed, that it could have been one hell of a lot worse."

She chuckled, very coldly. "You may sneer at quarterstaffs, but my husband doesn't. And I think, by the end of the day, you won't be sneering either."

She straightened, assuming as tall a stance as she could. Which wasn't much, but quite enough.

"You have your orders. *Follow them.*"

Hermogenes and Ashot left then, very hastily. An unkind observer might have said they scurried. An instant later, Zeno followed. His pace, however, was slower. Very proud, that stride was.

Euphronius, also, began to leave. But after taking three steps, he stopped. He fidgeted, then turned around.

"Yes?" asked Antonina.

The Syrian cleared his throat. "My grenadiers are also not trained to do anything other than—uh, slaughter people. And grenades are even more indiscriminate than arrows. I don't understand how you expect me to—"

Antonina laughed. "Euphronius! Relax!"

She walked over, smiling, and placed a reassuring hand on his arm.

"First of all, you're not going to be dealing with a crowd. You're going to be dealing with *gangs*. There won't be any innocent onlookers in *that* mob, believe me. Hippodrome thugs, they'll be, looking to pillage the Jews. Robbers, rapists, murderers—nothing else."

The smile vanished. Her next words were almost snarled.

"Kill as many of them as you can, Euphronius. *The more, the better.* And then have Triphiodoros and his infantry hang whatever prisoners you take. On the spot. No mercy. *None.* If you wind up draping the outskirts of the Delta Quarter with intestines, blood, brains, and corpses, you'll make me a very happy woman."

Euphronius gave out a little sigh of relief. "Oh," he said. Then, with a sudden, savage grin:

"We can do that. No problem."

Now he, too, was hurrying out of the room. Antonina was left alone with Theodosius.

For a moment, she and the new Patriarch stared at each other. Theodosius had said nothing, during the preceding discussion. But his anxiety had been obvious to Antonina. The anxiety was gone, now. But she was uncertain what emotion had replaced it. Theodosius was giving her a very odd look.

"Is something troubling you, Patriarch?"

"Not at all," replied Theodosius, shaking his head. "I was just—how can I explain?"

He smiled, fluttering his hands. "I suppose you could say I was contemplating God's irony. It's an aspect of the Supreme Being which most theologians miss entirely, in my experience."

Antonina frowned. "I'm afraid I don't—"

Again, the fluttering hands. "When the fanatic Paul calls you the Whore of Babylon, he demonstrates his ignorance. His stupidity, actually. The essence of Christ is his mercy, Antonina. And who, in this chaos called Alexandria, could find that mercy—other than a woman who understands the difference between sin and evil?"

Antonina was still frowning. Theodosius sighed.

"I am not explaining myself well. Let me just say that I am very glad that you are here, and not someone else. Someone full of their own self-righteousness. I will leave it at that."

Her frown faded, replaced by a half-rueful little smile. "I suppose I've adopted my husband's crooked way of looking at things."

"Crooked? Perhaps." The Patriarch turned to go. "But I would remind you, Antonina, that a grapevine is also crooked. Yet it bears the world's most treasured fruit."

When she was finally alone, Antonina walked slowly back to her chair and took a seat. She would not be able to enjoy that rest for long, for she intended to take her place with the cataphracts backing the Knights Templar. Within minutes, she would have to don her own armor. And wear it, throughout the day, under the hammering sun of Egypt. She grimaced, thinking of the sweltering heat that armor would bring.

But she needed that moment, alone. To remember the crooked mind—and the straight soul—of her absent husband.

"Be safe, love," she whispered. "Oh, please—be safe."

Chapter 32
THE EUPHRATES
Autumn, 531 A.D.

"This is ridiculous!" snarled Belisarius. "This isn't 'safe'—it's absurd!"

"We gave our oath, general," said Anastasius solemnly.

"To the Persian Emperor himself," added Valentinian, trying—and failing quite miserably—to look suitably lugubrious.

Belisarius glared at both of them. Then, transferred the glare onto the enemy, some distance away.

Quite some distance away. Belisarius, along with Anastasius and Valentinian, were standing on top of the huge pile of stones which the Kushans had dug out of the Nehar Malka. The Syrian infantrymen who defended that man-made hill had constructed an observation platform from which Belisarius could watch the progress of the battle. They had also built a narrow, winding road—more of a path, really—which led up to the summit from the protected northern side of the rockpile.

As a vantage point from which to observe the battle, Belisarius could find no fault with the thing. Even without his telescope, the rock-hill's elevation gave him an excellent view of the enemy's dispositions on the south side of the Euphrates and the Nehar Malka. The telescope enabled him to pick out even small details of the enemy's formations.

But—

"God damn it," he growled, "I'm too far away. By the time a courier gets up here and back again—no way to ride a horse up that so-called road—I might as well have given orders for yesterday's breakfast."

It's safe, insisted Aide.

Before Belisarius could make a reply, one of the Malwa rockets fired at the Roman troops defending the dam below veered wildly off course. For a moment, it seemed as if the missile was heading directly for the rockpile. Close enough, at least, that Valentinian and Anastasius began to take cover behind the low wall surrounding the platform.

Growling with satisfaction, Belisarius stood as erect as possible.

Get down! Get down!

Belisarius, sarcastically:

"Safe," remember? "Safe," you said.

And, in truth, safe it was. With typical unpredictability, the rocket suddenly swerved to the east. A few seconds later, it exploded harmlessly over the middle of the Nehar Malka.

Wisely, Aide refrained from comment.

Belisarius took a deep breath, controlling his temper. There was no point in trying to force the issue, at the moment. Valentinian and Anastasius were obviously ready and willing to enforce a strict compliance with their vow to Emperor Khusrau. For that matter, *all* of Belisarius' officers had made clear their own agreement with Khusrau's position. Belisarius had been shocked, actually, when he realized how adamant his commanders were that he stay out of the direct line of fire in the coming battle.

"There's no need for you in the front line, sir," Agathius had argued, at the command meeting on the eve of the battle. "No need—and a lot to be lost if you're killed or injured. This is just going to be a slugging match, at least in the beginning."

On that point, Agathius had been correct.

It was late afternoon, and the battle had been raging for hours. The Malwa had made their first probes at dawn, on both sides of the Euphrates. Encountering the large body of Persians guarding Ormazd's camp on the south bank, the Malwa had early on decided to take a purely defensive stance there. They were obviously more than happy to let Ormazd and his twenty thousand heavy cavalry sit on the sidelines while they concentrated their attack on the Roman forces.

Those Roman forces would have been their principal target, in any event. It was the Romans, not Ormazd's Persians, who were forted up on the dam across the Euphrates. It was the Romans, also, who were positioned to guard the dam from any attack coming up the Nehar Malka.

A slugging match, the first day—with the Romans in position to outslug the Malwa.

The defensive position of Belisarius' army was excellent. With the desert to the west and Ormazd's twenty thousand lancers encamped on the south bank of the Euphrates, the Malwa had no choice but to advance up the riverbed and along the narrow strip of land between the Euphrates and the Nehar Malka. As that strip of land approached the point where the Royal Canal branched directly east from the east-by-southeast-flowing Euphrates, it narrowed down to a mere spit. The tip of that triangle was guarded by well-built Roman fieldworks—complete with timber brought all the way down the Euphrates by barges. Buttressed with rocks and tamped earth, the walls of that palisade were guarded by Syrian dragoons. When needed, the dragoons were backed up by all of the Constantinople cataphracts, ready to sally at a moment's notice. Which they had, over and again, as the day wore on, waiting until the Syrians had worn out another Malwa assault before driving them back in defeat.

Nor could the enemy outflank the fieldworks to the east. To do so would require crossing the rapid flow of the Nehar Malka, in the face of another Roman barrier. The giant pile of rocks on the north bank of the Royal Canal which the Kushans had excavated had been turned into an impromptu fortress, anchoring the Roman left flank. More Syrian troops were stationed on that rockpile, under the command of Coutzes, along with the Callinicum garrison. So far, those soldiers had had an easy day. The Malwa had not yet made any attempt to cross the Nehar Malka and attack the dam from the north bank of the Royal Canal. They had concentrated their efforts on the dam itself, especially its eastern anchor, trying to hammer their way to victory.

Yes, on *that* point, Belisarius could not argue. The first day was a slugging match, nothing else, just as Agathius had predicted.

And, it was true, the general would have been able to play no particularly useful role on those front lines.

But Belisarius knew that would not last. The Romans were not facing the normal run of Malwa generals here. He had seen, with his telescope, the arrival of a howdah-bearing elephant with the enemy's army. A small mob of servants had been splashing that howdah with pails of water drawn from the river—a crude but effective way of cooling the howdah's interior.

Link itself was here. He was as certain of it as he was of his own name.

I must get closer, he thought to himself. Soon enough, this simple slugging match of Agathius' is going to start unraveling.

I must be closer.

Suddenly, hearing a change in the distant shouts of the enemy's forces, Belisarius cocked his head. The battle was so far away that he found himself forced to rely on his hearing as much as his eyesight.

"We're beating off the attack," he said.

Anastasius and Valentinian copied his stance. Listening with the trained ear of veterans.

"I think you're right," agreed Valentinian.

Anastasius nodded. Then asked: "What's that make? Five assaults?"

"Four," replied Belisarius. "That first one, just after dawn, was more in the way of a reconnaissance. There've only been four mass charges."

"Crazy bastards," sneered Valentinian. "Do they really think they can hammer their way onto that dam—without siege guns? Jesus, that must be a slaughter down there. The onagers and scorpions would be bad enough, backed up by Bouzes and his dragoons. But they've got to face Maurice and the Illyrians, too."

He gave his general an approving glance. "That was a great idea, that road you had the Kushans build."

Belisarius smiled crookedly. "I can't take credit for it, I'm afraid. I stole the idea from Nebuchadrezzar."

Inspired by the design of Babylon's fortifications, Belisarius had ordered a road built just behind the crest of the dam. A stone wall had then been hastily erected on the very crest. The road and the wall were jury-rigged, to be sure. The road was just wide enough and sturdy enough to allow the Thracian and Illyrian cataphracts to rush to any part of the dam which was under heavy attack. The wall was just thick enough, and just high enough, to shelter them from most missile fire. At the same time, it allowed the mounted archers to shoot their own bows over the wall at the Malwa soldiers trying to slog their way forward.

Combined with the torsion artillery mounted all along the dam, and the dismounted Syrians' archery and grenades, the result had been murderous. Most of the enemy troops had been forced to charge the dam up the riverbed of the Euphrates. Not only did that muddy terrain slow them down, but it also broke up the cohesion of their formations. The Euphrates had not dried up completely. The dam had diverted most of its water into the Nehar Malka, but there was still enough seeping through to produce a network of small streams and pools. Eventually, those streams converged and produced a small river—but not for several miles. Below the dam itself, the riverbed was an attacker's nightmare—mud, reeds, sinkholes, pools, creeks.

As far as possible, the Malwa had concentrated their efforts against the eastern end of the dam. There, the enemy troops could advance along the dry land which had once been the left bank of the Euphrates. But Belisarius had expected that, which was why he'd positioned the Constantinople troops on that end of the dam, backed up by the katyusha rockets. He had spent the night before the battle with Agathius and his men, exhorting them to stand fast. The Greeks, he explained, were the anchor of the entire defensive line. They would take the heaviest blows, but—so long as they held—the enemy could not prevail. When Belisarius finished, they gave him a cheer and vowed to hold the line.

Hold it they had, through four savage assaults. But they had driven back each charge, and added their own heavy charges onto the enemy's butcher bill.

The sounds of battle were fading rapidly now. It was obvious that the Malwa were retreating. Within a minute, Belisarius could see streams of enemy soldiers retreating from the dam. They were bearing large numbers of wounded with them, chased on their way by rocket volleys fired from the katyushas.

Belisarius glanced up at the sky. The sun was beginning to set.

"There'll be a night attack," he predicted. "A mass assault all across the line." He pointed to the eastern anchor. "The crunch will come there. Count on it."

"Agathius'll hold them," said Anastasius confidently. "Come what may, Agathius will hold."

Valentinian grunted his agreement.

Belisarius glared at the distant enemy. Then, glared at his bodyguards. If he could have turned his eyes inside out, he would have glared at Aide.

"I'm too far away!" he roared.

The attack began two hours after dusk, and it lasted halfway through the night. The worst of it, as Belisarius had predicted, came on the eastern anchor of the dam.

Hour after hour, the general spent, perched on his cursed observation platform. Leaning over the wall, straining to hear what he could.

Cursing Khusrau. Cursing Valentinian and Anastasius. Cursing Aide.

He got a little sleep in the early hours of the dawn, after the enemy assault had been clearly beaten off. At daybreak, Valentinian awakened him.

"A courier's coming," announced the cataphract.

Belisarius scrambled to his feet and went over to the side of the platform where the path came up from below. Peering down, he could see an armored man making his laborious way up that narrow, twisting trail through the rocks.

"I think that's Maurice," said Anastasius.

Startled, Belisarius looked closer. He had been expecting one of the young cataphracts whom Maurice had been using to keep the general informed of the battle's progress—not the chiliarch himself.

But it was Maurice, sure enough. Belisarius stiffened, feeling a chill in his heart.

Valentinian verbalized his thought. "Bad news," he announced. "Sure as taxes. Only reason Maurice would come himself."

As soon as Maurice made his way to the crest, Belisarius reached down and hauled him over the wall.

"What's wrong?" he asked immediately. "From the sound, I thought they'd been beaten off again."

"They were," grunted Maurice. He took off his heavy helmet and heaved a sigh of relief.

"God, it's like being in a furnace. Forgotten what fresh air tastes like."

"God damn it, Maurice! *What's wrong?*"

The chiliarch's gray eyes met Belisarius' brown ones. Squarely, unflinchingly. Sternly.

"The same thing that's usually wrong in a battle, whether it's going well or not. We're hammering the bloody shit out of them, sure, but they get to hammer back. We've taken heavy casualties—especially the Greeks."

Maurice drew in a long, deep breath.

"Timasius is dead. He led the Illyrians in a charge against some Malwa—Kushans, worse luck—who made it over the wall. Horse got hamstrung and gutted, and—" Maurice shrugged, not bothering to elaborate. There were few things in a battle as certain as the fate of an armored cavalryman brought down by infantry. Timasius wouldn't have survived ten seconds after hitting the ground.

"Liberius?" asked Belisarius.

"He's taken command of the Illyrians," replied Maurice. "He's doing a good job, too. He organized the counter-attack that drove the Kushans back down the dam."

Belisarius studied Maurice's grim face. He felt his chill deepen. Maurice hadn't climbed all the way up that hill just to tell him that a dull, dimwitted commander had been succeeded by a more capable subordinate.

"I'm sorry about Timasius," he said softly. "He was a reliable man, if nothing else. His family'll get his full pension—I'll see to it. But that's not what you came here to tell me. So spit it out."

The grizzled Thracian wiped his face wearily. "It's Agathius."

"*Damn,*" hissed Belisarius. There was a real anguish in that hiss, and the three cataphracts who heard it understood that it was the pain of a man losing a treasured friend, not a general losing an excellent officer.

"Damn," he repeated, very softly.

Maurice shook his head. "He's not dead, general." Grimacing: "Not quite, anyway. But he's lost one leg, for sure, and I don't know as how he'll still be alive tomorrow."

"What happened?"

Maurice swiveled, staring back at the dam. "They really pushed hard this time, especially at the eastern anchor. Solid Ye-tai, that was—fighting on their own, not just chivvying Malwa regulars."

Still looking to the southwest, the chiliarch muttered an incoherent curse. "They're mean, tough, gutsy bastards—I'll give 'em that. I don't even want to think how many casualties they took before they finally broke through."

He turned back to Belisarius. "The Syrian dragoons couldn't hold them, so Agathius led a lance charge. In pitch dark, can you believe it? Man's got brass balls, I swear he does. That broke the Ye-tai—crushed 'em—but he got hit by a grenade blast. Took off his right leg, clean, just above the knee. Mangled his left foot, too. It'll have to be amputated, I think. Beyond that—" He shrugged. "Shrapnel tore him up pretty fierce. He's lost a lot of blood."

"Get him off the dam," commanded Belisarius. He turned and pointed to the small fleet of barges anchored in the middle of the Euphrates about a mile to the north.

"Get him to one of the ambulance barges."

Maurice rubbed his face. "That's not going to be easy. He's still conscious, believe it or not." A half-wondering, half-admiring chuckle. "Still wants to fight, even! When I left the dam, he was yelling at the doctor to tie up the one leg and cut off the fucking useless foot on the other so he could get back on a horse."

Valentinian and Anastasius laughed. Belisarius couldn't help smiling himself.

"Hit him over the head, if you have to, Maurice. But I want him out of there."

Again, he pointed to the barges. "There's better medical care available in the ambulance barges. And his wife's on one of those boats, too. I don't know which one, but I'll find out. She'll probably be more help keeping him alive than anyone else."

Maurice's eyes widened. "His wife? Sudaba's here? What in the world is that young girl doing on a battlefield? That's the craziest—"

He broke off, remembering. Belisarius' own wife, Antonina, had had the habit of accompanying her husband on campaign also. All the way to the battlefield.

Belisarius clasped Maurice's shoulder firmly.

"I want him alive, Maurice. Get him out of there. Now. Put Cyril in command of—"

"Already done it," gruffed Maurice.

Belisarius nodded, took a deep breath. "All right. What else?"

The chiliarch scowled. Strangely, the expression cheered Belisarius up. Maurice—scowling morosely—meant a problem. Which was not the same thing as *bad news*.

"They're going to change tactics," Maurice announced. "Even the Malwa won't keep throwing troops away like this forever."

"They might," countered Belisarius mildly, "if they think they're wearing us down fast enough."

Maurice shook his head. "They're not. We're taking pretty heavy casualties, sure, but we're giving out four or five to every one we take. At that rate, attrition will chew them up before it does us." His scowl darkened. "And I'm sure they know it, too. I'll tell you something, general. Whoever's running the show on their side is no fool. The frontal attacks have been beaten off, but that's because the terrain favors us and we're on the defensive. The attacks themselves have been organized and directed as good as you could ask, given that Godawful riverbed they have to plow through. There's been none of their usual cocksure stupidity, thinking they can roll over everybody just with their numbers. Ye-tai and Kushans have been leading every attack, and the Malwa regulars have been backing them up the way they should."

A thought came instantly from Aide:

Link. Link itself is here.

I know, replied Belisarius.

Maurice was shaking his head again.

"They tried the straight-up tactic, to see if it would work. Pressed it home, hard. But now that we've proven to them that they can't just roll over us, they'll try a flank attack. I'm sure of it."

Belisarius scratched his chin, nodded. "I'm not arguing the point, Maurice. As it happens, I agree with you."

He glanced across the river. Upstream of the dam, just before the river diverted into the narrower channel of the Nehar Malka, the Euphrates was still a mile wide. But he could see the Persian camp where Ormazd's army had forted up throughout the day's battle.

"Any signs of movement over there?" he asked.

Maurice snorted. "About as much as a crocodile, waiting in the reeds. The only thing moving over there is Ormazd's nostrils, taking in the sweet air of opportunity."

Belisarius smiled. "Well, unless they want to hammer away at twenty thousand dehgans, that only leaves the Malwa one other option."

Maurice grimaced skeptically. He turned and pointed down the slope, to the Nehar Malka. "Do you have any idea how hard it would be for them to get across? The Nehar Malka's no shallow, placid river like the Euphrates was, General. It's narrower and deeper. The water's moving through there fast, and there aren't any fords within four days' march. They'll have to build a pontoon bridge, using those little barges they've got a few miles downriver."

He turned back, shaking his head. "While Coutzes and his boys on this rockpile piss pain all over them, and the katyushas come up to the riverbank and fire rockets at point-blank range, and me and Cyril and Liberius bring up all the cataphracts to hammer whichever poor bastards *do* manage to stagger across a rickety little pontoon bridge."

He jerked his head, pointing with his face at Ormazd's camp. "Personally, I'd rather take on the dehgans. If the Malwa can clear the right bank of the Euphrates, they can move upstream and cross back over damn near anywhere. We'd be trapped here. Have to abandon the dam and race back to Peroz-Shapur. Join forces with Kurush and try to hold out a siege."

Belisarius' smile was very crooked.

Maurice glared at him. "Are you *really* that sure of yourself?" he demanded.

Belisarius made a mollifying gesture with his hands. A gentle little patting motion.

Maurice was not mollified. "What's that?" he demanded. "Soothing the savage beast? Or just petting the dog?"

Belisarius left off the motion. Then, grinning:

"Yes, Maurice—I am that sure of myself. So sure, in fact, that I'm going to predict exactly how this next attack is going to happen."

He pointed down the slope of the rockpile to the Nehar Malka below. "I predict they'll start building their pontoon bridge today, in the late afternoon. The attack will begin after dark. You know why?"

"So they might have a chance of getting across the bridge," snorted Maurice. "Never do it in daylight."

Belisarius shook his head. "No. That's not why."

He gave Maurice a hard stare. "You say they've had Ye-tai and Kushans leading every attack?"

Maurice nodded.

"Not this next one, Maurice. You watch. Malwa regulars is all you'll see crossing that pontoon bridge—or would see, if it weren't dark. The reason they're going to attack at night is so that we can't see that none of their Ye-tai or Kushans are participating in the assault. *Those* troops—"

He turned his head, nodding toward the river.

"—will be crossing over to the right bank of the Euphrates, about a mile downstream from the dam. Out of our sight, especially since we'll be preoccupied with the attack on the Nehar Malka. By dawn, just when we think we've beaten off another assault, the Malwa army's best troops will come at us from behind. Like you said, they can find any number of places to ford the Euphrates upstream."

Maurice's scowl was ferocious, now. "You can't be positive that Ormazd will pull out and give them that opening," he protested.

Belisarius shrugged.

"Positive, no. But I'll bet long odds on it, Maurice. Ormazd knows that the only loyal Persian troops Khusrau has up here are Baresmanas and Kurush's ten thousand. They're forted up in Peroz-Shapur—"

"I wish they were here," grumbled the chiliarch. "We could use them."

"Don't be stupid! If they were here, Peroz-Shapur would be a pile of ashes. As it is, the Malwa expedition had to skirt the town and leave troops to guard against a sally. Just sitting in Peroz-Shapur, Kurush is a threat to them."

He waved his hand. "But let's not change the subject. To go back to Ormazd—this is his best chance to move against Khusrau. If the Malwa destroy us here, they'll return to Babylon. Keep Khusrau penned up while Ormazd takes over all of northern Mesopotamia. The only thing that kept him from doing that before was our intervention—that, and our victory at Anatha. If we're gone, he's got a clear hand."

"How's he going to explain that to his dehgans?" demanded Maurice.

Belisarius laughed. "How else? Blame it on us. Stupid idiot Romans insisted on a hopeless stand. Fortunately, he was too wise to waste his men's lives defending a canal which was obviously just a Roman scheme to reinvade Persia like they did in Julian's day."

"That's pretty tortuous reasoning," muttered Maur-ice, shaking his head.

Again, Belisarius barked a laugh. "Of course it is! So what? It'll serve the purpose."

Maurice was still shaking his head. "What if you're wrong?" Maurice growled, "Dammit, I *hate* tricky battle plans."

Belisarius smiled. "If I'm wrong, Maurice—so what? In that case, Ormazd will have to fight the Malwa who cross the Euphrates. They may defeat him, but after fighting twenty thousand dehgans I don't think they'll be in any shape to hit us on the flank. Do you?"

Maurice said nothing. Then, sighed heavily. "All right. We'll see how it goes."

The chiliarch started to turn away. Belisarius restrained him with a hand on his shoulder.

"Wait a moment. I'm coming with you."

Maurice gave him a startled look. Valentinian and Anastasius started to squawk. Aide began to make some mental protest.

Belisarius rode them all down.

"Things have changed!" he announced gaily. "The battle's reaching its turning point. I *have* to be down there, now. Ready—at a moment's notice—to fulfill my vow to Emperor Khusrau."

Maurice smiled. Valentinian and Anastasius choked down their squawks. Aide sulked.

"Safe," sneered Belisarius. He took a moment to don his armor.

"Safe," he sneered again, as he began the long trek down the hill.

Behind him, Maurice said, "Do be a little careful, will you? Going down that miserable path, I mean. Be a bit absurd, it would, you breaking your fool neck climbing down a pile of rocks."

"Safe," sneered Belisarius.

Two eager steps later, he tripped and rolled some fifty feet down the hill. When he finally came to a halt, piling up against a boulder, it took him a minute or so to clear his head.

The first thing he saw, dizzily, was Maurice leaning over him.

"Safe," muttered the gray-bearded veteran morosely. "It's like asking a toad not to hop."

He reached down a hand and hauled Belisarius back onto his feet. "Will you mind your step, from here on?" he asked, very sweetly. "Or must we have Anastasius carry you down like a babe in swaddling clothes?"

"Safe," Belisarius assured one and all. None of whom believed him for a moment.

Chapter 33

ALEXANDRIA
Autumn, 531 A.D.

Alexandria was famous throughout the Mediterranean world for the magnificence of its public thoroughfares. The two greatest of those boulevards, which intersected each other west of the Church of St. Michael, were each thirty yards across. The intersection itself was so large it was almost a plaza, and was marked by a tetrastylon—four monumental pillars standing on each corner.

The buildings which fronted on the intersection were likewise impressive. On the north stood a huge church, measuring a hundred yards square. The edifice was hundreds of years old. Originally built as a temple dedicated to the crocodile god Sobek, it had been converted into a Christian church well over a century earlier. Most of the pagan trappings of the temple had been discarded—the crocodile mummies in the crypts had been unceremoniously pitched into the sea—but the building itself still retained the massive style of ancient Egyptian monumental architecture. It loomed over the intersection like a small mountain.

Across from it, on the south, stood a more modern building: the gymnasium which marked Greek culture everywhere in the world. And, next to it, the public baths which were a hallmark of the Roman way of life. The eastern side of the intersection was taken up by another archetypal public structure, a large theater in which

389

the city's upper crust was entertained by dramatists and musicians. Only on the west were there any private buildings—three stately mansions, as similar as peas in a pod.

Taken as a whole, the entire effect was one of grandeur and magnificence.

But Antonina, studying that intersection from her vantage point atop the steps of her palace, was not impressed. She had grown up in a part of the city which was very different from the Greek aristocracy's downtown splendor. She had been born and raised in the native Egyptians' quarter, which still bore its old name of Rhakotis. There, the streets were neither wide nor well-paved. They were dirt alleys, which doubled as open sewers. The buildings in Rhakotis were ancient only in the sense that the collapsed mud-brick of one house served its successors as a cellar. There were no gymnasiums—no schools of any kind. As for public baths—

She snorted, remembering. The human population density in Rhakotis was bad enough. The animal population was even worse. The quarter teemed with cattle, pigs, donkeys, camels, goats—and, of course, the ubiquitous pigeons. And their pigeon shit.

The snort became an outright laugh. Zeno, standing next to her, eyed her quizzically.

"I was just thinking of the provisions of a typical Alexandrian rental agreement. For a house or an apartment. You know, the one about—"

Zeno smiled, nodding. "Yes, I know." His voice took on a sing-song cadence: " 'At the end of the term, the tenant shall return the house to the lessor free of dung.' "

He laughed himself, now. "It was so embarrassing for me, the first time I rented an apartment in Constantinople. I was puzzled by the absence of that provision in the contract. When I inquired, the landlord looked at me as if I were crazy. Or a barbarian."

Antonina began to say something, but broke off.

"They're coming!" she heard someone shout. One of the Knights Hospitaler, she assumed.

The entire boulevard in front of her was packed with them. A thousand Knights were arrayed there, in rigid formation. They stood in lines of twenty men, covering the entire width of the boulevard, and fifty lines deep. Each man carried a quarterstaff in his hand, held erect. Their only armor, as such, were leather caps reinforced by an iron strip across the forehead. But thick quilted jerkins and shoulder-pads lay under the white tunics emblazoned with the red cross of their order, providing added protection against blunt weapons. And most of the Knights had wound heavy linen around their forearms, as well.

The majority of the other Knights were positioned in the various side-streets debouching onto the main thoroughfare, but Zeno had crammed hundreds below the street itself. Familiar with Alexandria, the Knights' commander had taken advantage of the labyrinth of cisterns which provided the great city with its water supply. If necessary, those men could either pour out onto the street from the basements of nearby houses, or they could move surreptitiously elsewhere. Zeno had twenty couriers standing nearby, ready to carry his orders when the time came.

All in all, Antonina was more than satisfied with Zeno's dispositions. It remained to be seen, of course, how well the Knights would do in an actual fray. But Zeno, at least, seemed fully confident of their capabilities.

"There they come!" came another shout.

Peering at the distant intersection, Antonina saw that a huge mob was pouring into it from the east. Within two minutes, the intersection itself was packed with people, and the first contingents of the crowd were advancing down the boulevard toward her palace.

"Ten thousand, I make it," murmured Zeno. "Not counting those who are still out of sight."

As it drew near, the mob began to eddy and swirl. Seeing the stern-looking and disciplined formation of the Knights Hospitaler filling the street—not to mention the much scarier sight of armored cataphracts behind *them*—the faint-hearted members of the crowd began trying to get out of the front line. Pushing their way to the rear, or simply standing in one place uncertainly, they created obstacles to their more fanatical and determined compatriots.

For a minute or so, Antonina even hoped that the mob would grind to a stop and retreat. But that hope vanished. Soon enough, the disparate elements which made up the huge crowd had separated themselves out. Those who were timid, or vacillating, or merely curious, fell to the rear or pressed themselves against the walls of the various shops which lined the boulevard. The diehards surged to the fore.

The great majority of them were monks, thought Antonina. It was impossible to be certain, since the custom of monks wearing distinctive habits was still in the future. The uniform of the Knights Hospitaler was another of Belisarius' innovations. But Antonina knew the breed well. Only fanatic monks, as a rule, were quite as disheveled, shaggy-maned, and just generally dirty-looking as most of the men leading the mob. And the practiced, familiar way in which they handled their clubs and cudgels reinforced her supposition.

Antonina smiled ruefully, remembering Belisarius' description of a vision Aide had once given him of the monastic orders of the future, a time which would be called the Middle Ages. He had described to her the good works and gentle demeanor of the Benedictines and the followers of a man who would be called St. Francis of Assisi.

His Alexandria-born-and-bred wife had goggled at the description. The monks *she* knew from her youth bore as much resemblance to St. Francis as a rabid wolf to a lamb. In the Egypt of her day, the monastic orders (orthodox and Monophysite alike) were as prone to street-fighting as the thugs of the Hippodrome factions—and probably better at it. Certainly more savage.

A particularly beefy monk in the very forefront of the mob caught sight of her, standing on the steps of the palace. He raised his thick club and bellowed, "Death to the Whore of Babylon!"

Whether by predeliberation or simple spontaneous enthusiasm, the call was immediately taken up as the mob's warcry.

"Death to the whore! Death to the whore!"

The front lines of the mob charged the Knights Hospitaler barring the way. There was neither hesitation nor halfheartedness in that ferocious rush. The monks in the van were veteran brawlers. They had no fear whatever of the bizarrely-accoutered Knights, and even less of their quarterstaffs.

What the hell's the use of a six-foot-long club, anyway? No room to swing it in a street fight. Silly buggers!

Knowing what was coming, Antonina held her breath. Quarterstaffs, too, were one of Belisarius' innovations—at least, used in this manner. Shepherd's staffs were known, of course, and had featured in many a village brawl. But no-one had ever placed them in the hands of an organized force, who had been systematically trained in their use.

When the monks were just a few feet away, the captain of the front line called the command. In unison, the twenty Knights flipped their quarterstaffs level and drove them into the oncoming monks like spears. Expecting club-blows to the head, the monks were taken completely by surprise. The iron ferrules of the heavy quarterstaffs crushed into their unguarded chests and bellies.

The damage done was horrendous. Two monks died instantly, their diaphragms ruptured. Another, his sternum split and the bone fragments driven into his heart, died within seconds. The rest collapsed, tripping the ones piling up from behind. Some wailed with pain. Most didn't—broken ribs and severely lacerated bellies produce groans and hisses of agony, not loud shrieks.

Instantly, the spear-thrusts were followed by two quick, swirling, pivoting side-blows all across the line. Iron ferrules slammed into heads and rib cages, breaking both.

The captain cried out the command. Again, the stabbing quarterstaffs. Again, the scythe-like follow-on blows. A dozen more were struck down.

The mob piled higher, pushing forward, floundering on fallen bodies. Some managed to force their way through the first line of Knights, only to be mercilessly dealt with by the line which followed.

Again, the command. Again, the spear thrusts. Some of the mob, this time, knew what to expect. Tried to protect their midsections.

The Knights had expected that. This time, many of the iron-shod quarterstaff butts went into faces and heads. Skulls broke, jaws broke, teeth shattered. One throat was crushed. One neck broken.

The mob staggered. Eddied. Hesitated.

Zeno bellowed an order. Immediately, the front line of the Knights swiveled and stepped back. The second line moved forward.

The captain of that line used the forward momentum to drive through the next thrust savagely. The front of the mob reeled back—but only a few steps. The press from behind was too great. The monks in the very fore were trapped, now. Stumbling on fallen bodies, jammed up, unable to swing their own clubs—which were too short to reach the Knights, anyway—they were simply targets.

Command. Thrust; strike; strike. Command. Thrust; strike; strike.

Again, Zeno bellowed. The second line of Knights swiveled, moved back. The third line stepped forward.

Command. Thrust; strike; strike. Command. Thrust; strike; strike.

Zeno bellowed. Third line back. Fourth line up.

Command. Thrust; strike; strike. Command. Thrust; strike; strike.

Zeno was silent. The machine-like routine was established, automatic. Practiced—over and again—on grain ships. Now, tested and proven in action.

Fifth line. Sixth line. Seventh line.

The boulevard was awash in blood. The monks forced up by the surging mob behind them were like sausages pressed into a meat grinder. Their frenzied club swings could only, at best, deflect a thrusting quarterstaff—into the monk jammed alongside, more often than not. Until the next quarterstaff drove through. Then—downed, or staggering. Dead, often enough; crippled or maimed; or simply stunned or unconscious.

As the eighth line moved forward, the great mob of monks were seized by a sudden frenzy. They had seen enough to understand that their only hope was to surge over the Knights by sheer brute mass, damn the cost.

Shrieking and howling, at least two hundred fanatics lunged forward, trampling right over the bodies of the monks in front of them. They weren't even trying to use their cudgels, now. They were simply trying to close with the Knights and grapple—anything to get through that horrible zone where the quarterstaffs reigned supreme.

The surge hammered the line back. Several Knights were driven down, knocked off their feet. One was seized by the ankles and dragged into the mob, where he was savagely stomped to death. Another was pinioned by two monks while a third crushed his skull with three vicious cudgel blows.

But this, too, had been foreseen. Zeno bellowed a new command. The ninth line immediately sprang forward, bracing the eighth. Both lines locked their quarterstaffs, forming a barricade across the street. The mob slammed into that barricade, pushed it back, slowly, slowly—

The tenth line strode forward, drove their quarterstaffs through the gaps. Head-thrusts, these—there was no room for body blows.

Skulls cracked. Jaws shattered. Noses flattened. Eyes were gouged out. Teeth went flying everywhere.

Thrust. Thrust. Thrust.

Swivel. Step back. Eleventh line forward.

Thrust. Thrust. Thrust.

The lines holding back the mob were tiring now, and suffering casualties. Again, Zeno bellowed. The twelfth and thirteenth lines stepped forward and took their place, forming the barricade.

This maneuver was ragged, uneven. Switching places with a man forming a barricade is awkward, even when the man isn't bleeding and half-dazed—which many of them were. But the mob was in no position to take advantage of the momentary confusion. The monks in the fore of that mob were completely dazed, and a lot bloodier.

Soon enough, the hammering resumed.

Standing next to Antonina, Ashot whispered, "Jesus, Son of God. Mary, Mother of Christ."

Antonina's face was pale, but her stiff, cold expression never wavered.

"I told you," she stated harshly. "I told you."

She took a deep breath, almost a shudder. "Belisarius predicted this. He told me—told Zeno and the Knights' captains, too—that if they learned to use their quarterstaffs in a disciplined and organized way they could shatter any mob in the world. Easily."

Ashot shook his head. "I'm not sure the casualties in that mob are going to be much less than if we did it."

"Doesn't matter, Ashot. People don't look at clubs—which is all a quarterstaff is, technically—the same way they do edged weapons. A sword or a knife is an instrument of murder, pure and simple. Whereas a club—" She smiled wryly, and spread her hands in a half-comical little gesture.

"Tavern brawls, casual mayhem," continued Ashot, nodding. "Not *really* a deadly weapon."

He chuckled, very grimly. "Yeah, you're right. If a thousand monks got sabred, or lanced, they'd be martyrs. But if that same thousand just gets the living shit beaten out of them—even if half of them die from it—people will just shrug it off. What the hell? Fair fight. The monks had clubs too, and they've never been shy about using them. Just too bad if this new bunch of monks is a lot tougher."

Seventeenth line, now. *Thrust. Thrust. Thrust.*

"A *whole* lot tougher."

As the eighteenth line stepped forward, the mob finally broke. More accurately, the monks in the van broke. The crowd itself—the great thousands of them—had already begun edging away from the brutal battle. Edging, edging, walking, striding. Running.

There was room to retreat, now. Once they realized it, the battered fanatics suddenly lost all their fight. Within seconds, they were running away themselves, driving the onlookers before them.

Instinctively, the Knights Hospitaler began to pursue. But Zeno, without waiting for Antonina's command, bellowed again. The Knights halted immediately. Stopped, leaned on their staffs, drew in deep gasping breaths.

Antonina turned to Ashot.

"I want you and your cataphracts to ride through the city's center. Break up into squads."

She gave him a hard stare. *"Don't attack anybody.* Not unless you're attacked yourselves, at least. I just want you to be seen. Put the fear of God in that crowd. By nightfall, I want everyone who came out on the street today to be huddling in their villas and apartments. Like mice when the cats are out."

Ashot nodded. "I understand." Instantly, he trotted toward his nearby horse.

She turned to Zeno. "Call out all the Knights you had in reserve. Divide half of them into your—" She hesitated, fumbling for the word. "What did you decide to call that? Your two-hundred-man groups?"

"Battalions."

"Yes. That should be big enough for anything you'll face now. Send each battalion marching through the streets. The big thoroughfares, only. Don't go into the side streets. And stay out of the purely residential quarters."

He nodded. "We're doing the same thing as the cataphracts. Scaring everybody."

"Hell, no!" she snarled. "I want *them* to avoid trouble. I want you to *look* for it."

Scowling, she pointed with her chin at the bodies of dead and unconscious monks which littered the boulevard.

"Think you can recognize them? Pick them out from simple residents?"

"Sure," snorted Zeno. "Look for a pack of men who'd put any mangy alley curs to shame."

"Right." She took a breath. "Hunt them down, Zeno. Don't go into any side streets—I don't want to risk any ambushes in narrow quarters. And stay out of the areas where orthodox Greek citizens live. But hunt the monks down in the main thoroughfares. It's open season, today, on Chalcedon fanatics. Hunt 'em down, bring 'em to bay, beat 'em to a pulp."

She fixed him with a hot gaze. "I want it *bloody*, Zeno. I don't want those fucking monks huddling in their cells, tonight. I want them lying in the streets. Dead, bruised, maimed, broken—I don't care. Just so long as they're completely terrorized."

"Be a pleasure," growled Zeno. He cast a cold eye at the bloody street below. Not all of the bodies lying there were those of ultra-orthodox Chalcedon monks. Here and there, he could see a few wearing the white tunic with the red cross. Already, their comrades were picking through the casualties, hoping to find one or two still alive.

There wouldn't be any, Zeno knew. Not many Knights had been pulled into the crowd. But those who had could not possibly have survived.

"Be our *pleasure*," he growled again. Then, calming himself with a breath, asked, "And what of the other half? What do you want those Knights to do?"

"They'll be coming with me," replied Antonina, "along with Hermogenes and his infantry."

"Where are we going?"

"First, to the Delta Quarter. I want to see what happened there. Then—assuming that situation's under control—we'll be heading for Beta Quarter."

She swiveled, facing Theodosius. Throughout the street battle, the new Patriarch had stood quietly a few feet behind her, along with three of his deacons.

His face was very pale, she saw. Wide-eyed, he and his deacons were examining the carnage on the street below. Sensing her gaze, the Patriarch jerked his head away and stared at her.

"What's the name of that monastery?" she demanded. "I know where it is, but I can't remember what the bastards call it."

Theodosius pursed his lips, hesitating.

Antonina's face was as hard as steel. Her green eyes were like agates. "*You know the one, Patriarch.*"

He looked away, sighing.

"The House of St. Mark," he murmured. Then, with a look of appeal: "Is that really necessary, Antonina?" He pointed down to the street below. "Surely, you've made your point already."

"I'm not in the business of 'making points,' Theodosius," she hissed. "I'm not a schoolteacher, instructing unruly students."

She took three quick steps, thrusting her face into the Patriarch's beard. For all her short stature, it seemed as if it was the Patriarch looking up, not she.

"I am the rod of authority in Alexandria. I am the axe of the Empire."

She stepped back a pace. Waved toward the city's main intersection. "It's good enough to simply intimidate the average orthodox citizen. That's what Ashot and his cataphracts will be doing, now that the crowd is already broken up. But those—those—those—"

All the pent-up hatred of a woman reviled all her life by self-proclaimed holy men erupted.

"Those *stinking filthy putrid monks* are a different story altogether!"

She ground her teeth. Glared at the bodies lying on the street.

"Whore of Babylon, is it?"

When she turned back, the hot hatred was under control. Ice, now. Ice.

The agate eyes fixed on Zeno.

"The monastery called the House of St. Mark is the largest monastery in Alexandria. It's also the center of the city's most extreme Chalcedonians. Ultra-orthodox down to the cockroaches in the cellars. Before they made him Patriach, Paul was its abbot."

Zeno nodded.

"That monastery is *history*," grated Antonina. "By nightfall, it's nothing but rubble. And any monk who hasn't fled by the time we get there is on his way to Heaven."

The hate flared up anew: "Or wherever eternity calls for him. I have my own opinion."

Zeno moved away, then, rounding up his captains and explaining their new orders. Theodosius, for his part, fell back into silence. Long accustomed to the ferocious debate of a high church council, he recognized a hopeless argument when he saw one. And, even if he hadn't had the benefit of that experience, he could not misunderstand the meaning of the phrases which, now and again in the minutes which followed, came hissing out of Antonina's mouth like steam from a volcano. As she stared at the bloody street below, her face filled with cold fury.

Whore of Babylon, is it?
I'll show you the whore.
Come back to my home town, I have.
And, of course, again and again:
Fuck Alexandria.

When Antonina and her escort of Knights Hospitaler and Syrian infantry reached Delta Quarter, by midafternoon, they were immediately met by Euphronius. The commander of the Theodoran Cohort trotted up to her, along with Triphiodoros, the officer whom Hermogenes had placed in charge of the grenadiers' infantry support.

As he peered up at the woman perched on her saddle, looking a bit like a half-broiled little lobster in her armor, the young Syrian's expression was odd. Half-apologetic, half-accusing.

"I'm sorry," he said, "but—"

He gestured at the surrounding area. Looking up and down the street which marked the boundary of the Jewish quarter, Antonina could see perhaps two dozen bodies lying here and there. Hippodrome thugs. All Blues, from their garments. Killed by gunfire, for the most part, although she could see one storefront which had obviously been caved in by a grenade blast, with three bodies mixed in with the rubble.

Her eyes scanned the roofs. Six of the heavy wooden beams which braced the mudbrick construction were festooned with hanged corpses. No more.

"They ran away," complained Euphronius. "As soon as we fired the first volley." He turned, pointing to the shattered storefront. "Except that bunch. They tried to hole up in there. After we tossed in a couple of grenades, the half-dozen survivors surrendered." A self-explanatory wave at the grisly ornaments on the crossbeams.

Then, apologetically:

"We couldn't catch the rest. They ran too fast."

Then, accusingly:

"You didn't give us any cavalry."

"Can't catch routed men without cavalry," chimed in Triphiodoros. The sage voice of experience: "Men running for their lives always run faster than men who are just wanting to kill them."

Sage voice of experience: "Got to have cavalry, to really whip an enemy."

Antonina laughed. Shook her head, half-regretfully, half-ruefully. "I'll remember that!"

She turned her eyes to the Delta Quarter itself, just across the wide thoroughfare. That side of the street was lined with Jews. Young men, mostly, armed with cudgels, knives and the occasional sword or spear. As Hermogenes had predicted, the Jews had been quite ready to fight it out with the Hippodrome mob. Wouldn't have been the first time.

But, just as obviously, the tension of the moment had passed. Even the young bravos were relaxed, now, exchanging half-amicable words with Syrian grenadiers. And she could see women and children, too, here and there, as well as old folks. The children, filled with eager curiosity. The women, beginning to banter with the Syrian wives. And the old folks, of course—not for them this useless time-wasting—were already setting up their foodcarts and vending stalls. Life comes; life goes. Business is here today.

"Very good," Antonina murmured. "Very good."

Euphronius tried to maintain an officer's dignity, but his quiet relief at her approval was evident.

She smiled down at him. "Leave half your grenadiers here, Hermogenes. Along with Triphiodoros and his infantry. Just in case. Doesn't look as if the Greens showed up today. Maybe that's because they usually side with the Monophysites, but maybe it's because they're just dithering. If they change their minds, I want grenadiers here to change it back."

Euphronius nodded.

"Meanwhile, I want you and the rest to come with me."

She cocked her head, admiring the collapsed storefront. Her smile turned positively feral.

"I need some demolition experts."

By nightfall, the House of St. Mark was a pile of rubble. Buried beneath that mound of wooden beams and sundried brick were the bodies of perhaps a hundred ultra-orthodox monks. Nobody knew the exact number. From the rooftop and the windows, the monks had shrieked their defiance at the surrounding troops. Vowing never to surrender. They had particularly aimed their words at the figure of the small woman in armor sitting on a horse.

We will not yield to the Whore of Babylon!

And other phrases—considerably more vulgar—to that effect.

Antonina had not minded. Not in the least. She would not have accepted their surrender even if it had been offered. So, cheerfully, she waited for several minutes before ordering the grenadiers into action. Establishing, for the public record, that the monks had brought their doom onto themselves.

Murmuring, under her breath, a gay little jingle, as the grenades drove the monks into the interior of the huge monastery:

She's back, she's back!

The whore is back!

Chuckling quietly, as the sappers set the charges:

Alas, Alexandria!

Thy judgement has come!

Chortling aloud, as the walls came tumbling down:

How are the righteous fallen!

Chapter 34

Antonina rose before dawn the next morning, at an hour which normally found her fast asleep. But she was determined to drive through her re-establishment of imperial control without allowing the opposition a moment to regain their equilibrium.

Her servants bustled about, preparing her breakfast and clothing. When the time came to don her armor, Antonina was amused by the way her maid ogled the cuirass.

"The thing's obscene, I'll admit," she chuckled.

She walked over and examined the cuirass lying on an upholstered bench against the far wall of her sleeping chamber. Jutting into the air.

"Especially since my reputation must have grown in the telling, by the time the armorer got around to shaping his mold."

Firmly: "My tits are *not* that big."

The maid eyed her hesitantly, unsure of how to respond. The girl was new to Antonina's service. Antonina's regular maid had become ill at sea, and this girl had been hastily rounded up by her head servant Dubazes from the staff of the palace's former occupant.

There had been few of that staff left, when they arrived. Upon the arrival of Antonina's fleet, and the destruction of the naval forces which tried to block her way into the Great Harbor, the former owner had fled Alexandria. He was a Greek nobleman with close ties to Paul and Ambrose's faction, and had apparently decided that discretion was the better part of valor. He would wait out the storm at his estate in far-off Oxyrhynchos.

Antonina thought about that nobleman, as her maid helped her into the armor. Not about *him* so much—she didn't even know the man's name—but about what he represented. He was not alone in his actions. A very large part of Alexandria's Greek nobility had done likewise.

By the time she was buckling on the scabbard which held her cleaver, a task for which the maid was no use at all, she had made her decision. Two decisions, actually. Possibly three.

First, there would be no repercussions against the nobles who had stepped aside and remained neutral in the battle. Not even those who had fled outright. She was simply trying to establish firm imperial control over the city. Many—most—of the orthodox Greek nobility, especially in Alexandria, would remain hostile to the dynasty no matter what she did. So long as that hostility remain muted—a thing of whispers in the salons, rather than riots in the streets—she would ignore it.

Second—a lesser decision flowing from the first—she would instruct Dubazes to make sure the palace was in pristine condition when she left to take up her new residence at the Prefect's palace. The new Prefect had been officially installed the previous evening. There had been no opposition. His predecessor, along with the deposed Patriarch Paul, had fled to the military quarter at Nicopolis to take refuge with Ambrose and his Army of Egypt.

She snorted quietly. When the nobleman, whoever he was, eventually crept back into his palace, he would be surprised to discover it had not been ransacked and vandalized. The discovery would not dispose him any more favorably to the imperial authority, of course. But the calm certitude behind that little act of self-discipline might help strengthen his resolve to keep his head down.

Good enough.

Finally, a small thing, but—

She turned to her maid, and examined the girl. Under that scrutiny, the maid lowered her head timidly.

Egyptian. Not twenty years of age. From the Fayum, I'm willing to bet. Her Greek is good, but that accent is unmistakable.

"What is your name?" she asked.

"Koutina," said the maid.

"You are Monophysite?"

Koutina raised her eyes, startled. Antonina did not miss the fear hidden there.

She waved her hand reassuringly. "It means nothing to me, Koutina. I simply—" *Want to know your loyalties. An Egyptian Monophysite from the Fayum. Yes.*

She switched from Greek to the girl's native tongue. Antonina's own Coptic was still fluent, even if her long residence in Constantinople had given it a bit of an accent.

"I'll be leaving here today, Koutina. My regular maid will not recover from her illness soon. In fact, I will be sending her back to Constantinople to be with her family. So I will need a new maid. Would you like the job?"

Koutina was still staring at her uncertainly. The question about her religious loyalties had obviously unsettled the girl. Paul's persecution had been savage.

"I would *prefer* a Monophysite, Koutina." She smiled, patting the heavy cuirass. "I'm not wearing this grotesque thing for protection from heretics, you know."

Koutina began to return the smile. "You are very famous," she said softly. "I was frightened when you came." Her eyes flitted to the blade buckled to Antonina's waist. "We all heard about the Cleaver, even here in Alexandria."

"It has never been used against any but traitors."

"I know," said Koutina, nodding. "Still—"

Suddenly, all hesitation fled. "I would be delighted." She was beaming now. "It would be so exciting! You are going to fight the Malwa, everyone says so. Can I come there too?"

It was Antonina's turn to be startled. She had only intended to keep the girl in her service during her stay in Alexandria. But now, seeing the eagerness in Koutina's face, she began to reconsider. The young Egyptian was obviously not worried about the risks involved. Boredom, not danger, was the girl's lifelong enemy.

It was an enemy which Antonina herself well remembered, from her own girlhood. The grinding, relentless, tedious labor of a woman born into Egypt's poor masses. Koutina had probably left the Fayum seeking a better life in Alexandria—only to find that she had exchanged the toil of a peasant for the drudgery of a domestic servant.

She could not refuse that eager face. True, the girl might find her death, in Antonina's company. But she would not be—*bored.*

And besides, I need servants whose loyalty I can absolutely trust. Dubazes is not enough. I am certain the Malwa have infiltrated spies into my expedition. I must be certain they don't penetrate my own household.

Koutina, from the Fayum. Yes. I know that breed. The Malwa will have nothing to offer her except money, and I—

She laughed. Belisarius had not turned over *all* of the fortune he garnered in India to finance Shakuntala's rebellion. Nor had he given more than *half* of his war booty to his cataphracts.

And I am richer than any Malwa spymaster.

She grinned. "Done, Koutina. I will pay you well, too. Much better than your former employer."

Koutina's expression was an odd mixture of emotions. Pleasure at the thought of a sudden increases in wages; anger at the thought of her former employer. The man had been a cheapskate, obviously. And had combined that miserliness, Antonina was quite certain, with frequent solicitations. Koutina was pretty as well as young.

Smiling: "And I won't be rattling your door latch, either, late at night, trying to get into your room."

"That bastard!" hissed Koutina.

It was time to go. Time to crush a military rebellion. But Antonina had long since learned to savor all her victories—small ones, as well as large. So she took the moment to exchange a warm look with her new servant. Binding loyalty with her eyes, far more than her purse.

The maid broke the moment.

"You must go, you must go!" Koutina began bustling Antonina out of the room, fussing over the scabbard which held the cleaver. "Ambrose must be brought to heel!"

Out into the corridor, bustling her mistress along. Fussing, now, with the straps that held the cuirass. "He probably won't fight you, anyway. His soldiers will be blinded by the sun, shining off your brass boobs. You must be a giantess, they're so huge! They'll be terrified and run away!"

The stern-faced officers who awaited her in the entryway to the palace were startled, then. Startled—and mightily heartened. Appearing before them was the leader of their grim and perilous mission—a woman, and small at that—howling with laughter. As gay a laughter as they had ever heard. At any time, much less on the morning of a battle.

They took courage from the thought. Stern faces grew sterner still.

And Antonina kept laughing, and laughing, all the way out to her horse waiting in the courtyard. She wasn't sure what amused her most—the thought of her brass breasts, which made her laugh, or the way her laughter so obviously boosted the morale of her men.

Either way, either way. Doesn't matter. Out of small victories come great ones.

As her army marched through the streets of Alexandria, heading toward the suburb of Nicopolis where the Roman garrison had been stationed since the early days of imperial rule, Antonina took the opportunity to assess the city's mood. The streets were lined with people, watching the procession. Most of them were Egyptians and poor Greeks. Both were cheering—the Egyptians with loud enthusiasm, the Greeks with more restraint.

Word had already spread through the city that Theodosius had been installed as the new Patriarch. That news had been greeted by the Egyptian Monophysites with wild acclaim. Theodosius was one of their own. True, he was an adherent of the Severan school, whose moderate and compromising attitude toward the official Church was out of step with the more dogmatic tradition of Egyptian Monophysitism. But the Egyptian residents of Alexandria did not look on these things the same way as the fanatic Monophysite monks of the desert. They had had enough of street brawls, and persecution. Doctrinal fine points be damned. The Empress Theodora was one of them, and she had placed another in the Church of St. Michael.

Good enough—more than good enough!—to declare a holiday.

The Greek residents who watched Antonina pass—and cheered her on—took less pleasure in the news. Many of Alexandria's Greek population, of course, had adopted Monophysitism themselves. All of the religious leaders of that dogma were Greek, in fact, even if they found their popular base in the Coptic masses of Egypt. But most Greeks, even poor ones, had remained true to orthodoxy.

Still, they were not nobles. Tailors, bakers, linen-makers, glass-blowers, sailors, papyrus workers—almost all the Mediterranean world's paper was made in Alexandria—shopkeepers, merchants, domestic servants, fishermen, grain handlers: the list was well nigh endless. Some were prosperous, some merely scraped by; but none were rich. And all of them, even here in Alexandria, had come to accept the general opinion of the Roman Empire's great masses with regard to the imperial power.

That opinion had crystallized, in Constantinople itself, with the defeat of the Nika insurrection. From there, carried by the sailors and merchants who weaved Roman society into a single cloth, the opinion had spread to every corner of the Empire. From the Danube to Elephantine, from Cyrene to Trebizond, the great millions of Rome's citizens had heard, discussed, quarreled, decided.

The dynasty which ruled the Empire was *their* dynasty.

It never occurred to them, of course, to think of the dynasty as a "people's dynasty." Emperors were emperors; common folk were common folk. The one ruled the other. Law of nature.

But they did think of it as *theirs*. Not because the dynasty came from their own ranks—which it did, and they knew it, and took pleasure in the knowing—so much as they were satisfied that the dynasty understood *them*; and based its power on *their* support; and kept at least one eye open on behalf of *their* needs and interests.

Common folk were common folk, emperors were emperors, and never the twain shall meet. That still leaves the difference between a good emperor and a bad one—a difference which common folk measure with a very different stick than nobility.

The taxes had been lowered, and made more equitable. The haughtiest nobles and the most corrupt bureaucrats had been humbled, always a popular thing, among those over whom the elite lords it—even *executed*. Wildly popular, that. Stability had been restored, and with it the conditions which those people needed to feed their families.

And, finally, there was Belisarius.

As she marched through the streets, Antonina was struck by how often her husband's name made up the cheer coming from the throats of the Greek residents. The Egyptians, too, chanted his name. But they were as likely to call out her own or the Empress Theodora's.

Among the Greeks, one name only:

Belisarius! Belisarius! Belisarius!

She took no personal umbrage in that chant. If nothing else, it was obvious that the cheer was the Greeks' way of approving her, as well. She was Belisarius' wife, and if the Greek upper crust had often sneered at the general for marrying such a disreputable woman, it was clear as day that the Greek commoners lining the streets of Alexandria were not sneering at him in the least.

The Greeks had found their own way to support the dynasty, she realized. Belisarius might be a Thracian himself, and might have married an Egyptian, and put his half-Egyptian, half-who-knows-what bastard stepson on the throne, but he was still a *Greek*. In the way which mattered most to that proudest of Rome's many proud nations.

Whipped the Persians, didn't he? Just like he'll whip these Malwa dogs. Whoever they are.

Hermogenes leaned over to her, whispering: "The word of Anatha's already spread."

Antonina nodded. She had just gotten the word herself, the day before. The semaphore network was still half-finished, but enough of it had been completed to bring the news to Antioch—and from there, by a swift keles courier ship, to Alexandria.

There had been nothing personal, addressed to her, in the report. But she had recognized her husband's turn of phrase in the wording of it. And had seen his shrewd mind at work, in the way he emphasized the decisive role of Greek cataphracts in winning the great victory over Malwa.

That word, too, had obviously spread. She could read it in the way Greek shopkeepers grinned, as they cheered her army onward, and the way Greek sailors hoisted their drinking cups in salute to the passing soldiers.

Thank you, husband. Your great victory has given me a multitude of small ones.

The fortress at Nicopolis where the Army of Egypt lay waiting was one of the Roman Empire's mightiest. Not surprising. The garrison was critical to the Empire's rule. Egyptian grain fed the Roman world—Constantinople depended upon it almost entirely—and the grain was shipped through Alexandria's port. Since Augustus, every Roman Emperor had seen to it that Egypt was secure. For centuries, now, the fort at Nicopolis had been strengthened, expanded, modified, built up, and strengthened yet again.

"We'll never take it by storm," stated Ashot. "Not with the forces we've got. Even grenades'd be like pebbles, against those walls."

He looked up at the battlements, where a mass of soldiers could be seen standing guard.

"Be pure suicide for sappers, trying to set charges."

Ashot, along with Antonina and Hermogenes and the other top officers of the expedition, was observing the fortress from three hundred yards away. Their vantage point was another of the great intersections which dotted Alexandria itself. Very similar to the one at the city's center, if not quite as large, down to the tetrastylon.

Originally, the fortress had been built outside the city's limits. But Alexandria had spread, over the centuries. Today, the city's population numbered in the hundreds of thousands. The fortress had long since been engulfed within the suburb called Nicopolis.

It was a bit jarring, actually, the way that massive stone structure—so obviously built for war—rose up out of a sea of small shops and mudbrick apartment buildings. Comical, almost. In the way that a majestic lion might seem comical, if it were surrounded by chittering mice.

Except there were no chittering mice *that* day. The shops were boarded up, the apartments vacant. Nicopolis' populace had fled, the moment news came that Antonina was advancing against Ambrose. All morning, a stream of people had poured out of the suburb, bearing what valuables they owned in carts or haversacks.

Antonina turned to Hermogenes. "Do you agree?"

Hermogenes nodded instantly. "Ashot's right. I know that fortress. I was stationed in it for a few months, shortly after I joined the army. You can't believe how thick those stone walls are until you see them."

He twisted in his saddle and looked back at Menander.

"Could you take it with siege guns? You're the only one of us who's observed them in action."

Seeing himself the focus of attention, the shy young cataphract tensed. But there was no faltering or hesitation in his reply.

"Yes, I could, if we had them. But John told me just yesterday that he doesn't expect to produce any for months. Even then, it'd take weeks to reduce those walls."

Very shyly, now: "I don't know as Antonina can afford to wait that long."

"Absolutely not," she said firmly. "The longer this drags on, the more likely it is that revolt will start brewing in other parts of Alexandria. The rest of Egypt, for that matter. Paul has plenty of supporters in every one of the province's Greek towns, all the way up to Ombos and Syene, just below the First Cataract. Antinoopolis and Oxyrhynchos are hotbeds of disloyalty. Not to mention—"

She fell silent. The top officers surrounding her knew the strategic plan which she and Belisarius had worked out, months earlier, to carry the fight to Malwa's exposed southern flank. But the more junior officers didn't. Antonina had no reason to doubt their loyalty, but there was still the risk of loose talk being picked up by Malwa spies.

So she bit her tongue and finished the thought only in her mind:

Not to mention that I don't have weeks—months!—to waste in Alexandria. I've got to get to the Red Sea, and join forces with the Axumites. By early spring of next year, at the latest.

And the next one, full of anguish: Or my husband, if he's not already, will be a dead man.

But nothing of that anguish showed, in her face. Simply calm resolution.

"No, gentlemen, we've got to win this little civil war *quickly*."

Ashot tugged his beard and growled. "I'm telling you, it'll be pure slaughter if we try to storm that place."

Antonina waved him down. "Relax, Ashot. I'm not crazy. I have no intention of wasting lives in a frontal attack. But I don't think it's necessary."

Hermogenes, too, was tugging his beard.

"A siege'll take months. A year, probably, unless we get siege guns. That fortress has enough provisions to last that long, easily. And they've got two wells inside the walls."

Antonina shook her head. "I wasn't thinking of a siege, either."

Seeing the confusion in the faces around her, Antonina had to restrain a sigh.

Generals.

"You're approaching the situation upside down," she stated. "This is not really a military problem. It's *political*."

To Ashot: "Weren't you the one who was telling me, just yesterday, that the reason Ambrose couldn't intervene while we were suppressing the mob was because he needed the day to win over his troops?"

The commander of her Thracian bucellarii nodded.

She grinned. "Well, he's had a day. Just how solid do you think he's made himself? With his troops?"

Frowning.

Generals.

She pointed at the fortress. "How long have those men—the soldiers, I mean—been stationed here? Hermogenes?"

The young merarch shrugged.

"Years. Most of the garrison—the troops, anyway—spend their entire term of service in Egypt. Even units that get called out for a campaign elsewhere are always rotated back here."

"That's what I thought. Now—another question. Where do those men *live?* Not in the fortress, I'm sure. Years of service, you said. That means wives, children, families. Outside businesses, probably. Half of those soldiers—*at least* half—will have married into local families. They'll have invested their pay in their father-in-laws' shops. Bought interests in grain-shipping."

"The whole bit," grumbled Ashot. "Yeah, you're right. Fucking garritroopers. Always takes weeks to shake 'em down on a campaign. Spend the first month, solid, wailing about their declining property values back home."

The light of understanding came, finally, to her officers.

Or so, at least, she thought.

"You're right, Antonina!" cried Hermogenes excitedly. "That'll work!"

He cast eager eyes about, scanning the immediate environment of the fortress. "Most of 'em probably live right here, right in Nicopolis. We'll start by burning everything to the ground. Then—"

"Find their wives and daughters," chipped in his executive officer, Callixtos. "Track 'em down wherever they are and—"

"Won't need to," countered Ashot. "Any women'll do. At this distance, the garrison won't be able to make out faces anyway. Just women being stripped naked in the street with us waving our dicks around and threatening to—"

Antonina erupted. *"Stupid generals!"*

Startled, her horse twitched. Antonina drew back on the reins savagely. Wisely, the horse froze.

"Cretins! Idiots! Morons—absolute morons—the whole lot! You want me to end a small civil war by starting a big one? What the fuck is wrong with you?"

They shrank from her hot eyes. Antonina turned in her saddle and transferred the glare back to Menander.

"*You!* Maybe you're not too old to have lost all your wits! *Maybe.* How would *you* handle it?"

For a moment, Menander was too stunned to speak. Then, clearing his throat, he said, "Well. Well. Actually, while you were talking I was thinking about how the general—Belisarius, I mean—handled the situation with the Kushans. The *second* situation with the Kushans, I mean—not the first one where he tricked Venandakatra out of using them as guards—but the other one, where he—well, they were guarding us but didn't know the Empress—Shakuntala, I mean, not Theodora—was hidden in—well."

He stopped, floundering. Drew a deep, shaky breath.

"What I mean is, I was struck by it at the time. How the general used honey instead of vinegar."

Antonina sighed. Relaxed, a bit.

"You're promoted," she growled. "*Tribune* Menander, you are."

The eyes which she now turned on her assembled officers were no longer hot.

Oh, but they were very, very cold.

"*Here—is—what—you—will—do.* You *will* find the wives and daughters—and the sons and fathers and mothers and brothers and for that matter the second cousins twice-removed—of those soldiers forted up in that place."

Deep breath. *Icy* cold eyes.

"*More precisely*, you and your cataphracts will *escort* the Knights Hospitaler while *they* do the actual finding. You and your soldiers will stand there looking as sweet and polite as altar boys—or I'll have your guts for breakfast—while the Knights Hospitaler *convince* the soldiers' families that a potentially disastrous situation for their husbands and fathers and sons and brothers—and for that matter third cousins three times removed—would be resolved if the families would come back to their homes and reopen the shops. And—most important—would cook some meals."

"*Cook meals?*" choked Hermogenes.

A wintry smile.

"Yes. *Meals*. Big meals, like the ones I remember from my days here. Spicy meals. The kind of meals you can smell a mile away."

She gazed at the fortress, still smiling.

"Let the soldiers smell those meals, while they're chewing on their garrison biscuits. Let them think about their warm beds—with their wives in them—while they sleep on the battlements in full armor. Let them think about their little shops and their father-in-laws' promises that they'll inherit the business, while Ambrose gives speeches."

"They'll *never* agree to it," squeaked Ashot. "Their wives and daughters, I mean. And their families."

He squared his shoulders, faced Antonina bravely. "They won't come back. Not with us here. Hell, *I* wouldn't, come down to it."

An arctic smile. "That I can believe. Which is why you *won't* be here. Not you, not your cataphracts. Not Hermogenes, nor his infantry regulars. *I'll* be here, as a guarantee. Their own hostage, if they want to think of it that way."

"*What?*" demanded Hermogenes. "*Alone?*"

Suddenly, Antonina's usual warm smile returned. "Alone? Of course not! What a silly idea. My grenadiers will stay here with me. Along with *their* wives, and *their* children."

All the officers now stared at Euphronius. The young Syrian met that gaze with his own squared shoulders. And then, with a grin.

"Great idea. Nobody'll worry about *us* raping anybody." A shudder. "God, my wife'd kill me!"

Ashot turned back to Antonina. The short, muscular Armenian was practically gobbling.

"What if Ambrose sallies?" he demanded. "Do you think your grenadiers—*alone*—can stand up to him?"

Antonina never wavered. "As a matter of fact—*yes*. Here, at least."

She pointed down the thoroughfare to the fortress. "We're not on an open field of battle, Ashot. There's only two ways Ambrose can come at me. He can send his men through all the little crooked side streets—and I will *absolutely* match my grenadiers against him in *that* terrain—"

All the officers were shaking their heads. No cataphract in his right mind would even think of driving armored horses through that rabbit warren.

"—*or*, he can come at me with a massed lance charge down that boulevard. Which is what he'll do, if he does anything. Down that beautiful boulevard—which is just wide enough to tempt a horseman, but not wide enough to maneuver."

She bestowed a very benign, approving smile upon the boulevard in question.

"And *yes*, on *that* terrain, my grenadiers will turn him into sausage."

She drew herself up in the saddle, sitting as tall as she could. Which was not much, of course.

"Do as I say."

Her officers hastened to obey, then, with no further protest.

Possibly, that was due to the iron command in her voice.

But possibly—just possibly—it was because when she drew herself up in the saddle the blazing sun of Egypt reflected off her cuirass at such an angle as to momentarily blind her generals. And make a short woman seem like a giantess.

By noon of the next day, the first families began trickling back into Nicopolis. Antonina was there to greet them, from the pavilion she had set up in the very middle of the boulevard.

The first arrivals approached her timidly. But, finding that the legendary Antonina—*she of the Cleaver*—was, in person, a most charming and sweet-tempered lady, they soon began to relax.

By nightfall, hundreds had returned, and were slowly beginning to mingle with the grenadiers. All of the Syrians could speak Greek now, even if many of them still spoke it badly. So they were able to communicate with the soldiers' families. Coptic was the native language of most of those folk, but, as was universally the case in Alexandria, they were fluent in Greek as well.

By morning of the day after, the soldiers' families were quite at ease with the grenadiers. True, the men were a bit scary, what with their bizarre and much-rumored new weapons. But their wives were a familiar thing, even if they were foreign Syrians, as were their children. And it is difficult—impossible, really—to be petrified by a man who is playing with his child, or being nagged by his wife.

By the end of that second day, half of Nicopolis' residents had returned. Antonina's presence and assurances, combined with worry over their businesses and properties, proved irresistable.

On the morning of the following day, Antonina called for a feast. At her own expense, foodstuffs were purchased from all over the city. The great thoroughfare—not three hundred yards from the fortress—was turned into an impromptu, gigantic, daylong picnic.

As the picnic progressed, some of the wives of the garrison soldiers began to approach the fortress. Calling up to their husbands.

The first negotiations began, in a matter of speaking. Soldiers on the battlements began lowering baskets tied to ropes. Foodstuffs went up, to relieve the tedium of garrison biscuits. With those delicious parcels went wifely words, shouted from below. Scolding words, in some cases. Pleading words, in others. Downright salacious promises, in not a few.

Watching from her pavilion, Antonina counted every basket as a cannonball struck. Every wifely word, as a sapper's mine laid.

She leaned back easily in her couch, surrounded by the small horde of Nicopolis' housewives who had adopted her as their new patron saint, and savored the moment.

Great victories out of small ones.

Generals. Ha!

On the fifth day of the "siege," the first real trouble began. As one of the wives approached the fortress—this had now become a daily occurrence, almost a ritual—a small crowd of officers forced their way through the mob of soldiers standing on the battlements.

Threats were exchanged between officers and men. Then, one of the officers angrily grabbed a soldier's bow and took it upon himself to fire an arrow at the wife standing on the street below.

The arrow missed its mark, badly. The startled, squawking, outraged housewife was actually in much greater danger of being struck by the next missile hurled from the walls.

The officer himself, half-dead before he even hit the ground, fifty feet below.

The shaken housewife squawled, now, as she was spattered by his blood. Shrieked, then, covering her head and racing from the scene, as six more officers were sent on the same fatal plunge.

The rest of the day, and into the night, the crowd standing outside the fortress could hear the sounds of brawling and fighting coming from within. Antonina herself, even from the pavilion's distance, could hear it clearly.

By now, Antonina had relented enough to allow Ashot and Hermogenes to return to Nicopolis. Some of Hermogenes' soldiers had been allowed in, as well—just enough to provide her grenadiers with an infantry bulwark in the event of a battle. But she still kept the cataphracts well out of sight.

She stood in the entry of her pavilion next to her two officers, gauging the sounds.

"It's not a full battle, yet," opined Hermogenes.

"Not even close," agreed Ashot. "What you're hearing is about a hundred little brawls and set-tos. Ambrose is losing it completely."

Hermogenes glanced sideways at Antonina. "He'll sally tomorrow. Bet on it."

Ashot nodded. "He's got to. He can't let Antonina sit out here, rotting his army out from under him."

"How many will he still have, do you think?" she asked.

Ashot shrugged. "His cataphracts. The most of them, anyway. Those aren't Egyptians. They're a Greek unit, from Paphlagonia. Been here less than a year. They won't have much in the way of local ties, and all of their officers—down to the tribunes—were handpicked by Ambrose."

He tugged his beard. "Six hundred men, let's say. Beyond that—"

Tug, tug. His eyes widened. "Mary, Mother of God. I think that's *it*."

Eagerly, now: "I could bring up the Thracian bucellarii. Those fat-ass garritrooper shits'd never have a chance! We'd—"

"*No.*"

The gaze which she bestowed on Ashot was not icy, not in the least. The past few days, if nothing else, had restored her good temper. But it was still just as unyielding.

"My grenadiers I said it would be. My grenadiers it is."

Ashot sighed, but did not argue the point. Anton-ina was wearing her armor at all times, now, except when she slept. True, the sun was down. But the many candles in her pavilion still shined off her cuirass, making her seem—

Jesus, he thought, how can any woman have tits that big?

As the night wore on, the sounds of fighting within the fortress waned. Then, at daybreak, a sudden outburst erupted. Rapidly escalated to the sounds of a pitched battle.

Antonina had prepared the grenadiers the night before. By the time the battle within the fortress was in full swing, Antonina was already out on the street, in armor, on horseback. Ashot and Hermogenes sat their horses alongside her.

Ahead of them, drawn up and ready for battle, stood the Theodoran Cohort.

Three hundred of them were now armed with John of Rhodes' new handcannons. The handcannons had barrels made of welded wrought-iron staves, hooped with iron bands, mounted on wooden shoulder stocks. The barrels were about eighteen inches long, with a bore measuring approximately one inch in diameter.

The guns were loaded from reed cartridges with a measured charge in one end of the tube and a fiber wad and lead ball in the other. A hardwood ramrod recessed into the front of the stock was used to ram the charges down the barrel. The handcannons had no trigger. The charges were ignited by a slow match—tow soaked in saltpeter—held in a pivoting clamp attached to the stock.

As handheld firearms go, they were about as primitive as could be imagined. John of Rhodes had wanted to wait until he had developed a better weapon, but Belisarius had insisted on rushing these first guns into production. From experience, he had known that John would take forever to produce a gun he was finally satisfied with. The Malwa would not give them that time. These would do, for the moment.

Primitive, the guns were. Their accuracy was laughable—and many a bucellarii did laugh, during the practice sessions in Rhodes, watching the Syrian gunners miss targets at a range that any self-respecting Thracian cataphract could have hit with an arrow blind drunk. But it was noticeable that none of the scoffing cataphracts offered to serve as a target. Not after watching the effects of a heavy lead bullet which *did* happen to strike a target. Those balls could drive an inch into solid pine—and with far greater striking power than any arrow.

The formation into which the Cohort was drawn up was designed to take advantage of the hand-cannons. Half of the gunners were arrayed at the Cohort's front, in six lines stretching across the entire width of the boulevard, twenty-five men to a line. Squads of Hermogenes' infantry were interspersed between each line of gunners, ready to use their long pikes to hold off any cavalry who made it through the gunfire.

The other hundred and fifty gunners were lining the rooftops for fifty yards down both sides of the boulevard, ready to pour their own fire onto the street below. The rest of the Cohort, armed with grenades, stood in back of the gunners, their slings and bombs in hand.

The sounds of the fighting within the fortress seemed to be reaching a crescendo. For a moment, the gates of the fortress began to open. Then, accompanied by the steel clangor of swords on shields, swung partially shut.

"Christ," muttered Ashot. "Now that poor bastard Ambrose has to fight his way *out* of the fortress. What a mess that's got to be in there!"

Suddenly, the gates of the fortress opened wide. Seconds later, the first of Ambrose's cataphracts began spilling out into the street.

It was immediately obvious that the enemy cataphracts were totally disorganized and leaderless.

"That's not a sally!" exclaimed Hermogenes. "They're just trying to get out of the fortress."

"Fuck 'em," hissed Antonina. *"Euphronius!"*

The Cohort commander waved, without even bothering to look back. The nearest cataphracts were not much more than two hundred yards away. Well within range for his best slingers.

"Sling-staffs!" he bellowed. "Volley!"

Twenty grenadiers standing in the rear wound up, swirled in the peculiarly graceful way of slingers, sent the missiles on their way.

His best grenadiers, those twenty, with the most proficient fuse-cutting wives. Only three of the grenades fell short. None fell wide. Only two burst too late; none, too soon.

The crowd of cataphracts jostling their way out of the fortress—perhaps four hundred, by now—were ripped by fifteen grenades bursting in their midst. Then, a moment or so later, by the belated explosions of the two whose fuses had been cut overlong.

The casualties among the cataphracts themselves were fairly light, in truth. Their heavy armor—designed to fend off dehgan lances and axes—was almost impervious to the light shrapnel of grenades. And while that armor provided little protection against concussion, a man had to be very close to a grenade blast in order to be killed by the pure force of the explosion itself.

But their *horses*—

The armor worn by the cavalry mounts was even heavier. But it was concentrated entirely on their heads, chests, and withers. The grenades—especially the ones which exploded near the ground—shattered their legs and spilled their intestines. And, most of all, threw even the unwounded beasts into a frenzied terror.

Ambrose's cataphracts had been nothing but a mob, anyway. Now, they were simply a mob desperately trying to get out of the line of fire. More cataphracts piled out of the gates, adding to the confusion. Another volley sailed their way. More horses were butchered.

Another volley of grenades landed in their midst.

Ambrose's loyalists dissolved completely, then. There was no thought of anything but personal safety. Breaking up into small groups—or simply as individuals—the cataphracts raced their horses down the streets of Nicopolis.

Going where? Who knows? Just—somewhere else.

Anywhere else.

Anywhere common soldiers weren't rising in mutiny.

Anywhere grenades didn't rupture their bodies.

Anywhere the hot sun of Egypt didn't blind them, glancing off the great brass tits of a giantess.

Anywhere else.

Antonina captured the would-be Emperor two days later. In a manner of speaking.

After negotiating safe passage, a small group of Ambrose's subordinates rode up to the Prefectural Palace where Antonina now made her headquarters, accompanied by perhaps a dozen cataphracts.

And a corpse, wrapped in a linen shroud.

Ambrose, it was. The former commander of the Army of Egypt had been stabbed in the back. Several times.

He made us do it.

Loyal Romans, we are. Honest.

He made us do it.

And we'll never do it again, neither.

Nevernevernevernever.

We promise.

Antonina let it pass. She even welcomed the "loyal officers" back into the ranks of the Army of Egypt. Reduced in rank, naturally.

But even that punishment, she sweetened. Partly, with an explanation that room needed to made for the *new* officers whom the *new* commander had brought with him. Mostly, with a peroration on the subject of the future riches of Roman soldiers, from Malwa booty.

The officers made no complaint. They were glad enough not to be hanged.

The only grumbling at her lenient treatment of Ambrose's cataphracts, ironically enough, came from the other soldiers in his army. They were disgruntled that the same louts they had battled in the fortress—the stinking bums who had threatened their wives, even *shot arrows* at one of them—were let off so lightly.

But they didn't do more than grumble—and rather quietly, at that. Their own position, after all, was a bit precarious.

Best to let bygones be bygones. All things considered.

Someone, of course, had to pay the bill. Ambrose himself being dead—which didn't stop Antonina from hanging his corpse, and leaving it to sway in the wind from the fortress' battlements—the bill was presented to Paul and the former Prefect.

Both men had been found, after the cataphracts fled, huddling in one of the fortress' chambers. Paul, still defiant; the Prefect, blubbering for mercy.

Antonina hanged the Prefect immediately. His body swayed in the wind at the great intersection at the center of the city, suspended from one of the tetrastylon pillars.

Paul—

"No martyrs," she pronounced, waving down the bloodthirsty chorus coming from all her advisers except Theodosius. "An executed prefect is just a dead politician. Nobody gives a damn except his cronies, and they won't grieve for more than a day. A religious leader, on the other hand—"

She straightened in the chair which, for all intents and purposes, served as her throne in the audience chamber of the Prefectural Palace. Officially, of course, authority was in the hands of the new Prefect. In the real world—

He was standing in the crowd before her. One among many.

Her officers almost winced, seeing that erect, chest-swelling motion. But there was no blinding flash, this time. Antonina had stopped wearing her cuirass. Just the firm posture of a small woman. Voluptuous, true. But no giantess.

Not that the sight of that familiar, very female form led them to think they could oppose her will. Giantess or no, brass tits or no, on *that* matter the question was settled.

Seated on her "throne," Antonina decreed.

"No martyrs."

Theodosius sighed with relief. Seeing the little movement, Antonina turned her gaze onto him.

"What do you recommend, Patriarch?" she asked, smiling now. "A long stay on the island of Palmaria, perhaps? Tending goats. For the next fifteen or twenty years."

"Excellent idea!" exclaimed Theodosius. Piously: "It's good for the soul, that sort of simple manual labor. Everyone knows it. It's a constant theme in the best sermons."

Off to Palmaria, then, Paul went. The very same day. Antonina saw him off personally. Stood on the dock until his ship was under sail.

He was still defiant, Paul was. Cursed her for a whore and a harlot all the way to the dock, all the way out to his transport, and from the very stern of the ship which took him to his exile.

Antonina, throughout, simply responded with a sweet smile. Until his ship was halfway to the horizon.

Then, and only then, did the smile fade. Replaced by a frown.

"I feel kind of guilty about this," she admitted.

Standing next to her, Ashot was startled.

"About Paul? I think that bastard's lucky—"

"Not *him*," she snorted. "I was thinking about the poor goats."

Chapter 35
THE EUPHRATES
Autumn, 531 A.D.

"So where's your flank attack?" demanded Maurice. "You remember—the one you predicted was going to happen that very night. About a week ago."

Belisarius shrugged. Reclining comfortably against the crude rock wall of one of the artillery towers on the dam, he returned Maurice's glower with a look of complacence.

"I forgot about the negotiations," he explained.

"What negotiations?"

Belisarius stuck his thumb over his shoulder, pointing southwest.

"The ones that Ormazd has been having with the Malwa, these past few days." He reached down and brought a goblet to his lips, sipping from its contents.

Maurice eyed the goblet with disfavor.

"How can you drink that stuff? You're starting to go native on me, I can tell. A Roman—sure as hell a Thracian—should be drinking wine, not that—that—that Persian—"

Belisarius smiled crookedly. "I find fresh water flavored with lemon and pomegranate juice to be quite refreshing, Maurice. I thank Baresmanas for introducing me to it."

He levered himself into an upright position. "Besides," he added, "if I drank wine all day—day after day, stuck on this misbegotten dam—I'd be a complete sot by now."

"Anastasius and Valentinian drink wine," came the immediate riposte. "Haven't noticed them stumbling about."

Belisarius cast a cold eye on his two bodyguards, not four yards away. Like Belisarius, Anastasius and Valentinian were lounging in the shade provided by the artillery tower.

"With his body weight," growled the general, "Anastasius could drink a tun of wine a day and never notice." Anastasius, hearing, looked down at his immense frame with philosophical serenity. "And as for Valentinian—ha! The man not only looks like a weasel, he can eat and drink like one, too." Valentinian, hearing, looked down at his whipcord body with his own version of philosophical serenity. Which, more than anything, resembled a weasel after gorging itself in a chicken coop.

Suddenly, Belisarius thrust himself to his feet. The motion was pointless, really. It simply expressed the general's frustration at the past week of immobility. Stuck on a dam with his army while they fought it out, day after day, with an endless series of Malwa probes and attacks.

For all practical purposes, the battle had become a siege. Belisarius was a master of siegecraft—whether on offense or defense—but it was a type of warfare that he personally detested. His temperament led him to favor maneuver rather than simple mayhem.

He had not even had the—so to speak—relief of personal combat. On the first day after joining his army on the dam itself, Belisarius had started to participate directly in repelling one of the Malwa attacks. Even before Anastasius and Valentinian had corraled him and dragged him away, the Syrian soldiers manning that section of the wall had fiercely driven him off. Liberius and Maurice, riding up with their cataphracts to bolster the Syrians, had even cursed him for a damned fool.

The general's cold and calculating brain recognized the phenomenon, of course, and took satisfaction in it. Only commanders who were genuinely treasured by an army had their personal safety so jealously guarded by their own soldiers. But the man inside the general had chafed, and cursed, and stormed, and railed.

The general bridled the man. And so, for a week, Belisarius had reconciled himself to the inevitable. He had never again attempted to directly participate in the fight at the wall, but he had spent each and every day riding up and down the Roman line of fortifications.

Encouraging his soldiers, consulting with his officers, organizing the logistics, and—especially—spending time with the wounded.

Valentinian and Anastasius had grumbled, Aide had chafed—**rockets! very dangerous!**—but Belisarius had been adamant. His soldiers, he knew, might take conscious satisfaction in the knowledge that their commander was out of the direct fray. But they would—at a much, much deeper human level—take heart and courage from his immediate presence.

In that, he had been proven right. As the week wore on, his army's battle cry underwent a transformation.

Rome! Rome! it had been, in the first two days.

By the third day, as he rode up and down the fortifications, his own name had been cheered. That was still true, even more so, a week after the battle started. But his name was no longer being used as a simple cheer. It had become a taunt of defiance hurled at the enemy. The entire Roman army using that single word to let the Malwa know:

You sorry bastards are fucked. *Fucked.*

Belisarius! Belisarius!

Belisarius drained his goblet and set it down on the wall with enough force to crack the crude pottery.

He ignored the sound, swiveling his head to the west.

His eyes glared. It being late afternoon, the sun promptly glared back. He raised a hand to shield his face.

"Come on, Ormazd," he growled. "Make up your mind. Not even a God-be-damned Aryan prince should need a week to decide on treason."

Maurice turned his own head to follow Belisarius' gaze.

"You think that's what's been going on?"

"Count on it, Maurice," said Belisarius softly. "I can guarantee you that every night, for the past week, Malwa emissaries have been shuttling back and forth between Ormazd's pavilion and—"

For a moment, he began to turn his head to the south. Squinting fiercely, as if by sheer forth of will he could peer into the great pavilion which the Malwa had erected on the left bank of the Euphrates, well over a mile away. The pavilion where, he was certain, Link exercised its demonic command.

Maurice grunted sourly. "Maybe you're right. I sure as hell hope so. If this damned siege goes on much longer, we'll—ah." He made a vague gesture with his hand, as if brushing dung off his tunic.

Belisarius said nothing. He knew Maurice was not worried that the Malwa could take the dam by frontal assault. Nor was the chiliarch really concerned that the Malwa could wear out the Romans. The steady stream of barges coming down from Callinicum kept the defenders better supplied than the attackers. The Romans could withstand this kind of semi-siege almost indefinitely.

But—it was wearing. Wearing on the body, wearing on the nerves. Since the ferocious Malwa assaults of the first day and night, which they had suspended in favor of constant probes and quick pinprick attacks, casualties had been relatively light. But "light" casualties are still casualties. Men you know, dead, crippled, wounded. Day after day, with no end in sight.

"I hope you're right," he repeated. Sourly.

Belisarius decided a change of subject was in order. "Agathius is going to live," he announced. "I'm quite confident of it, now. I saw him just yesterday."

Maurice glanced upriver, at the ambulance barges moored just beyond range of the Malwa rockets. "Glad to hear it. I thought sure—" He lapsed into another little grunt. Not sour, this one. The inarticulate sound combined admiration with disbelief.

"Never thought he'd make it," he admitted. "Especially after he refused to go to Callinicum."

Belisarius nodded. Most of the Roman casualties, after triage, had been shipped back to Callinicum. But Agathius had flat refused—had even threatened violence when Belisarius tried to insist. So, he had stayed—as had his young wife. Sudaba had been just as stubborn toward Agathius' demands that she leave as he had been toward Belisarius. Including the threats of violence.

In truth, Belisarius was grateful. Cyril had succeeded to the command of the Constantinople troops, and had done very well in the post. But Agathius' stance had done wonders for the army's morale, and by no means simply among the Greeks. For the past week, a steady stream of soldiers—Thracians, Syrians, Illyrians and Arabs as much as Greeks—had visited the maimed officer on his barge. Agathius was very weak from tremendous loss of blood, and in great pain, what with one leg amputated at the knee and the other at the ankle. But the man had borne it all with a stoicism which would have shamed Marcus Aurelius, and had never failed to take the occasion to reinforce his visitors' determination to resist the Malwa.

A quiet thought came from Aide:

◇   ◇   ◇

**"Think where man's glory most begins and ends
And say my glory was I had such friends."**

"Yes," whispered Belisarius. "Yes."
**It's from a poet whose name will be Yeats. Many centuries
from now.**
Belisarius took a deep breath.
*Let us give mankind those centuries, then. And all the millions
of centuries which will come after.*

Chapter 36

In its pavilion, at the very moment when Belisarius made that silent vow, the thing from the future which called itself Link made its catastrophic mistake.

It had calculated the possibilities. Analyzed the odds. Gauged the options. Most of all, it had assessed the capabilities of the enemy commander so accurately, and so correctly, and in so many ways, that Belisarius would have been stunned had he ever known how well he had been measured.

Measured, however, only as a general—for that was all that Link understood. The being from the future, with its superhuman intelligence, had burrowed to the depths of the crooked mind of Belisarius. Down to the very tips of the roots.

And had missed the man completely.

"ORMAZD HAS AGREED, THEN?"

Link's top subordinates, four officers squatting on cushions before the chair which held the shape of an old woman, nodded in unison.

"Yes, Great Lady Holi," said one. "He will pull his troops out of position three hours after sundown."

Link pondered, gauged, calculated, analyzed.

Assessed the crooked, cunning brain of the great General Belisarius.

From long experience, the four officers sat silently throughout. It never occurred to them to offer any advice. The advice would not have been welcome. And, if Link had none of the explosive temper of the late Lord Jivita, the being was utterly merciless. The officers weren't especially afraid of the huge tulwar-bearing men who squatted between them and Great Lady Holi. Those were simply guards. But they had only to turn their heads to see the line of silent assassins who waited, as motionless as statues, in the rear of the pavilion. Link—Great Lady Holi—had used those assassins three times since the expedition began. To punish failure, twice. But there had also been an officer who couldn't learn to restrain his counsel.

Finally, Link spoke.

"THERE IS A POSSIBILITY. IT IS NOT LIKELY. WERE THE ENEMY LED BY ANY OTHER COMMANDER I WOULD DISMISS IT OUT OF HAND. BUT I CANNOT. NOT WITH BELISARIUS."

Silence followed again, for well over a minute. The Malwa officers did not ask for an explanation of those cryptic words. None would have been given if they had.

Gauged, analyzed, assessed. Made its decision.

"SEND THE KUSHANS FIRST. ALL OF THEM. ON FOOT."

The officers were visibly startled, now. After a moment, one of them ventured to ask:

"On *foot*?"

Silence. The officer cleared his throat.

"But—Great Lady Holi, it is essential that the maneuver be made with great speed. Belisarius will realize what we are doing by sunrise at the latest. Quite possibly earlier. It is almost impossible—even with the harshest orders—to keep such a large body of men from making *some* noise. And we have no control over the Persians, in any event."

Another interjected, "We *must* get the flanking column upriver as fast as possible. So that they can ford the Euphrates before Belisarius can block their way. That requires *cavalry*, Great Lady Holi."

"BE SILENT. I UNDERSTAND YOUR ARGUMENT. BUT THERE IS A POSSIBILITY, IF BELISARIUS IS CUNNING ENOUGH. I CANNOT TAKE THE CHANCE. THE YE-TAI,

AFTER THEY CROSS, CAN RACE UPRIVER TO SEIZE A
BRIDGEHEAD. THE REGULAR CAVALRY, FOLLOWING,
CAN BRING THE KUSHANS' HORSES WITH THEM. THEY
SHOULD STILL BE ABLE TO REACH THE YE-TAI IN TIME
TO HOLD THE CROSSING."

The officers submitted, of course. But one of them, bolder than
the rest, made a last protest:

"It will take the Kushans *so much time*, if they cross the river
on foot."

"THAT IS PRECISELY THE POINT.

"NOW, DO AS I COMMAND."

All opposition fled. The officers hastened from the pavilion,
spreading the command throughout the great army encamped
below the dam.

Alone in its pavilion, Link continued to calculate. Gauge.
Analyze.

Its thoughts were confident. Link was guided not simply by its
own incredible intellect, but also by intelligence—in the military
sense of the term. Roman prisoners had been taken, here and
there, in the days of fighting. Interrogated. Those of them with
personal knowledge of Belisarius had been questioned under torture, until Link was satisfied that it had squeezed every last item
necessary to fully assess the capabilities of its enemy.

It would have done better, had it been in Link's power, to have
interrogated a Persian survivor of the battle of Mindouos. The man
named Baresmanas.

But, perhaps not. Link would not have asked the right questions.
And Baresmanas would certainly not have volunteered the information, not even under the knife.

But he could have. He could have. He could have warned the
Malwa superbeing that mercy can have its own sharp point. Keener
than any lance or blade; and even deadlier to the foe.

Chapter 37

"Finally," hissed Belisarius.

The general was practically dancing with impatience, waiting for his horse to be brought up to the artillery tower where he had made his headquarters for the past week.

He was already in full armor. He had begun donning the gear the moment he heard the first katyusha volleys. As he had predicted, the Malwa were attempting to cross the Nehar Malka on a pontoon bridge. He was convinced that the maneuver was a feint, but, like all well-executed diversions, it carried real substance behind it. Thousands of Malwa troops were involved in the crossing, supported by most of their rocket troughs. By now, an hour into the battle, the scene to the east was a flashing cacophony. Katyusha rockets crossed trails with Malwa missiles. The Syrian soldiers on the rockpile added their own volleys of fire-arrows, aimed at the boats on the canal. The Nehar Malka was lit up by those flaming ships.

In the darkness ahead, he could make out the looming shape of his horse. Maurice, he realized, was the man holding it.

"How long ago?" were his first words.

He could barely make out Maurice's shrug.

"Who's to know? The Persians are being damned quiet. Much quieter than I would have expected, from a lot of headstrong dehgans. But Abbu's scouts report that they've already moved out at least half of their forces. Due west, into the desert."

Sourly: "Just as you predicted."

Belisarius nodded. "We've some time, then. Is Abbu—"

Maurice snorted. "Be serious! Of course he's in position. The old Arab goat's even twitchier than you are."

As Anastasius heaved him into the saddle, Belisarius grunted. "I am *not* twitchy. Simply eager to close with the foe."

" 'Close with the foe,' " mimicked Maurice, clambering onto his own mount. "My, aren't we flowery tonight?"

Securely in his saddle, Belisarius grinned. It was obvious that the prospect of action—*finally!*—had completely restored his spirits.

"Let's to it, Maurice. I do believe the time has come to reacquaint the Malwa with the First Law of Battle."

He tugged on the reins, turning his horse.

"The enemy has arrived. And I intend to fuck them up completely."

"What?" he demanded.

Maurice took a breath. "You heard me. Abbu's courier reports that they're sending the Kushans across first. On foot, all of them. They even dismounted the Kushan cavalry. They've got their Yetai battalions massed on the bank, mounted, but they aren't crossing yet. Behind them, Abbu thinks they're forming up kshatriya and Malwa regulars, but he's not sure. He can't get close enough."

Belisarius turned and stared into the darkness, raising himself up in the stirrups in order to peer over the wall. He was on the road at the eastern end of the dam, just behind the front fortifications. For a moment, he plucked at his telescope, but left off the motion almost as soon as it started. He already knew that the device was no help. It was a moonless night, and the Malwa crossing the almost-empty riverbed were a mile south of the dam. He could see nothing, not even with his Aide-enhanced vision.

"Kushans first, and without horses," he murmured. "That makes no sense at all."

He scratched his chin. "Unless—"

"Unless what?" hissed Maurice.

Scratched his chin. "Unless that *thing* is even smarter than I thought."

Maurice shook his head. "Stop being so damn clever! Maybe they want to make sure they don't make any noise crossing the Euphrates. Kushans on foot will be as silent as any army could be."

Belisarius nodded, slowly.

"That's possible. It's even possible that they made arrangements with Ormazd to have horses left for them. Still—"

A little noise drew their attention. An Arab courier was trotting toward them from the western end of the dam.

"Abbu says now!" the scout exclaimed, as soon as he drew up. "Almost all the Kushans are in the riverbed. At least eight thousand of them. Probably all of them, by now. Their first skirmishers will have already reached the opposite bank."

Belisarius scratched his chin.

"God damn it to hell!" snarled Maurice. "What are you waiting for? We can't let those men cross, general! After all our casualties, we don't have much better than eight thousand left ourselves. Once they get on dry land—on the south bank—they can ford upstream any one of a dozen places. We'll have to face them on—"

"Enough, Maurice." The chiliarch clamped shut his jaws.

Scratched the chin.

The general thought; gauged; calculated; assessed.

The man decided.

His crooked smile came. He said, very firmly:

"Let the Kushans cross. All of them."

To the scout:

"Tell Abbu to send up the rocket when the Ye-tai are almost across. And tell that old maniac to make sure he's clear first. Do you understand? I want him clear!"

The Arab grinned. "He will be clear, general. By a hair, of course. But he will be clear."

An instant later, the man was gone.

Belisarius turned back to Maurice. The grizzled veteran was glaring at him.

"Look at it this way," Belisarius said pleasantly. "I've just given you what you treasure most. Something else to be morose about."

Glaring *furiously*. To one side, Valentinian muttered: "Oh, great. Just what we needed. Eight thousand Kushans to deal with."

Belisarius ignored both the glare and the mutter. He began to scratch his chin, but stopped. He had made his decision, and would stick with it.

It was a bad decision, perhaps. It might even, in the end, prove to be disastrous. But he thought of men who liked to gamble, when they had nothing to gamble with except humor. And he remembered, most of all, a man with an iron face. A hard man who had, in two lives and two futures, made the same soft decision. A decision which, Belisarius knew, that man would always make, in every life and every future.

He relaxed, then. Confident, not in his decision, but in his soul.

"Let them pass," he murmured. "Let them pass."

He cocked his head, slightly. "Basil's ready?"

"Be serious," growled Maurice.

Belisarius smiled. A minute later, he cocked his head again. "Everyone's clear?" he asked.

"Be serious," growled Maurice.

"Everybody except us," hissed Valentinian. "We're the only ones left. The last Syrians cleared off five minutes ago."

"Let's be off, then," said Belisarius cheerfully.

As he and his three cataphracts walked their horses off the dam—moving carefully, in the dark—Belisarius began softly reciting verses.

The men with him did not recognize the poem. There was no way they could have. Aide had just given it to him, from the future. That future which Belisarius would shield, from men who thought themselves gods.

Those masterful images because complete
Grew in pure mind but out of what began?
I must lie down where all the ladders start
In the foul rag and bone shop of the heart.

Chapter 38

The moment the signal rocket exploded, Link knew.

Its four top officers, standing nearby on the platform of the command tower overlooking the river, were simply puzzled. The rocket, after bursting, continued to burn like a flare as it sailed down onto the mass of soldiers struggling their way across the bed of the Euphrates. Ye-tai, in the main, swearing softly as they tried to guide their horses in the darkness through a morass of streamlets and mucky sinkholes. But there were at least five thousand Malwa regulars, also, including a train of rocket-carts and the kshatriya to man them.

The flare burned. The officers stared, and puzzled.

But Link knew at once. Understood how completely it had been outwitted, although it did not—then or ever—understand how Belisarius had done it.

But the being from the future was not given to cursing or useless self-reproach. It recognized only necessity. It did not even wait for the first thundering sound of the explosions to give the order to its assassins.

Across the entire length of the dam blocking the Euphrates, the charges erupted. Almost in slow motion, the boulder-laden ships which formed the base of the dam heaved up. The sound of the eruption was huge, but muffled. And there was almost no flash given off. The charges, for all their immensity, had been deeply buried. Even Link, with its superhuman vision, could barely see the disaster, in the faint light still thrown off by the signal flare.

The officers saw nothing. Then, or ever. The first assassin's knife plunged into the back of the first officer, severing his spinal cord. A split second later, the other three died with him. Still staring at the rocket. Still puzzled.

Link had failed, but its failure would remain hidden. Its reputation was essential to the Malwa cause, and the cause of the new gods who had created Malwa. The officers would take the blame.

The mass of soldiers in the bed of the Euphrates—perhaps fourteen thousand, in all—froze at the sound. Turned, stared into the darkness. Puzzled. The night was dark, and the dam was a mile away. They, too, could see nothing. But the noise was ominous.

Then the first breeze came, and the smartest of the trapped soldiers understood. Shrieking, cursing—even sabring the slower-witted men who barred their way—they made a desperate attempt to scramble their horses out of the riverbed.

The rest—

The wall of water which smote the Malwa army came like a mace, wielded by a god. Untold tons of hurtling water, carrying great boulders as if they were chips of wood. Smashing in the sides of the old riverbed, gouging channels as it came, ripping new stones to join the old.

By the time the torrent struck, all of the doomed men in that riverbed understood. The sound was no longer a distant thunder. It was a howling banshee. Shiva's shriek. Kali's scream of triumph.

All of them, now, were fighting to get out. Their horses, panicked as much by the terror in their riders' voices as the thunder coming from the north, were scuttling through the mud, skittering past the reeds, falling into sinkholes, trampling each other under.

But it was hopeless. Some of the Malwa soldiers—less than a thousand—were far enough from the riverbed's center to reach the banks. Others, caught by the edges of the tidal wave, were able to save their lives by clinging to reeds, or boulders, or ropes thrown by their comrades ashore.

A few—a very, very small few—even survived the flood. A gigantic, turbulent mass of water such as the one which hammered its way down the riverbed is an odd thing. Fickle, at times. Weird, in its workings.

The Euphrates, restored to its rightful place, raged and raged and raged. But, here and there, it took pity. One soldier, to his everlasting amazement, found himself carried—gently, gently—to the riverbank. Another, too terrified to be amazed, was simply tossed ashore.

And one Malwa soldier, hours later and fifty miles downriver, waded out of the reeds. The Euphrates had nestled him in a bizarre and permanent little eddy—like a chick cupped in a man's hand—and carried him through the night. A simple man, he was—simple-minded, his unkind former comrades had often called him—but no fool. It was noted, thereafter, that the previously profane fellow had become deeply religious. Particularly devoted, it seemed, to river gods.

But for the overwhelming majority of the Ye-tai and Malwa regulars caught in Belisarius' trap, death came almost instantly. They did not even drown, most of them. They were simply battered to death.

Twelve thousand, one hundred and forty-three men. Dead within a minute. Another nine hundred and six, crippled and badly wounded. Most of those would die within a week.

Ten thousand and eighty-nine horses, dead. Two thousand, two hundred and seventy-eight camels, dead. Thirty-four rocket carts, pulverized. Almost half of the expedition's gunpowder weapons, destroyed.

It was the worst military disaster in Malwa's history.

And Link knew it. The superbeing was already examining its options, before the wall of water had taken a single life. Throughout the horror which followed, the creature named Great Lady Holi sat motionless upon its throne. Utterly indifferent to the carnage—those dying men and animals were simply facts—it went about its business.

Calculating. Gauging. Assessing.

The officers would take the blame. Link would take the credit for salvaging what could be salvaged.

Calculating. Gauging. Assessing.

Which was not much.

By the time the next rank of officers crept their timid way onto the command tower, Link had already made its decisions.

"WE MUST RETREAT. BEAT THE DRUMS."

"ORGANIZE RATIONING. WE WILL BE FORCED TO RETREAT THROUGH THE DESERT, WITH FEW CAMELS. WE CANNOT RISK A BATTLE ON THIS SIDE OF THE RIVER. BELISARIUS WILL HAVE ALSO COLLAPSED THE STONES INTO THE NEHAR MALKA, RESTORING THE OLD DAM. HE WILL BE ABLE TO CROSS EASILY. AND THERE ARE STILL TEN THOUSAND PERSIANS IN PEROZ-SHAPUR. OUR FORCES THERE MUST KEEP THOSE PERSIANS PENNED IN WHILE WE MAKE OUR RETREAT."

Even with the grim reminder of the slaughtered officers lying on the platform, some of Link's new top subordinates dared to protest.

Through the desert? Many will die, in such a retreat.

"AT LEAST FOUR THOUSAND, BY MY ESTIMATE. THEY CAN BE REPLACED."

And what about the Kushans? There are eight thousand of them in position to attack!

"POINTLESS. THEY HAVE NO HORSES. NO SUPPLIES. AND WE HAVE NO MEANS OF SUPPLYING THEM. OUR OWN SUPPLIES ARE LIMITED.

"BELISARIUS WILL NOT FIGHT, HE WILL SIMPLY ELUDE THE KUSHANS AND WAIT FOR THEM TO DIE OF HUNGER. A WASTE OF EXCELLENT TROOPS—WHOM WE NEED OURSELVES. WE MUST BEGIN THE RETREAT IMMEDIATELY. SEND COURIERS TO THE KUSHANS. THEY MUST GUARD OUR REAR AS WE MARCH BACK TO BABYLON."

The officers bowed their heads. They began to scurry out, but Link commanded them to remain. There were still some calculations to be made.

The officers waited, silently, while Link gauged and assessed.

It did not take the superbeing more than five minutes to reach another conclusion. A human commander, faced with that bitter logic, would have screamed fury and frustration. Link simply gave commands.

"SEND WORD TO OUR FORCES IN BABYLON. TELL THE COMMANDERS TO AWAIT OUR ARRIVAL, BUT THEY MUST BEGIN THE PREPARATIONS FOR LIFTING THE SIEGE OF BABYLON."

A last protest:

Lift the siege of Babylon? But—

"WE HAVE NO CHOICE. BELISARIUS HAS SAVAGED US THIS YEAR, DUE TO THE INCOMPETENCE OF MALWA'S GENERALS. OUR SUPPLY FLEET WAS ALREADY STRETCHED TO THE LIMIT. THIS NEW DISASTER WILL DESTROY MORE SHIPS. WE HAVE LOST TOO MANY MEN, TOO MANY SUPPLIES, TOO MUCH EQUIPMENT. WE CANNOT MAINTAIN THE SIEGE. WE MUST RETREAT TO CHARAX, AND BEGIN AGAIN NEXT YEAR.

"DO IT."

When the wall of water reached Peroz-Shapur, in the middle of the night, more Malwa lives were lost. Not many—simply those unlucky men among the forces guarding against a sally who had chosen the wrong moment to relieve themselves in the riverbed, away from the foul latrines of a siege camp.

Above, on the walls of the fortified town, Baresmanas and Kurush listened to the river. The Euphrates was back, and with it, hope.

"He has done it," whispered Kurush. "Just as he promised." He turned away, moving with his quick and nervous stride. "I must ready the troops. We may be able to sally, come dawn."

After he was gone, Baresmanas shook his head. "How can such a warm and merciful man be so ruthless?" he whispered. "So cold, so cruel, so pitiless?"

There was no accusation in those words. Neither condemnation, nor reproach. Simply wonder, at the complexity and contradiction that is the human soul.

Elsewhere within the walls of Peroz-Shapur, in the slave quarters where war captives were held, two thousand Kushans also listened to the sound of Malwa's destruction.

Friendly guards were questioned. Soon enough, answers were given.

The Kushans settled their bets.

Those who had won the wager—all but one—celebrated through the night. They had the means with which to celebrate, too. Their guards were in a fine mood, that night. Wine was given out freely, even by stingy Persians.

Only Vasudeva refrained from the festivity. When questioned, the Kushan commander simply smiled and said, "You forget. I made another bet. Enjoy yourselves, men."

Grinning, now, and pointing at the amphorae clutched in his soldiers' hands. "Soon, everything you own will be mine."

By the end of the next day, the Malwa guarding Peroz-Shapur began their retreat. Kurush—against Baresmanas' advice—tried a sally. His dehgans bloodied the enemy, but they were driven off with heavy casualties. The Malwa lion was wounded, and limping badly, but it still had its teeth.

The day after that, the Kushans were sent out to clear the riverbanks of the multitude of corpses which had washed ashore. Bury them quickly—no sanctified exposure to the elements for *those* foul souls—so that the stench would not sicken the entire city.

The Kushans did their work uncomplainingly. They had another bet to settle.

By the end of the day, the count had been made to every Kushan's satisfaction. And Vasudeva won his bet.

Many bodies had been buried, and their identities noted. There was not a single Kushan among them.

Vasudeva was rich, now, for he had been the only Kushan to dare that gamble. Rich, not so much in material wealth—his soldiers had had little to wager, after all—but in the awe and esteem of his men. Kushans admire a great gambler.

"How did you know?" asked one of his lieutenants.

Vasudeva smiled.

"He promised me. When we gave our oath to him, he swore in return that he would treat Kushans as men. Executed, if necessary. But executed as men. Not hanged like criminals, or beaten like dogs."

He pointed to the river below Peroz-Shapur. "Or drowned, like rats."

The lieutenant frowned. "He made that vow to us, not—" A gesture with his head upriver. "—to *those* Kushans."

Vasudeva's smile was quite like that of a Buddha, now.

"Belisarius is not one to make petty distinctions."

The commander of the Kushan captives turned away.

"Your mistake was that you bet on the general. I bet on the man."

◇   ◇   ◇

Two days later, at Babylon, Khusrau Anushirvan also basked in the admiration of his subordinates. Many of them—*many*—had questioned his wisdom in placing so much trust in a Roman general. Some of them had even been bold enough, and honest enough, to express those reservations to the Emperor's face.

None questioned his wisdom now. They had but to stand on the walls of Babylon to see how wise their Emperor had been. The Malwa fleet had been savaged when Belisarius lowered the river. It had been savaged again, when he restored it. A full quarter of the enemy's remaining ships had been destroyed in the first few minutes. Tethered to jury-rigged docks, or simply grounded in the mud, they had been lifted up by the surging Euphrates and carried to their destruction. Some were battered to splinters; others grounded anew; still others, capsized.

And Khusrau had sallied again. Not, this time, with dehgans across a pontoon bridge—no-one could have built a bridge across the roaring Euphrates on that day—but with sailors aboard the handful of swift galleys in his possession. The galleys had been kept ashore until the river's initial fury passed. As soon as the waters subsided to mere turbulence, the galleys set forth. Down the Euphrates they rowed, adding their own speed to the current, and destroying every Malwa ship they encountered which had managed to survive the Euphrates' rebirth.

There was almost no resistance. The galleys passed too swiftly for the enemy's cannons to be brought to bear. And the Malwa soldiers on the ships themselves were too dazed to put up any effective resistance.

Down the Euphrates the galleys went, mile after mile, until the rowers were too weak to pull their oars. They left a trail of burning ships thirty miles behind them, before they finally beached their craft and began the long march back to Babylon. On the west bank of the river, where the Malwa could no longer reach them.

Between the river and the Persian galleys, over half of the remaining Malwa fleet was destroyed. Not more than two dozen ships eventually found their way back to Charax, of the mighty armada which had set forth so proudly at the beginning of the year.

Other than sending forth the galleys, Khusrau made no attempt to sally against the Malwa encamped before Babylon. He was too canny to repeat Kurush's mistake at Peroz-Shapur. The Malwa lion had been lamed, true. It had not been declawed. There were still a hundred thousand men in that enemy army, with their siege guns loaded with cannister.

The Emperor simply waited. Let them starve.

The siege of Babylon had been broken, like a tree gutted by a lightning bolt. It had simply not fallen yet, much like a great tree will stand for a time after it is dead. Until a wind blows the hollow thing over.

That wind arrived twelve days later. Emperor Khusrau and his entourage, from the roof of Esagila, watched the survivors of the Malwa expedition drag their mangled army back into the camps at Babylon. That army was much smaller than the one which had set out a few weeks since. Smaller in numbers of men, and horses, and camels, positively miniscule in its remaining gunpowder weapons.

Two days later, the entire Malwa army began its long retreat south. By nightfall, the camps which had besieged Babylon for months were empty.

Khusrau spent all of that day, also, on top of Esagila. Surrounded by his officers, his advisers, his officials, a small horde of sahrdaran and vurzurgan, and a young girl named Tahmina.

Khusrau's more hot-headed officers called for a sally. Again, the Emperor refused.

Malwa was lamed, but still a lion.

And besides, the Persian Monarch had other business to attend to.

"Ormazd," he hissed. "Ormazd, first. I want his head brought to me on a pike, by year's end. Do it."

His officers hastened to obey. Surrounded by the rest of his huge entourage, the Emperor remained on Esagila. For a time, he stared at the retreating Malwa. With satisfaction, hatred, and anticipation.

"Next year," he murmured. "Next year, Malwa."

Then, he turned and began striding to the opposite wall of the great, ancient temple. His entourage began to follow, like a giant millipede, but Khusrau waved them back.

"I want only Tahmina," he commanded.

Disgruntled, but obedient, his officials and nobles and advisers obeyed. Timidly, hesitantly, the girl did likewise.

Once they were standing alone on the north wall of the temple, Khusrau's gaze was fixed on the northwest horizon. There was nothing to see, there, beyond a river and a desert. But the Emperor was looking beyond—in time, even more than in space.

His emotions now, as he stared northwest, were more complex. Satisfaction also, of course. As well as admiration, respect—even, if the truth be told, love. But there was also fear, and dread, and anxiety.

"Next year, Malwa," he murmured again. "But the year after that, and after that, and after that, there will be Rome. Always Rome."

He turned his head, and lowered his eyes to the girl standing at his side. Under her Emperor's gaze, the girl's own eyes shied away.

"Look at me, Tahmina."

When the girl's face rose, Khusrau smiled. "I will not command you in this, child. But I do need you. The Aryans need you."

Tahmina smiled herself, now. Timidly and uncertainly, true, but a smile it was. Quite a genuine one, Khusrau saw, and he was not a man easily fooled.

"I will, Emperor."

Khusrau nodded, and placed a hand on the girl's shoulder. Thereafter, and for the rest of the day, he said nothing.

Nor did he leave his post on the northern wall of Esagila, watching the northwest. The Malwa enemy could limp away behind his contemptuous back. Khusrau of the Immortal Soul was the Emperor of Iran and non-Iran. His duty was to face the future.

Chapter 39

Days later, Belisarius and Maurice surveyed the Nehar Malka from what was left of the rockpile on its north bank. Most of those rocks, so laboriously hauled out by the Kushans, were back where they came from. Once again, the Royal Canal was dry—or almost so, at least. The crude and explosive manner in which Belisarius had rebuilt the dam did not stop all the flow.

The Roman army was already halfway across what was left of the Nehar Malka. On their way back to Peroz-Shapur, now. After destroying the dam, Belisarius had retreated north, in case the Malwa made an attempt to pursue his still-outnumbered army. He had not expected them to make that mistake—not with Link in command—but had been prepared to deal with the possibility.

Once it became clear that the enemy was retreating back to Babylon, Belisarius had followed. They had reached the site of the battleground just two hours before.

"Enough," he said softly. "The Nehar Malka's dry enough. I don't think Khusrau will complain."

"Shouldn't think so," muttered Maurice. The chiliarch was not even looking at the Nehar Malka, however. He was staring at the Euphrates.

Not at the river, actually. The Euphrates, to all appearances, was back to its usual self—a wide, shallow, sluggishly moving mass of muddy water.

No, Maurice was staring at the banks of the river. Where the Malwa had abandoned their dead. It was not hard to spot the corpses—hundreds, thousands of them—even hidden in the reeds. The vultures covered the area like flies.

"Jesus," he whispered. "Forgive us our sins."

Belisarius turned his eyes to follow Maurice's gaze. No expression came to his face. He might have been a simple village blacksmith, studying the precision of his work.

When he spoke, his voice was harsh. "A man told me once that war is murder. Organized, systematic murder—nothing more, and nothing less. It was the first thing that man said to me, on the day I assumed command as an officer. Seventeen years old, I was. Green as the springtime."

"You were never as green as the springtime," murmured Maurice. "Day you were born, you were already thinking crooked thoughts." He sighed. "I remember, lad. It was true, then, and it's true now. But I don't have to like it."

Belisarius nodded. Nothing further was said.

A few minutes later, he and Maurice turned their horses and rode down to the bank of the Nehar Malka, ready to join the army in its crossing.

The job was not finished, not yet. Neither of them knew when it might be. But they knew when a day's work was done.

Done well. They could take satisfaction in that, at least, if not in the doing.

Craftsmen at their trade.

Epilogue
A THRONG AND ITS THOUGHTS

From her position on the dais against the east wall, Antonina surveyed the scene with satisfaction. The great audience chamber of the Prefectural Palace was literally packed with people. Servants carrying platters of food and drink were forced to wriggle their way through the throng like so many eels. The noise produced by the multitude of conversations was almost deafening.

"Very gratifying," pronounced Patriarch Theodosius, seated on a chair next to her.

"Isn't it?" Antonina beamed upon the mob below them. "I think the entire Greek aristocracy of Alexandria showed up tonight. As well as most of the nobility from all the major Delta towns. Even some from the valley. The Fayum, at least, and Antinoopolis."

A slight frown came.

"Actually, I'm a bit puzzled. Hadn't really expected such a massive turnout. I thought for sure that a good half of the nobility would boycott the affair."

Theodosius' eyes widened. "Boycott? A public celebration in honor of the Emperor's ninth birthday? God forbid!" The Patriarch smiled slyly. "Actually, Antonina, I am *not* surprised. Left to their own devices, I'm quite sure that half of Egypt's Greek noblemen would never have come. But their wives and daughters gave them no choice."

He nodded toward the middle of the great room, where the crowd was thickest. At the very center of that incredible population

density, a cup of wine in one hand, stood a handsome young
Roman officer.

"Egypt's most eligible bachelor," stated the Patriarch. "The merarch of the Army of Egypt. Newly elected to the Senate—and
already quite rich on his own account, due to his share of the spoils
from Mindouos."

Antonina stared at Hermogenes. A bit of sadness came to her,
for a brief moment, thinking about Irene. The host of women who
surrounded Hermogenes were all younger than Irene, and—with
perhaps one or two exceptions—considerably prettier.

"Put all their brains together," she muttered, "and they could
maybe match Irene. When she's passed out drunk. Maybe."

"What was that, Antonina?" asked Theodosius.

Antonina shook her head.

"Never mind, Patriarch. I was just thinking about a dear friend."
Sigh. "Who will never, I fear, find a husband."

"Too pious?" asked Theodosius.

Antonina bit off a laugh. "No, no. Just too—*much*."

She rose from her seat. "I will take my leave, now. The event
is clearly a roaring success. I think we can safely conclude that
Alexandria and Egypt have been returned to the imperial fold. But
I'm tired, and I don't think *that* crowd will object to my absence."

Theodosius suppressed his own humor, now, until after Antonina had walked out. Then he did laugh, seeing the mob below
heave a great collective sigh of relief.

The Patriarch was quite certain he could read their minds, at
that moment.

Thank God! She's gone!

No real woman has tits that big.

Satan's spawn, that's what she is.

The Whore From Hell. Ba'alzebub's Bitch.

But they kept those thoughts to themselves. Oh, yes. Discreet,
they were. Reserved.

"Very proper folk," said Theodosius approvingly, turning to the
man seated to his right. "Very polite. Very noble. Don't you think
so, Ashot?"

A charitable interpretation, from a man of God.

Less charitable was an Armenian cataphract's response.

"Scared shitless, that's what they are."

A KING AND HIS FEARS

"You are not thinking of *marrying* that woman?" demanded the negusa negast of Axum. The sovereign of Ethiopia leaned forward on his royal stool, his thick hands planted firmly on powerful knees, his massive jaw clamped shut. He frowned ferociously upon his youngest son.

Prince Eon bolted erect on his own stool. His jaw sagged. Dropped. Plummeted like a stone.

Standing behind him, Ousanas burst into laughter.

"Excellent idea, King of Kings!" cried the dawazz. "Certain to shrink overconfident fool boy's head into a walnut!"

Eon finally caught his breath. Enough, at least, to choke out, "Marry—*Irene?*"

He goggled at his father. The father glowered back.

"You seem much taken by this woman," accused the negusa nagast.

Eon's eyes roamed about the royal chamber, as if seeking rhyme or reason lurking somewhere in the stone recesses of heavy Axumite architecture.

"I *like* her, yes," he said. "Very much. I think she is incredibly capable and intelligent. And very witty. She often makes me laugh. A wonderful ally in our struggle. Even—" His eyes almost crossed, contemplating absurdity. "—Yes, even attractive. In her way. But—but—*marry* her?"

He fell silent. Again, his jaw sagged.

Satisfied, the negusa nagast leaned back in his stool. He fixed Ousanas with a stern gaze.

"Good thing for you, dawazz. Any other answer and I would have you beaten."

Ousanas looked smug. "Can't. Dawazz not subject to royal authority. Only answers to Dakuen sarwe."

The King of Kings snorted. "So? You think the regiment would hesitate? Just last night, the demon woman took half their monthly stipend, answering all their riddles. This morning, she took the rest. When they couldn't answer any of hers, even after she gave them all night to think it over." The negusa nagast glared. "Dawazz be a bloody pulp, Prince give any other answer. Be sure of it."

The negusa nagast smacked his heavy thigh. "I am satisfied. The Prince is foolish as a rooster, true. Headstrong like a bull. Who else would get me in a war with Malwa? But at least you have kept him sane, dawazz. Sane enough. Delusions of grandeur can be tolerated, in a King, so long as they are merely political. Never delusions in a wife!"

His heavy shoulders twitched, as if a sudden shiver had run down his spine.

"God save us from that fate! Never marry a woman smarter than you. Too dangerous, especially for a King. *That* woman! Smarter than Satan."

He turned his head, looking through the entryway to the room beyond. His library, that was.

"Best collection of books south of Alexandria," he noted proudly. "I have instructed my slaves to make a precise count. They will count them again, before I allow that woman to leave for India."

Eon cleared his throat. "We must leave soon, father."

The negusa nagast nodded his head. The gesture was slow, but certain. As solid as the head which made it.

"Yes. You must. Important to follow up on Garmat's successful mission, and quickly. Give all support to Empress Shakuntala and her cause. Give Malwa no time to think."

Again, the little shiver in the shoulders.

"*Essential* to get that woman on the other side of an ocean."

AN EMPRESS AND HIS MARRIAGE

"The time has come, Shakuntala," stated Holkar firmly. The peshwa leaned forward and lifted a scroll lying on the carpet before his cushion.

"This was brought by courier ship this morning. From Tamra-parni."

Dadaji unrolled the scroll, scanning it in the quick manner with which a man reads over a document he had already committed to memory. An odd little smile came to his face.

"Out of illusion, truth," he murmured.

He rolled the scroll back up and handed it to his Empress. Shakuntala stared at the harmless object as if it were a cobra.

"What is it?" she demanded.

Dadaji's smile faded. "It is a letter from the King of Tamraparni. Offering us an alliance—a *partial* alliance, I should say—against Malwa." He shrugged. "The offer is couched in caveats and riddled with qualifications. But, at the very least, he makes a firm promise of naval and logistical support. Possibly some troops."

He paused, taking a deep breath. Shakuntala eyed him suspiciously.

"And what else?"

"The offer—this is not said in so many words, but the meaning is obvious—is conditional upon your marriage to one of his sons." A wry smile. "His youngest son, needless to say. The King of Tamraparni is willing to risk something, to keep the Malwa at bay. But only so much. Not the heir."

He stopped, studying the young woman who was Andhra's Empress. Shakuntala was sitting very erect, her back as stiff as a board. Her face, if possible, was even stiffer.

Holkar tapped the scroll with a finger. "The King makes allusion to the false way in which we bandied his name about, in Muziris. But he does not complain, not formally. It is quite clear that your seizure of Suppara has changed the situation drastically. You are no longer an 'Empress-in-exile.' You have reestablished yourself on Andhra soil. With a port, here, and one of Majarashtra's largest cities—Deogiri—under the control of your forces. That gives you something far beyond formal legitimacy, which you already had. It gives you power."

He chuckled dryly. "Not much, not much, but some. Enough, at least, that the ruler of Tamraparni is willing to use you to keep Malwa as distant from his island as possible."

He paused. Shakuntala's face was still expressionless.

Dadaji suppressed a sigh.

"Empress, we must consider this offer very seriously. A dynastic marriage with one of south India's most powerful kingdoms would greatly strengthen your position. It might well make the difference between Andhra's survival and its downfall."

Still expressionless.

Now, Holkar did sigh. "Girl," he said softly, "I know that this matter pains you. But you have a duty, and an obligation, to your people."

The peshwa rose and strode to an open window, overlooking the harbor. From below, the sounds of celebration wafted into the palace. The governor's palace, once. The Malwa official languished in prison, now. Shakuntala had taken the building for her own.

Watching the festive scene below, Holkar smiled. Suppara was still celebrating, two weeks after its liberation from the Malwa heel. Dadaji knew his countrymen well. The Marathas would have celebrated even if the city were in ruins. As it was, they could also celebrate an almost bloodless victory. Once the cannons which Kungas had seized opened fire, the Malwa warships had been turned into wrecks within an hour. By the time Shakuntala and her cavalrymen disembarked on the docks, the Malwa garrison had fled the city.

Celebrate, celebrate, celebrate.

Malwa is gone. Andhra has returned.

The Empress herself is here.

Shakuntala! Shakuntala! Shakuntala!

Holkar pointed down to the city. "If you fall, girl, those people will fall with you. You brought them to their feet. You cannot betray that trust."

Behind him, Shakuntala's face finally broke. Just a bit. Just a flash of pain, a slight lowering of the head. A slow, shuddering breath.

But it was all very quick. Within seconds, she had raised her head. "You are correct, Dadaji. Draft a letter to the King of Tamraparni, telling him that I accept—"

A new voice cut in.

"I think this is quite premature."

Startled, Holkar turned from the window. "Premature? Why, Kungas?"

The Kushan was seated on his own cushion, to Shakuntala's right. He had said nothing, thus far, in this meeting of Shakuntala's closest advisers.

"Because," he rasped, "I do not think we should jump at the first offer." He spread his hand. "There will be others. The Cholas, for a certainty, now that Shakuntala has shown she is a force to be reckoned with. And I think their offer will have fewer caveats and qualifications."

He flipped his hand dismissively, almost contemptuously. "Tamraparni is an island. The Cholas share the mainland with the Malwa beast. They have less room to quibble. Their offer will be more substantial."

Holkar restrained his temper. "*If* they offer! I do not share your boundless optimism, Kungas. True, the Malwa press them close. But that is just as likely—more likely, in my opinion—to make them hesitate before offering the Malwa any provocation. Kerala *also* shares the mainland with Malwa, and we all know how that fact led Shakuntala's own grandfather to betray—"

"I agree with Kungas," interrupted Shakuntala forcefully. "We should wait. Not accept this first offer. We should wait. Longer."

Holkar blew out his cheeks. He knew that tone in Shakuntala's voice. Knew it to perfection.

No point in further argument, not now. So, he desisted; even did so graciously. Although he could not help casting an angry glare at Kungas.

No point in that either, of course. As well glare at an iron mask.

"What are you playing at?" Holkar demanded, after he and Kungas left the Empress' chamber. "You know how critical this question is! You and I have spoken on the matter before—many times."

Kungas stopped abruptly. Dadaji did likewise. The two men stood in the corridor for a moment, staring at each other. The peshwa, angry. The Bhatasvapati—amused, perhaps.

"Not quite, Dadaji," came the mild response. "*You* have spoken *to* me on this matter, that is true. Many times. But all I ever said was that I agreed that Shakuntala's marriage—whenever and however it comes—will be a decisive moment for our struggle."

Holkar frowned. "Yes. And so?"

Kungas twitched his shoulders. It might have been called a shrug.

"So—that does not mean I agree that she should marry the youngest son of the King of Tamraparni. I think she can do better."

Holkar, scowling: "With whom? Chola? *If*, of course, the Cholas even—"

"Who is to say, who is to say?" interrupted Kungas. Again, that little vestige of a shrug. The Bhatasvapati took his friend by the arm. "You should have more confidence in the Empress, Dadaji. When the time comes, she will know what to do. I am sure of it."

Silence followed, as the two men resumed their progress down the corridor. On the part of Kungas, it was an inscrutable sort of silence. On the part of Holkar, an irritable one.

Had the peshwa known the thoughts of the Bhatasvapati, at that moment, he would have been considerably more than irritated.

Dig in your heels, girl, dig in your heels. Stall. Make excuses. Dither. I will help, I will help. When the question of marriage is finally posed, you will know what to do. Then, you will know.

The Bhatasvapati shook his head, slightly, thinking of the strange blindness in the people around him.

So obvious!

A GENERAL AND HIS OFFICER

Within a minute of his arrival in Agathius' room, Belisarius knew that the crippled officer was preoccupied with something. The cataphract was plucking at the sheets of his bed, as if distracted. The motion seemed to make his wife nervous. Or perhaps it was just that the young girl was fussing over her injured husband, the way she kept fluffing his pillows and stroking his hair.

Belisarius decided that he should come to the point. He began pulling a scroll from his tunic.

At that moment, however, Agathius turned to his wife and said, "Would you leave us for a moment, Sudaba? I have something I must discuss privately with the general."

Sudaba nodded. Then, after a last fluff of the pillows and a quick smile at Belisarius, scurried from the room. Belisarius was struck by the way Agathius watched her as she went. Odd, really. He seemed like a man trying to burn an image into his memory.

Once the Persian girl was gone, Agathius took a deep breath and looked to the general.

"I need your advice," he said abruptly. "I will have to divorce Sudaba, now, and I want to make sure—if it can be done—that the divorce does not cause problems for you. With your alliance with the Persians, I mean."

He spoke the sentences quickly, but clearly, in the way a determined man announces a decision which he does not like but must carry out.

Belisarius' jaw dropped. It was the last thing he had been expecting to hear.

"Divorce Sudaba?" His eyes wandered about, for an instant, as if searching for rhyme and reason hidden away in a corner of the room.

"But—*why*?"

Agathius' face grew pinched. With a sudden, quick flip of his muscular wrist, the cataphract twitched aside the blankets covering his body. From the hips and above, that body was still as broad-shouldered and thick-chested as ever. A bit wasted, perhaps, from his long weeks of bed-ridden recovery, but not much.

His legs, however—even that part of his legs which still remained—were pitiful remnants of the powerful limbs which had once gripped a warhorse in the fury of a battlefield.

"Look at me," he said. Not with anger so much as resignation.

Belisarius frowned. Scratched his chin. "It does not seem to me that Sudaba cares, Agathius. Judging from what I can see, I think she is not put off—"

"Not *that*," growled Agathius. The man's usual good humor made a brief re-entry. "Far as that goes, I think she's happier than ever," he chuckled. "I'm here all the time now, where she can get her hands on me. And there's nothing wrong with my—"

He broke off, sighing. "The problem's not with her, general. Or with me, for that matter. It's—it's—" He waved a hand, weakly. "It's the way things are, that's all. She's a Persian noblewoman. I'm a fucking baker's son with a battlefield rank in the military nobility."

Agathius glanced around the luxurious chamber, for a moment, as if assessing its value.

"I've still got plenty of booty left, from Anatha—a damn little fortune, by my old standards. But it's really not going to last more than a year or two. Not the way I have to live, if I'm to meet her expectations—and, even more, the expectations of her family.

"I've got to face facts, general. I'm a legless cataphract—which is the most ridiculous thing in the world—whose only other skill is baking bread. There's no way I can—"

He gaped, then, seeing his general burst into riotous laughter.

Gaped. That was the last reaction he had been expecting.

With a fierce struggle, Belisarius forced his laughter down. "Oh, God, I *am* sorry," he said weakly, wiping his eyes. "I feel so guilty, now. I wanted the pleasure of telling you myself. I had to come to Peroz-Shapur anyway, to refit the army, and so I thought I'd bring the news personally instead of just sending it by courier."

Agathius' face was a study in confusion. "News? What news?"

Belisarius was grinning now. And there was not a trace of crookedness in that expression, not a trace.

He hauled out the scroll. "As soon as it was clear that we'd driven the Malwa back to Charax, I sent—well, 'recommendations' is hardly the word. Emperor or no, he's still my kid. I gave Photius firm and clear instructions, and, I'm pleased to say, the marvelous boy followed them to perfection."

He handed over the scroll. "Here you are. The official document will arrive by courier, some weeks from now. This is a copy sent over the semaphore line. Doesn't matter. It's as good as gold."

Gingerly, Agathius took the scroll. In an instant, Belisarius' quick mind understood the expression on the man's face.

"You can't read," he stated.

Agathius shook his head. "No, sir. Not really. I can sign my name well enough, as long as I've got some time. But—"

He fell silent. Not from embarassment so much as frustration.

The embarassment, in that moment, was entirely Belisarius'. The general should have remembered that a man of Agathius' background was almost certain to be illiterate.

The general waved his hand, as if brushing aside insects.

"Well, that'll have to change. Right off. I'll send word to Patriarch Anthony to send one of his best monks to be your tutor. Two of them, now that I think about it. Sudaba's probably not literate, either. Not a dehgan's daughter."

Grinning:

"Can't have that. Not in the wife of a Roman Senator, recently enrolled in the ranks of the Empire's *illustres*. By unanimous acclaim, mind you. I also got a private message from Sittas. He tells me the Emperor's nomination was extremely—ah, *firm*. Sittas himself took the occasion to appear before the Senate in full armor. In recognition—or so he told those fine aristocratic fellows—of the valor of the Greek cataphracts at Anatha and the Nehar Malka."

Grinning:

"The Emperor also saw fit to give the new Senator a grant of royal land, in keeping with his exalted status. An estate you've got now, Agathius, in Pontus. Quite a substantial one. Annual income's in the vicinity of three hundred solidi. Tax-exempt, of course. As an imperial grant, it's *res privata*."

Grinning, grinning:

"Oh, yes. There's real soldier business, too, in addition to all the Senatorial fooferaw. You've been promoted. You're the new *Dux* of Osrhoene. That post carries an excellent salary, by the way. Another four hundred solidi. In addition to the troops stationed in that province, you have complete authority over all Roman military units serving in Persian Mesopotamia which are not directly under my command. You report only to me, in my capacity as *magister militum per orientem*."

Grinning, grinning, grinning:

"As you can see, I've picked up a few new titles of my own. As Dux of Osrhoene, your official headquarters will be located at the provincial capital of Edessa. But I'd really prefer it if you based yourself here, in Peroz-Shapur. I've already discussed the matter with Baresmanas and Kurush, and they have no objection whatsoever. Quite the contrary, actually. They're even hinting that Khusrau will insist on presenting you with a palace. I think they would feel a lot more secure in Rome's allegiance if the commander of the Roman forces was planted right in their own territory. Along with his Persian wife and—"

Grinning, grinning, grinning, grinning:

"—soon enough, I've no doubt, a slew of children."

The grin finally faded, replaced by something which was almost a frown. "God in Heaven, Agathius! Did you really think I'd let one of the finest officers I've ever had go back to baking bread? On account of his *legs*?"

Agathius was speechless.

Belisarius rose, smiling crookedly.

"You're speechless, I see. Well, that's good enough for today. But make sure you've got your wits about you by tomorrow—*Duke*. I'll be coming by, first thing in the morning. We've got a new campaign to plan, against Malwa. You won't be riding any horses in that campaign—you'll be staying right here in Peroz-Shapur—but I'll be relying on you to organize the whole Roman effort to back me up."

"I won't fail you," whispered Agathius.

"No," agreed Belisarius. "I don't imagine you will."

He turned away. "And now, I'll go tell your wife she can come back in. Best thing for you, I think."

He left, then, murmuring a little verse.

"Think where man's glory most begins and ends
And say my glory was I had such friends."

A CAPTOR AND HIS CAPTIVES

Two hours later, Belisarius was enjoying a cup of wine with Vasudeva in the barracks where the Kushan captives were quartered. A very small cup of wine.

"The Persians are back to their stingy habits," groused Vasudeva. The Kushan commander cast a sour look around the dingy room. He, along with fifteen of his top officers, were crammed into a space that would have comfortably fit six.

"Crowded, crowded," he grumbled. "One man uses another for a pillow, and yet another for a bed. Men wail in terror, entering the latrines. Leaving, they blubber like babes."

Glumly:

"Nothing to wager on, except whether we will eat the rats or they, us. Every Kushan is betting on the rats. Ten-to-one odds. No takers."

Philosophically:

"Of course, our misery will be brief. Plague will strike us down soon enough. Though some are offering odds on scurvy."

Belisarius smiled. "Get to the point, Vasudeva."

The Kushan commander tugged his goatee. "It's difficult, difficult," he muttered. "There are the proprieties to consider. People think we Kushans are an uncouth folk, but they are quite mistaken. Naturally, we have no truck with that silly Rajput business of finding a point of honor in the way you trim your beard, or peel a fruit. Still—" He sighed. "We are slaves. War captives taken in fair battle. Bound to respect our position, so long as we are not belittled."

From lowered eyelids, he gave Belisarius a keen scrutiny. "You understand, perhaps?"

The Roman general nodded. "Most certainly. As you say, the proprieties must be observed. For instance—" He drained his cup, then, grimaced. "Nasty stuff! I've gotten spoiled on that good Roman campaign wine, I suppose."

He wiped his lips, and continued, "For instance, if I were to bring you along on my next campaign as a slave labor force, the situation would be impossible. War captives used for labor must be closely guarded. Everyone knows that."

All the Kushans in the room nodded solemnly.

"Unthinkable to do otherwise," agreed Vasudeva. "Foolish for the captor, insulting to the captive."

"Yes. But since I will be undertaking a campaign of rapid maneuvers—feints, forced marches, counter-marches, that sort of thing—it would be impossible to detail any troops to waste their time overseeing a lot of surly, disgruntled slaves. Who would slow us down enormously, in any event, since they'd have to march on foot. Can't have slaves riding horses! Ridiculous. They could escape."

"Most improper," intoned Vasudeva. "Grotesque."

Belisarius scratched his chin. "It's difficult, difficult."

He raised his hand.

"A moment, please, while I consider the problem."

He lowered his head, as if in deep contemplation. Sent a thought inward.

Aide?

Piece of cake.

When Belisarius raised his head, a familiar expression had returned to his face. Seeing that crooked smile, the Kushans grinned.

He gave Vasudeva—and then, the other Kushan officers—a keen scrutiny of his own.

"You have heard, perhaps, that I have some small ability to see the future."

Vasudeva snorted. "You are a witch! Everyone knows that. Not even thumb-sucking Persians will take our wagers on *that* subject. And we offered very excellent odds. Twelve-to-one."

Belisarius chuckled.

"Slavery is an interesting condition, Vasudeva. It takes many forms. Different in the past than in the present. And different still, in the future. Many forms."

He leaned forward. Sixteen Kushans did likewise.

"Let me tell you about some slaves of the future."

Leaned forward. Leaned forward.

"They will be called—*Mamelukes.*"

A MESSAGE AND A PROMISE

When Antonina opened the door, Koutina hurried into her bedroom.

"I was hoping you'd still be awake," said the maid, "even though you left the birthday celebration so early."

Her young face was eager, almost avid. She held out a sheet of papyrus.

"It's a message! A message! For you! They say it came by the semaphore network—all the way from Mesopotamia!"

As she passed the paper over, Koutina added, "I think it's from your husband. I'm not sure. I can't read."

Uncertainly:

"Though it seems awfully short."

Antonina studied the message. Koutina was quite right, she saw. It was a very short message.

Just long enough. Her heart soared.

Next year, love. Next year.

"Yes," she whispered. "I will be there. I promise."

AN EMPEROR AND HIS PEOPLE

The morning after his birthday party, Emperor Photius made his way to the servant quarters of his palace.

Trudge, trudge, trudge.

Some of the nine-year-old boy's gloom came from simple weariness. The birthday party had been a tense, unhappy, and exhausting affair. What with the huge crowd, and the presentation of the Senators, and the ever-critical eye and tongue of the Empress Regent, Photius had enjoyed himself about as much as a sheep enjoys its shearing. Or a lamb, its slaughter.

Mostly, though, his black and dispirited thoughts came from The News.

Theodora had told him last night, just before the party began. Much as Photius imagined a farmer tells his piglet, "How marvelous! Aren't you just the fattest little thing?"

Reaching his destination, Photius knocked on the door. That was the only door which the Emperor of Rome ever knocked upon. All others were opened on his command.

The door to the modest apartment in the palace's servant quarters swung open. A young woman stood in the doorway. She was quite a pretty woman, despite the scars on her face.

"Oh, look! It's Photius!"

She smiled and stepped aside.

"Come in, boy, come in."

As he stepped through the door, Photius felt his melancholy begin to lift. Entering the living quarters of Hypatia and her husband Julian always cheered him up. It was the only place in the world where Photius still felt like himself. Hypatia had been his nanny since he was a toddler. And, though Julian had only become his chief bodyguard recently, Photius had known him for years. Julian had been one of Belisarius' bucellarii.

Julian himself now appeared, emerging into the small salon from the kitchen. He held a cup of wine in one hand.

Grinning cheerfully. The same cheerful grin the man had worn the first time Photius met him, at the estate in Daras. Photius had been six years old, watching wide-eyed from his bed while a burly cataphract climbed through his window and padded over to the door leading to Hypatia's quarters. Cheerfully urging the boy to keep quiet. Which Photius had, that night and all the nights which followed.

"Welcome, Emperor!" boomed Julian.

"Don't call me that," grumbled Photius.

Julian's grin widened.

"Feeling grouchy, are we? What's the matter? Did your tutors criticize your rhetoric? Or did the Empress Regent find some fault with your posture?"

"Worse," moaned Photius. "Terrible."

"Well, lad, why don't you come into the inner sanctum and tell us all about it?" Julian placed a large hand on the boy's shoulder and guided him into the kitchen. Hypatia followed on their footsteps.

The room—the largest in the apartment, by a goodly measure—was crowded, as usual. Two of Julian's fellow cataphracts were lounging about the huge wooden table in the middle of the kitchen. Wine cups in hand, as usual. Their wives and mothers busied about preparing the midday meal, while a small horde of children scampered in and out of the room, shrieking in play.

As usual.

"Hail, Photius! Rex Imperator!" cried out one of the cataphracts, lifting his cup. Marcus, that was.

The other, Anthony by name, matched the gesture. And the words, though he slurred them badly.

Julian plunked himself down at the table and said, "Ignore them, lad. They're already drunk. As usual, on their day off."

" 'S'our right," muttered Anthony. "A whole day wit'out 'avin' to listen t'a fuckin' tutor natterin' a' th'puir boy."

"*Photius* has to listen to them nattering seven days a week," said Hypatia. Primly: "Don't see him blind drunk two hours after sunrise."

" 'Course not!" snorted Anthony. " 'E's only eight years—no, by God! Nine years old, 'e is! Birt'day's yesserday!"

He lurched to his feet. "Hail Photius! Emperor of Rome!"

"*Don't call me that!*" shrilled the boy. "I'm sick of it!"

"Bein' called Emp'ror?" queried Marcus, bleary-eyed.

"No," groused Photius. "I'm sick of *being* Emperor!" He let out a half-wail. "I never asked them to!" And then a full wail. "They made me do it!"

The three cataphracts peered at the boy owlishly.

"Dissagruntled he is," opined Marcus.

"Downhearted'n downcast," agreed Anthony.

Julian bestowed a sage look upon his comrades. "Photius says he has terrible news to report."

It came out in a rush:

"They're going to make me marry somebody!" shrilled Photius. "Next year!"

Very owlish peers.

"A'ready?" queried Marcus. "Seems a bit—ah—ah—"

"Early," concluded Anthony. His eyes crossed with deep thought. "Ten years old, 'e be then. Still too early for'is pecker to—"

"Don't be vulgar!" scolded his wife, turning from the stove.

Anthony shrugged. "Speakin' fact, tha's all."

Hypatia sat down on the bench next to Photius. "Who are you supposed to marry?" she asked.

"Somebody named Tahmina," he replied sourly. "She's Persian. A Princess of some kind. I think she's the daughter of Baresmanas, the Persian ambassador who was here last spring."

"The *Suren?*" hissed Julian. His easy, sprawling posture vanished. He sat bolt upright. An instant later, Anthony and Marcus did the same.

The three cataphracts exchanged stares with each other. Then, suddenly, erupted into a frenzy of table-thumping, wine-spilling exhilaration.

"He did it! He did it!" bellowed Julian, lunging to his feet.

"Here's to the general!" hallooed Anthony, raising his wine cup and downing it in one quaff. The fact that he had already spilled its contents did not seem to faze him in the least.

Marcus simply slumped, exhaling deeply. His wife came over and enfolded him in her plump arms, pressing his head against her breasts.

All the women in the kitchen were standing around the table, now. They did not match the sheer exuberance of the cataphracts, but it was obvious that their own pleasure in the news was, if anything, greater.

"Why is everybody so happy about it?" whined Photius. "I think it's terrible! I don't want to get married! I'm only nine years old!"

His plaintive wail brought silence to the room. Everyone was staring at Photius.

Gently, Hypatia turned the boy to face her. "Do you understand what this means?" she asked. "For *me?* For *us?*"

Uncertainly, Photius shook his head.

Hypatia took Photius' hands in her own. "What it means, Emperor, is—"

"Don't call me that!"

"Be quiet, Photius. Listen to me." She took a deep breath. "What it means, *Emperor*, is that your father has ended the long war with Persia. No Persian—not a *Suren*, for sure—has ever married a Roman Emperor. That peace will last our lifetimes, Photius. And more, probably."

She turned her head, looking at Julian. "What it means, *Emperor*, is that my husband will not die somewhere, on a Persian lance. Our children will not grow up fatherless."

She looked around the room. "What it means, *Emperor*, is that Anthony's mother over there will not have to bury her own son before she dies. And Marcus' wife and children will enjoy a comfortable retirement, instead of grinding poverty on a cripple's dole."

When she turned back to face Photius, her eyes were leaking tears. "Do you understand?"

Staring up at her scarred face, Photius remembered a night when that face had been covered with blood instead of tears. A horrible, terrifying night, when a boy barely four years old had hidden in a closet while Hypatia's pimp savaged her with a knife for refusing a customer.

He had been helpless, utterly helpless. Had only been able to cower, listening to her shrieks. Powerless, to stop the torment of the woman who had raised him while his mother was gone. Powerless.

He lifted his little shoulders, then. Squared them.

He was powerless no longer. He was the Emperor of Rome.

True, the pimp Constans was beyond his reach. Years ago, when Maurice and Anastasius and Valentinian had come to bring Photius and Hypatia to the estate in Daras, they had paid a little visit on Constans. Two years later, after he married Hypatia, Julian and several of his cataphract friends had tendered their own regards to the crippled ex-pimp.

Constans was beyond his reach or any man's, now. But much else was not.

Powerless no longer. He had never, quite, thought of it that way. Had never, quite, realized what that meant. To *other* people. *His* people.

"Okay," he said. "I'll do it."

A new round of celebration erupted, in which, this time, Photius participated cheerfully. He even drank three cups of wine with his cataphracts, and got a bit drunk himself.

And why should he not? He was the Emperor of Rome, after all. *Their* Emperor.

A FAREWELL AND A PARTING THOUGHT

Baresmanas and Agathius saw him off at the gates of Peroz-Shapur. As his army marched past, Belisarius and his two companions spoke briefly on the prospects for his coming campaign.

Briefly—and more out of habit than anything else. It was a subject they had already discussed at great length.

The time came when friends made their farewells, knowing it might be for the last time. Agathius was gruff and hearty. Baresmanas was flowery and profusive.

Belisarius was simply cheerful.

"Enough," he said. "We'll meet again—be sure of it! I don't intend to lose, you know."

Quick, final handclasps, and the general trotted away to join his army.

Damn right, spoke Aide. Then—

Belisarius broke into laughter.

"What was that last?" he asked. "Sounded like 'those sorry bastards are fucked.' Terrible language! But, maybe not. Maybe you just said—"

Mutter, mutter, mutter.

Fortune's Stroke

To John & Becky

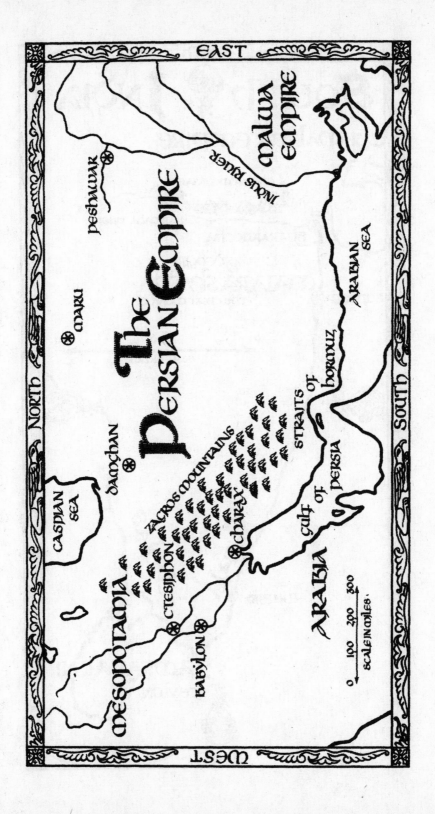

Prologue

The best steel in the world was made in India. That steel had saved his life.

He stared at a drop of blood working its way down the blade. Slowly, slowly. The blood which covered that fine steel was already drying in the sun. Even as he watched, the last still-liquid drop came to a halt and began hardening.

He had no idea how long he had been watching the blood dry. Hours, it seemed. Hours spent staring at a sword because he was too exhausted to do anything else.

But some quiet, lurking part of his battle-hardened mind told him it had only been minutes. Minutes only, and not so many of those.

He was exhausted. In mind, perhaps, even more than in body.

In a life filled with war since his boyhood, this battle had been the most bitter. Even his famous contest against one of India's legends, fought many years before, did not compare. That, too, had been a day filled with exhaustion, struggle, and fear. But it had been a single combat, not this tornado of mass melee. And there had been no rage in it, no murderous bile. Deadly purpose, yes—in his opponent as much as in himself. But there had been glory, too, and the exultation of knowing that—whichever of them triumphed—both their names would ring down through India's ages.

There had been no glory in this battle. His overlords would claim it glorious, and their bards and chroniclers give it the name. But they were liars. Untruth came as naturally to his masters as breathing. He thought that was perhaps the worst of their many crimes, for it covered all the rest.

His staring eyes moved away from the sword, and fixed on the body of his last opponent. The corpse was a horror, now, what with the mass of flies covering the entrails which spilled out from the great wound which the world's finest steel had created. A desperate slash, that had been, delivered by a man driven to his knees by his opponent's own powerful sword-stroke.

The staring eyes moved to the stub still held in the corpse's hand. The sword had broken at the hilt. The world's finest steel had saved his life. That and his own great strength, when he parried the strike.

Now, staring at the man's face. The features were a blur. Meaningless. The life which had once animated those features was gone. The man who stared saw only the beard clearly. A heavy beard, cut in the square Persian style.

He managed a slight nod, in place of the bow he was too tired to make. His opponent had been a brave man. Determined to exact a last vengeance out of a battle he must have already known to be lost. Determined to kill the man who led the invaders of his country.

The man who stared—the *invader*, he named himself, for he was not given to lies—would see to it that the Persian's body was exposed to the elements. It seemed a strange custom, to him, but that was the Aryan way of releasing the soul.

The man who stared had invaded, and murdered, and plundered, and conquered. But he would not dishonor. That low he would not stoop.

He heard the sound of approaching footsteps behind him. Several men. Among those steps he recognized those of his commander.

He summoned the energy to rise to his feet. For a moment, swaying dizzily, he stared across the battlefield. The Caspian Gates, that battlefield was called. The doorway to all of Persia. The man who stared had opened that doorway.

He cast a last glance at the disemboweled body at his feet.

Yes, he would see to it that the corpse was exposed, in the Persian way.

All of the enemy corpses, he thought, staring back at the battlefield. The stony, barren ground was littered with dead and dying men. Far beyond the grisly sight, rearing up on the northern horizon, was the immense mountain which Persians called Demavend. An extinct volcano, its pure and clean lines stood like some godly reproach to the foul chaos of mankind.

Yes. All of them.

His honor demanded it, and honor was all that was left to him. That, and his name.

Finally, now, he was able to stand erect. He was very tall.

Rana Sanga was his name. The greatest of Rajputana's kings, and one of India's most legendary warriors.

Rana Sanga. He took some comfort in the name. A name of honor. But he did not take much comfort, and only for an instant. For he was not a man given to lies, and he knew what else the name signified. Malwa bards and chroniclers could sing and write what they would, but he knew the truth.

Rana Sanga. The man—the legend, the Rajput king—who led the final charge which broke the Persians at the Caspian Gates. The man who opened the door, so that the world's foulest evil could spill across another continent.

He felt a gentle touch on his arm. Sanga glanced down, recognizing the pudgy little hand of Lord Damodara.

"Are you badly injured?"

Damodara's voice seemed filled with genuine concern. For a moment, a bitter thought flitted through Sanga's mind. But he dismissed it almost instantly. Some of Damodara's concern, true, was simply fear of losing his best general. But any commander worthy of the name would share that concern. Sanga was himself a general—and a magnificent one—and knew full well that any general's mind required a capacity for calculating ruthlessness.

But most of Damodara's concern was personal. Staring down at his commander, Sanga was struck by the oddity of the friendship in that fat, round face. Of all the highest men in the vast Malwa Empire, Damodara was the only one Sanga had ever met for whom he felt a genuine respect. Other Malwa overlords could be capable, even brilliant—as was Damodara—but no others could claim to be free of evil.

Not that Damodara is a saint, he thought wryly. *"Practical," he likes to call himself. Which is simply a polite way of saying "amoral." But at least he takes no pleasure in cruelty, and will avoid it when he can.*

He shook off the thought and the question simultaneously.

"No, Lord Damodara. I am exhausted, but—" Sanga shrugged. "Very little of the blood is mine. Two gashes, only. I have already bound them up. One will require some stitches. Later."

Sanga made a small gesture at the battlefield. His voice grew harsh. "It is more important, this moment, to see to the needs of honor. I want all the Persians buried—exposed—in their own manner. *With* their weapons."

Sanga cast a cold, unyielding eye on a figure standing some few feet away. Mihirakula was the commander of Lord Damodara's Ye-tai contingents.

"The Ye-tai may loot the bodies of any coin, or jewelry. But the Persians must be exposed with their weapons. Honor demands it."

Mihirakula scowled, but made no verbal protest. He knew that the Malwa commander would accede to Sanga's wishes. The heart of Damodara's army was Rajput, unlike any other of the Malwa Empire's many armies.

"Of course," said Damodara. "If you so wish."

The Malwa commander turned toward one of his other lieutenants, but the man was already moving toward his horse. The man was Rajput himself. He would see to enforcing the order.

Damodara turned back. "There is news," he announced. He gestured toward another man in his little entourage. A small, wiry, elderly man.

"One of Narses' couriers arrived just before the battle ended. With news from Mesopotamia."

Sanga glanced at Narses. There was sourness in that glance. The Rajput king had no love for traitors, even those who had betrayed his enemies.

Still—Narses was immensely competent. Of that there was no question.

"What is the news?" he asked.

"Our main army in Mesopotamia has suffered reverses." Damodara took a deep breath. "*Severe* reverses. They have been forced to lift the siege of Babylon and retreat to Charax."

"Belisarius," stated Sanga. His voice rang iron with certainty.

Damodara nodded. "Yes. He defeated one army at a place called Anatha, diverted the Euphrates, and trapped another army which came to reopen the river. Shattered it. Terrible casualties. Apparently he destroyed the dam and drowned thousands of our soldiers."

The Malwa commander looked away. "Much as you predicted. Cunning as a mongoose." Damodara blew out his cheeks. "With barely ten thousand men, Belisarius managed to force our army all the way back to the sea."

"And now?" asked Sanga.

Damodara shrugged. "It is not certain. The Persian Emperor is marshalling his forces to defeat his brother Ormazd, who betra—who is now allied with us—while he leaves a large army to hold Babylon. Belisarius went to Peroz-Shapur to rest and refit his army over the winter. After that—"

Again, he blew out his cheeks.

"He marched out of Peroz-Shapur some weeks ago, and seems to have disappeared."

Sanga nodded. He turned toward the many Rajput soldiers who were now standing nearby, gathering about their leader.

"Does one of you have any wine?" He lifted the sword in his hand. "I must clean it. The blood has dried."

One of the Rajputs began digging in the pouch behind his saddle. Sanga turned back to Damodara.

"He will be coming for us, now."

The Malwa commander cocked a quizzical eyebrow.

"Be sure of it, Lord Damodara," stated Sanga. He cocked his own eye at the Roman traitor.

Narses nodded. "Yes," he agreed. "That is my assessment also."

Listening to Narses speak, Sanga was impressed, again, by the traitor's ability to learn Hindi so quickly. Narses' accent was pronounced, but his vocabulary seemed to grow by leaps and bounds daily. And his grammar was already almost impeccable.

But, as always, Sanga was mostly struck by the sound of Narses' voice. Such a deep voice, to come from an old eunuch. He reminded himself, again, not to let his distaste for Narses obscure the undoubted depths to the man. A traitor the eunuch might be. He was also fiendishly capable, and an excellent advisor and spymaster.

"Be sure of it, Lord Damodara," repeated Rana Sanga.

His soldier handed him a winesack. Rajputana's greatest king began cleaning the blade of his sword.

The finest steel in the world was made in India.

He would need that steel. Belisarius was coming.

Chapter 1

PERSIA

Spring, 532 A.D.

When they reached the crest of the trail, two hours after daybreak, Belisarius reined in his horse. The pass was narrow and rocky, obscuring the mountains around him. But his view of the sun-drenched scene below was quite breathtaking.

"What a magnificent country," he murmured.

Belisarius twisted slightly in the saddle, turning toward the man on his right. "Don't you think so, Maurice?"

Maurice scowled. His gray eyes glared down at the great plateau which stretched to the far-distant horizon. Their color was almost identical to his beard. Every one of the bristly strands, Maurice liked to say, had been turned gray over the years by his young commander's weird and crooked way of looking at things.

"You're a lunatic," he pronounced. "A gibbering idiot."

Smiling crookedly, Belisarius turned to the man on his left. "Is that your opinion also, Vasudeva?"

The commander of Belisarius' contingent of Kushan troops shrugged. "Difficult to say," he replied, in his thick, newly learned Greek. For a moment, Vasudeva's usually impassive face was twisted by a grimace.

"Impossible to make fair judgement," he growled. "This helmet—" A sudden fluency came upon him: "Ignorant stupid barbarian piece of shit helmet designed by ignorant stupid barbarians
with shit for brains!"

A deep breath, then: "Stupid fucking barbarian helmet obscures
all vision. Makes me blind as a bat." He squinted up at the sky.
"It is daylight, yes?"

Belisarius' smile grew more crooked still. The Kushans had not
stopped complaining about their helmets since they were first
handed the things. Weeks ago, now. As soon as his army was three
days' march from Peroz-Shapur, and Belisarius was satisfied there
were no eyes to see, he had unloaded the Kushans' new uniforms
and insisted they start wearing them.

The Kushans had howled for hours. Then, finally yielding to
their master's stern commands—they were, after all, technically
his slaves—they had stubbornly kept his army from resuming its
march for another day. A full day, while they furiously cleaned and
recleaned their new outfits. Insisting, all the while, that invented-
by-a-philosopher-and-manufactured-by-a-poet-civilized-fucking
caustics were no match for hordes of rampaging-murdering-rap-
ing-plundering-barbarian-fucking lice.

Glancing down at Vasudeva's gear, Belisarius privately admitted
his sympathy.

He had obtained the Kushans' new armor and uniforms, through
intermediaries, from the Ostrogoths. Ironically, although the work-
manship—certainly the filth—of the outfits was barbarian, they
were patterned on Roman uniforms of the previous century. As
armor went, the outfits were quite substantial. They were sturdier,
actually, than modern cataphract gear, in the way they combined
a mail tunic with laminated arm and leg protection. That weight,
of course, was the source of some of the grumbling. The Kushans
favored lighter armor than Roman cataphracts to begin
with—much less this great, gross, grotesque Ostrogoth gear.

But it was the helmets for which the Kushans reserved their
chief complaint. They were accustomed to their own light and
simple headgear, which consisted of nothing much more than a
steel plate across the forehead held by a leather strap. Whereas
these—these—these great, heavy, head-enclosing, silly-horse-tail-
crested, idiot-segmented-steel-plate fucking barbarian fucking
monstrosities—

They obscured their topknots! Covered them up completely!

"Which," Belisarius had patiently explained at the time, "is the point of the whole exercise. No one will realize you are Kushans. I must keep your existence in my army a secret from the enemy."

The Kushans had understood the military logic of the matter. Still—

Belisarius felt Vasudeva's glare, but he ignored it serenely. "Oh, surely you have some opinion," he stated.

Vasudeva transferred the glare onto the countryside below. "Maurice is correct," he pronounced. "You are a lunatic. A madman."

For a moment, Vasudeva and Maurice exchanged admiring glances. In the months since they had met, the leader of the Kushan "military slaves" and the commander of Belisarius' bucellarii—his personal contingent of mostly Thracian cataphracts who constituted the elite troops of his army—had developed a close working relationship. A friendship, actually, although neither of those grizzled veterans would have admitted the term into their grim lexicon.

Observing the silent exchange, Belisarius fought down a grin. *Outrageous language,* he thought wryly, *from a slave!*

He had captured the Kushans the previous summer, at what had come to be called the battle of Anatha. In the months thereafter, while Belisarius concentrated on relieving the Malwa siege of Babylon, the Kushans had served his army as a labor force. After Belisarius had driven the main Malwa army back to the seaport of Charax—through a stratagem in which their own labor had played a key role—the Kushans had switched allegiances. They had never had any love for their arrogant Malwa overlords to begin with. And once they concluded, from close scrutiny, that Belisarius was as shrewd and capable a commander as they had ever encountered, they decided to negotiate a new status.

"Slaves" they were still, technically. The Kushans felt strongly that proprieties had to be maintained, and they had, after all, been captured in fair battle. Their status had been proposed by Belisarius himself, based on a vision which Aide had given him of military slaves of the future called "Mamelukes."

Vasudeva's eyes were now resting on him, with none of the admiration those same eyes had bestowed on Maurice a moment earlier. Quite hard, those eyes were. Almost glaring, in fact.

Belisarius let the grin emerge.

Slaves, of a sort. But we have to make allowances. It's hard for a man to remember his servile status when he's riding an armored horse with weapons at his side.

"How disrespectful," he murmured.

Vasudeva ignored the quip. The Kushan pointed a finger at the landscape below. "You call this magnificent?" he demanded.

Snort. The glare was transferred back to the plateau. The rocky, ravine-filled landscape stretched from the base of the mountains as far as the eye could see.

"If there is a single drop of water in that miserable country," growled Vasudeva, "it is being hoarded by a family of field mice. A small family, at that."

He remembered his grievance.

"So, at least," he added sourly, "it appears to me. But I am blind as a bat because of this fucking stupid barbarian helmet. Perhaps there's a river—even a huge lake!—somewhere below."

He cocked his head. "Maurice?"

The Thracian cataphract shook his head gloomily. "Not a drop, just as you said." He pointed his own accusing finger. "There's not hardly any vegetation at all down there, except for a handful of oak trees here and there."

Maurice glanced for a moment at the mountains which surrounded them. A thin layer of snow covered the slopes, but the scene was still warmer than the one below. As throughout the Zagros range, the terrain was heavily covered with oak and juniper. The rainfall which the Zagros received even produced a certain lushness in its multitude of little valleys. There, aided by irrigation, the Persian inhabitants were able to grow wheat, barley, grapes, apricots, peaches and pistachios.

He sighed, turning his eyes back to the arid plateau. "All the rain stays in the mountains," he muttered. "Down there—" Another sigh. "Nothing but—"

He finally spotted it.

Belisarius smiled. He, with his vision enhanced by Aide, had seen the thing as soon as they reached the pass. "I do believe that's an oasis!" he exclaimed cheerfully.

Vasudeva's gaze tracked that of his companions. When he spotted the small patch of greenery, his eyes widened. *"That?"* he choked. "You call *that* an 'oasis'?"

Belisarius shrugged. "It's not an oasis, actually. I think it's one of the places where the Persians dug a vertical well to their underground canals. What they call their *qanat* system."

The clatter of horses behind caused him to turn. His two bodyguards, Anastasius and Valentinian, had finally arrived at the mountain pass. They had lagged behind while Valentinian pried a rock from one of his mount's hooves.

Belisarius turned back and pointed to the "oasis." "I want to investigate," he announced. "I think we can make it there by noon."

Protest immediately erupted.

"That's a bad idea," stated Maurice.

"Idiot lunatic idea," agreed Vasudeva.

"There's only the five of us," concurred Valentinian.

"Rest of the army's still a day's march behind," added Anastasius. The giant cataphract, usually placid and philosophical, added his own glare to those of his companions.

"This so-called 'personal reconnaissance' of yours," rumbled Anastasius, "is pushing it already." A huge hand swept the surrounding mountains. A finger the size of a sausage pointed accusingly at the plateau below. "Who the hell knows what's lurking about?" he demanded. "That so-called 'plateau' is almost as broken as these mountains. Could be an entire Malwa cavalry troop hidden anywhere."

"An entire *army*," hissed Valentinian. "I think we should get out of here. I *certainly* don't think we should go down—"

Belisarius cleared his throat. "I don't recall summoning a council," he remarked mildly.

His companions scowled, but fell instantly silent.

After a moment, Maurice spoke quietly. "Are you determined on this, lad?"

Belisarius nodded. "Yes, Maurice, I am. I've been thinking about these qanats ever since Baresmanas and Kurush described them to me. They've been figuring rather heavily in my calculations, in fact." He pointed to the distant patch of greenery. "But it's all speculation until I actually get to inspect one. This is my first chance, and I don't intend to pass it up."

Having established his authority, Belisarius relented a moment. His veterans were entitled to an explanation, not simply a command.

"Besides, I don't think we need to worry about encountering Damodara's forces yet. The battle where they took the Caspian Gates was bloody and bitter. By all accounts, Damodara simply left a holding force at the Gates while he retired his main army to Damghan for the winter. By now, they'll have refitted and recuperated—they're probably back through the Gates, maybe even as far into Mah province as Ahmadan—but that's still almost fifty miles from here."

Vasudeva cleared his throat. "Is your assessment based on reports from spies, or is it—"

Belisarius smiled. "Good Greek logic, Vasudeva."

Nothing was said. But the expression on the faces of his Thracian and Kushan companions spoke volumes concerning their opinion of "good Greek logic." Even Anastasius, normally devoted to Greek philosophy, was glowering fiercely.

Belisarius spurred his horse into motion and began picking his way down the trail. Silently, his men followed.

More or less silently, that is. Valentinian, of course, was muttering. Belisarius did not ask for a translation. He was quite sure that every phrase was purely obscene.

Halfway down the slope, a new voice entered its protest.

This is a bad idea, came the thought from Aide.

Et tu, Brute? responded Belisarius.

Very bad idea. I have been thinking it over, and Maurice is correct. And Vasudeva and Valentinian and Anastasius. This is too much guesswork. There are only five of you. You should leave this off and rejoin your army. You can investigate that oasis later, with a much larger force.

Belisarius was a bit startled by the vehemence in Aide's tone. The crystalline being from the future had been with him for years now, ever since it was brought to him by the monk, Michael of Macedonia. Over the course of that time, in fits and starts, Belisarius and Aide had worked out their relationship. Aide advised him, and guided him, and often educated him, on matters pertaining to history and broad human affairs. And the "jewel" was also an almost inexhaustible fount of information. But, from experience, Aide had learned not to outguess Belisarius when it came to problems of strategy and tactics. In that realm, the crystalline being had learned, Belisarius was supreme. Which was why it had come here from the future, after all. To save itself and its crystal race from slavery or outright destruction, Aide had come back to the past searching for the great Roman general who might thwart the attempt of the "new gods" to change all of human history.

But, though Belisarius was startled, he was not swayed. If anything, Aide's echo of his companions' protests simply heightened his resolve.

And so it was, as Belisarius and his little troop worked their way down the slopes of the Zagros mountains onto the plateau of Persia, that another voice was added to Valentinian's muttering.

Stubborn Thracian oaf was the only one of those half-sensed thoughts which was not, technically, obscene.

Chapter 2

The trap was sprung when the Romans were less than three hundred yards from their destination. That was the only mistake the Rajputs made.

But they could hardly, in good conscience, be faulted for that error. Sanga had warned them of Belisarius' quickness and sagacity. But Sanga knew nothing of Aide, and of the way in which Aide enhanced Belisarius' hearing as well his eyesight. So his men sprang the trap at the moment when, logically, they had the Romans isolated from any retreat or shelter.

Belisarius heard the clattering of horses set into sudden motion before any of his comrades—before, even, the lurking enemy appeared out of the ravines in which they were hidden.

"It's an ambush!" he hissed.

Valentinian reacted first. He began reining his horse around.

"No!" shouted Belisarius. He pointed, with both hands, to their side and rear. "They waited until they could cut us off from the mountains!"

He spurred his horse forward, now pointing ahead. "Our only chance is to fort up!"

His comrades, from long experience, did not argue the matter. They simply followed Belisarius' galloping horse, as their commander charged forward.

Belisarius scanned the terrain ahead of him. The small "oasis" toward which they were heading was not much more than a grove of trees. Spindly fruit trees—apricots, mostly, with a handful of peaches.

Useless.

But, a moment later, his uncanny eyesight spotted what he was hoping for.

"There's a building! In the grove!" Belisarius cast a quick glance over his left shoulder. He could see the enemy now.

Damnation! Rajputs.

Perhaps a dozen. A glance over his right shoulder. *Same.*

His quick mind flashed back over his experiences in India. *The standard for a Rajput cavalry platoon is thirty. Which means—*

He turned his head back around, scanning the grove ahead. In less than two seconds, he saw what he was expecting.

"There are Rajputs in the grove, too!" he shouted. "Probably half a dozen!"

Belisarius made no attempt to draw his bow. He was not a good enough archer to handle it at a full gallop. None of his companions were, except—Valentinian already had his bow out. In less time than Belisarius would have imagined possible, the cataphract had fired an arrow. The missile sped ahead of the galloping cluster of Romans and plunged into the trees. Instantly, a cry of pain went up. Almost as instantly, five Rajputs drove their horses out of the grove, pounding toward the oncoming Romans. Belisarius could see a sixth Rajput, but the man was sliding off his horse, clutching at an arrow in his shoulder.

This was lance work, now. All of the Romans except Valentinian already had their heavy lances in position. So did Valentinian, by the time the Rajputs arrived. With his weasel-quick reflexes, the cataphract even managed to slide his bow back in its sheath before taking up his lance. Almost any other man in the world would have been forced to simply drop the weapon.

The contest, under the circumstances—a head-on collision between an equal number of Roman cataphracts and Rajput lancers—was no match at all. Even without stirrups, the heavier Roman cavalry would have triumphed. With them, and the much heavier and longer lances the stirrups made possible, Belisarius and his men almost literally rode right over their opponents. For a few seconds, the general's world was a cacophony of shouts. The clangor of lance against shield covered but could not disguise the more hideous sounds of splitting flesh and bone. Battle cries became shrieks, fading into hissing death.

Three of the Rajputs were killed almost instantly, their bodies torn by the great spears. A fourth would die within minutes, from the blood pouring out of a half-severed thigh.

The only one who survived, suffering nothing worse than bruises, was the Rajput who faced Vasudeva. Though the Kushan was a skilled warrior, he had little experience with stirrups and lanceplay. But he was a veteran, and had the sense not to try matching the prowess of his companions. Instead of finding the gaps between armor, he simply drove his lance into his opponent's shield. The impact knocked the man right off his horse.

The Romans rode on. Belisarius could now see more of the building through the trees. It was a farmhouse, typical of the sort erected by large Persian families. Square in design, the structure was single-storied and measured approximately thirty feet on a side. The walls were heavy and solid, constructed out of dry stone. He couldn't see the roof clearly, but he knew it would be made of wooden beams covered with soil.

Except—

There was something odd about the shape of the farmhouse. The trees obscured his vision, but it seemed as if the building sloped on one side.

A thought came from Aide. **This is earthquake country. That building is half-collapsed.**

Belisarius nodded. They were entering the small grove which surrounded the farmhouse, and he could see that the fruit trees were poorly tended. The place had all the signs of an abandoned farm.

Earthquake, probably, just like Aide says. Then—war comes. The survivors would have fled.

Belisarius cast a last glance over his shoulder. Their pursuers, he saw, were spreading out. Realizing that they had missed their chance at an immediate ambush, the Rajputs intended to surround the grove and trap the Romans in the farmhouse.

Grimly, he turned away. Five men against most of a Rajput cavalry platoon was bad odds. Very bad. But at least they'd have the advantage of being forted up rather than caught in the open.

A moment later they were through the grove and reining up next to the farmhouse.

If you can call this a "fort," he thought ruefully, examining the structure.

"There's only the one door," pointed out Maurice. "Maybe one in back, but I doubt it. Not if this is like most Persian farmhouses."

"You call that a 'door'?" demanded Valentinian. His expression was that of a man who had just eaten a basket of lemons.

Maurice managed the feat of shrugging while he climbed off his horse. "It'll do, it'll do. We can probably shore it up with beams." He glanced up at the half-collapsed roof. "Be plenty of them lying around, I should think."

Valentinian left off further comment, although his continued sour expression made clear his opinion of "forts" with collapsed roofs.

Once all five Romans were dismounted, they pried open the door and led their mounts into the farmhouse. The half-dark interior of the farmhouse was filled, for a minute or so, with the noise and dust thrown up by skittish horses, still blowing from exertion and prancing nervously. Vasudeva occupied himself with calming and tying up the mounts while his four companions spread out and investigated the place.

The investigation was quick, but thorough.

Maurice summed it up. "Could be worse. Walls are thick. The stones were well placed. Roof'll be a problem, but at least"—he pointed to the rubble filling the northern third of the farmhouse—"when it collapsed it brought down the adjoining walls. One or two Rajputs could squeeze in there, but there's no way they could do a concerted rush."

Hands on hips, he made a last survey of their fort.

"Not bad, actually. Once we brace the door—"

He smiled thinly, watching Anastasius match deed to word. The giant simply picked up a beam and jammed it against the door. Then, as casually as it were but a twig, he did the same with another.

Maurice finished: "—we'll be able to hold them off for quite a bit."

Valentinian's expression was still sour. Sour, sour, sour. "That's great," he snarled. "You *have* noticed there's no way out of here? You *have* noticed there's no food in the place?"

Gloomily, he watched Belisarius pry the cover off what appeared to be a well in the southeast corner.

"At least we've got water," he grumbled. "Maybe. If that well isn't dry."

Belisarius spoke, then, with astonishing good cheer. "Better than that, Valentinian. Better than that. I do believe this leads to a qanat." He pointed down into the well. "See for yourself."

Valentinian and Maurice hurried over.

"Make it quick," commanded Vasudeva. The Kushan was peering through a small chink in the western wall. "The Rajputs are into the grove."

"Same on this side," added Anastasius, peering through a similar chink in the opposite wall. "They've got us surrounded." A moment later: "They're dismounting, now, going to charge us on foot." His tone grew aggrieved. "I thought Rajputs never got off their horses, even rode them into the damned latrines."

"Not Sanga's Rajputs," commented Belisarius idly, still staring down into the well. "He's just as stiff-necked as any Rajput when it comes to his honor, but that doesn't extend to any silliness when it comes to military tactics."

Suddenly, Vasudeva hissed. "They've got grenades!" he exclaimed.

Belisarius' head jerked up from his examination of the well.

"You're certain?" he demanded. But he didn't wait for a reply before reconsidering his plans. Vasudeva was not the man to make such a mistake.

"I thought the Malwa never let anyone but their kshatriyas handle gunpowder weapons," complained Valentinian.

"So did I," mused Belisarius, scratching his chin. "Looks like Damodara decided to relax the rules."

He resumed studying the well. "Not surprising, I suppose. He's rumored to be far and away their best field commander, and his army's based on Rajputs. Sanga's Rajputs, to boot."

As he continued his scrutiny of the well, his voice grew thoughtful. "That explains this ambush, I think. I forgot how good Sanga is. Got too accustomed to those arrogant Malwa in Mesopotamia. He knows me. He probably figured I'd do my own reconnaissance, and set traps all along the foothills."

Belisarius looked up, finished with his examination. When he spoke, the iron tone in his voice indicated that he had reached a decision.

"No point in forting up, now," he announced. "They won't waste lives trying to force their way through the door. They'll just blow out the walls of the farmhouse."

"They're already moving in," agreed Vasudeva. "Three men, on this side, carrying grenades. I can't even fire on them. Chink's big enough to peek through, but not for an arrow."

"I've got two on my side," said Anastasius. "Same thing."

Belisarius pointed down the well. "We'll make our escape through here. Strip off your armor. It's a long, narrow climb, and I've no idea how much room we'll have below."

"What about the horses?" demanded Valentinian.

Belisarius shook his head. "No way to get them down. We'll use them for a diversion. But first—" He strode over to the horses. "Pull out our own grenades. I want to set them against all the walls. We'll do the Rajputs' work for them. Bring the whole place down. It might cover our escape."

He began digging grenades out of his saddlebags. An instant later, Maurice and Valentinian were doing the same.

"I've got fuse-cord," announced Maurice. "We can tie together all the grenades. Set them off at once."

Belisarius nodded. He carried a handful of grenades over to the west wall and began placing them, while Valentinian did the same on the east. Maurice followed, quickly tying the fuses to a length of fuse-cord.

Suddenly, Vasudeva shouted. *"Get down! Now!"*

All five Romans flopped onto the dirt floor of the farmhouse. An instant later, a series of explosions rocked the building. On the west wall, not far from Vasudeva, a small hole was blown out. Everywhere else the walls stood, although they were noticeably shakier.

"God bless good stonework," muttered Anastasius. "Always admired masons. A saintly lot, the bunch."

The horses reared up, whinnying with fear, fighting the reins which tied them to a fallen beam. Maurice, the best horse handler among them, rushed to quiet them down.

"Are they preparing a charge?" demanded Belisarius.

Vasudeva, back at his chink, shook his head. "No. They're too canny. They're putting together another batch of grenades. They won't charge until the place is a pile of rubble. Let the falling stones do their work for them." He grunted approvingly. "Good soldiers. Smart."

Belisarius nodded. "That gives us a couple of minutes." He pointed to the door. "Anastasius—pull those braces away. Then get ready to knock down the door. Maurice, as soon as the door goes, drive the horses through. That'll stop the Rajputs for a moment. They'll think we're trying a rush, and besides"—he smiled cheerfully—"Rajputs love good horses. They won't be able to resist taking the time to catch these."

He turned. Seeing that Valentinian had quietly gone about finishing the task of tying together all the grenades, he nodded with satisfaction.

"That's it, then. Vasudeva, you go first. Then Valentinian. Maurice and Anastasius, as soon as you drive the horses out, you follow. I'll go last."

Belisarius seized the heavy well cover and lifted it back onto the low stone wall which surrounded the well. Then, using a short beam, he propped it open. When the time came, he would be able to drop the cover back onto the well by knocking aside the beam.

He began stripping off his armor. Before he was half finished, Vasudeva was out of his own armor and already clambering into the well. The Kushan grabbed a wooden peg fixed into the stonework of the shaft—the first of many which served as a ladder—and began lowering himself.

"At least I've got rid of that miserable stupid ignorant barbarian helmet and that—" The rest of his words were lost as he vanished into the darkness.

Valentinian handed Belisarius the end of the fuse cord as he began his own descent into the well. He had nothing to say. Nothing coherent, at least. He *was* muttering fiercely.

Belisarius looked up. Maurice and Anastasius were in place. They, too, had already stripped off their armor.

"Do it," he commanded. Then, remembering an undone task, shouted: "Wait! I need a striker!"

Maurice scowled, and hastily dug into one of the saddlebags. A moment later, he came up with the device and pitched it to Belisarius. As soon as Anastasius saw that Belisarius had caught the striker, the huge Thracian heaved one of the beams aside. A moment later, the other followed. And then, a moment later, Anastasius kicked open the door. One powerful blow was enough to send the half-splintered thing flying into the farmyard beyond.

That done, Anastasius lumbered toward the well while Maurice, shouting and cursing, began driving the horses through the door.

The well was a tight fit for Anastasius, but he took the problem philosophically. "There's much to be said for the Cynic school," he commented, as he began the awkward task of lowering his great form down the narrow stone shaft. "Unfairly maligned, they are."

An instant later, Maurice practically leapt into the well. "Make it quick, lad," he hissed. "None of your fancy perfect timing crap. The Rajputs are already coming." He began dropping down the shaft. "Just blow it. *Now.*"

Well said, chimed in Aide.

Belisarius was not inclined to argue the point. He just waited long enough to be certain that Maurice was far enough ahead that he wouldn't be climbing down onto his head before he struck flame to the fuse. He took a second to make sure the fuse was burning properly before tossing it onto the floor. Then, after climbing into the well and lowering himself a few feet, he reached up and knocked aside the beam. The heavy wooden cover slammed back down over the shaft opening. Belisarius barely managed to jerk his hand out of the way, saving himself from broken fingers.

The interior of the well was completely dark, now. Hastily, feeling for the wooden pegs, Belisarius began lowering himself.

He was twenty feet down when the charges went off. The force of the explosion shook the walls of the shaft. For a moment, Belisarius froze, listening intently. He could hear the slamming of stones and heavy beams on the well cover above him, and he feared that it might give way. An avalanche of rubble would sweep him off the peg ladder. He had no idea how far he would fall.

Far enough, said Aide gloomily. **Too far.**

In the event, it would have been forty feet.

When he finally reached the end of the well-shaft, his feet flailed about for a moment, searching for pegs which weren't there. A hand grabbed his ankle.

"That's it, General," came Valentinian's voice out of the darkness. "Anastasius, get him down."

Huge hands seized Belisarius' thighs. The general relinquished his grip on the pegs, and Anastasius lowered him easily onto a floor. A gravel floor, Belisarius thought, from the feel of it.

He began to stand up straight, then flinched. He couldn't see the roof, and feared crashing his head.

That brought to mind a new problem. "Damn," he growled. "I forgot it would be pitch-black down here."

"I didn't," came Maurice's self-satisfied reply. "Neither did Vasudeva. But I hope you had the sense to bring that striker down with you. It's the only one we've got."

Belisarius dug into his tunic and withdrew the striker. His hand, groping in the darkness, encountered that of Maurice. The Thracian chiliarch took the device and struck it. A moment later, Maurice had a taper burning. It was a short length of tallow-soaked cord, one of the field torches which Roman soldiers carried with them on campaign.

The smoky, flickering light was enough to illuminate the area. Belisarius began a quick examination, while Maurice lit the taper which Vasudeva was carrying.

Valentinian, staring around, whistled softly. "Damn! I'm impressed."

So was Belisarius. The underground aqueduct they found themselves in was splendidly constructed—easily up to the best standards of Roman engineering. The aqueduct—the qanat, as the Persians called it, using the Arabic term—was square in cross section, roughly eight feet wide by eight feet tall. The central area of the tunnel, about four feet in width, was sunk two feet below the ledges on either side. That central area, where the water would normally flow except during the heavy runoff in mid-spring, was covered with gravel. The ledges were crudely paved with stone blocks, and were just wide enough for a man to walk along.

Except for a small trickle of water seeping down the very center, the qanat was dry. It was still too early in the season for most of the snow to begin melting.

"What do you think the slope is, Maurice?" asked Belisarius. "One in three hundred? That's the Roman standard."

"Do I look like an engineer?" groused the chiliarch. "I haven't got the faintest—"

"One in two hundred," interrupted Vasudeva. "Maybe even one in a hundred and fifty."

The Kushan smiled seraphically. In the flickering torchlight, he looked like a leering gargoyle. "This is mountain country, much like my own homeland. No room here for any leisurely Roman slopes." He pointed with his torch. "That way. The steep slope makes it easy to see the direction of the mountains. But we've a long way to go."

He set off, pacing along the ledge on the right. Cheerfully, over his back: "Long way. Tiring. Especially for Romans, accustomed to philosopher slopes and poet-type gradients." He barked a laugh. "One in three hundred!" Another laugh. "Ha!"

An hour later, Valentinian began complaining.

"There would have been room for the horses," he whined. "Plenty of room."

"How would you have lowered them down?" demanded Anastasius. "And what good would it have done, anyway?"

The giant glanced up at the stone ceiling. Unlike his companions, Anastasius had chosen to walk on the gravel in the central trough of the qanat. On the ledges, he would have had to stoop.

"Eight feet, at the most," he pronounced. "You couldn't possibly *ride* a horse down here. You'd still be walking, and have to lead the surly brutes by the reins."

Mutter, mutter, mutter.

"So stop whining, Valentinian. There's worse things in life than a long, uphill hike."

"Like what?" snarled Valentinian.

"Like being dead," came the serene reply.

They passed a multitude of vertical shafts along the way, identical to the one down which they had lowered themselves. But Belisarius ignored them. He wanted to make sure they had reached the mountains before emerging.

Three hours after beginning their trek, they reached the first of the sloping entryways which provided easier access to the qanat. Belisarius fought off the temptation. He wanted to be well into the mountains before they emerged, away from any possible discovery or pursuit.

Onward. Valentinian started muttering again.

Two hours later—the slope was *much* steeper now—they reached another entryway. This one was almost level, which indicated how high up into the mountains they had reached.

Again, Belisarius was tempted. Again, he fought it down.

Further. Onward.

Valentinian's muttering was nonstop, now.

◇   ◇   ◇

An hour or so later, they reached another entryway, and Belisarius decided it was safe to take it. When they emerged, they found
themselves in the very same pass in the mountains from which
they had begun their descent to the plateau. Night had fallen, but
there was a full moon to illuminate the area.

It was very cold. And they were very hungry.

"We'll camp here," announced Belisarius. "Start our march
tomorrow at first light. Hopefully, some of Coutzes' cavalry will
find us before too long. I told him to keep plenty of reconnaissance
platoons out in the field."

"Which could have done what we just did," grumbled Maurice.
"A commanding general's got no business doing this kind of work."

Quite right, came Aide's vigorous thought.

"Quite right," came the echo from Valentinian, Anastasius and
Vasudeva.

Seeing the four men glaring at him in the moonlight, and sensing
the crystalline glare coming from within his own mind, Belisarius
sighed.

*It's going to be a long night. And a longer day tomorrow—if
I'm lucky, and Coutzes is on the job. If not—*

Sigh.

*Days! Days of this! Slogging through the mountains is bad
enough, without having every footstep dogged by reproaches and
"I-told-you-sos."*

"I told you so," came the inevitable words from Maurice.

Chapter 3

"I told you so," murmured Rana Sanga. The Rajput king strode over to the well and peered down into the shaft.

Pratap, the commander of the cavalry troop, suppressed a sigh of relief. Sanga, on occasion, possessed an absolutely ferocious temper. But his words of reproach had been more philosophical than condemnatory.

He joined the king at the well.

"You followed?" asked Sanga.

Pratap hesitated, then squared his shoulders. "I sent several men to investigate. But—it's pitch-black down there, and we had no good torches. Nothing that would have lasted more than a few minutes. By the time we finally cleared away the rubble and figured out what had happened, the Romans had at least an hour's head start. It didn't seem to me—"

Sanga waved him down. "You don't have to justify yourself, Pratap. As it happens, I agree with you. You almost certainly wouldn't have caught up with them and, even if you had—"

He straightened, finished with his examination of the well. In truth, there wasn't much to see. Just a stone-lined hole descending into darkness.

"From your description of the giant Roman, I'm sure that was one of Belisarius' two personal bodyguards. I've forgotten his name. But the other one is called Valentinian, and—"

From the corner of his eye, he saw Udai wince. Udai was one
of his chief lieutenants. Like Sanga himself, Udai had been present
at the Malwa emperor's pavilion after the capture of Ranapur. The
emperor, testing Belisarius' pretense at treason, had ordered him
to execute Ranapur's lord and his family. The Roman general had
not hesitated, ordering Valentinian to do the work.

For a moment, remembering, Sanga almost winced himself.
Valentinian had drawn his sword and decapitated six people in less
time than it would have taken most soldiers to gather their wits.
Sanga was himself accounted one of India's greatest swordsmen.
Valentinian was one of the few men he had ever encountered—the
very few men—who he thought might be his equal. To meet such
a man down *there*—

"Just as well," he stated firmly. "In the qanat, with no way to
surround them, the advantage would have been all theirs." He
turned away from the well, and began picking his way across the
mound of rubble.

"The ambush failed, that's all. It happens—especially against an
opponent as quick and shrewd as Belisarius."

Seeing Ajatasutra standing before him, at the edge of the stone
pile which had once been a farmhouse, Sanga stopped and drew
himself up.

"I will not have my men criticized." The Rajput's statement was
flat, hard, unyielding. His brows lowered over glaring eyes.

Ajatasutra smiled, and spread his hands in a placating gesture.
"I didn't say a word." The assassin chuckled dryly. "As it happens,
I agree with you. The only thing that surprises me is that you came
as close as you did. I didn't really think this scheme of yours was
more than a half-baked fancy. Generals, in my experience, don't
conduct their own advance reconnaissance."

"I do," rasped Sanga.

"So you do," mused Ajatasutra. The assassin eyed the Rajput
king. His lips twisted humorously. "You were right, and Narses was
wrong," he stated. "You assessed Belisarius better than he did."

Again, Ajatasutra spread his hands. "I will simply report the
facts, Sanga, that's all. The ambush was well laid, and almost succeeded. But it failed, as ambushes often do. There is no fault or
failure imputed."

Sanga nodded. For a moment, he studied the man standing
before him. Despite himself, and his normal fierce dislike for

Malwa spies, Sanga found it impossible not to be impressed by Ajatasutra. Ajatasutra was one of the Malwa Empire's most accomplished assassins. A year earlier, he had been second in command of the mission to Rome which had engineered the attempted insurrection against the Roman Empire. Narses had been the Malwa's principal co-conspirator in that plot. The insurrection—the Nika revolt, as the Romans called it—had failed, in the end, due to Belisarius. But it had been a very close thing, and the Malwa Empire had not blamed Ajatasutra or Narses for its failure. The two men had warned Balban, the head of the Malwa mission, that Belisarius and his wife, Antonina, were playing a duplicitous game. That, at least, had been their claim—and the evidence seemed to support them.

So, held faultless for the defeat, Narses had been assigned by Emperor Skandagupta to serve Lord Damodara as an adviser. The eunuch, from his long experience as one of the Roman Empire's chief officials, possessed a wide knowledge of the intricate politics of the steppe barbarians and the semibarbarian feudal lords who ruled Persia's easternmost provinces. He had been a great help to the campaign, as Damodara and Sanga fought their way into the Persian plateau.

Ajatasutra had accompanied Narses. He served the Roman traitor as his chief lieutenant—and as his legs and eyes. The old eunuch was still spry and active—amazingly so, given his years. But for things like this sudden twenty-mile ride to investigate a failed ambush, Ajatasutra usually served in his stead. The assassin would observe, and assess, and report.

Sanga relaxed. In truth, he had found Ajatasutra guiltless of the self-serving "reports" for which Malwa spies were notorious among their Rajput vassals. He would never be fond of Ajatasutra—he had no more liking for assassins than he did for traitors, even ones on his side—but he could not honestly find any other fault in the man.

"You're lucky, in fact," remarked Ajatasutra, "that you didn't suffer worse casualties."

"Four of my men were killed!" snarled Pratap. "Two others wounded, and yet another half-crushed when the farmhouse blew up. He will lose both his legs."

Ajatasutra shrugged. The gesture was not callous so much as one of philosophical resignation. "Could have been a lot worse.

Most of the stonework collapsed inward, when Belisarius blew the walls. Fortunately, he was just trying to cover his escape. If he'd been forced to make a last stand, I guarantee that half your men would be dead. And precious few of the survivors uninjured."

Pratap's eyes smoldered resentfully. "I didn't realize you were well acquainted with the man." Then, with a sneer: "Other than suffering a defeat at his hands in Constantinople."

Ajatasutra studied Pratap's angry face. His own expression was relaxed, almost bland.

"Actually, I'm not. My own contact with Belisarius came at a distance. But I am quite well-acquainted with his wife, Antonina. Balban set a trap for her, too, you know—in Constantinople, right at the end."

The anger faded from Pratap's features, replaced by curiosity.

"I never heard about that," he stated.

"Neither did I!" snapped Sanga. The Rajput king glared at the Malwa assassin. "You tried to take revenge on Belisarius by murdering his *wife*?"

Sanga's famous temper was surfacing, now. Again, Ajatasutra made the placating gesture with his hands. "Please, Rana Sanga! It was Balban's doing, not mine. And you can't even blame him—the orders came directly from Nanda Lal."

Far from placating Sanga, mention of Nanda Lal brought his outrage to the surface. But at least, Ajatasutra saw, the tall and fearsome Rajput's fury was no longer directed at him. There was no love lost, he knew, between Rana Sanga and the Malwa Empire's spymaster.

The assassin spread his hands wide. "I thought it was a bad idea, myself. And I warned Balban that he was underestimating the woman."

The hot glare in Sanga's eyes faded, as the implication registered. "The ambush failed," he stated. "Belisarius' wife survived."

Ajatasutra laughed harshly. " 'Survived'? That's one way of putting it. It'd be more accurate to say that she set her own ambush and butchered most of Balban's thugs."

By now, all of the Rajputs at the scene were clustering about—Sanga's own contingent as well as Pratap's cavalry troop. Like warriors everywhere, they enjoyed a good tale. Ajatasutra, seeing his audience—and the easing fury in Sanga's face—relaxed. He held out his hand, perhaps five feet above the ground.

"She's quite small, you know. This tall, no more. Gorgeous woman. Beautiful, voluptuous—" He paused dramatically.

"*But*—" He grinned. "Her father was a charioteer. He was reputed to have taught her how to use a blade. And I'm quite certain her husband trained her also. Probably had that man of his—that killer Valentinian—polish her skills."

Ajatasutra paused, to make sure he had his audience's rapt attention. Then: "When she realized Balban had set a pack of street thugs after her, she forted herself up in the kitchen of a pastry shop. I wasn't there, myself—I watched from outside—but she apparently poured meat broth over the lot and began hacking them with a cleaver. Killed several herself, before one of Belisarius' cataphracts came to her rescue. After that—"

He shrugged. "One cataphract—against a handful of street toughs."

The Rajput cavalrymen surrounding him, veterans all, grunted deep satisfaction. Roman cataphracts were their enemy, of course, but—

Street toughs—against a *soldier*?

"A woman did all that?" queried one of the Rajputs. The air of satisfaction was absent, now. He seemed almost aggrieved. "A *woman?*"

Ajatasutra smiled. Nodded. Held out his hand again. "A little bitty woman," he said cheerfully. "No taller than this."

The assassin glanced at Rana Sanga. He saw that the anger in the Rajput king's face had completely faded. Replaced by something which almost seemed sadness, thought Ajatasutra.

Odd.

Abruptly, Sanga turned away and began striding toward his horse. "Let's go," he commanded. "There's nothing more to be done here. I want to make it back to the army by nightfall."

Once astride his horse, he gave the scene a last quick survey. "The ambush failed," he announced. "That's all."

That night, standing before his tent in the giant camp of Damodara's army, Rana Sanga studied the mountains looming to the west. The full moon bathed them in a silvery beauty. But there was something ominous about that pale shimmer. Liquid, almost, those mountains seemed. As difficult to pin down as the man who lurked somewhere within them.

"I wish we had killed you," whispered Sanga. "It would have made things so much easier for us. And then again—"

He sighed, turned away, pulled back the flap to his tent. He gave a last glance at the moon, high and silvery, before stooping into the darkness. He remembered another night he had done the same, after the massacre of rebel Ranapur. Remembered his thoughts on that night. The same thoughts he had now.

I wish you were not my enemy. But—

I swore an oath.

That same moment, staring down onto the plateau from the mountain pass, Belisarius studied the flickering fires of the far-distant Malwa army camp. It was the day after the ambush, and his own army had arrived. The Roman troops were camped just half a mile below the crest of the mountains.

He was no longer estimating the size of the enemy army. He was done with that. He was simply contemplating one of the men he knew was among that huge host.

It was very nicely done, Sanga. Sorry to have disappointed you.

The thought was whimsical, not angry. Had he been in Sanga's place, he would have done the same. And he mused, once again, on the irony of the situation. There were few men in the world he dreaded as much as Rana Sanga. A tiger in human flesh.

And yet—

He sighed and turned away. He would meet Sanga again.

Picking his way down the trail in the semidarkness, he remembered the message which the Great Ones had once given Aide and his race. The secret—part of it, at least—which those awesome beings of the future imparted to the crystals they had created, when those crystals found themselves threatened by the "new gods."

Guided by that message, the crystals had sent Aide back in time to find "the general who is not a warrior." But the Great Ones had understood the entirety of the thing. Descended from human flesh—though there was no trace of that flesh remaining in them—they understood all the secrets of the human soul, and its contradictions.

Aide, in a soft mental message, spoke the words: **See the enemy in the mirror.**

A sudden deep sadness engulfed Belisarius.

The friend across the field.

Chapter 4

AXUM

Spring, 532 A.D.

Antonina shook her head, partly in awe, partly in disbelief. "Was anyone killed when it fell?" she asked.

Next to her, Eon lifted his massive shoulders in a small shrug.

"Nobody knows, Antonina." For a moment, the Prince of Axum's dark face was twisted into a grimace of embarrassment. "We were still pagans, at the time. And the workmen would have all been slaves. We Ethiopians kept many slaves, back then"—his next words came in a bit of a rush—"before we adopted the teachings of Jesus Christ."

Antonina fought down a smile. The semi-apology in Eon's response was quite unnecessary, after all. It was not as if Roman rulers—

"Please, Eon! You don't need to apologize for the barbarity of your pagan ancestors. At least your old kings didn't stage gladiatorial contests, or feed Christians to lions."

Alas. She could tell immediately, from Eon's expression, that her attempt at reassurance had failed of its mark.

"Not Christians, no," mumbled Eon. "But—" Another shrug of those incredible shoulders. "Well . . . There are a lot of big animals here in Africa. Lions, elephants. And it seems that the old kings—"

There came yet another shrug. But the gesture, this time, contained neither apology nor embarrassment. It was the movement of the powerful shoulders of a young prince who, when all was said and done, was not really given to self-effacement.

"It's over, now," he stated. "We instituted Christian principles of rule two hundred years ago." He pointed to the enormous thing in front of them. "We keep that here as a reminder to our kings. Of the pagan folly of royal grandiosity."

Antonina's eyes returned to the object in question. Eon had brought her here, from the royal compound a mile to the southwest—the Ta'akha Maryam, it was called—as part of his sight-seeing tour of Ethiopia's capital city. He had started off, in the morning, by showing her the magnificent churches which adorned the city. The churches, especially the cathedral which the Ethiopians had named the Maryam Tsion, were the pride of Axum. But then, in mid-afternoon, the prince had insisted on showing her this as well.

It was an obelisk, lying on its side, broken into several pieces. The huge sections were crumpled over the tombs of pre-Christian kings, leaving the obelisk a rippling monument to ancient folly. More than anything else, to Antonina, it resembled an enormous stone snake, making its serpentine way across the landscape of the Ethiopian highlands.

The obelisk had fallen, Eon explained, as it was being erected. Staring at it, Antonina could well believe the tale. It was difficult to judge, because of its position, but she thought the obelisk was far larger than any created even by the ancient Egyptians. Only a king possessed by delusions of grandeur could have thought of ordering mortal men to erect such a preposterous structure.

She shivered slightly, thinking of the men who must have been trapped by the obelisk in its ruin. When the thing fell, it crushed several of the tombs beneath it. The blood and mangled flesh of slaves, for a time, would have decorated the sepulchres where royal bones lay buried.

Eon misinterpreted the motion. "You are cold!" he exclaimed. "I have been thoughtless. I forgot that you are not accustomed—"

She waved down the apology. "No, no, Eon. I'm not really cold. I was just thinking—"

She stopped, shivering again. She *was* cold, she suddenly realized. She had always thought of Africa as the quintessential land of warmth. But the heartland of Axum lay in the Ethiopian high-lands. True, the capital city was situated in the broad, fertile plain called Hatsebo, well below the mountains which towered all about in stark majesty. But it was still over a mile above sea level.

"Perhaps we should return to the Ta'akha Maryam," she admit-ted. A bit hurriedly, to stave off another apology: "Your father will be growing impatient with our long absence."

Actually, she knew, Eon's father—the *negusa nagast*, "King of Kings," as he was titled—would not be in the slightest bit impa-tient. She was quite certain that King Kaleb had welcomed her daylong absence from the royal compound. It gave him time to consult with his advisers, before making a response to the Roman Empire's proposals.

Antonina and her entourage had arrived in the Ethiopian city of Axum a week earlier. Axum—the capital had given its name to the Ethiopian kingdom, just as had Rome—had never received such a high-level delegation from the Roman Empire. Since Ethio-pia's conversion to Christianity under the tutelage of the missionar-ies who were revered as the "Nine Saints," the Axumites had maintained cordial relations with the great empire to their north. But, except for trade matters, there had been very little in the way of official diplomatic exchange. Until Antonina came, at the head of a small army, armed not only with the strange new gunpowder weapons but with a barrage of proposals from the Emperor of Rome.

As they began picking their way through the broken stones of ancient kings, Antonina found herself, once again, fighting down a smile. She could well understand how King Kaleb would have wanted a day—at least!—to mull over the Roman Empire's pro-posals.

Those proposals were, after all, hardly what you'd call vague and meaningless diplomatic phrasery.

Rome accepts Axum's offer of an alliance against the Malwa Empire. To further our joint aim of crushing that monstrous realm, we propose:

Rome will supply Axum with gunpowder weapons, and the tech-nicians to train you in their use and manufacture.

Axum will provide the fleet necessary to keep the rebellion in southern India alive. Axumite ships will run the Malwa blockade

of the Majarashtra coast, carrying arms and supplies provided
by Rome.

Axum will also provide the fleet necessary to—

Her thoughts broke off. She and Eon were almost out of the
ruins. As they picked their way around yet another half-crumbled
structure, she caught sight of the figure lounging against one of
the tombs at the very edge of the field of monuments.

Ousanas, for once, was not grinning. Indeed, he looked positively disgruntled.

Antonina made no attempt to fight down her smile, now.
"What's the matter, Ousanas?" she called out. "Has your philosophical composure abandoned you, for the moment? Shame,
shame! What would the Stoics say?"

Ousanas shook his head. "The Stoics advocated serenity in the
face of life's tragedies and great misfortunes." Scowling: "They did
not intend their precious teachings to be wasted on petty annoy-
ances. Such as having to waste half a day while a fool boy prince
shows a frivolous woman with too much time on her hands the
inevitable results of self-aggrandizement, a lesson which"—deep
scowl—"any child learns the first time they sass their elders."

Antonina and Eon reached the edge of the field. Ousanas thrust
himself erect from his semi-reclined posture. There was nothing
of a lurch in that movement, as there would have been for most
men. On one of his powerful forearms, Ousanas bore the scar left
by a panther he had slain years earlier. The tall African had triumphed in that encounter, as he had in so many others, because
he shared the sinuous grace and power of the great feline hunters
of the continent. For all that Ousanas derided royalty—which, as
Prince Eon's dawazz, was his duty and obligation—the man was a
majestic figure in his own right.

Antonina's grin was still on her face. She pointed over her shoulder with a thumb to the great field of monuments behind her.

"I would have thought you'd approve of this display," she said.
"An aid to your task, showing the results of excessive royal self-
esteem."

Ousanas cast a sour look at the stone ruins in question. "Nonsense," he replied forcefully. "Maintaining this grotesque and useless field is itself a testament to royal idiocy. Who but cretin kings
would need to waste so much good land for such a trivial purpose?

A child requires no more than the memory of his last set of bruises."

He began stalking off, headed toward the Ta'akha Maryam. "We'd do better just to haul the negusa nagast out of his palace, once or twice a year, and thrash him soundly." He repeated Antonina's gesture, pointing with his thumb at the ruins over his shoulder. "Then we could turn this into good farmland. Raise crops for needy children. Feed poor dawazz, weak from his endless labor like Sisyphus."

Antonina glanced at Eon, walking alongside her. She was expecting to see the prince's face twisted into a scowl, hearing Ousanas' outrageous proposals. But, to her surprise, Eon's expression was one of sly amusement.

The dawazz, it seemed, had done his work well.

"And just who would do all that work, Ousanas?" asked the prince. "Hauling great stones, thousands of them, out of that field. Backbreaking work, day after day after day. Take years, probably. *You?*"

Ousanas' snort was answer enough.

"Thought not," mused Eon. "No sane man would. No *free* man, that is. So we'd have to reinstitute mass slavery. Give the King of Kings a whole army of slaves—*again*—just like in the old days."

Eon's grin did not quite match those which his dawazz usually employed, but it came close.

"So," he concluded cheerfully, "in order to accomplish your goal of abasing royalty, we'd have to elevate royalty to its grandiose status of old. Good thinking, Ousanas!" The prince shook his head in a gesture of exaggerated chagrin. "I'm ashamed of myself! All these years, I thought your obsession with philosophy was a waste of time. But now, I see—"

Ousanas interrupted: "Enough!" He stopped abruptly, and stared at the distant mountains which surrounded the Hatsebo plain. His expression, from a scowl of irritation, faded into one of thoughtfulness.

"You see those mountains?" he asked softly. "Impossible to reach, the greatest of them. Just so do men stare at justice and righteousness. An unattainable goal, but one which we must always keep in our sight. Or we will drown in the madness of the pit."

He puffed his cheeks, and then blew out the breath slowly. "It's a pity, all things considered, that democracy doesn't work," he mused. "But the Greeks proved that, along with so much else. Smartest people in the world, Greeks. Who else would be deluded enough to try running a country with no king?"

He shook his head sadly. "All they ever did was fight and bicker and squabble. Endless wars between petty states—never could run more than a city, at best!—and all for nothing. Ruin and destruction—just read Thucydides." Another shake of his head. "Finally, of course, sensible people like the great Philip of Macedon put an end to the silly business."

Still staring at the mountains, Ousanas sighed heavily. "Got to have kings, and emperors, and the whole lot of puffed-up pigeons. No way around it. Somebody's got to give the orders."

He turned to face the young prince who had been placed in his charge so many years before. Now, he smiled. A rare expression that was, for the dawazz. A beaming grin was often found on his face. But Antonina, watching, could not remember ever having seen such a simple, gentle smile on the face of the man named Ousanas.

"You are a good boy, Eon," said the hunter. "Tomorrow you will be proclaimed a man, and I will no longer be your dawazz. So I will say this now, and only this once."

Ousanas bowed his head, just slightly. "It has been a privilege to be your dawazz, and a pleasure. And I do not really think, when all is said and done, that my labor has been that of Sisyphus."

Eon stared up at the tall figure of the man who had guided him, and taught him, and—most of all—chastened and chastised him for all those years. There was a hint of moisture in his eyes.

"And I could not have found," he replied, "not anywhere in the world, a better man to be my dawazz."

Tentatively, almost timidly, Eon reached out his hand and placed it on Ousanas' arm. "You have nothing to fear tomorrow," he said softly.

The normal and proper relation between dawazz and prince returned. Ousanas immediately slapped Eon on his head. Very hard.

"Fool boy!" he cried. "Of course I have something to fear! Entire Dakuen sarwe—half of it, anyway, and that's more than enough to do for my poor bones!—will be standing in judgement. Of *me*, not you!"

He turned to Antonina, his face twisting into a grimace. His eyes were almost bulging. "Axumite sarwen most pitiless creatures in universe! Soldiers—cruel and brutal! And this—this—" He pointed an accusing finger at Eon. "This *idiot prince* says I have nothing to fear!"

He threw up his hands. "I am lost!" he cried. "Years of work—for nothing. Boy still as mindless as ever!" Again, he began stalking off. Over his shoulder: "Royalty stupid by nature, as I've always said. The Dakuen sarwe will do what it wills, cretin-maybe-someday-king! Pay no attention to *you*."

Antonina and Eon began following him. Faintly, they could hear Ousanas' grumbling.

"Idiot Ethiopians and their imbecile customs. Had any sense, they'd beat the prince instead of the poor dawazz." A low, heartfelt moan. "Why did I ever do this? Could have stayed in central Africa. Doing simple safe work. Hunting lions and elephants, and other sane endeavors."

Antonina leaned over and whispered: "Is he really worried, Eon? About the judgement, tomorrow?"

Eon smiled. "I do not think so, not really. But you know Ousanas. All that philosophy makes him gloomy." His expression changed, a bit. "And he is right about the one thing. Only the Dakuen sarwe's opinion will matter, come tomorrow morning. It is not a public ceremony. No one else will be there—not even the king himself. Only the soldiers of my regiment."

Antonina started with surprise. "But—why then was *I* invited? Wahsi asked me to come, just yesterday. He was quite insistent about it—and he's now the commander of the regiment."

Eon cocked his eye at her. "You are not a guest, Antonina. You will be there as a *witness*."

When the Ta'akha Maryam was looming before them, Antonina shook off her pensive thoughts and remembered her mission. With a few quick steps, she caught up with Ousanas.

"I really think we should go visit the Tomb of Bazen," she said, "before we return to the royal compound. And the rock-cut burial pits nearby! Eon's told me all about them."

Ousanas stopped dead in his tracks and stared down at her.

"What for?" he demanded, scowling. "They're just more graves, for ancient men possessed by ridiculous notions of their importance in the scheme of things." With a snort: "Besides, they're empty. Robbers—sane men!—plundered them long ago."

Patiently, Antonina explained.

"*Because*, Ousanas, I really think the negusa nagast would appreciate a full day to consult with his advisers, without the presence of the Roman Empire's ambassador. Two full days, actually—since I'll be tied up all day tomorrow at the Dakuen sarwe's ceremony."

Ousanas was not mollified. Rather the contrary, in fact.

"Marvelous," he growled. "I'd forgotten. One of the witnesses for the prince's sanity is a madwoman herself. Come to Axum to propose all-out war against the world's most powerful empire, for no good reason except that her husband has visions."

He resumed his stalking, headed now toward the Tomb of Bazen to the east. Antonina and Eon followed, a few steps behind.

After they had gone a few yards in their new direction, Antonina turned her head toward Eon. She was about to make some jocular remark about Ousanas, but a movement near the Ta'akha Maryam caught her eye.

Three men were racing away from the royal compound, as if being chased by a lion. Two of them were Ethiopian, but the third—

She stopped, hissed. Eon turned his head to follow her gaze.

The third of the three men fleeing the Ta'akha Maryam caught sight of them. He stumbled to a halt and stared. At the distance—perhaps fifty yards—Antonina couldn't make out his features clearly, but two things were obvious.

First, he was Indian. Second, he was cursing bitterly.

An instant later, the man resumed his flight.

"Ousanas!" called out Eon.

But the hunter had already spotted the men. And, quicker than either of his two companions, deduced the truth. Ousanas sprang on Eon and Antonina like a lion, swept them up, one in each arm, and tackled them to the ground.

The impact knocked the wind out of Antonina. The incredible explosion which followed stunned her half-senseless.

She watched, paralyzed, as the royal compound erupted. At first, because of shock, she didn't realize what she was seeing. A paralyzing noise—rapid series of noises, actually, blurring together—was followed by a huge cloud of billowing dust. Then, within a split second, she saw great stones moving. Some of the smaller pieces were flung high into the sky, but most of the massive slabs which made up the Ta'akha Maryam simply heaved up. Seconds later, the compound began to collapse. The building which held the throne room was the first to go, buckling like a broken bridge. That set off a chain reaction, in which the toppling walls of one room or building caused its neighbor to cave in as well. The sound of screams was buried beneath the uproar of collapsing masonry. By the time the process ground to a halt, perhaps a minute later, over a third of the Ta'akha Maryam was nothing but a heap of rubble. The noise of destruction faded into a chill silence—except for one faint shriek of agony, spilling across the dust-clouded landscape like a trail of blood.

Long before that time, Antonina realized what had happened. The first billowing gust had brought a sharp and familiar smell to her nostrils.

Gunpowder. *Lots* of gunpowder.

The Malwa Empire had struck. King Kaleb, the negusa nagast of Ethiopia, was lying somewhere under those stones. So was his older son, Wa'zeb, the heir. And so—if she hadn't insisted on a last-minute change of plans—would have been Antonina herself and Eon. She realized—dimly; still half-dazed—that the men who lit the fuse had waited until they were sure that she and Eon were about to enter the royal compound.

Painfully, Antonina levered herself up. They wouldn't know until the rubble was searched, but she strongly suspected that Eon was the sole survivor of the royal dynasty. And he was not even a man yet, by the customs of his people—not until the morrow's ceremony.

Eon Bisi Dakuen, Prince of Axum, was already on his feet. He was staring at the figure of Ousanas. The dawazz, his great spear in hand, was racing after the three men who had emerged from the Ta'akha Maryam. They had a two-hundred-yard lead on Ousanas, and were running as fast as they could, but it only took Antonina a moment to gauge the outcome.

Eon, apparently, reached the same conclusion. He took two steps in that direction, as if to follow, but stopped. "Ousanas is the greatest hunter anyone in Axum ever saw," he murmured. "Those are dead men."

He turned, stooped, and helped Antonina to her feet. His face seemed far older than his years. Bleak, and bitter.

"Are you all right?" he asked. "I must organize the search for my father and brother." A wince of pain came. "And Zaia, and our daughter Miriam, and Tarabai. And my adviser Garmat. All of them were in there."

She nodded. "I'll help. Some of my people were in the Ta'akha Maryam, too."

Eon's eyes scanned the rubble. "The Roman delegation should be safe. The section of the royal compound where you were housed is still standing."

They began making their way toward the shattered compound. Noise was returning, now, in the form of shouting commands and pleas for help. People were already moving about the ruin, beginning to pluck at the crumpled stones. One of those men, catching sight of them, cried out with joy and began sprinting in their direction.

His joy was no greater than Antonina's, or Eon's. That man was named Wahsi, and he was the commander of the Dakuen sarwe.

The prince's regiment, once. Now, in all likelihood, the royal regiment.

Wahsi reached them and swept the prince into his embrace. Other soldiers of the Dakuen sarwe were following, and their own joy was quite evident.

Antonina heard Eon's muffled voice: "Gather the regiment, Wahsi. And the Lazen and the Hadefan sarawit, if my father and brother are dead. They must sit on Ousanas' judgement also, if I am to be the negusa nagast."

He pried himself loose from Wahsi's clasp. Then, his face still cold and bleak, he issued his commands: "First, we must search the ruins. Then we will have the ceremony, as soon as possible. There is no time to waste. This will not be Malwa's only blow. We are at war, and I intend to give them no respite. *And no quarter.*"

Wahsi nodded. His own expression was fierce. So were those on the faces of the soldiers standing around.

Antonina found herself seized by a sudden—and utterly inappropriate—urge to giggle. She fought it down savagely.

Bad move, Malwa. If you'd gotten Eon also—

But, you didn't. Bad move. Bad, bad, bad move.

Chapter 5

DEOGIRI

Spring, 532 A.D.

Nanda Lal, the Malwa Empire's chief spymaster, studied Deogiri. The walled city was two miles away from the hilltop where Nanda Lal was standing, just a few yards from Lord Venandakatra's pavilion. Venandakatra had placed his headquarters on the only hill in the area which approached Deogiri's elevation. The men who built Deogiri, centuries earlier, had designed the city for defense.

And designed it very well, he thought sourly.

Deogiri, upon whose ramparts Rao's rebels held Malwa at bay, was one of the best-fortified cities in India. The upper fortress, built on a conical rock at the top of a hill that rose almost perpendicularly from the surrounding plain a hundred fifty yards below. The outer wall of the city was nearly three miles in circumference, and three additional lines of fortification lay between it and the upper fortress. Throughout, the stonework was massive and well made.

Emperor Skandagupta had sent Nanda Lal here to determine why Lord Venandakatra was having so much difficulty subduing the Deccan rebellion. The task had not taken the spymaster long in the doing. An hour's study of Deogiri was enough, coming on top of the days which Nanda Lal had spent travelling here from

509

Bharakuccha. Days, protected by a large escort of Rajputs, creeping through the hills of Majarashtra. Days, expecting a Maratha ambush—and fighting three of them off.

His gloomy thoughts were interrupted by a shrill scream, coming from somewhere behind him. Nanda Lal did not turn his head. He knew the source of that shriek of agony. The first of the Maratha guerrillas which his Rajput escort had captured during the last ambush was being fitted to the stake.

For a moment, the sound cheered him up. But only for a moment. Every town in Majarashtra had corpses fitted onto stakes. Still, the rebellion swelled in strength.

Silently, Nanda Lal cursed the Great Country. Silently, he cursed Raghunath Rao. Silently, he cursed the "Empress" Shakuntala. But, most of all—

Hearing the approaching footsteps, he cursed their cause.

But most of all—curse you, Venandakatra! If you hadn't let Belisarius maneuver you into giving Rao his chance, Shakuntala would never have become such a thorn in our side.

He sighed, and turned away from Deogiri. The thing was done. Much as he would have liked to curse Venandakatra aloud—fit *him* to a stake, in truth—the unity of the Malwa dynastic clan had to be maintained. That, above all, was the foundation of Malwa's success.

"You see?" demanded Venandakatra, when he reached Nanda Lal's side. The Goptri of the Deccan pointed at Deogiri. "You see? Is it not just as I said?"

Nanda Lal scowled. "Do not push the matter, cousin!" he snapped. "Deogiri was just as strong when *you* held it."

Venandakatra flushed. But the color in his flabby cheeks was due more to embarrassment than anger. His eyes fell away from Nanda Lal's level gaze.

Nanda Lal, as was his way, twisted the blade. "Before *you*—through your carelessness, Venandakatra—allowed Rao and his rebels to take Deogiri by surprise." The spymaster sneered. "No doubt you were preoccupied, raping another Maratha hill girl instead of attending to your duty."

Venandakatra clenched his jaws, but said nothing. His thin-boned, fat-sheathed frame was practically shaking from fury. But, still, he said nothing.

Nanda Lal allowed the silence to linger, for perhaps a minute. Then, with a little shrug, he let the tension ease from his own shoulders. Thick shoulders, those were. Heavy with muscle.

"Good," he murmured. "At least you have not lost your wits." Coldly: "Do not let your kin proximity to the emperor blind you to certain realities, Venandakatra. My bloodline is equal to your own, and I am second in power only to Skandagupta himself. Do not forget it."

Nanda Lal clapped a powerful hand on Venandakatra's shoulder. Under the fat, the thin bones felt like those of a chicken. The Goptri of the Deccan flinched, as much from the force of that "friendly" gesture as surprise.

"Enough said!" boomed Nanda Lal. With his hand still on Venandakatra's shoulder, he steered the Goptri toward the pavilion.

As they neared the pavilion's entrance, their progress was interrupted by another shriek of agony. The first Maratha captive had apparently expired, and the second was being fitted onto a stake.

Venandakatra found the courage to speak. "You should have used shorter stakes," he grumbled.

Nanda Lal chuckled. "Why bother?" He stopped, in order to examine the execution. The ground surrounding Venandakatra's pavilion had been packed down. Alongside the road which led north to Bharakuccha, six stakes had been erected. The first Maratha was dead, draped over his stake. The second was still screaming. The remaining four captives were bound and gagged. The gags would not be removed until the last moment, so that the Yetai conducting the execution would not be subject to curses.

"Why bother?" he repeated. "The terror campaign is necessary, Venandakatra, but do not put overmuch faith in it. The Great Country is littered with skeletons on stakes. How much good has it done?"

Venandakatra opened his mouth, as if to argue the point. But, again, discretion came to his rescue.

Nanda Lal took a deep breath, and blew it out slowly through his nose. "The emperor and I will tolerate your sadism, Venandakatra," he murmured softly. "Up to a point. That point ends when your lusts interfere with your duty."

Throughout, Nanda Lal's hand had never left Venandakatra's shoulder. Now, with a shove, he forced the Goptri into the pavilion.

The pavilion's interior was lavish with furnishings. Thick carpets covered every inch of the floor. The sloping cotton walls were lined with statuary, silk tapestries, and finely crafted side tables bearing an assortment of carvings and jewelry.

With another shove, Nanda Lal pushed Venandakatra toward the great pile of cushions at the center of the pavilion. A third shove sent the Goptri sprawling onto them. Venandakatra was now hissing with outrage but, still, he spoke no words of protest.

Satisfied that he had cowed the man sufficiently, Nanda Lal scanned the interior of the pavilion. His eyes fell on a cluster of Maratha girls in a corner. They ranged in age from ten to thirteen, he estimated. All of them were naked and chained. The current members of Venandakatra's harem. Judging from their scars and bruises, and the dull fear in their faces, they would not survive any longer than their many predecessors.

That should finish the work, thought Nanda Lal. He turned his head to the Rajput officer standing guard by the pavilion's entrance.

"Take them out"—he pointed to the girls—"and kill them. Do it now."

Seeing the rigidity in the Rajput's face, Nanda Lal snorted. "Behead them, that's enough." The Rajput nodded stiffly and advanced on the girls. A moment later, he was leading them out of the pavilion by their chains.

The girls did not protest, nor make any attempt to struggle. Nanda Lal was not surprised. Marathi-speaking peasant girls, from their look. They probably didn't understand Hindi and, even if they did—

His eyes fell on Venandakatra, gasping with outrage.

I probably did them a favor, and they know it.

Nanda Lal waited until the sound of a sword cleaving through a neck filtered into the pavilion.

"So, Venandakatra, let us deal with your duty. With no further distractions. Now that I have investigated the situation, I will recommend to the emperor that your request for siege guns be granted."

The spymaster nodded toward the north. "But you will have to be satisfied with the guns at Bharakuccha. Six of them—that should be enough. And there will be no other reinforcements. The war in Persia has proven more difficult than we foresaw, thanks to Belisarius."

He shrugged. "It would take too long to bring siege guns across the Vindhyas, anyway. As it is, hauling the great things here will take months, even from Bharakuccha."

Venandakatra's face lost its expression of outrage. Anger came, instead—anger and satisfaction.

"At last!" he exclaimed. "I will take Deogiri!" He clenched his bony fingers into a fist. "Rao will be mine! He and the Satavahana bitch! I will stake them side by side!"

Nanda Lal studied him for a moment. "Let us hope so, Venandakatra."

He turned away and strode to the pavilion entrance. There, the spymaster filled his nostrils with clean air.

Let us hope so, Venandakatra. For the sake of the Empire. Were it not for that, I would almost wish for your failure.

His eyes fell on the execution ground. The six Maratha rebels were all dead, now. Their bodies were draped over the stakes. Their heads lolled, as if they were mourning their sisters sprawled on the ground in front of them. Five heads, and five headless corpses, naked in a spreading lake of blood.

You would look good on a stake, Venandakatra. Splendid, in fact.

Chapter 6
SUPPARA
Spring, 532 A.D.

Irene Macrembolitissa, the Roman Empire's ambassador to the rebels of south India, strode down one of the corridors in Empress Shakuntala's small palace, head deep in thought. The Empress of Andhra—it was a grandiose title, for a young girl leading a rebellion against Malwa, but one to which she was legitimately entitled—had requested Irene's presence in the imperial audience chamber. It seemed that Kungas had finally returned from his long journey to the rebel-held city of Deogiri. Shakuntala wanted Rome's envoy present, to hear his report.

Irene had never met Kungas. She knew of him, of course. Kungas was one of the top military commanders of Shakuntala's small army. He bore the resplendent titles of *Mahadandanayaka* and *Bhatasvapati*—"great commandant" and "lord of army and cavalry." He was also the head of Shakuntala's personal bodyguard, an elite body made up entirely of Kushans.

Before she left Constantinople, Belisarius had provided Irene with a full and thorough assessment of Kungas. He knew the Kushan from his trip to India, and was obviously taken by him. Without quite saying so, Belisarius had left Irene the impression that Kungas' advice and opinions should be given the utmost care and consideration.

Privately, Irene had her doubts. She was one of the Roman Empire's most accomplished spymasters—an unusual occupation for a woman, especially a Greek noblewoman—and she had generally found that male military leaders were too heavily influenced by the martial accomplishments of other men. That Kungas was shrewd and cunning on the battlefield, Irene did not doubt for a moment. That did not necessarily translate into the kind of skills which were necessary for an imperial adviser.

Head down, striding along in her usual brisk and long-legged style, Irene tightened her lips. The upcoming session, she thought, would be difficult.

The young empress doted on Kungas, so much was obvious. Knowing the history of Shakuntala and Kungas' relationship, Irene did not find the girl's attitude odd. Kushans were Malwa vassals, and Kungas had been the man assigned as Shakuntala's guard and captor after the Malwa had conquered her father's empire of Andhra. He had saved her from rape, at the sack of Amaravati. Had held her safe, until Belisarius and Rao rescued her—and had then, learning the secret of that rescue, held his tongue and kept the secret from his Malwa masters. In the end, he and his men had thrown off their loyalty to Malwa and smuggled Shakuntala to south India. Since then, they had saved her life more than once from Malwa assassination teams.

The fact remained, he was nothing more than a semibarbarian warlord. Not even literate, by all accounts.

Irene was not looking forward to the upcoming session. *She would have to steer a delicate course between offending the empress and—*

Paying no attention to anything but her thoughts, Irene swept into a junction with another corridor and crashed into an unseen obstacle.

For a moment, she almost lost her footing. Only a desperate hand, reaching out to clutch the object into which she had hurtled, kept her from an undignified landing on her backside.

Startled, she looked up and found herself gazing into the statue of a steppe warrior. Into the face of the statue, more precisely. A bronze and rigid mask, apparently part of a single casting. Stiff, still, unmoving. Extremely well done, she noted, all the way down to the lifelike armor and horsehair topknot.

But the artistry of the piece did not leave her mollified.

"What idiot left a statue in the middle of a corridor?" she hissed angrily. Then, after a brief second scrutiny: "Ugly damned thing, too."

The statue moved. Its lips, at least. Irene was so startled she actually jumped.

"Horses think I'm pretty," said the statue, in heavily accented but understandable Greek. "Why else do they give me such playful nips?"

Irene gasped, clasping a hand over her mouth. She stepped back a pace or two. "You're *real!*"

The statue gazed down at its body. "So I am told by my scholarly friend Dadaji," the thing rasped. "But I am not a student of philosophy, myself, so I can't vouch for it."

For all that she was startled, Irene's quick mind had not deserted her. "You must be Kungas," she stated. "You fit Belisarius' description."

At first, Irene thought she was several inches taller than he. But closer examination revealed that Kungas was not more than an inch below her own height. It was just that the man was so stocky, in a thick-chested and muscular fashion, that he looked shorter than he actually was. Beyond that, his whole body—especially his face—looked as if it were made of metal, or polished wood, rather than flesh. She did not think she had ever seen a human being in her life who seemed so utterly—*hard*.

His features were typically Kushan. Asiatic, steppe features: yellowish complexion, flat nose, eyes which seemed slanted due to the fold in the corners, a tight-lipped mouth. His beard was a wispy goatee, and the mustache adorning his upper lip was no more than a thin line of hair. Most of his scalp was shaved, except for a clot of coarse black hair gathered into a topknot.

Kungas returned Irene's scrutiny with one of his own. His next words startled her almost as much as the collision.

"You have beautiful eyes," he announced. "Very intelligent. And so I am puzzled."

Irene frowned. "Puzzled by what?"

"Why are you wearing such a stupid costume?" he asked, gesturing to the heavy Roman robes. "In *this* climate?"

Kungas' lips seemed to twitch. Irene thought that might be a smile. She wasn't sure.

"I grant you," he continued, "many of the Indian customs are ridiculous. But the women are quite sensible when it comes to their clothing. You would do much better to wear a sari, and leave your midriff bare."

Irene grinned. "I'm a diplomat," she explained. "Got to maintain my ambassadorial dignity. Especially since I'm a woman. Everybody looks at these absurd robes instead of me. So all they see is the Roman Empire, rather than the foreign *female*."

"Ah." Kungas nodded. "Good thinking."

"You must be on your way to the audience chamber yourself," said Irene. She cocked her head to the side. "The empress will be delighted to see you. She has missed you, I think. Although she says nothing."

Now, finally, Kungas did smile. "She never does. Lest people see the uncertain girl, instead of the ruler of Andhra."

He made a slight bow. "Envoy from Rome, I must give my report to the empress. May I escort you to the audience chamber?"

Irene bowed in return, and nodded graciously. Side by side, she and Kungas headed toward the great double doors at the end of the corridor.

From the corner of her eye, Irene studied Kungas. She was a bit fascinated by the way he moved. Silently, and surely—more like a cat than a thick, stocky man. But, mostly, she was fascinated by Kungas himself. Such a thick, hard, rigid statue, he seemed. But she had not missed the warm humor lurking inside the bronze casting, nor the intelligence.

Then, turning her eyes to the front, she gave her head a little shake.

You're the envoy from Rome, she reminded herself. For a moment, her fingers plucked at her heavy robes. *So just forget it, woman. Besides, the man can't even read.*

"How long does Rao think it will take Venandakatra to bring up the siege guns?" asked Shakuntala. The empress, seated on a plush cushion, leaned forward from her lotus position. Her brow was wrinkled, as if she were a schoolgirl straining to understand a lesson.

Irene was not fooled by Shakuntala's resemblance to a young student. *That is one very worried monarch,* she thought, watching from her vantage point against the east wall of the small audience chamber.

Irene's translator leaned over, whispering, but she stilled him with a gesture. Her Hindi had improved well enough that she was able to follow the discussion. Irene had an aptitude for languages—that skill was a necessity for a spymaster in Rome's polyglot empire—and she had been tutored by Belisarius before leaving Constantinople. In the months since her arrival at Suppara, she had been immersed in Hindi. *And* Marathi. As was true of most Indian monarchs, Shakuntala used Hindi as the court language, but Irene had begun learning the common tongue of Majarashtra as well.

"How long?" repeated the empress.

Seated easily in his own lotus position, Kungas shrugged. "It is difficult to say, Your Majesty. Many factors are involved. The siege guns were at Bharakuccha. Venandakatra has thus been forced to haul them across the Great Country. Very difficult terrain, as you know, through which to move huge war engines. And Rao has been harassing the Malwa column with his mountain fighters."

"Can he stop them?" demanded Shakuntala. "Before they can bring the guns to Deogiri?"

Kungas shook his head. As with all the man's gestures, the movement was slight—but emphatic, for all that.

"Not a chance, Your Majesty. He can slow it down, but he does not have the forces to stop it. Venandakatra has reinforced the column's escort with every spare military unit at his disposal. He cannot reduce Deogiri without those guns—and *with* them, he cannot fail. Any one of those cannons is big enough to shatter Deogiri's walls, and he has six of them."

Shakuntala winced. For a moment, Kungas' face seemed to soften. Just a tiny bit.

"There is this much, Your Majesty," he added. "The Vile One has been forced to end the punitive raids in the countryside. He cannot spare the men. Every cavalry troop he has, beyond the ones investing Deogiri, are assigned to guard the column bringing the cannons."

Shakuntala rubbed her face. For all her youth, it seemed an old, tired gesture. Venandakatra's atrocities in the Maratha countryside, Irene knew, had preyed heavily on her soul. Even by Malwa standards, Venandakatra was a beast. The man's official title was Goptri of the Deccan—the "Warden of the Marches," assigned by the Malwa emperor to subjugate his most unruly new province. But by Marathas themselves, the man was called nothing but the Vile One.

Shakuntala's face rubbing ended, within seconds. Her natural energy and assertiveness returned.

"It is up to us, then," she pronounced. "We must organize a relief column of our own."

The two Maratha cavalry officers seated next to Kungas stirred, and glanced at each other. The senior of them, a general by the name of Shahji, cleared his throat and spoke.

"I do not think that is wise, Empress. We have been able to hold Suppara, and the coast, but our forces are still not strong enough to relieve Rao at Deogiri."

"Unless we took our whole army," qualified Kondev, the other Maratha general. "But that would leave Suppara defenseless."

Shakuntala's face tightened. Kondev drove home the point:

"You have a responsibility here also, Your Majesty."

"I can't simply let Rao be destroyed!" snapped the empress. She glared angrily at the two Maratha cavalry generals.

Shakuntala's chief adviser, Dadaji Holkar, intervened. As always, the scholarly *peshwa*—"premier," Irene translated the term—spoke softly and calmly. And, as always, his tone calmed the empress.

Although, thought Irene, his words did not.

"There is the *other* alternative, Your Majesty."

Holkar's statement seemed to strike Shakuntala like a blow, or a reprimand. The young empress' face grew pinched, and Irene thought she almost recoiled.

Holkar's lips tightened, for a moment. To Irene, his eyes seemed sad.

Sad, but determined.

"If we insist, as a condition to the marriage," he continued, "I am quite certain that the Cholas will send an army. A large enough army to relieve Deogiri, without requiring us to abandon Suppara."

Holkar glanced quickly at Kungas. "At the time, I thought Kungas was unwise, to urge you to decline the offer of marriage from the Prince of Tamraparni. But his advice proved correct. The Cholas *did* make a better offer."

His gaze returned to the empress. Still sad, but still determined.

"*As you know,*" he stated, gently but emphatically. "I read you the text of their offer last week. You said that you wanted to think about it. I suggest that the time for thinking is over."

Again, Holkar glanced at Kungas. More of a lingering look, actually. Irene, watching, was puzzled by Holkar's stare. It seemed more one of anger—irritation, perhaps, and apprehensiveness—than admiration and approval. And she noticed that the empress herself was staring at Kungas rather oddly. Almost as if she were beseeching him.

For his part, Kungas returned their gazes with nothing beyond masklike imperturbability.

Something's going on here, thought Irene.

As other advisers began speaking, also urging the marriage on the empress, Irene's quick mind flitted over the situation. She knew of the Chola king's offer of his oldest son in marriage to Shakuntala. Irene had learned about it almost as soon as Shakuntala herself. The Greek spymaster had begun creating her own network of informants from the moment she arrived in India. But Irene had simply filed the information away for later consideration.

Irene had realized, weeks ago, that the subject of Shakuntala's possible dynastic marriage was a source of considerable tension in the palace. Such a marriage would produce an immediate improvement in the position of the young empress. Yet, she was obviously unhappy at the prospect, and avoided the subject whenever her advisers raised it.

At first, Irene had ascribed Shakuntala's hesitation to the natural reluctance of a strong-willed female ruler to give up any portion of her power and independence. (An attitude which Irene, given her own temperament and personality, understood perfectly.) As the weeks passed, however, Irene had decided that more was involved.

The young empress never discussed the subject, except in political and military terms, but Irene suspected that her feelings on Deogiri were personal as well. Deogiri—and, more specifically, the man who was in command of the rebel forces there.

Irene had never met Raghunath Rao, no more than she had Kungas. But Belisarius had spoken about him many times, also—and at even greater length than on the subject of Kungas. To her astonishment, Irene had eventually realized that Belisarius was a bit in awe of the man—an attitude which she had never seen the Roman general take toward anyone else in the world.

Raghunath Rao. She rolled the glamorous, exotic-sounding name over a silent tongue, her mind only half-following the enthusiastic jabberings of the junior advisers. (Every one of whom, she noted, agreed with the peshwa Dadaji Holkar. But Kungas had not spoken yet.)

The Panther of Majarashtra. The Wind of the Great Country. The national hero of the Marathas, and a legend throughout all of India. The only man who ever fought the Rajput king Rana Sanga to a draw, after an entire day spent in single combat.

Raghunath Rao. One of India's greatest assassins, among other things. The man who slaughtered—single-handedly, no less—two dozen of her captors in the Vile One's palace in order to rescue Shakuntala from captivity, after Belisarius, through a ruse, saw to the removal of Kungas and her Kushan guards.

Rao, the supreme Andhra loyalist, did so in order to rescue the legitimate heir of the dynasty. Yes, of course. But he was also rescuing the girl whom he had raised since the age of seven, after her father, the Emperor of Andhra, had placed the child in the Maratha chieftain's care. The mutual devotion between Rao and Shakuntala was something of a legend itself, by now.

To all outward appearances, it was the attachment of a young woman and her older mentor. But Irene suspected that under the surface lay much more passionate sentiments. Sentiments which were perhaps all the fiercer, for never having been spoken or acted on by either person.

The junior advisers were still jabbering, so Irene continued her ruminations. Irene had her own opinion regarding the question of Shakuntala's possible dynastic marriage. That opinion was still tentative, but it seemed to her that Shakuntala's advisers were missing—

Her thoughts broke off. Kungas was finally speaking.

"I disagree. I think this is all quite premature." His words were all the more forceful for the quiet manner in which he spoke them. Kungas' voice exuded the same sense of iron certainty as his mask of a face. "The Chola offer, as I understand it, is filled with quibbles and reservations."

Holkar began to interrupt, but Kungas drove on.

"If the empress breaks the siege of Deogiri," he stated, "and thereby proves that she can hold southern Majarashtra, there will certainly be a better offer. From someone, if not the Cholas."

Holkar threw up his hands. "*If! If!*" He lowered his hands and, with an obvious effort, brought himself under control. Irene realized that—unusually, for the mild-mannered peshwa—the man was genuinely angry.

"*If*, Kungas," he repeated, through teeth that were almost clenched. "*If*." Holkar leaned forward, slapping the rug before him emphatically. "But that is precisely the point! We do not have the troops to simultaneously relieve Deogiri and hold Suppara and the coast."

Holkar sprang to his feet and strode over to a window in the west wall. He stared out at the ocean lying beyond. From her vantage point on the opposite side of the chamber, Irene could not see the ocean itself, but she knew what the peshwa was looking at.

Malwa warships, dozens of them. Holding position, as they had for weeks, just out of range of the three great cannons protecting Suppara's harbor. Each of those warships had a large contingent of marines, ready to land at a moment's notice.

The Malwa had made no attempt to storm Suppara for months now. But in the first few weeks after Irene was smuggled through the blockade on an Axumite vessel, she had watched while they made three furious assaults. Each of those attacks had been beaten off, but it had taken the efforts of all of Shakuntala's soldiers—as well as the four hundred Ethiopian sarwen under Ezana's command—to do so.

Holkar turned away from the window. He gave Kungas a hard, stony look, before turning his eyes to Shakuntala. "Shahji and Kondev are correct, Empress. We cannot relieve the siege of Deogiri without leaving Suppara defenseless. I do not therefore see—"

"We do not have to *relieve* Deogiri," interrupted Kungas. "We simply have to destroy the siege guns."

Holkar froze. Still standing, he frowned down at Kungas.

The Kushan warrior's shoulders seemed to twitch, just a bit. Irene, learning to interpret Kungas' economical gestures, decided that was a shrug. With just a hint of irony, she thought. Perhaps some amusement.

What an interesting man. Who would have expected so much subtlety, in such an ugly lump?

"Explain, Kungas," said Shahji.

Again, Kungas' shoulders made that tiny twitch.

"I discussed the situation with Rao. The problem is not the siege itself. Rao is quite certain that he can hold Deogiri from the Vile One's army. You are Maratha, Shahji. You know how strong those walls are. Deogiri is the most impregnable city in the Great Country."

Shahji nodded. So did Kondev.

"Water is not a problem," continued Kungas. "Deogiri has its own wells. Nor is Rao concerned about starvation. Venandakatra simply doesn't have enough troops to completely seal off Deogiri. The Panther's men are all Maratha. They know the countryside, and have the support of the people there. Since the beginning of the siege, Rao has been able to smuggle food and provisions through the Vile One's lines. And he long ago smuggled out all of the civilians of the city. He only has to feed his own troops."

Kungas lifted his right hand from his knee and turned it over. "So, you see, the only problem is the actual *guns*. We don't have to relieve the siege. We simply have to destroy those guns, or capture them."

"And how will we do *that*?" demanded Holkar.

Before Kungas could respond, Kondev threw in his own objection. "And even if we do, Venandakatra will simply bring in more."

Irene hesitated. Her most basic instinct as a spymaster—*never let anyone know how much you know*—was warring with her judgement.

I'm the envoy from Rome, she reminded her instinct firmly. She leaned forward in her chair—Shakuntala had thoughtfully provided them for the Romans, knowing they were unaccustomed to sitting on cushions—and cleared her throat.

"He can't," she said firmly. "He's stripped Bharakuccha of every siege gun he has. Those cannons—there are only five of them left, Kungas, by the way; one of them was destroyed recently, falling off a cliff—are the only ones the Malwa have in the Deccan. To get more, they'd have to bring them from the Gangetic plain, across the Vindhya mountains. That would take at least a year. And Emperor Skandagupta just informed Venandakatra, in a recent letter, that the Vile One will have to rely on his own resources for a while. It seems the war in Persia is proving more difficult than the Malwa had anticipated."

She leaned back, smiling. "He was quite irate, actually. Most of his anger was directed at Belisarius, but some of it is spilling over on Venandakatra. Emperor Skandagupta does not understand, as he puts it, why the 'illustrious Goptri' is having so much difficulty subduing—as he puts it—'a handful of unruly rebels.' "

Everyone was staring at her, eyes wide open. Except Kungas, she saw. The Kushan was looking at her also, but his gaze seemed less one of surprise than—

Interest? Irene lowered her own eyes, plucking at her robes. For a moment, looking down, she caught sight of her nose.

Damn great ugly beak.

She brushed back her hair and raised her head. *Envoy from Rome*, she reminded herself firmly.

The wide-eyed stares were still there.

"Is your spy network really *that* good?" asked Holkar, a bit shakily. *"Already?* You've only been here for—"

He broke off, as if distracted by another thought.

Irene coughed. "Well . . . *Yes*, peshwa, it is that good."

She gave Shakuntala an apologetic little nod. "I was intending to give you this latest information at our next meeting, Your Majesty." The empress acknowledged the apology with a nod of her own.

Irene turned her gaze back to Kungas.

"So that objection to the Bhatasvapati's proposal is moot," she said. "But I confess that I have no idea how he intends to destroy the existing guns."

Kungas began to explain. Irene listened carefully to his plan. She was required to do so, not simply by her position as the envoy of Rome, but by the nature of the plan itself. At one point, in fact, the meeting was suspended while Irene sent for one of the Syrian gunners who had accompanied her to India, in order to clarify a technical problem.

So, throughout the long session, Irene was attentive to Kungas' proposal. But there was a part of her mind, lurking far back, which focused on the man himself.

When the session was over, and she was striding back to her rooms, she found it necessary to discipline that wayward part.

The envoy of Rome! Besides, it's absurd. I'm the world's most incorrigible bookworm, and he's an illiterate. Ugly, to boot.

◇   ◇   ◇

Not long after arriving in her quarters, a servant announced the arrival of the peshwa.

Irene put down her book, a copy of the *Periplus Maris Erythraei,* and rose to greet her visitor. She had been expecting Dadaji Holkar, and she was quite certain why he had come.

The peshwa was ushered into her chamber. The middle-aged scholar seemed awkward, and ill at ease. He began to fumble for words, staring at the floor.

"Yes, Dadaji," said Irene. "I will instruct my spies to search for your family."

Holkar's head jerked up with surprise. Then, lowered.

"I should not ask," he muttered. "It is a private matter. Not something which—"

"You did not ask," pointed out Irene. "I volunteered."

The demands of her profession had trained Irene to maintain an aloof, calculating stance toward human suffering. But, for a moment, she felt a deep empathy for the man in front of her.

Dadaji Holkar, for all the prestige of his current status as the peshwa of India's most ancient and noble dynasty, was a low-caste scribe in his origins. After the Malwa had conquered Andhra, Dadaji—and his whole family—had been sold into slavery. Belisarius had purchased Holkar while he was in India, in order to use the man's literary skills to advance his plot against Venandakatra. In the end, Holkar had been instrumental in effecting Shakuntala's escape and had become her closest adviser.

But his family—his wife, son, and two daughters—were still in captivity. Somewhere in the vastness of Malwa India.

It was typical of Holkar, she thought, that he would even hesitate to ask for a personal favor. Most Indian officials—most officials of *any* country, in her experience—took personal favors as a matter of due course.

She smiled, brushing back her hair. "It's not a problem, Dadaji. It will be an opportunity, actually. To begin with, it'll give my spies a challenge. The Malwa run an excellent espionage service, but they have grown too confident and sure of themselves. Quite easy to penetrate, actually. Whereas finding a few Maratha slaves, scattered across India, will test their skills."

She pursed her lips, thinking for a moment, before adding: "And there's more. I've been thinking, anyway, that we should start probing the sentiments of the lower classes in Malwa India. A very good way to do that is to have my spies scouring India looking for some Maratha slaves."

"Can you find them?" he asked, in a whisper.

"I can promise you nothing, Dadaji. But I will try."

He nodded, and left. Irene returned to her chair. But she had not read more than a page of the *Periplus* when the servant announced another visitor.

The Bhatasvapati was here.

Irene rose again. She was interested—and a bit annoyed—to find that her emotions were unsettled. She was even more interested—and not annoyed at all—to realize that she had no idea why Kungas had come.

I like surprises. I get so few of them.

When Kungas came into her chamber, Irene got her first surprise. As soon as he entered, he glanced over his shoulder and said: "I saw Dadaji leaving, just a minute ago. I don't think he even noticed me, he seemed so preoccupied."

Kungas swiveled his head back to face her. "He came to speak to you about his family," he stated. "To ask you for your help in finding them."

Irene's eyes narrowed. "How did you know?"

Kungas made the little shoulder-twitch which served him for a shrug. "There are only two reasons he would come here, right after the session in the imperial audience chamber. That is one of them. Like everyone else, he was impressed by your spy network."

"And the other reason?"

Kungas seemed to be examining her carefully. "The other reason would be to discuss with you the question of Empress Shakuntala's marriage prospects. He is much concerned with that subject, and would want to enlist the support of the Roman envoy."

Kungas' looked away for a moment, in a quick scrutiny of the chamber. The furniture he gave no more than a glance, but his gaze lingered on a chest in the corner. The lid was open, and he could see that it was full of books.

When his eyes returned to Irene, she thought there was some impish humor lurking within them.

She got her second surprise.

"But I knew that couldn't be it. He would not have left so soon. You do not agree with him, I think, and so he would have stayed to argue."

"How do you know my opinion?" she demanded.

Again, the little shoulder-twitch. "It is—not obvious, no. Nothing about you is obvious. But I do not think you agree that the empress should make a dynastic marriage with one of the independent south Indian monarchies."

Irene studied Kungas for a moment, in silence.

"No, I don't," she said slowly. "I am not certain of my opinion yet, mind you. But I think . . . " She hesitated.

Kungas held up his hand. "Please! I am not prying, envoy from Rome. We can discuss this matter at a later time, when you think it more suitable. For the moment—"

A very faint smile came to his lips. "Let me just say that I suspect you look at the thing as I do. A monarch should marry the power which can uphold the throne. And so the thing is obvious—to any but these idiot Indians, with their absurd fetishes."

Irene suppressed her little start of surprise. But Kungas' eyes were knowing.

"So I thought," he murmured. "Very smart woman."

He turned away, heading for the door. "But that is not why I came," he said. "A moment, please. My servant is carrying something for me."

Irene watched while Kungas took something from the servant who appeared in the doorway. When he turned back, she got her third surprise. Kungas was carrying a stack of books.

He held them out to her. "Can you read these?"

Hesitantly, Irene took the top book and opened it. She began to scan the first page. Then stopped, frowning.

"This isn't Greek," she muttered. "I thought it was, but—"

"The lettering is Greek," explained Kungas. "When we Kushans conquered Bactria, long ago, we adopted the Greek alphabet. But the language is my own."

He fumbled with the stack of books, drawing out a slim volume buried in the middle.

"This might help," he said. "It is a bilingual translation of some of the Buddha's teachings. Half-Greek; half-Kushan." His lips twitched. "Or so my friend Dadaji tells me. He can read the Greek part. I can't read any of it. I am not literate."

Irene set the first book down on a nearby table and took the one in Kungas' outstretched hand. She began studying the volume. After a few seconds, without being conscious of the act, she moved over to her chair and sat down. As ever, with true bibliophiles, the act of reading had drawn her completely out of her immediate surroundings.

Two minutes later, she remembered Kungas. Looking up, she saw that the Kushan was still standing in the middle of the room, watching her.

"I'm sorry," she said. She waved her hand at a nearby chair.

Kungas shook his head. "I am quite comfortable, thank you." He pointed to the book. "What do you think?"

Irene looked down at the volume in her lap. "I *could*, yes." She looked up. "But why should I? It will be a considerable effort."

Kungas nodded. Then, slowly, he moved over to the one window in her room and stared out at the ocean. The window was open, letting in the cooling breeze.

"It is difficult to explain," he said, speaking as slowly as he had moved. He fell silent for a few seconds, before turning back to her rather abruptly.

"Do you believe there is such a thing as a soul?" he asked.

Somehow, the question did not surprise her. "Yes," she replied instantly. "I do."

Kungas fingered his wispy beard. "I am not so sure, myself." He stared back through the window. "But I have been listening to my friend Dadaji, this past year, and he has half convinced me that it exists."

Again, Kungas fell silent. Irene waited. She was not impatient. Not at all.

When Kungas spoke again, his voice was very low. "So I have decided to search for my soul, to see if I have one. But a man with a soul must look to the future, and not simply live in the present."

He turned his eyes back to her. He had attractive eyes, Irene thought. Almond colored, as they were almond shaped. Such a contrast, when you actually studied them, to the dull armor of his features. The eyes were very clear, and very bright. There was life dancing in those eyes, gaily, far in the background.

"I have never done that before," he explained. "Always, I lived simply in the present. But now—for some months, now—I have found myself thinking about the future."

His gaze drifted around the room, settling on a chair not far from Irene's own. He moved over and sat in it.

"I have been thinking about Peshawar," he mused. "That was the capital of our Kushan kingdom, long ago. It is nothing but ruins, today. But I have decided that I would like to see it restored, after Malwa is broken."

"You are so confident of breaking Malwa?" asked Irene. As soon as she spoke the words, she realized they were more of a question about Kungas than they were about the prospects of war.

Kungas nodded. "Oh, yes. Quite certain." His masklike face made that little cracking movement which did for a smile. "I am *not* so certain, of course, that I myself will live to see it. But there is no point in planning for one's own death. So I keep my thoughts on Peshawar."

He studied her carefully. "But to restore Peshawar, I would have to be a king myself. So I have decided to become one. After the fall of Malwa, Shakuntala will no longer need me. I will be free to attend to the needs of my own Kushan people."

Irene swallowed. Her throat seemed dry. "I think you would make a good king," she said, a bit huskily.

Kungas nodded. "I have come to the same conclusion." He leaned forward, pointing to the volume in her lap. "But a king should know how to read—certainly his own language!—and I am illiterate."

He leaned back, still-faced. "So now you understand."

Again, Irene swallowed. "You want me to learn Kushan, so that I can teach you how to read it."

Kungas smiled. "And some other languages. I should also, I think, know how to read Greek. And Hindi."

Abruptly, Irene stood up and went to a table against the wall. She poured some wine from an amphora into a cup, and took a swallow.

Without words, she offered a cup to Kungas. He shook his head. Irene poured herself another drink.

After finishing that second cup, she stared at the wall in front of her.

"Most men," she said harshly, "do not like to learn from a woman. And learning to read is not easy, Kungas, not for a grown man. You will make many mistakes. You will be frustrated. You will resent my instructions, and my corrections. You will resent—me."

She listened for the answer, not turning her head.

"Most men," said Kungas softly, "have a small soul. That, at least, is what my friend Dadaji tells me, and he is a scholar. So I have decided, since I want to be a king, that I must have a large soul. Perhaps even a great one."

Silence. Irene's eyes were fixed on the wall. It was a blank wall, with not so much as a tapestry on it.

"I will teach you to read," she said. "I will need a week, to begin learning your language. After that, we can begin."

She heard the faint sounds of a chair scraping. Kungas was getting up.

"We will have some time, then," came his voice from behind her. "Before I have to leave on the expedition to destroy the guns."

Silence. Irene did not move her eyes from the wall, not even after she heard Kungas going toward the door. He did not make much sound, as quietly as he moved. Odd, really, for such a thick-looking man.

From the doorway, she heard his voice.

"I thank you, envoy from Rome."

"My name is Irene," she said. Harshly. Coldly.

She did not miss the softness in Kungas' voice. Or the warmth. "Yes, I know. But I have decided it is a beautiful name, and so I did not wish to use it without your permission."

"You have my permission." Her voice was still harsh, and cold. The arrogant voice of a Greek noblewoman, bestowing a minor favor on an inferior. Silently, she cursed that voice.

"Thank you . . . Irene."

A few faint sounds of footsteps came. He was gone.

Irene finally managed to tear her eyes away from the wall. She started to pour herself another cup of wine, but stopped the motion midway. With a firm hand, she placed the cup back on the table and strode to the window.

Leaning on the ledge, she stared out at the ocean, breathing deeply. She remained there for some time, motionless, until the sunset.

Then, moving back to her chair, she took up the slim volume and began studying her new-found task. She spent the entire evening there, and got her final surprise of the day. For the first time in years, she was not able to concentrate on a book.

Chapter 7

PERSIA

Spring, 532 A.D.

"You're right, Maurice," said Belisarius, lowering his telescope. "They're *not* going to make a frontal assault."

Maurice grunted. The sound combined satisfaction with regret. Satisfaction, that his assessment had proven correct. Regret, because he wished it were otherwise.

The chiliarch examined the fieldworks below them. From the rise where he and Belisarius were standing, the Roman entrenchments were completely bare to the eye. But from the slope below, where the Rajput cavalry was massed, they would have been almost invisible.

Almost, but not quite. Again, he grunted. This time, the noise conveyed nothing but regret. "Beautiful defenses," he growled. "Damn near perfect. Pure killing ground, once they got into it." His gaze scanned the mountainous terrain around them. "Doesn't look like too bad a slope, not from below. And this is the only decent pass within miles."

Belisarius' eyes followed those of Maurice. This stretch of the Zagros range was not high, measured in sheer altitude, but it was exceptionally rugged. There was little vegetation on the slopes, and those slopes themselves, for all their rocky nature, were slick

531

and muddy from the spring runoff. Little rills and streams could be seen everywhere.

Impossible terrain, for cavalry—except for the one pass in which Belisarius had positioned his army. He had designed his defenses carefully, making sure that their real strength was not visible from the plateau below.

The temptation, for an enemy commander, would be almost overwhelming. A powerful, surging charge—clear the pass—the road to Mesopotamia and its riches would lie wide open. The only alternative would be to continue the grueling series of marches and countermarches which had occupied both the Roman and the Malwa armies for the past several weeks.

Almost overwhelming—for any but the best commanders. Like the ones who, unfortunately, commanded the Malwa forces ranged against them.

"You were right," Belisarius pronounced again. He cocked an eye at his chief subordinate, and smiled his crooked smile. "Think I've gotten sloppy, do you, from dealing with those Malwa thick-heads in Mesopotamia?"

Maurice scowled. "I wasn't criticizing, General. It was a good plan. Worth a try. But I didn't think Sanga would fall for it. Lord Damodara might have, on his own. Maybe. But it's been obvious enough, the past month, that he listens to Sanga."

Belisarius nodded. For a moment, his eyes were drawn to a pavilion on the plateau below. The structure was visible to the naked eye. But, even through a telescope, it wasn't much to see.

For two days now, while the Malwa army gathered its forces below the pass, Belisarius had scrutinized that pavilion through his telescope. The distance was too great to discern individual features, but Belisarius had spotted Sanga almost immediately. The Rajput king was one of the tallest men Belisarius had ever met, and he had no doubt of the identity of the towering figure that regularly came and went from the pavilion. Nor of the identity of the short, pudgy man who often emerged from it in Sanga's company.

That would be Lord Damodara, the top commander of the Malwa army in the plateau. One of the *anvaya-prapta sachivya*, as the Malwa called the hereditary caste that dominated their empire. Blood kin to Emperor Skandagupta himself.

From the moment Belisarius had first seen that pavilion, he had been struck by it. It was nothing fancy, nothing elaborate, and, by

Malwa standards, positively austere. The structure was completely unlike the grotesque cotton-and-silk palace which Emperor Skandagupta had erected at the siege of Ranapur. And Belisarius was quite certain that Lord Venandakatra, the anvaya-prapta sachivya whom the Roman general knew best, would have disdained to use it for anything other than a latrine.

Beyond the nature of the pavilion itself, Belisarius had been just as struck—more so, perhaps—by the use to which it was put. In his past experience, Malwa headquarters were the scenes of great pomp and ceremony. Such pavilions—or palaces, or luxury barges—were invariably surrounded by a host of elite bodyguards. Visitors who arrived were accompanied by their own resplendent entourages, and with great fanfare.

Great fanfare. Kettledrums, heralds, banners—even trained animals, prancing their way before the mighty Lords and Ladies of Malwa.

Not Damodara's pavilion. There had been a steady stream of visitors to that utilitarian structure, true enough. But they were obviously officers—Rajputs, in the main, with the occasional Ye-tai or kshatriya—and they invariably arrived either alone or in small groups. Not a bodyguard to be seen, except for the handful posted before the pavilion itself. And those—for a moment, Belisarius was tempted to use his telescope again, to study the soldiers standing guard before Damodara's pavilion. But there would be no point. He would simply see the same thing he had seen for the past two days. The thing which had impressed him most about that pavilion.

Rajput guards—always. Never Ye-tai. That single, simple fact had told him more than anything else.

The Ye-tai were barbarians. Half a century earlier, they had erupted into the plains of north India and begun conquering the region, as they had already done with the Kushan territories to the northwest. But when they came up against the newly rising Malwa realm, an offshoot of the collapsing Gupta Empire, their advance was brought to a halt. Already, Belisarius now knew, the being from the future called Link had armed the Malwa with gunpowder technology. With their rockets, cannons, and grenades, the Malwa had defeated the Ye-tai. But then, instead of simply subjugating the barbarians, the Malwa had incorporated them into their own power structure. Had, in fact, given them a prized and prestigious place—just below that of the anvaya-prapta sachivya themselves. Ye-tai clan chiefs had even been allowed to marry into the elite castes.

The move was extraordinarily shrewd, commented Aide, **and quite beyond the capacity of normal Hindu rulers to even envision. The instructions must have come from Link itself. The Ye-tai are not part of the caste-and-class structure of Hindu society—what Indians themselves call the varna system. By giving such heathen barbarians a place in the elite, Link has provided a powerful and reliable Praetorian guard for the Malwa dynasty which is its creature.**

Mentally, Belisarius nodded his agreement. That was how the Malwa invariably used their Ye-tai forces. The barbarians were ferocious warriors in their own right. But the Malwa, instead of using them as spearhead troops, used them as security and control battalions.

Except—for Damodara.

Again, Belisarius made that mental nod. Damodara had placed his Ye-tai contingents with his fighting forces, and relied solely on Rajputs for his own protection. The Rajputs were treasured by the Malwa for their military skills, just as was true of their Kushan vassals. But they were not trusted.

Except by Damodara, Aide, just as you say. The Rajputs form the bulk of his army, and he's obviously decided to weld them to himself by giving them his final trust.

Belisarius sighed, faintly. *All of which tells me a great deal. None of which I'm happy to know.*

This had been Belisarius' first opportunity to study his opponent at close hand. Roman and Malwa contingents had clashed several times in the weeks which had elapsed since his narrow escape from the ambush at the oasis, but the forces involved had been small. For the most part, the Romans and the Malwa had kept their distance, as each army tried to outmaneuver the other through the labyrinth of the Zagros range.

The Romans had had the best of it, in a narrow sense. Belisarius was simply trying to block the Malwa from passing through the Zagros onto the open plain of Mesopotamia. He had succeeded in doing so, true. But Damodara and Sanga handled their own forces extremely well. They had not dislodged the Romans blocking their way, but they had, slowly, succeeded in forcing them back.

The Zagros was a wide range, but it was not inexhaustible. Sooner or later, Belisarius would run out of room to maneuver. So he had decided to fight a battle on his own chosen terrain. If he could badly bloody the Malwa, he would gain more time—possibly even regain some lost ground.

Against the normal run of Malwa commanders, his plan would have worked. Against Damodara, and his Rajputs, it had failed. Just as Maurice had predicted.

Belisarius raised his telescope and studied Damodara's pavilion, trying to discern anything inside the dark interior. It was a vain enterprise, more born from habit than anything else.

But, suddenly and surprisingly, Aide spoke urgent words. **There's a telescope in there! I can just barely make it out.**

Belisarius focused his own eyesight, but even with Aide's help he could not see the telescope which was apparently hidden within the pavilion. He was not surprised, however. Aide could often detect things through Belisarius' eyes which the general himself could not.

Big, clumsy damned thing, came Aide's mental sniff.

Still—nothing. Belisarius knew that Aide was using his own crystalline version of what the "jewel" called *computer image enhancement.*

Is this important? asked Aide.

In and of itself—not especially. If that telescope's as big and awkward as you say, it's not going to be much of a help on the battlefield. But the fact that Damodara has one is interesting, nonetheless. It's a reminder to us not to underestimate the Malwa.

Belisarius folded up his telescope. As so often before, in doing so, he was struck by the clever design of John of Rhodes' device. But, for all that, his motion was sharp and decisive.

"That's it, then," he announced, turning away. "Pass the word, Maurice. We'll leave a unit here on guard, but get the army ready for another march." He gestured with his head toward the enemy below. "They'll be moving out themselves, sometime tonight. Make sure Abbu and his scouts are close enough to see which route they take."

"Won't be very close," replied Maurice grimly. "Not with Rajput flankers."

Belisarius began striding toward his own tent, some fifty yards down the trail. Over his shoulder, he said, "I'm well aware of that.

Just close enough, Maurice, that's all. Just close enough. If that army ever breaks contact with us, we'll be in a sea of trouble."

A few steps away, hearing the exchange, Valentinian scowled.

"I was afraid this was going to happen. God, I'm sick of marching." He cast a half-hoping, half-skeptical eye at the Malwa army on the plateau below. "You think if I tried taunting them again—?"

Next to him, Anastasius snorted sarcastically. "And just what do you think that'll accomplish? Besides making you look like an idiot? *Again.*"

Two miles away, at the entrance to his pavilion, Lord Damodara straightened up from his own telescope. Then, feeling the usual ache, the Malwa general grimaced. "Wish I had one of *his* telescopes," he grumbled.

Standing next to him, Rana Sanga cast a glance at the optical device in question. The Malwa telescope, quite unlike the slender, handheld artifact which he had seen in Belisarius' hands, was an ungainly thing. As in many areas—steelmaking was one outstanding exception—Indian craftsmanship was not the equal of Greek. The Malwa approach to optics was much like their approach to shipbuilding: *Since we can't make it elegant, we'll make it big and sturdy.*

Big and sturdy the Malwa telescope certainly was. So big, unfortunately, that it had to be supported on a rigid framework which could only be adjusted with great difficulty. The end result was that anyone who used the thing was forced to stoop in an awkward posture which, after a period of time, invariably resulted in back pain.

For a moment, Sanga was tempted to point out that Damodara, as short as he was, suffered less from the problem than did Sanga himself. But he restrained the impulse. Lord Damodara maintained an easy and informal bearing around his top subordinates, but he *was* anvaya-prapta sachivya. There were limits.

Instead, he opted for the bright side. "It's a better telescope than he has," he pointed out. "At least as far as its strength goes."

Judging from his snort, Damodara was not mollified.

"And so what?" he demanded. He gestured through the open flap of the pavilion. "So I can discern his features, where he can't mine. On the rare occasions when he happens to wander into my field of view, that is. While he, for his part, can look anywhere he wants. *Without* breaking his spine in the process."

Damodara rubbed his back, still grimacing. "I'd trade with him in a minute! And so would you, Rana Sanga—so stop trying to cheer me up."

Sanga said nothing. After a few seconds, Damodara stopped scowling. The young Malwa lord's innate good humor returned.

"There's this much," Damodara said cheerfully. "I'm quite sure he doesn't know we have a telescope. We didn't have them when he was in India, and I'm positive he hasn't spotted mine." He glanced around his headquarters. The telescope was positioned ten feet inside the entrance, well within the gloom of his pavilion's interior. Damodara had kept it there at all times, despite the limited field of view which the position provided, precisely in order to keep Belisarius from spotting the device.

For an instant, the scowl returned. "I'm not sure that makes any difference, of course. But—" He shrugged. "With Belisarius, I'll take any advantage I can get."

Damodara turned away from the telescope and moved toward the large table located at the very center of the pavilion. Sanga, without being asked, immediately followed.

At the edge of the table, Damodara planted his pudgy hands and leaned over, intently examining the huge vellum map which covered most of it. His gaze, now, was one of satisfaction rather than disgruntlement. Whatever they lacked in optical craftsmanship, no one could fault the skill of Malwa mapmakers. He was especially pleased with the topographical information which his chief cartographer managed to include.

Damodara peered into a corner of the dimly lit pavilion. As always, his cartographer was waiting patiently, seated on a small cushion. Narses was also in the corner, available in case Damodara needed his advice. The eunuch, following Roman custom, sat in a chair.

"It is up to date, Lord Damodara," said the mapmaker. "Just this morning, I incorporated the latest information brought in by the Pathans."

Damodara nodded, and turned back to the map. For a time, he was silent, examining the terrain shown thereon. At his side, Rana Sanga did the same. Then, Lord Damodara reached out and placed his finger on a location some fifteen miles to the south.

"There, perhaps?" he asked. "Judging from the map, it seems like an obscure pass. Very narrow, but it might be enough."

Sanga studied the pass in question for a moment, before shaking his head. The gesture was more one of slow consideration, however, than firm judgement. "I don't think so, Lord." He hesitated, tugging at his rich beard. "I am not sure of this, you understand, but it seems to me that Belisarius has been especially keen to thwart us from making any headway to the *south*. I suspect that he already has scouts watching the approaches to that pass."

Damodara looked up, his eyes widening. He seemed slightly startled.

"To the south—*especially*? I hadn't—" He frowned, thinking; then, chuckled ruefully. "It seemed more to me that he was thwarting us *anywhere* we went."

Sanga's shoulders lifted in a small shrug. "That is true, Lord. But I still think that he has been quickest of all to prevent us from going south."

Damodara spread his hands on the table, staring at the map. It was obvious to Sanga, watching the movement of his eyes, that Damodara was retracing every step of the past month's maneuvers.

"I think you're right," he murmured, after a minute or two. Damodara straightened up, staring now at the bare leather of the pavilion wall across from him.

"Why is that, do you think?" he mused thoughtfully. His gaze turned to Sanga. "It doesn't make any sense. What difference does it make, whether we bypass him to the north or the south? So long as he can keep us from making westward progress, he keeps us out of Mesopotamia. Tied up here, in these miserable mountains."

Damodara's eyes returned to the map. "If anything," he added slowly, "I would think he'd prefer to maneuver us south. That way he can keep us following the Zagros range—all the way to the Gulf." He pointed to the southern reaches of the mountains shown on the map. "In the end, we might find ourselves emerging into Mesopotamia down at the delta. Near Charax."

He laughed sarcastically. "Where he already has our main army bottled up! With Emperor Khusrau and his lancers to keep the cork in the bottle."

Sanga's beard-tugging grew more vigorous. "There *is* one possible explanation. Especially dealing with Belisarius."

Lord Damodara cocked his head, peering up at the tall Rajput next him. "A trap," he stated. Sanga nodded.

Damodara began pacing back and forth slowly. His hands, in one of the Malwa lord's characteristic gestures, were clasped in front of him as if he were in prayer. But the short, jabbing, back-and-forth motion of the hands conveyed concentration rather than piety.

"You could be right," he mused. A sudden bark—half-humorous, half-exasperated. "Subtle bait! But that is the way the man thinks."

Damodara suddenly stopped his pacing and turned to face Sanga squarely. "What do you advise?" he demanded.

Sanga stopped his beard-tugging, and took a deep breath.

"Go north," he said firmly. "It may be a trap, Lord Damodara. He may be laying an ambush for us. But traps can be turned against the trapper. A trap designed for a wolf will not necessarily hold a tiger. Our troops are excellent, and our army outnumbers his by two-to-one."

Damodara nodded. "Closer to three-to-one, I think." The Malwa lord's eyes grew a bit vacant. Again, his hands were clasped before him in the gesture of prayer. But there was no emphatic jabbing, this time. The hands were still, except for a slight flexing of the fingers.

Sanga, recognizing the signs, waited. As usual, Damodara did not take long to make his decision.

"I agree," the Lord said firmly. "We will go north." He barked another laugh. "With our eyes wide open! And—"

There was a sudden commotion at the entrance to the pavilion. Damodara and Sanga turned. They saw that two of the Lord's Rajput guards were barring the way of a Ye-tai who, for his part, was expressing his anger in no uncertain terms.

It was General Mihirakula, the commander of Damodara's Ye-tai troops.

"Let him in!" called out Damodara. The guards stepped aside, and Mihirakula stormed into the pavilion. He cast an angry glance at Rana Sanga before coming to a halt in front of Lord Damodara.

"What is this nonsense I hear?" demanded Mihirakula. "I was just informed by one of your"—another angry glance at Sanga—"Rajput dispatch riders that we are to make preparations for a march. *Is this true?*"

The question was obviously rhetorical. Mihirakula did not wait for an answer before gesturing angrily at the mountains visible through the open flap of the pavilion.

"Why are we not charging the stinking Romans?" he demanded. "We will brush them aside like flies!" Again, Mihirakula glared at Sanga. "If the Rajputs are too fearful, then my Ye-tai will lead the way!"

The Ye-tai general was a big man, heavy in the shoulders and thick in the chest, but Sanga was as much taller than he as Mihirakula was than Damodara. The Rajput drew himself up to his full towering height. His hands were clasped tightly behind his back, but it was obvious from the tension in Sanga's powerful arms that he was barely controlling his anger.

Damodara intervened quickly. He placed a slight, restraining hand on Sanga. To the Ye-tai general, he stated firmly: "The orders were mine, General Mihirakula." Damodara made his own gesture toward the mountains. "The Roman fieldworks here are too powerful. *But*," he added, overriding the Ye-tai's gathering splutter of protest, "my scouts tell me that we may find a way to the north."

Again, he overrode Mihirakula's protest. This time, saying with a cheerful smile: "The scouts think there will be opposition, of course. So I was thinking of using you and your men as my vanguard element in the next march."

The smile Damodara was bestowing on Mihirakula was positively a beam, now. "To clear the way for us, of course. So that we can finally be done with these damned mountains."

Mihirakula relaxed, a bit. He glanced at Sanga, once again, before replying to Damodara. But the glance had more of satisfaction in it than anger.

"Soon, do you think? My men are very restless."

Damodara shrugged. "Soon enough. Within a week, I imagine." He made a little, apologetic grimace. "Marching through these mountains, as you know, is not a quick business."

All apology and goodwill vanished. Damodara's next words were spoken in a tone of steel: "And *now*, General Mihirakula, you will carry out my commands. *At once*."

The Ye-tai commander knew that tone. For all his barbarous nature, Mihirakula was not a fool. He bowed his head, stiffly, and departed from the pavilion.

After he was gone, Sanga let out a short, angry grunt. "My Rajputs can lead—" he began, but Damodara waved him silent.

"I am well aware of that, Sanga. But the Ye-tai *are* getting restless." He gave Sanga a shrewd glance. "So are your Rajputs, for that matter, even if they control their impatience better."

Damodara pointed at the map. His finger made little wandering gestures, as if retracing the tortuous route of the past weeks. "Good soldiers grow impatient with this kind of endless maneuvering. Sooner or later, they will demand action. You know that as well as I do."

Grudgingly, Sanga nodded.

Damodara spread his hands. "So let the Ye-tai lead the way, for now. If there is a trap, they will spring it. To be frank, I'd rather see them bloodied than you."

It was plain enough, from the look on his face, that Sanga found his commander's cold-bloodedness distasteful. But Damodara took no offense. He simply chuckled.

"I am Malwa, Rana Sanga, not Rajput. *Practical.*"

Two days later, Belisarius was studying a map spread across a table in his own field headquarters. All of his top commanders were joining him in the enterprise. Those included, in addition to Maurice and Vasudeva: Cyril, who had succeeded Agathius in command of the Greek cataphracts after Agathius had been crippled at the Battle of the Nehar Malka; and Bouzes and Coutzes, the two young Thracian brothers who commanded the Syrian contingents in Belisarius' army.

Abbu entered, pushing his way through the leather flaps which served as an entrance. The chief of Belisarius' Arab scouts did not wait for an invitation to speak before advancing to the center of the tent and giving his report.

The old bedouin did not give the map so much as a glance. Abbu was a stern traditionalist. Despite his deep (if unspoken) admiration for Belisarius, the Arab considered the map an alarming omen—either of the Roman general's early senility, or of his rapid descent into modern decadence.

"The Malwa are heading north," he announced, "toward that saddle pass I told you about. It is obvious they are expecting an ambush. They have their Ye-tai contingents leading the way." Abbu grunted approvingly. "He's no fool, that Malwa commander. He'll feed the barbarians into the fire—good riddance—before following through with his Rajputs."

"Before *trying* to follow through," said Cyril.

Abbu shook his head. The bedouin's countenance, always dour, grew positively gloomy. "They will succeed. The pass is too wide, and the slopes on either side not steep enough. The north slope is especially shallow. They will be able to use their numbers against us. It won't be easy, but they'll force their way through."

Cyril began to bridle at the Arab's easy assumption of defeat, but Belisarius intervened.

"That's just as well," he stated forcefully. "I *want* to steer them north. So we'll put up a stiff resistance at the pass itself, but withdraw before our men get mangled." He bent over, studying the map; then pointed with his finger.

"If this is accurate, once they get through the pass their easiest route will be to follow this small river to the northwest." He cocked an eye at Abbu. The Arab scowled fiercely, but said nothing—which was his way of admitting that the newfangled absurdity could not be faulted.

Belisarius kept his eye on Abbu. "And if I'm reading this map correctly," he added, "when we fall back and set our positions *southwest* of the pass, our fieldworks will be too strong for the Malwa to take any other direction."

Abbu's scowl deepened. But, again, he said nothing.

"If you don't want to hold the pass, general," asked Bouzes, frowning, "then why even put up a fight at all? Seems like a waste of good soldiers." The young Thracian did not bother to add: *which is not your usual style*. Like all of the men in that tent, he had become very familiar with Belisarius' tactical methods. One of those methods—a very important one—was to be sparing with his men's lives, whenever possible.

Belisarius shook his head. "I don't have any choice, Bouzes. I can't afford to make it *too* easy, not for commanders like Damodara and Sanga. If we fight like lions whenever they move south, but stand aside when they move north, they'll start to wonder why. Doesn't make sense. Strict military logic would be the other way around—I should be more than happy to steer them down the Zagros, toward Pars." He winced. "I do *not* want Sanga and Damodara spending much time contemplating my bad logic."

Maurice interrupted. His own expression did not exude any great happiness. "They're probably already doing that," he growled.

Belisarius heaved a sigh. "Yes, I'm sure they are. But as long as they don't think too much about the qanats, and don't know about the Kushans, I think we'll be all right."

He cast a quick glance at the helmet which Vasudeva had placed upon the table. As always, the Kushan had removed the detested monstrosity as soon as he entered the tent and was safe from spying eyes. Belisarius' expression resumed its usual calm serenity. He even managed a crooked smile.

"My plan *is*, after all," he said cheerfully, "a bit on the crazed side."

That announcement did not seem to bring any great cheer to the other men in the tent. But they did not protest—not, at least, beyond thinking private dark thoughts. Those men were all very familiar with Belisarius' tactical principles and methods. Many of those methods struck them as bizarre, but not the one which—*always*—stood at the very center.

Win the war. That's all that matters.

Chapter 8

AXUM

Spring, 532 A.D.

Eon's regimental ceremony did not take place until days after the bombing of the Ta'akha Maryam. Initially, the prince had insisted on doing it at once. But calmer voices—older ones, at least—prevailed.

Foremost among those voices had been that of Wahsi, the commander of the regiment itself.

"There is no time now, King of Kings," he insisted.

"I am not the negusa nagast!" roared Eon. "I cannot be—not until I am accepted into the Dakuen sarwe!"

The prince—king, now; his father and brother's corpses had already been found—rose from his labors. Eon had worked through the night, along with his soldiers and most of Axum's populace, clearing away the rubble and debris. It was now mid-morning of the next day, and there was still much work to be done. The royal quarters themselves had been excavated, but the Malwa explosives had shattered well over a third of the great complex. Hundreds of corpses had been found, and as many survivors. The rescue workers could hear the faint moans of a few victims who were still alive, buried beneath the stones.

Wahsi placed a gentle hand on Eon's shoulder. "The Dakuen can wait, King."

The Dakuen commander gestured with his head, indicating the knot of soldiers standing just a few feet behind him. Those men were all of the officers of the regiment, other than the ones who were with Ezana in India. "None of us are concerned about the matter."

Hearing Wahsi's words, the regimental officers growled their agreement. Several of them glanced at the figure of Ousanas. The dawazz was just a few yards away, oblivious to the exchange. He was too busy pulling away stones.

Not even Eon failed to miss the obvious approval in those glances.

"There is no need," repeated Wahsi softly. Then, very softly, in words only Eon could hear: "No need, Eon. There is no question of the regiment's approval of Ousanas, and you."

Wahsi chuckled but, again, so softly that only Eon could hear. "They will have harsh words to say, of course, about the hunter's ridiculous philosophies, and will relish every detail of your childhood follies. But that is just tradition." He cast a glance at the distant figure of Antonina, who was directing her own soldiers in the rescue operation. All of the Roman troops had survived the explosion, and they had immediately pitched into the work. "They are especially looking forward to hearing about all the times Ousanas was forced to slap you silly, until you finally learned not to ogle the wife of Belisarius."

Eon managed a smile. It wasn't much of a smile, but Wahsi was still relieved to see it. For just a fleeting instant, Eon's was the face of a young man again. For hours, since the bodies of Zaia and Tarabai had been found, his face had been that of an old man broken with grief. Zaia had been his concubine since Eon was thirteen years old. If the passion had faded, some, from their relationship, he had still loved her deeply. And he had been almost besotted with Tarabai, since he met her in India.

"You lost everyone yesterday, Eon," said Wahsi gently. "Your women and your only child, along with your father and brother. No man in the world—prince or peasant, it matters not—can think clearly at such a time, or deal with anything beyond his grief. So let us simply concentrate on the work before us. There will be time, soon enough, for the ceremony."

He stepped back a pace, and raised his voice slightly.

"For the moment, you are the negusa nagast. That is the opinion of the Dakuen sarwe, as well as the Lazen and the Hadefan."

Wahsi gestured toward two of the officers in the cluster. They were named Aphilas and Saizana and were, respectively, the commanders of the Lazen and the Hadefan sarwe. The Lazen had been the regiment of Kaleb; the Hadefan, that of Wa'zeb. Along with the Dakuen, they constituted the current royal regiments of the Ethiopian army.

"That is correct, King," said Aphilas. Saizana nodded, adding: "And we have spoken to all of the other sarawit. The soldiers are of one mind on this matter. All of them."

Then, almost in a snarl: "We will have our vengeance on Malwa. And you are the King of Kings who will lead us to it."

Eon wiped his face with a hand, smearing dirt and rock dust. It was a weary, weary gesture. "How is Garmat?" he asked. "Will he survive?"

Wahsi broke into a smile of his own. And not a thin one, either.

"Be serious, King! If twenty great stones falling on that old Arab brigand couldn't kill him outright, do you really think he would die of lingering wounds?"

One of the officers—an older man, well into his fifties—laughed. "I remember when we were chasing that bandit through the desert, years ago. Never could catch him, no matter how many ambushes we laid."

Another officer, also middle-aged, grinned. "Personally, I think he's malingering. Lazy half-breed! Just doesn't want to haul stones."

A little laugh swept the small crowd. Even Eon joined in the humor, for a moment.

Finding Garmat had been the only brightness in a long, dark night. The adviser had apparently been standing some distance away from the throne, when the bombs went off. The Malwa saboteurs, of course, had set the main charges in the walls near the throne itself. When the explosion took place, King Kaleb and all of the people in his immediate vicinity—including his oldest son and heir, Wa'zeb—had been pulverized by the great blast. The rest of the people in the throne room, except for Garmat and a servant, had been crushed by the falling roof and walls. But, by a freak of fortune, some of the Ta'akha Maryam's great stones, in their collapse, had formed a sort of shelter for Garmat and the servant. The servant, in fact, had been almost unharmed, other than being frightened half out of her wits. Garmat's injuries had been severe—several broken bones, along with innumerable bruises and lacerations—but his life had been spared.

The news of Garmat's survival, as it spread, brought cheer to everyone—especially to the sarwen. Partly, that was due to fondness for the man himself. King Kaleb's rule had been good, so far as the people of Axum were concerned. Much of that they ascribed to the sage, and usually gentle, advice of Garmat.

But, mostly, the news brought cheer to the soldiers laboring in the wreckage because it stirred flame in their fierce hearts. The sarwen had not forgotten that Garmat was the same wily half-Arab bandit who had eluded the Ethiopian army for years—until, finally, he had accepted their offer to become Kaleb's own dawazz, when Eon's father was still a boy. After Kaleb succeeded to the throne, Garmat had been his chief adviser for years, until Kaleb assigned him to serve Eon in the same post.

Gentle, the man Garmat had often been, in his advice to Ethiopian royalty. But always shrewd, always cunning, and—when he felt it necessary—as savage and pitiless as the Arabian desert which had shaped him. More than one Axumite soldier, hearing the news that Garmat still lived, silently repeated Antonina's own thought.

Bad move, Malwa. Bad news, you bastards. You'd have done better to toy with a scorpion, after tweaking its tail.

Ten days after the explosion, the regimental ceremony was finally held. The fact that the Ta'akha Maryam was a ruin did not impede the proceedings. By tradition, the ceremony was never held in the royal compound. It was always held on the training fields where, Ethiopians never forgot, the real power of Axum was created. The army's training fields were located about half a mile west by northwest of the royal compound, at the base of one of the two great hills which overlooked the capital. This hill, which formed the eastern boundary of Axum, was called the Mai Qoho. The one on the north, the Bieta Giyorghis.

Standing to one side, in the group of witnesses who were not members of the regiments, Antonina surveyed the scene. She was impressed, more than anything, by the open—almost barren—nature of the grounds. Other than the row of open-air thrones on the north end of the field, butted against the slope of the Mai Qoho, the training grounds were completely bare except for a handful of wooden spear targets.

That was the Axumite way of looking at things, she realized. When she first arrived in Ethiopia, Antonina had not noticed the absence of fortifications until the officers of her army began pointing it out to her. They had been quite impressed. None of Axum's towns—not even the capital city of Axum itself, nor the great seaport of Adulis—were surrounded by walls. Not one of the many villages through which they passed, on their long trek upcountry, had so much as a small fortress to protect it.

The ancient Athenians had placed their faith in the wooden walls of their ships. The Axumites, in the spears of their regiments.

That was not from lack of ability. Axumites were quite capable of massive stonework. The Ta'akha Maryam and, especially, the glorious cathedral of Maryam Tsion, were testimony to the skill and craftsmanship of Ethiopian masons. But those edifices were for pomp, display, ceremony, and worship. They had nothing to do with *power*.

Power came from the regiments. They, and they alone.

She brought her eyes back to the thrones at the north end of the field. Those, too, she thought, testified to the same approach.

The structures were identical, and quite small—nothing like Kaleb's great throne in the Ta'akha Maryam had been. Each throne rested on a granite slab not more than eight feet square. A smaller slab atop the first provided the base for the throne itself, which was a solid but simple wooden chair. Four slender stone columns, rising from each corner of the upper slab, supported a canopy which sheltered the occupant from the sun. A gold cross—very finely made; Axumite metalsmiths were as skilled as their masons—surmounted the entire structure, but the canopy itself was made of nothing fancier than woven grass.

Those thrones were for the commanders of the Axumite sarawit, the regiments into which their army was organized. It was typical of Axumite notions of rule that those commanders, taken as a collective group, were called "nagast"—kings.

None of them, as individuals, enjoyed that title. Unlike the vassal states of the Ethiopian Empire, whose rulers retained their royal trappings (so long, of course, as they acknowledged the suzerainty of the King of Kings), the regimental commanders derived their authority entirely from the army itself. But, in the real world, the attitude of the regiments was considered far more important than the vagaries of sub-kings.

Only three of the thrones were occupied, this day. Even that was unusual. According to tradition, one man alone should be sitting on a throne today—the commander of the Dakuen sarwe. Even the king himself, though he was not present, was required to vacate his throne in the royal compound until his son's regiment had passed its judgement.

But Wahsi had bent the custom, today. With the murder of Kaleb and Wa'zeb, the Lazen and the Hadefan sarawit had lost their own royalty. Wahsi had offered, and they had accepted, to share the prince. For the first time in Axumite history, a man would ascend the throne with the approval—and the name—of three regiments.

The ceremony was beginning. Eon was taking his own place, standing alone to one side. At the very front, before the assembled regiments themselves, Ousanas was being brought forward.

Antonina struggled mightily against a giggle. The dawazz was positively festooned with chains and manacles. The servile devices looked about as appropriate on him as ribbons on a lion.

And probably, she thought, eyeing Ousanas' tall and heavily muscled figure, *just about as effective, if he decides he's tired of the rigmarole.* Belisarius had told her once, after returning from India, that Ousanas was probably the strongest man he had ever met in his life. Even stronger, he suspected, than the giant Anastasius.

But Antonina's humor faded quickly enough. The chains and manacles might seem absurd, but there was nothing absurd-looking about the squad of soldiers who surrounded Ousanas. There were eight of them, and all were holding weapons in their hands. These were not the usual stabbing spears and heavy, cleaverlike swords with which Axumites went into battle, however. The soldiers were holding clubs, inlaid with iron studs.

Weapons to beat a slave who had failed in his duty. Beat him to death, easily enough, if he had failed badly.

Antonina, staring at those cruel implements, had no trouble with giggles. Not any longer. She knew the clubs were not ornaments. It had happened, over the past two centuries, that a regiment had beaten a dawazz savagely—fatally, on two occasions—because they judged that he had failed in his duty to educate his prince.

She tore her eyes away, and looked at Eon. The sight of the young royal's upright and square-shouldered stance reassured her. The calmness in his face, even more so.

Not today. Not that prince.

A minute later, the ceremony itself got underway.

Five minutes later, Antonina was fighting giggles again.

Ten minutes later, she stopped trying altogether, and joined in the general hilarity. She spent most of the day, in fact, laughing along with everyone else.

Antonina had forgotten. There was a serious core—deadly serious—at the heart of that ceremony. But Axumites, when all was said and done, did not hold solemnity in any great esteem. The best armor against self-aggrandizement and pomposity, after all, is always humor.

By and large, the ceremony proceeded chronologically. Eon's prepubescent follies were dismissed quickly enough. Everyone wanted to get to the next stage.

Antonina learned, then, the reason for the other women standing in her group. All of them, it seemed—except for three old crones whose testimony had to do with Eon's pranks in the royal kitchen—had been seduced by the young prince at one time or another.

It was quite a crowd. Antonina was rather impressed.

But she was more impressed, *much* more, by what followed. Most of the women were—or had been—servants in the royal compound, while Eon was in his teens. The kind of women, in every land, who were the natural prey of young male nobles feeling the first urges of budding sexuality.

But they were not there, it developed, to press any grievances against the prince. They simply recounted—either volunteering the information, or responding to one of the many questions shouted out by soldiers in the ranks—the ways in which Eon had finagled his way into their beds. Their statements were frank, open, usually jocular—and often at the expense of Eon himself. It became clear soon enough that, especially in his earlier years, the prince's skill at working his way into their beds had not been matched by any great skill once he got there.

Several of the tales were downright hilarious. Antonina was especially entertained by the account of a plump, older woman who had once been a cook in the royal compound. The woman—she must have been a good twenty years older than Eon—recounted in lavish detail her patient, frustrated attempts to instruct a headstrong fifteen-year-old prince in the basic principles of female anatomy. Not with any great success, it seemed, until she discovered the secret: *slap the fool boy on his head!*

That produced a gale of laughter, sweeping across the entire training field. The soldiers guarding Ousanas grinned at him with approval.

Unfortunately, Antonina could not follow all of the woman's tale. Her own knowledge of Ge'ez, the Axumite language, was still very poor. Menander, one of the cataphracts who had accompanied Belisarius on his trip to India, was serving as her translator. He had become good friends with Wahsi and Ezana during that long journey, and was quite fluent in the language.

Alas, Menander was also young, and he still bore the imprint of his conservative village upbringing. So, whenever the story got especially juicy, he fumbled and stumbled and—Antonina had no doubt—was guilty of excessive abridgement.

"And what was *that* about?" Antonina demanded, once the roaring laughter had subsided a bit.

Menander fumbled and stumbled. Abridged.

"Ah," said Antonina, nodding her head wisely. "Yes, of course. It *is* difficult to teach a thick-headed male how to use his tongue for something more useful than boasting."

But, for all its salacious humor, there was still a deadly serious purpose to the business. As she listened to the questions which the soldiers asked of the women, Antonina understood that they were probing for something quite important.

The soldiers were not concerned—not in the least—with Eon's amatory habits. Young lads, of any rank in society, are always randy. A prince, because of his prestigious position and the self-confidence which that position gives him, will be much more successful than most teenage boys in the art of seduction. That much was inevitable, natural, and no concern of the soldiers. Rather the contrary, in fact—no one wanted a shy, self-effacing king in charge of a country, especially one who might have difficulty perpetuating the royal line.

And if a particular prince proved to be particularly adept at the skill—as Eon obviously was—so much the better. A glib tongue was a useful attribute for a good monarch.

What the soldiers *were* concerned about were Eon's methods. Charm is one thing; bullying is another. If Eon could use his prestige as a prince to sweet-talk his way into a hundred servant girls' beds, that was a source for nothing beyond amusement. But if he used that royal position in order to threaten his way to the goal, that *was* regimental business. A prince who would rape his servants would not hesitate, as a king, to rape his country.

But there was no trace of that in Eon's past. The questioning of the women went on as long as it did, Antonina decided, simply because everyone was enjoying the affair. Everyone except Eon, at least, although Antonina noticed that the prince himself was not reluctant to join in the laughter, even when he was the butt of the joke.

Soon enough, it was Antonina's turn to be a witness. Wahsi led the questioning, as he had since the beginning of the ceremony.

It did not take him more than a minute to clarify the issue involving Antonina. A randy prince was fine, so long as he could keep it under control. But a prince who would jeopardize important political affairs because of his unbridled lust would make a disastrous ruler.

Here, Wahsi glowered fiercely, leaning forward in his throne.

Isn't it true that during his trip to Constantinople, the fool boy prince could not stop ogling the wife of Rome's greatest general?

Antonina was not even tempted to deny the charge. Wahsi himself, along with Ezana, had been Eon's bodyguards during that time. But she managed to toss the thing off easily enough.

Well, yes, I suppose, for the first few days. But I was not offended. It's not as if I'm unaccustomed to it, after all—

Here, she drew herself erect, swelling her chest a bit. Antonina had deliberately worn the most revealing costume she had brought with her on this expedition. The outfit was not really very provocative, in all truth—nothing like the costumes she had worn in her days as a courtesan—but it didn't need to be. With her figure, she could attract men wearing a sackcloth.

An appreciative murmur rose from the ranks of the watching soldiers.

—and Eon was perfectly courteous in his actual conduct. A most proper young prince.

So much for that.

Menander was summoned next. The questioning here had no sexual overtone, but the issue was the same. Wasn't it true, during Eon's trip, that he behaved overbearingly toward Roman soldiers? Mention was made, in particular, of an arm-wrestling match in which the arrogant prince could not resist showing off his grotesque musculature.

Menander did not handle the thing as smoothly as Antonina. But, in its own way, his stubborn and vehement—almost resentful—defense of Eon was even more effective. No one watching the young foreign soldier, stammering his admiration for the prince, could fail to be impressed with the way in which Eon had obviously won over his allies, whatever might have been his initial blunders. And, again, laughter swept the field when Menander described Ousanas' methods of correcting Eon's behavior.

The rest of the ceremony was much of a piece. Every aspect of Eon's character was probed—with humor, more often than not, but relentlessly nonetheless. The dawazz was on trial, not the prince. But the real issue was Eon's suitability to assume the throne.

By mid-afternoon, the question was settled. In truth, Antonina realized, it had never really been at issue. The soldiers in the gathered regiments had followed the tradition scrupulously, but they had long since made their own private judgements. And it was not difficult for her, watching those soldiers, to come to the conclusion that they would not only accept Eon as their monarch, but were fiercely looking forward to his rule.

Bad move, Malwa.

The ceremony ended. The shackles were removed from Ousanas. Following custom, Wahsi offered the former dawazz a choice. He could return to his homeland, laden with riches; or he could choose to stay in Axum, where the new king would doubtless find a suitable post for his talents.

Ousanas' answer brought the last roar of laughter to the field—and a roar of fury with it.

"I shall stay here," he announced. "My own folk are too practical. Here, I will have great opportunity to contemplate philosophy. Especially the dialectic, which teaches us that all things are a contradiction."

He gave Eon a stony look. "As the fool boy king will prove soon enough."

When the laughter faded, he said: "But the dialectic also teaches us that all things change. *As the Malwa are about to discover—even quicker!*"

Chapter 9

The following day, Eon began his duties as negusa nagast. By tradition, he would have spent the evening carousing with his soldiers and the townsfolk of Axum. But Eon had been in no mood for festivity. His personal losses were too recent, and too deeply felt. His soldiers understood, and did not begrudge their new King of Kings spending the night in the cathedral of Maryam Tsion, praying for the souls of his family.

But by the morning, Eon had assumed his post. Whatever grief he still felt—and no one doubted it was there—he kept it locked away. The struggle against Malwa took center stage.

As it must. Just as Eon had predicted, the Malwa had struck again.

"Abreha is leading the rebellion," stated Wahsi. Sitting on his little stool, the Dakuen commander planted his hands on his knees. "And apparently the entire Metin sarwe has decided to accept their commander's claim to being the new King of Kings."

"The Falha sarwe has done the same," chimed in Saizana. The commander of the Hadefan leaned forward on his own stool, adding: "But they will only support Abreha as the king of Yemen. According to our spy, at least, they will not support Abreha if he tries to cross the Red Sea and invade Ethiopia itself."

Garmat, lying on an elevated pallet near Eon, raised his head. "What of the Halen?" he whispered. The old adviser was on his way to recovery, but he was still very weak. "And do we know what happened to Sumyafa Ashwa?"

"The Halen regiment," replied Saizana, "is apparently torn by dissension. They are forted up in Marib, and—so far—seem to be adopting a neutral stance." He shrugged. "As for Sumyafa Ashwa, his fate is unknown at the moment. But I think we must assume he was murdered. The viceroy was resident in Sana, after all, which is the hotbed of the rebellion."

Garmat lowered his head. For a few seconds, his eyes closed. There was no visible expression on his face, but Antonina, seated next to him, thought that Garmat was allowing himself a moment of sorrow. She knew that Sumyafa Ashwa had been a close friend of Garmat's for many years. It had been at Garmat's recommendation, after Axum conquered southern Arabia, that King Kaleb had appointed the Christian Arab as viceroy of Yemen.

Others in the room apparently shared her assessment. No one spoke, allowing Garmat to grieve in peace.

Antonina used that moment to inspect the room, and its occupants. Eon had begun the session by asking her to present the Roman Empire's proposals. Preoccupied with that task, and with the discussion which had immediately followed concerning the rebellion in Arabia, she had not had the opportunity to assess the new circle of royal advisers.

It was a small circle. Except for Garmat, none of the Ethiopian kingdom's top advisers had survived the bombing. The royal council was being held in the only audience chamber of the Ta'akha Maryam which had escaped unscathed. The room was quite large. Even the heavy wooden columns which were scattered throughout, supporting the stone ceiling, could not disguise the fact that most of the chamber was empty.

Antonina's eyes, scanning the room, fell on one of the windows which were situated along the eastern wall. The window was sturdily built, in the square stone-and-timber style favored by Axumites. There was no glass in that window. The cool highland breeze came into the chamber through the stone crosses which were the window's structure and decoration. Antonina's view of the Mai Qoho and the mountains looming beyond was filtered through the symbol of the Christian faith.

She found strength in that symbol, even more than the majesty of the mountains, and turned her eyes back to the circle of advisers.

Small, yes. But rich otherwise.

Garmat was there, after all. And all of the regimental commanders except the three who had been stationed in Yemen. And—most
important of all, Antonina suspected—Ousanas was there.

Her gaze came to rest on Ousanas. In times past, the former
dawazz would have squatted on a stool behind the prince. Ready
to chastise him, when necessary, but otherwise keeping his place.

Ousanas was no longer a slave, however. He had no title, now.
But Antonina did not miss the significance of his position in the
circle. Axumites, like Romans, reserved the place by a monarch's
right hand as the place of ultimate respect. And there Ousanas
sat—on a cushion, not a stool, in that peculiar cross-legged position
which he had learned in India. "The lotus," he called it, claiming
that it was an aid to meditation.

A bizarre man, in so many ways, given to fancies and philosophies. But Antonina was reassured by his presence.

Eon cleared his throat, indicating a resumption of the discussion.
The young king squared his shoulders against the wooden back of
the massive chair which was serving him as a throne, and turned
to Antonina.

"We will have to deal with this rebellion first," he stated. "You
know I agree with Rome's proposals, but I cannot—"

Eon spoke in Ge'ez, but Antonina did not wait for Menander's
interpretation. She understood enough of the words, and she had
been expecting the sense of them anyway.

Waving her hand in a gesture of agreement, she said: "Of course,
Your Majesty. Axum must set its own house in order, before it can
even think of striking at Malwa. Besides, this rebellion was certainly inspired and organized by the Malwa espionage service. It
is no accident that the rebellion broke out *the very same day* that
the Ta'akha Maryam was destroyed. There is no way the rebels in
Yemen could have known about the bombing, unless they had
been told in advance. It takes at least a week to travel from Axum
to Sana, using the fastest horses and ships."

After Menander interpreted, she continued. "I do not think the
Malwa suspect my husband's strategy. But they had good reason
to strike at Axum, anyway. Ethiopians played a key role in rescuing
the Empress Shakuntala and setting in motion the rebellion in the
Deccan. The Malwa obviously decided to pay Axum back in the
same coin—and throw in regicide for good measure."

She nodded at Eon. "So far as I am concerned, crushing the rebellion in Yemen is part of the war against Malwa. My own army is therefore at your disposal, for that purpose."

One of the officers—Gabra, commander of the Damawa regiment—began to protest. "This is an internal affair. I am not sure that using foreign troops wouldn't make the problem worse. The Halen regiment has stayed neutral, this far. If we use—"

Ousanas interrupted him. "Be damned to all that! Abreha and his rebels are using foreign troops, aren't they? According to our spy"—he glanced to a corner of the room, where the man recently arrived from Sana was standing—"Abreha is surrounded by half a dozen Malwa agents, everywhere he goes. He is publicly boasting that Malwa military units will soon be arriving in Yemen."

The hunter slapped the floor. "And most of his forces *now* are not Axumite! Abreha's regiment and the Falha—put together—are less than two thousand men." His eyes swept the room, scanning the row of regimental commanders seated before the negusa nagast. "On their own, they would stand no chance. So—according to our spy—most of Abreha's forces consist of Arabs. Bedouin tribesmen from the interior."

Again, he looked in the corner. The regimental commanders twisted their heads, following his gaze. Seeing all eyes upon him, the spy stepped forward a few paces.

"Most of them," the man stated. "Some of the Arabs of the towns have declared for Abreha. But most of his support comes from the bedouin."

Garmat levered himself up. "What about the Quraysh?" he asked.

The spy made a fluttering motion with his hand. "So far, Mecca has remained loyal. That could change, of course—*will* change, soon enough—if the rebellion is not crushed."

Hearing this news, several of the commanders grunted. The sounds were inarticulate, but full of import.

Antonina understood the meaning. The great Arab tribes centered in Mecca and the other towns of western Arabia—among which the Quraysh were dominant—were traders, not bedouin. It was they, not the nomads of the interior, who chafed most under Ethiopian rule. The bedouin of the interior did not really care who ruled fertile Yemen. Those nomads who had given their allegiance to Abreha would have done so for immediate bribes—and the hope of possible loot, if Abreha set out to conquer Ethiopia.

But the commercial interests of the tribes in Mecca often clashed with those of Axum. Axum's control of the great trading route which passed through the Red Sea rested on its navy's ability to suppress piracy. The Quraysh, on the other hand, *depended* on piracy. It was not that they themselves were pirates—although the accusation was often made—so much as the simple fact that no one used their more expensive camel caravans unless the sea route was infested by pirates.

For years now, since Axum under King Kaleb had conquered southern Arabia and clamped the iron grip of its navy on the Red Sea, the traders of Mecca had suffered greatly. By all logic, it should have been they—not bedouin nomads—who were flocking to Abreha's banner. The fact that they weren't—

"They've always been smart," said Garmat, now sitting erect. For the first time since the session began, the old adviser's face was animated and eager. He seemed like the Garmat of old, and Antonina was not the only one in the room who felt their spirits rise.

"Mecca is the key," said Garmat emphatically. "Mecca and Yathrib, and the whole of the Hijaz. I have said this before, and I will say it now again: control of Yemen depends on our control of the western coast."

Garmat stuck out his thumb. "We will always have the allegiance of the Arab townsmen of Yemen. Most of them, at least. Those people are farmers. They want stability and order, and no power in this region can provide it as well as Axum. True, they chafe a bit, because we are foreign. But not much, because Ethiopians are not *very* foreign, and—" He made a quick little flip of his hands, indicating himself. A small laugh rose in the chamber. Garmat was the product of a liaison between an Arab woman and an Ethiopian trader.

The adviser grinned. "I am by no means the only half-breed in Arabia—or in Axum." The assembled commanders grinned back. From their appearance, at least two of them had obvious Arab ancestry. Antonina, knowing of the long and intimate contact between Ethiopia and Arabia, suspected that most Axumites had Arabs perched in their family trees. Whole flocks of Arabs, more often than not.

Garmat continued. "The towns of Yemen will support us, given a choice. The bedouin mean nothing. They will bow to whoever has the power, and will not rebel so long as their customs are not meddled with." He shrugged. "Of course, their allegiance is casual. If there is unrest, they will look to take advantage. But so long as Axum is firmly in control of Yemen—*and the Hijaz*, the western coast—the bedouin will tend to their own affairs."

He leaned forward, looking intently at Eon.

"I said this to your father, and I will say it to you. *Mecca is the key*. Weld the Hijaz to Ethiopian rule, and you will hold all of southern Arabia in a solid grip. But so long as the Quraysh are discontent, your rule is based on sand."

For a moment, his eyes closed. "I was never quite able to convince Kaleb. He did not disagree, exactly, but—" The eyes reopened. "He was never willing to pay the price."

Garmat's tone hardened. *"The price must be paid. Now."*

A murmur of protest began to rise from the military officers. Garmat eyed them stonily.

Antonina hesitated. She agreed with Garmat, but was unsure if she was in position to intervene in what was a delicate matter for Ethiopians.

Her hesitation was made moot, almost at once.

"What is your advice, Ousanas?" asked Eon.

The former dawazz spoke forcefully. "Pay the price. Immediately—*and in full*. I agree completely with Garmat."

The murmur of protest was swelling. Ousanas fixed the assembled regimental commanders with his eyes. If the gaze of Garmat was stony, his was that of a basilisk.

"These sounds of protest you hear, King of Kings," said Ousanas, indicating the officers with an accusing finger, "are the sounds of petty greed. Nothing more."

The officers—most of them, at least; not Wahsi—glared at Ousanas. The former dawazz glared back. And made instantly clear, whatever his official status was now, that a former slave was not hesitant to clash with army commanders.

"Stupid boys," he sneered, "coveting their stupid little marbles, and unwilling to share them with the other boys on the playground."

Antonina took a deep breath. She understood what lay beneath this quarrel. She had been well-briefed by her own excellent advisers, one of whom—the Armenian cataphract Ashot—was very familiar with Ethiopia and the complexities of Red Sea trade and politics.

Unlike Rome, Axum made no distinction between its army and its navy. Each of the regiments had its own fleet of ships, which were manned by its soldiers. For all that they were highland-born-and-bred, Ethiopia's soldiers were as much seamen as they were infantry. Seamen—and traders. Whenever the navy was not at war, or not on patrol, the regiments' ships carried trade goods. *And* took a percentage of the profits from civilian ships, on the grounds that their suppression of piracy was all that enabled civilian merchants to prosper.

Ethiopia's army, in short, had an immediate and vested interest in maintaining the supremacy of seaborne trade in the Red Sea—which was precisely the condition that squeezed the camel caravans of the Quraysh and the other trading tribes of Mecca and the Hijaz.

Antonina realized that she was holding her breath. This quarrel had the potential to erupt into a bitter brawl which could be disastrous for her plans. Belisarius' strategy depended on the support of a strong—and united—Axum.

When Eon spoke, his voice was low. Like a lion, growling at cubs.

"You—will—obey—me."

Startled by the majesty in that voice, the eyes of the officers left Ousanas and settled on the negusa nagast.

Eon sat in his throne, almost unmoving. In the time which followed, he used no grand gestures to give emphasis to his words. It was quite unnecessary. The words themselves seemed carved in stone.

"Do not forget, commanders of the sarawit, why Ethiopia is ruled by me—and not you. You are the nagast, but I am the *negusa* nagast. King of Kings. Our ancestors realized that kings are prone to folly, and thus they instituted the dawazz and required the approval of the regiments before a prince could become a king. But they also realized that officers—nobles of all stripes—are prone to a different folly. They forget to think of the kingdom, and think only of their own little piece of the realm. And thus the *negusa* nagast was set above you."

He stared down at them, like a sphinx. "You think only of your profits, as if they were the sum of things. But I was at Ranapur, where Malwa butchered two hundred thousand people. Flayed them, fed them to animals, trampled them under elephants, tore them apart with oxen."

He was stone, stone: *"Two hundred thousand*. Can you comprehend that number—you *coin-counters*? All the towns in Ethiopia and Arabia, put together, do not contain half so many people. You think Malwa will not do the same to Axum and Sana? Do you?"

Finally, he moved. A finger lifted from the arm of the throne and pointed to Ousanas.

"My dawazz, at my command, took the Talisman of God in his own hand and saw Axum's future, if Malwa is not crushed. By the time of his death in battle, we were nothing but refugees fleeing into central Africa—and with no great hope of finding a haven there."

He leaned forward, just a bit. "What use will your treasure be in central Africa, *merchants*? Do you plan to buy the finest grass huts, and sleep on the best dirt?"

Eon stared at his commanders. After a moment, they lowered their heads.

All but Wahsi, who growled: "I was at Ranapur, also. I did not try to count Malwa's murders. I could not even count the rivers of blood."

Eon let the silence last for a full minute, before he spoke again. Stone became iron.

"There will be no quarrel over this matter. I will tolerate no dispute. I will order the immediate execution of any officer who so much as utters a word of protest in private conversation with his soldiers. I will perch the heads of every commander of every regiment on the crosses of their thrones in the training field. If you doubt me—if you think the sarwen will follow you rather than the negusa nagast—then test me now. Before I smash rebellion in Arabia, I will smash it here."

Silence. Eon let it stand, for two full minutes.

Iron became steel.

"My commands are as follows. We will send a delegation to Mecca immediately, riding the fastest horses in Axum and taking the fastest ship in Adulis. If Garmat is strong enough for the journey, he will lead the expedition. If he is not—"

"I am well enough, King of Kings," said Garmat.

Eon nodded; continued: "Our delegation will meet with the leaders of the Quraysh and all the other tribes of the Hijaz. They will offer the following. Henceforth, the tribes will be entitled to a share of the profits from the seaborne trade. They will also be granted access to all caravan trade anywhere in the realm of Axum—here in Ethiopia as well as in Arabia. And finally—"

The young king took a little breath of his own. For just a second, a shadow seemed to cross his face.

"The delegation will offer marriage to the negusa nagast—to me—for one of their princesses. Whichever one they select. The blood of Arabia will henceforth flow into Axum's ruling dynasty."

Eon smiled, finally. It was a small, wan smile. "Legally, and officially. It has already flowed into it often enough otherwise."

Antonina was not fooled by that smile. She understood how little Eon cared, so soon after the death of Tarabai and Zaia, to even think of marriage. But the young king, here also, was showing that he could put the needs of his kingdom first.

"*Negusa nagast,*" she murmured, under her breath.

Or so she thought. Perhaps she spoke louder than she intended, because the words were almost instantly echoed by others in the room. By all in the room, within seconds.

"*Negusa nagast,*" repeated the regimental commanders. The two words, alone, were the token of their submission.

Ethiopia's new King of Kings had established his rule. In what mattered, now, not in the formalities of ritual and custom. The regiments had raised him to the throne, but he had shown that he could break them to his will.

At first, as she carefully studied the faces of the commanders of the sarawit, Antonina was surprised that she could see no signs of resentment. To the contrary—for all their impassivity, she was sure she detected an underlying sense of satisfaction in those hard, black faces.

But, after a time, she realized that she had misunderstood those men. Traders and merchants they might be, in some part of their lives. But at the heart of those lives lay spears, not coins. When all was said and done, those warriors counted victory as the greatest treasure of all. And, like all such men, they knew that triumph was impossible without sureness of command.

Sureness of which they had just been given evidence. With their own heads offered, if need be, as the proof.

There was no need. In the hours which followed, as the session relaxed and delved into the specifics of war, and campaigns, and negotiations, and trade privileges, Antonina witnessed the forging of Ethiopia's new leadership. It centered on Eon, of course; but Ousanas was there also, and Garmat and Wahsi, and, by the end of the day, every single commander of the sarawit except those in rebellion in Arabia.

Watching the easy confidence with which those men planned their next campaign—participating in it fully, in fact, for her own forces were integral to the plans—Antonina found herself, again and again, forced to suppress an urge to giggle.

Bad move, Malwa. Oh—bad, bad move.

Chapter 10

DEOGIRI

Spring, 532 A.D.

Raghunath Rao finished his bowl of rice and set it down on the stone floor of the rampart. Still squatting on his heels, he leaned back against the outer wall. His head, resting against the rough stones, was only inches from one of the open embrasures in the crenellated fortification. The breeze coming through the gap in the wall helped to ease the heat. It was the middle of *garam*, India's dry season, and the land was like an oven.

Rao exuded satisfaction. "It's nice to get rice for a change," he commented. "I get sick of millet."

Squatting next to him, Maloji nodded cheerfully. "We should have enough for several days, too. That was a big shipment smuggled in from the coast."

Rao turned his head, peering through the embrasure at the distant lines of the Malwa besieging Deogiri. "Was there any trouble?"

Maloji grinned. "Not the least." He jerked his head toward the Malwa. "Half of those wretches, by now, are simply trying to stay alive. The Vile One isn't sending out many patrols any longer, and most of those keep their eyes closed. We let them pass unmolested, they don't see anything. That's the unspoken agreement."

Rao smiled. His eyes scanned the enemy trenches and field-works. That was simply habit. The Malwa besiegers were not trying to advance their lines any longer. They were simply waiting for the siege guns to arrive and break Deogiri's huge walls.

The walls of Deogiri had shrugged off Venandakatra's light field artillery, and they had been the doom of thousands of Malwa soldiers. The enemy had not tried to assault the city for weeks, now. Not even Venandakatra, who cared as much for the lives of common soldiers as he did for insects, would order any more charges.

Maloji continued. "If the Rajputs were still here, of course, we'd have a problem. But they've all been sent north. Our spies in Bharakuccha say the Malwa are having nothing but grief with the Romans in Persia." He spit on the floor. "Not even the Vile One's Ye-tai can force the regular rabble to conduct serious patrols any longer."

Both men fell silent, for several minutes. Then, clearing his throat, Maloji spoke again.

"Have you received word from the empress?"

Rao nodded. "Yes. A letter arrived yesterday. But she said nothing concerning the siege guns. I didn't expect her to. If Kungas was able to convince her of our plan, she would not send any message to us. For fear of interception. The plan can only succeed if absolute secrecy is maintained."

Maloji hesitated, then scowled. "I still don't like it. How can you trust that man so much? He betrayed Malwa once. Why would he not betray us? Everything depends on him, and his fellow traitors."

Rao's eyes left the enemy and settled on Maloji. His expression was utterly serene.

"Words, Maloji. Those are just words. The veil of illusion. How can the man be accused of betraying Malwa, when he never gave his loyalty to them in the first place? He was born into their world, he did not choose it freely."

"He worked for them," countered Maloji stubbornly. "All the Kushans did."

Rao smiled. "Tell me, Maloji. Did you ever catch wild animals—cubs—when you were a boy, and keep them in a pen?" His friend and subordinate nodded. "Did they escape?"

Maloji chuckled. "The mongoose did."

Rao nodded. "And then? Did you denounce the mongoose for a traitor?"

Maloji laughed. After a moment, he made a little gesture with his hand, opening the palm. It was not the first time in his life he had made that gesture, nor, he knew, would it be the last. The student, acknowledging the master.

Rao's eyes grew slightly unfocused. "I know that man, Maloji. Better, perhaps, than I know any other man alive. I spent weeks studying him, outside the walls of the Vile One's palace, while he was still Shakuntala's captor. My enemy, he was then. I hated him with a pure fury. But I never misunderstood him."

Rao rolled his shoulders against the stone wall, pointing to the south.

"I will never forget the day I saw Kungas coming through that gate, bringing word from the empress that she had taken Suppara. I fell to my knees, I was so stunned. I knew Belisarius must have found Indian allies, to smuggle Shakuntala out of captivity, but I had no idea it was him."

Rao's eyes closed, as he savored the memory.

"On my knees. He came up to me and extended his hand, but I refused the offer. I stayed on my knees for several minutes, not because I was still shocked, but because I was praying."

He opened his eyes and stared at the blinding sky of India. "I understood, then—*I knew*—that God has not forsaken us. I *knew* the asura was doomed."

He brought down his eyes to meet those of his friend. "Trust me in this, Maloji. If the thing can be done, Kungas will do it."

Silence reigned for several minutes. Then, with a little shake of his head, Rao spoke again. His voice was perhaps a bit harsh.

"The empress wrote the letter to ask for my advice. The Cholas have offered marriage to her. The eldest son of the dynasty."

Maloji studied Rao intently. "And what did you say?"

Rao flexed his hands. He spent a few seconds examining the opening and closing fingers, as if they were objects of great fascination.

"I urged her to accept," he said forcefully. "The Cholas are the most powerful independent kingdom of south India. Their proposal was full of quibbles, of course, but they are still offering a genuine alliance. A marriage between Shakuntala and the Cholas

would strengthen us like no other. I am in full agreement with
Dadaji Holkar on that matter, and I told her so very clearly."

Maloji looked away. "That must have been a difficult letter for
you to write," he said softly.

Rao's eyes widened. "Why?"

Maloji snorted. A moment later, he brought his gaze back to
Rao. It was a sad gaze.

"Old friend, you cannot fool me. Others, perhaps. But not *me*."

He said nothing else. For a moment, Rao tried to meet Maloji's
level gaze with one of his own. But only for a moment.

"It is dharma, Maloji," he murmured, studying his flexing fingers. "I have lived my life by duty, and discipline. And so has—"

He took a deep, almost shuddering breath. A faint sheen of
moisture came to his eyes.

"And so has she." Another breath—he made no attempt to control the shudder, now—and he finally, to another man, spoke the
words. "She is the treasure of my soul, Maloji. But I have my duty,
and she has hers. We will both be faithful to our dharma."

His fingers became fists. "That is the way it must be. *Will* be."

Maloji hesitated. He was perhaps Rao's closest friend, but this
was a subject they had never discussed. With a little shrug, he
decided to widen the crack.

"Have you ever spoken to her?"

Rao's back stiffened. "Never!" he exclaimed. "That, alone, would
be a betrayal of my trust. She was given into my care by the
Emperor of Andhra himself, to safeguard the dynasty. It would be
the foulest treason for me to betray that trust."

Maloji shook his head. "You are not her father, Rao. Much older
than she, true. So what? If I remember right, the oldest son of
Chola is no younger than you."

Rao made a short, chopping motion. "That has nothing to do
with anything. She is the purest blood of India. The heir of ancient
Satavahana. I am a Maratha chieftain." For a moment, he managed
a grin. "It is true, I am considered kshatriya—by Marathas, at least.
But my mother's father was a peasant, and no one even knows the
name of my paternal grandfather, although he is reputed to have
been a tinker."

His powerful hands relaxed. A great sigh loosened his muscular
body. "The world is what it is, Maloji. We must be true to our
dharma, or we lose our souls."

His whole body seemed to ooze against the stones of the wall, as if he were seeking to find oneness with the universe.

"We must accept, that is all." Rao turned his eyes to his friend. The moisture was gone, along with any outward sign of pain. Suddenly, he grinned.

"It has been difficult, I admit. I remember, the first time—" He chuckled wryly. "She was thirteen, perhaps fourteen years old. She had done especially well in one of the exercises I set her to, and I praised her. She laughed and embraced me, pressing herself close. Suddenly—it struck me like a bolt of lighting, I will never forget the moment—I realized she was a woman now. And not just any woman, but—"

He groped for words. Maloji provided them: "She has been called the Black-Eyed Pearl of the Satavahanas since she was twelve. There is a reason for it, which goes far beyond her eyes. I have not seen her since Amaravati, but even then she was beautiful."

Rao closed his eyes again. "I try not to think about it," he whispered. "It is difficult, but I manage. Since that day, years ago, I have kept myself from looking at the beauty of her body. Other men may do so, but not I." His eyes reopened. "But I cannot blind myself to the real beauty. I have tried—so very hard—but I cannot. I simply try not to think about it." He smiled. "Perhaps that is why I meditate so often."

Abruptly, he rose. "Enough. We will not speak of this again, Maloji, though I thank you for your words." He stared at the Malwa enemy over the battlements. "We have a war to fight and win. A dynasty to return to its rightful place. An empress to shield and protect—and cherish. That is our dharma."

He pushed himself away from the stones and turned toward the stairs leading to the city below. "And now, I must be about my tasks. I have my duty, she has hers. She will marry Chola, and I will dance at her wedding. The best dance I ever danced."

Seconds later, he was gone. Maloji, watching him go, bowed his head. "Not even you, Raghunath Rao," he whispered. "Not even you—the Great Country's best dancer as well as its soul—can dance that well."

Chapter 11
PERSIA
Spring, 532 A.D.

The first Malwa barrage came as an unpleasant surprise to the Roman troops dug in on the crest of the saddle pass. Instead of sailing all over the landscape, a majority of the Malwa rockets landed uncomfortably near their entrenchments. And the fire from the small battery of field guns which Damodara had placed on a nearby hilltop was fiendishly accurate. The Roman fieldworks were partially obscured by small clouds of dust and flying dirt.

There was not much actual damage, however. Two cannon balls landed in trenches, but they caused only one fatality. Solid cannon shot was designed for field battles, where a ball could bounce through the packed ranks of advancing infantry. Even when such a solid shot struck a trench directly, it usually did nothing more than bury itself in the loosened dirt. The man killed just had the misfortune of standing on the wrong patch of soil. His death was almost silent, marked only by a sodden thud; and then, by the soft and awful sounds of blood and intestines spilling from a corpse severed at the waist.

Worse casualties were created by the single rocket which hit directly in a trench. Rocket warheads were packed with gunpowder and iron pellets. When such a warhead exploded in a crowded trench, the result was horrendous.

"*Damn,*" hissed Maurice, watching the survivors in the trench frantically trying to save the wounded. The shouts of the rescuers were drowned beneath the shrieks of dying and injured men. "They've got impact fuses."

Belisarius nodded. "*And* they've refitted their rockets with proper venturi," he added. "You can tell the difference in the sound alone, leaving aside the fact they're ten times more accurate."

Frowning, he swiveled his telescope to point at Damodara's pavilion, erected just a few hundred yards behind the front lines of the Ye-tai who were massing for a charge.

Through the telescope, Belisarius could see Damodara standing on a platform which had been erected in front of the pavilion. The platform was just a sturdy framework of small logs, but it was enough to give the Malwa commander a good field of view. It was typical of Damodara, thought Belisarius, that he had not even bothered to have the logs planed. Most anvaya-prapta sachivya would have insisted on polished planks, covered with rugs.

"How did he do it?" the Roman general muttered. "I knew the Malwa would come up with impact fuses and venturi soon enough. But I didn't expect to see them appear in Damodara's army, as isolated as they are from the manufactories in India."

Belisarius lowered the telescope, still frowning.

"They must have hauled them here," said Maurice. The gray-haired veteran frowned as well. "Hell of a logistics route! I'd hate to be relying on supplies that have to be moved through the Hindu Kush and—all that."

The last two words were accompanied by a vague little wave of Maurice's hand, indicating the entire broken and arid terrain between the lush plains of north India and the Zagros range. Mountains, hills, deserts—some of the roughest country in the world, that was. More suited for mountain goats than supply trains.

"It *could* be done," mused Belisarius. "Trade caravans have made it all the way to China, when you think about it. But not often, and not carrying anything more cumbersome than luxury goods."

Aide amplified. **Gold coins, crystal and red coral from the Roman Empire, in exchange for silk from China. Some jewelry, both ways.**

Belisarius scratched his chin, as he invariably did when deep in thought. "Damodara would have one advantage," he added slowly. "He wouldn't have to worry about brigands. No hill bandit in his right mind would attack a Malwa military caravan."

"Pathans would," countered Maurice, referring to the fiercest of the mountain tribes. "Those bastards—*down!*"

He and Belisarius hastily crouched in their trench. Nearby, Anastasius and Valentinian did the same. A volley of Malwa rockets sailed overhead, passing no more than ten feet above them. A few seconds later, they heard the explosive sounds of the rockets landing somewhere on the back slope of the saddle pass.

As soon as Belisarius was certain that the volley had ended, he rose and peered behind him. He had taken position in a trench at the very crest of the pass, allowing him as good a view of the back slope as the foreground. Leaning over the log parapet, he studied the scene intently.

His brow was creased with worry. Belisarius had positioned his handcannon troops just behind the crest of the pass. They would—he thought—be out of danger there until he needed them. *And* out of sight of the enemy. The handcannons were Belisarius' own little surprise for the Malwa. He had not used them yet, in this campaign, and he hoped that Damodara and Sanga were still unaware of their existence.

Maurice joined him. The chiliarch, after one quick look, verbalized Belisarius' own thoughts.

"No damage. The rockets passed over them too." Maurice's face broke into a grin. That was a rare expression, on *his* face. Belisarius was amused to see that it was probably the least humorous grin in the world. Wintry, you might call it.

"But I'll bet they're not whining anymore about all the digging you make them do," chuckled Maurice. He and Belisarius could see the first heads of the handcannon troops popping up from their trenches. Those soldiers were not more than fifty yards away, and their expressions caused Belisarius to break into his own grin. Worry, fear—combined with more than a dose of outrage.

What the hell is this? *Here we were, enjoying a pleasant moment of relaxation, engrossed in cursing that damn fool General Pick-and-Shovel who makes us dig trenches every time we take two steps, and—*

What the hell's going on? It's not fair!

Still grinning, Belisarius turned around and resumed his study of the enemy. After a moment, he picked up the broken thread of their conversation.

"Pathans wouldn't attack Damodara's supply trains. Don't forget, Maurice, those caravans would be protected by Rajput troops. *Sanga's* Rajputs, to boot. And I'm sure Sanga would see to it that the information was passed on to the tribesmen. He has his own Pathan trackers, you know."

Belisarius looked at the large body of Rajput cavalry that formed the right wing of the enemy's formation. There were a smaller number of Rajputs on the Malwa left wing, but Belisarius had spotted Sanga earlier through his telescope. In this coming battle, the Rajput king had been assigned to the right. With his naked eyes, Belisarius couldn't distinguish Sanga any longer from the thousands of other Rajputs massed on that side of the battlefield. But he was certain that Sanga was still there.

"Sanga led the last punitive expedition which the Rajputs sent against the Pathans," he said, speaking softly. "That was years ago. There haven't been any since because Sanga ravaged them so badly—" Belisarius broke off, with a little grimace. "Bloody business, that is."

Maurice gave his commander a quick, shrewd glance. Belisarius, in the past, had led his own punitive expeditions against barbarians. In the trans-Danube, several times; and, once, against the Isaurians in Asia Minor. Even as young as he'd been then—and Belisarius was still shy of thirty—his campaigns had already been marked by sagacity and cunning.

They'd also been brutal and savage, as campaigns against barbarians always were. Belisarius had a detestation of cruelty which was unusual in soldiers of the time. Some of that aversion, thought Maurice, was simply due to the man's nature. But that natural inclination had been hardened and tempered by the sight of Goth and Isaurian villages visited by his own troops.

Seeing beneath Belisarius' now-expressionless face, Maurice turned his eyes away. He was quite sure, in that moment, that he knew what Belisarius was thinking. An image came to Maurice, as vividly as if it had just happened yesterday. He remembered seeing Belisarius standing over the body of a child in one of those villages. The young commander—still in his teens, he'd been—had just arrived, with Maurice and some of his Thracian cataphracts. The village was in flames, but the main body of the army had already passed through, rampaging on ahead.

Judging by the size of the pitiful little corpse, the Goth had been not more than five years old. Belisarius' soldiers had set a sharpened stake in the ground, impaled the boy, castrated him—and cut off his penis for good measure—amputated his arms, and then, mercifully, cut his throat. But neither Belisarius nor Maurice, surveying the scene, doubted the sequence in which the soldiers had committed their atrocities. For minutes which must have seemed an eternity to their victim, Roman troops had subjected a helpless child to the cruelest tortures imaginable.

The naked and disemboweled body of a girl had been lying nearby. The boy's mother, perhaps, but more likely his sister. The corpse's face was nothing but a pulp, covered with half-dried, crusted blood. It was impossible to discern her features, but the body itself seemed not far past puberty. The girl had obviously been gang-raped before she was murdered.

Remembering, Maurice could still hear Belisarius' quiet and anguished words. *"And these men call themselves Christians?"*

Prior to that day, Belisarius had simply tried to restrain his army. Thereafter, he instituted the draconian policy regarding atrocities for which he was famous—notorious, from the viewpoint of some soldiers and all mercenary troops. As it happened, by good fortune, the men responsible for that particular atrocity had been identified and arrested within a week. Belisarius immediately ordered their execution. The army had almost mutinied, but Belisarius already had his corps of hand-picked Thracian bucellarii to enforce his orders.

Still, the atrocities continued, if not as often. It was almost impossible to restrain troops completely in war against barbarians, since so many of the soldiers in the campaigns were borderers. Barbarians were guilty of their own brutal practices, and the soldiers burned for vengeance. In the dispersed nature of such combat, troops soon learned to keep their savageries hidden.

Maurice banished the memory. Again, he glanced at Belisarius. The general's gaze was still on the Rajput troops, where Sanga commanded, and his lips were moving. Maurice could not hear the words he spoke, but he thought he knew what they were. Belisarius had told him of the message which the Great Ones of the future had given to Aide, to guide the crystal in its search for help in the ancient past of humanity.

Find the general who is not a warrior, had been part of that message. But there had also been: *See the enemy in the mirror, the friend across the field.*

Belisarius emitted a little sigh, and shook his head. The motion was quick and abrupt, as if he were tossing something off. When the general turned back to Maurice, there was no sign of anything in his brown eyes but the calm self-control of an experienced commander on a battlefield.

"We've got some time," Belisarius pronounced. As if to verify his words, the distant Malwa batteries erupted in new salvos. After a quick glance, Maurice ignored them. From their trajectories, none of the missiles would strike in their vicinity. He gave his attention back to the general.

"At least an hour," continued Belisarius, "before they start their first assault." He began walking toward the cross-trench which gave access to the back slope. From habit, Belisarius stayed in a semicrouch, but it was obvious from the casual way he looked back at Maurice that he had come to the same assessment of the current barrage's accuracy.

"Kurush should still be in the field headquarters. I want to talk to him." Belisarius pointed to the enemy. "There's a bit of a mystery here that I'd like to clear up, if we can. I don't like bad news of any kind, but I *especially* don't like surprises."

As Belisarius had hoped, Kurush was in the field headquarters. The young Persian nobleman had arrived just the day before, accompanied by three subordinate officers. He had been sent by Emperor Khusrau to reestablish liaison with the Romans. Since Belisarius had led his army into the Zagros, in hopes of delaying Damodara's advance while Khusrau set Mesopotamia in order, the Persian emperor had had no contact with his Roman allies.

Khusrau Anushirvan—Khusrau of the Immortal Soul, as the Aryans called him—had not chosen Kurush for the assignment by accident. Partly, of course, his choice had been dictated by the prickly class sensitivities of Aryan society. Kurush was a sahrdaran, the highest-ranked layer of the Persian aristocracy. To have sent a lesser figure would have been insulting—not to Belisarius, who didn't care—but to other members of the sahrdaran. Faced with his half-brother Ormazd's treasonous rebellion, Khusrau could not afford to lose the loyalty of any more Persian aristocrats.

But, for the most part, the Emperor of Persia had sent Kurush because of the man's own qualities. For all his youth, Kurush was an excellent military commander in his own right. And, best of all, he was familiar to Belisarius. The two men had worked together the year before, during Belisarius' campaign in northern Mesopotamia.

When Belisarius strode through the open flaps of the field headquarters' entrance, he saw that the four Persian officers were bent over the table in the center of the tent, admiring the huge map.

"This is marvelous!" exclaimed Kurush, seeing Belisarius. The nobleman strode forward, gesticulating, with the nervous energy that was always a part of him.

"Where did you get the idea?" he demanded. He shook his head vigorously. "Not the map itself. I mean the—" Kurush snapped his head around, looking toward the Syrian craftsman whom Belisarius had trained as a cartographer. "What did you call it? Tapo—*something*."

"Topography," said the mapmaker.

"Yes, that's it!" Kurush's head snapped back to Belisarius. "Where did you get the idea? I've never seen any other maps or charts which show elevation and terrain features. Except maybe one or two prominent mountains. And rivers, of course."

Belisarius shrugged. "It just came to me, one day." His words were abrupt, even a little curt.

Typical, groused Aide. **I never get any credit. Glory hound!**

Belisarius pursed his lips, trying not to smile. This was a subject he did not want broached. Belisarius had once told Kurush's uncle, the sahrdaran Baresmanas, the secret of Aide's existence. But he didn't think Kurush knew, and he saw no reason to change that state of affairs. The fact was that Aide had given him the idea, just as he had so many others that Belisarius had implemented.

Toil, toil, toil, that's all I do. A slave in the gold mines, while you get to prance around in all the finery. Good thing for you trade unions haven't been invented yet, or I'd go out on strike.

Wanting to change the subject—as much to keep from laughing as anything else—

The eight-hour day! For a start. Wages, of course. Not better wages, either—any wages. I'm not getting paid at all, now that I think about it. Exploiter! Then—

—Belisarius drove over Aide's witticisms—

—there's the whole matter of benefits. I'll let the medical slide, seeing as how the current state of medical practice makes me shudder, but—

—along with Kurush's onrushing stream of questions.

I demand a pension. Thirty-and-out, nothing less!

"Are any Persian towns in your eastern provinces centers of artisanship?" asked Belisarius. "Especially metalworking?"

Kurush's mouth snapped shut. For a moment, the Persian nobleman stared at Belisarius as if he were a madman. Then he burst into laughter.

"In the *east*?" he cried. Kurush's laughter was echoed by all three of his officers. One of them snorted. "Those hicks can barely manage to rim a cartwheel."

"Do they even *have* carts?" demanded another.

Kurush was back to vigorous headshaking. "The eastern provinces are inhabited by nothing besides peasants and petty noblemen. They know how to grow crops. And how to fight, of course—but even that, they do poorly."

He rocked his head back and forth, once, twice, thrice. The quick little gesture was by way of qualification. "I should be fair. The eastern dehgans are as good as any, in single combat. But their tactics—"

"*Charge*," sneered one of his officers. "If that doesn't work—*charge again*." His two fellows chortled agreement. "And if that doesn't work?" queried one. He shrugged. "Charge again. And keep doing it until your horse has the good sense to run away."

Kurush grinned. "If you want Persian artisans, Belisarius, you have to go to Mesopotamia or Persarmenia for them. Except in Fars province. There are some metalsmiths—armorers, mostly—in Persepolis and Pasargadae."

He cocked his head quizzically. "Why do you ask?"

Belisarius walked over to the table and stared down at the map, scratching his chin. "I ask because the gunpowder weapons Damodara's army is using are quite a bit more sophisticated than anything I expected them to have." He gestured with his head toward the east. The sound of the Malwa barrages carried clearly through the leather walls of the tent.

Still scratching his chin, he added: "I thought it might be possible that Damodara established a manufacturing center somewhere in Hyrcania or Khorasan. But that's not likely, if there are no native craftsmen to draw on. I doubt he would have brought an entire labor force with him all the way from the Gangetic plain. A few experts, maybe. But not the hundreds of skilled workers it would take to manufacture—"

Again, he gestured toward the east wall of the tent. Again, the sound of Malwa rocketry and cannon fire pierced the leather.

A new voice entered the discussion. "It *is* possible, General Belisarius. He could have set one up at Marv." Vasudeva rose from a chair in a corner of the tent and ambled toward the table. "Marv is a big enough town, and it's well located for the purpose."

Vasudeva reached the table and leaned over, pointing to Marv's location on the map. His finger then moved east to the river Oxus, and then, following the river's course, southeast to a spot on the map which bore no markings.

"Right about there is the city of Begram," said the Kushan general. "The largest Kushan city, after Peshawar. Our kings, in the old days, had their summer palaces at Begram." A bitter tinge entered his voice. "Peshawar is nothing but ruins, today. But Begram still stands. The Ye-tai did not destroy it, except for the stupas."

For all the calm in Vasudeva's voice, Belisarius did not miss the underlying anger—even hatred. When the Ye-tai conquered the Kushan kingdom, a century earlier, they had singled out Buddhism for particularly savage repression. All the monks had been murdered, and the stupas razed to the ground. Like most Kushans Belisarius knew, Vasudeva still considered himself a Buddhist. But it was a faith he practiced in fumbling secret, with no monks or learned scrolls to guide him.

Vasudeva's finger retraced the route he had indicated a few seconds earlier. "As you can see, travel from Begram to Marv is not difficult. Most of it can be done by river craft."

"And what's in Begram?" asked Kurush.

Vasudeva smiled thinly. "Kushans. What else?" The smile faded. "More precisely, Kushan *craftsmen*. Even in the old days, Begram was the center of artisanship in the Kushan realm. Peshawar was bigger, but it was the royal city. Full of soldiers, courtiers, that sort of thing." With a chuckle, as dry as the smile: "And a horde of bureaucrats, of course."

Vasudeva fingered his wispy goatee. "If Damodara had the good sense—*if*, General Belisarius; the Malwa, as a rule, don't think of Kushans as anything other than vassal soldiers—he could have easily transplanted hundreds of Kushan craftsmen to Marv. There, he could have built up an armament center. Close enough, as you can see from the map, to supply his army once it passed the Caspian Gates. But far enough away, in a sheltered oasis, to keep it safe from Persian raiders."

He's right! said Aide to Belisarius. **Marv would be perfect. The Seleucids walled the city eight hundred years ago. The whole oasis, actually. The Sassanids made it a provincial capital and a military center after they conquered the western part of the Kushan Empire. And Marv will become—would have become—the capital of Khorasan province after the Islamic conquest.**

The Persian officers were staring at Vasudeva as if he were babbling in an unknown tongue. One of them turned his head and muttered to another: "*I've* never thought of Kushans as anything but soldiers."

Vasudeva heard the remark. His smile returned. It was a *very* thin smile.

"Nobody does," he said. "The fact remains that Kushans have been skilled artisans for centuries. Appearances to the contrary, we aren't barbarian nomads." He looked down at his hands, flexing his fingers. "My father was a very good jeweler. I wanted to follow in his footsteps. But the Malwa had other plans for me."

Belisarius felt a sudden rush of empathy for the stocky Kushan mercenary. He, as a boy, had wanted to be a blacksmith rather than a soldier. Until the demands of his class, and Rome, decreed otherwise.

"Damodara is smart enough," he mused. He leaned back from the table. "More than smart enough."

Belisarius began slowly pacing around. His softly spoken words were those of a man thinking aloud. "*If* he had good enough intelligence, that is. The Malwa spymaster, Nanda Lal, is a capable man—very capable—but I never got the sense, in the many days I spent in his company, that he thought much about manufacturing and artisanry. His orientation seemed entirely political and military. So where would Damodara have learned—?"

Narses!

"*Narses,*" snarled Maurice. "He's got that stinking traitor working for him."

Belisarius stopped his pacing and stared at the Thracian chiliarch. His own eyes held nothing of Maurice's angry glare. They were simply calm. Calm, and thoughtful.

"That's possible," he said, after a few seconds. "I've never spotted him, through the telescope. But if he's with Damodara's army, Narses would be sure to stay out of sight."

Belisarius scratched his chin. "Possible, possible," he mused. "Narses was an expert on central Asia." He gave Kurush a half-rueful, half-apologetic glance. "We always let him handle that side of our affairs with the Aryans. He was—well, I've got to be honest: *superb*—when it came to bribing and maneuvering barbarians into harassing Persia's eastern provinces."

For a moment, Kurush began to glower. But, within a couple of seconds, the glower turned into a little laugh.

"I know!" he exclaimed. "The grief that man caused us! It wasn't just barbarians, either. He was also a master at keeping those damned eastern noblemen stirred up against imperial authority."

Kurush took four quick strides to the entrance. He stared out and up, toward the crest of the pass. To all appearance, he was listening to the sound of the Malwa barrage. But Belisarius knew that the man's thoughts were really directed elsewhere, both in time and space.

Kurush turned his head. "Assuming that you're right, Belisarius, what's the significance of it?"

"The significance, Kurush, is that it means this Malwa army is even more dangerous that we thought." The Roman general moved toward the entrance, stopping a few feet behind Kurush. "What it means is that *this* army could ravage Mesopotamia on its own, regardless of what happens to the main Malwa army in the delta."

Startled, Kurush spun around.

"They're not big enough!" he exclaimed. "If Emperor Khusrau wasn't tied up keeping the Malwa in Charax—" He stumbled to a halt; then, glumly: "And if we didn't have the traitor Ormazd to deal with in upper Mesopotamia—" His words trailed off again. Stubbornly, Kurush shook his head.

"They're still not big enough," he insisted.

"They *are*, Kurush," countered Belisarius. "*If* they have their own armament center—and I'm now convinced they do—then they are more than big enough."

He stepped up to the entrance, standing right next to Kurush. His next words the general pitched very low, so that only the Persian nobleman could hear.

"That's as good an army as any in the world, sahrdaran. Trust me. I've been fighting them for weeks, now." He hesitated, knowing Kurush's touchy Aryan pride, but pushed on. "And they've defeated every Persian army that was sent against them."

Kurush tightened his jaws. But, touchy or not, the Persian was also honest. He nodded his head curtly.

Belisarius continued. "I thought they'd be limited by the fact that Emperor Skandagupta sent Damodara and Sanga into eastern Persia with very little in the way of gunpowder weapons. But if that's *not* true—if they've created their own weapons industry along the way—then we are looking at a very different kind of animal. A tiger instead of a leopard."

Kurush frowned. "Would Skandagupta permit Damodara such freedom? I always got the impression, from what you told me of your trip to India, that the Malwa gunpowder industry was kept exclusively in their capital city of Kausambi—right under the emperor's nose."

Belisarius stared at the pass above them, as if he were trying to peer through the rock of the mountains and study the enemy on the other side.

"Interesting question," he murmured. "Offhand, I'd say—*no*. But what does Skandagupta know of things in far-off Marv?" Belisarius smiled himself, now—a smile every bit as thin as Vasudeva's had been.

"*Narses*," he said softly, almost lingering over the name. "If Damodara does have Narses working for him, then he's got one of the world's supreme politicians—and spymasters—helping to plan his moves. Narses is not famous, to put it mildly, for his slavish respect for established authority. And he worships no god but Ambition."

Kurush stared at Belisarius, wide-eyed. "You think—"

Belisarius' shoulders moved in a tiny shrug. "Who knows? Except this: if Narses is on the other side of that pass, then I can guarantee that he is spinning plans within plans. Never underestimate that old eunuch, Kurush. He doesn't think simply of the next two steps. He always thinks of the twenty steps beyond those."

Kurush's smile was *not* thin. "That description reminds me of someone else I know."

Belisarius did not smile in return. He simply nodded, once. "Well, yes. It does."

For a few seconds, the two men were silent. Then, after a quick glance into the interior of the tent to make sure no one could overhear, Kurush whispered: "What does this mean—in terms of your strategy?"

Again, Belisarius made that tiny shrug. "I don't know. At the moment, I don't see where it changes anything." He thrust out his chin, pointing at the enemy hidden from their sight by the pass above. "I can delay that army, Kurush, but I can't stop it. So I don't see that I have any choice but to continue with the plan we are already agreed on."

Belisarius gave his own quick glance backward, to make sure no one was within hearing range. Kurush was familiar with his plans, as were Belisarius' own chief subordinates, but he knew that none of the other Persian officers were privy to them. So far as they knew, Belisarius and his Roman army were in the Zagros simply to fend off Damodara's advance. He wanted to keep them in that happy state of ignorance.

"I do know this much," he continued, turning his eyes back to Kurush. "The rebellion in south India is now more important than ever. If our strategy works, here, and we drive the main Malwa army out of the delta—and *if* the rebellion in Majarashtra swells to gigantic proportions—then the Malwa will have no choice." Again, he pointed with his chin to the pass. "They will have to pull that magnificent army out of Persia. And use *it*, instead of Venandakatra's torturers, to crush the Deccan."

Kurush eyed him. He knew how much Belisarius liked and admired the Marathas and their Empress Shakuntala. "That'll be very tough on the rebels."

Belisarius winced, but only briefly. "Yes—and then again, maybe not."

He paused, staring at the mountains. "Those men are far better soldiers than anything Venandakatra has. And there's no comparison at all between their leaders and the Vile One. But that army is Rajput, now, at its core. And Damodara has welded himself to them. Rajputs have their own hard sense of honor, which fits their Malwa masters about as well as a glove fits a fish tail. I'm not sure how good they'll be, when the time comes for murder instead of war."

Kurush scowled. The expression made clear his own opinion. *Malwa was Malwa.*

Belisarius did not argue the point. He was not at all sure that Kurush was wrong. But, inwardly, he made another shrug. As much as Belisarius prided himself on his ability to plan ahead, he had never forgotten that the heart of war is chaos and confusion. Between the moment—now—and the future, lay the maelstrom. Who could foresee what combinations, and what contradictions, that vortex would produce? In the months—years—ahead?

Now intervened, breaking his train of thought. The sounds of the Malwa barrage abruptly ceased. Looking up the slope, Belisarius saw a courier racing toward the field headquarters. One of Bouzes' Syrians, he thought.

Belisarius did not wait for the man to arrive. He turned back into the tent and announced, to the Roman and Persian officers who had remained by the table: "Gentlemen, there's a battle to be fought."

Chapter 12

On his way back up the slope, Belisarius stopped when he came to the trenches where the handcannon soldiers were dug in. He turned to Maurice, waving his hand.

"Go on ahead, and see to the rest of the army. I want to go over our plans one last time with Mark and Gregory."

Maurice nodded, and continued plodding toward the crest of the pass. His progress was slow. The trench through which he was moving had been recently dug. The soil was still loose, making for unfirm footing. His biggest difficulty, however, came from the sheer weight of his weapons and armor. Cataphract gear was heavy enough, sitting on a horse. For a man on foot, climbing uphill, the armor seemed made of lead ingots instead of steel scale. The weapons weighed more than Nero's sins.

Belisarius felt a moment's sympathy for Maurice—but only a moment. He was wearing his own cataphract gear, and would be making that trek himself soon enough. If the war against Malwa dragged on for years, Belisarius thought the day would come when Roman soldiers could finally be rid of that damned armor. In visions which Aide had given him of gunpowder armies of the future, soldiers had worn nothing but a plate cuirass and a helmet. Just enough to stop a bullet, except at close range.

He sighed. That day was still far off. Belisarius had spent hours—and hours and hours—studying the great generals of the future, especially those of the first centuries of gunpowder warfare.

Aide knew all of human history, and the crystal had shown Belisarius the methods and tactics of those men. Jan Zizka; Gonzalo de
Cordoba and the Duke of Parma; Maurice of Nassau; Henry IV
of France; Tilly and Wallenstein, and Gustavus Adolphus; Turenne
and Frederick the Great; Marlborough; Napoleon and Wellington;
and many others.

Of all those men, the only one Belisarius truly admired was
Gustavus Adolphus. To some degree, his admiration was professional. Gustav II Adolf, King of Sweden, had reintroduced mobility
and fluid tactics into a style of war which had become nothing
more than brutal hammering. Massive squares of musket and pike
slamming into other such squares, like the old Greek phalanxes.

But, for the most part, Belisarius was attracted by the man himself. Gustavus Adolphus had been a king—a very self-confident
and ambitious king, in point of fact—who was by no means
immune from monarchy's vices. Still, he had been scrupulous
about consulting the various estates of his kingdom, as he was
required to do by Swedish law. He had managed to win the firm
loyalty of his officers and soldiers by his fair and consistent conduct.
He was as good a king as he was a general—Sweden was, by far,
the best administered realm of his time. He had been the only
king of his day who cared a fig for the needs of common folk. And
his troops, when they entered the Thirty Years War under his
command, had been the only soldiers who did not ravage the
German countryside.

I would have liked to meet that man, he mused.

Aide's voice came into his mind. The crystal's thoughts were
hesitant, almost apologetic.

**He will never exist, now. Whatever happens. If Malwa wins
this war, and Link establishes its domination over mankind,
there will be no kings like that. Not ever.**

Belisarius' face tightened. Link, the secret master of the Malwa
dynasty, was an artificial intelligence sent back in time by the "new
gods" of the future. Belisarius had met the creature, once, when
he was in India. It had taken the form of Great Lady Holi, the
aunt of the Malwa emperor. Aide called it a cybernetic organism.

Belisarius' eyes drifted across the landscape of the Zagros, as if
that rugged mountain range was a metaphor for human destiny.
The slopes of those mountains were rocky, treacherous, and at
least half-hidden by spurs and crests. Belisarius had learned much,

over the past four years, about mankind's future—it would be better to say, *futures*, because the "new gods" had their own plans for shaping human destiny. But he still did not know much about the "new gods" themselves. Aide, he was sure, was not withholding information from him. The crystal was simply incapable of understanding such mentalities.

Belisarius thought he understood them. They reminded him of religious fanatics he had met. Orthodox or Monophysite, it mattered not. All such men were imbued with the certainty that they—and they alone—understood the Will of God. Those who opposed them were not simply in error, they were the minions of Satan. To be scourged, that others might be cleansed.

That was the vision, he thought, which animated the "new gods" of the future. Outraged by the chaotic kaleidoscope of humanity, as it spread through the stars, they were seized by a determination to *purify the race*.

There had been no conceivable way to accomplish that goal, in their future time. Humanity had settled throughout the galaxy, and all the galaxies nearby. Isolated by incredible distances and the speed of light, each human planet went its own way. The human species was evolving in a million different directions, like the branches of a great tree, with nothing to bind it but a common heritage and the slender threads of the Great Ones in their travels.

So, the "new gods" had sent Link back in time, to alter history when humanity was still living on a single planet. To crush the mongrel empire called Rome, and to build a world state centered in north India. The "new gods" intended to use the Hindu caste system as the germ for what they called a "eugenics program." They would *purify the race*—and if, in the doing, they slaughtered millions, they cared not the least. Those were cattle, at best, if not outright vermin. Only the "new gods," and those they would shape in their image, were truly human.

Aide was right. If Malwa won, there would be no kings in the future like Gustavus Adolphus.

And if we win? he asked. But he knew the answer, before Aide even gave it.

Then you will have changed history also. The course of it will remain, like a broad river, but the banks will be altered. There may not even be a country called Sweden, in that future. There certainly won't be a man named Gustavus

Adolphus. Or, if there is, he's as likely to be a peasant or a glassmaker as a king.

For a moment, the thought saddened Belisarius. The Roman general had no doubt of the righteousness of his cause. None at all. But even the most just war causes destruction. Saving that great, flowering tree of humanity's future, Belisarius would crush many of its buds. There would be no Gustavus Adolphus. No Shakespeare; no Cervantes; no Spinoza and Kant; no Sir Isaac Newton.

The moment passed. *But there will be others, like them.*

Yes, came Aide's reply. Quietly: **And there will be a place, too, for others like me. We are also people, with our own rightful place in that great tree.**

Belisarius' musings were interrupted by a voice.

"How soon do you want us ready, general?"

Belisarius snapped out of his reverie and focused his eyes on the speaker. It was Mark of Edessa, the commander of Belisarius' new unit of handcannon soldiers.

An idle thought crossed Belisarius' mind. *I have got to come up with a new name for them. "Handcannon soldiers" is just too much of a mouthful.*

Belisarius took a moment to examine the man. Mark was in his early twenties. He was a Syrian, of predominantly Arab ancestry. That was useful, given that most of his men were of similar stock. Like all Roman soldiers, the men spoke Greek—or learned to, at least, shortly after enlisting. But Mark's fluency in Arabic and several of the Aramaic dialects had proven valuable many times.

But that was not the principal reason Mark had been given this new command. The young officer, during the course of the previous year's campaign in Mesopotamia, had shown himself to be resourceful and reliable. He also—this was quite unusual for a cavalryman—had no objection to fighting on foot, and had proven to have a knack for the new gunpowder weapons.

Belisarius remembered the first time he met Mark, almost four years earlier. The general had just taken command of the army at Mindouos. His predecessor had let that army rot, and Belisarius had found it necessary to purge many of the existing officers. A number of men had been promoted from the ranks. Mark had been one of them, recommended by Belisarius' cataphract, Gregory.

He saw two more figures scuttling up the trench.

"Speak of the devil," he murmured. Gregory himself was arriving. He and Mark had become good friends, and had shown they could work together well in combat. That was one of the reasons that Belisarius had put Gregory in command of another new unit, the pikemen who served as a bulwark for the handcannon soldiers.

Call them "musketeers," came Aide's thought. Technically, it would be more accurate to call them arquebusiers, but—

"Arquebusiers" is ridiculous. Musketeers it is!

Belisarius broke into a smile. The new name was a minor triumph, true. Picayune, perhaps. But he was a firm believer in the axiom that large victories grow out of a multitude of small ones.

Gregory had arrived, now. He and Mark were eyeing their general quizzically, wondering why he was smiling. Almost grinning, in fact.

"I've got a new name for your men, Mark," he announced. "From now on, we'll call you musketeers."

Mark and Gregory looked at each other. It was almost comical the way each began mouthing the word.

"I like it," pronounced Gregory, after a moment's experimentation. Mark nodded his head. "So do I!"

The third man came up, and now Belisarius did break into a grin.

"And what have we here?" he asked. "The three musketeers?"

Oh, that's gross! There followed a mental, crystalline version of a raspberry. **Low, low.**

Gregory gave the new man, whose name was Felix Chalcenterus, an unkind look. The same little glare was transferred to Mark of Edessa.

"Give me a break, general," he growled. "You won't find me fighting with these new-fangled gadgets. Cold steel, that's still my business."

Mark and Felix matched Belisarius' grin. "He's hopeless, General," stated Mark. "Set in his ways, like an old village woman."

Belisarius chuckled at the quip, even though it was quite unfair. For the past year, Gregory had served as Belisarius' chief artillery officer. In this campaign of fluid maneuver, Belisarius had left his cumbersome artillery behind, so Gregory had been free to take on another assignment. The main reason Belisarius had put the man in charge of the new unit of pikemen was that Gregory was one of those officers who seemed almost infinitely flexible. He was one of the very few Thracian cataphracts who didn't squeal like a stuck pig when asked to fight on foot, with a pike instead of a lance. The pikemen were an elite unit, true, but Gregory had still been hard-pressed to find enough Thracians to volunteer. In the end, he had relied heavily on the new Isaurians who were enlisting into the general's corps of bucellarii.

Belisarius got down to business. "Are *you* ready?" he asked. The question was directed at all three men simultaneously. Felix Chalcenterus served Mark as his executive officer.

"We're set, general," came Mark's reply. Gregory and Felix nodded their agreement.

"Good. Remember—don't start up the slope until I signal for you." Belisarius made a little head toss toward the east. "You can be damned sure that Sanga will have some of his Pathan scouts perched on the nearby hilltops, watching everything we do. They'll have some means of signaling Damodara—mirrors, if the sun's right. If not, they'll have something else. Banners, maybe smoke. It's essential that they can't see you until the time comes for your countercharge."

Belisarius gave the three men a quick scrutiny. Satisfied that they understood the point, he added: "You'll have to come up the hill in a hurry, mind. I won't give the signal until the last minute. In a hurry—*and* in good formation. Can you do it?"

There was no verbal reply. Just three self-confident smiles and nodding heads.

"All right," said Belisarius. He gave out a little sigh. "The moment's come, then. It's my turn to climb that damned hill."

He turned and set off, slogging his way. Every step forward was marked by half a step backward, sliding in the loose soil. Progress was marked by the soft, crunching sounds of semifutility. Within a few yards, his armor and weapons felt like the burden of Atlas.

"Some day," he muttered. "If this war goes on long enough. I'll be skipping through the meadows with nothing but a helmet and a linen uniform. Not a care in the world."

Except frying in napalm, or being shredded by high explosive shells, came Aide's unkind thought. **Not to mention being**

picked off at five hundred yards by a sniper armed with a high-velocity rifle. And while we're at it, let's not forget—

Not a care in the world! insisted Belisarius. His thought was perhaps a bit surly. *Death is a feather. Cataphract gear is the torment of Prometheus.*

Then, very surly: *Spoilsport.*

By the time he reached the trench at the crest of the pass, Belisarius was exhausted. He half-collapsed next to Maurice. Valentinian and Anastasius were still in the trench, a few feet to his right.

Maurice gave him no more than a cursory glance before resuming his study of the enemy troops on the slope below. "You'll get over it soon enough," he said. The words were unkind but the tone was sympathetic. "You'd better," added Maurice grimly. "The Ye-tai aren't wasting any time."

Wearily, Belisarius nodded. Fortunately, his exhaustion was simply due to heavy, but brief, exertion. It was not the kind of fatigue produced by hours of relentless labor. He knew from experience that his well-toned muscles would recover in a few minutes—even if, at the moment, he didn't feel as if he could ever walk again.

The general's head was below the parapet, resting against the sloped wall of the trench. He was too tired to lift it. He could hear the faint sounds of orders being shouted in Hindi, coming from far down the slope.

"What are they doing, Maurice?" he asked.

"The Ye-tai will be making the main assault. Nothing fancy, just a straight charge up the slope. On foot. They've just about finished dressing their lines." He gave a little half-incredulous grunt. "Good lines, too. Way better than I've ever seen barbarians do before."

"They're not exactly barbarians," said Belisarius. He made a brief attempt at raising his head, but gave it up almost instantly. "They act like it, sure enough. The Malwa encourage them to behave barbarously, not that the Ye-tai need much encouragement. But they've been an integral part of the Malwa ruling class for three generations, now. All of their sub-officers, to give you an idea, are literate. Down to a rank equivalent to our pentarchs."

Maurice emitted another grunt. From Belisarius' other side came Valentinian's half-incredulous (and half-disgruntled) exclamation: "You've got to be kidding!"

Belisarius smiled. Valentinian's attitude was understandable. Even in the Roman army, with its comparatively democratic traditions, not more than half of the sub-officers below the rank of hecatontarch could read and write.

Valentinian himself carried the rank of a hecatontarch. That was the modern Greek equivalent of the old Latin "centurion"—commander of a hundred. But in his case, the rank was a formal honor more than anything else. Valentinian didn't command anyone. His job, along with Anastasius, was to keep Belisarius alive on the battlefield.

Valentinian was literate, just barely. He could sign his name without help, and he could pick his way through simple written messages. But he had never even thought of trying to read a book. If someone had ever suggested it to him—

"You should read a book sometime," commented Anastasius mildly. "Be good for you, Valentinian."

"You've got to be kidding," came the instant, hissing response.

He's got to be kidding, echoed Aide.

Listening to the exchange, Belisarius' smile widened. Anastasius *was* literate—and not barely. The giant Thracian cataphract read any book he could get his hands on, especially if it dealt with philosophy. But his attitude, for a Roman soldier, was unusual—it might be better to say, extraordinary.

Anastasius himself ascribed his peculiarity to the fact that he had a Greek father. But Belisarius thought otherwise. There were plenty of Greek soldiers in the Roman army who were as illiterate—and as uninterested in literacy—as any Hun. Belisarius suspected that Anastasius' obsession with philosophy was more in the nature of a personal rebellion. The man was so huge, and so strong, and so brutal in his appearance, that Belisarius thought he had turned to reading as a way of assuring himself that he was a man and not an ogre.

The thought of ogres brought his mind back to the moment. Literate they might be, but the Ye-tai were the closest human equivalents to ogres that Belisarius had ever met.

Speaking of which, muttered Aide, **you'd better gird your loins, grandpa. The ogres are coming.**

Belisarius heard the sound of kettledrums. "They're coming," said Maurice. He spoke softly, as he usually did, but his tone was as grim as a glacier. "Fierce bastards, too. Nobody's got to drive *them* forward. They're coming on like starving wolves after a crippled antelope."

Belisarius had recovered enough. With a little grunt of effort, he heaved himself half-erect and looked over the parapet.

He gave the Ye-tai charging up the mountain pass no more than a quick, almost perfunctory, study. He had seen Ye-tai in action before, and was not surprised by anything he saw—neither the vigor of their charge, nor the way they still managed to keep their lines reasonably well dressed even while storming up a rock-strewn slope. It was impressive, to be sure. But there was nothing in the world as sheerly *impressive* as a charge of Persian heavy cavalry. Belisarius had faced Persian charges, in the past, and broken the armies who made them.

He spent a little more time gauging the kshatriyas who were accompanying the Ye-tai. In the Malwa Empire, unlike other Hindu realms, the warrior caste was devoted almost exclusively to gunpowder weapons and tactics. Except in Damodara's army, in fact, they had a monopoly on such weapons.

There were a number of kshatriyas dispersed through the ranks of the oncoming Ye-tai. All of them were carrying grenades—one in the hand, with several more slung from bandoliers. Their free hands held the strikers to light the fuses.

None of the kshatriyas, of course, were in the first few ranks. As lightly armored as they were, the grenadiers could not hope to match Roman soldiers in hand-to-hand combat. But Belisarius was impressed to see that the kshatriyas were not, as he had observed in other Malwa armies, hanging far back in the rear.

Here, too, Damodara's style of leadership was evident. Over time, Malwa's pampered kshatriyas had lost much of the martial rigor which that warrior caste possessed in other Hindu societies. They were held in open scorn by Rajput kshatriyas. Damodara, it seemed, had reinstituted the old traditions. Those grenadiers storming up the hill alongside the sword-wielding Ye-tai bore no resemblance to the arrogant idlers whom Belisarius had seen while he was in India.

But there were still not many of them, he was relieved to see. Not enough to change the equation in the immediate battle. No more than one in twenty of the enemy soldiers in the oncoming charge were carrying grenades. That was an even smaller percentage than usual. Whatever armaments complex Damodara had succeeded in creating, it was apparently still small. Belisarius suspected that Damodara was doing what he would have done himself—*had* done, in fact, when Belisarius created his own weapons industry. Concentrate on quality, not quantity. Build a few good cannons, and improve the rocketry, rather than try to churn out simple grenades.

So, the general's eyes were soon drawn to the enemy's flanks, where the Rajput cavalry were massed. *That* was the real threat. Belisarius was confident that he could handle the Ye-tai charge. He had his own surprise waiting, on the back side of the slope. But, no more than Damodara, had Belisarius been able to produce gunpowder weapons in great quantity. His one thousand musketeers could break the Ye-tai but—

Aide's voice interrupted his train of thought. There was a tinge of annoyance in the crystal's words. A tinge of annoyance—and more than a tinge of worry.

They're *not* musketeers. Not really. Eighteenth-century musketeers could fire three volleys a minute. But they had flintlocks. You don't even have arquebuses as good as Gustavus Adolphus' soldiers, and they couldn't fire more often than—

Aide broke off, with the mental equivalent of a sigh of exasperation. He and Belisarius had already had this argument. As always, when the dispute involved purely military affairs, Belisarius' opinion had carried the day.

The general did not bother with a reply. He was too preoccupied with studying the Rajputs.

Not to his surprise, Belisarius saw that most of the Rajput cavalry—two out of three, he gauged—were now concentrated on the enemy's right flank, under Sanga's command. The pass in which Belisarius was making a stand was saddle-shaped. The flanks of the pass were not sheer cliffs, but rounded slopes. The slope on Belisarius' left was almost gentle. If the Ye-tai could pin the Roman center, Sanga would have no real difficulty leading a mass cavalry charge against the Roman left.

Belisarius, of course, had read the terrain the same way as Damodara and Sanga. And so he had positioned his heaviest troops, the Greek cataphracts under Cyril's command, on his left. He would hold the center and the right with the lighter Syrian forces, and the new units of musketeers and pikemen.

The fact remained that he was badly outnumbered, and the ground was open enough that the Malwa could bring all their forces to bear. Not easily; not quickly—but surely, for all that.

Belisarius shook his head a little, reminding himself that he was not trying to *win* this battle. He just needed to put up enough of a fight so that his retreat to the south, when the time came, would not seem too puzzling to his opponents. Belisarius could afford the tactical setback involved in giving up this battlefield, as long as his troops weren't badly mauled. He could *not* afford the strategic defeat which would be certain, if Damodara or Sanga—or Narses, if the canny eunuch was with them—ever figured out what Belisarius was planning for, months from now.

Maurice verbalized Belisarius' own thoughts.

"It's going to be a bit touch-and-go," growled the chiliarch. "More than a bit, if your little surprise doesn't work as well as you think it will. Which it probably won't," he added sourly. "Nothing ever works the way it's supposed to, on a battlefield."

Belisarius started to respond, but fell silent. The Ye-tai were almost close enough—

Time. Belisarius gave the hand signal, and the small group of cornicenes just a few yards away immediately began blowing on their horns.

The peal of the cornicens immediately brought thousands of Greek cataphracts and Syrian archers to their feet, standing hip-high in their trenches with bows already nocked. A volley of arrows swept down the slope.

Like a scythe, came the simile to Belisarius' mind, but he knew it was inappropriate. Plunging fire was difficult. He was not surprised to see many of the arrows sail right over the approaching mass of Ye-tai. And it was often ineffective even when it struck, against experienced troops.

The Ye-tai were veterans, and had been expecting the volley. As soon as they saw the cataphracts rearing up, the Ye-tai crouched and sheltered behind their shields. The shouted orders of their officers were quite unnecessary. Because of the angle, they presented smaller targets to begin with, and each Ye-tai was experienced enough to keep his shield properly slanted.

Those were good shields, as good as Roman ones. Laminated wood reinforced with iron—nothing like the flimsy wicker shields with which the Malwa Empire armed its common soldiers. Most of the Roman arrows which hit their targets glanced off harmlessly.

The Ye-tai immediately resumed their charge, bellowing their battle cries. Another volley; another shielded crouch; another upward surge. They lost men, of course—plenty of them—but not enough. Not for *those* warriors. Ye-tai had many vices; cowardice was not one of them.

"Not a chance," grunted Maurice. There was no amazement in those words. Not even a trace of surprise. Maurice sounded like a man remarking that there was no way a sandcastle was going to hold back the tide.

The chiliarch glanced at Belisarius. "You'd better see to your gunmen. We're going to need them."

Belisarius was already turning. As he began giving the new signal, he heard Maurice mutter: "Oh, marvelous. The Rajputs are already starting *their* charge. God, I hate competent enemies." A few seconds later, hissing: "*Shit.* I can't believe it!"

Belisarius had been watching the musketeers climbing up the slope. Hearing the alarm in Maurice's voice, he immediately turned around.

Seeing the speed with which the Rajput cavalry was charging up that side of the saddle, Belisarius understood Maurice's shock. Belisarius himself had never seen cavalry move that quickly in mountainous terrain.

Silently, he cursed himself for an idiot. He had forgotten—it might be better to say, never understood in the first place. Belisarius was accustomed to Roman and Persian heavy cavalry, whose gear and tactics had been shaped by centuries of war on the flat plains of Mesopotamia. But the Rajputs were *not* heavy cavalry—not, at least, by Roman and Persian standards—and they were unfazed by rough terrain.

Rajputana is a land of hills, chimed in Aide. **The Rajput military tradition was forged in expeditions against Pathan mountaineers, and battles fought against Marathas in the volcanic badlands of the Great Country.**

"Like a bunch of damned mountain goats," growled Maurice. He cocked his head. "You do realize, young man, that your fancy battle plan just flew south for the winter." For all the grimness of the words, there was a trace of satisfaction in the voice. Maurice

was one of those natural-born pessimists who took a strange pleasure in seeing the world live down to their expectations.

Belisarius had already reached the same conclusion. The weak-
est part of his tactical plan had been its reliance on close timing.
The Rajputs had just kicked over the hourglass. Shattered it to
pieces, in fact. Sanga's forces would strike the Roman left long
before Belisarius had expected them to.

"Get over there quick, Maurice," he commanded. "Work with
Cyril to get the Greeks reoriented. They'll have to hold off Sanga
now, as long as they can. Forget about any countercharge against
the Ye-tai." He pointed to the large force of Thracian cataphracts
positioned halfway down the back slope, as a reserve. "And send
a dispatch rider to the bucellarii, telling them to move left. We're
going to need them."

"What about the Mamelukes?" asked Maurice. He looked southwest, to where the Kushans were holding the fords at the river
half a mile below. "Do you want them up here, with you?"

Belisarius shook his head. "Not unless I'm desperate. I can't risk
having any of them captured. Even a dead Kushan body could give
the game away."

Maurice gave a skeptical glance at the musketeers who were
nearing the crest.

"Do you really you think you can hold—" he started to say, but
broke off. A second later, the chiliarch was scuttling down the
trench, toward the Roman left. For all Maurice's frequent sarcasms
on the subject of Belisarius' "fancy damned battle plans," the Thracian veteran was not given to arguing with him in the midst of
actual combat. A general's willingness to *command*—instantly and
surely—was more important in a battle than whether the command
itself was wise. Maurice had seen battles won, more than once,
simply because the commander had stood his ground and given
clear and definite orders. *Any* orders, just so long as the troops
felt that a steady hand was in control.

Belisarius peered over the parapet. The Ye-tai were very close,
now. Their battle cries filled the air, thick with confidence, heavy
with impending triumph. They had been bloodied by the Roman
archery, but not badly enough. Several thousand would still reach
the crest, where outnumbered and lightly armed Syrian infantry
would be no match for them.

He rose, half-standing, and looked over the other parapet. The musketeers and the pikemen were almost at the crest, just a few yards down the slope. They had stopped, actually, to make a final dress of their lines. Belisarius saw Mark of Edessa watching him, calmly waiting for the general's order.

Here goes, thought Belisarius.

He gave the signal. Again, the cornicens blew. As he turned back to face the enemy, Belisarius saw small figures on nearby hilltops frantically waving banners. The Pathan scouts had caught sight of the new Roman unit surging forward, and were signaling Damodara.

Too late.

Belisarius took a deep breath, and gave a small prayer for the soul of a man he had never met, and never would. A general of a future that would never be. A man he didn't much care for, as a human being, but who had been one of history's greatest generals.

May your soul rest in peace, wherever it is, Iron Duke. I hope this works as well for me as it did for you at Busaco.

Aide's words, when they came, surprised Belisarius. He had been half-expecting some muttered reproaches. Something to the effect that *Wellington*'s men could fire three volleys a minute; or that *Wellington* had the massive fortifications of the Lines of Torres Vedras to fall back on; or even—Aide had a bit of the pedant in him—that the title "Iron Duke" was an anachronism, in this context. The nickname was political, not military. It had been given to *Prime Minister* Wellington by English commoners, years after the fall of Napoleon, when he responded to a mob breaking his windows by installing iron shutters on his mansion in London.

But all that came, instead, was reassurance.

It will. The reverse-slope tactic was Wellington's signature. It worked at Salamanca, too. And even against Napoleon at Waterloo.

Belisarius was grateful for that quiet voice of confidence. He needed it. This battle was shaping up to be the worst fight of his life, rather than the simple cut-and-run he had anticipated. Once again, he had underestimated the Rajputs.

The musketeers reached the crest of the pass, and leveled their handcannons at the Ye-tai storming forward. Belisarius rose to join in his world's first use of a musket volley in battle, but not before giving himself a small curse.

Don't ever do that again, you jackass. Just because you've got brains, and a friend who can show you the future, don't ever forget that other men have brains too. And damned good ones, with the will to match.

The muskets roared, all across the line. Instantly, the crest of the pass was shrouded in gunsmoke. It was impossible to see more than a few feet through those acrid billows. Impatiently, while his musketeers went through the practiced drill with their clumsy muzzle loaders, Belisarius waited for the smoke to clear.

There was a good breeze coming through the pass. The clouds of gunsmoke were swept away within seconds. And Belisarius, seeing the havoc wreaked by a thousand .80–caliber smoothbores firing at close range, felt himself relax. Just a bit. The Ye-tai army was like a bull, half-stunned by a hammer blow between the eyes.

He raised his eyes, staring across the mounded heaps of Ye-tai corpses to his opponent's distant pavilion. Belisarius had just sent his own message—to himself, as well as Damodara. Reminding them both that if Belisarius had no monopoly on intelligence, neither did he have a monopoly on overconfidence.

And don't underestimate me *again, Lord of Malwa,* he thought. *Better yet—do underestimate me again.*

The Ye-tai, stubborn and courageous, were pushing forward. They clambered up and over the corpses and hideously shattered bodies of their wounded comrades, roaring with rage and hefting their swords. The Ye-tai were no longer trying to maintain formation. They were just a mob of enraged berserks, burning to reach their tormentors. The bull was half-stunned, but it was still a bull.

The second line of musketeers stepped forward and fired. While the smoke cleared, the third line took their place. Behind, the first line had already finished reloading and was preparing for a second volley.

It was true that Belisarius' musketeers, with their awkward matchlocks, could not match Wellington's three volleys a minute. The guns themselves were not much better than sixteenth-century arquebuses. John of Rhodes, working with sixth-century technology, couldn't possibly match the precision of nineteenth-century gunmaking. But Belisarius had all of Aide's encyclopedic knowledge to draw upon, so he had been able to leap over centuries of military experimentation in other ways. It *was* within the capacity of the Roman Empire to manufacture the prepared cartridges

which Gustavus Adolphus had introduced. The muzzle loaders
themselves were clumsy things, but there was nothing clumsy
about the way they were being used.

His musketeers couldn't manage more than one volley a minute,
but Belisarius could *rely* on that rate. And, as the smoke cleared,
and he saw the carnage which the second volley had created, Belisarius knew that would be enough.

**Wellington's reverse-slope tactic depended as much on
the shock of surprise as it did on rates of fire,** said Aide.

Belisarius nodded. An enemy storming forward in expectation
of furious victory had its spirits shattered, along with its bodies,
when it was struck down by a hail of bullets. Not even warriors
like the Ye-tai could withstand such a blow.

No more than Napoleon's Imperial Guard at Waterloo.

The third line stepped forward, their weapons ready. There was
no need for plunging fire, now. The vanguard elements of the Ye-
tai had reached the crest and were not more than ten yards from
the trenches. Felix Chalcenterus, the executive officer, was in
charge of fire control. He called out the orders, in sure sequence.

Level! The guns came up like so many blunt lances.

There was no command to aim. Belisarius' musketeers, like Wellington's, were simply trained to fire in the general direction of
the enemy. The weapons were so inaccurate, beyond fifty yards,
that marksmanship was pointless.

Fire! The handcannons erupted. Another cloud of smoke
obscured everything.

Obscured sight, that is, not sound. Belisarius could hear the
bullets slamming into the struggling mass of Ye-tai. The sounds
had a metallic edge, where bullets impacted armor, but he knew
the armor was irrelevant. At that range, the murderous lead pellets
punched through the finest plate armor as if it were mere cloth.
The muzzle velocity of a matchlock arquebus was extremely
high—supersonic, more often than not. The high-velocity rifles
which would replace them in the future would do no more than
double that, even after centuries of arms development and
refinement. An arquebus' round shot lost its muzzle velocity very
quickly, of course—far sooner than the spinning bullets of rifles.
But at *this* range, the heavy-caliber arquebuses were probably even
more effective than rifles.

The shrieks of wounded Ye-tai began to fill the pass, like the wail of a giant banshee. The Ye-tai were tough—as tough as any soldiers Belisarius had ever seen. But no soldiers are *that* tough.

The bull was on its knees, now. Bellowing, still, but dying for all that.

Their bloody work done, the third line retired. Even with the breeze, the pass was still half-obscured with smoke. But Belisarius could hear Felix commanding the first line back to the front. Chalcenterus' voice still had the timbre of his youth, but the voice itself was relaxed and confident.

I didn't make any mistake there, at least, Belisarius consoled himself. Felix had first caught the general's eye at the battle of the villa near Anatha, the previous year. Belisarius had been impressed by the Syrian soldier's alert calmness when the Roman army was subjected to its first experience with rocket fire. He had kept an eye on the youth, and seen to his rapid promotion.

The first line, back in position, went through the sequence. Another roar of handcannon fire. The pass was completely shrouded in smoke. Even with their clumsy weapons, the men could still keep up a rate of fire that outmatched the breeze.

The sound of bullets slamming into the enemy had a sodden quality, now. Belisarius was thankful that he couldn't actually see the results. This was sheer slaughter. He knew that the rear elements of the Ye-tai would already be staggering back in defeat. But the barbarian soldiers trapped at the front were helpless. Immobile targets. The bull was no longer even bellowing. It was just a dying beast, dumbly waiting for another blow of the hammer.

The second line returned, and the blow came. Belisarius heard Gregory calling out an order. His pikemen had been in position since the first line of musketeers stepped forward, ready to fend off any Ye-tai who made it through the gunfire. But they had not even been needed. Gregory had obviously come to the conclusion that they wouldn't be, and so he had called on his men to use their grenades.

The pikemen lowered their twelve-foot spears and plucked grenades from their bandoliers. Each pikeman carried only two of the devices. More would have impeded them in performing their principal duty. But these were special grenades. The pikemen had been equipped with the new grenades which John of Rhodes had developed—the ones with impact fuses.

The grenades had a simple "potato-masher" design. A strip of cloth was attached to the butt of the wooden handle. Like the cloth strips often attached to javelins, it would stabilize the grenade in flight and ensure that the weapon would strike in the proper orientation to set off the fuse. There was no need to fumble with a striker, or cut a fuse to proper length. Each pikeman simply yanked out the pin which armed the device, and sent it sailing down the slope.

The grenades disappeared into the clouds of smoke which were wafting down the pass. Before they hit, Felix had ordered another round of gunfire. Not more than a second after that roaring lightning, Belisarius heard the sharp claps of the grenades exploding down the slope. The sounds harmonized like music composed by a maniac. A homicidal maniac. Those Ye-tai at the rear, trying to retreat, were being savaged by the grenades even while their comrades at the front were being hammered into pulp by the guns.

For an instant, Belisarius was seized by a savage urge to order a countercharge. That had been his plan from the beginning. The Ye-tai were already broken—as badly as any army could be, driven back from an assault. A rush of pikemen now would complete their destruction. The fierce army which had charged up the slope not minutes earlier would be as thoroughly beaten as any army in human history.

Mark and Gregory were at his side now, awaiting the order. Their faces were tense and eager. They knew as well as Belisarius that they were on the verge of total victory.

Fiercely, Belisarius restrained himself. Yes, the enemy was beaten *here*. But—

Distantly, he could hear wails from another direction. To his left. Wails of pain, and the steel clash of weapons. He couldn't see anything through the wafting clouds of gunsmoke, but he knew the Rajputs were already hammering his left flank.

All ferocity and sense of satisfaction fled. His counterstroke at the saddle had worked, just as it had worked in another future for a man named Arthur Wellesley. But battles are rarely neat and tidy affairs which go according to plan. Not against well-led enemies, at least.

This battle could still wind up a disaster, came Aide's forceful thought.

Belisarius had won the struggle at the center, true. But if he didn't withdraw his army quickly, and in good order—which was the most difficult maneuver of all, in the face of the enemy—Sanga and the Rajputs would roll up his flank.

"No," he commanded, pointing toward the slope of the saddle to their left. Only the crest of the pass was still visible, due to the gunsmoke, but they could see hundreds of Rajput cavalry pouring across the terrain. Ten times that number would be hidden in the clouds below, on the lower part of the slope. *Twenty* times, more likely. There had been at least ten thousand Rajputs massed on the Malwa right, under Sanga's command.

Mark began to argue—respectfully, but still vehemently, but Gregory restrained him with a firm shake of the shoulder. The Thracian cataphract was older than the Syrian, more of a veteran—and more familiar with Belisarius.

"Shut up, youngster," he growled. "The general's right. If we charge down that slope, we'll be completely out of position when the Rajputs hit us. They'll turn us into sausage."

Belisarius didn't pick his officers for reticence and timidity. The young Syrian flushed, a bit, from Gregory's rebuke, but plowed on. "The Greeks'll hold them! Those are Cyril's men—and Agathius', before him. The same cataphracts who broke the Malwa at Anatha, and then at—"

"There are only three thousand of them, Mark," said Belisarius mildly. He wasn't going to spend more than a few seconds, arguing with a subordinate in the middle of a battle. But he *was* prepared to spend those seconds. There was no other way to train good officers.

"They're facing four times their number—probably five," he continued. "They're splendid troops, yes. But they don't have as good a position as we did here in the center. There's no one protecting *their* flank. Sanga will just send enough men to keep them pinned while he sweeps around them. He won't even try to crush the Greeks, not now. He'll bypass them and fall on us."

He pointed to the line of musketeers. The men had ceased firing now, and the pikemen had used up all their grenades. The center of the battlefield was almost quiet, except for the cries of wounded Ye-tai.

"How do you expect to form a defensive line against that charge—*here*? Straddling a mountain pass, with the enemy coming *down* the slope?"

Mark fell silent. His face still had a stubborn look to it, but Belisarius knew that the young Syrian was—not convinced, perhaps, but ready to obey.

Satisfied with that, Belisarius turned to Gregory and said: "Fall back southwest, toward the river. Upstream." He pointed to a location where the narrow river below the pass broadened a bit. "Where Vasudeva's guarding the fords. Set your men, and the musketeers, to hold the river after I get the rest of the army across."

Gregory nodded. A moment later, he and Mark were shouting commands to their men.

And now, thought Belisarius, looking toward his left flank, *I've got to try to get those men out of here. Which is not going to be easy. Sanga will be like a tiger, with me trying to pry meat from his jaws.*

Belisarius heard Valentinian and Anastasius stirring behind him. As the general's personal bodyguards, they hadn't been expecting to do much in this current battle beyond looking grim and fearsome. But they were veterans, and could recognize a battle plan in tatters when they saw one.

"Looks like we're going to have to work, after all," groused Valentinian. Anastasius was silent. "What's the matter, large one?" came Valentinian's sarcastic voice. "No philosophical motto for the occasion? No words of wisdom?"

"Don't need 'em," rumbled Anastasius in reply. "Even a witless weasel can see when he's in a fight for his life."

Chapter 13

By the time Belisarius reached his left flank, where the Greeks were holding back the Rajputs, his bucellarii were already arriving. He was deeply thankful for their speed in responding to his orders, but he took a moment to give himself a mental pat on the back.

His tactics for this battle were at least half ruined, but Belisarius thought he could still pull his army out before disaster struck. If he did, it would be because of his past foresight. His Thracian cataphracts rode the finest heavy chargers in the world. Half the money for those magnificent and expensive warhorses was provided by Belisarius out of his own purse. Only the best steeds in the world, coming from halfway down the slope and carrying their own armor and armored cataphracts, could have reached the crest so quickly.

And they would be needed. It took only the sight of Cyril's exhausted face for Belisarius to know that his Greek cataphracts were on the verge of collapse. They'd held off the Rajput charges, so far. But they would break under the next one, or the one after that. Sanga had taken full advantage of his numerical superiority on the Roman left. His Rajputs outnumbered the Greeks five- or six-to-one, and Sanga had sent them up in swirling waves—one after another, with hardly a moment's pause.

The Rajput king had not made the mistake of trying to hammer the Greeks under. The cataphracts were more heavily armed and armored than Rajputs, and they were fighting dismounted from behind fieldworks. If the Rajputs had tried a simple and direct assault, their numbers would have been nullified by the inevitable jamming up at the fieldworks. Instead, Sanga had used his own variation of "Parthian tactics," except that his sallies were as much lance-and-sword work as archery. Cut, slash, and whirl away. Repeat; repeat; repeat; repeat; repeat.

With his advantage in numbers, Sanga had been able to rotate his units. His cavalrymen had had time to rest and tend to their wounded. But for the Greeks defending, there had been no respite at all. It was like holding back waves from the ocean. As soon as one ebbed, another came.

The best soldiers in the world are only flesh and blood, and muscle. The Greeks were so weary that it was an effort to even lift a sword—much less swing it properly. Men at that stage of exhaustion are almost helpless against a good opponent. Lance thrusts strike home, that could have been parried by fresh arms. Sword strokes kill, that should have been easily deflected with a shield.

Half the Greeks had dropped their shields, by now. They needed both hands to hold their weapons. And the hands themselves, often enough, were trembling with fatigue.

"Get them out, Cyril!" called Belisarius. "Pull them out of the fieldworks—*now.*" He twisted in his saddle and pointed to the river below. Vasudeva and his Kushans were clearly visible, in well-ordered formations, guarding the fords.

"Get them across the river," he commanded. "Don't even try for an orderly retreat. Just get them mounted and down there, as fast as you can. The Syrians will cover your flank and the musketeers will hold the river against any Malwa pursuit."

Cyril reached between the flanges of his helmet with a thumb and two fingers, wringing the sweat off his brow and down his nose. He staggered half a pace.

"The Rajputs'll be coming again," he started to protest. "In a minute, no more. You'll need us—"

"I'll take care of the Rajputs with my Thracians," snapped Belisarius. "*Do as I say, Cyril.* Get your men out of here!"

The Greek commander stopped arguing. As Cyril began calling out orders to his men, Belisarius took the time for a quick study of the enemy.

The Rajputs massed on the northern flank of the pass had paused in their attacks, he saw. They had seen the Thracians coming, and were taking the time themselves to gauge the new situation. The reinforcements would strengthen the Roman left, but—

Not enough. That would be Sanga's conclusion, Belisarius knew, within less than five minutes. He was certain the Rajput king was already organizing a new wave of attacks. Sanga was not one to waste time at the climactic moment of a battle.

Neither was Belisarius. Five minutes would be enough. More than enough—and less. Before that time was up, Sanga would realize the truth. Belisarius had no intention of shoring up his left flank. He was going to use his Thracians to cover a general retreat.

Once Sanga understood what Belisarius was doing, all hell would break loose. There would be no careful, calculated sallies. Just a great smash of armies, as Sanga tried to shatter the Roman army's last shield—using fifteen thousand Rajputs against less than three thousand Thracian cataphracts.

The bucellarii were pouring up onto the crest, now. Maurice was already organizing the charge, without waiting for Belisarius' command.

Belisarius took another moment to study the rest of the battlefield. The gunsmoke had all cleared away, and he could see the center. For one of the few times in his bloody life, Belisarius saw a battleground that was literally covered with bodies. The Ye-tai had been shattered. Hundreds of them—perhaps even as many as two thousand—were staggering away down the slope toward their own camp. But those men were out of the battle. Satan himself couldn't have rallied them, not after that butchery.

The Roman right wing, and the enemy facing them—not more than five thousand Rajputs, now—had hardly fought at all. A few probes and skirmishes, nothing more. The southern flank of the pass was much steeper than the northern one. Sanga—or Damodara—had not made the mistake of trying to duplicate the Malwa charges which had been so successful on their right. The Rajput left wing had been there simply to keep the Romans from counterattacking.

Not that Belisarius had ever intended to send his lightly armed Syrians in a counterattack, unless by wild fortune the entire battle had turned into a Malwa rout. He had stationed them there to do the same thing as their opponents—keep them from reinforcing the other flank.

That was another part of Belisarius' tactics which had not worked as well as he had planned. Judging from what he could see, Belisarius thought Damodara had steadily drawn troops from his left in order to reinforce Sanga's hammer blows on the right. The Malwa lord had judged Belisarius' Syrians correctly. They would be fearsome opponents, defending a steep slope against cavalry. But almost useless, in a sally. So he had moved thousands of his Rajput cavalrymen from one end of the battlefield to the other. Belisarius could see large contingents of them cantering across the small valley below the pass, going to reinforce Sanga. And even as he watched, another unit of five hundred Rajputs broke away from their lines on his right and did the same.

Belisarius almost laughed, then. He had never seen a better illustration of Maurice's conviction that battles are by nature an unholy, contradictory mess, in which nothing ever works the way it's supposed to. This time, however—*and thank God for that!*—it was his enemy who had fallen into the quagmire.

Ironically, Damodara's best move was also his worst. *If* Belisarius had been planning to make a stand, Damodara's transfer of forces would have been a masterstroke. But the Roman general had no intention of doing so. Instead, he was going to pivot his army in a retreat to the southwest, using his right flank as the hinge. His biggest fear had been that Damodara would break the hinge. But now, having depleted his left wing, Damodara had not a chance of storming the Syrians on the southern slope of the pass. Bouzes and Coutzes would be able to withdraw their men in an orderly manner, after covering the retreat of the rest of the army.

Marvelous, marvelous—assuming, of course, that Belisarius could blunt Sanga's coming charge with his Thracians. And that—

He eyed the huge mass of Rajput cavalry on the northern slope. *That's going to be—*

"This is going to be fucking dicey," growled Maurice. Belisarius turned in his saddle. Unnoticed, Maurice had already brought his horse alongside.

"It's still a mountain pass, broad and shallow as it is, Maurice," pointed out Belisarius. "It's not a level plain. Sanga won't be able to send more than five thousand at a time. Six at the most."

Peering between the cheekplates of his helmet, Maurice's eyes did not seemed filled with great cheer at this news. He could count just as well as Belisarius. The Thracians were still facing two-to-one odds, against an enemy with plenty of reserves.

"If we didn't have stirrups," said the chiliarch bleakly, "this'd be pure suicide." He frowned. "Now that I think about it—why *don't* the Malwa have stirrups? You'd think they would, by now." Maurice glanced at Belisarius' chest plate, below which Aide nestled in a leather pouch. "They've got their own visions of the future, don't they?"

Belisarius shrugged. "Link's mind doesn't work like Aide's. Aide is a—an *aide*. Link is the Supreme Commander of the Universe. I suspect the thing is so bound up with its great plans for future weapons that it didn't think to build on the little possibilities which are already here. It certainly wouldn't have thought to consult with its human tools—any more than you'd ask a hammer's opinion if you were wielding it properly."

Not likely, remarked Aide. **For Link, people barely even qualify as tools. Just so much raw material.**

Belisarius began to add something, but broke off. He could see the Greeks were ready to mount. And all of his Thracians were here, and in formation.

"May as well do it," said Maurice, anticipating his general's thought. Belisarius nodded. A moment later, Maurice passed on the command. The cornicens began to wail.

The Greeks surged out of the trenches and began clambering aboard their horses. They were tired, tired, but they found the strength regardless. *They* were getting out of here, and only had to make it down to the river below.

The Thracians began moving forward, toward the Rajputs. They were slowed a bit, making their way through the narrow spaces between the fieldworks which had been left open for sallies. By the time the bucellarii made it onto the open and relatively flat northern part of the saddle, Sanga had realized the truth. His own horns began blowing. The sound was different, in pitch and timbre, from that made by Roman cornicens. But Belisarius did not mistake their meaning.

Attack! Now! Everyone!

The huge mass of Rajput cavalry surged toward them. Belisarius ordered his own charge. There was no room here for the usual

Roman tactic of preceding a lance charge with a murderous volley of arrows. No room—and no time. The Thracians were so badly outnumbered that Belisarius could only try to use their greater weight in a single blow of the hammer. The saddle was wide and shallow, for a mountain pass, but it was still not a level plain. If his cataphracts, with their heavier armor and lances—and stirrups—could smash the front ranks of the Rajputs into a pulp, that would stymie the rest. Long enough, hopefully, for the Thracians to be able to beat their own retreat.

The distance between the two armies vanished in seconds. The hammer fell.

The Rajputs did not break—quite.

Belisarius had shattered a Malwa army once before, with such a charge, on the first day of the battle at Anatha. But that Malwa army had been arrogant, and unfamiliar with Roman heavy cavalry tactics.

For the Rajputs, too, this was their first time facing Roman cataphracts in a lance charge. But *this* Malwa army had fought its way across the entire Persian plateau, against Aryan dehgans. They had faced heavy cavalry before, and won. Every time.

Still . . . The Persians had not been equipped with stirrups, and that was the deciding difference. A long, heavy lance braced by feet in stirrups is simply a far more effective weapon than the shorter, much lighter spear used by cavalrymen without stirrups. In the relatively narrow confines of the saddle pass, the Rajputs could not avoid those lances. And the lances ripped them apart.

But not completely. Not enough to allow the Romans to simply turn and break away. Hundreds of Rajputs in the front ranks survived the first clash, and were immediately tying up the cataphracts with their swordplay. Within seconds, the saddle pass was filled with the sounds of steel meeting steel.

We can't afford this, thought Belisarius, as he jerked his lance out of the belly of a Rajput cavalryman. For a moment, he was able to survey the battle scene in reasonable safety. Anastasius and Valentinian were keeping most of the enemy in his vicinity from getting near him.

It took less than five seconds for Belisarius to make his decision. *Enough. It's more ragged than I would have liked, but—enough.*

He shouted new orders to the small unit of cornicenes who were trailing him. The horns began blowing the call for retreat. The Thracians obeyed immediately, even though—for the moment—they were winning the battle. Maurice had long since purged the ranks of Belisarius' bucellarii of any arrogant hotheads. *If the general says you retreat, then you retreat. Forget about the guy in front of you, and the fact that you're beating him into a pulp. The general sees the whole battle. You do what he says. At once.*

Belisarius himself began moving away from the front line. He swept his eyes back and forth, gauging the progress of his troops. It was uneven—there were still knots of Romans and Rajputs flailing at each other with swords—but most of the cataphracts were falling back well enough. The Rajputs were trying to pursue, of course, but the piled-up bodies of the men and horses driven under in the hammersmash were delaying them badly. Badly enough, Belisarius thought, for most of his men to make their escape.

Within seconds, in fact, Belisarius realized that he and his little cluster of soldiers were almost at the very rear of the Roman retreat. A bit isolated, actually. He had been so preoccupied with watching the rest of the army that he hadn't paid attention to his own situation.

Valentinian brought the point home. "We're sticking out like a thumb, general. Everyone's ahead of us. We ought to pick up the pace a little or—"

A swirl of motion caught the corner of Belisarius' eye. He turned his head and saw that a small group of Rajputs had forced their way over the barricade of bodies. The enemy was charging toward them, now, with not more than thirty yards to cover.

Belisarius didn't even think of fleeing. Against enemies like these, running was sure death. He reined his horse around and set his lance. Alongside him, he sensed Valentinian and Anastasius doing the same.

The Rajput in the lead was very tall. As he reared up, holding his spear in the overhead position of stirrupless lancers, he loomed like a giant.

Belisarius looked up—and up—at the man's face. Rajput helmets were visorless, beyond a narrow noseguard.

The face was Rana Sanga's.

Belisarius' own helmet was a German Spangenhelm. The heavy, curving cheekplates covered much of his face, but there was no noseguard. And so, in that instant, he knew that Sanga recognized him as well.

The friend across the field. But the friend had crossed the field, now, and was no friend here. Belisarius was about to fight a man who was counted one of the greatest warriors of India.

He braced his feet, set the lance, and spurred his charger forward. Valentinian rode alongside, perhaps a pace behind. Anastasius tried to do the same, but was intercepted by two other Rajputs.

Two seconds later, Belisarius learned why Sanga was a legend.

Since he first discovered stirrups, Belisarius had never failed to defeat an enemy lancer without them. Until Sanga. The Rajput king avoided the longer and heavier Roman lance by a quick twist in the saddle, and then plunged his own lance downward with all the power of his mighty arm.

Into the neck of Valentinian's horse. The spear tip penetrated unerringly between two plates in the armor and ruptured arteries. The horse coughed blood and collapsed, spilling Valentinian to the ground.

As always in battle, Aide was augmenting Belisarius' senses and reflexes. The general's mind seemed to move as quickly as lightning. But it was ice, not fire, which coursed through his nerves now. Sanga's stroke, he realized, had been completely purposeful. The Rajput king had seen Valentinian in action, and had obviously made his own estimate of which enemy needed to be taken out first.

Which does not, thought Belisarius grimly, *speak well for* my prospects.

The Roman general reined his horse around. In the corner of his eye, he saw that Anastasius was now facing three Rajputs. The giant was hammering one of them down, but he would be no immediate help to Belisarius.

Sanga was also wheeling around, ready to charge. He was too close for the heavy lance to be more than a hindrance. Belisarius dropped the weapon and drew his long cavalry saber. He spurred his mount forward.

An instant later, his sword stroke was deflected by Sanga's shield. Belisarius barely managed to get his own shield up in time to meet Sanga's counterstrike.

The power of that blow was shocking, especially coming from a man riding a horse without stirrups. Unlike Belisarius, Sanga could only grip his horse with his knees. That incredible sword stroke had been delivered with upper-body strength alone.

Belisarius was a strong man himself, but he knew at once that he was hopelessly outmatched. Fortunately, most very powerful men are slow, and Belisarius hoped—

The next stroke came so quickly that even Belisarius' Aide-augmented senses could barely react in time to block it. The third blow—Belisarius was not even trying to strike back—was aimed at his thigh. Only Aide's help allowed Belisarius to interpose his shield quickly enough to keep from having his leg amputated. But the leg went numb. Sanga's sword had driven the shield into his thigh like a sledge. And had also, judging by the sound, cracked the shield itself.

The next sword cut broke his shield in half. Only the iron outer rim was still holding it together.

Finally, Belisarius swung his own blade. Sanga blocked the cut with his shield and then, with a flashing sweep, hammered the sword right out of Belisarius' hand. In the backstroke, the Rajput king drove Belisarius half out of the saddle. The Roman's shield was practically in tatters, now.

Never in his life had Belisarius faced such an incredible opponent. He saw another stroke of that terrible sword coming, and knew he was a dead man. Off balance, with a shredded shield, he had no hope of blocking it.

His mind, Aide-augmented, was still racing. His body could not react in time, but everything seemed to move as slowly as blood in winter. He even had time to find it odd, that his last thought should be:

I can't believe Raghunath Rao faced this man—for an entire day!

The sword descended. But, at the last instant, veered aside. Not much, but enough to simply knock Belisarius off his horse instead of cutting him in half. The shield absorbed most of the blow, splintering completely, but Belisarius knew his arm was broken. He was half-stunned before he even hit the ground, and that impact dazed him completely.

His eyes were still open. But his mind, for a few seconds, was blank.

He saw Sanga's horse buckle. Saw the lance jutting into the mount's throat. Saw Valentinian, on foot, holding the lance and bringing the beast down. Saw Sanga leap free before the horse could pin him, sword still in hand. Saw Valentinian's first sword stroke, quick as lightning. Saw Sanga parry it, just in time. Saw—

Nothing more, but a horse's flank. A huge hand seized him by the collar of his tunic and hauled him up. Hercules plucking a fruit. He was hanging across a saddle like a sack of flour.

His brain began to work again. *Anastasius' saddle*, he realized. He realized, too—dimly—that he could hear Maurice's shouting voice. And the voices of other Thracians. He could hear the sound of pounding hooves, and feel the horse beneath him break into a gallop.

"Valentinian," he croaked.

"Valentinian will have to do for himself," rumbled Anastasius. "I'm *your* bodyguard, not his."

"Valentinian," he croaked again.

The giant's sigh was audible even over the sound of thundering horses. Then: "I'm sorry, general. I'll miss the bastard. I surely will, not that I'd ever say it to him."

Then, only: "Not that I'll ever have the chance. He's on his own now, against that demon Sanga and twenty thousand of his Rajputs."

Chapter 14

Valentinian did not have to face twenty thousand Rajputs. Only their greatest king.

By the time the battle between Rana Sanga and Valentinian ended, every one of the Rajputs in Damodara's army was on the crest of the saddle, watching. All except the men too badly injured to be moved—and many of those, in later years, counted that loss worse than their scars and severed limbs.

In the annals of Rome, it would be named the *Battle of the Pass*. But for the Rajputs, it would always be known as the Battle of the Mongoose.

In part, the name was given in Belisarius' honor. The Rajputs had won the battle, insofar as possession of the field counts as victory. (Which it does, in every land.) But even on their day of triumph, they knew that the Roman general had yielded little but the blood-soaked ground itself. A pittance, really, when the disparity in numbers was counted—and the butcher's bill paid.

True, they had driven him off, and seized the pass, and cleared their way to yet another range within the Zagros. But there were many more passes to come, before they finally broke through to Mesopotamia. And the Roman general had shown them, in rack and ruin, just how steep a price he would charge for that passage.

For the most part, however, the name was given in honor of Valentinian.

Indians have their own way of looking at animals, and incorporating their spirits into legend. Western folk, seeing Valentinian, were often reminded of a weasel. But there are no weasels in India. There are mongoose, instead. As quick; as deadly—but admired rather, for their cunning, than feared for their bloodlust.

Like Westerners, Indians are familiar with snakes. But they do not share the occidental detestation for serpents. Rather the opposite. There are few of God's creatures, in their eyes, as majestic as the king cobra.

It was those eyes which watched the battle, and gave it the name. Valentinian, much smaller and less powerful than the great king, was the quickest and most agile swordsman any of those Rajputs had ever seen. A battle which most of them expected to last for three minutes—if that long—lasted instead for three hours.

The Roman army watched also, from a much greater distance. By the time the battle was well underway, every surviving Roman soldier had forded the river. On the relative safety of the far bank, Belisarius' officers drew the army into formation while the general himself had his broken arm tended to.

At first, the Roman troops were tense. They were half expecting the enemy to launch a new attack. There was still time, after all—it was no later than mid-afternoon—and this Malwa army had proven its mettle.

Tense, but not worried. The Roman soldiers, in fact, were almost hoping their enemies would try to force their way across the river. They were quite confident of their ability to beat back the assault, and with heavy losses.

But, soon enough, it became obvious that the Rajputs had no intention of making any such foolish gesture. They were too battlewise, first of all. And, secondly, they were completely preoccupied with watching the single combat on the crest between Sanga and Valentinian.

By the time Belisarius emerged from his tent, his arm splinted and bound to his chest, the Roman troops themselves had settled into the relaxation of watching the match. More accurately, they listened to the news brought by dispatch riders. Only Maurice, using Belisarius' telescope, was actually able to see much.

When Belisarius came up to Maurice, the chiliarch lowered the telescope.

"You heard?" he asked. Belisarius nodded.

"Craziest damned thing I've ever seen," muttered Maurice.

His attitude did not surprise Belisarius. Nor Aide:

The custom of single combat between champions is no longer part of Graeco-Roman culture. Hasn't been, for over a millennium—not since the days of Homer. But it's still a living part of India's traditions, at least among Rajputs. Not even two decades of Malwa rule has broken that romantic notion of chivalry.

Belisarius' eyes studied the pass above. There seemed to be Rajputs covering every inch of the slopes which provided a view of the battle. Even the Rajput units standing guard, assigned to watch for a possible enemy counterattack, had their heads turned away from the Roman army.

If anything, added Aide, **their time in the Malwa yoke is making them treasure this moment even more. There has been nothing like this in years, for Rajputana's warriors. Just the butchery of Ranapur, and Amaravati before that.**

Maurice extended the telescope to its rightful owner.

Belisarius shook his head. "One of two men I treasure is going to die, today. I have no desire to watch it."

Aide's voice, soft: **I am sorry for it, too.**

Maurice brought the telescope back to his eye and resumed observing the battle. He had expected Belisarius' response. His offer of the telescope had been more in the way of a formality than anything else.

But he was still astonished by the Malwa commander.

"Craziest thing I've ever seen," he repeated. "What the hell is Damodara thinking?" He pulled the telescope a few inches from his eye and used it to point at the huge force of Rajputs covering the entire pass. "All he has to do is give the order, and Valentinian is a pincushion. You couldn't see him, for all the arrows sticking out of his body."

Belisarius shook his head. "No Rajput would obey that order, and Damodara knows it. If he sent anyone else, the Rajputs would kill them. And Damodara himself, most likely, if they thought he'd given the command. Besides—"

Belisarius stared across the river, and up the slope. He was not trying to watch the battle between Sanga and Valentinian. He was simply searching, in his mind's eye, for Damodara.

Aide verbalized his thoughts. **A man who rides a tiger long enough begins to think like a tiger himself.**

"This is utter madness!" snarled the Malwa spymaster. He glared down at Damodara, and pointed to the enemy army across the river half a mile distant. "While you waste time in this frivolity, the Romans are making their escape!"

The Malwa commander, squatting comfortably on a cushion, did not respond for a few seconds. His eyes remained fixed on the two men battling fiercely a few dozen yards away. When he did reply, his tone was mild.

"It's a moot point, Isanavarman." Damodara glanced down the slope. "Under no circumstances would I order my army to force the river against *that* opponent." His tone hardened. "I certainly have no intention of giving such an order today. Not after the losses we've taken, from those infernal handcannons."

His eyes moved to the spymaster. They were hard, cold eyes. "Of whose existence I was not informed, by men whose duty it is to know such things."

The spymaster did not flush. But he looked away. Behind him, his three top subordinates tried to make themselves as inconspicuous as possible.

"The best spies in the world," muttered Isanavarman, "cannot discover everything."

The spymaster gave Narses a sour look. The eunuch was squatting on his own cushion next to Damodara. At Damodara's *left* hand—the position allotted, by Indian custom, to a lord's chief civilian adviser. "Did your Roman pet warn you?" demanded Isanavarman, almost snarling. "He has his own spies."

"Not more than a few," responded Damodara. The Malwa commander was back to watching the battle. "Nothing like the horde of spies which Nanda Lal placed at your disposal."

The spymaster gritted his teeth, but said nothing. What was there to say?

Nanda Lal was the chief spymaster for the entire Malwa Empire, and considered Isanavarman his best agent. Nanda Lal had assigned him to be the spymaster for Damodara's army for that very reason. By the simple nature of geography, Damodara was operating an independent command. His was the only army not under the immediate and watchful eye of Malwa's rulers. So Nanda Lal had sent Isanavarman—with many spies, if not quite a horde—as much to keep an eye on Damodara as his enemies.

So what was there to say?

Damodara found words. "Make yourself useful for a change, Isanavarman. Interview the surviving Ye-tai. Find out as much as you can about the handcannons."

Isanavarman began to say something, but Damodara cut him short. "*Do it*. I am the commander of this army, spymaster, not you."

The Malwa lord lifted his finger in a little gesture at the troops surrounding them. Rajputs, all of them, except a few hundred kshatriyas—those whose proven valor had made them welcome. Most of the kshatriyas were in the camp, knowing full well the Rajputs would not permit their presence.

Isanavarman scanned the mass of soldiers. There were perhaps a thousand Ye-tai there also. But the spymaster did not fail to notice that the Ye-tai were scattered through the mass of Rajputs in small groups. Individuals, often enough, chatting amiably with their Rajput companions. Rajputs had a certain scorn for Ye-tai barbarity. But this was a day of manliness, and no one questioned Ye-tai courage.

"Do it," repeated Damodara. Again, cold eyes went to the spymaster. "Leave now, Isanavarman. This is not a place for you."

The spymaster left, then, trailed by his three subordinates. Nanda Lal's agents did not flee, exactly, but neither did they amble. They were not oblivious to other hard, cold eyes upon them. The eyes of thousands of Rajput warriors, who had no love for Malwa spies at any time or place—and certainly not here, on this day of glory.

When they were gone, Damodara leaned toward Narses. The commander's eyes were still fixed on the combat between Valentinian and Rana Sanga, but his gaze seemed a bit unfocused. As if Damodara's thoughts were elsewhere.

"I trust he no longer has a horde of spies," he murmured.

Narses' sneer, as always, was magnificent. "He's got the three who came with him, and two others. The rest are on my payroll."

Damodara nodded. "Tonight, then. I think that would be best."

"It'll be perfect," agreed Narses. "A pitched battle was fought today. A great victory for Malwa, of course, but not without its cost. The cunning Roman general sent a cavalry troop raiding into our camp. Terrible carnage. Great losses."

Narses crooked his finger. Ajatasutra, squatting ten feet away, rose and came over.

"Tonight," whispered Narses. "Do it yourself, if possible."

Ajatasutra did not sneer. He never did. That was one of the reasons, oddly, why Narses had grown so fond of him. But the assassin's thin smile had not a trace of humor in it.

"Those arrogant snobs haven't used a dagger in years," he said softly. "Years spent lounging in Kausambi, reading reports, while poor downtrodden agents like me were having hair-raising adventures with tired old eunuchs."

Narses had a fine grin, to match his sneer. It was not an expression often seen on his reptilian face—and no more reassuring, come to it, that a cobra's yawning gape. But the grin stayed on his face, for minutes thereafter.

He was amused, thinking not of serpents but of different animals. Tigers, and men who choose to ride them.

He glanced at Damodara. The Malwa commander's eyes were riveted on the combat, now, and there was nothing unfocused in the gaze.

He might as well have stripes himself, thought Narses.

In the tales of bards, and the lays of poets, truth takes on a rosy tinge. More than a tinge, actually. The reality of a single combat between two great warriors becomes something purely legendary.

There is little place, in legends, for sweat. Even less for thirst and exhaustion. And none at all for urination.

But the fact remains that two men do not battle each other, for hours, without rest. Not even if they were fighting half-naked, with bare hands—much less encumbered by heavy armor and wielding swords. Single combat between champions, other than a glancing encounter in the midst of battle, is by nature a formal affair. And, like most formalities, has a practical core at the center of its rituals.

After the first five minutes, Sanga and Valentinian broke off, gasping for breath. By then, the area was surrounded by Rajputs. Sanga's cavalrymen were still astride their mounts, holding their weapons. One of them, seeing the first open space between the two combatants, began edging his horse toward Valentinian. The man's lance was half-raised.

Sanga bellowed inarticulate fury. The Rajput shied away.

Sanga planted his sword tip in the ground—carefully, making sure there were no stones to dull the blade—and leaned upon it. After gasping a few more breaths, he pointed at Valentinian.

"Give the man water," he commanded. "Wine, if he prefers." The Rajput king studied his opponent, for a few seconds. Valentinian was still breathing deeply, and leaning on his own sword, but Sanga saw that he was no longer gasping.

"And bring us food and cushions," added Sanga. He smiled, quite cheerfully. "I think we're going to need them."

For the next few minutes, while Sanga and Valentinian rested, the Rajputs organized the necessities. A dozen Rajputs clustered around Sanga. Four began moving toward Valentinian, after lowering their weapons. One of them carried a winesack; another, a skin full of water; the third, a rolled-up blanket to serve Valentinian as a cushion whenever he rested; the fourth, some dry bread and cheese.

Sanga nodded toward them, while keeping his eyes on Valentinian. "They will assist you," he called out to the Roman. "Anything you need."

Sanga straightened. "You may surrender, of course. At any time."

For a moment, Valentinian almost gave his natural response—*fuck you, asshole!*—but restrained the impulse. He simply shook his head. A gesture which, at the end, turned into a little bow. Even Valentinian, hardbitten and cynical as he was, could sense the gathering glory.

In the hours which followed, as a lowborn Roman cataphract fought his way into India's legends, the man's mind wondered at his actions.

Why are you doing this, you damned fool?

All his life, Valentinian had been feared by other men. Feared for his astonishing quickness, his reflexes, his uncanny eye—most of all, for his instant capacity to murder. Precious few men, in truth, can kill at the drop of a hat. Valentinian, since the age of ten, could do it before the hat was touched.

And so men feared him. And found, in his whipcord shape and narrow face, the human image of a vicious predator.

Because I'm tired of being called a weasel, came the soul's reply.

The end came suddenly, awkwardly, unexpectedly—almost casually. As it usually does, in the real world. The bards and poets, of course, would have centuries to clean it up.

Sanga's foot slipped, skidding on a loose pebble. For a moment, catching his balance, his shield swung aside. Valentinian, seeing his opening, swung for the Rajput's exposed leg. No Herculean stroke, just Valentinian's usual economic slice. The quick blade cut deeply into Sanga's thigh.

The Rajput fell to one knee, crying out in pain. Pain—and despair. His leg was already covered with blood. It was not the bright, crimson spurting of arterial blood, true, but it was enough. That wound would slay him within half an hour, from blood loss alone. Sooner, really. Within minutes, pain and weakness would cripple him enough for his enemy to make the kill.

Then—

All other men, watching or hearing of that battle in years to come, would always assume that Valentinian made his only mistake.

But the truth was quite otherwise. For hours, Valentinian had avoided matching strength with Sanga. He had countered the king's astonishing power with speed, instead. Speed, cunning, and experience. He could have—*should* have—ended the battle so. Circling the Rajput, probing, slashing, bleeding him further, staying away from that incredible strength, until his opponent was so weak that the quick death thrust could be driven home. Killing a king, like a wolf brings down a crippled bull. Like a weasel kills.

Something inside the man, buried deep, rebelled. For the first time since the battle began—for the first time in his life, truth be told—Valentinian swung a heroic blow. A mighty overhand strike at the Rajput's head.

Sanga threw up his sword, crosswise, to block the cut. Valentinian's sword, descending with the power of his own great strength, met a blade held in Rajputana's mightiest hand.

The finest steel in the world was made in India. The impact snapped the Roman sword in half, leaving not more than a six-inch stub in Valentinian's fist.

Six inches can still be enough, in a knife fight. Valentinian never hesitated. Weasel-quick, he flung himself to his own knee and drove the sword stub at Sanga's throat.

The Rajput king managed to lower his helmet in time. The blade glanced off the noseguard and ripped a great tear in Sanga's cheek. More blood gushed forth.

It was not enough. No cry of despair escaped his lips, but Valentinian knew he was finished. Facing each other at close distance, both on their knees, the advantage now was all Sanga's.

Sanga was never one for hesitation himself. Instantly, the Rajput king swung a blow. Valentinian interposed his shield. The shield cracked. Another blow. The shield broke. Another blow, to the head, knocked the Roman's helmet askew. The final blow, again to the helmet, split the segmented steel and sent Valentinian sprawling to the ground. Senseless, at the very least. Probably dead, judging from the blood which began pouring through the sundered pieces of the Spangenhelm.

Sanga raised his arm, to sever Valentinian's neck. But he stopped the motion, even before the sword finished its ascent.

He had won a glorious victory, this day. He would not stain it with an executioner's stroke.

Sanga sagged back on his heels. In a daze, he stared up at the sky. It was sunset, and the mountains were bathed in purple majesty. Around him, vaguely, he heard thunderous cheers coming from thousands of Rajput throats. And, seconds later, felt hands laying him down and beginning to bind his wounds.

A glorious victory. He had not felt this clean—this Rajput pure—for many years. Not since the day he fought Raghunath Rao, and first entered himself into Indian legend.

In the river valley below, the Romans also heard the cheer. The mountains seemed to ring with the sound.

Maurice lowered the telescope. "That's it," he said softly.

Belisarius took a deep breath. Then, turning to Coutzes: "Send a courier, under banner of truce. I want to know if Valentinian's dead, so that the priests can do the rites."

"And if he's alive?" asked Coutzes.

"See if they'll accept a ransom." Belisarius' crooked smile made a brief appearance. "Not that I think I could afford it, even as rich as I am. Not unless Damodara's truly lost his mind."

◇   ◇   ◇

"Not for all the gold in Rome," was Damodara's instant reply. "Do I look like a madman?"

When Coutzes brought back the news, Belisarius lowered his head. But his heart, for the first time in hours, soared to the heavens.

"He might still die," cautioned Coutzes. "They say he's lost a lot of blood. And his skull's broken."

Anastasius snorted. So did Maurice.

"Not Valentinian," said Belisarius. He lifted his head, smiling as broadly as he ever had in his life. "Not *my* champion. Not that great, roaring, lion of a man."

The following morning, the Malwa army began moving along the river. To the northwest, away from the Romans. Belisarius' army, still holding the fords, made no effort to block them.

Not a single soldier, on either side, thought the matter odd.

"Let's hear it for maneuvers," said a Rajput to a Ye-tai. The barbarian nodded quick agreement.

"God, I love to march," announced a Greek cataphract. His eyes swept the mountains. "Gives us a chance to admire the scenery. For weeks, if we're lucky. Maybe even months."

"Beats staring at your own guts," came a Syrian's response. "Even for a minute."

Chapter 15
YEMEN
Spring, 532 A.D.

"It'll be tonight, for sure," stated Menander.

Ashot wobbled his hand back and forth, in a gesture which indicated less certainty. "Maybe. Maybe not."

Menander stood his ground. "It'll be tonight," he repeated confidently. The young cataphract took two steps to the entrance of the field headquarters and pulled back the flap. The Roman army's camp had been set up half a mile east of a small oasis. Menander was staring in that direction, but his eyes were on the horizon rather than the oasis itself.

A moment later, Euphronius joined him. The young Syrian—he was Menander's age, in his early twenties—took one look at the sky and nodded.

"Sundown in less than an hour," he said. "Moonshine, after that, until midnight. The Arabs will wait until the moon goes down. Then they'll attack."

Antonina, seated in a chair near the center of the tent, found herself smiling. As soon as she realized what she was doing, she removed the expression. But not soon enough for it to have escaped Ashot's attention.

Ashot grinned at her. She returned the grin with a look of stern admonition, like a prim schoolteacher reproving an older boy in a classroom when he mocked the youngsters.

With about the same success. True, Ashot had the grace to press his lips together. But he still looked like the proverbial cat who swallowed a canary.

Ashot commanded the five hundred cataphracts whom Belisarius had sent along with Antonina on her expedition. Her husband had selected the Armenian officer for the assignment because Belisarius thought Ashot—after Maurice, of course—was the best field commander among his bucellarii. For the most part, Belisarius' decision had been due to Ashot's innate ability. But he had also been influenced by the man's experience. Even though Ashot was only in his mid-thirties, the Armenian was a veteran of more battles and campaigns than any other officer in Belisarius' household troops. (Again, of course, leaving aside Maurice.)

From her own experience over the past year, Antonina had come to understand why Belisarius had counted that so heavily in his decision. She was still herself something of a novice in the art of war. Time and again, Ashot's steadying hand had been there, when Antonina's assumptions proved incorrect.

The enemy didn't do what you expected them to do? Yeah, well, they usually don't. No problem. We'll deal with it.

Euphronius and Menander turned away from the entrance. With the absolute surety possessed only by young men, they made their pronouncements.

"Tonight," predicted Menander.

"Right after the moon goes down," decreed Euphronius.

"The main attack will come from the east," ruled Menander.

Euphronius nodded his head. Solon approving a judgement by Hammurabi. "Only possible direction. They'll be able to use the setting moon to guide them in the approach. And they won't get tangled up in the oasis."

Antonina squared her shoulders. "Very well, then. See to the preparations."

The two young officers swept out of the tent, brushing aside the flap as if they were the trade winds. When they were gone, Antonina eyed Ashot. The Armenian's grin was back in full force.

"All right," she growled, "now tell me what *you* think."

Still grinning, the Armenian shrugged. "I don't know. And for that matter, I don't care. The attack *might* come tonight—although I'm skeptical—so we need to be prepared anyway. It'll be good drill, if nothing else."

Ashot pulled up a chair and lounged in it. His grin faded into a smile of approval. "I like cocky young officers," he said. "As long as they're men of substance—which those two certainly are." He shrugged again. "They'll get the silly crap knocked out of them soon enough. In the meantime, I can count on them to stand straight in the storm. Whenever it comes, from whatever direction."

Antonina lifted a cup from the table next to her chair and took a sip. The vessel was filled with water from the nearby oasis, flavored with just a dash of wine.

"Why don't you think it'll be tonight?" she asked.

Ashot stroked his cheek, running fingers through his stiff and bristly beard. "It just doesn't seem likely to me, that's all. We'll be facing bedouin nomads. They're quite capable of moving fast, once they've made their decision. Fast enough, even through the desert, that they *could* be in position by tonight."

He leaned forward, planting elbows on knees. "But I know that breed. I can almost guarantee that they'll spend two or three days quarreling and bickering before they decide what to do." He chuckled. "That's the whole point of this exercise. That's why we landed north of Sana, instead of right at the coast with Eon and his sarawit."

Antonina nodded. The tactics of this campaign had been primarily worked out by Ashot and Wahsi. Antonina and Eon, of course, had approved the plan. But neither had felt themselves qualified to develop it in the first place.

And if they had, she knew, they wouldn't have thought to come up with *this* plan. Ashot and Wahsi, veterans of campaigns and not just battles, had immediately seen the weakness in the traitor Abreha's strategic position. His problem was political, more than purely military.

Abreha was holding Yemen with only two rebel regiments from the Ethiopian army. Those two regiments, the Metin and the Falha, were forted up in the provincial capital of Sana. The third regiment stationed in Arabia, the Halen at Marib, was still maintaining neutrality in the civil war.

The bulk of Abreha's forces, therefore—well over three-fourths of them—consisted of Arab irregulars. Warriors from the various bedouin tribes in southern Arabia, under the shaky command of an unstable cluster of war chiefs. As individuals, the Arab nomads were ferocious fighters. But their discipline was almost nonexistent, and their concept of war was essentially that of brigands and pirates. They had flocked to Abreha's banner, not because they cared which faction of Axum ruled southern Arabia, but because they saw a chance for loot.

So, Antonina was offering them a juicy plum—her small army of Romans, detached and isolated from the main body of Ethiopian sarwen who had landed on the coast near Sana. Rome was the land of wealth, in that part of the world. What few gold coins the Arabs possessed were solidii minted in Constantinople. The streets of the fabled city, capital of the Roman Empire, were reputed among those tribesmen to be paved with gold. (There were a few skeptics in their midst, of course, who thought the tales unlikely. Silver, certainly, but not gold.)

Now, this day, ready to be plucked, was a force of rich Romans not more than two thousand strong. Less than that, really, in the eyes of the bedouin. At least five hundred of those Romans were *women.*

And that, of course, was another inducement to attack. The tribesmen would capture concubines along with treasure. Roman women, to boot, who were reputed to be the most beautiful women in the world. (Again, of course, there were skeptics. But they were all women themselves, driven by spite and jealousy.)

It was a cunning plan. Even if Abreha tried to restrain them, his Arab irregulars would ignore his orders. But Ashot and Wahsi thought that Abreha, in all likelihood, would not object. From a purely military standpoint, attacking the Romans would seem to be a good move. By approaching Sana from the north, in a separate column, the Romans were isolated from the Axumite army under Eon. Abreha would see the chance to defeat his enemy in detail.

A cunning plan—and risky. There were at least five thousand bedouin under Abreha's banner. They would outnumber the Roman forces by a factor of almost three-to-one.

Antonina's eyes drifted to a corner of the tent. There, resting on a small table, was her own handcannon. Much as she detested the thing, the sight of the weapon helped to restore her confidence.

The handcannon was smaller than the heavy smoothbores carried by her Cohort, and much more finely crafted. John of Rhodes had made it for her personally. It was the prototype of a line of weapons he planned to develop for cavalrymen. He called it a *pistol*.

"An over-and-under double-barreled caplock, to be precise," he'd told her, when he handed her the weapon a week before her departure from Alexandria. "It's the first gun made using the new percussion caps. Beautiful piece, isn't it?"

Antonina, handling the device, had privately thought the term "beautiful" was absurd. To her, the grotesque-looking weapon was ugly, awkward—and God-awful *heavy*. Her small hand could barely hold the grip.

"No, no, Antonina!" John exclaimed. "You've got to hold it with *both* hands. Here—put your left hand under the stock. That's why the wood's there." His expression shaded from pride to half-apology. "It's not really a true handgun, yet, except for a big man. But it's the best I could come up with this soon."

Despite her private reservations, Antonina had thanked John for the gift. Quite profusely, at the time he gave it to her. Two days later, after spending several hours on the practice range—John had been adamant on the point—her thanks were less heartfelt. She had no doubt the damned thing would do its lethal duty, if and when the time came. But her hands ached and her butt was bruised from the times she had been knocked off her feet by the recoil. She darkly suspected, moreover—damn what the doctors said—that at least one of her shoulders was dislocated. Permanently, from the feel of it.

Ashot's eyes followed hers.

"Ugly damned thing," he grunted. "Glad I don't have to shoot a handcannon. Even that one, much less the bonebreakers the Cohort uses."

For all the sourness of the words, however, his expression was cheerful enough. He leaned back in his chair and planted his hands on his hips.

"Relax, Antonina. The plan'll work. It looks a lot riskier than it really is, unless we screw up."

Antonina blew out her cheeks. "You're that confident in the handcannons?" she asked.

Ashot snorted. "Antonina, I don't have any confidence in *any* weapons. Weapons are just tools, I don't care how newfangled and fancy they are. No better than the men who use them."

He waved his hand. "I *do* have confidence in those Syrian boys out there. And their wives. But most of all, I've got confidence in the general."

"The general," to Ashot, meant Belisarius. Like most of the bucellarii, it was a title which Ashot bestowed on no one else. So Antonina was surprised, when Ashot added: "*Both* generals."

She gazed at him quizzically. Ashot chuckled.

"Didn't your husband ever mention him to you? I'm sure he must have."

Antonina understood the reference, then. Belisarius had done much more than "mention" that other general to her, in point of fact. In the weeks leading up to his departure for Persia, the year before, Belisarius had spent half his time preparing his wife for her own expedition. He had drilled her for hours, day after day, in that other general's tactics. He had even insisted—the only time he ever did so—that she take Aide in her hand and enter the crystal's world of visions.

She almost shuddered, remembering those scenes of ghastly slaughter. But she took heart, as well, remembering the battle of Waterloo. Where the French cavalry broke—again and again—against Wellington's infantry at the ridge of La Haye Sainte.

"Maybe tonight," she heard Ashot murmur. "And maybe not. Doesn't matter. We'll break the bastards, whenever they come."

He barked a harsh laugh. "The only thing I know for sure is this, Antonina. A month from now, those bedouin hotheads will be sulking in their tents. Calling you the Iron Dyke."

Chapter 16

The attack came two nights later, long before the moon went down, and from the south. Menander and Euphronius were both exceedingly disgruntled. The tactics of their enemies made no sense at all!

They got over it, quickly enough. Very quickly. Whatever the Arabs lacked in the way of tactical acumen, they made up for in other ways.

Ashot was not surprised—neither by the Arabs' tactics nor by the vigor of their attack. The timing was about what he had guessed, so far as the day was concerned. He had not really expected bedouin irregulars to be patient enough to wait until midnight. South was the direction from which they had come, and they had the advantage of moonlight to guide them. True, the same moonlight made them easier targets, but the desert warriors sneered at such unmanly concerns. There was a hill to the south, moreover, almost next to the Roman camp. The hill would disguise the Arabs' approach, and give them the advantage of charging downhill.

None of it, as Ashot had foreseen, made any difference. The Theodoran Cohort was prepared, as they had been for three days. As soon as the sun went down, the troops were on full alert. The matchlocks were loaded and the matches themselves were lit. The musketeers buckled on their short swords. The wives laid out the grenades, cut the fuses, prepared the cartridges. Sharpened stakes were set in the ground at eighteen-inch intervals, making for additional protection for the musketeers. The Thracian cataphracts, dismounted, took up their pikes.

The smell of smoldering slow match blew across the camp on the ceaseless breeze. The cataphracts and the Cohort waited. Ashot waited. Menander and Euphronius polished their certainties. Antonina mouthed a silent prayer for the soul of a general she had never met and never would, wherever that soul might be.

Two hours after sundown, the attack started. With a sudden whoop, several thousand Arabs on camelback surged over the hilltop and began charging down onto the camp. Most of them were holding swords, but many brandished torches.

"What the hell?" demanded Menander.

"What's wrong with those stupid—" began Euphronius. But the young commander of the Cohort broke off. He had immediate duties to attend to.

"Sling-staffs!" he shouted. "To the south! As soon as the enemy's in range!" He raced off, seeing to the disposition of the musketeers.

Menander stayed behind, standing next to Antonina and Ashot. He was in direct charge of the cataphract pikemen, but he really had nothing to do. The cataphracts, veterans all, were no more surprised by the illogic of the enemy's attack than Ashot. And, unlike the musketeers, they did not have cumbersome supplies and equipment to move around. The units, without waiting for orders, simply shifted their positions slightly.

They didn't have far to go. Ashot had set the camp in such a way that the Roman troops formed a tightly packed square. The musketeers formed the front line, on all four sides, protected by the palisade of sharpened stakes. The pikemen took position just a few yards behind, ready to form an additional bulwark where needed. The grenadiers, along with the hundred cataphracts whom Ashot was keeping as a mounted reserve, were positioned in the center of the camp.

"Range," for grenadiers wielding sling-staffs, meant a hundred and fifty yards. By the time the first wave of Arabs reached that distance, the wives had cut and lit the fuses. The grenades were sent on their way.

Ashot mounted up. He managed the task unassisted, and with relative ease. Like the rest of the cataphracts, he was wearing half-armor instead of full gear. He had felt that would be enough, against lightly armed irregulars. Mobility would be more important than protection and weight of charge, in this battle.

Ashot was not planning any thunderous sallies, in any case. His relative handful of cavalrymen would be swallowed up in a sea of swirling bedouin, if they ever left the safety of the camp. Their role was to provide a sharp, quick counterpunch wherever the enemy might threaten to break through the front lines.

Menander and Euphronius, of course, had argued with him.

"Can't destroy an enemy without cavalry pursuit," Menander had sagely pointed out. Euphronius nodded firm agreement.

"Don't need to," had been Ashot's sanguine reply. "We're not facing disciplined regulars, who'll regroup after a defeat. The bedouin haven't got any staying power. They'll attack like maniacs, but if they bounce off, good and bloodied, they'll decide the whole business is not favored by the gods. They'll melt into the desert and go back to tending their flocks. That's good enough, for our purposes. Abreha won't have them, at his side, when Eon and Wahsi storm into Sana."

Menander and Euphronius, of course, had not been convinced. But the youngsters had satisfied themselves, in the days thereafter, with lengthy exchanges on the subject of senility.

Antonina did less than anyone, waiting for the charge. She simply followed Ashot's advice—say better, *instructions*—and stood firmly in her place. Right at the center of the camp, where everyone could see and hear her.

"Your job," Ashot had explained cheerfully, "is simply to give the troops confidence. That's it, Antonina. Just stand there, looking as resolute as Athena, and shout encouragement. And make sure you wear that obscene breastplate."

Antonina donned the cuirass, with the help of her maid, Koutina. Looking down at her immense brass mammaries, she had her usual reaction.

Ashot's good cheer faded. "And *try* not to giggle," he grumbled. "That looks bad, in a commander, during desperate battle."

Antonina giggled.

Now, as she waited for the charge, Antonina had no trouble restraining her giggle. She maintained her outward composure, but she was quite scared. Terrified, if truth be told.

Ashot could make his veteran pronouncements, and her young officers could decree the certain future. But all Antonina could see, staring at the horde of shrieking nomads coming down the hill like an irresistible force of nature, was a wave of rape and murder.

Cursing at the weight of her awkward firearm, she shifted the strap which held the thing over her shoulder. Her hand groped for the hilt of her "sword." Once her fingers curled around the plain wood of the blade's utilitarian handle, she felt her confidence return. She had used that cleaver before—and used it successfully—to defend herself against rape and murder, when Malwa-paid thugs attacked her in Constantinople. Maurice had purchased the cleaver, afterward, and given it to her for her personal weapon in the battle at the stadium.

Ask any veteran, Antonina, he'd told her at the time. *They'll all tell you there's nothing as important in a battle as having a trusty, tested blade.*

The cleaver brought confidence. And so, even more, did Ashot's whispered words: "It's just another knife fight in a kitchen, Antonina. Like you've done before."

The grenades began landing among the Arabs. Few of them missed. The Syrian slingers were combat veterans themselves, now. The confidence which that gave them, added to their own skill, made for a murderous volley.

As before, against cavalry, the main effect of the exploding bombs was moral. Not many of the Arabs themselves were killed, or even seriously injured, by the crude devices. Most of the casualties were sustained by their mounts, and even the camels did not suffer greatly. The year before, when used against Ambrose's rebel cataphracts on the paved streets of Alexandria, shrapnel from exploding grenades had wreaked havoc on the unarmored legs of their horses. But here, on desert sand, there were no ricochets to multiply the damage.

The camels did not suffer greatly from *physical* damage, that is. But the beasts were completely unaccustomed to artillery fire, and immediately began to panic. The sound and fury of the explosions caused most of that terror. But even the sputtering flare of a burning fuse caused camels to stumble and shy away.

Camels are large animals, heavier than horses. Once started on a charge down a hill, they were impossible to stop. But the charge, as hundreds of camels either collapsed from wounds or simply stumbled from fear, turned into something more in the nature of an avalanche. An avalanche is a fearsome thing, true. But it has no brains at all. By the time thousands of bedouin piled up at the foot of the hill, not fifty yards from the Roman front lines, they had about as much coordination and conscious purpose as a snowdrift blown by the wind.

Euphronius gave the order. *Level!* Antonina held her breath. *Fire!*

Fifty yards was within range of the smoothbore arquebuses. Some of the bullets went wide, and many simply buried themselves in the sand. But of the hundreds of rounds fired in that first volley, almost a fourth found a human target.

It mattered hardly at all whether the bullets struck a head, a torso, or a limb. Round shot loses muzzle velocity quickly. But, within fifty yards, the loss was not enough to offset the weight of the .80–caliber lead drop shot. The heavy projectiles, at that range, caused terrible wounds—and struck with incredible force. Arms were blown off, not simply wounded. Thigh bones were pulverized. Men died from shock alone.

The first line of musketeers stepped back, replaced by the second. Antonina expected Euphronius to give the order to fire immediately, but the Syrian waited for the dense cloud of gunsmoke to clear away. She began dancing impatiently, until she realized what she was doing and forced herself to stand still.

Restraint was difficult, even though Antonina understood Euphronius' inaction. It was impossible to see more than a few yards from the front line—and would have been, even in broad daylight. Even the crest of the hill was obscured by the gunsmoke. Until the smoke cleared, the musketeers would be guessing at their target.

A few gaps began appearing in the clouds. Enough, apparently. Euphronius gave the order, and the arquebuses roared again.

The second line stepped back, and the third line came forward. By now, Antonina saw, the first line was already reloaded and ready to fire again.

She felt a certain female smugness. *Her* troops could manage a much better rate of fire, she knew, than those of her husband. Despite the fact that they were using the same type of firearms, *her* troops had wives, standing with the men. The Theodoran

Cohort carried twice as many handcannons as they had gunners. The women kept the spares ready and loaded. As soon as the men stepped back, a freshly loaded gun was in their hands, while their wives set to work reloading the fired pieces.

With that advantage, Antonina's cohort could manage a rate of fire which approached that of Wellington's men. As a battle wore on, of course, the rate would drop quickly. After a few rounds had been fired through the crude arquebuses, gunpowder residues fouled the bores. The weapons had to be cleaned before they could be reloaded, and even efficient Syrian wives could not do that instantly.

Still—

Fire! she heard Euphronius shout. The third line discharged their pieces.

The only reason her troops were not maintaining a faster rate of fire was simply to let the clouds of gunsmoke clear away sufficiently to aim. Had there been a strong wind blowing, they could have been hammering the Arabs almost ceaselessly.

Antonina cursed the light desert breeze. The curse seemed to be effective. A sudden gust blew a great hole in the clouds.

The gap was closed, within seconds, by the first rank's second round of fire. But in those seconds, Antonina saw the carnage.

By now, just as she had experienced in her fight in the kitchen, Antonina was feeling nothing beyond controlled fury. But even with battle-lust burning in her veins, she was glad that the scene was filtered through dim moonlight. The shrieks coming out of that murky mass of struggling men were bloodcurdling enough.

That's got to be pure horror.

The thought was at the edge of her mind, however. At the forefront came recognition that the enemy had recovered enough to change tactics. Wails of agony were overridden by frantic shouts and commands. Murky movement blurred, poured to the sides.

"They're going to the flanks!" bellowed Ashot, loud enough to be heard all through the Roman camp. On the heels of that baritone shout, Antonina heard Menander's high tenor. The young cataphract was shifting his pikemen, shoring up all four sides of the camp.

Seconds later, Euphronius did the same. The commander of the Cohort had concentrated half his musketeers on the southern flank of the camp, facing the hill. Now, he began moving units to the other three sides.

Within two minutes, the Roman formation was that of a classic infantry square, bristling like a hedgehog with muskets and pikes. The Arabs were swirling all around the camp, attacking on every side in small lunges and sallies.

For the first time, the pikemen went to work. Euphronius, for all his youth, was too canny to waste entire salvoes on small clots of enemy cavalry. The threat of those shattering salvoes, in the long run, was all that was holding the enemy at bay. If the Roman musketeers fired too often, their weapons would become hopelessly fouled.

So he waited, patiently, until he saw a large enough cluster gathering. Then, and only then, did the gunsmoke clouds fill the air. In the meantime, the pikes were busy, keeping at bay the small groups of Arabs—sometimes one man alone—who tried to rush the Roman lines.

"Keeping busy" meant, for the most part, simply standing their ground. Not often were the blades of the pikes actually needed.

That was not due to cowardice on the part of the men facing those pikes. No one doubted the courage of the bedouin, or their willingness to hurl themselves onto the Roman lines. But it is a simple fact, often glossed over by historians and *always* by poets and bards, that horses and camels—level-headed, sensible, sane, rational creatures—can not be forced onto a wall of spears. Any number of camels, either from accident or from being half-crazed by wounds, did stumble against the pikes. The pikes brought them down, and their riders with them. But the great mass of the beasts shied away, despite the shrieking commands of their supposed masters.

Antonina, after a few minutes, felt her tension easing. She had been told—*assured*—by her husband, and by Maurice and Ashot, that this would be true. Still, seeing is believing.

Stand your ground, love, her husband had told her. *Just stand your ground, with pike and handcannon. No cavalry in the world will be able to break you, unless they break your will. Artillery could, but you won't be facing that where you're going.*

Many things about herself Antonina had doubted, over the years. Never her will. She was a small woman, but she had a spine to match Atlas.

So, as the battle raged, Antonina found herself doing exactly what Ashot—and her husband and Maurice before him—had told her to do. Just stand there, looking calm and confident. Shout the occasional words of encouragement; whistle a tune; whatever—as long as it's not a giggle.

She only had to fight down a giggle once. Her maid, Koutina, having no duties of her own in battle, had still insisted on staying at Antonina's side. The time came when Koutina nodded sagely, as if some inner suspicion had been confirmed.

"I knew it," she said. The young Egyptian maid glanced at the wall of pikes and muskets, dismissing them serenely. "They're scared of your giant tits, is what it is. That's why they won't come any closer."

At the very end, Antonina learned another lesson. Her husband—and Maurice, and Ashot—had told her of this one, too. But she had forgotten, or never quite believed.

Battles are unpredictable things. Chaos incarnate.

The bedouin finally broke, screaming their frustration. Thousands of Arabs pounded away from the camp, fleeing into the desert. But, by some strange eddy, a large cluster of enemy cavalrymen suddenly hammered into the southern flank of the Roman square.

Since the first few moments of the battle, when the soldiers facing the hill had borne the brunt of the attack, their fight had been easy. If nothing else, the great mound of human and camel bodies in front of them kept most of the Arabs at bay. Now, coming from God-knows-where-or-how, a knot of some twenty bedouin thundered at the line.

The line had been thinned, too far. The Roman flank did not break, but it did crack. Three bedouin made it into the camp itself. Ashot's cataphracts, mounted and held in reserve, started moving toward them.

Before the cataphracts could reach them, two of the Arabs were felled by gunshots. The third Arab's mount was brought down by a pike. The bedouin warrior sprang off the collapsing camel, like a nimble acrobat, and rolled to his feet.

Not six yards from where Antonina was standing, alone except for Koutina.

The maid screamed and scuttled behind Antonina. Drawn by the sound, the nomad turned his head. An instant later, he bounded toward them, his curved sword held high. The man was shrieking like a berserk.

Antonina never even thought to draw her cleaver. Against street thugs, that trusty blade had done wonders. But it would be as effective as a whittling knife against the man charging her now.

She snatched the handcannon off her shoulder. For a moment, she fumbled with the dual hammers and triggers, until John of Rhodes' endless hours of training bore fruit. With her finger firmly on the rear trigger, she cocked the left-side hammer, leveled the gun, and fired.

As always, the blast was deafening and the recoil half-spun her around. But she ignored the pain—was not even aware of it, in truth.

Frantically, she brought the weapon to bear again. She was astonished to see that the Arab was still standing. Her first shot had smashed his rib cage. The man's right side was covered with blood. Antonina could *see* a jagged rib protruding, glistening in the moonlight.

The bedouin did not even grimace. He had stopped shrieking, now. His face seemed calm, like a death mask. The man reached across his body with his left hand and pressed the horrible wound, holding his ruptured side in place. Then he began plodding toward her. His sword was still in his right hand.

For an instant, Antonina was paralyzed by the incredible sight. Then she went berserk herself.

"Fuck you!" she screamed. She sprang forward and jammed the muzzle against the Arab's chest. The fury of her charge was so great that the small woman actually forced the man back two paces. Driving him with the handcannon by rage of body, while her mind—as cold as a kitchen icebox—went through the trained sequence.

The bedouin raised the sword. *Finger on front trigger. Cock the right-side hammer.*

She pulled the trigger. Again, the recoil hammered her aside.

Antonina was oblivious to the pain. Still shrieking obscenities, she spun back and swung the heavy barrel at the Arab's head.

The gun swept through thin air. The momentum of the frenzied swing spun Antonina clear around. She stumbled, off balance, and fell on her butt. The heavy cuirass drove her down.

She stared at her opponent. The man was lying on his back, just a few feet away. She had swung at nothing, she realized. The second shot had ruptured the Arab's heart, and probably his spine with it. He had fallen even before she spun around.

Finally, pain registered. Her hands hurt. Her arms hurt. Her shoulders hurt. Her ass hurt. Even her breasts hurt, where the brass armor had impacted them in her fall.

"Ow," she muttered. A moment later, Koutina was at her side, kneeling, clutching her. The clutch, unfortunately—the desperate squeeze of a terrified kitten—was right across her breasts, pressing the armor further into the poor bruised things.

"*Ow.*" Almost desperate herself, she tried to pry Koutina loose. Or, at least, to shift the girl's anaconda grip a little lower down.

Ashot loomed above her. Antonina stared up at him.

"Well, the battle's won," announced the cataphract. "Total victory. We won't see those Arabs again. Neither will Abreha."

Ashot did not seem ecstatic at the news. To the contrary. His expression was grim and condemnatory.

"I *told* you so," he snarled, glaring at the body of the dead Arab.

Two more cataphracts came up behind Ashot. They seemed to loom over the stubby Armenian as much as he loomed over Antonina. Huge men.

Antonina recognized them. They were named Matthew and Leo. They were the two cataphracts whom Ashot had proposed as her bodyguards, when the expedition left Alexandria.

Antonina had spurned the proposal. She had not been able to explain why, at the time, even to herself. Or had not wanted to, at least. She knew that her husband had bodyguards. Valentinian and Anastasius, as a matter of fact, who were universally considered the best fighters in the Thracian bucellarii. But for Antonina—

No. It had not been necessary, she felt. Unlike Belisarius, who led his men in combat, Antonina had no intention of actually fighting. And there was a stubborn, mulish part of her which had resented the idea.

What am I, a little girl who needs chaperones?

"Does that offer still stand?" she croaked.

Ashot snorted. He gave Matthew and Leo a wave of the hand. "You've got a new job, lads."

" 'Bout time," she heard Matthew mutter.

Leo said nothing. He almost never did. He just reached down his bear-paw-sized hand and lifted Antonina to her feet.

Antonina stared up at him. Leo was the ugliest, scariest-looking, most brutish man she—or anyone else—had ever seen. His fellow cataphracts called him "the Ogre." When they weren't calling him "the Ox," that is, on account of his extremely limited intellect.

But they never called him either name to his face.

Such a handsome man, thought Antonina. *I can't think of better company.*

Antonina's maid was still clutching her. Leo had lifted both of the women, with one hand. Koutina's grip shifted again.

"*Ow*," hissed Antonina. But she didn't pry the girl off. She just patted her hand reassuringly, while she took her own comfort staring at an ogre.

Her ogre.

Chapter 17

KAUSAMBI

Summer, 532 A.D.

"You are disturbed, Nanda Lal," said Great Lady Sati. The young Malwa noblewoman leaned back in her plush, well-upholstered chair. Her ring-heavy fingers stroked the armrests, but her austerely beautiful face was completely still. "Something is troubling you."

The Malwa emperor started, hearing those words. Skandagupta rolled his fat little body side to side on his ornate throne, shifting his eyes from Lady Sati to Nanda Lal. As always when the Malwa Empire's highest council met, the room was unoccupied except for those three people and the special guards. The guards, recruited exclusively from the distant land of the Khmers, were all devotees of Link's cult. Seven of them were giant eunuchs, kneeling in a row against a far wall of the chamber. Their immense bodies were naked from the waist up. Each held a bare tulwar in his hands. The remaining two guards were assassins. Those, garbed in black shirts and pantaloons, stood on either side of the chamber's entrance.

Nanda Lal was frowning, but silent. Emperor Skandagupta prompted him. "If something is troubling you, cousin, speak up," he commanded. "I can't imagine what it is."

Skandagupta reached for the cup of tea resting on a side table next to his throne. "Best news we've had in months. Belisarius has finally been beaten!"

Lady Sati shook her head. The gesture carried a certainty far beyond her years—as if she were already possessed by the divine being which would someday inhabit her body. But the certainty was simply born of habit and training. Sati had spent more time in the company of Link than any other person in the world. (Other than her aunt Holi, of course. But Great Lady Holi was no longer a human being. Holi was nothing, now, beyond Link's sheath.)

"He has not been *beaten*," she said. "Simply driven off, for a time. There is a difference."

Finally, Nanda Lal spoke. "Quite a difference," he growled in agreement. The spymaster took a deep breath. "But it is not Belisarius who concerns me, at the moment. It is Damodara."

The emperor's eyes widened. Lady Sati's did not. "You are concerned about the arms complex in Marv," she stated.

Nanda Lal extended a thick hand, wobbling it back and forth. "In itself—no. Not much, anyhow. We discussed that matter weeks ago, you recall, when we first discovered the fact."

"Yes, we did," interrupted the emperor. "And we agreed that it was not worth making an issue over." Skandagupta shrugged. "It is against Malwa law, true. But we gave Damodara a most thankless task, and can hardly complain when he improved his odds."

The emperor fixed narrow, fat-shrouded eyes on Nanda Lal. "So why the sudden concern?" Forcefully: "I myself am very partial to Damodara. He is far and away our best military commander. Energetic and practical."

"Which is *precisely* what bothers me," countered Nanda Lal. "Your Majesty," he added, almost as a casual afterthought.

Nanda Lal reached to another side table and picked up a scroll. He waved it before him.

"This is a report from a man named Pulumayi, which supplements Lord Damodara's account of the recent battle in the Zagros where Belisarius was beaten."

The emperor frowned. "Pulumayi? Who is he? Never heard of him." He raised his cup toward his mouth.

Nanda Lal snorted. "Neither had I! I had to check my records, to verify his claim." He drew air into his nostrils. "Apparently, Pulumayi is now my chief spy in Damodara's army."

Skandagupta's cup paused before reaching his lips. "What happened to Isanavarman?" he demanded.

"He is dead," came Nanda Lal's harsh reply. "Along with all my top agents. Pulumayi succeeded to Isanavarman's post because he is the most highly ranked survivor—" Again, that deep-drawn breath. "It seems that Belisarius' cavalry raided Damodara's camp during the battle."

Nanda Lal tapped the scroll in the palm of his left hand. "So, at least, this report claims. I do not doubt the claim—not insofar as the casualties are concerned, that is. Their actual cause may be otherwise."

Lady Sati's fingers came to a stop. They did not clench the armrests. Not exactly. But the grip was very firm.

"You suspect Damodara," she stated. Her quick, Link-trained mind sped beyond. "Narses."

"Yes. The entire affair is too convenient." Again, Nanda Lal lifted the scroll. "This, combined with the arms complex, is making me uneasy."

Abruptly, Skandagupta drained his cup and set it down, rattling, on the side table. "I still think it's nonsense! I've known Damodara since he was a toddler. That's a practical man if you'll ever meet one. And he's not given to ambition, beyond a reasonable measure."

Slowly, Nanda Lal shook his head. "No, Emperor, he is not. But practicality is a malleable thing. What is impractical one day, may be practical on the morrow. As for ambition—?" He sniffed. "That, too, changes with the tide."

When Sati spoke, her voice was low and calm. "Your fear is for the future, then. Not the immediate present. A possibility."

"Yes." Nanda Lal paused. "Yes, that. I do not propose to take action, at the moment. But I think we should not close our eyes to the—possibility, as you call it."

Lady Sati shrugged. "It's a simple enough matter." She leaned toward the Emperor. "Bestow great honors on Damodara, Skandagupta. And riches. Hold a ceremony within a week. Among those riches will be a mansion here at the capital. Very near to this palace." She smiled, thinly. "Among those honors will be the expectation that Damodara's entire family will take up residence therein. And stay there."

Skandagupta squinted; then, smiled his own thin humor. "Hostages. Yes. That should do nicely. Damodara dotes on his children."

Still, Nanda Lal seemed unhappy. But, after a moment, he shook off the mood. His next words were almost cheerful: "Venandakatra's siege guns should be arriving at Deogiri very soon. Within two weeks, three at the most."

"Finally!" exclaimed the emperor. His eyes narrowed. "That should do for Raghunath Rao. I look forward to seeing his skinsack suspended in my feast hall." Fat folded further; the eyes became mere slits. "*And* Shakuntala's. I will hang her right next to her father."

"Shakuntala will take a bit of time," cautioned Sati. "Even after we take Deogiri."

She looked to Nanda Lal. "We must tighten the blockade of Suppara. Make sure the rebel empress does not make her escape."

The spymaster scowled. "I'm afraid that's impossible. We don't have the naval forces available—not with Axum to contend with."

"A pity," muttered Skandagupta, "that we didn't catch Prince Eon with the rest." He shrugged. "But I don't see where it matters. Even if Shakuntala escapes after we take Deogiri, where can she go? Only to Ethiopia, or Rome. Where she will be nothing but an impoverished exile."

The emperor nodded toward Sati. "Just as Link said, long ago. Without Majarashtra, Shakuntala is nothing but a nuisance."

Sati nodded grudging agreement. "True. Although I *would* prefer to see her flayed."

"Whatever we do," sneered Nanda Lal, "we certainly won't make the mistake of handing her over to Venandakatra again. Dead—or exiled. That's it."

The spymaster reached up and stroked his nose. As always, the feel of that crushed and mangled proboscis stirred his fury. Belisarius had done for that.

Since there was no way, at present, to vent his feelings for Belisarius, Nanda Lal transferred his cold rage elsewhere. "One last point," he snarled, "before we end this meeting. The rebel bands in Bihar and Bengal are growing bolder. I recommend—"

"More impalings!" snapped the emperor. "Line every road with the bandits!"

"I agree," chimed in Great Lady Sati. "The male ones, anyway. Better to turn their women over to the soldiers, before auctioning them to the whoremasters. Add defilement to destruction. That will cow the peasants."

Nanda Lal's snarl of fury slid into something resembling a leer. "Not enough," he demurred. "It's too hard to catch the bandits in the forests."

He bestowed the leer on the emperor. "Since all the news is good—Belisarius defeated; Deogiri about to fall—I see no reason that half your Imperial Guard can't be released for a campaign."

The emperor smiled. Grinned. "Excellent idea! The Ye-tai are getting restless, anyway, from garrison duty here in Kausambi. A campaign in Bihar and Bengal would do them good."

Skandagupta leaned forward, planting his hands on his knees. "What do you have in mind? A punitive campaign, right through the countryside?" He barked a laugh. "Yes! Sweep everything, like a knife. Cut a swath twenty miles wide—from Pataliputra to the Bay of Bengal. The hell with hunting for bandits! Just burn everything, kill everyone." Another barked laugh. "Except the women, of course. My Ye-tai will have a better use for those."

Nanda Lal leaned forward to match gazes with the emperor. "I was thinking of two swaths, actually. One—just as you say—starting at Pataliputra. The other—"

There came a knock on the door. Nanda Lal paused. One of the assassins opened the door and peered through. A moment later, he turned to the emperor and announced: "Sire, your lunch is here."

"Ah!" exclaimed Skandagupta. "Excellent." He smacked his hands together. "Let us eat. We can develop our plans over the meal."

"Food will sustain us," concurred Sati. "This will be a long session."

Nanda Lal's leer returned. "Yes—but the discussion will season the meal. I like my food hot and spicy."

Chapter 18

MAJARASHTRA
Summer, 532 A.D.

Irene stared nervously at the Malwa milling around the impromptu field camp which Ezana's soldiers had set up alongside the road to Deogiri. There appeared to be thousands of them—especially leering Ye-tai, who were making no attempt to hide their ogling of her. Muttered phrases swelled from the mob. The content of those coarse words was not quite audible, but their meaning was more than clear enough—like surf, frothing lust. Ezana's four hundred sarwen, standing guard with their spears in hand, reminded her of a pitiful dike before a surging ocean. A child's sand castle, with the tide about to come in.

Why did I ever agree to do this? Irene demanded of herself.

Herself babbled reassurance: "Seemed like a good idea at the time."

That was then; this is now.

"Get a grip on yourself, woman. The whole idea was to distract them, which has definitely been done."

Sure has. I'll bet they'll be even more distracted when all four thousand of them start gang-raping me. Wonderful!

"You and your husband, Ezana, are supposed to be envoys from the King of the Vandals, seeking an alliance against Rome. Surely they wouldn't—"

645

Surely, my ass! Do those drooling thugs look like diplomats to you? Whoever came up with this insane scheme?

"Well, actually—*you* did."

Thanks for reminding me. I forgot I'm an idiot.

"It's a good plan," herself repeated stubbornly. Herself reminded Irene of one child reassuring another that there really aren't any monsters, as the ogre stuffs them into his gullet.

I'm an idiot. Idiot—idiot—idiot! This is the stupidest plan—

Ezana entered the small pavilion—not much more than a canopy, really, shielding the richly garbed "Vandal" noblewoman from the blistering sun. Her "noble African husband" had to stoop, in order to keep his elaborate ostrich-plume headdress from being swept off.

"Good plan!" he grunted, as soon as he straightened. Ezana gazed placidly on the Malwa soldiery swarming around them. In the far distance, to the north, the first of the siege guns in the column was now visible, being painfully hauled another few feet south to Deogiri.

"Will you look at that rabble?" he demanded. "They make bedouin look like a Macedonian phalanx. The officers are worse than the men."

"Don't remind me," snarled Irene. She glanced apprehensively at the cluster of officers sitting their horses nearby. The officers were perched a few yards up a slope, giving them a better view of Irene than that enjoyed by the common troops. Behind them reared the crest of one of Majarashtra's multitude of ridges.

The officers were ogling her even more openly than the Yetai. She saw one of them say something, followed by a round of leering laughs.

"What is *wrong* with these animals?" she demanded, half-angrily and half-nervously. "Haven't they ever seen a woman before? If I looked like Antonina, I might understand it. She could make the sun stop in its tracks. But I'm—"

She gestured at herself. Again, anger was mixed with apprehension. "I'm not ugly, I suppose. But with my big nose—"

Ezana chuckled. "You are quite an attractive woman, Irene, in my opinion. But it really doesn't matter."

He hooked a thumb toward the Malwa. "This is why we agreed to the plan, Irene. If you hadn't volunteered to come, we never would have considered it. Kungas and I both knew what would happen, if the Malwa encountered a large party of foreigners claiming to have been shipwrecked on the coast. They are not diplomats. They would have just attacked us, on general principle. Even if they weren't guarding their precious siege guns."

He gazed at her with approval. "But with *you* here, all dressed up in such finery—" His gaze, falling on her bosom, became very approving. "Such *provocative* finery—scandalous, the way foreign women dress! And they're all sluts, those heathens, everybody knows it."

Irene scowled. "Those monkeys know as much about Vandals as I do about—" She groped for a simile, but couldn't find an appropriate one. With her voracious reading habits, Irene couldn't think of any subject that she didn't know more about than Ye-tai and Malwa soldiers did about the people and politics of North Africa.

Ezana grinned. "They know Africa is a land of black people." He cupped his hand under his chin, as if presenting his ebony face. "And if the woman is pale, and beautiful, so much the more exotic!"

"I am *not* beautiful," insisted Irene.

Ezana, still grinning, shook his head. Then, nodding toward the Malwa soldiers gawking at her: "You look beautiful to *them*, woman. After weeks on the road, struggling through India's heat and dust, you look like Aphrodite herself."

Again, he admired her bosom. "Especially your tits."

Even as nervous as she was, Irene couldn't help but chuckle. She glanced down at the objects in question, which were almost entirely visible due to the cut of her tunic. She had overseen the seamstresses in Suppara herself, blending Roman style with what she remembered of the costumes of Minoan women painted on vases. The small amount of skin still covered—a fifth, at most—simply framed, supported, presented, and emphasized the splendid remainder.

"It *is* impressive, isn't it? Makes me look like Antonina, almost."

Ezana's grin faded to a simple smile. "It was bound to happen, Irene. You've never been a soldier, on a long and arduous march. Even disciplined sarwen or Roman cataphracts would be ragged in their ranks, with every man eager to get a look. Hot, tired, aching feet and butts—most of all, *bored.* Especially since Rao stopped attacking the column many days ago."

The smile became a sneer, cheerfully bestowed on the mob surrounding the Ethiopian camp. *"Those* soldiers? Ha!"

He rubbed his hands with satisfaction. "No, no. It worked just like you planned. Four hundred sarwen, some Syrian gunners disguised as slaves, and one Roman woman have completely distracted an army ten times their number. Stopped them in their tracks, diverted their attention, disintegrated their formations—"

His eye caught movement to the north. He barked a laugh. "Look! Even some of the troops dragging the guns are trotting our way."

"Oh, marvelous," hissed Irene. Gloomily: "At least I'm not a virgin." She eyed the leering mob, and the artillery soldiers hastening down the road to join them. "Step aside, Messalina," she muttered. "I think I'm about to exceed your exploits. Put them completely in the shade, in fact."

Ezana chuckled. "I'm not sure who Messalina was, but if—" Humor remained, in his eyes, but Ezana's face was suddenly stern and solemn.

"You are a bold woman, Irene Macrembolitissa. Hold fast to that courage, and set aside your fears. No one will harm you. Kungas would never have agreed to this, if he did not think we Ethiopians could shield you when the hammer falls." The stiff face became a black mask; as hard and unyielding as Kungas' own. "Which it will, and very soon."

Irene's eyes began to move toward the ridge above them, but she forced them aside.

Ezana, seeing the movement, nodded. "He will be there, Irene. Kungas will come."

Irene, trying to settle her nerves, fastened on that image. Kungas, and his hard face, coming toward her. Kungas, smiling with his eyes as she corrected his grammar. The little twitch in his lips, before he made a jest about thick-headed Kushans, even though she herself had been astonished by his ability to learn anything quickly. Kungas, day after day after day, sitting by her side in a chamber, learning to read. Never complaining, never grumbling, never angry at her for his own shortcomings.

The memory of a hard face, and clear almond eyes, and a heart beating hidden warmth and humor, and a mind like an uncut diamond, steadied her. She took a few deep breaths. *Kungas will come.* A few more breaths. *He will.* A few more. *Kungas.*

She felt herself return. To the memory of a hard face she added her own irrepressible humor.

"What do you think, Ezana?" she asked, gesturing with her chin toward the cluster of officers not more than thirty yards away. The Malwa were still staring at her, exchanging unheard quips. "Will they start the seduction with fine wine? Some music, perhaps?"

Ezana chuckled. Irene snorted. "Not likely, is it?" Her sour gaze fell on one particularly gross Malwa officer. The man had his tongue sticking out, wagging it at her.

"Will you look at—"

The officer's eyes bulged. Blood coughed out of his mouth, coating the obscene tongue. An arrowhead was protruding through his throat.

An instant later, the clustered officers were swept off their horses as if struck by a giant sickle. Irene gaped. Part of her mind identified the objects which had turned men into shredded meat. Arrows. But most of her brain simply went blank.

Dimly, she heard Ezana shouting. Her mouth still wide open from shock, she turned her head. The Syrian gunners had abandoned their servile toil and were already hurling grenades. The missiles were joined in mid-flight—and then overtaken—by four hundred javelins. Ethiopia's spearmen were also in action.

The javelin volley swept the front ranks of the Malwa mob like another great sickle. The second volley was on its way before the grenades even landed. Again, Death swung its sickle—and then *again*, as the grenades began exploding in the packed crowd. Some of the grenades were smoke bombs. Within seconds, the bloody scene began to disappear behind streaked and wafting clouds.

She was in a daze. Irene had never been in a battle before. She had never been *near* a battle before. Part of her shock and confusion was produced by simple fear. But most of it was an even simpler collapse of intelligence.

Irene's well-trained, logical mind stumbled and tripped, trying to find order and reason in the bedlam around her. Everything seemed pure chaos. An inferno of unreason. Through the eddying smoke, she caught glimpses of: men dying; sarwen locking their shields; the flight of arrows and javelins, and grenades; yelling Kushans charging down the slope; bellowing Ye-tai, desperately trying to rally confused troops. Shouts of confusion; shrieks of agony; screams of death and despair; cries of victory and triumph.

Noise, noise, everywhere. Steel and wood and flesh breaking. She clapped her hands over her ears, in her own desperate struggle to rally intelligence. Half in a crouch, sheltered under a canopy, she forced her eyes to watch. Desperately—*desperately*—trying to find a place where reason could set its anchor.

The anchor scraped across stone, finding no place.

How can men stand this? she wondered. Her eyes recognized purpose in the chaos. Her eyes saw the discipline of the sarwen, the way their shield wall held like a dike—and no pitiful child's castle of sand, this, against the coming tide. Her eyes saw—she had been told, but had never really believed—how the Malwa broke against those shields and spears. Men—enemies, yes, but still men—using their own flesh like water, trying to break the reef. Flesh became red ruin; blood everywhere; a severed arm, here; a coil of intestines, there; a piece of Malwa brain, crushed under an Ethiopian sandal.

Irene's eyes watched Satan spread his carpet across a dusty road in India. She *saw*, but her mind could not encompass the seeing.

A powerful hand seized her shoulder and drove her to her knees.

"*Down*, woman!" Her ears heard Ezana's voice, shouting further commands. Her eyes saw five sarwen, surrounding her like a wall. Her mind understood nothing. She was no more than a child, now, recognizing shelter.

She closed her eyes and pressed her hands over her ears. Finally, darkness and relative quiet brought back a modicum of reason. In that small eye of the storm, Irene sought herself.

After a time—seconds? minutes? hours?—she began to recognize herself.

Courage, foundation of all virtues, came back first.

I will not do this. Firmly, she opened her eyes and removed her hands from her ears.

She could see nothing, on her knees, except a few glimpses through the legs of the sarwen standing guard over her. And what little she could see was still obscured by smoke. After a moment, she stopped trying to make sense of the battle. She simply studied the legs of the soldiers shielding her.

Excellent legs, she concluded. Under the black skin, powerful muscles flexed calves and thighs. The easy movement of men watching, not fighting themselves, but ready to spring into action at an instant's notice. Human leopards. Horny, calloused feet rested firmly in sturdy sandals. Toes shaped in Ethiopia's mountains fit stony Majarashtra to perfection.

She listened to their banter. Her Ge'ez was good enough, now, to understand the words. But her mind made no attempt to translate. Most of the words were profanity, anyway—nothing more than taunting curses hurled down on the invisible enemy. She simply listened to the confidence in those voices. Human leopards, growling with predator satisfaction.

Two phrases, only, did she ever remember.

The first, howled with glee: "And will you look at those fucking Kushans? God—*damn!*"

And the response, growling bemused wonder: "I'm glad Kungas is on our side, boys. Or we'd be so much dog food."

So am I. Oh, dear God, so am I.

In the time which followed, as a Malwa army was ripped to pieces between Ethiopia's shield wall and a Kushan avalanche, Irene went away. This was not her place. She had no purpose here.

She needed to find herself, again. For perhaps the first time in her life.

Herself appeared, and demanded the truth. *Don't ask why you came, woman. You know the answer. And don't tell me lies about clever stratagems, and ruses, and battle plans. Tell others, but not me. You know why you came.*

"Yes," she choked, closing her eyes. Tears leaked through the lids. "I know."

A sarwen, hearing the soft sobs, glanced down at her. For a moment, no more, before he looked away. A woman, her wits shattered. Nothing to puzzle over. Women were fragile by nature.

But he was quite wrong. The tears streaking Irene's cheeks were tears of happiness, not fear. Fear there was, of course, and fear aplenty. But it was not fear of the moment. No, not at all. It was the much greater fear—the deep terror, entwined with joy—of a human being who had finally, like so many others before her, been able to give up a hostage to fortune. A woman who, finally, understood her friend Antonina and could—finally—make the same choice.

"He would have gone into the fire, anyway," she whispered to herself. "No matter what I did."

Herself nodded. *And you could not bear the thought. Of staying behind, staring at a horse.*

◇   ◇   ◇

Then, he was there. She saw the legs of the sarwen around her ease and stretch. Saw them move aside. Heard the shouts of greeting and glee. In the distance, a muted roar. The first of the Malwa guns was being destroyed—overcharged powder blowing overcharged shot, rupturing the huge weapon like a rotten fruit.

He squatted next to her, where she knelt. "Are you all right?"

Irene nodded. Smiled. He placed a hand on her shoulder.

He had never touched her before. She reached up and caressed the hand with her own. Feeling, with her long and slender fingers, the short ones, heavy with flesh and sinew, which held her shoulder so gently.

She pressed her face into his thick chest. His hand slid down her arm, his arm became a shield, his touch an embrace. Suddenly, fiercely, she pressed open lips against his muscular neck. Kissing, nuzzling. Her breath came quick and short. She flung her arms around him and drew him half-sprawling across her. Her left leg, kicking free of the long tunic, coiled down his out-thrust right leg. Her sandal scraped the bare skin of his calf.

For a moment—pure heat, bolting out of a stable like a wild horse—Irene felt Kungas respond. His hard abdomen pressed her own, desire meeting desire. But only for a moment. Kungas chuckled. The sound carried more delight than humor. Much more. *Much* more. It was the choked laugh of a man who discovers, unexpectedly, that an idle dream has taken real form. Yet, despite that little cry, his strong arms and body went rigid, pinning her—not like a wrestler pins an opponent, but simply like a man restrains a child from folly. Seconds went by, while his lips nuzzled her lovely, thick, chestnut hair. Irene felt his breath; heavy, hot at first, but cooling quickly.

She chuckled herself, then, as his restraint brought her own. "I guess it's not a good idea," she mumbled. "The Ethiopians would probably insist on watching."

"Worse, I'm afraid," he responded dryly, still kissing her hair. "They'd accompany us with drums. Placing bets, all the while, on when we'd stop."

Irene laughed outright. The sound was muffled against his chest.

"No," whispered Kungas gently. "Not for us, and not now. Passion always comes, after death's wings flap away. But it is cheap, and gone with the morrow. And you will wonder, afterward, whether it was you or your fear."

He chuckled again. Delight was still in that sound, but it was warm rather than ecstatic. "I know you, Irene. You would resent me. And what's worse, you would study books trying to find the answer."

"Think I couldn't find it?" she demanded.

She heard his soft laugh, rustling through her hair. Felt the little movement of his chest. Knew the economic subtlety she had come to cherish so. "I don't doubt you would. But reading takes so much time. I don't want to wait *that* long."

Smiling, she raised her head. The clear brown eyes of Greek nobility, looking past a long and bony nose, stared into eyes of almond, in a flat and barbarous face. "How long, then?" she asked.

Another muted roar swept the pavilion; and then another. But the Kushan's eyes never left her own. The destruction of Venandakatra's guns—the rubble of Malwa's schemes—the salvation of a dynasty—these were meaningless things, in that moment, for those two people embracing on a road.

"First, I must learn to read," he said. "Not before." His face was stiff, and solemn, but Irene did not miss the little twitch in his lips.

She smiled. "You are a good student, you know. Amazingly good."

Kungas' smile could have been recognized by anyone, now. "With such an incentive, who could fail?"

There was another roar, as a siege gun ruptured; and another. This time, Kungas did look.

"That's the last of them," he said. "We must be off, now, before they rally and Venandakatra sends more. We can make the coast, if we don't dawdle."

With easy grace, he rose to his feet and extended his hand. A moment later, Irene was standing at his side.

The realities of war had returned. Irene could see the sarwen and the Kushan troops forming their columns in preparation for the forced march to the sea, and the Ethiopian ships waiting there to carry them back to Suppara.

But Kungas did not immediately relinquish his grip on her hand. He took the time to lean over and whisper: "We will know."

Irene, grinning, squeezed his hand. "Yes. We will always know."

She burst into laughter, then. Riotous, joy-filled laughter. Ethiopian and Kushan soldiers nearby, hearing that bizarre sound on a bloody battlefield, looked her way.

For a second or two, no more. A woman, her wits frayed by the carnage. Nothing to puzzle over. Women were fragile by nature.

Chapter 19

PERSIA
Summer, 532 A.D.

"Can you disguise the entrance afterward?" asked Belisarius. He waved his hand, in a gesture which encompassed the valley. "The whole area, actually. Keep in mind, Kurush, there'll be more than ten thousand soldiers passing through here—*and* as many horses."

The Roman general turned his head, looking down at the river. The river flowed west by northwest. Like the valley itself, the river was small and rather narrow. The pass where it exited the valley was barely more than a gorge. They were almost in the foothills of the western slope of the Zagros, but the surrounding mountains seemed to have lost none of their usual ruggedness.

"I assume you'll be taking the horses out that way," Belisarius said, pointing toward the gorge. "By the time they pass through, the whole valley will be churned into mush. No way to disguise the tracks."

Kurush shook his head, smiling. "We won't try to hide the tracks, Belisarius. Quite the opposite! The more Damodara's mind is on that gorge, the more he'll be diverted from the real exit."

Belisarius scratched his chin. "I understand the logic, Kurush. But don't underestimate Damodara and Sanga—*and* their scouts. Those Pathan trackers can trail a mouse. They won't simply trot after the horses, salivating. They'll search the entire valley."

Belisarius turned his head and studied the entrance to the qanat. The timber-braced adit was located about a hundred yards up the mountainside, not far from the small river which had carved out this valley. The sloping ramp, after a few feet, disappeared into darkness.

He hooked a thumb in that direction. "There'll be tracks there too," he pointed out. "No way to disguise *them*, either. Even if you collapse the entrance, the tracks will be all over the area. Ten thousand troops leave a big trail."

Kurush's smile widened. He shook his head. "You're worrying too much. We can cover the soldiers' tracks by running the horses through afterward. Everywhere except this immediate area. Then—"

The Persian nobleman leapt onto a small rock a few feet away. From that perch, he leaned over and pointed along the steep slope of the mountain. "This is mining country, Belisarius. Silver, mostly. There are small deposits in this valley."

He spread his hands apologetically. "Nothing more than traces, really, according to the miners I brought with me. But the miners will be gone before Damodara arrives. And I doubt very much if an army of Rajput cavalrymen will be able to tell him that the ore in the area isn't worth mining."

Aide made a mental snort. ***Rajputs?***

Belisarius chuckled. "Hardly! And their Pathans, outside of hunting, consider all forms of labor to be women's work."

The Roman general nodded. "Yes, that'll work. After we pass through, you'll have this whole slope turned into a mining operation. Cover our tracks with tailings." He pointed at the adit. "And I assume that you'll have your miners cover our tracks well into the qanat. Fifty yards should do it. Pathans are outdoorsmen. They won't be comfortable more than a few feet into that blackness."

Again, Belisarius studied the gorge at the far end of the valley. "All that will be left, after a few days," he mused, "are the tracks of Roman horses. Passing, by pure coincidence, through a mining area on their way into Mesopotamia."

He paused, thinking. "One thing, however. Those Pathans know their business, Kurush. You'll have to make sure—"

Kurush was grinning. "Yes, yes!" he interrupted. "I'll have the horses carrying sacks filled with dirt. Weighing about what a Roman soldier does. Their tracks will be deep enough."

Belisarius returned the grin with one of his own. "You've thought of everything, I see."

Kurush shrugged. Belisarius almost laughed. The modest gesture fit the Aryan sahrdaran about as well as a curtsy fits a lion.

His humor faded. "You understand, Kurush, that the hammer will fall on you? Once Damodara understands what has happened—and it won't take him long—he won't waste time trying to chase after me. He'll strike directly into Mesopotamia."

Kurush shrugged again. The gesture, this time, did not even pretend at modesty. It was the twitch of a lion's shoulders, irritated by flies.

"That is only fair, Roman, after all you've done for the Aryans."

Kurush sprang off the rock and strode over to Belisarius. He jabbed his chin toward the south, using his stiff Persian-cut beard as a pointer. "As soon as he gets the word, the emperor will begin retreating toward Babylon. He's on the verge of doing it, anyway, so it won't seem odd at all." Kurush scowled. "The Malwa have been pressing him very hard."

Belisarius eyed the sahrdaran. The Roman general had no difficulty interpreting Kurush's frowning face. He could well imagine the casualties which Emperor Khusrau's soldiers had taken over the past months. While Belisarius had been maneuvering with Damodara in the Zagros mountains all through the spring, Khusrau had been keeping the huge main army of the Malwa invasion penned up in the Tigris-Euphrates delta. The task would have been difficult enough, even without—

He decided to broach the awkward subject.

"Has the rebellion—?"

Khusrau's frown vanished instantly. The Persian nobleman barked a laugh.

"The head of the emperor's half-brother has been the main ornament of his pavilion for two weeks, now." Kurush grimaced. "Damn thing was a mass of flies, by the time I left. Stinky."

His good humor returned. "Ormazd's rebellion has been crushed. *And* that of the Lakhmids. We took Hira almost two months ago. Khusrau drove the population into the desert and ordered the city razed to the ground."

Belisarius let no sign of his distaste show. He had never been fond of "punitive action" against enemy civilians, even before he met Aide and was introduced to future standards of warmaking.

But he did not fault Khusrau. By the standards of the day, in truth, driving the population of Hira out of the city before destroying it was rather humane. The Lakhmids had been Persian vassals before they gave their allegiance to the Malwa invaders. Most Persian emperors—most Roman ones, for that matter, including Theodora—would have repaid that rebellion by ordering the city's people burned inside it.

And let's not get too romantic about the Geneva Convention and the supposedly civilized standards of future wars, either, remarked Aide. **They won't prevent entire cities being destroyed, with their populations. Purely for "strategic reasons," of course. What difference does that make, to mangled children in the ruins of Coventry? Or to thousands of Korean slave laborers incinerated at Hiroshima?**

Kurush was pointing with his beard again, this time to the west.

"The emperor has instructed me to defend Ctesiphon, while he retreats to Babylon. I will have ten thousand men. That should be enough to hold our capital city, for a few months. Damodara does not have siege guns."

Kurush turned his eyes to Belisarius. There was nothing in the Persian's gaze beyond a matter-of-fact acceptance of reality.

"In the end, of course," he said calmly, "we will be doomed. Unless your thrust strikes home."

Belisarius smiled crookedly. "It is said that an army marches on its belly, you know. I will do my best to drive a lance into the great gut of Malwa, once you have drawn the shield away."

Kurush chuckled. " 'An army marches on its belly,' " he repeated. "That's clever! I don't recognize the saying, though. Who came up with it?"

Good move, genius, said Aide sourly. **This will be entertaining, watching you explain to a sixth-century Persian how you came to quote Napoleon.**

Belisarius ignored the quip. "I heard it from a Hun. One of my mercenaries, during my second campaign in the trans-Danube. I was rather stunned, actually, to find such a keen grasp of logistics in the mind of a barbarian. But it just goes to show—"

Father of lies, father of lies. It's a good thing my lips are sealed, so to speak. The stories I could tell about you! They'd make even Procopius' *Secret History* look like sober, reasoned truth.

◇ ◇ ◇

Lord Damodara leaned back in his chair, studying Narses' scowling face.

"So what is it that bothers you, exactly?" he asked the eunuch.

"Everything!" snapped Narses. The old Roman glared around the interior of the pavilion, as if searching its unadorned walls for some nook or cranny in which truth lay hidden.

"None of what Belisarius is doing makes any sense," stated Narses. "Nothing. Not from the large to the small."

"Explain," commanded Damodara. The lord waved his pudgy little hand in a circular motion. The gesture included himself and the tall figure of the Rajput king seated next to him. "In simple words, that two simpletons like myself and Rana Sanga can understand."

The good-humored quip caused even Rana Sanga to smile. Even Narses, for that matter, and the old eunuch was not a man who smiled often.

"As to the 'large,' " said Narses, "what is the purpose of these endless maneuvers that Belisarius is so fond of?" The eunuch leaned forward, emphasizing his next words. "Which are not, however—*and cannot be*—truly endless. There is no way he can stop you from reaching Mesopotamia. The man's not a fool. That must be as obvious to him, by now—" Narses jabbed a stiff finger toward the pavilion's entrance "—as it is to the most dim-witted Ye-tai in your army."

"He's bought time," remarked Sanga.

Narses made a sour face. "A few months, at most. It's not been more than eight weeks since the battle of the pass, and you've already forced him almost out of the Zagros. Your army is much bigger than his. You can defeat him on an open battlefield, and you've proven that you can maneuver through these mountains as well as he can. Within a month, perhaps six weeks, he'll have to concede the contest and allow you entry into Mesopotamia. At which point he'll have no choice but to fort up in Ctesiphon or Peroz-Shapur, anyway. So why not do it now?"

"I don't think it's odd," countered Damodara. "He's used the months that he kept us tied up in the Zagros to good advantage, according to our spies. That general of his that he left in charge of the Roman forces in Mesopotamia—the crippled one,

Agathius—has been working like a fiend, these past months. By the time we get to Ctesiphon, or Peroz-Shapur, he'll have the cities fortified beyond belief. Cannons and gunpowder have been pouring in from the Roman armories, while we've been counter-marching all over these damned mountains."

Sanga nodded. "The whole campaign, to my mind, has Belisa-rius' signature written all over it. He always tries to force his enemy to attack him, so that he can have the advantage of the defensive. By stalling us for so many months here in the mountains, he's been able to create a defensive stronghold in Mesopotamia. It'll be pure murder, trying to storm Peroz-Shapur."

Narses stared at the two men sitting across the table from him. There seemed to be no expression at all on the eunuch's wizened, scaly face, but both Damodara and Sanga could sense the sarcasm lurking somewhere inside.

Neither man took offense. They were accustomed to Narses, and his ways, by now. There was a bitterness at the center of the eunuch's soul which was ineradicable. That bitterness colored his examination of the world, and gave scorn to his every thought.

Thoughts, however—and a capacity to examine—which they had come to respect deeply. And so a kinsman of the Malwa dynasty, and Rajputana's most noble monarch, listened carefully to the words of a lowborn Roman eunuch.

Narses leaned over and pointed with his finger to a location on the great map which covered the table.

"He will make his stand at Peroz-Shapur, not Ctesiphon," pre-dicted Narses. "Belisarius is a Roman, when all is said and done. Ctesiphon is Persia's capital, but Peroz-Shapur is the gateway to the Roman Empire."

Damodara and Sanga both nodded. They had already come to the same conclusion.

Narses studied the map for a few seconds. Then:

"Tell me something. When the time comes, do you intend to hurl your soldiers at the walls of Peroz-Shapur?" He almost—not quite—sneered. "You don't have too many Ye-tai left, either, so the soldiers you'll use up like sheep at a slaughterhouse will all be Rajput."

Rana Sanga didn't rise to the bait. He simply chuckled. Damo-dara laughed outright.

"Not likely!" exclaimed the Malwa lord. He leaned over the table himself. The months of arduous campaigning had shrunk Damodara's belly enough that the movement was almost graceful.

Damodara's finger traced the Tigris river, from Ctesiphon upstream toward Armenia.

"I won't go near Peroz-Shapur." Another laugh. "Any more than I'd enter a tiger's cage. I won't try to besiege Ctesiphon either. I'll simply use the Tigris to keep my army supplied and move north into Assyria. From there, I can strike into Anatolia—or Armenia—while most of Khusrau's army is tied up fighting our main force on the southern Euphrates."

He leaned back, exuding self-satisfaction. "Belisarius will have no choice," pronounced Damodara. "All that work he's done to fortify Peroz-Shapur will be wasted. He'll have to come out and face me, somewhere in the field."

Narses' eyes left Damodara and settled on Rana Sanga. The Rajput king nodded his agreement with Damodara's explication.

"Ah," said Narses. "An excellent strategy. I am enlightened. *Except*—why hasn't Belisarius figured the same thing out himself? The man has never, to put it mildly, been accused of stupidity."

Silence. Damodara squirmed a bit in his chair. Sanga maintained his usual stiff composure, but the very rigidity of the posture indicated his own discomfort.

Narses sneered. "Ah, yes. You've wondered that yourselves, haven't you? Now and again, at least."

The eunuch relinquished the sneer, within a few seconds. He was too canny to risk offending the two men across the table from him. And, if the truth be told, he had a genuine respect for them.

"Let's leave that broad problem, for a moment, and move on to some seemingly minor questions. Of these, there are three that stand out."

Narses held up a thumb. "First. Why has Belisarius, since the very beginning of this campaign in the Zagros, always been willing to let us move north?"

Narses nodded toward the Rajput. "As Rana Sanga was the first to point out, many weeks ago." He gave another nod, this time at Damodara. "As you yourself remarked at the time, Lord, that makes no sense. It should be the other way around. He should be fighting like a tiger when we move north, and put up only token resistance when we maneuver to the south. That way, he would be keeping us from threatening Assyria."

Silence.

Narses held up his forefinger alongside the thumb.

"The second small problem. In all the skirmishes we've fought over the past months—even during the battle at the pass when his situation was desperate—Belisarius has never used his mercenaries. *Why?* He's got two thousand of the Goth barbarians, but he handles them like they were the only jewels in his possession."

Sanga cleared his throat. "Doesn't trust them, I imagine." The Rajput king scowled. "I don't trust mercenaries either, Narses."

The eunuch snorted. "Of course you don't!" Narses slapped his hand down on the table. The sharp sound seemed to fill the confines of the tent.

"*Belisarius has never trusted mercenaries,*" hissed Narses. The eunuch's eyes were fixed on Sanga like a serpent's on its prey. "He never has. He is well known for it, in the Roman army—which, as you know, is traditionally an army which uses mercenaries all the time. But Belisarius never uses them except when he has no choice, and *then* he only uses mercenaries as auxiliaries. Hun light cavalry, for the most part."

Narses jabbed at the map. "So why would he bring two thousand Goth heavy cavalry with him, in a campaign like this one? There's nothing in this kind of campaign which would keep a mercenary's interest. No loot, no plunder. Nothing but weeks and weeks of arduous marches and countermarches, for nothing beyond a stipend."

The eunuch laughed sarcastically. "Belisarius never would have brought Goth mercenaries along with him for the good and simple reason, if no other, that he would have known they'd desert within two months. Which brings me—"

He held up a third finger.

"Point three. Why *haven't* those mercenaries deserted?" Another sarcastic, sneering laugh. "Goths are about as stupid as the horses they ride, but even horses aren't that stupid."

Narses planted both hands on the table and pushed himself against the back of his chair. For just an instant, in that posture, the small old eunuch seemed a more regal figure than the Malwa dynast and the Rajput king who faced him.

"So. Let's put it all together. We have one of history's most cunning generals—who *always* subordinates tactics to strategy—engaged in a campaign which, for all its tactical acumen, makes no sense at all strategically. In the course of this campaign, he drags along a bunch of mercenaries he has no use for, and which have no business being there on their own account. What does that all add up to?"

Silence.

Narses scowled. "What it adds up to, Lord and King, is—*Belisarius*. He's up to something. Something we aren't seeing."

"What?" demanded Damodara.

Narses shrugged. "I don't know, Lord. At the moment, I only have questions. But I urge you"—for just an instant, the eunuch's sarcastic, sneering voice was filled with nothing beyond earnest and respectful pleading—"to take my questions seriously. Or we will find ourselves, in the end, like so many of Belisarius' opponents. Lying in the dirt, bleeding to death, from a blow we never saw coming."

The silence which now filled the tent was not the silence of a breath, held in momentary suspense. It was a long, long silence. A thoughtful silence.

Damodara finally broke it.

"I think we should talk to him," he announced. "Arrange a parley."

His two companions stared at him. Both men were frowning.

Narses was frowning from puzzlement. "What do you hope to accomplish? He'll hardly tell you what he's planning!"

Damodara chuckled. "I didn't imagine he would." The Malwa lord shrugged. "The truth? I would simply like to meet the man, after all this time. I think it would be fascinating."

Damodara shifted his eyes to Rana Sanga. The Rajput king was still frowning.

Not from puzzlement, but—

"I am bound to your service by honor, Lord Damodara," rasped Sanga. "That same honor—"

Damodara raised a hand, forestalling the Rajput. "Please, Rana Sanga! I am not a fool. Practical, yes. But practical in *all* things." He chuckled. "I would hardly plan a treacherous ambush, in violation of all codes of honor, using Rajputs as my assassins. *Any* Rajputs, much less *you*."

Damodara straightened. "We will find a meeting place where ambush is impossible. A farmhouse in open terrain, perhaps, which Belisarius' scouts can search for hidden troops."

He nodded at Rana Sanga. "And you, King of Rajputana, will serve as my only bodyguard at the parley itself. That should be enough, I think, to protect me against foul play—and *will* be enough, I am certain, to assure Belisarius that he has nothing to fear. Not once he has *your* word of honor, whatever he thinks of my own."

The frown faded, somewhat, from Sanga's brow. But the quick glance which the Rajput king gave Narses still carried a lurking suspicion.

Damodara chuckled again. "Have no fear, Rana Sanga. Narses won't be within miles of the place."

"Not likely!" snorted the eunuch.

A week later, Damodara's dispatch rider returned with Belisarius' response.

"The Roman general wrote it out himself," the Rajput said, as he handed over the sealed sheet. The man seemed a bit puzzled. Or, perhaps, a bit in awe. "He didn't even hesitate, Lord Damodara. He wrote the reply as soon as he finished reading your message. I watched him do it."

Damodara broke the seal and began reading. He was surprised, but not much, to see that Belisarius' message was written in perfect Hindi.

When he finished, Damodara laughed.

"What's so amusing?" asked Narses.

"Did he agree?" asked Rana Sanga.

Damodara waved the letter. "Yes, he agreed. He says we can pick the location, and the time. As long as Rana Sanga is there, he says, he has no concerns about treachery."

The Rajput's face was stiff as a board. Damodara smiled, knowing how deeply Sanga was hiding his surge of pride.

He transferred the smile to Narses.

"As for the amusement—Belisarius *did* add a stipulation, Narses. He insists that you must be at the parley also."

The eunuch's face almost disappeared in a mass of wrinkles. Damodara's smile became an outright grin. The Roman traitor, in that moment, was not even trying to hide his own emotions. That great frown exuded *suspicion*, the way a glacier exudes chilliness.

"*Why me?*" demanded Narses.

Damodara shrugged. "I have no idea. You can add that to your list of unanswered questions."

Chapter 20

ADULIS

Summer, 532 A.D.

Seated on his throne, in what had been the viceroy's audience hall at Sana, Eon stared down at the crowd. Other than the dozen or so sarwen standing guard against the walls, and his immediate advisers—Antonina, Garmat and Ousanas—the people who packed the large chamber were all Arabs. The Arabs were gathered in clusters. Each cluster consisted of several middle-aged or elderly men, a middle-aged woman serving as a chaperone, and—

"Christ in Heaven," muttered Eon, "there's a *horde* of them. Did every single Arab in Mecca bring his daughter?"

Garmat, standing at Eon's left hand, whispered, "Don't exaggerate, King. That's not a horde of young women. Merely a large mob. As to your question—what did you expect? There are many tribes in the Hijaz, and each is comprised of several clans. They couldn't agree on a single choice, so every one of those clans sent its favorite daughter."

Eon's jaw tightened. "This is no time for humor, old man. How am I supposed to choose one? Without offending the others?"

Garmat hesitated. From Eon's other side, Ousanas whispered: "Have Antonina make the choice. She is from Rome. The Empire is very respected, but also very distant. The Arabs will accept her decision as being impartial."

Standing next to Ousanas, Antonina's eyes widened with startlement. Before she had time to register any protest, however, Garmat weighed in with his concurrence.

"That's an excellent idea. And because she's a woman, she can spend time alone with the girls before making her choice. That gives better odds of making a good selection than for you to just guess, looking at a sea of veils."

Eon looked up at Antonina. Whatever protest she might have made died under the silent appeal in those young brown eyes. An appeal, she realized, which was as much personal as political. So soon after the loss of his two beloved concubines, Eon was in no mental state to select a wife.

She nodded. "If you wish, King of Kings. But I would like to have several days to make the decision. As Garmat said, I can spend the time getting acquainted with the girls."

"Take as much time as you need," said Eon. The King rose from his throne. The faint murmurs in the room died away.

"As all of you know," he said, speaking in a voice loud enough to be heard throughout the chamber, "Axum has formed an alliance with the Roman Empire against the Malwa." Eon nodded imperiously toward Antonina. "This woman, Antonina, is the wife of the great general Belisarius. She is also an accomplished leader in her own right and is the head of the Roman Empire's delegation."

The room was silent. The absence of any whispers indicated the fact that everyone in the room was already quite familiar with Antonina's position. Eon had suspected as much, but wanted to give emphasis to her importance.

"I wish to have her select my wife from among your daughters," he announced. "There can be no suspicion of any favoritism, if the choice is made by Rome's envoy. She will spend a few days in the harem, in order to meet the girls, before making her decision."

Now, the room *was* filled with whispers. Antonina, listening carefully to the emotional undertone of the hubbub, decided that Eon's announcement was meeting with general favor.

Since the negusa nagast was clearly prepared to let the crowd's quiet little discussion continue for a bit, Antonina took the opportunity to inspect her surroundings. She had been rushed into the audience chamber the moment she arrived in Sana.

The viceroy's palace, judging from the evidence, suffered more damage from Eon's recapture of Sana than the city itself. The heavy stone architecture was still intact—Eon had used no gunpowder in his assault, simply the spears of the sarawit—but most of the walls were scorched. The palace walls had been adorned with tapestries, which were now nothing but ashes. Fortunately, the flames had been extinguished before they could do more than slightly char the heavy beams supporting the roof.

The rebel Abreha had made his last stand here. It hadn't been much of a stand, from the reports Antonina received. Once his Arab auxiliaries had been drawn away from Sana by Antonina's bait, Abreha's two rebel regiments had been forced to face the loyal Ethiopian sarawit unaided. Even sheltered behind Sana's walls, they had had no great stomach for the task.

When word came, from fleeing bedouin, that the Romans had shattered the Arab army at the oasis, most of Abreha's troops had mutinied. Only two hundred men from his own Metin regiment had remained loyal to him. The rest, and the entire Falha sarwe, had negotiated surrender terms with Eon.

The negusa nagast, filled with youthful fury, had not been inclined to grant anything beyond their lives. But Garmat's advice prevailed. The Falha sarwe had been reaccepted as a unit, with no repercussions. Even the men from Abreha's regiment who surrendered had gone unpunished, except that new officers had been appointed. The old ones were cashiered in disgrace.

Abreha and his remaining two hundred rebels had forted up in the viceroy's palace. The fighting had been ferocious, for about an hour, as spears flashed in rooms and corridors. But Abreha's two hundred had been overwhelmed by the loyal sarwen pouring through the palace's many entrances.

There had been no quarter given. Not even Garmat had recommended mercy, after the body of his friend, Sumyafa Ashwa, had been found. The former viceroy had been tortured by the Malwa agents who had advised Abreha in his rebellion. Whatever information the Malwa had extracted from the man had not come easily. Sumyafa had died under the knife.

The Malwa agents had been captured, along with Abreha himself, in the very audience chamber where Antonina was now standing. They had not been tortured, exactly. Ethiopians were not given to lingering forms of death-dealing. Still, the traditional Axumite way of punishing treason was savage enough. The traitors had been disemboweled and then strangled with their own guts. The latter was simply a gruesome flourish, since intestines are too soft to serve as a proper garrote.

Antonina wrinkled her nose. The stench had faded, but it was still powerful. Most of the stone floor, even after hours of scrubbing, was stained with brown marks. Flies were buzzing about everywhere. They seemed to cover every inch of floor where someone was not standing.

Antonina stared at the crowd of Arab tribesfolk. All of them were standing on those brown stains—men, women, and young girls alike—with not a trace of squeamishness. Oblivious to the smell, so far as Antonina could determine. Occasionally, casually, they swatted away flies buzzing around their faces, but they ignored the insects crawling on the floor.

Those people were merchants, not bedouin—Meccans, mostly, although some were from Yathrib and Jidda—but they were still Arabs. Arabia was the land of the desert, and its people, over the centuries, had been formed by its harsh regimen. Those folk were much given to poetry, and could spend hours in town squares and bedouin camps engaged in cheerful banter and argument. And they could often be the most generous and hospitable people in the world. But they were not squeamish, not in the least. Ethiopia had repaid rebellion in the traditional coin. The Arab merchants standing before the King of Kings were simply congratulating themselves for having had the good sense to avoid the business.

Eon, apparently, decided that the Arabs had had enough time to think.

"If anyone has an objection, speak now," he commanded. The room fell silent. Eon waited, for at least a minute. There was no voice of protest. Antonina, watching for the little body twitches which might indicate uneasiness, could see none.

"Good idea, Ousanas," she murmured.

"I am a genius," agreed the former dawazz. "It is well known, in educated circles." Garmat snorted. "Not, of course, among decrepit former bandits."

He began to add something else, but fell silent. Eon was speaking again.

"Send your girls to the harem. Servants will show you the way. Antonina will join them shortly."

A moment later, the crowd was filing out of the room. The eyes of several dozen veiled young women were now peeking at Antonina. All of those eyes were curious. Some were shy; some bold. Some seemed friendly; some uncertain; a few, perhaps even hostile.

Those last eyes, she suspected, belonged to particularly comely girls. Vain creatures, who were filled with dark suspicion that an unveiled Roman woman, herself a beauty, would not be swayed by their good looks.

You've got that right, my fine fillies, she thought sardonically. *Forget all that nonsense. I'm looking for a young man's wife. That's a different business altogether.*

Antonina's task was simplified, from the very beginning, by her unspoken decision to seek a wife only among the clans of the Quraysh. All the tribes in the Hijaz had sent girls, but that was mainly a matter of pride. The Quraysh, sensibly, had neither objected nor made any demand for precedence. Still, the fact remained that the Quraysh dominated western Arabia. To pick a wife from any other tribe would offend them deeply. And, on the other hand, none of the other tribes would take it amiss if Antonina chose a Quraysh girl. They were expecting her to, in truth. They simply wanted their own precious daughters to be given formal consideration.

Which Antonina did. She was careful to spend as much time with girls from the other tribes as she did with those from the various clans of the Quraysh. That was not simply a matter of show, either. Concubinage was respected practice among Arabs. She intended to select several concubines for the negusa nagast, from among the non-Quraysh girls. She had not discussed the matter with Eon prior to entering the harem. Antonina knew the young King was not even looking forward to a wife, much less a gaggle of concubines. But he would yield to political necessity, when the time came.

◊   ◊   ◊

Her name was Rukaiya, and she was from the Beni Hashim clan of the Quraysh.

Antonina dismissed her, at first. The girl was much too pretty—downright stunning, in fact—and, what was worse, very slender. Eon was the sole survivor of the Axumite dynasty, and Antonina wanted to take no chances with the royal line. Her friend, the empress Theodora, was also a slender woman. Theodora had almost died in childbirth, because of her narrow hips. The baby *had* died, and Theodora had never had another.

Antonina wanted a girl with big hips. Intelligent, also, and with a good temperament. But she wanted a girl who could produce royal heirs without a hitch. Lots of them.

But, as the hours went by on the first day, in conversations with the various prospects, she found her eyes being drawn toward Rukaiya. That was not because the Beni Hashim girl was *trying* to draw her attention. Rather the contrary. If anything, Rukaiya seemed almost to be avoiding her.

There was no way to do so, of course. Not in the harem which, other than its sleeping chambers, consisted of a single large room. The roof was open, and the center of the room was occupied by a shallow pool. The girls—almost fifty of them—were seated on benches. The majority were packing the benches which fronted the pool, where they would be most visible. But there were perhaps two dozen seated on benches ranged against the far walls.

At first, Antonina had thought those were the shy ones. But, as she became introduced to all of them, she realized that most of the girls on the rear benches were from the non-Quraysh tribes. They knew perfectly well that they would not be chosen, and they had seen no reason to gasp for breath in the crush at the pool.

All except Rukaiya—who, though Quraysh, had clearly not chosen that self-effacing position because of any shyness. Antonina's attention was drawn to her, in fact, because she began noticing how often other girls, as the day went on, would scurry over and exchange words with Rukaiya.

Antonina could not hear those exchanges, but it didn't take her long to understand what was happening.

In the first few hours, anxious girls went to Rukaiya to settle their nerves. A few words spoken by a calm and friendly face seemed to do the trick. The girls would resume their seats at the pool, a bit more relaxed.

As the day wore on, Antonina noticed several other girls surreptitiously scurrying over to Rukaiya's bench. These, she thought, were downcast because they were not very pretty, and were looking for reassurance. The most beautiful girl in the room seem to give it to them. With words, for the most part. But Antonina also noticed the little hugs, and the hair-stroking, and the time Rukaiya held a softly weeping fifteen-year-old girl in her arms for several minutes. The girl, with her lumpy face and figure, obviously felt she was too unattractive to be a king's wife.

Which, in truth, she was. Antonina was not looking for beauty, first and foremost. But whoever she selected would have to be pretty enough to arouse the king's interest. Axum needed a stable dynasty. That meant heirs, which a homely queen might not provide.

But, although Antonina was impressed by Rukaiya, she continued to rule her out. For a while, as she listened to one or another girl chatter at her, Antonina mulled over the possibility of selecting Rukaiya for one of Eon's concubines. But she decided against that, as well. The daughter of the Beni Hashim was just *too* beautiful. Too attractive in all respects, for that matter. After hours in the harem, observing with her keen eyes and mind, Antonina couldn't fail to notice Rukaiya's ease of manner and excellent temperament.

All of which, of course, argued against her.

She's too skinny for a queen and too dazzling for anything else. Antonina didn't want to risk a situation where the King of Kings produced no legitimate heirs because he was besotted with a concubine.

She went to bed, the first night, with that conclusion firmly drawn. By the end of the second day, the firm conclusion was getting ragged around the edges.

The second day was a day for culling. In the course of it, Antonina—as gently as possible—made clear to most of the girls she talked to that they were no longer under consideration. Many of them took the news cheerfully enough, especially those who were not of the Quraysh. But there were others, of course, who were upset.

At least half of those, Antonina couldn't help but notice, immediately made a beeline for Rukaiya's bench. By mid-afternoon, the daughter of the Beni Hashim was surrounded by a cluster of other girls. It was, by far, the most cheerful group of girls in the harem.

Whatever tears had tracked down those young cheeks were dried, and the girls were laughing at one of Rukaiya's soft-spoken jests. The girl seemed to have quite a wit, on top of everything else.

Antonina had still not exchanged a word with her. She had ruled Rukaiya out from the very start, and Rukaiya herself had made no attempt to get Antonina's attention. But the Roman woman knew full well what was happening at that bench.

There are people in this world who have the knack for it. People who draw others around them, like a lodestone draws iron filings. The kind of people whom others, when they stumble and fall, automatically look to for help and guidance.

The kind of people, in short, that you like to see sitting on a throne—and rarely do.

Antonina shook her head. *Too skinny.*

By the morning of the third day, Antonina had narrowed her selection to three girls. She decided to spend the entire day in private conversations with those final prospects.

Rukaiya was not among them. Yet, when the time came for Antonina to make her announcement to the assembled girls in the harem, her tongue seemed to have a will of its own. After she finished naming the three finalists, the rebellious organ kept talking.

"And Rukaiya," her tongue blurted out.

Across the room, Rukaiya's head jerked up. The girl was staring at Antonina, wide-eyed. That was due to surprise, and—something else. Rukaiya, strangely, seemed distressed by the announcement.

That's odd, thought Antonina. Then, firmly, to her tongue: *And she's still too skinny.*

Antonina interviewed Rukaiya last of all. It was already late in the afternoon by the time the Beni Hashim girl entered the small sleeping chamber in the harem which Antonina was using for her private meetings.

As Rukaiya took a seat on a bench across from her, Antonina admired the grace in the girl's movements. There was something almost sinuous in the way Rukaiya walked, and slid herself onto a couch. Even the way the girl sat, with her hands modestly folded in her lap, had a feline poise to it. And her clear brown eyes, watching Antonina, had little in them of a sixteen-year-old girl's uncertainty and awkwardness.

Antonina returned Rukaiya's stare in silence, for a good minute or so. She was studying the girl carefully, but could read nothing in her expression. That beautiful young face might as well have been a mask. Antonina could detect none of the quick-witted liveliness which she had noticed for two days, nor the startled apprehension which had shone in Rukaiya's eyes the moment she heard herself named as one of the four finalists.

Let's clear that mystery up first, she decided.

"You seemed startled, when I named you," Antonina stated. "Why is that?"

The girl's answer came with no apparent hesitation. "I was surprised. You had seemed to pay no attention to me, the first two days. And I was not expecting to be selected. I am too skinny. Two men—their parents, actually—have already rejected me as a wife. They are worried I will not be able to bear children."

The statement was matter-of-fact, relaxed—almost philosophical. That was its own surprise. Most Arab girls, rejected by a suitor's parents, would have been heartsick.

The problem was not romantic. Marriage among upper-class Arabs was arranged by their families. Often enough, the man and woman involved did not even know each other prior to their wedding. But marriage was the destiny and the highest position to which an Arab girl could aspire. To be rejected almost invariably produced feelings of unworthiness and shame.

Yet Rukaiya seemed to feel none of that. Why?

Antonina was alarmed. One obvious explanation for Rukaiya's attitude was that the girl was so egotistical—so enamored of her own beauty and grace—that she was simply incapable of accepting rejection. She might be the kind of person who, faced with disappointment, always places the blame on others.

In the long history of the Roman Empire, Antonina reminded herself, there had been more than one empress with that mentality. Most of them had been disastrous, especially the ones whose noble birth reinforced their egotism. Antonina's friend Theodora, in truth, had the same innate temperament. But Theodora's hard life had taught the woman to discipline her own pride. A girl like Rukaiya, born into Arabia's elite, would have nothing to teach her to restrain arrogance.

"You do not seem upset by the fact," Antonina said. The statement had almost the air of an accusation.

For the first time since she entered the chamber, life came back to Rukaiya's face. The girl chuckled. Her face exuded a cheerful acceptance of the world's whimsies. The expression, combined with the little laugh, was utterly charming.

"My family is used to it. All the women, for generations, have been skinny. My mother's thinner than I am, and she was rejected four times before my father's family decided to take a chance on her."

Rukaiya gave Antonina a level gaze. "I am her oldest daughter. She has had three more, and two sons. One of my sisters, and one of my brothers, died very young. But not at childbirth. My grandmother had nine children. None died in childbirth, and six survived into adulthood. *Her* mother—my great-grandmother—had twelve children. She died before I was born, but everyone says she had the hips of a snake."

Rukaiya shrugged. "It just doesn't seem to matter, to us. My mother tells me that it will be very painful, the first time, but not so bad after that. And she is not worried that I will die."

Well, so much for that problem, thought Antonina wryly. *But I'm still puzzled—*

"You did not simply seem surprised, when you heard me call out your name. You also seemed upset." Again, Antonina's statement had the air of an accusation.

The mask was back in place. Rukaiya opened her lips, as if to speak. It was obvious, to Antonina, that the girl was about to utter some sort of denial. But, after a moment, Rukaiya lowered her head and murmured: "I was not upset, exactly. It would be a great honor, to become the wife of the negusa nagast. My family would be very proud. But—"

She paused, then raised her head. "I have enjoyed my life. I am very happy, in my father's house. My father is a cheerful man. Very kind, and very intelligent."

Rukaiya hesitated, groping for words. "I have always known, of course, that someday I would be married and have to leave for another man's house. And there is a part of me that looks forward to that day. But not—" She sighed unhappily. "Not so soon."

Her next words came out in a rush. The girl's face was full of life, now, and her hands gestured with animation.

"I don't know what I would *do*, in another man's house. I am so afraid of being *bored*. Especially if my husband was a severe man. Most husbands are very strict with their wives. Since I was ten years old, my father has let me help him with his work. He is one of Mecca's richest merchants, and he has many caravans. I keep track of most of his accounts, and I write almost all his letters, and—"

Antonina's jaw dropped. She didn't think there were more than two dozen women in all of Arabia—and they were invariably middle-aged widows—

"You can *read*?" she demanded.

Rukaiya's own jaw clamped shut. For an instant, her young face reminded Antonina of a mule. A beautiful mule, true, but just as stubborn and willful.

The expression was fleeting, however. Rukaiya lowered her head. Her quick-moving hands, once again, were demurely clasped in her lap.

"My father taught me," she said softly. "He insists that all women in his family must know how to read. He says that's because they might be widows, someday, and have to manage their husbands' affairs."

Again, the words started coming in a rush. "But I think he just says that to placate my mother. She doesn't like to read. Neither do my sisters. They say it's too hard. But I love to read, and so does my father. We have had so many wonderful evenings, talking about the things we have read in books. My father owns many books. He collects them. My mother complains because it's so expensive, but that's the one subject on which my father lays down the law in our house. Most of our books are Greek, of course, but we even have—"

She stopped talking, then, interrupted by Antonina's laughter. The laughter went on for quite a while. By the time Antonina finally stopped, wiping tears from her eyes, Rukaiya's expression of shock had faded into simple curiosity.

"What's so funny?" she asked.

Antonina shook her head. "The negusa nagast of Ethiopia is one of the world's champion bibliophiles. His father, King Kaleb, amassed the largest library south of Alexandria in his palace at Axum. In all honesty, I don't think Kaleb himself actually read any of those books. But by the time Prince Eon was fifteen, he had read all of them. I remember, when he came to Rome, how many hours he spent with my friend Irene Macrembolitissa—she *is* the world's greatest bibliophile—"

Antonina fell silent, staring at the girl across from her. Again, tears welled up in her eyes, as she remembered a friend she thought she would never see again.

Oh God, child, how much you remind me of Irene.

Memory made the decision. Memory of another woman—intelligent, quick-witted, active—whose own life had been frustrated, so many times, by the world's expectations.

Fuck it. We have souls, too.

"You will be happy, Rukaiya," predicted Antonina. "And you will never, I promise you, be bored." Again, she wiped away tears; and, again, laughed.

"Not as that man's wife! Oh, no. You'll be keeping track of the King of King's accounts, Rukaiya, and writing *his* letters. He's building an empire and he's at war with the greatest power in the world. Soon enough, I think, you'll find yourself longing for a bit of tedium."

Finally, finally, the face across from her was nothing but that of a young girl. A virgin, barely sixteen years of age. Shy, anxious, uncertain, apprehensive, eager, curious—and, of course, more than a little avid.

"Is he—? Will he—?" Rukaiya fumbled, and fumbled.

"Yes, he will like you. Yes, he will be kind. And, yes, he will give you great pleasure."

Antonina rose and walked over. She took Rukaiya's face in her hands and fixed the girl's eyes with her own.

"Trust me, child. I know King Eon very well. Put aside all doubts and fears. You will enjoy being a woman."

Rukaiya was beaming happily, now. Just like a bride.

Chapter 21

Garmat did *not* beam happily, when he first saw Rukaiya.

"She's too skinny," he complained. Standing in his place of honor on the lower steps of the palace entrance, he turned his head and hissed in her ear: "What were you *thinking*, Antonina?"

Antonina's humor was a bit frayed, because of the heat. Standing under the bare sun of southern Arabia, wearing the heavy robes of imperial formality, was not enjoyable. So, for an instant, the decorum of a Roman official was replaced by the response of a girl raised on the rough streets of Alexandria.

"Piss on you, old fart," she hissed back. Then, remembering her duty, Antonina relented.

"I checked the family history, Garmat. All the women are slender, but none of them have had problems with it. Rukaiya's mother—"

There followed a little history lesson. Not so little, rather. Antonina had expected the issue to arise, so she had supplemented Rukaiya's own account with a more thorough investigation. Happily, the girl had not been sugar-coating the truth. For as many generations as clan memory went—which, typical of Arab tribesmen, was a *long* way back—only two women in that line had died in childbirth. That was better than average, for the day.

Her history lesson concluded, with all the solemnity of a Roman official, the Alexandria street urchin returned.

"So piss on you from a dizzy height, old fart."

"Well said," came Ousanas' whisper. The former dawazz—he still had no official title—was standing right behind them, on a higher step.

Antonina cocked her head a quarter turn. "You're not worried?" she whispered over her shoulder. Sourly: "I expected every man within fifty miles to be crabbing at me about it."

Ousanas' gleaming grin made a brief appearance. "Such nonsense. It comes from too much exposure to civilization and its decadent ways. My own folk, proper barbarians, never fret over the matter. Women drop babies in the fields, just like elands and lions."

Garmat, still tight-faced, began to mutter again. He was giving his own lecture, now, on natural history. Explaining, to a bird-brained Roman woman and an ignorant Bantu savage, the difference between passing a large human skull through a narrow pelvic passage and the effortless ease with which mindless animals—

He fell silent, stiffening with formal rigidity. The King of Kings was finally entering the square before the palace, where his bride and her party were waiting.

It was quite an entrance. Antonina, even after her years of exposure to Roman imperial pomp, was impressed. Axumites, as a rule, were not given to formality. But, when occasion demanded, they threw themselves into it with the wild abandonment of a people shaped by Africa's splendor.

Eon was preceded by dancers, leaping and capering to the rhythm of great drums. The dancers were garbed in leopard skins and cloaks of ostrich feathers. The drummers were clothed less flamboyantly. They wore shammas, the multilayered togas which were the usual costume worn by Ethiopians in the highlands. But these shammas were for ceremonial occasions. The linen was richly dyed, and adorned with ivory and tortoiseshell studs.

Behind the dancers and drummers came Eon's ceremonial guard. This body consisted of the officers of his regiment, and was much larger than normal. Eon had been adopted by three regiments, not the customary one, and all of them were present. Wahsi, Aphilas and Saizana, as commanders of the Dakuen, Lazen and the Hadefan sarawit, led the procession.

Here, Axum's more typical practicality made its reappearance. True, the soldiers were wearing ostrich-plume headdresses which were far larger and more elaborate than anything they would have worn in battle. But the weapons and light armor were the same practical and utilitarian implements with which the Ethiopian army went to the field of slaughter.

The soldiers were there, not so much to protect their king from assassins, as to remind the huge crowd packing the square of a simple truth. *Axum rules by the spear, when all is said and done. Do not forget it.*

Studying the crowd, however, Antonina could detect no signs of resentment in the sea of mostly Arab faces. The people of the desert, for all their love of poetry, were not given to flights of fancy when it came to politics. That rulers will *rule*, was a given. That being so, best to have a strong rule, and a firm one. That makes possible—possible—a fair rule as well.

Antonina decided she was reading the crowd properly. All the faces she could see were filled with no expressions beyond satisfaction and the pleasure of people enjoying a great spectacle. The measures which Eon had taken, the concessions which he had given the Hijaz even more than his leniency toward the bedouin rebels, had gone a long way to mollify southern Arabia to Ethiopian rule. The marriage about to take place, she thought, would finish the job. Arabs were as famous for their trading ability as they were for their poetry and their incessant political bickering. They knew a good bargain when they saw one.

Eon entered the square, now, and splendiferous royal pomp soared to the heavens.

"Good God," whispered Antonina, "is that thing *solid gold*?"

Garmat smiled. His usual good humor was back. "Of course not, Antonina," he whispered in return. "A chariot made of solid gold would collapse of its own weight. The wheels and axle, anyway."

Garmat bestowed a look of admiration on the vehicle lumbering into the square. "But there's plenty of gold on it, believe me. Enough gold plate to make it seem solid, even on the undercarriage." He made a little pointing gesture with his beard. "Those elephants aren't there just for show. The beasts have their work cut out for them, hauling the thing."

"Not to mention their own costumes," murmured Antonina. The four elephants drawing the chariot were cloaked in a pachyderm version of ceremonial shammas, not battle armor, but Antonina didn't even want to guess at the weight of ivory and tortoiseshell decorations.

Eon was riding alone in the open-backed, two-wheeled chariot. The chariot itself was patterned after the ancient war chariots of Egypt, which were designed for two men—one to control the horses, while the other served as an archer. But Eon did not require assistance. He had no reins to hold. The elephants were controlled by four mahouts. Those men, Antonina was relieved to see, were wearing nothing beyond their usual practical gear. The four elephants drawing Eon's chariot were *war* elephants, with the temperament to match. God help the crowd if the mahouts lost control of them.

Eon's own costume, to Antonina's eye, was a bit odd at first, until she realized she was seeing the usual Axumite combination of splendor and practicality. On the one hand, his tunic was made of simple, undyed linen. A Roman emperor—any Roman noble-man, for that matter, above the level of an equestrian—would have worn silk. But the utilitarian cloth was positively festooned with pearls and beads of red coral, and the threads which held the garment together were inlaid with gold.

His tiara, unlike the grandiose crowns of Roman or Persian emperors, was nothing more than a silver band studded with carne-lian. The simplicity of the design, Antonina suspected, was to emphasize the importance of the four-streamered headdress which the tiara held in place. That was called a phakhiolin, by Ethiopians, and it was the traditional symbol of Axum's King of Kings.

She thought there was a subtle message in that headgear. Eon had already announced, the day before, that the capital of Axum was being moved to Adulis. The Arab notables gathered in the palace had reacted to the announcement with undisguised satisfac-tion. The decision to move the capital, those shrewd men knew, was the surest sign that their new ruler intended to weld them into his empire. The center of Axum, from now on, would be the Red Sea rather than the highlands—a center which was shared by Arabia along with Africa.

Today, gently, Eon was reminding them of something else. He still had the highlands, after all, and the breed of disciplined spear-men forged in those mountains. Their symbol, still, rode on the top of the negusa nagast's head.

His staff of office carried the same message. The shaft of the great spear was sheathed in gold, as was the Christian cross sur-mounting it. Sheathed in gold, and decorated with pearls. But the blade itself—the great, savage, leaf of destruction—was plain steel, and razor sharp.

The slow-moving chariot finally reached the center of the square. The mahouts brought the elephants to a halt, and Eon dismounted. In a few quick strides, he took his place next to his bride, and the wedding ceremony began.

The first part of the ceremony, and by far the longest, consisted of Rukaiya's conversion to Christianity. That went on for two hours. Long before it was over, Antonina, sweltering in her robes, was cursing every priest who ever lived.

In fairness, she admitted, the fault lay not principally with the priests. True, they were their usual long-winded selves, the more so when they basked in the warmth of such a gigantic crowd's attention. But most of the problem came from the sheer number of conversions.

Rukaiya was not converting alone. Everyone had known, of course, that the new Queen of Ethiopia would have to become a Christian (if she was not one already, as many Arabs were). Her own father, the day after Rukaiya's selection was publicly declared, had made his own announcement. He—and all his family—would convert also.

That had been a week ago. By the day of the wedding, well over half of the Beni Hashim had made the same decision, and a goodly portion of the other clans of the Quraysh as well. There were hundreds of people in the square—well over a thousand, by Antonina's guess—who were undergoing the rite alongside their new queen.

For all her sweltering discomfort, Antonina did not begrudge them that ceremony. True, she suspected that most of the converts were driven by less-than-spiritual motives. Canny merchants, seeing an angle. But not all of them. And not even, she thought, any of them—not completely, at least.

Arabia was a land where religion seethed, under the surface. Most Arabs of the time were still pagans, despite the great success which Jewish and Christian missionaries had found there. But even Arabia's pagans, she knew, had a sense that there was a supreme god ruling the many deities of their pantheons. They called that god Allah.

As the conversion ceremony wound its way onward, Antonina's mind began to drift. She recalled a conversation she had had with Belisarius, before he left for Persia.

Her husband had told her of a religion which would rise out of Arabia, in what had been the future of humanity. Islam, it would be called, submission to the one god named Allah. The religion would be brought by a new prophet not more than a century in the future. A man named Muhammad—

For a moment, she started erect, snapped out of her reverie by a specific memory of that conversation. Her eyes darted to Rukaiya, standing in the center of the square.

Muhammad will also be from the Beni Hashim clan of the Quraysh. And, if I remember right, will have a daughter named Rukaiya.

She realized that her choice of Rukaiya, in ways she had not even considered, had probably already changed history. The Beni Hashim of Muhammad's future had not been Christians, except for a few. After today, they would be. How would that fact affect the future?

She slipped back into memory.

"Will it still happen, now?" she had asked Belisarius. "After all that's changed?"

Her husband shrugged. "Who's to know? The biggest reason Islam swept the Levant, and Egypt, was because the Monophysites converted almost at once. Voluntarily, most of them. Muhammad's stark monotheism, I think, appealed to their own brand of Christianity. Monophysitism is about as close as you can get to Islam, within the boundaries of the Trinity."

Belisarius scowled. "And after centuries of persecution by orthodox Christians, I think the Monophysites had had enough. They saw the Arabs as liberators, not conquerors."

Antonina spoke. "Anthony's trying—"

"I know he is," agreed Belisarius. "And I hope the new Patriarch of Constantinople will be able to rein in that persecution." Again, he shrugged. "But who's to know?"

Standing in the square, sweating in her robes, Antonina could still remember the strange look which had come to her husband's face.

"It's odd, really," he'd said, "how I feel about it. We have already, just in what we've done these past few years, changed history irrevocably." He patted his chest, where Aide lay in his little pouch. "The visions Aide shows me are just that, now. I can still learn an enormous amount from them, of course, but they're really no more than illusions. They'll never happen—not the way he shows me, anyway."

His face, for a moment, had been suffused with a great sadness. "I don't think there will ever be a Muhammad. Not the same way, at least. He might still arise, of course, and be a prophet. But if Anthony succeeds, I think Muhammad will more likely be a force regenerating Christianity than the founder of a new religion. That was how he saw himself, actually, in the beginning—until orthodox Christians and the Jews rejected him, and he found an audience among pagans and Monophysites."

Antonina had been puzzled. "Why does that make you sad? I would think you'd prefer it. You're a Christian, yourself."

Belisarius' smile, when it came, had been very crooked. "Am I?"

She remembered herself gasping. And, just as clearly, could remember the warm smile in her husband's face.

"Be at ease, love. Christianity suits me fine. I've no intention of abandoning it. It's just—"

The look of strangeness, of strange *wonder*, was back on his face. "I've seen so much, Antonina," he whispered. "Aide has taken me millions of years into the future, to stars beyond the galaxy. How could the simple certainties of the Thracian countryside withstand such visions?"

She had been mute. Belisarius reached out and caressed her face.

"I am certain of only one thing," he said. "I can't follow half of Anthony's theology, but I know he's right. God made the Trinity so unfathomable because He does not want men to understand Him. It's enough that we look for Him."

His hand, leaving her cheek, swept the universe. "Which we will, love. Which we will. We are fighting this war, at bottom, so that people can make that search. Wherever the road leads them."

His gentle smile returned. "That's good enough. For a simple Thracian boy, raised to be a soldier, that's more than good enough."

◇   ◇   ◇

Finally, it was ending. Antonina almost sagged from relief. She felt like a melting blob of butter.

She watched as Eon turned to Rukaiya and removed the veil. Then, she fought down a grin. The King of Ethiopia, for the first time, saw his new wife's face. He seemed like an ox, struck between the eyes by a mallet.

A little gasp—not so little, actually—went up from the crowd. Some of that was caused by shock, at seeing a young woman unveiled in public. The Arabs had known it was coming, of course. Eon had made very clear that he was only willing to concede so much to Arab traditions. Ethiopian women did not wear veils, not even young virgins, and the King of Kings had stated in no uncertain terms that his new wife would follow Axumite custom in that regard. Still, the matrons in the square were shocked. Shocked, shocked! They could hardly wait to scurry home and start talking about the scandal of it all.

But most of the gasps came from Rukaiya's sheer beauty. The crowd had been expecting a pretty girl, true. But not—not *this*.

Within seconds, the gasps gave way to murmurs. Looks of shock and surprise were replaced by—

I will be damned, thought Antonina. *I didn't even think of that*.

"You are a genius yourself, Antonina," whispered Ousanas. "That is what a queen *should* look like. And will you look at the greedy bastards? Every one of those coin-counting merchants just realized there's no way the King of Kings is going to ignore his new Quraysh bride."

Garmat's opinion was otherwise. "She's too gorgeous," he complained. "We'll never be able to pry Eon out of bed." With a hiss: "What were you *thinking*, Antonina?"

Antonina ignored the old fart. She simply basked, a bit, in the admiring glances sent her way by the crowd. And she positively wallowed in the penumbra of another's admiration. Even at the distance, she could not misread Eon's face. That young face had been shadowed, ever since he found the mangled bodies of his concubines in the stones of the Ta'akha Maryam. Now, at last, she could see the shadow start to lift.

Like her husband before her, Antonina had come to love Eon as if he were her own son. She realized, now that it was over, that she been guided throughout by a mother's instinct—not the calculations of a diplomat. She trusted that instinct, far more than she trusted the machinations of politics.

Garmat still didn't understand, but Ousanas did. The tall hunter leaned over and whispered: "A genius, I say it again."

Antonina shrugged modestly. "It's a good match. The girl's father, I think, will make an excellent adviser in his own right. And Rukaiya herself is very intelligent. She'll—"

"Not that nonsense," snorted Ousanas.

He sneered at Garmat. Ousanas' sneer was as magnificent as his grin. "Politics is a silly business. Games for boys too old to grow up." The famous grin made its appearance. "Wise folk, like you and me, understand the truth. As long as the boy is happy, he will do well. Everything else is meaningless."

That evening, at the great feast in the palace, Eon sidled up to her. He began to fumble with words of thanks and appreciation.

Antonina smiled. "She's very beautiful, isn't she?"

Eon nodded happily. "She's smart, too. Did you know she can actually *read*? And she's funny. Even before I lifted the veil I thought I would be enamored. She told a little joke, while the priests were droning on and on. I almost died, trying not to laugh."

He was silent, for a few seconds, admiring his wife. Rukaiya was the center of attention for the crowd—and had been, since the feast started. At the moment, she was surrounded by many of the young girls who had spent the days in the harem with her. Antonina, watching the ease with which Rukaiya handled that little mob of admirers—who had, not so long ago, been her rivals— congratulated herself once again.

She'll make a great queen.

The final reward came. Eon took her hand and gave it a little squeeze.

"Thank you," he whispered. "You have been like a mother for me."

Toward the end of the feast, Rukaiya sought her out. The young queen drew Antonina aside, into a corner of the great chamber. She clutched Antonina's hands in her own.

"I'm so nervous," she whispered. "Eon and I will be leaving, very soon. For his private chamber. I am so nervous. So scared."

Antonina smiled reassuringly, almost placidly. The expression was hard to maintain. She was waging a ferocious battle—not against giggles, but uproarious laughter.

What a lot of crap! Do you think you can fool me, girl? You're not scared. You just can't wait to get laid, that's all.

But a mother's instinct came to the rescue, again.

"Relax, Rukaiya. Forget what you might have heard. Most men, believe it or not, don't mount their wives like a bull mounting a heifer. They actually talk, first."

Some of them, anyway. Eon will.

Rukaiya's eyes were boring into her own, like a disciple staring at a prophet.

Hell with it. Antonina did laugh.

"Relax, I say!" She pried loose one of her hands and stroked the girl's cheek. Humor faded away, under the intensity of Rukaiya's gaze. Half-dreading; half-hopeful; half-eager; half-curious; half— . . .

That's way too many halves. This girl's got too many emotions going on at once.

"Trust me, Rukaiya," she said softly. "When the time comes, Eon will be very gentle. But it may not come as soon as you think. Maybe not at all, tonight."

Rukaiya's mouth gaped wide.

Antonina's hand went from the girl's cheek to her lustrous, long black hair. Still stroking, she said: "Remember, girl, he recently lost concubines that he loved very much. It will be hard for him, too, when you are alone. He will be reminded of them, and be saddened. And he will be nervous himself. He's not a virgin, of course—"

She fought down a giggle. *To put it mildly!*

"—but he's still a young man. Not much older than you. In the beginning, I think, he will just want to talk."

Slowly, Rukaiya's mouth closed. The girl thought on Antonina's words for a time, as the Roman woman kept stroking her hair. The words, and the caresses, began to calm her.

"I know how to do *that*," Rukaiya announced. "I'm good at talking."

The next morning, at the breakfast feast, Garmat began grumbling again.

"What were you *thinking*, Antonina?"

The old adviser was sitting right next to her, in a position of honor near the head of the great table. Ousanas was seated on her other side. The two positions at the very head of the table, of course, were reserved for the King of Kings and his new queen. Judging from the fanfare of the drums, they were about to make their entrance.

"What were you *thinking*?" he repeated. "I just discovered the girl can read, on top of everything else. Wonderful. Two bookworms. They probably spent the whole night talking philosophy." He shook his head sadly. "The dynasty is doomed. There will be no heirs."

Eon and Rukaiya swept into the dining hall and took their seats. Ousanas took one glance at their faces and pronounced the obvious.

"You are a doddering old fool, Garmat. And Antonina is still a genius."

Yes, I am, she thought happily. *A true and certain genius.*

Chapter 22

PERSIA
Summer, 532 A.D.

"It looks like he's coming alone," said Damodara, squinting at the tiny figure in the distance. The Malwa lord cocked his head toward the tall Rajput standing next to him. "Am I right? Your eyes are better than mine."

Sanga nodded. "Yes. He's quite alone." The Rajput king watched the horseman guiding his mount toward them. The parley had been set on the most open patch of ground which Sanga's trackers had been able to find in this stretch of the Zagros. But the bleak, arid terrain was still strewn with rocks and small gullies.

"That is his way, Lord Damodara." Sanga's dark eyes were filled with warm admiration. "His way of telling us that he trusts our honor."

Damodara gave Sanga a quick, shrewd glance. For a moment, he felt a twinge of envy. Damodara was Malwa. Practical. He did not share Sanga's code of honor; nor, even, the prosaic Roman version of it possessed by Belisarius. But Damodara understood that code. He understood it very well. And he found himself, as he had often before, regretting that he felt no such certainty in the face of life's chaos.

Damodara was certain of nothing. He was a skeptic by nature—and had been, since his earliest memories as a boy. He was not even certain of the new gods which ruled his fate.

He did not doubt their existence. Like Sanga himself—the Rajput king was the only man who had ever done so beyond Malwa's dynasty—Damodara had spent time alone with Link. Damodara, like Sanga, had been transported into visions of humanity's future. He had seen the new gods, and the destiny they brought with them.

No, Damodara did not doubt those gods. He did not even doubt their perfection. He simply doubted their certainty. Damodara did not believe in fate, and destiny, and the sure footsteps of time.

Belisarius was close enough now for Damodara to make him out clearly. *That*, Damodara believed in. That, and the reality of the Rajput standing next to him in the shade of the pavilion. He believed in horsemen riding across stony ground, under the light of a mid-morning sun. He believed in the sun, and the rocks, and the cool breeze. He believed in the food resting on platters at the center of the low table in the pavilion. He believed in the wine which was in the beaker next to the food, and he believed in the beaker itself.

None of those things were perfect. Even the sun, on occasion, had spots. And they were very far from being certain, beyond the next few hours. But they were real.

Damodara was Malwa. Practical. Yet he had discovered, as so many practical men before him, that being practical was a lot harder than it looked. So, for a moment, he envied Sanga's certainties.

But only for a moment. Humor came to his rescue. Damodara had a good sense of humor. Practical men needed it.

"Well, we can't have that!" he proclaimed. "A commander should have a bodyguard."

Damodara turned his head and whispered something to Narses. The eunuch nodded, and passed the message to the young Rajput who was serving as their attendant in the pavilion. A moment later, the youth was on his horse and cantering toward the Rajput camp a short distance away.

And so it was, by the time Belisarius drew up his horse before the small pavilion in which the parley would be held, that he discovered he would have a bodyguard after all.

Valentinian helped him down. The cataphract was not wearing any armor, beyond a light Rajput helmet, but he was carrying a sword slung from a baldric. And, of course, knives and daggers. Belisarius could see three of them, thrust into a wide sash. He did not doubt there were as many more, secreted away somewhere. Most men counted wealth in coins. Valentinian counted wealth in blades.

"How are you feeling?" asked Belisarius.

Valentinian's narrow face grew even more pinched. "Not too well, sir, to be honest. I stopped seeing double, at least. But my head still hurts, more often than not, and I don't have much strength back."

Valentinian glanced at the Malwa sitting in the open pavilion. They were out of hearing range. Damodara had politely allowed Valentinian to meet Belisarius alone.

"I'll do my best," he whispered, "if there's any trouble. But I've got to warn you that I'm not my old self. Not yet, anyway."

Belisarius smiled. "There won't be any trouble. And if there is, we'll have Sanga to protect us."

Valentinian grimaced. "Pity *those* poor bastards. God, that man's a demon." Gingerly, he touched the light helmet on his head. "I don't ever want to do that again, I'll tell you for sure. Not without him tied up, and me using grenades."

Again, Valentinian glanced at the enemy in the pavilion. This time, however, it was a look of respect rather than suspicion.

"I've been well treated, general. Pampered like a lord, if you want to know the truth. Sanga himself has come to visit me, any number of times. Even Damodara." A look of bemusement came to his face. "He's actually a friendly sort of fellow, the fat little bugger. Odd, for a Malwa. Even got a sense of humor. Pretty good one."

Belisarius shrugged. "Why is that odd? The Malwa are humans, Valentinian, not gods." Belisarius gave his own quick glance at the pavilion. "Which is the reason, when the dust settles, that the new gods will find Malwa has failed them. They're trying to make perfection out of something which is not only imperfect by nature, but *must* be. Only imperfect things can grow, Valentinian. Striving for perfection is as foolish as it is vain. You can only create a statue—a thing which may look grand, on a pedestal, but will not stand up so well on the field of battle."

Belisarius brought his eyes back to Valentinian. "You swore an oath, I assume."

Valentinian nodded. For a moment, he seemed uncomfortable. Not ashamed, simply . . . awkward, like a peasant in the company of royalty. Men of Valentinian's class and station did not swear solemn oaths with the same practiced ease that nobility did.

"Yes, sir. They stopped putting a guard over me. But I had to swear that I would make no attempt to escape and that I wouldn't fight, except in self-defense. And I'll have to go back with them, of course, after this parley."

Valentinian's feral, weasel grin made its appearance. "On the *other* hand, they didn't make me swear I'd keep my mouth shut." Another glance at the pavilion. "I've learned some things, General. Real quick: you were right about Damodara's arms complex. It's in Marv, just like Vasudeva thought it might be. They'll have their own handcannons soon enough. The Malwa have already started making them, in Kausambi. But Damodara's boasting that he'll have his own, made in Marv."

Belisarius shook his head. "He wasn't boasting, Valentinian—and he didn't tell you by accident. He knows you'll pass on the information. He wants me to have it."

Valentinian frowned. "Why would he do that?"

"Because he's a very smart man. Smart enough to understand something which few generals do. Sometimes a secret given away can serve as well as a secret kept. Or even better. He's probably hoping I'll try to make a raid on Marv, once he forces me out of the Zagros, rather than retreating into Mesopotamia. The city's in an oasis, and I'm sure he's got it fortified like Satan's jaws. We'd be eaten alive, trying to storm the place, and the few table scraps would be snapped up in the desert."

Valentinian squinted at him, as if he were seeing double. His hand, again, touched his helmet gingerly.

"Christ," he muttered. "How can you stand to think all crooked like that? My head hurts, just trying to follow." He made a little hiss. "And I *still* don't understand why Damodara would do it. He can't really think you'd fall for it."

Belisarius shrugged. "Probably not. But you never know. It's worth a try." He scratched his chin. "The man's a lot like me, I believe. In some ways, at least. He likes an oblique approach, and he keeps his eye on all the angles."

Another hiss came from Valentinian. "God, my head hurts."

Belisarius took Valentinian by the arm and began leading him toward the pavilion. As they neared, walking slowly, Valentinian remembered something else.

"Oh, yeah. Maurice was right about Narses, too. He's—"

Belisarius nodded. He had already spotted the small figure of the old eunuch in the shade of the pavilion.

He smiled crookedly. "I imagine, by now, that Narses is running the whole show for Damodara."

Valentinian grinned. It was an utterly murderous expression.

"Would you believe how successful that raid was? You know—the cavalry raid against the Malwa camp that you must have ordered, even though I never knew about it and I was right by your side the whole time."

Belisarius grinned himself. "A brilliant stroke, that was. So brilliant that my own memory is blinded."

Mine too, concurred Aide. Firmly: **But I'm sure you must have ordered it. And I'm *quite* sure the raid was a roaring success.**

"Killed every one of Damodara's top spies," murmured Valentinian. They were almost at the pavilion. "Vicious Romans slit their throats, neat as you could ask for."

They were entering the pavilion, now. Valentinian moved aside and Belisarius strode to the low table at the center. Damodara and Sanga nodded a greeting. Damodara was smiling; Sanga, stiff and solemn. Narses, sitting far back from the table, was glaring. But he, too, managed a nod.

Gracefully, with the practiced ease of his time in India, Belisarius folded himself into a lotus and took a seat on one of the cushions.

He saw no reason to waste time on meaningless diplomatic phrasery.

"What is the purpose of this parley?" he asked. The statement, for all the brusqueness of the words, was not so much a demand as a simple inquiry. "I can't see where there's any military business to discuss." He waved at Valentinian. "Unless you've changed your mind about his ransom."

Damodara chuckled. Belisarius continued.

"So what's the point of talking? You're trying to get into Mesopotamia, and I'm trying to stop you. Slow you down, more precisely. You've managed to drive me almost out of the Zagros—we're not so many miles from the floodplains, now—but I kept you tied up for months in the doing. That's bought time for Emperor Khusrau, and time for my general Agathius to build up the Roman forces in Mesopotamia."

Belisarius shrugged. "I'm going to keep doing it, and you're going to keep doing it. Sooner or later—sooner, probably—I'll give up the effort and retreat to Peroz-Shapur. Maybe Ctesiphon. Maybe somewhere else. Then we'll fight it out in the open. I imagine you're looking forward to that. But you won't enjoy it, when the time comes. So much, I can promise."

Damodara shook his head, still smiling. "I did not ask for this parley in order to discuss military affairs. As you say, the matter is moot."

Still smiling; very cheerfully, in fact: "And I don't doubt for a minute that you'll make it just as tough for us on flat ground as you have in the mountains."

Sanga snorted, as a man does when he hears another man announce that the sun rises in the east.

"I asked for this parley, Belisarius, simply because I wanted to meet you. Finally, after all these months. And also—"

The Malwa lord hesitated. "And, also, because I thought we might discuss the future. The *far* future, I mean, not the immediate present."

Bull's-eye. Am I a genius, Aide?

A true and certain genius, came the immediate response. **But I still don't understand how you figured it out.**

Belisarius leaned forward, preparing to discuss the future. *Because Lord Damodara is a man. The best man of the Malwa, because he's the only one who doesn't dream of being a god. He follows the Malwa gods, true. But he is beginning to wonder, I think, how well his feet of clay will stand the march.*

"Lord Damodara—" began Belisarius. The general reached up and began unlacing his tunic. Beneath the cloth, nestled in a leather pouch, the future lay waiting. Like a tiger, hidden in ambush.

You're on, Aide.

There was no uncertainty in the response. Neither doubt, nor puzzlement.

I'll clean their clocks. Scornfully: **Polish their sundials, rather.**

Damodara—almost—took Aide in his hand when Belisarius made the offer. But, at the end, the Malwa lord shied away from the glittering splendor. Partly, his refusal was based on simple, automatic distrust. But not much. He didn't really think Belisarius was trying to poison him with some mysterious magical jewel. He believed, in his heart of hearts, that Belisarius was telling the truth about the incredible—*gem?*—nestled in his hand.

No, the real reason Damodara could not bring himself to take the thing, was that he finally realized that he did not want to know the future. He would rather make it himself. Poorly, perhaps; blindly, perhaps; but in his own hands. Pudgy, unprepossessing hands, to be sure. Nothing like the well-formed sinewy hands of a Roman general or a Rajput king. But they were *his* hands, and he was sure of them.

Sanga was not even tempted.

"I have seen the future, Belisarius," he stated solemnly. "Link has shown it to me." The Rajput pointed to Aide. "Will that show me anything different?"

Belisarius shook his head. "Not at all. The future—unless Link and the new gods change it, with Malwa as their instrument—is just as I'm sure Link showed it to you. A place of chaos and disorder. A world where men are no longer men, but monsters. A universe where nothing is pure, and everything polluted."

Belisarius lifted his hand, his fingers spread wide. Aide glistened and coruscated, like the world's most perfect jewel.

"This, too, is a thing of pollution. A monster. An intelligent being created from disease. The worst disease which ever stalked the universe. And yet—"

Belisarius gazed down at Aide. "Is he not beautiful? Just like a diamond, forged out of rotting waste."

Belisarius closed his fingers. Aide's glowing light no longer illuminated the pavilion. And a Roman general, watching the faces of his enemies, knew that he was not the only one who missed the splendor.

He turned to Damodara. "Do you have children?"

The Malwa lord nodded. "Three. Two boys and a girl."

"Were they born perfectly? Or were they born in blood, and your wife's pain and sweat, and your own fear?"

A shadow crossed the Roman's face. "I have no children of my own. My wife Antonina can bear them no longer. In her days as a courtesan, after she bore one son, she was cut by a man seeking to become her pimp."

Those coarse truths, spoken by a man about his own wife, did not seem odd to his enemies in the pavilion. They knew the story—Narses had told them what few details the Malwa espionage service had not already ferreted out. Yet they knew as well, as surely as they knew the sunrise, that the Roman was oblivious to any shame or disgrace. Not because he was ignorant of his wife's past, but simply because he didn't care. Any more than a diamond, nestled with a pearl, cares that the pearl was also shaped from waste.

The shadow passed, and sunlight returned. "Yet that boy—that bastard, sired by a prostitute's customer—has become my own son in truth. As dear to me as if he were born of my own flesh. Why is that, do you think?"

Belisarius stared down at the beauty hidden in his fist. "This too—this monster—has become like a son to me. And why is *that*, do you think?" When he raised his head, the face of the Roman general was as serene as the moon. "The reason, Lord of Malwa and King of Rajputana, was explained to me by Raghunath Rao. In a vision I had of him, once, dancing to the glory of time. *Only the soul matters, in the end.* All else is dross."

Belisarius turned to Rana Sanga. "My wife is a very beautiful woman. Is yours, King of Rajputana?"

Sanga stared at the Roman. Belisarius had never met Sanga's wife. For a moment, angrily, Sanga wondered if Rome's spies had—

He shook off the suspicion. Belisarius, he realized, was simply making a shrewd guess. Looking for any angle from which to drive home the lance.

"She is plump and plain-faced," he said harshly. "Her hair was already gray by the time she was thirty."

Belisarius nodded. He opened his hand. Beauty reentered the pavilion.

"Would you trade her, then, for my own?"

Sanga's powerful fingers closed around the hilt of his sword. But, after an instant, the gesture of anger became a simple caress. A man comforted by the feel of an old, familiar, trusted thing. The finest steel in the world was made in India. That steel had saved him, times beyond counting.

"She is my life," he said softly. "The mother of my children. The joy of my youth and the certainty of my manhood. Just as she will be the comfort of my old age."

Sanga's left hand reached up, gingerly stroking the new scar which Valentinian had put on his cheek. The scar was still angry-looking, in its freshness, but even after it faded Sanga's face would remain disfigured. He had been a handsome man, once. No longer.

"Assuming, of course, that I reach old age," he said, smiling ruefully. "And that my wife doesn't flee in terror, when she sees the ogre coming through her door."

Again, for a moment, the fingers of his right hand clenched the sword hilt. Powerful fingers. Sanga's smile vanished.

"I would not trade her for a goddess." The words were as steely as his blade.

"I didn't think so," murmured Belisarius. He slipped Aide back into his pouch, and refastened the tunic.

"I didn't think so," he repeated. He rose, and bowed to Damo-dara. "Our business is finished, I believe."

Belisarius was a tall man. Not as tall as Sanga, but tall enough to loom over Damodara like a giant. He was a big man, too. Not as powerful as Sanga, to be sure, but a far more impressive figure than the short and pudgy Malwa lord sitting on a cushion before him.

It mattered not at all. Lord Damodara returned the Roman general's gaze with the placidity of a Buddha.

"Yes, I believe it is," he agreed pleasantly. Damodara now rose himself, and bowed to Belisarius. Then, he turned slightly and pointed to Narses. "Except—"

Damodara smiled. The very image of a Buddha.

"You requested that Narses be present. I assume there was a reason."

Belisarius examined the eunuch. Throughout the parley, Narses had been silent. He remained silent, although he returned Belisa-rius' calm gaze with the same glare with which he had first greeted him.

"I would like to speak to Narses alone," said Belisarius. "With your permission."

Seeing the distrust in Damodara's eyes, Belisarius shook his head.

"I assure you, Lord Damodara, that nothing I will discuss with Narses will cause any harm to you."

He waited, while Damodara gauged the thing. Measured the angles, so to speak.

That was a beautifully parsed sentence, said Aide admiringly.

I had an excellent grammarian. My father spared no expense on my education.

Damodara was still hesitating. Looking for the oblique approach, wherever the damn thing was. That it was there, Damodara didn't doubt for an instant.

"I will give you my oath on it, if you wish," added Belisarius.

Oh, that's good. You're smart, grandpa. Don't let anybody tell you different.

Belisarius almost made a modest shrug. But long experience had taught him to keep his conversations with Aide a secret from those around him.

I am a man of honor. But I've never seen where that prevents me from using my honor practically. We Romans are even more practical than the Malwa. Way more, when push comes to shove.

The offer seemed to satisfy Damodara. "There's no need," he said pleasantly. Again, he bowed to Belisarius. Then, taking Sanga by the arm, he left the pavilion.

Belisarius and Narses were alone. Narses finally spoke. "*Fuck you.* What do you want?"

Belisarius grinned. "I just want to tell you your future, Narses. I think I owe you that much, for saving Theodora's life."

"I didn't do it for *you*. Fuck you." The old eunuch's glare was a thing of wonder. As splendid, in its own way, as Aide's coruscating glamour. Sheer hostility, as pure as a diamond, forged out of a lifetime's malice, envy and self-hatred.

"And what do I care?" demanded the eunuch. Sneering: "What? Are you going to tell me that I'm an old man, right on the edge of the grave? I already know that, you bastard. I'll still make your life as miserable as I can. Even while they're fitting me for the shroud."

Belisarius' grin was its own thing of marvel. "Not at all, Narses. Quite the contrary." He tapped the pouch under his tunic. "The future's changed, of course, from what it would have been. But some things will remain the same. A man's natural lifespan, for instance."

Narses glared, and glared. Belisarius' grin faded, replaced by a look of—sorrow?

"Such a waste," he murmured. Then, more loudly: "I will tell you the truth, Narses the eunuch. I swear this before God. You will outlive me, and I will not die young."

His crooked smile came. "Not from natural causes, anyway. In this world, which we're creating, who knows what'll happen? But in the future that would have been, I died at the age of sixty. You were still alive."

Narses jaw dropped. "You're serious?" For a moment, a lifetime's ingrained suspicion vanished. For that moment—that tiny moment—the scaled and wrinkled face was that of a child again. The infant boy, before he had been castrated and cast into a life of bitterness. "You're really telling me the truth?"

"I swear to you, Narses, before God Himself, that I am speaking the truth."

Suspicion returned, like a landslide. "Why are you telling me this?" demanded Narses. "And don't give me any crap. I know how tricky you are. There's an angle here." The eunuch's angry eyes scanned the interior of the pavilion, and the landscape visible beyond, as if looking for the trap.

"Of course there's an angle, Narses. I should think it's obvious. *Ambition.*"

Narses' eyes snapped back to Belisarius.

"Such a waste," repeated Belisarius. Then, firmly and surely: "I forgive you your treason, Narses the eunuch. Theodora won't, because she cannot abandon her spite. But I can, and I do. I swear to you now, before God, that the past is forgiven. I ask only, in return, that you remain true to the thing which brought you to treason. Your ambition."

Belisarius spread his hands, cupped, like a giant holding an invisible world. "Don't think small, Narses. Don't satisfy yourself with the petty ambition of bringing *me* down. Think big." His grin returned. "Why not? You've still got at least thirty more years to enjoy the fruits of your labor."

Narses' quick eyes glanced at Rana Sanga. The Rajput king was standing outside, perhaps forty feet away. He and Damodara were chatting amiably with Valentinian.

"Don't be *stupid*," he hissed. "I cleaned up Damodara's nest, sure. He was sick and tired of Nanda Lal's creatures watching his every move. But—more than that?"

The great sneer was back in force. "This is a *Rajput* army, Belisarius, in case you haven't noticed. Those crazy bastards are as likely to violate an oath as you are. They swore eternal allegiance to the Malwa emperor, and that's that."

Belisarius scratched his chin, smiling crookedly. "So they did. But I suggest, if you haven't already, that you investigate the nature of that oath. Oaths are specific, you know. I asked Irene, last year, to find out for me just exactly what the kings of Rajputana swore, at Ajmer, when they finally gave their allegiance to Malwa."

The smile grew as crooked as a root. "They swore eternal allegiance to *the Emperor of Malwa*, Narses." Belisarius began to leave. At the edge of the pavilion, just within the shade, he stopped and turned around.

"There was no mention of Skandagupta, by the way. No name, Narses. Just: *the Emperor of Malwa.*"

He almost laughed, then, seeing Narses' face. Again, it was the face of a young boy. Not the face of trusting innocence, however. This was the eager face of a greedy child, examining the cake which his mother had just placed before him in celebration of his birthday.

With many more birthdays to come. Lots of them, with lots of cake.

On the way back, riding through the badlands, Aide spoke only once.

Deadly with a blade, is Belisarius.

Chapter 23

The minute Belisarius entered the headquarters tent, he knew. The grinning faces of his commanders were evidence enough. Maurice's deep scowl was the proof.

He laughed, seeing that morose expression.

"What's the matter, you old grouch?" he demanded. "Admit the truth—you just can't stand it, when plans go right, that's all. It's against your religion."

Maurice managed a smile, sort of. If a lemon could smile.

" 'T'ain't natural," he grumbled. "Against the laws of man and nature." He held up the scroll in his hand and offered it to Belisarius. Then, shrugging: "But, apparently, it's not against the laws of God."

Eagerly, Belisarius unfolded the scroll and scanned its contents.

"You read it." It was a statement, not a question.

Maurice nodded, gesturing to the other officers. "And I gave them the gist."

Belisarius glanced at the faces of Cyril, Bouzes and Coutzes, and Vasudeva. A Greek, two Thracians, and a Kushan, but they might as well have been peas in a pod. All four men were beaming. Satisfaction, partly, at seeing plans come to fruition. Sheer pleasure, in the main, because they were *finally* done with maneuvers. Except for one last, long, driving march, of course—but that was a march to battle. That the march would end in triumph, they doubted not at all. Theirs was the army of Belisarius.

Not *quite* peas in a pod. The Kushan's grin was so wide that it seemed to split his face. Belisarius gave him a stern look and shook the scroll admonishingly.

"The helmets stay on until we're well into the qanat, Vasudeva. Any Kushan who so much as sheds a buckle, before we're into the passage—I'll have him impaled. I swear I will."

Vasudeva's grin never wavered. "Not to fear, General. We are planning a religious ceremony, once we're in. A great mounded pile of stinking-fucking-stupid-barbarian crap. We will say a small prayer, condemning the shit to eternal oblivion." He spread his hands apologetically. "By rights, of course, we should set it all afire. But—"

Coutzes laughed. "Not likely! Not unless you want to smother all of us in smoke. It'll be hard enough to breathe, as it is, with over ten thousand men humping through a tunnel. Even sending them through in batches, we'll be half-suffocating."

Satisfied, Belisarius resumed his examination of the scroll. He was not really reading the words, however. The message was so short that it did not require much study. Simply a date, and a salutation.

His gaze was fixed on that salutation, like a barnacle to a stone. Two words.

"Thank God, we're done with these mountains," stated Bouzes. "*And* those tough Rajput bastards!" agreed his brother happily.

Tears welled into Belisarius' eyes. "This message means something much more precious to me," he whispered. He caressed the thin sheet. "It means my wife is still alive."

Seeing the sheer joy in Belisarius' face, his commanders fell silent. Then, after clearing his throat, Cyril muttered: "Yes, sir. Very probably."

Belisarius gave the Greek cataphract a shrewd glance. Cyril's expression, he saw, was mirrored on the faces of the brothers and Vasudeva. Uncertainty; hope, for the sake of their general; but—but—

"Shit happens, in war," stated Belisarius, verbalizing their unhappy thoughts. "Maybe Antonina's dead. Maybe Ashot sent the message, telling us when the fleet would sail from Adulis."

He looked at Maurice. The chiliarch was grinning, now, as hugely as Vasudeva had done earlier. There was not a trace of veteran pessimism in that cheerful expression.

Belisarius smiled. "Tell them, Maurice."

Maurice cleared his throat. "Well, it's like this, boys. I only told you the gist of the message itself. Ashot might have sent *that*, sure enough. Could have sent it, standing over Antonina's bleeding corpse. But I really doubt the stubby bastard would have addressed the general as—and I quote—*'dearest love.'* Even if he is an Armenian."

The tent erupted with laughter. Belisarius joined in, freely, but his eyes were back on the scroll.

Dearest love. The two words poured through his soul like wine. Standing in a tent, in the rocky Zagros, he felt as if he were soaring through the heavens.

Dearest love.

They broke for the south two days later. Belisarius waited until the next cavalry encounter was over. Just a quick clash between thirty Romans and their equivalent number of Rajputs, in a nearby valley. No different from a dozen others—a hundred others—which had taken place over the past few months.

The encounter, as had usually been the case since the Battle of the Pass, was almost bloodless. Neither side was trying to hammer the other any longer. They were simply staying in touch, making sure that each army knew the location of its opponent.

No Roman was killed. Only one was seriously injured, but he swore he could make the march.

"It's just my arm, general," he said, holding up the heavily band-aged limb. "Just a flesh wound. Didn't even lose much blood."

Belisarius had his doubts. But, seeing the determination in the cataphract's face, he decided to bring him along. The army had just been informed, at daybreak, of their new destination. The wounded cataphract wanted to stay with his comrades. At worst, the man would not lose his strength for several days. That was good enough.

The general straightened up from his crouch. "All right," he said. He gave the cataphract a look which was not grim, simply stoic. "Worst comes to worst, you'll be in Rajput hands."

The cataphract shrugged. He was obviously not appalled by the prospect. Nor had he any reason to be. The conflict between the two armies, even before the battle in the pass, had been civilized. Thereafter, it had been downright chivalrous. The Rajputs would treat the man as well as Belisarius' soldiers had treated their own Rajput captives.

Remembering those captives, Belisarius shrugged himself. "Comes to it," he said, "I'll just leave you behind with the prisoners. Far enough into the qanat that Damodara won't find you until it's too late, and with plenty of food. You won't need water, of course."

The cataphract grimaced, slightly, at the mention of water. The spring runoff was long over, but the qanat was still at least a foot deep. For all their eagerness to quit the mountains, none of the soldiers were looking forward to a long march through a tunnel. Walking along narrow ledges on the sides, lest their feet become soaked by the water pouring through the center passage.

Maurice came up. "Now," he said. "Couldn't ask for a better time."

Belisarius nodded. It was only mid-morning of the day after the cavalry clash. The Rajput horsemen would have returned to their own army, bringing Damodara the news of the Roman whereabouts. They would not return for at least a day, probably two.

Long enough.

"Are the men—?"

"Mounted up, and ready," came Maurice's immediate reply. "They're just waiting for the order."

Belisarius took a deep breath, filling his lungs.

"*Now,*" he said. Quickly, while the clean air of the mountains buoyed him up and stiffened his resolve. Soon enough, he would be gasping and sweating in damp, smoky darkness. One of thousands of men, stumbling through a tunnel eight feet wide, their steps barely illuminated by a few torches.

The Roman camp, within minutes, was a beehive of activity. Long files of mounted soldiers started down the valley, headed for another small valley two days' ride away. That valley was also a beehive of activity. Kurush and his miners had been preparing the deception for weeks, now.

Belisarius waited until the very end, before he mounted up and followed. It was odd, he realized, how much he was going to miss the mountains. Odd, when he thought of the many times he had cursed them. But the Zagros had been good to him, when all was said and done. And he was going to miss the clean air.

He drove out all regrets. Aide helped.

Think of the sea breeze. Think of gulls, soaring through blue skies. Think of—

The hell with all that! came Belisarius' cheerful retort. *All I want to think about is Venus rising from the waves.*

And that was the thought that held him, through the miserable days ahead. His wife, coming to meet him from across the sea.

Dearest love.

At a place called Charax. A place where Belisarius would lance a dragon's belly; and show the new gods that they too, for all their dreams of perfection, still needed intestines.

Charax. Belisarius would burn that name into eternity.

But the name meant nothing to him. It was just the place where his Venus would rise from the waves. A name which was only important because a man could remember embracing his wife there, like so many men, over so many years, at so many places, had embraced their wives after a long separation. Nothing more.

So is eternity made, said Aide gently. **Out of that simple clay, and no other.**

Chapter 24

MAJARASHTRA

Summer, 532 A.D.

Irene whispered a few words into her agent's ear. The man nodded, bowed, and left the room. Irene closed the door behind him.

Kungas had ignored the interchange. Bent over the reading table in Irene's outer chamber, carefully writing out the assignment she had given him, Kungas had seemed utterly oblivious to the spy's arrival or his whispered conversation with Irene. But, the moment the spy was gone, Kungas raised his head and cocked an eye toward her.

Seeing the expression on her face, he turned away from the table completely.

"Is something wrong?" he asked.

Irene stared at him, blank-faced. Kungas rose from the chair. A faint frown of worry creased his brow.

"What is wrong?" he demanded.

Irene shook her head. "Nothing," she replied. "Nothing is *wrong.*"

With the air of a woman preoccupied by something, she drifted toward the window. Kungas remained in place, following only with his eyes.

Once at the window, Irene placed her hands on the sill. She leaned into the gentle breeze coming from the ocean, closing her eyes. Her thick, lustrous, chestnut hair billowed gently in the wind.

Behind her, unseen, Kungas' hands moved. Coming up, cupping, as if to stroke and caress. But the movement was short-lived. In seconds, his hands were back at his side.

Irene turned away from the window. "I need your advice," she said softly.

Kungas nodded. The gesture, as always, was economical. But his eyes were alert.

For a moment, as her mind veered aside into the hot place in her heart, Irene reveled in her own words. *I need your advice.* Simple words. But words which, except for Belisarius and occasionally Justinian, she had never spoken to a man. Men, as a rule, did not give advice to women. They condescended, or they instructed, or they babbled vaingloriously, or they tried to seduce. They rarely simply advised.

She could not remember, any longer, how many times she had said the words to Kungas. And how many times, in the weeks since the battle where they destroyed the guns, he had simply advised.

By sheer force of will, she jerked her mind back from that place in her heart. The fire was there, but it was banked for a time.

She shook her head, smiling.

"What is so amusing?" asked Kungas.

"I was just remembering the first time I met you. I thought you were quite ugly."

His lips made the little movement which stood Kungas for a grin. "No longer, I hope?"

She gave no answer. But Kungas did not miss the little twitch of her hands. As if she, too, wanted to stroke and caress.

Irene cleared her throat. "There is news. News concerning Dadaji's family. The location of his son has been found. The location where he *was,* I should say. It seems that several months ago Dadaji's son was among a group of slaves who escaped from his master's plantation in eastern India. The ringleader, apparently. Since then, according to the report, he has joined one of the rebel bands in the forest."

Kungas smacked his hands together. For an instant, the mask vanished. His face shone with pure and unalloyed delight.

"How wonderful! Dadaji will be ecstatic!"

Irene raised a cautioning hand. "He is in great danger, Kungas, and there is nothing I can do to help him. The Malwa have been pouring troops into the forests, since they finally realized they can no longer dismiss the rebels as a handful of brigands."

Kungas shrugged. "And so? The boy dies, arms in hand, fighting the asura who ravages his homeland. That is the worst. You think that would break Dadaji's heart? You do not really understand him, Irene. Beneath that gentle scholar is a man of the Great Country. He will do the rites, weeping—while his heart sings with joy."

Irene stared at him. Skeptically, at first. Then, with a nod, she deferred to his judgement. (And reveled, also, in that deferral.)

"There is more," she added. "More than news." She took a deep breath. "My spies found his wife, also. A slave in a nobleman's kitchen, right in Kausambi itself. Following my instructions, they decided it would be possible to steal her away. In Malwa's capital," she snorted, half-chuckling, "noblemen do not guard their mansions too carefully."

Kungas' eyes widened. In another man, they would have been practically bulging.

Irene laughed. "Oh, yes. She is *here*, Kungas. In Suppara." She nodded toward the door. "In this very house, in fact. My man has her downstairs, in the salon."

Now, even Kungas' legendary self-control was breaking. "*Here?*" he gasped. He stared at the door. Then, almost lunging, he began to move. "We must take her to him at once! He will be so—"

"*Stop!*"

Kungas staggered to a halt. For a moment, staring at Irene, he frowned with incomprehension. Then, his expression changed, as understanding came. Or so he thought.

"She has been disfigured," he stated. "Dishonored, perhaps. You are afraid Dadaji will—"

Irene blew out a breath—half-laugh, half-surprise. "No—no." She smiled reassuringly. "She is quite well, Kungas, according to my agent. Very tired, of course. He says she was asleep within seconds of reaching the couch. The journey was long and arduous, and her life as a slave was sheer toil. But she is well. As for the other—"

Irene waved her hand, as if calming an unsettled child. "My spy says she was not abused, not in that manner. Not even by her master. She was not a young woman, you know. Dadaji's age."

She looked away, her jaw tightening. "With so many young slaves to rape, after the conquest of Andhra, men simply beat her until she was an obedient drudge." Her next words were cold, filled with the bitterness of centuries. Greek women had been raped, too, often enough. And listened to Greek men, and Greek poets, boasting of the Trojan women. "Not even Dadaji will count that as pollution."

"*That is not fair,*" said Kungas harshly.

Irene took a deep breath, almost a shudder. "No, it is not," she admitted. "Not with Dadaji, at least. Although—" She sighed, shaking her head. "How can any man as intelligent as he be so stupid?"

It only took Kungas a second, perhaps two, to finally understand her concern.

"Ah." He stared out the window for a moment. "I see."

He looked down at his hands, and spread wide his fingers. "Tonight, the empress has called a council. She will finally decide, she says, which offer of marriage to accept."

The fingers closed into fists. He looked up at Irene. "You will state your opinion, then, for the first time. And you do not want Dadaji to refrain from arguing his, because he feels himself so deeply in your debt."

She nodded. Kungas chuckled. "I never imagined Rome's finest spymaster would hold herself to such a rigid code of honor."

Irene made an inarticulate, sarcastic noise. "I hate to disillusion you, Kungas. I do this not from honor, but from simple—" She paused. When she spoke again, the acid-tinged sarcasm was gone from her voice.

"Some, yes. Some." She sighed. "It is difficult to manipulate Dadaji, even for someone like me. It's a bit too much like maneuvering against a damned saint."

She reached up and wiped her face, restoring the spymaster. "But that is still not my reason. My reason is cold-blooded statecraft. Whatever decision the empress makes will be irrevocable. You know Shakuntala, Kungas. She is as intelligent, I think, as Justinian."

She barked a laugh. "She *certainly* has the willpower of Theodora." Then, shaking her head: "But she is still a girl, in many ways. If she discovers, in the future, that one of her closest advisers—he is like a father to her, you know that—withheld his advice on such a critical matter—" The headshaking became vigorous. "No, no, no. That would shake her self-confidence to the very roots. And *that* we cannot afford. She may make the wrong decision. Rulers often do. But her confidence must never waver, or all will be lost."

Kungas eyed her, head aslant. "Have I ever told you that you were a very smart woman?"

"Several times," she replied, smiling. She cocked her own head, returning his look of amusement with questioning eyes.

"You still have not asked," she said softly. "What my opinion is. We have never discussed the matter, oddly enough."

He spread his hands. "Why is that odd? I know your opinion, just as surely as you know mine."

He dropped his hands and lifted his shoulders. "It is obvious. I even have hopes, once we explain, that Dadaji will be convinced."

Irene snorted. Kungas smiled, but shook his head.

"You are too skeptical, I think." The thick, heavy shoulders squared. "But we will know soon."

He began to move toward the door, his head turned away. "I think it would be best, Irene, if you spoke first."

"I agree. It will strike the harder, coming from an unexpected source. You will follow, of course, when the time is right."

He did not bother to reply. There was no need. For a moment, never speaking, the man and woman in the room reveled together in that knowledge.

Kungas had reached the door. But Irene spoke before he could open it.

"Kungas." He turned his head. Irene gestured at the writing table. "You can read, now. Kushan, rather well, and your Greek is becoming passable. Your writing is still very crude, but that is merely a matter of practice."

His eyes went to the table, lingering there for a moment. Then, closed shut.

"Why, Kungas?" she asked. Her voice was calm, but tinged with anxiety. And, yes, some pain and anger. "My bed has always been there for you. But you have never come. Not once, in the weeks since the battle."

Kungas reopened his eyes. When he looked at Irene, his gaze was calm. Calm, and resolute.

"Not yet."

Irene's own gaze was not so calm. "I am not a virgin, Kungas," she said. Angrily, perhaps—or simply pleading.

The Kushan's mask of a face broke in half. Irene almost gasped. She had never seen Kungas actually *grin*.

"I did not imagine you were!" he choked out. He lowered his head, shaking it back and forth like a bull. "Shocking news. Most distressing. I am chagrined beyond belief. Oh, what shall I do?"

As tense as she was, Irene couldn't restrain her laughter. Kungas raised his head, still grinning.

But the question remained in her eyes. He took a few steps forward, reached out his hand, and drew her head into his shoulder.

"I have this to do first, Irene," he said softly, stroking her hair. "I cannot—" Silence, while he sought the words. "I cannot tend to my own needs, while hers are still gaping. I have guarded her for too long, now. And this struggle, I think, is perhaps her most desperate. I must see her through it safely."

She felt his chest heave slightly, from soft laughter. "Call it my own dharma, if you will."

Irene nodded, her head still nestled in his shoulder. She reached up and caressed the back of his neck. Slender fingers danced on thick muscle.

"I understand," she murmured. "As long as I understand." She laughed once herself, very softly. "I may need reassurance, again, mind you. If this goes on and on."

She knew he was smiling. "Not long, I think," she heard him say. "The girl *is* decisive, you know."

Irene sighed, and ceased caressing Kungas' neck. A moment later, her hands placed firmly on his chest, she created a space between them.

"So she is," she murmured. "So she most certainly is."

Pushing him away, now. "Go, then. I will see you tonight, at the council meeting."

He bowed ceremoniously. "Prepare to do battle, Irene Macrembolitissa. The dragon of Indian prejudice awaits your Roman lance."

Gaiety returned in full force. "What a ridiculous metaphor! It's back to the books for you—*barbarian oaf!*"

Chapter 25

It was late in the night before Irene spoke. The council had already gone on for hours.

Irene craned her neck, twisting her head back and forth. To all outward appearance, it was the gesture of someone simply stretching in order to remain alert in a long, long imperial council.

In reality, she was just trying not to smile at the image which had come to her mind.

This isn't a "council." It's a—down, smile, down!—damned auction.

Her eyes, atop a rotating head, fell on the empress. Shakuntala was sitting, stiff and straight-backed, on a cushion placed on her throne. The throne itself was wide and low. In her lotus position, hands at her side, Shakuntala reminded Irene of the statue of a goddess resting on an altar. The girl had maintained that posture, and her stern countenance, throughout the session—with no effort at all, seemingly. That self-discipline, Irene knew, was another of Raghunath Rao's many gifts to the girl.

Irene's head twisting became a little shake.

Stop thinking of her as a "girl." That is a woman, now. Not more than twenty, yes, and still a virgin. But a woman nonetheless.

In the long months—almost a year, now—since Irene had come to India, she had grown very fond of Shakuntala. In private, Shakuntala's imperious demeanor was transmuted into something quite different. A will of iron, still, and self-assuredness that would shame an elephant. But there was also humor, and quick intelligence, and banter, and a willingness to listen, and a cheerful acceptance of human foibles. And that, too, was a legacy of Raghunath Rao.

Not one of Shakuntala's many advisers doubted for a moment that the empress, should she feel it necessary, could order the execution of a thousand men without blinking an eye. And not one of those advisers—not for instant—ever hesitated to speak his mind. And that, too, was a legacy of Rao.

Irene's eyes now fell on the large group of men sitting before the empress, on their own plush cushions resting on the carpeted floor.

The bidders at the auction.

The envoys from every kingdom in India still independent of Malwa were there. Tamraparni, the great island south of India which was sometimes called Ceylon, was there. And, in the past two weeks, plenipotentiaries from every realm in the vast Hindu world had arrived also. Most of those envoys had brought soldiers with them, to prove the sincerity of their offers. The Cholan and Tamraparni units were quite sizeable. Suppara was packed like a crate, with soldiers billeted everywhere.

Whether smuggled through the blockade of the coast, or, more often, marching overland from Kerala, they had come. Kerala, ruled by Shakuntala's grandfather, was there too, despite his treacherous connivance the year before with a Malwa assassination plot against her. Shakuntala had practically forced its representative Ganapati to grovel. But, in the end, she had allowed Kerala to join the bidding.

Irene had never fully realized, until the past few weeks, the true extent of the Hindu world. She had always thought of Hinduism, and its Buddhist offspring, as religions of India. But, like Christianity, those religions had spread their message over the centuries. And, more often than not, spread their entire culture along with it.

Representatives from Champa were there, and Funan, and Langkasuka, and Taruma, and many others. The faces of those envoys bore the racial stamp of southeast Asia and its great archipelagoes but, beneath the skin, they were children of India in all that mattered. Nations sired by Indian missionaries, suckled by Indian custom, nurtured by Indian commerce, and educated in Sanskrit or one of its derivatives.

Even China was there, in the form of a Buddhist monk sent by one of the great kingdoms of that distant land. He, unlike the others, had not come to bid for Shakuntala's hand in marriage. He had come simply to observe. But men—not royal envoys, at least—do not travel across the sea in order to observe a stone. They come to study a comet.

Shakuntala's rebellion had shaken Malwa. The world's most powerful empire was still on its feet, and still roaring its fury. But it was locked in mortal combat with adversaries from the mysterious West—enemies who had proven far more formidable than the Hindu world had envisioned. And now, rising from the stony soil of the Great Country, Shakuntala's rebellion was hammering the giant's knees. If those knees ever broke—

The independent kingdoms of the Hindu world, finally, had shed their hesitation. They feared Malwa, still—were petrified by the monster, in fact—but Shakuntala had shown that the beast could be bloodied. Not beaten, perhaps. That remained to be seen. But even the vacillating, timid, fretful kingdoms of south India and southeast Asia had finally understood the truth.

Andhra had returned. Great Satavahana, the noblest dynasty in their world, was still alive. That empire, and that dynasty, had shielded south India and the Hindu lands beyond for centuries. Perhaps it could do so yet.

All of them had come, and all of them were bidding for the dynastic marriage. And the bidding had been fierce. In the weeks leading up to the council, the canny peshwa Dadaji Holkar had matched one proposal against another, scraping quibble against reservation, until nothing was left but solid offers of alliance. At the council meeting itself, in the course of the hours, Dadaji had compressed those solid offers into so many bars of iron.

Irene repressed a grin. Dadaji Holkar, low-born son of polluted Majarashtra, had outwitted and outmaneuvered and outnegotiated the Hindu world's most prestigious brahmin diplomats. Had any of them been told, now, that Dadaji himself was nothing but a low-caste vaisya—a mere sudra, in truth, in any land of India outside the Great Country—they would have been shocked from the tops of their aristocratic heads to the soles of their pure brahmin feet. Distressed also, of course, at the thought of the pollution they had suffered from their many hours of intimate contact with the man. For the most part, however, they would have simply been stunned.

It is not possible! He is one of the most learned men in India! A scholar, as well a statesman!

She could picture them gobbling their disbelief. *It is not possible! He is the peshwa of Andhra! How could great Satavahana—India's purest kshatriya—have been fooled by such a man? Not possible!*

Irene's fight to restrain her humor became transformed into something much grimmer. Something cold, and calculating, and—in its own way—utterly ruthless. She, too, could be an executioner.

Studying the brahmin diplomats seated before the empress, Irene's eyes began to glint. *I will show you what is* possible. *Fools!*

It was time. The envoys had presented their offers. Dadaji had summarized the situation. It only remained for the empress to make her decision.

Irene could not have explained the little movements she made, of head and hands and eyes, which drew Shakuntala's attention. Neither could the young empress herself. But the two women had spent many hours in private and public discourse. Irene knew how to signal the empress, just as surely as the empress understood how to interpret those signals.

Shakuntala's head turned to Irene. The empress' eyes seemed as bright as ever, probably, to most observers. But Irene could sense the dull resignation in that imperial gaze.

"I would like to hear from the envoy of Rome," stated Shakuntala. As always in public council, the empress' voice was a thing to marvel at. Youthful, true, in its timbre. But a fresh-forged blade is still a sword.

A faint murmur arose from the diplomats.

Shakuntala's eyes snapped back to them. "Do I hear a protest?" she demanded. "Is there one among you who cares to speak?"

The murmurs fled. Shakuntala's eyes were like iron balls. The Black-Eyed Pearl of the Satavahanas, she was often called. But black, for all its beauty, can be a terrifying color.

Black iron smote clay. "You would *protest*?" she hissed. *"You?"* The statue moved, slightly. A goddess, with a little gesture of the hand, dismissing insects. "After Malwa conquered Andhra, and flayed my father's skin for Skandagupta's trophy, what did *you* do?"

The statue sneered. "You trembled, and quailed, and whimpered, and tried to hide in your palaces." The goddess spoke. "Rome—*only Rome*—did not cower from the beast."

Shakuntala's next words were spoken through tight teeth. "Doubt me not in this, you diplomats. If Malwa is slain, the lance which brings the monster down will be held in Roman hands. Not ours. Alone—not if all of us united—could we do the deed. Our task is to shield the Deccan, and do what we can to lame the beast."

The diplomats bowed their heads. Those brahmins, for all their learning, were insular and self-absorbed to a degree which Irene, accustomed to Roman cosmopolitanism, often found amazing. But even they, by now, knew the name of Belisarius. A bizarre name, an outlandish name, but a name of legend nonetheless. Even in south India—even in southeast Asia—they had heard of Anatha. And the Nehar Malka, where Belisarius drowned Malwa's minions.

Shakuntala kept her eyes on their bowed heads, not relenting for a full minute. Black iron is as heavy as it is hard.

During that long minute, while Indian diplomats—again—quailed and hid their heads, Irene sent a mental message to a man across the sea. He would not receive it, of course, but she knew he would have enjoyed the whimsy. That man had spent hours and hours with her, in Constantinople—days, rather—counseling Irene on her great task. Explaining, to a woman of the present, the future he wanted her to help create.

Well, Belisarius, you wanted your Peninsular War. I do believe you've got it. And if we don't have Wellington, and the Lines of Torres Vedras, we have something just as good. We have Rao, and the hillforts of the Great Country, and—

Her eyes fell on a hard, harsh, brutal face.

—and we've got my man, too. Mine.

She gathered the comfort in that possessive thought, and transformed softness into hard purpose.

"Speak, envoy of Rome," commanded Shakuntala.

Irene rose from her chair and stepped into the center of the large chamber. Dozens of eyes were fixed upon her.

She had learned that from Theodora. The Empress Regent of Rome had also counseled Irene, before she left for India. Explaining, to a spymaster accustomed to shadows, how to work in the light of day.

"Always sit, in counsel and judgement," Theodora had told her. "But always stand, when you truly want to lead."

Irene, as was her way, began with humor.

"Consider these robes, men of India." She plucked at a heavy sleeve. "Preposterous, are they not? A device for torture, almost, in this land of heat and swelter."

Many smiles appeared. Irene matched them with her own.

"I was advised, once, to exchange them for a sari." She sensed, though she did not look to see, a pair of twitching lips. "But I rejected the advice. Why? Because while the robes are preposterous, what they represent is not."

She scanned the crowd slowly. The smile faded. Her face grew stern.

"What they represent is Rome itself. Rome—*and its thousand years.*"

Silence. Again, slowly, she scanned the room.

"*A thousand years,*" she repeated. "What dynasty of India can claim as much?"

Silence. Scan back across the room.

"The greatest empire in the history of India, the Maurya, could claim only a century and half. The Guptas, not more than two." She nodded toward Shakuntala. "Andhra can claim more, in years if not in power, but even Andhra cannot claim more than half Rome's fortune."

Her stern face softened, just slightly. Again, she nodded to the empress. The nod was almost a bow. "Although, God willing, Andhra will be able to match Rome's accomplishment, as future centuries unfold."

Severity returned. "*A thousand years.* Consider *that*, noble men of India. And then ask yourself: how was it done?"

Again, she smiled; and, again, plucked at a heavy sleeve.

"It was done with these robes. These heavy, thick, preposterous, unsuitable robes. These robes contain the secret."

She paused, waited. She had their complete attention, now. She took the time, while she waited, to send another whimsical, mental message across the sea. Thanking a harsh, cold empress named Theodora, born in poverty on the streets of Alexandria, for training a Greek noblewoman in the true ways of majesty.

"The secret is this. These are the robes *of* Rome, but they are not Roman. They are Hun robes, which we took for our own."

A murmur arose. *Huns? Filthy, barbarous—Huns?*

"Yes. Hun robes. We took them, as we took Hun trousers, when our soldiers became cavalrymen. Just as we took, from the Aryans, the armor and the weapons and the tactics of Persia's horsemen. Just as we took from the Carthaginians—eight hundred years ago—the secrets of war at sea. Just as we took, century after century, the wisdom of Greece, and made it our own. Just as we took the message of Christ from Palestine. Just as we have taken everything we needed—*and discarded anything we must*—so that Rome could endure."

She pointed her finger toward the north. "The Malwa call us mongrels, and boast of their own purity. So be it. Rome shrugs off the name, as an elephant shrugs off a fly. Or, perhaps—"

She grinned. Or, perhaps, bared her teeth.

"Say better, Rome *swallows* the name. Just as a huge, half-savage, shaggy, mastiff cur of the street wolfs down a well-groomed, purebred house pet."

A tittering laugh went through the room. Irene allowed the humor to pass. She pointed now to Shakuntala.

"The empress said—and said rightly—that if the monster called Malwa is slain, the hand which holds the lance will be Roman. I can give that hand a name. The name is Belisarius."

She paused, letting the name echo through the chamber.

"*Belisarius.* A name of glory, to Rome. A name of terror, to Malwa. But, in the end, it is simply a name. Just like this"—she fingered a sleeve—"is simply cloth. So you must ask yourself—why does the name carry such weight? Where does it come from?"

She shrugged. "It is a Thracian name, first. Given to his oldest son by a minor nobleman in one of Rome's farming provinces. Not three generations from a peasant, if the truth be told."

She fixed cold eyes on the crowd. "Yet that *peasant* has broken armies. Armies more powerful than any of you could face. And why is *that*, noble men of India?"

Her chuckle was as cold as her eyes. "I will tell you why. It is because Belisarius has a soul as well as a name. And whatever may have been the flesh that made the man, or the lineage that produced the name, the *soul* was forged on that great anvil which history has come to call—*Rome*."

She spread her arms wide, trailing heavy sleeves. "Just as I, a Greek noblewoman wearing Hun robes, was forged on that same anvil."

Irene could feel Theodora flowing through her now, like hot fire through her veins. Theodora, and Antonina, and all the women who had birthed Rome, century after century, back to the she-wolf who nursed Remus and Romulus.

She turned to Shakuntala.

"You asked, Empress of Andhra, my advice concerning your marriage. I am a Roman, and can give you only Roman advice. My friend Theodora, who rules Rome today, has a favorite saying. *Do not trample old friends, in your eagerness to make new ones.*"

She scanned the faces in the crowd, watching for any sign of understanding.

Nothing. The faces were transfixed, but blank with incomprehension. Except—Dadaji Holkar's eyes were widening.

Drive on, drive on. Strike again.

"Whom should you marry? To a Roman, the answer is obvious. You are a monarch, Shakuntala, with a duty to your people. *Marry the power*—that is the Roman answer. Marry the strength, and the courage, and the devotion, and the tenacity, which brought you to the throne and can keep you there. Wed the strong hand which can shield you from Malwa, and can strike powerful blows in return."

Scanned the faces. Transfixed, but—still nothing. Except Holkar. A wide-eyed face, almost pale with shock, as he began to understand.

Again, the hammerstroke. Even prejudice, in the end, will yield to iron.

"Do not wed a man, Empress. Wed a people. Marry the people—the *only* people—who never failed you. Marry the people who carried Andhra on their shoulders, when Andhra was bleeding and broken. Marry the men who harry Malwa in the hills, and the women who smuggle food into Deogiri. Marry the nation that sent its sons into battle, not counting the cost, while all other nations cowered in fear. Marry the boys impaled on the Vile One's stakes, and their younger brothers who step forward to take their place. Wed *that* folk, Shakuntala! Marry that great, half-savage, shaggy mastiff of the hills, not—"

She pointed accusing fingers at the assembled representatives of the Hindu world's aristocracy.

"Not these—these purebred *lapdogs.*"

Accusing fingers curled into a fist. She held the fist out before her.

"*Then*—! Then, Shakuntala, you will hold power in your hand. True power, real power—not its illusion. Steel, not brittle wood."

She dropped her fist, flicking dismissive fingers. The gesture carried a millennium's contempt.

"Marry the Roman way, girl," she said. Gently, but with the assurance of Rome's millenium. "Wed Majarashtra. Find the best man of that rough nation, and place your hand in his. Let *that* man dance your wedding dance. Open the womb of India's noblest and most ancient dynasty to the raw, fresh seed of the Great Country. Let the sons born of that union carry Andhra's fortune into the future. If you do so, that fortune will be measured in centuries. If you do otherwise, it will be measured in years.

"As for the rest . . . " She shrugged. "As for what people might say, or think . . . " She laughed, now. There was no humor at all in the sound. It carried nothing beyond unyielding, pitiless condemnation. Salt, sown into soil.

"Let them babble, Shakuntala. Let them cluck and complain. Let them whimper of purity and pollution. Let them sneer, if they will. What do you care? While their thrones totter, yours will stand unshaken. And they will come to you soon enough—trust me—like beggars in a dusty street. Pleading that you might let the uncouth husband sitting by your side, and lying in your bed, lead their own armies into battle."

Finally—*finally*—everyone in the room understood. The envoys were gaping at her like so many blowfish. Dadaji's face, she could not see. The peshwa's head was bowed, as if in thought. Or, perhaps, in prayer.

She turned back to Shakuntala. The empress, though she was not gaping, seemed in a pure state of shock. She sat the throne, no longer like the statue of a goddess, but simply like a young child. A schoolgirl, paralyzed by a question she had never dreamed anyone would ever ask.

The Roman teacher smiled. "Remember, Shakuntala. Only the soul matters, in the end. All else is dross. That is as true of an empire as it is of a man."

Quietly, then, but quickly, Irene took her seat. In the long silence which followed, while envoys gasped for breath and a peshwa bowed his head—and a schoolgirl groped for an answer she already knew, but could not remember—Irene simply waited. Her hands folded in her lap, breathing easily, she simply waited.

Prejudice would erupt, naturally. Soon, the room would be filled with outrage and protest. She did not care. Not in the least.

She had done her job. Quite well, she thought. Holding the tongs in firm hands, she had positioned the blade to be forged. Prejudice would sputter up, of course, just as hot iron spatters. But the hammer, held in barbarous thick hands, would strike surely. And quench the protest of purity in the greater purity of tempering oil.

Kungas did not wait for the protest to emerge. Kushans were a folk of the steppes, and swift horses.

"*Finally!*"

He was standing in the center of the room, before anyone saw him rise.

"*Finally.*"

He let the word settle, ringing, as that word does. Then, crossing muscle-thick arms over barrel chest, he turned his head to the empress.

"Do as she says, girl. It is obvious. *Obvious.*"

The first mutters began to arise from the crowd of notables. Kungas swung his head toward them, like a swiveling cannon.

"*Be silent.*" The command, though spoken softly, brought instant obedience. The mask was pitiless, now. As pitiless, and as uncaring, as steppe winter.

"I do not wish to hear from *you.*" The mask twisted, just slightly. But Satan, with his goat lips, would have been awed by that sneer.

"*You?* You would *dare?*" The snort which followed matched the sneer. Pure, unalloyed contempt.

Kungas swiveled his head back to Shakuntala. "I will tell you something, girl. Listen to me, and listen well. I was your captor, once, before I was your guardian. I knew the truth, then, just as surely as I know it now. The thing is obvious—*obvious*—to any but fools blinded by custom."

Again, he snorted. Contempt remained, augmented by cold humor.

"All those months in the Vile One's palace, while I held you captive. Do you remember? Do you remember how carefully I set the guards? How strictly I maintained discipline? You had eyes to see, girl, and a mind which was trained for combat. Did you see?"

He stared at the empress. After a moment, Shakuntala nodded. Nodded, not imperiously, but like a schoolgirl nods, when she is beginning to follow the lesson.

Kungas jerked his head at the notables.

"Against whom was I setting that iron guard, girl? *Them?*"

He barked a laugh so savage it was almost frightening.

"*Them? Those purebred pets?*"

The laugh came again, baying like a wolf.

"I did not fear *them*, girl. I did not watch so carefully because I was worried about *Chola*. Or Tamraparni, or Kerala, or—"

He broke off, waving a thick hand.

"I was your enemy then, Shakuntala. And as good an enemy, as I have been a friend since. I knew the truth. I always knew. I knew who would come for you. I knew, and I feared the coming."

For a moment, his eyes moved to Dadaji. The peshwa's face was still hidden. Kungas made a little nod toward that bowed head, as if acknowledging defeat in an old argument. "My soul knew he was there. I could sense his own, lurking in the woods beyond the palace. I never spotted him, not once, but I *knew*. That is why I set the guards, and held the discipline, and never wavered for a second in alertness. I never feared anything, except the coming of the panther. One thing only, I knew, could threaten my purpose. The Wind of the Great Country—that, and that alone, could sweep you out of Malwa's grasp."

His eyes returned to the empress. Clear, bright almond eyes, in a face like bronze. "And that Wind alone, girl, is what can keep you from the asura's claws."

He uncrossed his arms, and dropped his hands to the side. "Do as the Roman woman tells you, Shakuntala. Do that and no other. Hers is the advice of an empire which, for a thousand years, has never lost sight of the truth. While *these*—"

Again, the stiff, contemptuous fingers. "*These* are nothing but envoys from kingdoms long lost to illusion."

And now he too took his seat. And silence reigned again. The envoys did not even murmur. The lapdogs had been cowed.

Irene held her breath. One voice, alone, remained to be heard. One voice, alone in that room, which could still sway the empress to folly. She dreaded that voice, and found herself praying that the man she had come to love had read another man's soul correctly. For perhaps the first time in her life, Irene prayed she was in error.

Shakuntala's face was as stiff as a statue's. But the exterior rigidity could not disguise—not from Irene; not from anyone in the room—the turmoil roiling beneath.

Irene was swept with pity. The girl's mind—and the empress *was* a girl, now—was locked tight. Sheer, utter paralysis. Shakuntala's deepest, most hidden wish was at war with her iron sense of duty—and now, a foreign woman had turned duty against desire. Cutting loose one with the other, true. But still leaving behind, to a girl who had never once seen their connection, nothing but a tangled web of doubt and confusion.

Shakuntala did what she could only do, then. She turned to the man who, more than any other, she had come to rely on to find the threads which guided her life.

"Dadaji?" she said softly, pleadingly. "Dadaji? You must tell me. What should I do?"

Irene's jaws tightened; her lips were pursed. That question had not been asked of an adviser, by an empress. That had been the question a daughter asks her father. A loving daughter, turning to a trusted father—seeking, not advice, but direction.

It was Holkar's decision, now. Irene knew that for a certainty. In her current state of paralysis and confusion, Shakuntala would obey the peshwa as surely as a daughter will obey her father.

Irene saw Dadaji's shoulders rise and fall, taking a deep breath. He lifted his head. For the first time since Irene had read understanding in his eyes, she saw Dadaji's face.

The relief was almost explosive. She had to fight to let her breath escape in silence.

Before Holkar said his first word, Irene knew the answer. That was the face of a father, not a peshwa. A loving father who, like millions before him, could chide and train and discipline his daughter. But who could not, when the time finally came, deny her what she truly wished.

Dadaji Holkar began to speak. Irene, listening, knew that Kungas had read the man's soul correctly, and she had not. When all was said and done, and the trappings and learning were stripped away, Dadaji Holkar remained what he had always been. A simple, modest, kindly man from a small town in Majarashtra, trying to raise a family as best he could. Malwa had savaged his family, and torn his own daughters away. He would not, could not, do the same to the girl he had taken in their place.

Holkar's face had brought relief. Relief so great, that Irene barely listened to his first words. But after a few seconds, she did. And then, less than a minute later, was struggling not to laugh.

The soul of Dadaji Holkar was that of a father, true. But the mind still belonged to the imperial adviser. Once again, great Satavahana's lowborn peshwa would outmaneuver brahmins.

"It is difficult for you, Empress, I realize." Dadaji raised his hand, as if to ward off the peril which threatened his monarch. As best he could, that is—which, judging from the feebleness of the gesture, was precious little. "Your own purity—" He broke off, sighed, plowed forward. "But you must put the needs of your people first. As difficult as the choice may be, for one of your sacred lineage."

The peshwa, twisting sideways on his cushion, turned toward Irene and bowed.

"I listened carefully to the Roman envoy's words. As carefully as I could, even though my heart was beating rebellion. But my mind could not deny the words. It is true, what she says." Again, he sighed, as a man does when he cedes preference to duty. "If you place your obligation to your people above all else, thrusting aside your personal concerns, then you must indeed do as the Roman says. If you would marry power, Empress, then marry the man from the Great Country."

A faint murmur of protest began to rise from the envoys seated nearby. The barbarous Kushan had intimidated them, with his savage derision. The scholarly peshwa—a brahmin like themselves; or so, at least, they thought—could perhaps be reasoned with.

Dadaji thrust out his hand, palm down. The gesture, in its own way, was as contemptuous as Kungas' sneer. A sage, stilling the ignorant babble of village halfwits.

"*Be silent.*" Holkar fixed cold eyes on the gathered envoys. "What do *you* know of power?"

The peshwa was well into middle age, but he was still an active man. Dadaji rose from the cushion, as easily as a youth. He stared down at the envoys for a moment, before he began pacing back and forth. Hands clasped behind him, head tilted forward—the master, lecturing schoolboys. "You know nothing. The true ways of power are as mysterious to you as the planets."

Pace, pace, back and forth. "No country in India—not all of us put together—can field an army which could defeat Malwa in the field. That task is for the Romans, led by Belisarius. But he, too, cannot do it alone. Belisarius can lance the asura, but only if the demon is hamstrung. And *that*, we *can* do. But the doing will be difficult, and bloody, and costly. It will require courage and tenacity, above all other things."

He stopped, gazing down on Chola's envoy. "When Shakuntala's father, years ago, asked you for your help against Malwa, what did you do?" He waited for the answer. None came, beyond a head turned aside.

He looked upon Ganapati. "What did Kerala do?" he demanded. Ganapati, also, looked away.

Holkar's bitter eyes scanned the envoys. Most looked aside; some bowed their heads; a few—those from distant southeast Asia—simply shrugged. Their help had not been asked by Shakuntala's father.

But Holkar did not allow them that easy escape and, after a time, they looked away also. They knew the truth as well as he. Had Andhra asked, the answer would have been the same. *No.*

He flared his nostrils. "Power!" he snorted. "What you understand, *diplomats*, is how to manipulate power. You have no idea how to create it. Tonight, I will tell you. Or, rather—"

Again, he bowed to Irene. "I will simply repeat her words. Power comes from below, noble men of India. From that humble place, and no other. An empire, no matter how great—no matter how large its armies or well-equipped its arsenals—has no more power than the people upon whom it rests give to it. For it is they—*not you*—who must be willing to step forward and die, when the time comes. It is that low folk—*not you*—who have the courage to crawl upon a demon's haunch and sever its tendons."

He turned his back to them. Scornfully, over his shoulder: "While you, consulting your soothsayers and magicians, try to placate the beast in the hope it will dine elsewhere."

His hands were still clasped behind his back. For a moment, they tightened, and his back stiffened.

"Do not forget, noble men of India, that I am also Maratha. I know my people, and you do not. You scorn them, for their loose ways and their polluted nature. But you are blind men, for all your learning. As the Kushan says, lost in illusion."

He took a deep breath, and continued. "Today, Majarashtra trembles on the brink. Maratha sympathies are all with Shakuntala, and many of its best sons have come to her side. But most Maratha are still waiting. They will smuggle food, perhaps, or spy; or hide a refugee. But no more. Not yet. The heel of Malwa is upon their neck. The Vile One's executioners have draped their towns with the bodies of rebels."

Another deep breath; almost a great sigh. "It is not fear which holds them back, however, if you plunge into their hearts. It is simply doubt. They remember Andhra, true, and are loyal to that memory. But Andhra failed them once before. Who is to say it will not again?"

He turned his head to the northeast, peering intently at the walls of the chamber, as if he could see the Great Country beyond. "What they need," he said softly, "is a pledge. A pledge that the dynasty they have supported will never abandon them. And what pledge could be greater—than for the Empress of Andhra to make the dynasty their own? No Maratha has ever sat upon a throne. A year from now, the child of Majarashtra's greatest champion will *be* the dynasty."

His own face—soft, gentle, scholarly—was now as hard a mask as that of the Kushan.

"It will be done," he pronounced. "The empress, I am sure, will find her way to her duty. As will Rao." Then, spinning around, he confronted the envoys again. "But it will be done *properly.*"

His smile, when it came, was as savage as Kungas'. "The empress will wed Rao in Deogiri, not here. She will dance her wedding dance in the Vile One's face, in the midst of a siege. Hurling defiance before Malwa, for all to see. And *you*, noble men of India—you of Chola and Kerala and Tamraparni—will attend that wedding. And will provide the troops to escort her through the Vile One's lines."

The envoys erupted in protest. Outraged babble piled upon gasping indignation.

Holkar ignored them serenely. He turned back to his empress. Shakuntala was staring at him—blank-faced, to all appearances. But Holkar could sense her loosening self-control.

From the side of the chamber, Irene sent him an urgent thought. *End it, Dadaji. Give her space and time, before she breaks. The rest can be negotiated tomorrow.*

Apparently, telepathy worked. Or perhaps it was simply that two people thought alike.

"Marry Rao, Empress," decreed Dadaji Holkar. Then, in words so soft that only she could hear: "It is your simple duty, girl, and nothing else. Your dharma. Let your mind be at ease."

Those father's words removed all doubt. Shakuntala was fighting desperately, now, to maintain her imperial image. Beneath the egg-thin royal shell, the girl—no, the woman—was beginning to emerge.

Dadaji turned, but Kungas was already on his feet, clapping his hands.

"Enough! Enough!" the Kushan bellowed. "It is late. The empress is very weary. Clear the chamber!"

No envoy, outraged or no, wanted to argue with that voice. The rush for the door started at once. Within a minute, the chamber was empty except for Irene, Kungas, and Dadaji. And the empress, still sitting on her throne, but already beginning to curl. As soon as the heavy door closed, she was hugging her knees tightly to her chest.

Years of discipline and sorrow erupted like a volcano. Shakuntala wept, and wept, and wept; laughing all the while. Not the laughs of gaiety, these, or even happiness. They were the deep, belly-emptying, heaving laughs of a girl finally able—after all the years she had swallowed duty, never complaining once of its bitter taste—to wallow in the simple joys and desires of any woman.

Kungas stepped to her side and embraced her. A moment later, squirming like an eel, Shakuntala forced him onto the throne and herself onto his lap. There she remained, cradled in the arms of the man who had sheltered her—as he had again that day—from all the world's worst perils. Since the day her father died, and Malwa made her an orphan, Kungas had never failed her. The child found comfort in his lap, the girl in his arms, the empress in his mind. But the woman, finally out of her cage, only in his soul. Choked words of love and gratitude, whispered between sobs, she gave him in return. And even Kungas, as he stroked her hair, could not maintain the mask. His face, too, was now nothing but a father's.

Dadaji began to move toward the empress, ready to share in that embrace. But Irene restrained him with a hand.

"Not now, Dadaji. Not tonight."

Holkar looked back, startled. "She will want—need me—"

Irene shook her head, smiling. "Her wants and needs can wait, Dadaji. They are well-enough satisfied, and Kungas is there for her tonight. He will shelter her through her joy, just as he guarded her through despair. Tonight, Dadaji, you must give to yourself."

He frowned, puzzled. Irene began pulling him toward the door. "There is someone you must see. Someone you have been seeking, since the day she was lost. She should already be in your chambers."

By the time she opened the door, Dadaji understood. By the time she closed the door, he was already gone. She could only hear his footsteps, pounding down a corridor. It was odd, really. They sounded like the steps of a young man, running with the wind.

The lamps were lit, when Irene entered her own chambers. Her servants, knowing her odd tastes from months of experience, had prepared her reading chair. Tea was ready, steeping in a copper kettle. It was lukewarm, by now, but Irene preferred it so.

As always, her servants had taken several books from the chest and placed them on the table next to the lamp. The books had been chosen at random, by women who could not read the titles. Irene preferred it so. It was always pleasant, to see her choices for the night. Irene enjoyed surprises.

She sat and took a sip of tea. Then, for a few minutes, she weighed Plato against Homer, Horace against Lucretius.

None, in the end, fit her mood. Her eyes went to the door of her bedroom. A flush of passion warmed her. But that, too, she pushed aside. Kungas would not come, that night. Not for many nights still, she knew.

There was regret in that knowledge, and frustration, but neither anger nor anxiety. Irene knew her man, now. She did not understand him, not entirely. Perhaps she never would. But she did know him; and knew, as well, that she could accept what she did not understand. The same stubborn determination that had kept an illiterate to his books, week after week after week, would keep him away from her bed, for a time. Not until an empress was wed to a champion, and he gave away his girl to the man she had chosen, would Kungas be satisfied that he had done his duty.

So the man was. So he would always be. Irene, comparing him to other men she had known, was well content in her choice.

She arose and moved to the window. Felt the breeze, enjoyed the sound of surf. She was happy, she realized. As happy as she had ever been. That understanding brought with it an understanding of her mood. And frustration anew.

She laughed. "Oh, damn! Where are you, Antonina? I want to get blind, stinking drunk!"

Chapter 26

THE ARABIAN COAST
Autumn, 532 A.D.

"How could I have been so *stupid*?" demanded Antonina, glaring over the stern rail of her flagship. She rubbed her face angrily, as if she might squeeze out frustration by sheer force. "I should have known they'd follow us, the greedy bastards. And we were bound to be spotted, once we came within sight of land. There's only one obvious reason a fleet of Ethiopian warships would be cruising along the southern coast of Arabia—we're going to pillage the Malwa somewhere. Damned carrion-eaters!"

Wahsi, standing next to her, was matching her glare with one of his own. Even Ousanas, on her other side, had not a trace of humor in his face.

"None of us thought of it, Antonina." Ousanas twisted his head, as if searching the deck of the Ethiopian warship for a missing person. Which, in a way, he was.

"I wish Garmat were here," he grumbled. "If there's anyone who knows how a bandit thinks, it's him." Ousanas gestured at the Arab dhows which were trailing in the wake of Antonina's fleet. "He might figure out how to talk them into going away."

"I doubt it," said Antonina, wearily. She stopped rubbing her face and stared at the small armada. The dhows reminded her of buzzards following a pack of wolves. "The problem is, Ousanas, they're not really pirates. Just dirt-poor fishermen and bedouin, smelling the chance for loot."

"They'll ruin all our plans!" snarled Wahsi. "There'll be no way to keep this expedition a secret, with that gaggle of geese following us. Assuming they don't just sell the information to the Malwa outright."

Antonina was back to rubbing her face. With only one hand, this time, slowly stroking her jaw. Without realizing it, she was half-imitating her husband's favorite mannerism when he was deep in thought.

"Maybe not," she mused. "Maybe—"

She glanced up, gauging the time of day. "It'll be sundown, soon." She pointed to a small bay just off the port bow. "Can we shelter the fleet there, tonight?" she asked Wahsi.

The Dakuen commander examined the bay briefly. "Sure. But what for? You said you wanted us to stay out of sight of land once we got halfway down the Hadrawmat. We're there. We should be putting further out to sea. Make sure we're over the horizon during daylight, until we reach the Strait of Hormuz."

Antonina shrugged. "That was for the sake of secrecy. With them following us"—she pointed to the fleet of dhows—"there's no point. We have to keep *them* out of sight, too. No way to do that without talking to them. That's why I want to anchor in the bay. The dhows will follow, and I think I can set up a parley."

"A *parley*?" choked Wahsi.

Antonina smiled. "Why not?"

Wahsi was glaring at her, now. "Are you insane? Do you really think you can *reason* with those—those—"

Ousanas' laugh cut him off. The laugh, and the huge grin which followed. "Of course she doesn't think that, Wahsi!"

The tall hunter beamed down at the short Roman woman. "She's not going to appeal to their 'reason,' man. Just their greed."

"Well spoken," murmured Antonina. She smiled demurely at Wahsi. "I'm a genius, remember?"

It took hours, of course. Long into the night, negotiating with a small horde of Arab chieftains and subchieftains. Each little dhow had its own independent captain, and each of them had an opinion of his own. Four or five opinions, as often as not.

"We cannot board those great Malwa beasts," snarled one of the village-notables-turned-pirate-captain. He spoke slowly, and emphatically, so that Antonina could follow him. Her command of Arabic was only middling. "The one time we tried—" He threw up his hands. "Butchered! Butchered! Only two ships came back."

"Butchered, butchered," rose the murmur from the crowd. The pavilion which Antonina had ordered erected on the beach was packed with Arab chieftains. All of them joined in the protest, like a Greek chorus.

Antonina responded with a grin, worthy of a bandit.

"That was my husband's ship, I imagine."

The statement brought instant silence. Seventeen pairs of beady eyes were examining her, like ferrets studying a hen. Except this hen had just announced that she was mated to a roc.

Antonina nodded toward Ousanas. The hunter was squatting out of the way, in a corner of the tent. He had been there since the Arabs first entered. After a glance, none of them had paid him any attention. The Roman woman's slave, obviously; beneath their notice.

Ousanas grinned and rose lazily. The tall hunter reached behind him and drew forth his great stabbing spear. Then, hefting it easily, he began rattling off some quick sentences in fluent Arabic. Antonina could only follow some of it, but the gist was not hard to grasp.

Simple concepts, really. *Yeah, that's right, you mangy fucks. I was there too.* (Here, two of the chieftains hissed and tried to edge their way back into the crowd. No translation was needed—they remembered Ousanas, clearly enough.) *It was almost funny the way you pitiful amateur pirates scuttled over the sides—the few of you who still could, that is, after we gutted and beheaded and disemboweled and maimed and mangled and slaughtered—*

And so on, and so forth. Fortunately, Ousanas concluded on a happier note.

So let's not hear any crap about what can and can't be done. You couldn't do it, for sure. But nobody's asking you to. We'll do the serious work. All you've got to do is haul away the spoils.

The fishermen/bandits had taken no offense at Ousanas' grisly taunts. But they were deeply offended by his last statement.

Again, Antonina had no difficulty interpreting the gist of their hot-tempered remarks.

What? Do we look like fools? Why would you do all the danger-ous work and let us take the loot? Snort, snort. *Do you take us for idiots? Lies, lies.*

Antonina decided to interject the voice of sweet, feminine reason.

"Nobody said you'd get *all* the loot, you stupid oafs. Do we look like fools, ourselves?" She pointed imperiously at the fleet of Ethiopian warships moored in the bay. The ships were quite visible in the moonlight, since the tent flaps had been pulled aside to allow the cooling breeze to enter.

"*Those*, you ignorant dolts, are what are called *warships*." Snort, snort. "As different from your pitiful canoes as a lion from a sheep." Sneer, sneer. "You *do* know what a sheep is, don't you? You should. You've fucked them often enough, since you're too ugly to seduce a woman and too clumsy to catch one."

The Arabs laughed uproariously. Then, settling comfortably on their haunches, they readied for some serious bargaining. Clearly, the Roman was a woman they could do business with. A marvelous command of insult, even if her words were stumbling and prosaic. But allowances had to be made. Arabic was not her native tongue, after all.

Antonina clapped her hands, like a schoolteacher commanding the attention of stupid and unruly students. The Arabs grinned.

"The Axumite warships are quite capable of bringing down the Malwa vessels. The problem is—they're fighting ships. Not much room, with all the soldiers, to carry off loot." Her next words, Antonina spoke very slowly, so that imbeciles might be able to follow her simple reasoning.

"We . . . will . . . take . . . what . . . we . . . can. You . . . get . . . the . . . rest. Do . . . you . . . understand?"

Suspicion came back, in full force.

Why would you offer us charity? Are we fools? A trap! A trap! One of them began warning his fellows that the treacherous Romans and Ethiopians were trying to steal their dhows, but he was silenced by scowls. Insulting, that was, to their intelligence. The Arabs knew perfectly well the Ethiopians were about as inter-ested in patched-together dhows as they were in camel dung. Still—

Why?

"We are at war with Malwa," was Antonina's reply. "We will strike their convoy, but we are not seeking loot as such. After we are done, we will sail east, to storm their fortress at Barbaricum. Burn it to the ground. In war, you must move quickly. We will not have time to plunder the entire convoy and make sure it is completely destroyed. We simply cripple it, take what we can—quickly—and be on our way. You will finish them off."

She leaned back, gazing on them serenely. Like a schoolteacher, satisfied that she had—*finally*—hammered home the simple lesson. "With your help, we strike the hardest blow at Malwa. With our help, you get much plunder. That's the bargain."

It took two more hours. But it was not really difficult. Most of the time was spent haggling over the peripheral details.

The Arabs would stay out of sight of land, like the Ethiopians. They would obey the orders of the flotilla commander. (Here, Antonina pointed to Ousanas; the hunter began honing his spear.) They would not wander off if they spotted a lone merchant ship. And so on, and so forth.

Not difficult. Those men knew a good bargain when they saw one. Even if they weren't geniuses.

Chapter 27
THE TIGRIS
Autumn, 532 A.D.

"You seem unhappy, Sanga," commented Damodara. "Why is that?"

The Malwa lord had drawn up his horse next to the Rajput king, on a slope of the foothills. Damodara gestured at the floodplain below them. A large river was clearly visible, a few miles in the distance, wending its slow way to the sea. "I should think you'd be delighted at the sight of the Tigris. *Finally*."

Rana Sanga rubbed the scar on his left cheek. Then, realizing what he was doing, drew away the hand. He was a king of Rajputana. Battle scars should be ignored with dignity.

Still frowning, Sanga twisted in his saddle and stared back at the mountains. The peaks of the Zagros front range loomed behind them, like unhappy giants. They, too, seemed creased with worry.

"Something's wrong," he muttered. Sanga brought his gaze back, staring down at the slope before them. The rolling ground was sprinkled with Rajput cavalrymen. Each cavalry platoon was accompanied by a Pathan tracker, but the presence of the trackers was redundant. The huge trail left by the Roman army would have been obvious—quite literally—to a blind man. Ten thousand horses, and as many pack mules, tear up soil like a Titan's plow.

"Why do you say that?" asked Damodara. "Are you still concerned that our advance scouts haven't made contact with Belisarius?" The Malwa lord shrugged. "I don't find that odd. Once Belisarius made the decision to retreat into Mesopotamia, he had every reason to move as quickly as possible. We, on the other hand, have been moving cautiously and slowly. He might have been laying an ambush."

Damodara pointed to the floodplain, sweeping his hand in a wide arc. "There's no way to set an ambush *there*, Rana Sanga. That land is as flat as a board. You can see for miles."

The Malwa commander eased back in his saddle. "We don't know where he is, that is true. Ctesiphon. More likely Peroz-Shapur. Somewhere else, perhaps. But that he is in the floodplain cannot be doubted. You could hardly ask for a clearer trail."

Sanga's lips twisted. "No, you couldn't. And that's exactly what bothers me." Again, he twisted in the saddle, staring back at the mountains. "In my experience, Lord Damodara, Belisarius is most to be feared when he seems most obvious."

Damodara felt a moment's irritation at Sanga's stubborn gloom, but he squelched it. He had learned not to dismiss Sanga's presentiments. The Rajput king, for all his aristocratic trappings, had the combat instincts of a wild animal. The man was as fearless as a tiger, but without a tiger's assumption of supremacy.

Damodara almost laughed at the image which came to him. A mouse the size of a tiger, with a tiger's fangs and claws, wearing Sanga's frowning face. Furious worry; fretting courage.

Sanga was still staring at the mountains. "I cannot help remembering," he said slowly, "another trail left by Belisarius." He jerked his head slightly, motioning to the floodplain below. "Just as obvious as that one."

He settled himself firmly in the saddle. Then, turning to Damodara, he said: "I would like your permission to retrace our steps. I would need several of my Pathan trackers and my own clansmen. You can spare five hundred cavalrymen for two weeks."

For the first time, a little smile came to Sanga's face. "For what it's worth, I don't think you need fear an ambush." The smile vanished. "I have a feeling that Belisarius is hunting larger game than us."

Frowning with puzzlement, Damodara cocked his head southward. "The only bigger game is Great Lady Holi's army." The

Malwa lord, in Sanga's presence, did not bother with the fiction that Great Lady Holi was simply accompanying the Malwa Empire's main force in Mesopotamia. Sanga knew as well as Damodara that "Great Lady Holi" was a human shell. Within the exterior of an old woman rested the divine creature from the future named Link. Link, and Link alone, commanded that huge army.

"There are more than a hundred and fifty thousand men in that army, Rana Sanga," protested Damodara. "Even now that they have left the fortifications of Charax, and are marching north along the Euphrates, they can have nothing to fear from Belisarius. Military genius or not, the man's army is simply too small to threaten them."

Sanga shrugged. "I do not claim to have any answers, Lord Damodara. But I am almost certain that *that*"—he pointed to the trail left by the Roman army—"is a knife-cut on a horse's hoof."

Damodara did not understand the last remark, but he did not press Sanga for an explanation. Nor did he withhold his permission. Why should he? On the open plain, Belisarius posed no real threat to his army either. He could afford, for two weeks, to lose the services of Rana Sanga and five hundred Rajput cavalrymen.

"Very well," he said. Damodara paused, rubbing his lower back. "Probably just as well. The army is weary. While you're gone, we'll make camp by the Tigris. After six months of campaigning, the soldiers could use some rest."

Chapter 28
THE STRAIT OF HORMUZ
Autumn, 532 A.D.

Wahsi had been skeptical, at first. But, by the time the fleet reached the Strait of Hormuz, even he was satisfied that the Arabs would not give away the secret.

"Not until they discover they've been tricked, at least," he said to Antonina. The Dakuen commander pressed his shoulders against the mainmast, rubbing them back and forth to relieve an itch. The feline pleasure he seemed to take in the act matched poorly with the unhappy scowl on his face.

Wahsi had been gloomy since the start of the expedition. Like Maurice, Wahsi viewed "clever plans" with a jaundiced eye—especially plans which depended on timing and secrecy. Synchronization is a myth; stones babble; and nothing ever works the way it should. Those, for Wahsi as much as Maurice, were the Trinity.

"Doesn't really matter, I suppose," he grumbled sourly. "I'm sure half the crowd who watched us sail from Adulis were Malwa agents, anyway."

"Please, Wahsi!" protested Antonina. Smiling: "You exaggerate. Not more than a third of the crowd, at the most."

If anything, Wahsi's scowl deepened. Sighing, Antonina decided to retread old ground.

738

"Wahsi, they saw us sail *north*. Carrying the Theodoran Cohort back to Egypt."

"They won't believe—"

"Of course they won't!" snapped Antonina. "That's why I had my Syrians babble cheerfully in the markets that we had a secret plan to disembark at Aila and march into Mesopotamia. The Malwa will be looking for the truth beneath the illusion, and that should satisfy them. Especially when they see Ashot and the cataphracts—and the whole Cohort except for the gunners—unload from the ships and march inland." She giggled. "Koutina looked perfect, too, wearing that obscene replica of my obscene cuirass."

Wahsi was still scowling. Antonina sighed again.

Exasperated, now: "Do you really think Malwa spies in Aila are going to match numbers with Malwa spies at the other end of the Red Sea in order to make sure they have the same count of the ships in that huge fleet? Do you really think anyone saw twelve ships come about, after nightfall, and sail back? Do you really think Malwa agents can see in the dark? We were out of sight of land when we passed Adulis, and we stayed out of sight until we reached the Hadrawmat." She concluded firmly: "The only ones who spotted us were the Arab fishermen of the coast, and we've got them with us now."

Wahsi had no argument. But his expression was still mulish.

Ousanas, lounging against the rail nearby, had been following the conversation. When he spoke, his own face was more serious than normal.

"Still, Antonina, Wahsi raises a good point." Ousanas gestured with his head toward the flotilla of Arab dhows trailing the Ethiopian warships. "What will they do, once they discover they've been swindled?"

Antonina shrugged. "They'll be very unhappy with me, I imagine. So what? They're hardly likely to attack *us*. Those flea-bitten bandits have no more stomach for taking on Ethiopian warships than Malwa ones."

Wahsi stopped rubbing his shoulders against the mast and stood erect. Hands planted on hips, he twisted and glared at the Arab dhows.

"I'll tell you what they'll do, Antonina. They'll be as grouchy as so many camels. And they'll be looking to get something out of all those windless days pulling on the oars. It won't happen until we're almost at Charax. The greedy bastards will keep hoping, till the last minute, that the Malwa convoy you promised them is just over the horizon. But by the time they finally realize that there is no Malwa convoy and never was, they'll also understand what you're really planning to do. They'll land and go looking for the first Malwa, to sell the information."

He turned back to Antonina, cocking his head. "Am I not right?" he demanded.

She responded with a cheerful grin "Yes, yes. *And then what?*"

Her question produced a moment's silence. Suddenly, Ousanas whooped a laugh.

"Of course! *Then*—" He whooped again. "*Then*, a bunch of dirt-poor Arabs, for whom haggling is both art and sport, spend twenty-eight years bargaining with a snotty Malwa official over the price. *Before* they tell the Malwa anything. By which time—" He beamed on Antonina approvingly. "It's all over, one way or the other."

He transferred the beaming grin to Wahsi. "The woman's a genius. I said it before; I say it again."

Even Wahsi managed a smile. "She's tricky, I give you that." Grudgingly: "Maybe. Maybe it'll work."

Then, back to scowling: "I *hate* clever tactics." For a moment, his eyes caressed the sight of his stabbing spear, propped against the rail nearby. He sighed, scratching his scalp. "You know what I wish? I wish—"

There was a sudden cry from the lookout perched in the bow. A stream of words followed, by way of explication. An instant later, Wahsi was capering about, cackling with glee.

Ousanas leapt onto the port rail, holding himself by a stay. Once he verified the lookout's claim with his own eyes, his grin erupted.

"Thy wish is granted, commander of the Dakuen!" he shouted gaily.

Even if she had been standing on the rail, Antonina would have been too short to see. "Is it really—?"

"Indeed so! Take heart, Antonina. Your name will not be cursed, in villages of the Hadrawmat, for a trickster and a cheat." Ousanas pointed dramatically at the northern horizon. "The Malwa convoy has arrived—just as you promised!"

Chapter 29

It was blind luck, of course. The westbound monsoon season, which would bring hordes of ships bearing supplies to the Malwa in Charax, would not begin for several weeks. At this time of the year, with the eastbound monsoon breathing its last, Antonina had not expected to encounter any ships sailing back to India.

It was even bad luck, in some ways. On balance, Antonina would have preferred to encounter no Malwa ships at all on her way into Charax. There was always the danger that her own flotilla would be too badly mauled in a sea battle to carry out her task. Had the Arab dhows not attached themselves to her fleet, she would have been tempted to let the Malwa convoy pass unmolested.

But when she muttered her misgivings to Wahsi, the Dakuen commander shook his head.

"That'd be pointless, Antonina. Those Malwa spotted us as soon as we spotted them. Sooner, probably, if they're keeping lookouts on those huge masts. They would have sent a warning back to Charax, on one of the galleys. We'd have had to attack them in any event."

The Malwa convoy was completely in sight, now. The convoy had been sailing from west to east, before the wind. The Axumite fleet, approaching from the south with the wind on the beam, was intercepting them at a ninety-degree angle.

Wahsi studied the enemy ships. The hulls of the great cargo vessels had emerged over the horizon, and they could see the sails of the two smaller galleys which were serving the convoy as an escort. The galleys were already furling their sails and unlimbering their oars, in preparation for battle.

"Arrogant shits," he snarled. "*Two* galleys? For a convoy that size?" His Axumite *amour propre* was deeply offended.

Ousanas chuckled. "They probably never expected to face Ethiopian warships, Wahsi. Not this year, at least." He hooked a thumb over his shoulder, pointing to the Arab ships. The dhows were already falling back and spreading out. The Arabs intended to stay well clear of the fighting, but be ready to swoop in for the spoils. "And two galleys are more than enough, to protect against that rabble. We beat off a fleet just as big with a single unguarded cargo vessel."

He studied the five cargo ships. "Big brutes, aren't they?"

"So what?" said Wahsi, shrugging. "We're not planning to board those wooden cliffs." He cast approving eyes on the Roman gunners readying their guns. "We'll just pound them into splinters, and let the Arabs do the rest."

Privately, Antonina thought Wahsi was being overly sanguine. Like most people who had little experience with cannons, Wahsi tended to have an inflated idea of their effectiveness. But she said nothing. This was no time for doubts. Not less than two hours before a pitched battle at sea.

She brought her own eyes to bear on the men and women of the Theodoran Cohort who were struggling to ready the cannons. But, unlike Wahsi's unalloyed admiration, hers was a knowledgeable gaze.

Too few. That was her main concern. The Ethiopian war galleys, unlike the ship which John of Rhodes had constructed a year earlier, were not designed for cannons. In the time allowed, before they left Adulis, her Syrian gunners had done what they could. But there was no way to overcome the basic design problem of the ships themselves.

Like almost all warships of the time, the Axumite craft were built for speed and maneuver. Only the prows were well braced. The rest of the ships were lightly built. And even the prows, on Axumite warships, were relatively flimsy. Ethiopian naval tactics were based on boarding. Their ships had no rams.

To make matters worse, the ships were built using the method which was common to the Mediterranean and the Erythrean Seas.

Instead of starting with a sturdy skeleton of keel and ribs—that method, in Antonina's day, was only used by north Europeans—the Ethiopian ships were built of planks pegged or sewn together, with only a modicum of internal bracing added at the very end. The ships were not much more than wooden shells, really. The recoil from broadsides fired by five-inch guns would start breaking up the hulls after a few volleys.

Antonina's gunners had compromised by simply bracing the hulls directly amidships. Each Axumite craft had four guns, two on a side. Fearsome weapons, true, especially within a hundred yards. But two guns do not a broadside make.

For a moment, Antonina felt a deep regret that she had not brought John's gunship with her. At the moment, she would trade half the Ethiopian flotilla for the *Theodora*. But—

She made a mental shrug. Her decision had been the right one. The problem had not been technical. It would have been possible, though very difficult, to portage the *Theodora* from the Nile to the Red Sea. But there would have been no way to do it in secret, not with the huge workforce the job would have required. The Malwa would have been alerted to her plans. The only reason to haul the *Theodora* into the Red Sea would be to go after Malwa ships in the Persian Gulf. The Malwa probably wouldn't have deduced her ultimate goal—the idea of attacking Charax by sea was insane; it was the most fortified harbor in the world. But they would have surely beefed up the patrols in the Gulf, which would be enough to stymie her purpose.

A cry from the lookout cut through her half-reverie. After a few seconds, Antonina saw the cause. The two Malwa galleys were emerging from the enemy convoy, bearing directly on the Ethiopians.

"They're brave bastards," she said, half-admiringly.

Wahsi glanced at her, then sneered. "Brave? No, Antonina. They're just swaggering bullies, who've never faced Axumites at sea."

The Dakuen commander's gaze returned to the cannons. For just an instant, admiration was replaced by something which was almost resentment. Antonina choked down a laugh. Wahsi, she thought, was half-tempted to leave the cannons unused—just so he could prove to the Malwa how hopelessly outclassed they were.

But Wahsi was a veteran. Within seconds, he had apparently repressed the childish impulse. He turned to Ousanas and said: "I recommend that we simply blow them apart on our way into the convoy. But the decision is yours, *aqabe tsentsen*."

The term "aqabe tsentsen" meant "keeper of the fly-whisks." To Antonina's Roman sensibilities, it was a peculiar title for a man who was second only to the negusa nagast in authority. But the fly-whisk, along with the spear, was the traditional emblem of Axumite royalty. Three days after his marriage, the King of Kings had bestowed the title on Ousanas. Other than the forces in Ethiopia itself, and the troops which Garmat commanded as the new viceroy of Arabia, Ousanas was now Axum's top military officer as well as the king's chief adviser.

Ousanas grinned. "Please, Wahsi! I am still the uncouth barbarian hunter of old. I know as much about sea battles as a hippopotamus knows of poetry." He made a grand, sweeping gesture. "I leave everything in your capable hands."

Wahsi grunted. "All that philosophy has not been wasted, after all." A moment later, he was shouting orders at his crew.

The flagship continued on its northerly course, still under sail. The other Axumite warships followed the lead. Antonina was surprised. She had expected Wahsi to order the sails reefed, and to unlimber the oars. Like all such craft of the time, Ethiopian warships usually went into battle with oars rather than sails.

At first, she assumed that Wahsi had given the order because he was leery of his ships' rowing capacity. One of the problems with fitting the ships with cannons was that a large section of the oarbanks was taken out of action. But then, as she saw the grim satisfaction on Wahsi's face, she had to choke down a laugh.

Wahsi was too much of a veteran to indulge himself in the childish fancy of fighting without cannons. But she thought he had found a substitute. He would defeat his enemy without even bothering to use his oars—much as a boy boasts that he can whip another with one hand tied behind his back.

As the galleys neared, Antonina's amusement faded. Apprehension came in its place. As superior as Ethiopian ships were, compared to Malwa vessels, there was still no way they could outmaneuver galleys while under sail.

She gave Ousanas a look of appeal. He simply grinned. So, reluctantly, she opened her mouth, preparing to urge caution on the headstrong Dakuen commander.

Whatever words she would have spoken were drowned by Wahsi's sudden bellow. *"Fall off the wind!"*

Within moments, the ship turned to starboard and was running with the wind. Behind, one ship following the other, the fleet copied the maneuver.

Antonina held her breath. They were now driving across the oncoming Malwa galleys at what seemed a blinding speed. Collision was almost upon them—and the Malwa vessels, unlike their own, had cruel rams splitting the waves.

Only at the last instant did she realize the truth. The Malwa, oared, might be more maneuverable. But they were no faster, not with the Ethiopians sailing before the wind. The Axum warships would cross their enemies' bows at point-blank range.

The Syrian gunners were excellent. And, if Antonina had not been able to bring the *Theodora*, she *had* been able to bring its gunnery officer. The best gunnery officer in the world.

Eusebius' high-pitched screech rang out. The two five-inch guns on the port side roared, heeling the ship.

When the smoke cleared—

Two five-inch marble balls, fired at thirty-yards range, had split the galley's bow wide open. Both rounds must have struck within inches of each other, right on the ship's prow.

Once shattered, the heavy bracing which secured the ram acted like so many pile drivers hammering the thin planks of the hull. The Malwa ship opened up like a hideous flower, spilling men and blood into the sea.

The gruesome sight fell behind. The second Malwa galley came up, also to port. Not enough time had elapsed for the gunners to have reloaded, so Wahsi simply sailed on. A few seconds later, Antonina heard the guns of the next ship. Then, the third; and then, the fourth.

She did not turn her head to watch the results. There was no need. Not when she had Ousanas' and Wahsi's cheerful faces to serve as her mirror.

"More food for the fish," Wahsi pronounced. He turned his eyes back to the front. Beyond the bow, he could see the five great cargo ships, less than a mile away.

"Soon, now." He pointed. "Look. They've already set up their rockets."

As if his pointing finger had been a signal, a volley of rockets soared away from one of the Malwa vessels. Of the six missiles, five skittered half-aimlessly before they plunged into the sea. But one of the rockets held a straight course until it, too, plowed harmlessly into a wave two hundred yards distant.

Antonina was not relieved by the distance of the miss. This first volley had been a mistake, undoubtedly ordered by a nervous and rattled captain. The range was still too great for rockets to have any real hope of success. But the steadiness with which that one rocket had held its course could only mean one thing.

They've fitted them with real venturi. Some of the rockets, anyway. Just as Belisarius predicted.

She took a breath. "I think—"

Wahsi was already shouting the orders. A moment later, the Ethiopian crew was swarming over the ship, erecting the new rocket shields. Each Axumite ship was carrying almost two hundred soldiers. Most of those men, under normal conditions, would have been busy at the oars. But with the ships under sail, they were free for other work. The shields were erected within minutes.

As she watched, Antonina gave herself a silent reproof. Wahsi's determination to fight under sail, she now realized, had not been the decision of a truculent male eager to show his mettle. The commander had foreseen the necessity to erect the shields quickly.

She glanced at Ousanas. The aqabe tsentsen, once again, was grinning at her. She grinned back, accepting the jeer in good humor.

I, too, when it comes to this, am nothing but an amateur. Let the professionals handle it.

She turned her eyes to the shields. Her own professional pride surfaced. She might not know anything about ships, but she *did* know gunpowder warfare. Better than anyone in the world, she thought. John of Rhodes might have a superior grasp of the theory, but not the practice.

Except my husband. After all these months fighting the Rajputs in Persia, I'm sure he's better than I am.

The thought combined pride and worry. Antonina had no idea if Belisarius was still alive. By now, he should have gotten the message she had sent him, telling Belisarius when she would leave Adulis for their rendezvous at Charax. That message would have been taken by fast horses to the nearest semaphore station, at Aila.

From there, flashing up and down the line of semaphore stations which she and Belisarius had constructed the year before, the message would have reached Ctesiphon within a day. Persian couriers would carry it to Belisarius' army in the nearby Zagros, again using the fastest horses available.

But there had been no way for a message to be returned. Belisarius had told Antonina, once, of the almost-magical communication devices of future centuries. "Radio," one was called. Such devices were far beyond the technological capability of her time—and would be, even with Aide to guide them, for decades to come.

She sighed unhappily. To shake off her anxiety concerning Belisarius, she resumed her study of the shields.

Antonina had designed the shields herself, before she left Constantinople the year before. Not, of course, without advice from Belisarius—and plenty of help, when the time came to translate theory into practice, from the Syrians of her Theodoran Cohort. The gunners and their wives, being borderers born and bred, were excellent blacksmiths, carpenters and tanners. And whatever they couldn't handle had been done by the Ethiopian artisans and craftsmen whom King Eon had put at her disposal in Adulis.

Each Axumite ship had been fitted with iron hoops on the rails near the bow. A heavy wooden ridgepole was affixed to the mainmast. The ridgepole ran parallel to the ship's hull, right down the center, its end stabilized in the stem.

As soon as Wahsi gave the order, the Syrian gunners and the Ethiopian sailors began erecting the shield. While Ethiopians furled the sails, the gunners set sturdy wooden braces in the iron hoops along the rails. Each hoop had a bar welded across the bottom to hold the brace butts. The top end of each brace had a hole drilled through it. As the gunners lowered the braces toward the ridgepole, the Ethiopian sailors began threading rope through the holes. Within minutes, the tops of the braces were bound tightly to the mast-and-ridgepole structure. The end result was a sloping A-frame which covered the bow of the ship.

Other sailors were already tossing ropes over the ridgepole and braces. Quickly, with the speed of experienced seamen, the ropes were drawn tight. The A-frame was now lashed down. The ropes provided further strength, along with a filled-in framework.

The wives of the gunners, meanwhile, had finished hauling the special armor out of the hold. The spans of boiled leather, already precut and punched with holes, were stitched onto the pole-and-rope framework with thinner cord. The sailors began dousing the leather armor with buckets of seawater.

Antonina moved to the bow along with Ousanas and Wahsi, admiring the handiwork. Wahsi did not share her enthusiasm. "Ugly," he groused. Through a viewing slit in the shield, the commander glared down at the bow-waves, which were noticeably smaller. "Slow. Clumsy."

"Ignore him, Antonina," said Ousanas serenely. The aqabe tsentsen pointed to the nearest Malwa vessel. The huge cargo ship was less than four hundred yards away. Kshatriyas could be seen scurrying about their rocket troughs. "Soon enough, he will be glad to have that shield."

Seconds later, the Malwa vessel was shrouded in rocket smoke. Six missiles came streaking across the water.

Five missed, most of them widely. But, again, the sixth missile sped straight and true. Antonina held her breath. She was about to discover if her inventor's pride was warranted.

It was. The rocket struck the sloping side of the shield and glanced off. The shield boomed like a giant kettledrum. The missile soared into the sky, exploding fifty yards overhead.

She blew out her breath, as a second relief came to reinforce the first.

No impact fuses, thank God. Belisarius didn't think they'd have them yet. Not for cargo vessels, anyway.

Theoretically, she knew, the shield should protect the ship even from rockets armed with impact fuses. Partially, at least. If the Malwa fuses were anything like the Roman ones, they were crude devices. A glancing impact might very well not be enough to trigger them—and, even if it did, most of the force would be spilled across the shield instead of punching through. The design would have been well-nigh useless, of course, against heavy cannon balls. But the Malwa had not yet equipped their ships with cannons. Not these ships, anyway.

"Good," grunted Wahsi. "It works." Grudgingly: "I didn't really think it would."

And why not? thought Antonina merrily. *It worked at Hampton Roads, didn't it?*

But she kept the thought to herself. Both Wahsi and Ousanas knew of Aide. Ousanas, in fact, was one of the few people in the world who had entered Aide's world of future vision. But they were not really comfortable with the knowledge. At the moment, in the midst of battle, they needed surety and solid ground. It was not the best time to launch into a discussion of visions.

Besides, I've got a reputation as a genius to maintain. Won't help that any, if I admit I got my design from a future ship called the Merrimac.

Another volley erupted from the Malwa ship. Then, seconds later, a flight of missiles soared off the deck of another enemy vessel.

Wahsi ignored the oncoming rockets. He stooped, sticking his head into the entrance of the shield, and bellowed orders. The orders were passed down to the steersman at the rear.

The Ethiopian ship began pulling toward the nearest enemy. Progress was slow, of course. The shield was not especially heavy, but it caught the wind like a giant drag. The oarsmen strained, grunting with every sweep of the oars, forcing the craft forward.

Fortunately, neither the seas nor the wind were heavy. Antonina had been told they wouldn't be, as a rule, this time of year. She was relieved to find the information accurate.

Slow progress is still progress. The Malwa convoy—all merchantmen, now that their escorts had been destroyed—were simply seeking to escape the Ethiopians. But the Malwa ships paid a price for their huge and ungainly design. They, too, crept along like snails.

Ousanas verbalized her own assessment. "We'll overtake them," he pronounced. "Soon, I think."

Chapter 30

"Soon" proved to be half an hour.

Half an hour after that, "soon" became "never."

Antonina, once again, discovered the First Law of Battle. Nothing ever works the way it should.

"Pull out, Wahsi!" she shouted, trying to make herself heard over the roar of the cannons and the shrieks of the rockets. "We can't sink them!"

Stubbornly, the Axumite commander shook his head. The headshake turned into a duck, as another flight of rockets soared overhead. But there was no damage. The Syrian gunners, after a few minutes of battle, had switched to cannister. The solid shot had proven ineffective, but the cannister kept the Malwa kshatriyas from the rail. They were not able to lower their rocket troughs far enough to bring the missiles to bear on the Ethiopian ships alongside.

"There's no point!" she shouted. "We could punch holes in that damned thing for a week, and it wouldn't make a difference. We can't sink it!"

Wahsi ignored her. He was leaning out of the shield, studying the rest of the battle. The huge Malwa cargo ships were like buffaloes being torn at by a dozen lean wolves. The roar of cannon fire, mingled with the shriek of rocketry, rippled over the waves. Each Axumite ship was wreathed in gunsmoke; every Malwa ship had holes punched in its hull—and none of them, plain as day, was in any danger of sinking. The battle was a pure and simple stalemate.

While she waited for Wahsi to make a decision, Antonina snarled her own frustration at the Malwa ship looming above her, not twenty yards off.

It was an incredible sight, in its way. The hull of the Malwa ship looked like a sieve. At least a dozen five-inch marble cannonballs had punched holes through the thin planks. But—

I was afraid this might happen. Belisarius warned me that wooden ships, in the days of sail, were almost never sunk by cannon fire. The Spanish Armada was wrecked by a storm, not English guns. The only ship at the battle of Trafalgar actually destroyed by gunfire was the Achille, *after fire spread to its magazines. The rest were captured by boarders or lost during the storm which followed. Still, I had hoped—those ships, after all, were heavily built northern European craft. Not these cockleshells. But it doesn't matter. Wood doesn't sink. It's as simple as that.*

Another volley of unaimed rockets shrieked overhead. The Malwa were simply venting their own frustration. The missiles plunged into the sea hundreds of yards past the two Axumite vessels drawn alongside.

Wahsi ducked back under the shield. The leather was ragged now, where a few Malwa rockets had struck early in the battle. But that, at least, had worked as Antonina hoped. Even the one rocket which exploded when it hit the shield had spent most of its fury harmlessly. Only five rowers had been injured, none seriously.

"We'll do it the old-fashioned way!" shouted Wahsi. He seized his spear and began bellowing new orders. The rowers drove the ship against the Malwa vessel. Grappling hooks were being dug out, and scaling equipment readied.

Antonina started to protest. This battle with the convoy had turned into an absurd distraction. They could break off now and still make it into Charax long before the convoy could bring the alarm. The last thing she wanted was to see the Ethiopian forces suffer heavy casualties in a boarding operation.

But the protest died on her lips. One look at Wahsi's face was enough. The Dakuen commander was in pure battle fury. He would have that convoy, by God—no matter what.

She glanced at Ousanas. The aqabe tsentsen shrugged.

The cannons, after firing a last volley of cannister to clear the rail, were being hastily drawn aside. With Wahsi in the lead, dozens of Axumite soldiers tossed their grappling hooks and began swarming up the side of the Malwa ship. Their battle cry—*Ta'akha Maryam! Ta'akha Maryam!*—rang with pure bloodlust.

"Forget it, Antonina," said Ousanas. "If Ezana were here—"

Ousanas glanced at the other Malwa ships. Already he could see other Ethiopian soldiers starting their own boarding operations. And, faintly, he could hear the same merciless words: *Ta'akha Maryam! Ta'akha Maryam!*

He turned back to Antonina. "Ezana was always the more cool-headed of the two. But I'm not sure even he would be able to restrain the sarwen. Not this far into the battle. Axum has the most ferocious navy in the Erythrean Sea. They didn't get that way by being timid."

Antonina sighed, and leaned against one of the poles bracing the shield. Her face was covered with sweat and the streaks left by gunsmoke. The interior of the shielded bow, under the heat of a mid-autumn afternoon, was a sweltering pit.

"Let's just hope, then," she muttered.

"Relax." Ousanas studied her with his intelligent eyes. "You're thinking about that other boarding operation, aren't you? Where we—Belisarius and his companions—slaughtered the Arab pirates who tried to storm our ship."

She nodded wearily. Ousanas gave her a reassuring little pat on the shoulder. "Relax, I say."

He paused for a moment, listening to the sounds of combat coming from the deck above. Then, very calmly: "Four things are different, here. First, the Arabs were facing a large force of Ye-tai escorting Lord Venandakatra. These cargo ships only have a handful of the murderous bastards. Second, the Arabs didn't have cannister to clear their way to the deck. Half of them died before they made it over the rail. Third, they were pirates, not Axumite marines. Finally—"

His great grin erupted. In the gloom of the shield's interior, it seemed to Antonina like a beacon. "And finally—fool woman!—*these* sorry Malwa bastards don't have your husband to save their hides."

"Or me," he added modestly, caressing the shaft of his spear. "*Especially* me, now that I think about it." He seized the great spear and began prancing about, feigning lunges and thrusts. "I was terrible! A fury! A demon from below!"

Antonina managed her own grin. Despite herself, Ousanas' antics were cheering her up. It was impossible to wallow in misery for very long around Ousanas.

There was a sudden surge in the battle clangor. Hurriedly, Antonina stuck her head out of the shield and peered up at the rail.

A moment later, a small flood of Malwa sailors and kshatriyas began diving overboard. Their own shouts of fear were pursued by the sounds of murder. *Ta'akha Maryam! Ta'akha Maryam!* One of the leaping Malwa, misjudging in his terror, landed on the rail of her ship. His body seemed to snap in half, not ten feet from her. The sound of the impact combined breakage and rupture—like sticks in a bag of offal, slammed against stone.

Antonina thought his back was broken. It was a moot point. Even before her bodyguards, Matthew and Leo, unlimbered their weapons, Ousanas pushed past her and stabbed the fallen sailor with his spear. The great leaf blade opened his chest and drove him over the side.

She craned her head up. Another—a Ye-tai warrior—had his back pressed to the rail, fighting an unseen opponent. Not two seconds after she spotted him, she saw a spear drive through his chest. The bloodied blade was sticking four inches out of his back.

The Ye-tai was driven half over the rail by the power of the blow. He toppled over, falling into the sea, the spear still sticking into his body.

Wahsi appeared at the rail, grabbing for the haft of the spear. Too late.

The Dakuen commander's face was contorted with rage. He shook his fist at the plunging body of the Ye-tai.

"That was my best spear!" he roared. "You stinking—"

Then, everything seemed to happen at once—and yet, to Antonina, as slowly as anything she had ever seen.

Wahsi's face was suddenly a mask of—not shock, so much as simple surprise. Then, he was flying through the air, soaring over the waves as if he were a bird. The Malwa rocket which had struck him right in the spine was carrying him out to sea like a gull. For a moment, his arms even seemed to be flapping. But Antonina, seeing the burning fury pouring out of his back, knew that the man was already dead.

The burning gunpowder reached the warhead. The rocket exploded thirty yards from the ship and half as many above the waves. The largest piece of Wahsi which struck the water was his right leg. The rest of the Dakuen commander was simply a cloud of blood and shreds of flesh and bone.

"God in Heaven," she whispered. She turned a shocked face to Ousanas.

The aqabe tsentsen clenched his teeth. Then, without a word, he took his spear and raced toward the grappling ropes amidships. Within seconds, Antonina saw him swarming onto the ship.

At first, she assumed that Ousanas was just venting his own fury and battle lust. But then, hearing his bellowing roars, she realized that he was doing the opposite. The aqabe tsentsen was taking command, and dragging the sarwen away from their pointless revenge.

Literally dragging, in some cases. She saw Ousanas personally pitch three Ethiopian marines onto the rail. He had to rap one of them on the skull with the haft of his spear before the man started climbing down the ropes.

Blood was beginning to drip over the sides of the Malwa ship above her. Antonina didn't want to think about the carnage up there. At the best of times, Axumite sarwen were murderous in battle. Now, with their regimental commander slain, they were fury incarnate.

"What a waste," she whispered. "What a pointless, stupid waste."

She stared out at the patch of ocean where Wahsi had disappeared—what was left of him. There would be no point, she knew, in searching for the pieces of his body. The fish would get them long before they could be retrieved.

She wiped her face, smearing sweat and smoke and more than a few tears.

"What a waste," she whispered again. "What a stupid, stupid, stupid waste."

It took Ousanas fifteen minutes to get the Ethiopian soldiers off the Malwa vessel. By then, any Malwa was long dead except for the few who might have found a hiding place in the hold below. Ousanas had to bully a dozen sarwen from wasting time searching the cargo.

At his order, the Ethiopian ships cast off and began rowing toward the other ships being boarded. Soon enough, the aqabe tsentsen was repeating his actions, bringing the battle to a halt.

That did not prove difficult. All five Malwa vessels had been stormed. As Ousanas had predicted, Malwa cargo ships were simply no match for Axumite marines.

Wisely, Ousanas said nothing of Wahsi's death until the Ethiopian fleet had resumed its course up the Persian Gulf. The five Malwa vessels were left behind, wallowing in the waves. Already, the Arab dhows were closing in.

When the news was passed, from one ship to another, Ousanas had to reestablish his authority anew. He was forced to personally visit one of the ships crewed by men of the Dakuen sarwe, to beat down what almost amounted to a mutiny.

"Stupid fools," he snarled to Antonina, after clambering back aboard the flagship. "They were bound and determined to go back and see that not a single Malwa was left alive."

She looked at the cluster of Malwa ships, now several miles astern. The Arab dhows were tied alongside, like lampreys.

She shook her head. "That's—"

"Stupid!" roared Ousanas. The aqabe tsentsen gestured angrily at the ships being plundered. "What do they think the Arabs won't do, that they would?" He glared astern. "Any Malwa cowering in a hold is having his throat slit, even as we speak."

Antonina grimaced. "Maybe not. They might capture them, in order—"

"Better yet!" bellowed Ousanas. "Better yet! We can lullaby ourselves to sleep, thinking of Malwa slaves hauling water for bedouin women."

He shook his head. "But they won't be so lucky, believe me. The ships were India-bound, Antonina. Loaded with booty from Persia. The sarwen grabbed some, but most of it was left behind. Those Arabs are now the richest men in the Hadrawmat. What do they want with some mangy Malwa slaves? They can buy better ones back home." He made a savage, slitting gesture across his throat. "Fish food, that's all."

Ousanas leaned on the rail, gripping the wood in his powerful hands. The anger faded from his eyes, replaced by sorrow.

"What a waste," he murmured. "What a stupid waste. All for a stinking convoy that was never anything more than an accidental diversion."

He shook his head sadly. "We cannot even do the rites. Nothing left."

Antonina placed her hand on Ousanas' shoulder and shook it firmly.

"That is also stupid. Of course we can do the rites. We are not pagans, Ousanas." What had become her husband's most treasured saying came to her mind. "Only the soul matters, in the end. We can pray for Wahsi's soul—and those of the other men who died."

Ousanas sighed, lowering his head. Then he snorted.

"*What* other men?" For a moment, his grin almost appeared. "Wahsi was the only casualty. The only fatality, at least."

Antonina's jaw sagged. Seeing the expression, Ousanas did manage a wan and feeble grin.

"I told you, woman." He tossed his head, sneering at the Malwa ships fading into the distance. "Sheep, in the hands of Ethiopian marines. Nothing but sheep. The only wounds were caused by Yetai, and even they could do no better. There are no soldiers in the world as good as Axumite sarwen, Antonina, in the close quarters of a boarding operation."

He rubbed his face. The gesture was sad, not weary. "Even the rocket which killed Wahsi was fired by accident. A gaggle of kshatriyas were trying to turn it around to face their attackers. The fuse was lit—one of them killed by a spear—he stumbled, fell, knocked the rocket trough askew—"

Ousanas waved his hand. "Stupid," he muttered. "Just one of those stupid, pointless deaths which happen in a battle. That's all it was."

Wahsi's death was far more than that, when the funeral ceremony was held the next day. By then, after hundreds of Ethiopian soldiers had whispered through the night, the sarawit had come to their own conclusions.

There was a part of Antonina, as she listened to the lays and chants—there were bards among the soldiers; amateurs, but good at their business—which thought the whole thing absurd. But that was only a part of the woman's soul, and a small one at that.

The soul which stood at her center did not begrudge the soldiers their myth. By the time the expedition returned to Ethiopia, she knew, Wahsi would have entered Africa's own warrior legends. His death, leading a great sea battle, would become a thing of glory.

She did not begrudge the sarwen those legends. She would not have begrudged them, even if she weren't the leader of an expedition to rescue her husband from destruction.

But, since she was, she *certainly* didn't intend to start spouting nit-picking, picayune, petty little truths. Leave that for antiquarians and historians of the future.

Ousanas spoke her thoughts aloud.

"Pity the poor Malwa at Charax," he said cheerfully, as he and Antonina listened to the chants. "That stupid death has turned a shrewd maneuver against enemy logistics into a crusade. They would storm the gates of Hell, now."

Chapter 31
CHARAX
Autumn, 532 A.D.

When the captain of the unit guarding Charax's northeastern gate was finally able to discern the exact identity of the oncoming troops, he was not a happy man.

"Shit," he cursed softly. "Kushans."

The face of his lieutenant, standing three feet away, mirrored the captain's own alarm. "Are you sure?"

The captain pulled his eye away from the telescope mounted on the ramparts and gave his lieutenant an irritated look. "See for yourself, if you don't believe me," he snarled, stepping away from the telescope.

The lieutenant made no move to take his place. The question had not been asked seriously. It was impossible to mistake Kushans for anyone else, once they got close enough for the telescope to pick out details. If for no other reason, no one in Persia beyond Kushans bound up their hair in topknots.

The captain marched over to the inner wall of the battlement and leaned over. A dozen of his soldiers were standing on the ground below, their heads craned up, waiting to hear the news.

"Kushans!" he shouted. The soldiers grimaced.

"Summon the commander of the watch!" bellowed the captain. Then, more loudly still: "And hide the women!" The latter command was unneeded. The soldiers were already scurrying about,

rounding up the slave women whom the guard battalion had dra-
gooned into their service.

Not that those women needed any chivvying. Except for the
cosmopolitan sprinkling typical of a great port, the women were
Persian and Arab. Some had been captured during the sack of
Charax when the Malwa first took the port. Others had been seized
by one or another of the raiding columns which the Malwa had
sent ravaging Mesopotamia over the past year and a half. They
detested their captors, true. But they had even less desire to be
seized by soldiers arriving at Charax after weeks on campaign. The
garrison troops were foul and brutal, but at least they were no
longer rampant.

Let the poor creatures in the military brothels handle these
new arrivals. The women in the guard compound were even more
determined than their masters to stay out of sight.

Satisfied that the necessary immediate measures were being
taken, the guard captain slouched back to his post. In his absence,
the lieutenant had manned the telescope.

"Good news," announced the lieutenant, his eye still at the telescope. "Most of that lot are prisoners. Must be ten thousand of
them."

The captain grunted with satisfaction. That *was* good news.
Excellent news, actually, and on two counts.

First, it meant that the Malwa had scored a big victory somewhere. The captain was relieved. Ever since the disaster at the
Nehar Malka, followed by a year of frustration, the commanders of
the Malwa army had been like so many half-lamed tigers, nursing
wounded paws and broken teeth, and venting their anger on subordinates. A victory, thought the captain, would help to ease the
sullen atmosphere.

Secondly, and more important for the immediate future, it
meant that the Kushans would be kept busy. The slave laborers
which the Malwa Empire's early victories in Mesopotamia netted
had long since been worked to death, except for the women kept
for the army's pleasure. Until the new prisoners were securely
fitted into slave-labor battalions and set to work expanding the
harbor, the Kushans would be needed to guard them. That meant
they wouldn't have idle time on their hands, to go looking for the
better women and wine which the garritroopers would have

stashed away. They would have to be satisfied with the hags in the brothels, and the vinegar which passed for wine in the barracks.

He could see that an advance party of Kushans was cantering toward the gate. The main body of Kushans and their captives was not more than two hundred yards away.

The captain turned, looking for the commander of the watch. The sot should have arrived by now, to order the opening of the gates. In turning, the captain caught a glimpse of the soldiers standing by a siege gun positioned on the great firing platform appended to the wall. As always, the gun was pointed toward the desert. By now, the gun crew would have loaded the weapon with cannister. One of the soldiers was removing the firing rod from the furnace. The bent tip of the rod was glowing red, ready to be inserted into the touchhole.

Angrily, the captain shouted at him. His words were not orders. They were not even particularly coherent. Just a string of profanities. Hastily, the soldier quenched the rod in a nearby bucket.

"Fucking idiots," snarled the captain. Next to him, the lieutenant shook his head. "Just what we need," he groused. "Some stupid jackass to fire a load of cannister into a couple of thousand Kushans."

The lieutenant made for the ladder and began scurrying down. "I'll get over there," he said. "Make sure there aren't any other imbeciles roaming around loose." His head disappeared below the wall. "Kushans!" came his voice.

Again, the captain looked for the watch commander. Seeing the soldier he had sent on the search standing below—alone—he cursed under his breath. The soldier looked up, spread his hands, shrugged.

Not even sundown, and the bastard's already drunk.

The captain sighed. He hated taking responsibility for anything, much less opening the city's gate. But—

He eyed the oncoming troops. *Kushans. Hot, tired, thirsty, horny*—and *they just won a victory. I don't get that gate open, they'll come over the walls and*—

The thought was too gruesome to contemplate further. The captain bellowed new commands. By the time the advance party of Kushans arrived, the gates were open. Wide enough, at least, to admit a dozen horsemen. It would take another full minute to swing the huge, heavy gates completely aside.

To the captain's surprise, the leader of the Kushans clambered up the ladder as soon as he dismounted. The captain had expected him to join his fellows at the well below. The guards were already circulating among the new arrivals, flavoring the well water with wine poured from amphorae. Doing what they could to assuage the new arrivals, who would know full well that the garritroopers had good wine hidden somewhere about. Hopefully, the Kushans would be satisfied with the hospitality, and not go searching in the cellars.

"So let's be hospitable," muttered the captain to himself. He went to greet the Kushan climbing onto the rampart, hands outstretched.

"A great victory!" he cried, beaming from ear to ear.

The Kushan returned the grin with one of his own. "Better than you think," he replied. Proudly, the Kushan pointed to the oncoming mass of prisoners. "Those are Romans. Belisarius' men! We smashed them not six days ago. Routed them! Even got their horses."

The captain had wondered a bit, seeing so many of the prisoners still mounted. The majority were marching on foot, manacled in long chains, but there were at least four thousand captives who were simply manacled to their saddles.

Then again, if I were one of those Romans I wouldn't try to escape either. Horse be damned. Just like those crazy Kushans to make a game out of hunting you down. Gut you along with your horse and then drag you with your own intestines. Drag the horse too, probably.

The Kushan leader seized the captain in a hearty embrace. Gasping for breath, but not daring to complain, the captain studied the nearest prisoners. The first ranks were now within thirty yards of the gates. At the very forefront were two tall men. One of them was so huge he was almost a giant.

The captain grimaced. *Glad I didn't have to catch that monster! Let's hear it for garrison duty.*

To the captain's relief, the Kushan drew away from the bear hug and gestured toward the nearby gun platform.

"You *did* quench the firing rods?" he demanded. The Kushan's smile thinned, became less friendly. "We don't want any accidents now, do we?" The smile became *very* thin. "We wouldn't even bother looking for your women. Time we were done, you could fit one of those siege guns up your ass."

The captain shook his head hastily. Reassurances began pouring out of his mouth. To his relief, the friendly grin returned.

"Enough said!" exclaimed the Kushan. He seized the captain's arms and squeezed them reassuringly.

The first prisoners had reached the gate. They were being marched in ten abreast, with Kushan guards flanking them on both sides. The huge one at the fore, noticed the captain, really was a giant. He positively dwarfed the man next to him, even though that man was big himself.

The captain made a quick decision.

"Listen," he said softly, conspiratorially. "You come—" He glanced at the horizon. The sun was almost setting. "Tonight, after dark. Bring a few of your officers, if you want."

He gave the Kushan a friendly leer. "We'll have some fresh young women for you." He started to make a jocular shrug, but the Kushan's hands were still on his arms. "Well, they're not all *that* fresh, of course."

The prisoners were pouring through now, spilling onto the flat expanse inside the walls. The column barely fit the gate, even as wide as it was. The Kushans were chivvying the captives mercilessly, driving them in like a human flood.

"But they're better than the broken-down cunts in the brothels." Cackling: "Last week, half the crew of a cargo ship got through one of the bitches before they noticed she was dead."

He cackled again. The Kushan joined in the humor, laughing uproariously. Apparently, he found the thing so funny that he couldn't stop squeezing the captain's arms. The Kushan was very strong. The captain began to wince.

The wince turned into a gasp. A horse had kicked him in the stomach. The captain couldn't understand where the horse had come from.

He was on his knees. He didn't understand how he'd gotten there. And he saw, but didn't understand, how a sword was in the Kushan's hand.

The sword moved. The captain's vision was blurred, for an instant, as if he were being tumbled about in a barrel. He heard vague and muffled sounds, like shouts and screams filtered through wool.

When the captain's eyes refocused, his cheek was pressed to the stone floor of the rampart. A few feet away, blood was pumping out of the neck of a headless corpse. The noise was soft, rhythmic. *Splash. Splash.*

He just had time, before everything went dark, to realize that he was staring at his own body.

Chapter 32

"I thought, at first, that you'd moved too quickly," said Belisarius. He finished cleaning the blood from his sword and tossed the rag into a corner of the room. The tattered piece of cloth, torn from a Malwa soldier's tunic, landed soddenly on a large pile of its fellows. From the grisly mound of linen, a pool of blood was spreading slowly across the stone floor, reflecting the light from the lamps on the walls.

It was a large floor. The room had once been the audience chamber of Charax's viceroy, before the Malwa turned it into their military headquarters. But even that floor was now half-stained. The blood pooling from the heap of bodies in one corner had almost joined that spilling from the rags.

Vasudeva shrugged. "I had planned to wait, until everyone was through the gates. But there was always the danger of someone spotting something wrong, and besides—"

He shrugged again. Coutzes, sitting at a nearby table with his feet propped up, laughed gaily. "Admit it, maniac of the steppes!" The young Syrian general lifted his cup, saluting the Kushan. "You just couldn't resist! Like a wolf, with a lamb in its jaws, trying to withstand temptation."

Coutzes downed the cup in a single gulp. Then grimaced.

"God, I hate plain water. Even from a well." But Coutzes didn't even glance at the amphorae lining the shelf on a nearby wall. Belisarius had given the most draconian orders, the day before, on the subject of liquor. The general had seen what happened to an army, storming a city, if it started to drink. Troops could be hard enough to control, at such times, even when they were stone sober. It was essential—imperative—that Charax stay intact until the Roman army was ready to leave. Drunken troops, among their multitude of other crimes, are invariably arsonists. Let fire run loose in Charax, with its vast arsenal of gunpowder, and ruin was the sure result.

Belisarius slid the sword back into its scabbard. "I wasn't criticizing," he said mildly. "Once I realized what caliber of opponent we were facing, I was only surprised that you'd waited so long."

Bouzes came through the door. His sword was still in his hand, but the blade was clean. A few streaks indicated that it had been put to use; but not, apparently, in the past few minutes.

Coutzes' brother was scowling fiercely. "Where did they find this garbage?" he demanded. "Did they round up every pimp in India and station them here?" He seemed genuinely aggrieved.

Maurice, leaning against a nearby wall, chuckled. "What did you expect, lad?" He tossed his head, northward. "Every soldier worth the name is marching along the Euphrates, ready to fight Khusrau. The Malwa must have figured they could garrison a place this well fortified with anybody who could walk."

"Some of them couldn't even do that!" snapped Bouzes. "Half the garrison was already drunk, before we even started the assault. The sun hadn't gone down yet!" His scowl became a thing purely feral. "They won't walk now, for sure. Not ever."

"I *would* like as many prisoners as possible, Bouzes," said Belisarius. As before, his tone was mild.

Yes, agreed Aide. **The more enemy soldiers we can shove out the gates, the more mouths Link will have to feed. With nothing to feed them with.**

Bouzes flushed under the implied reproof.

"I tried, General." He gave a quick, appealing glance at the other commanders in the room. "We all tried. But—"

Maurice levered himself off the wall with a push of the shoulder and took two steps forward. Bouzes gave a small sigh of relief.

"Forget it, General," said Maurice harshly. "If there's five hundred of that scum left tomorrow morning to push out into the desert, I'll be surprised. There'll be no mercy for Malwa, this night. Not after the men found the torture chambers, and the brothels.

Any Mahaveda priest or mahamimamsa who died by the blade can count himself lucky. The men are dragging most of them to the torture chambers, to give them a taste of their own pleasures."

"*Along* with any soldier they caught within sight of one of the brothels," growled Coutzes. "*Jesus.*"

Belisarius did not argue the matter. He had seen one of the brothels himself.

Roman soldiers were not, to put it mildly, the gentlest men in the world. Nor was "gallantry" a word which anyone in their right mind would ever associate with them. Any Roman veteran—and they were all veterans, now—had spent his own time in a military brothel, filing through a crib for a few minutes' pleasure.

But the scene in *that* brothel had been something out of nightmare. A nightmare which would have roused Satan from his sleep, trembling and shaken. Long rows of women—girls, probably, though it was impossible to determine their age—chained, spread-eagled, on thin pallets. On occasion, judging from residual moisture, they had been splashed with a pail of water to clean them off. All the women were sick; most suffered from bedsores; many were dying; not a few were already dead.

No, Roman soldiers were not what a later age would call "knights in shining armor." But they had their own firm concept of manhood, nonetheless, which was not that of pimps and sadists. The women in the brothels were all Persian, or Arab, just like the women those soldiers had been consorting with since they began their campaign in Persia. Many Roman soldiers had married their kinsfolk. Among Persians, since the Malwa invasion began, the name of Charax had been synonymous with bestiality. Their Roman allies—friends and husbands, as often as not—had absorbed that notion, over the past year and a half. Now, having seen the truth with their own eyes, they would exact Persia's vengeance.

And besides, mused Aide whimsically, **they've spent the last six months fighting Rajputs. Can't do that, not even the crudest brawler recruited in Constantinople's hippodrome, without some of the chivalry rubbing off.**

Belisarius' eyes fell on the pile of corpses in a corner. The body of the Malwa garrison's commander was on the very top. Belisarius himself had put the body there, with a thrust through the heart, after the man had failed to stutter surrender quickly enough.

For just an instant, Belisarius regretted that sword thrust. He could have disarmed the man. Saved him for the torture pits.

He shook off the thought. Took a deep breath, and forced down his own rage, seething somewhere deep inside. This was no time for rage. If he was having a hard enough time controlling his fury, he could well imagine the mental state of his troops.

That fury can't be stopped, but it must *be controlled.*

He turned his eyes back on his commanders. All of them were staring at him. Respectfully, but stubbornly.

He forced a smile. "I'm not arguing the point, Maurice. But if it gets out of control, if the men—"

"Don't worry about it," interrupted Maurice brusquely, shaking his head. He pointed to the row of amphorae lining the shelf. "To the best of my knowledge, that's the only liquor left in Charax which hasn't already been spilled in the streets. More often than not, the men do it themselves before they're even ordered. No one wants any Malwa to escape because some bastard was too drunk to spot them. As for the women—"

He shrugged. Coutzes lazed to his feet and strode over to the shelf. As he began plucking amphorae and tossing them through a nearby window, he said: "The only problem there, general, is that any woman in Charax who's managed to stay out of the brothels—hooking up with a garrison unit, usually, or an officer—is throwing herself at a Roman soldier tonight." The first sounds of shattering wine flasks came from the street below. "Can't blame them. They'll do anything to get out of here. So would I."

Finished with the last amphora, he turned back, grinning. "Even if meant being called Coutzes the Catamite for the rest of my life."

Belisarius chuckled, along with his officers. "All right," he said. "I don't care about that. I don't expect my soldiers to be saints and monks. By tomorrow, we'll have regular camp followers. As long as the women are treated decently enough, and the men are kept from liquor, I'll be satisfied. We'll take the women with us, when we leave. Those who want, we'll try to reunite with their families."

"Most of them don't have any families left," grated Bouzes.

"Except us," added Maurice. The chiliarch's gray eyes were as grim as death. He hooked a thumb toward the window. Now that the sounds of breaking amphorae had ended, the screams could be heard again.

"I'm telling you, General—*relax*. That isn't the sound of a city being sacked by troops raging out of control, raping, drinking and burning. That's just the sound of an executioner doing his duty."

After a moment, Belisarius nodded. He decided Maurice was right. The focused fury of an army, he could control.

He slapped his hands together. The sharp sound echoed in the room, snapping his officers alert.

"Let's get to the rest, then." He turned to Vasudeva. "Where does it stand with the ships?"

Vasudeva stroked his topknot. The pleasure he so obviously took in the act almost made Belisarius laugh. "The last word I got from Cyril—maybe half an hour ago—was that all of the cargo ships had been seized. Except one, which managed to pull free from the docks before the Greeks could get to it. Most of the galleys, of course, escaped also."

The Kushan shrugged. "No way to stop them, before they reached the screen of galleys in the outer harbor. Not without firing rockets or flame arrows. So Cyril let it be. He says we've got more ships than we need, anyway, and he didn't want to risk an explosion or a drifting fireship."

"God, no!" exclaimed Bouzes. The young officer shuddered slightly. Charax was a city made of stone and brick. It would not burn easily, if at all. But it was also, for all practical purposes, a gigantic powderkeg. The port had been the arsenal for Malwa's intended conquest of Persia.

"The Greeks hadn't searched the ships yet," continued Vasudeva. "Although I imagine by now they've probably—" He broke off, hearing footsteps. Then, waving his hand: "But let's let him tell us."

Cyril was marching through the door. As soon as he entered, his eyes fell on the pile of corpses in the corner.

"Got off too easy, the swine," he muttered. Turning to Belisarius, he said: "We've started the search. Everything looks good. Lucky for us, none of the priests were stationed aboard any of the craft."

That had always been Belisarius' deepest fear. Some of the huge ships moored at the dock had been loaded with gunpowder. A fanatic priest aboard one of them, if certain of capture, would have ignited its cargo. The explosion might well have destroyed the harbor, along with the Roman escape route.

"Nobody else?" he asked.

Cyril smiled. "The only ones aboard were sailors. After we stormed a few of the ships, the rest negotiated surrender. Once we were sure all of them were on the docks, and the ships were secured—"

His smile was as grim as Maurice's eyes. "We gave them new terms of surrender. They weren't happy about it, but—" He shrugged. "Their protests were short-lived."

Another laugh swept the room. Even Belisarius joined in. There would be no mercy for Malwa from anyone, that night. A dog, barking in Hindi, would have been slaughtered.

Belisarius turned to Bouzes. Without being prompted, the young Thracian officer moved back to the window and began pointing to the walls beyond. The gesture was a bit futile. It was still long before sunrise. The darkness was unbroken except by slowly moving Roman squads, holding torches aloft in their search for Malwa hideaways.

"All of the siege guns have been seized and manned. I talked to Felix just twenty minutes ago." He gave Cyril a half-apologetic glance over his shoulder. "Unlike the Greeks, who have plenty of seamen, Gregory doesn't have anyone who's fired guns that size. So he kept maybe two dozen Malwa gunners alive. Felix says they're babbling everything they know, faster than we can ask."

"Good," grunted his brother. "By tomorrow morning, we can fire a few test rounds. Using them for the shot."

Again, savage humor filled the room. And, again, Belisarius joined in.

Even Aide: **Why not? The British did, during the Indian Mutiny. Unlike them, we've even got a decent excuse.**

The bloodthirsty aura of that thought did not surprise Belisarius. He only wondered, for a moment, at the vastness of the universe. Which could produce, over the eons, such miracles as a crystal intelligence learning human wrath.

His eyes came back to Vasudeva. From experience with the Kushan since he entered the service of Rome, Belisarius had learned to use him as his executive officer in matters of logistics. Vasudeva was as proficient a lieutenant, in that complex work, as Maurice was on the battlefield.

Vasudeva tugged his goatee. "Everything's still a mess, of course. Will be, till at least tomorrow night. But I'm not worried about it."

He spread his arms, hands wide open, as if he were embracing a beloved but obese friend. "There were fifteen thousand men garrisoned here, permanently. Between their stores, and the huge stockpiles for the main army, the Malwa have bequeathed a treasure upon us. We don't really have to organize much of anything. Just grab what we need, load up the ships, and get ready to leave when the time comes. Won't take more than three days."

"The Malwa army should be back here by then," opined Cyril. "Their first elements, anyway. Enough to invest the city."

Maurice made a fist, and inspected his knuckles. "That'll be too late. Way too late. By the day after tomorrow, we'll be able to hold Charax against them. For three weeks, at the very least. A month and a half wouldn't surprise me. Although I don't want to think about our casualties, by then."

And now, all eyes were on Belisarius.

He smiled. Widely, not crookedly. All rage and fury vanished, as he remembered that other—much deeper—side of life.

"She'll come," he said. "She'll come."

Chapter 33
THE TIGRIS
Autumn, 532 A.D.

In the event, Lord Damodara lost Sanga's services for only nine days. On the morning of the tenth, the Rajput king strode into Damodara's pavilion and slammed the truth onto his commander's table.

Damodara stared at the object resting before him. At his side, he sensed Narses' start of surprise. A moment later, the eunuch hissed.

The "truth" was a helmet. A great, heavy, ungainly contraption of segmented steel plates. A Goth helmet, Damodara vaguely realized.

"We found a small mountain of the things," said Sanga, "along with all the other gear those mercenaries were wearing."

Damodara looked up. "Where?"

Sanga glowered at the helmet. "Do you remember that small valley we passed through, where the Persians had been mining?" He snorted. "I remember noticing how fresh the mine tailings were. I was impressed, at the time, by the courage and determination of the Persian miners—to have kept working till the last minute, with a war raging about their heads."

"The tunnel!" explained Narses. "There was a tunnel there. A mine adit."

Sanga shook his head. "That is no mine, Narses. They disguised the first few dozen yards to make it look like one, but it is really an entrance to a qanat." He pointed at the helmet. "We found those about fifty yards in. Piled in a heap, as I said. It took us an hour to move the stuff aside, and go beyond. Thereafter—"

He pulled up a chair and sat down heavily. "From that point on, the trail is as clear as the one we have been following. Belisarius' entire army—I am as certain of it as I am of my own name—took that route. Hidden from sight underground, they marched to the south. They probably emerged, miles away, in another valley. Their Persian allies would have had fresh horses waiting for them."

He slapped the map with his hand. "*That* is why Belisarius was always willing to let us move north, but was so stubborn an opponent to the south. He was protecting the location of the tunnel. It must have taken them weeks—months—to prepare everything, even with help from the Persians. He could not afford to have us stumble upon his secret by accident, in the course of our maneuvers."

Damodara's eyes were wide open. His next words were almost choked out.

"Are you telling me that—" He waved his hand, weakly, as if to encompass all of time and space. "Everything we've done, for months—all the maneuvers and the fighting—even the battle at the pass—was a *feint*?"

Sanga nodded. "Yes, Lord. It was all a feint. Belisarius was buying time, yes. But he wasn't buying time for Emperor Khusrau, or his man Agathius in Peroz-Shapur. He was buying it for himself. Until the time was right, and the preparations were finished, and he could finally strike at his true target. Now that Emperor Khusrau's retreat has drawn our main army out of Charax, the Roman can drive home the death stroke."

"*Here,*" said Sanga. His finger speared a point on the map. "*At Charax.*"

Damodara's eyes, already wide, were almost bulging.

"That's insane!" he cried. "Charax is the most fortified place in the world! Even without the main army there, the garrison is still the size of Belisarius' army. Bigger! There's no way on earth he could storm the place—not even if he had siege guns."

Narses interrupted. His voice was dry and cold, like arctic ice.

"Have you ever heard of the Trojan Horse, Lord Damodara?" he asked. The Malwa lord twisted his head, transferring the incredulous gaze to Narses.

The old eunuch chuckled humorlessly. "Never mind. I will tell you the tale some other time. But you can trust me on this, Lord. *That*—"

He jabbed a finger at the helmet resting on the table. "*That* is a Trojan helmet." Narses laughed. There was actual humor in that laugh, mixed with rueful admiration.

"God, has the world even seen such a schemer?" He laughed again. "Those helmets, Lord Damodara, tell you the truth. They were discarded by Belisarius' two thousand Goth mercenaries, now that they no longer needed them to maintain the disguise. For those men were never Goths to begin with."

Damodara's mind finally tracked the trail. His eyes remained wide. His jaws tightened. The next words came between clenched teeth.

"There were two thousand Kushans in the army which Belisarius destroyed at Anatha last year. We always assumed they were slaughtered along with the rest."

Rana Sanga ran fingers through his thick hair. Then he, too, laughed—and, like Narses, his laugh was mixed rue and admiration.

"He used the same trick against us in India," mused Sanga. "Turned the allegiance of Kushans, and then left a false trail, so that the Kushans could do his real work."

Damodara was back to staring at the map. After a moment, his eyes narrowed.

"This still doesn't make sense," he said softly. He tapped his finger on the location of Charax. "I can see where he might get into Charax, using Kushans as his entry. And, certainly, once he got in—" Damodara snorted. "His soldiers, against garrison troops, would be like wolves in a sheep pen."

Slowly, the Malwa lord rose up, leaning on the table. His eyes went back and forth from Sanga to Narses.

"But then—how does he get *out*?"

Again, Damodara's finger tapped the map. This time, very forcefully, like a finger of accusation.

"Our main force is still not more than a few days' march away from Charax. Before Belisarius could finish his work of destruction, he would be surrounded by the largest army in the world. No way to escape. He couldn't even sail out on the cargo ships in the harbor. He couldn't get through the screen of war galleys stationed in the outer harbor. And not even Belisarius—not even behind *those* fortifications—can hold more than a few weeks against fifteen-to-one odds. Two months, at the outside."

Again, the jabbing finger. "It's a suicide mission!" he exclaimed. "Impossible!"

Sanga shook his head. "Why so, Lord? Belisarius is as courageous as any man alive. I would lay down my life for my country and honor. Why would not he?"

Damodara was shaking his head before the Rajput even finished. "That's not the point, Sanga. For honor and country, yes. But for *this*?"

Sanga stared up at Damodara, as if he were gazing at a unicorn. Or a cretin.

"Lord Damodara," he said, speaking slowly, "do you understand what Belisarius will do? Once he is in Charax—"

Damodara slammed the table angrily. "I am not a fool, Sanga! Of course I know what he will do. He will destroy the entire logistics base for our invasion of Persia. He will leave a hundred and fifty thousand men stranded without food or supplies—*and* without means of escape. He will certainly destroy the fleet at anchor there. He will not be able to touch the war galleys outside the harbor, of course, but even if he could—" Damodara threw up his hands. "Those ships could not possibly transport more than two thousand men. Even including the supply ships on the Euphrates, we couldn't evacuate more than—"

Abruptly, Damodara sat down. His face was drawn. "It would be the worst military disaster in history. A death stroke, just as you said. Our army would have no choice. They would have to retrace the route taken by Alexander the Great, when he retreated from India to the west. Except they would have no provisions at all, and far more men to feed and water. Even for Alexander, that road was disastrous."

Gloomily, Damodara stared at the map. His eyes were resting on what it showed of the lands bordering the Persian Gulf. The map showed very little, in truth, because there was nothing there of military interest. Mile after mile after mile of barren, arid coastline.

His eyes moved up. "They can't even try to retrace the route we've taken, through the plateau. We're too far north. They'd have to fight their way through Khusrau's army. With no way to replenish their gunpowder."

"We could help," interjected Sanga quickly. "With us striking in relief, we could open a route for them into the Zagros. Then—" His words trailed off. Sanga, unlike Damodara, was not an expert in logistics. But he knew enough to realize the thing was hopeless.

"Then—*what*?" demanded Damodara. "An army that size—through the Persian plateau *and the Hindu Kush*? We had a difficult enough time ourselves, with a quarter that number of men and all the supplies we needed."

He was back to staring at the map. "No, no. If Belisarius drives home that stroke, he will destroy an army of one hundred and fifty thousand men. Not more than one in ten will ever find their way back to India. The rest will die of thirst or starvation, or surrender themselves into slavery."

Again, he slammed the table. This time, with both hands.

"If! If!" he cried. "It still doesn't make sense! Belisarius would not pay the price!"

Sanga began to speak but Damodara waved him silent.

"You are not thinking, Sanga!" Damodara groped for words, trying to explain. "Yes—Belisarius *might* commit suicide, to strike such an incredible blow. But I do not think—"

He paused, and took a few breaths. "One of the things I noticed about the man, these past months—noticed and admired, for it is a quality I like to think I possess myself—is that Belisarius does not throw away the lives of his soldiers. Some generals treat their men like so many grenades. Not he."

Damodara gave Sanga a piercing gaze. "You say you would give up your own life, King of Rajputana. For honor and country, certainly. But for the sake of a strategic masterstroke?" He waited. Sanga was silent.

Damodara shrugged. "Possibly. Possibly. *But would you condemn ten thousand other men as well?*"

Sanga looked away. "I didn't think so," said Damodara softly. "Neither would Belisarius."

Not a sound was heard, for perhaps half a minute. Then, Narses began to chuckle.

"What is so funny?" demanded Damodara angrily. Sanga simply glared at the eunuch.

Narses ignored Damodara. He returned Sanga's glare with a little smile, and a question.

"Whom do you trust most of all in this world, King of Rajputana? If your life depended on cutting a rope, in whose hands would you want the blade?"

"My wife," came the instant reply.

Narses grinned. A second later, the eyes of Sanga and Damodara were riveted back to the map. And, a second after that, moved off the map entirely—as if, somewhere on the floor, they could find the portion which displayed Egypt, Ethiopia, and the Erythrean Sea.

They barely registered Narses' words. Still chuckling: "Now we know—*now*, at last we understand. Why Belisarius put his own wife in charge of the Roman expedition to Egypt and Ethiopia. You remember? We wondered about it. Why risk her? Any one of his best officers could have commanded that expedition. But if your life depended on it—yours and ten thousand others—oh, yes. Then, yes. Then you'd want a wife, and no other."

"How can any man think that far ahead?" whispered Damodara. "And even if he could—how could they coordinate their movements?"

Sanga crossed his heavy arms, and closed his eyes. Then, speaking slowly: "As to the first, he did not have to plan everything down to the last detail. Belisarius is a brilliant tactician as well as a strategist. He would have relied on himself to create the openings, where needed. As to the other, they have their semaphore stations. And—"

All traces of anger left his face. His eyes reopened. "I have often noticed, from my own life, how closely the thoughts of a man and his wife can run together. Like the thoughts of no other person."

He took a deep breath and exhaled. "I believe Narses is right, Lord Damodara. At this very moment, I think Belisarius is destroying Charax. And—this very moment—his wife is bringing a fleet to clear away the war galleys and escort her husband and his men to safety."

The Rajput king stared at the map. "The question is—what do *we* do?"

He uncrossed his arms and leaned on the table. A long, powerful finger began tracing the Tigris. "We can do nothing to help the main army in the Delta. But the one advantage we have now is that Belisarius is no longer barring our way. We can strike north, into Assyria, and—"

"*No!*"

Startled, Sanga stared at Narses. The old eunuch rarely intervened in purely military discussions. And then, with diffidence.

Narses arose. "I say—*no*." He looked to Damodara. "This army is the best army in the Malwa Empire, Lord. Within a month—two, at the outside—it will be the *only* Malwa army worth talking about, west of the Indus. I urge you, Lord, not to throw that army away."

Narses pointed to the map. "If you go north to Assyria—then what? You could wreak havoc, to be sure. Possibly even march into Anatolia. But you are not strong enough, with your army alone, to conquer either Persia or Rome. And your army will suffer heavy casualties in the doing. Very heavy."

Damodara was frowning. "Then what do you suggest, Narses?"

The eunuch shrugged. "Do nothing, at the moment." He cast a glance at Sanga. The Rajput king was scowling, but there was no anger in the expression. He seemed more like a man puzzled than anything else.

"Do nothing, Lord," repeated Narses. "Until the situation is clarified. Who knows? The emperor may very well want you to return to India, as soon as possible. Not even the Malwa Empire can withstand the blow which Belisarius is about to deliver, without being shaken to its very roots. The Deccan rebellion rages hot. Others may erupt. You may be needed in India, very soon—not in Assyria. And, if so, best you should return to India—"

The last words were spoken with no inflection at all. Which only made them the more emphatic.

"—*with the best army in the possession of the Malwa dynasty. Intact, and in your hands.*"

Damodara's eyes seemed to widen, a bit. Then, his eyelids lowered.

"Narses raises a good point, Sanga," he murmured, after a moment's thought. "I think we must give it careful consideration."

His eyes opened. The lord straightened in his chair and issued commands.

"Have the men make camp, Rana Sanga. A strong camp, on the near bank of the Tigris. Not permanent, but no route-camp either. We might be here for several weeks. And begin the preparations for a possible march back across the plateau."

His eyes closed again. "It is true, what Narses says. Who knows what the future will bring? We might, indeed, be needed back in India soon."

Sanga hesitated, for perhaps a second or two. Then, with a little shrug, he rose and left the pavilion.

When he was gone, Lord Damodara opened his eyes and gazed at Narses. The gaze of a Buddha, that was.

"I have been thinking," he said serenely, "of what Belisarius said to me. When he swore that what he wished to discuss with you in private would cause no harm. To *me*, that is. As I think back, I realize it was a very carefully phrased sentence. Would you agree?"

Narses nodded immediately. His own face was as placid and expressionless as Damodara's. "Oh yes, Lord. That's the nature of oaths, you know. They are always very specific."

Damodara gazed at him in silence. Still, like a Buddha.

"So they are," he murmured. "Interesting point."

He looked away, staring at nothing. His eyes seemed quite unfocused.

"We will do nothing, at the moment," he mused softly. "Your advice is well taken, Narses. Nothing, at the moment. So that, whatever the future brings, Malwa's best army will be available for—whatever is needed."

"Nothing," agreed Narses. "At the moment."

"Yes. That is the practical course. And I am a practical man."

Chapter 34

CHARAX
Autumn, 532 A.D.

Belisarius peered between the shields which Anastasius and Gregory were holding up to shelter him. They themselves were crouching far enough below the battlements to be protected from the swarm of incoming arrows, but Belisarius had insisted on observing the siege personally. That meant sticking his head up, despite the unanimous disapproval of his officers.

"You were right, Gregory," he murmured. "They'll have their siege guns ready by tomorrow evening. But no sooner. As it is, they'll have to work through the night. If they try to fire them now, before they've laid stone platforms, the recoil will probably spill the guns."

Gregory refrained from any comment. Maurice, in his place, would have already been uttering sarcastic phrases. *I told you so* would have had been cheerfully tossed with *What? I am blind?* and *A commanding general has to risk his neck to play scout?*

But Maurice had a unique relationship with Belisarius. Gregory did not feel himself in a position to reprove his general. Even if the damned fool *did* insist on taking needless risks.

Belisarius ducked below the ramparts. Gregory and Anastasius lowered their shields, sighing with relief.

"We could sally," said Gregory. "Try to spike the guns. Probably couldn't get close enough, but we might be able to fire the carriages."

Belisarius shook his head. "It'd be pure suicide. The main body of the Malwa army hasn't arrived yet, but there are at least thirty thousand men out there. Ye-tai and Kushans, most of them, along with a few Rajput cavalry contingents."

Belisarius shook his head again. The gesture was almost idle, however. Most of the general's mind seemed to be concentrated elsewhere.

"Not a chance, Gregory. Not even if we sallied with every man we've got. The Malwa know as well as we do that those guns are the key to smashing their way into Charax quickly. That's why they cannibalized most of their supply ships in order to get them down here as quickly as they could. They probably hope they might retake the city before we destroy it completely."

Belisarius fell silent. His eyes were now turned completely away from the enemy beyond the walls. He was studying the interior of Charax. The city, like most great ports, was a labyrinth. Other than the docks themselves and the small imperial quarter where, in times past, the Persian viceroys had held court, Charax was a jumbled maze of narrow streets. At one time, from what he could tell, the city had been blessed with a few small squares and plazas. But over the years, the necessities and realities of commerce had made themselves felt. Charax was a city of tenements, warehouses, bazaars, entrepôts, hostels, inns, brothels, and a multitude of other buildings designed for handling sailors and their cargoes. The construction, throughout, was either mud brick or simple fill, plastered with gypsum.

Rubble, in short, just waiting to happen.

"If we can keep it from burning . . . " he mused. His thoughts ranged wide, traversing the centuries which Aide had shown him.

You are thinking of Stalingrad.

Belisarius scratched his chin. *Yes, Aide. How long did Chuikov's men hold out, in the ruins? Before the counteroffensive was finally launched?*

Longer than *we* will need. Fighting street by street is the most difficult combat imaginable, if you are not concerned with saving the city.

Belisarius grinned. The feral expression would have been worthy of Valentinian.

I'm planning to wreck it anyway. I was going to do it all at once, when we left. But there's no reason not to make a gala affair out of the business. Why settle for an evening ball, when you can hold dances every night? For weeks, if need be.

He made his decision, and turned to Gregory.

"How long would it take you to turn the siege guns around? *Our* siege guns, I mean—the ones facing the sea from the south wall. I want them facing into the city."

Gregory started. "What about—?" The cataphract paused. His eyes went to the south. From his elevation, on the ramparts of the northern wall, Gregory could see all the way across the city to the harbor beyond. The twenty Malwa galleys patrolling just outside the range of the seaward siege guns were clearly visible.

Gregory answered his own question. "Guess we don't really need them, against the galleys." He frowned for a moment or two, thinking.

"I'd need at least three days, general. Probably four, maybe five." Apologetically: "The things are huge. The only reason we could do it at all, in less than two weeks, is because I can use the dockside cranes—"

Belisarius patted his arm. "Five days is fine, Gregory. Take a week. You'll need to build new ramparts, don't forget. Protecting them from fire coming from *inside* the city."

Gregory's eyes widened. "You're going to let them in!"

Belisarius nodded. "They'll breach the walls, anyway, once the siege guns start firing. Rather than waste men trying to hold the wall against impossible odds, we'll just let them come in. Then—" He pointed to the rabbit warren of the city. "The more walls and buildings they shatter, the worse it'll get for them. We can set mines and booby traps everywhere. We'll retreat through the city, day after day, destroying it as we go. The Malwa will have to charge cataphracts and musketeers across the worst terrain I can think of. By the time they pin us on the docks, they'll have lost thousands of men. *Tens* of thousands, more like."

For a moment, Belisarius' normally calm face was set in lines of savage iron. "Even if Antonina never arrives, and we die here, I intend to gut this Malwa beast. One way or the other."

He rose up, in a half-crouch. "Let's do it," he commanded. "I'll have Felix replace you in command of the pikemen. He's due for another promotion, anyway. You concentrate on the siege guns. Once we get them turned around, it'll be the Malwa facing cannister. They'll never be able to get their own siege guns into the rubble."

Gregory studied the far-distant southern walls of the city, facing the sea. "They'll still have the range—"

Belisarius snorted. "With what kind of accuracy? Sure, a few rounds will hit the harbor. But most of them will miss, and those guns take forever to reload. Whereas the farther back they push us, the closer they get to our own artillery."

Gregory's grin became feral. "Yeah, they will. And before they get into cannister range—you know that idea you had, about chain shot?"

Belisarius had intended to leave immediately. But the enthusiasm on the gunnery officer's face was irresistible. And so, for a few pleasant minutes, a general and his subordinate discussed murder and mayhem. With great relish, if the truth be told.

Aide kept out of the discussion, more or less, other than the occasional remark.

Unwanted remarks, so far as Belisarius was concerned. He thought: **How did we crystals ever emerge from such protoplasmic thugs?** was snide. And **Can't we just learn to get along?** positively grotesque.

By the morning of the tenth day, the Malwa siege guns had completed their work of destruction. A stretch of Charax's northern wall two hundred yards wide was nothing but rubble. Twenty thousand Ye-tai stormed out of their trenches a quarter of a mile away and charged the breach. Squads of Kushans were intermingled with the Ye-tai battalions, guarding other squads of kshatriya grenadiers.

"They've finally learned," commented Maurice, studying the oncoming horde through a slit window. He was squatting next to Belisarius in a tower, less than two hundred yards from what had been Charax's northern wall. The elevated position gave both men a clear view of the battleground.

Belisarius was still breathing heavily from the exertion of his climb up the narrow stairs. He had arrived at the top of the tower just seconds earlier. Maurice had flatly refused to allow him up until the siege guns had ceased firing. The chiliarch hadn't wanted to risk a stray round killing the Roman commander.

Belisarius had tried to argue the point with his nominal subordinate, but Maurice had refused to budge. More to the point, *Anastasius* had refused to budge. The giant had made clear, in simple terms, that he was quite prepared to enforce Maurice's wishes by the crude expedient of picking Belisarius up and holding him off the ground.

"What's happening?" demanded Belisarius. The general put his eye to another window. For a moment, he was disoriented by the narrow field of vision. The slit window had been designed for archers. At one time, until Charax expanded, the tower he was perched in had been part of the city's original defensive walls.

"They've finally learned," repeated Maurice. He poked a stubby finger into the window slit. "Look at them, lad. The Ye-tai are leading the charge now, instead of driving regulars forward. And they're using Kushans as light infantry to cover the grenadiers." After a moment, he grunted: "Good formation. Same way I'd do it, without musketeers."

He turned and grinned at the general. "I'll bet that monster Link is kicking itself in its old woman's ass. Wishing it hadn't screwed up with the muskets."

Belisarius returned the grin. Three days before, in one of the warehouses by the docks, the Roman soldiers had found two hundred crates full of muskets. The weapons were still covered with grease, protecting them from the salt air of their sea voyage.

The Malwa Empire had finally produced handcannons, clear enough. And, just as clearly, hadn't gotten them to Mesopotamia in time to do Link any good. Belisarius suspected that Link had intended to start training a force of musketeers. Three of the crates had been opened, and the weapons cleaned. But the gunpowder *hadn't* arrived in Charax yet. At least, the Roman soldiers investigating the warehouses and preparing them for demolition hadn't discovered any.

The best laid plans of mice and men, said Aide. **I guess it applies to gods, too.**

Belisarius smiled. The muskets were all lying underwater, now, in Charax's harbor. The Roman musketeers had taken one look at the things and pronounced them unfit for use. Too crude. Too poorly made. Most of all—*not our stuff. Furrin' junk.*

In truth, Belisarius hadn't thought the Malwa devices were much inferior to Roman muskets. But he had allowed the musketeers their pleasant hour, pitching "furrin' junk" into the sea. He had as many muskets as he needed, anyway, and the escape ships would be crowded enough already. There were at least six thousand Persian civilians to be evacuated, along with the Roman troops.

The first wave of Ye-tai was already clambering over the rubbled wall. Volleys of grenades were sailing over their heads, clearing the way.

There was no way to be cleared, however. As soon as the siege guns began firing, Maurice had pulled back the troops on the wall. Those soldiers had long since taken up new positions.

"When?" asked Maurice.

Belisarius studied the assault through the slit window. What had been the northern wall was now an ant heap, swarming with Ye-tai. The soldiers were making slow progress, stumbling over the broken stones, but at least five hundred were now into the level ground inside the city.

If the Ye-tai hadn't been seized by the fury of their charge, they might have wondered about that level ground. An area fifty yards wide, just within the northern wall, had been cleared by Belisarius' troops. "Cleared," in the sense that the buildings had been hastily knocked apart. The sun-dried bricks hadn't been hauled away, simply spread around. The end result was a field of stones and wall stumps, interspersed with small mounds of mud brick.

They might have wondered about those mounds, too. But they would have no time to do so.

There were now at least a thousand Ye-tai packed into the level ground, along with perhaps two hundred Kushans and kshatriyas. The Malwa soldiers were advancing toward the first line of still-intact buildings. They were moving more slowly now, alert for ambush. Kshatriya grenadiers began tossing grenades into the first buildings.

"*Now,*" said Belisarius. Maurice whistled. A moment later, the small squad of cornicenes in a lower level of the tower began blowing their horns. The sound, confined within the stone walls of the tower, had an odd timbre. But the soldiers waiting understood the signal.

Dozens of fuses were lit. Fast-burning fuses, these. Three seconds later, the holocaust began.

The mud brick mounds scattered everywhere erupted, as the huge amphorae buried within them were shattered by explosive charges. The amphorae—great two-handled jugs—had been designed to haul grain. But they held naphtha just as nicely.

Some of the jugs were set afire by the explosions. Mud brick mounds became blooming balls of flame and fury, incinerating the soldiers crowded around them.

Most of the jugs did nothing more than shatter, spilling their contents. The naphtha they contained was crude stuff. Undistilled, and thick with impurities. Explosive charges alone were not usually enough to set it aflame. But the charges did send clouds of vapor and streams of smelly naphtha spewing in all directions. Within seconds, most of the Malwa soldiers packing the level ground were coated with the substance.

The next round of charges went off. Mines, disguised with rubble, had been laid against the walls of the nearest tenement buildings. They had been manufactured over the past few days by Roman troops working in the harbor's warehouses, smithies and repair shops.

The mines, too, were crude. Not much more than buckets, really, packed with explosives and laid on their sides. Some were copper kettles, but most were simply amphorae reinforced with iron hoops. Wooden lids held the charges from spilling out.

These mines were designed for incendiary purposes. As soon as the charges in the bases of the buckets were fired, combustible materials saturated with distilled naphtha spewed forth. Hundreds—thousands—of burning objects rained all over the ground before them, igniting the crude naphtha which already saturated the area.

Within seconds, hundreds of Malwa troops had been turned into human torches. All other sounds were submerged under a giant's scream.

"Jesus," whispered Maurice, peering through the slit. "Jesus, forgive us our sins."

Belisarius, after a few seconds, turned away. His face seemed set in stone.

"That should stop the charge," he said. "From now on, they'll advance like snails."

Maurice's gaze was still fixed on the human conflagration below. It could not be said that he turned pale, but his cheeks were drawn. He hissed a slow breath between clenched teeth.

Then, with a quick, harsh shake of the head, he too turned away.

He glanced at Belisarius. "Snails? They'll advance like trees growing roots, more like." Again, hissing: *"Jesus."*

Musketeers began to clamber onto the tower platform and take their places at the arrow slits. Belisarius and Maurice edged through the soldiers and started descending the stairs. Both men were silent.

Vocally, at least. Trying to shake off the horror, Belisarius spoke to Aide.

That was what you meant, isn't it?

Aide understood the question. His mind and Belisarius', over the years, had entwined their own roots.

Yes. Wars of the future will not really be civilized, even when the Geneva Convention is followed. More antiseptic, perhaps, in the sense that men can murder each other at a distance, where they can't see the face of the enemy. But, if anything, I think that makes war even more inhumane.

It did not seem strange—neither to the man nor the crystal—that Aide should use the word "inhumane" as he did. From the "inside," so to speak. Nor did it seem strange that, having used the word, Aide should also accept the consequence. If there had been any accusation in the word, it had been aimed as much at himself as the men who fired the naphtha. Had it not been Aide, after all, who showed Belisarius the claymore mines of the future?

The question of Aide's own humanity had been settled. The Great Ones had created Aide and his folk, and given them the name of "people." But, as always, that was a name which had to be established in struggle. Aide had claimed his humanity, and that of his crystal clan in the human tribe, in the surest and most ancient manner.

He had fought for it.

Chapter 35
DEOGIRI
Autumn, 532 A.D.

Irene chuckled sarcastically. "Well, Dadaji, what do you think they're saying now?" She draped her right elbow over the side of the howdah, leaned back, and looked at the elephants trailing them in the procession. The Keralan delegation was riding in the next howdah. The sight of Ganapati's face was enough to cause her to laugh outright.

Holkar did not bother to turn his head. He simply gazed upon the cheering crowds lining the road and smiled beatifically. "No doubt they are recognizing their error, and vowing to reapply themselves to their philosophical studies."

Irene, her eyes still to the rear, shook her head in wonder. "If Ganapati doesn't close his mouth a little, the first strong breeze that comes along will sweep him right out of his howdah."

She craned her neck a bit, trying to get a better glimpse of the elephants plodding up the road behind the Keralans. "Same goes for the Cholan envoys. And the Funanese, from what I can see." Again, she shook her head—not in wonder, this time, but cheerful condemnation. "O ye of little faith," she murmured.

She removed her elbow and turned back into her own howdah. For a moment, Irene's eyes met those of the woman sitting across from her, nestled into Holkar's arm. Dadaji's wife smiled at her.

The expression was so shy—timid, really—that it was almost painful to see.

Irene immediately responded with her own smile, putting as much reassurance into the expression as she possibly could. Dadaji's wife lowered her gaze almost instantly.

Poor Gautami! She's still in shock. But at least I finally got a smile from her.

Irene moved her eyes away from the small, gray-haired woman tucked under Holkar's shoulder. She felt a deep sympathy for her, but knew that any further scrutiny would just make Holkar's wife even more withdrawn. The problem was not that Gautami was still suffering any symptoms from her long captivity. Quite the opposite, in truth. Gautami had gone from being the spouse of a modest scribe in a Maratha town to a Malwa kitchen slave, and then from a slave to the wife of ancient Satavahana's peshwa. The latter leap, Irene thought, had been in some ways even more stressful than the first plunge. The poor woman, suddenly discovering herself in India's most rarified heights, was still gasping for breath.

Looking away, Irene caught sight of yet another column of Marathas approaching the road along which Shakuntala was making her triumphant procession toward Deogiri. The gentle smile she had bestowed on Gautami was transformed into something vastly more sanguine—a grin that bordered on pure savagery.

"Column," actually, was an inappropriate word. "Motley horde" better caught the reality. At the forefront, whooping and hollering, came perhaps two dozen young men. Five of them were on horseback, prancing forward and then back again—the self-appointed "cavalry" of whatever village had produced them. The rest were marching—half-charging, say better—on foot. All of them were bearing weapons; although, in most cases, the martial implements still bore the signs of recent conversion. Hoes, mostly, hammered into makeshift polearms by the local blacksmith. But Irene could see, here and there, a handful of real spears and swords.

Coming behind the rambunctious young men were other, older men—ranging through late middle age. They, too, were all carrying weapons of one sort or another. Some among them, astride horses, even had armor and well-made bows and swords. Those would be what passed for kshatriyas in that village, nestled somewhere in the Great Country's volcanic reaches. Behind them, marching more slowly, came perhaps two or three hundred people. Women, children, graybeards, the sick and infirm, priests—Irene did not doubt for an instant that the mob comprised every person in that village, wherever it was, who could move on their feet.

The column reached the road and began merging into the throng spilling along both sides, as far as the eye could see. Irene did not look back again, but she knew that many of those people, once Shakuntala's procession had passed, would join the enormous crowd following the empress toward Deogiri. The Greek noblewoman had stopped even trying to estimate their numbers.

I had no idea the Great Country held this many people. It seems like such a barren land.

Dadaji must have sensed something of her thoughts. "Many of us, aren't there?" he remarked. Holkar swiveled his head, examining the scene. "I had not realized, myself. Nor, I think, had anyone. And that too will give them courage, when they go back to their villages."

A sudden roar drifted back from the crowd ahead. Moments later, the procession staggered to a halt. Dadaji leaned over the side of the howdah and peered forward.

"She's giving a speech again." He shook his head, smiling. "If she keeps this up—"

A huge roar drowned his words; then, like an undulating wave, it rolled through the crowd lining the road. In seconds, as the people near the howdah joined in, the noise became half-deafening. Most of those people could not possibly have heard any of Shakuntala's words, but it mattered not in the least. They knew what she had said.

For days, as her expedition to Deogiri moved through southern Majarashtra, the Empress of Andhra had given a single short, simple, succinct speech. By now, every Maratha within a week's horseback ride—a fast, galloping ride—knew its content.

Andhra is Majarashtra's bride.
My army is my dowry.
My husband will break Malwa's spine.
My sons will grind Malwa's bones.

It was not even a speech, any longer. Simply a chant, every one of whose words was known by heart and repeated by untold thousands—untold *tens* of thousands—of Marathas. By them—and by many others. The Great Country, for centuries, had served as a haven for people fleeing tyranny and oppression. The Marathas, as a people, were the mongrel product of generations past who had found a sanctuary in its hills and badlands. The new refugees who had poured in since the Malwa Empire began its conquest of India simply continued the process. Many of the voices chanting Shakuntala's phrases did so, not in Marathi, but in dozens of India's many tongues.

The roar faded. The procession lurched back into motion. Irene cocked an eye at Holkar. "You were saying, Dadaji?"

The peshwa shook his head, still smiling. "If she keeps this up, she'll be so hoarse by the time she gets to Deogiri that she won't be able to propose to Rao at all." His smile widened, became quite impish. "He still hasn't said 'yes,' you know? And he's hardly the kind of man who can be browbeaten—not even by *her*."

Irene grinned in return. "You don't seem greatly concerned. Good God! What if he says 'no'? *Disaster!*"

Holkar made no verbal response. The expression on his face was quite enough.

Irene laughed. "You should model for sculptors, Dadaji—the next time they need to carve a Buddha."

Holkar squeezed his wife close. "So I keep telling Gautami." He chuckled. "Stubborn woman! She persists in denying my sainthood."

"Of course I do," came the instant response. Irene almost gasped, seeing the woman's eyes. Still shy, still half-downcast, but—yes! Twinkling!

"What kind of a saint snores?" demanded Gautami.

My God—she told a joke!

"The girl has gone mad, Maloji," growled Rao, glaring down at the elephant leading the enormous—and utterly bizarre—"relief column" which was almost at the huge gate in Deogiri's southern wall. From his perch atop that wall, Rao could see Shakuntala clearly. The empress was riding alone on the lead elephant, standing completely erect in full imperial regalia.

"Look!" he cried, pointing an accusing finger. "She does not even have a bodyguard in her howdah!"

Serenely, Maloji examined the army of polearm-wielding Maratha peasants who flanked the howdah, just beyond the stiff ranks of Kushans who marched directly alongside the empress. His gaze moved to the ostrich-plumed black soldiers who came behind her elephant.

Then, scanning slowly, Maloji studied the various military units which trotted all over the landscape south of the walled city, alertly watching for Malwa enemies. He recognized the Cholan and Keralan troops, but could only guess at the exact identity of the others. There were perhaps three thousand of them in all, he thought. It was difficult to make a good estimate, however, because of the huge crowd of Marathas which seemed to fill the landscape.

Rao started pounding the top of the wall with his hands. "What is Kungas thinking?" he demanded.

Maloji leaned back, sighing satisfaction. "I never realized how many nations there are in this world," he murmured. Then, casting his glance sideways at the fretful man by his side, he chuckled.

"Relax, Rao!" Another chuckle. "I really don't think she's in any danger from the Vile One's army."

Now, an outright laugh. Maloji jerked his head back and to the north. "Ha! The Vile One has all his troops surrounding *his* camp, while he cowers in his pavilion. For all intents and purposes, *he* is the one besieged this day."

Rao was still slapping the wall. Maloji snorted.

"Stop this, old friend!" He reached over and pinned Rao's hands to the stones. "You are being foolish, and you know it. Another report came in from Bharakuccha just this morning. More Malwa troops are stumbling into the city, seeking a haven. Entire garrisons, as often as not, from some of the smaller towns. The whole land is seething rebellion. The Great Country is coming to a boil. There is no chance in the world that Malwa will strike at the empress. Not today, for a certainty."

Rao stared at him. For a moment, he tried to pry his hands from under Maloji's. But there was no great conviction in that effort.

"She is still insane," he muttered stubbornly. "This whole scheme of hers is insane. It . . . it . . . " He took a breath. "She is endangering her purity—her sacred lineage—for the sake of mere statecraft."

For a moment, Rao's usual wit returned. "A masterstroke, I admit, from the standpoint of gaining Maratha allegiance." Wit vanished with the wind; the deep scowl returned. "But it is still—"

"*Stop it!*" commanded Maloji. Suddenly, almost angrily, he seized Rao's wrists and jerked the man away from the wall.

Startled, Rao's eyes went to his. Maloji shook his head.

"You do not believe any of this, Rao. You are simply afraid, that is all. Afraid that what you say is true. Afraid that the girl who comes to you today is not the girl you longed for, but simply an empress waging war."

After a moment, Rao's eyes dropped. He said nothing. There was no need for words.

Maloji smiled. "So I thought." He released Rao's wrists, but only to seize the man's shoulders and turn him toward the stairs leading down to the city below. Already, they could hear the sound of the great gates opening.

"Go, go! It's long past time the two of you spoke." He began pushing Rao ahead of him. Majarashtra's greatest dancer seemed to be dragging his feet.

"And let me make a suggestion." Maloji chortled. "I think you'd better stop thinking of her as a 'girl.' "

They were alone, now. Even Kungas had left the room, secure in the knowledge that his empress was in the care of a man who was, among many other things, one of India's greatest assassins.

Rao stared at Shakuntala. It had been three years since he saw her last. And then only for two hours.

"You have changed," he said. "Greatly."

Shakuntala's eyes began to shy away, but came back firmly.

"How so?" she asked, straightening her back. Shakuntala's normal posture was so erect that she always looked taller than she was. Now, she was standing like an empress. Her black eyes held the same imperial aura.

Rao shook his head. It was the slow gesture of a man in a daze, trying to match reality to vision.

"You seem—much older. Much—" He waved his hand. The gesture, like the headshake, was vague and hesitant. He took a breath. "You were a beautiful girl. You are so much more beautiful, now that you are a woman. I do not understand how that is possible."

There was perhaps a hint of moisture in Shakuntala's eyes. But her only expression was a sly smile.

"You have not changed much, Rao. Except there is some gray in your beard."

Rao stood as erect as the empress. Harshly: "That is only one of the reasons—"

"*Be quiet.*"

Rao's mouth snapped shut. For a moment, his jaw almost sagged. He had never heard Shakuntala speak that way. The Panther of Majarashtra was as stunned as any of the pampered brahmin envoys who had also been silenced by that ancient voice of great Satavahana.

When Shakuntala continued, her tone was cold and imperious. "I do not wish to hear anything about your age. What of it? It has never mattered to me. It did not matter to me when I was a girl, held captive by Malwa. It does not matter to me now, when I am the Empress of Andhra."

She snorted. "Even less! No untested young husband would survive Malwa, so I would still be a widow soon enough."

Rao began to speak again.

"*Be quiet.*" Again, Rao's mouth snapped shut.

"I will hear no argument, Rao. I will listen to no words which speak of age, or blood and purity, or propriety and custom. I have made my decision, and I will not be swayed."

Imperial hauteur seemed to crack. Perhaps. Just a bit. Shakuntala looked away.

"I will not force you into this, Rao. You have only to say—*no*. Refuse me if you wish, and I will bow to that refusal. But I will hear no argument."

"If I *wish*?" he cried. Shakuntala's gaze came back to him, racing like the wind. In that instant, she knew the truth.

There was no hint of moisture in her eyes, now. The tears flowed like rain. She clasped her hands tightly in front of her. Her shoulders began to shake.

"I never knew," she whispered. Then, sobbing: "Oh, Rao—I never *knew*. All those years—"

Rao's own voice was choked, his own eyes wet. "How could I—?" His legs buckled. On the floor, kneeling, head down: "How could I? I only—only—"

She was kneeling in front of him. Cradling him in her arms, whispering his name, kissing his eyes, weeping softly into his hair.

Eventually, humor returned, bringing its own long-shared treasure.

"You must be off," murmured Rao. "This is most unseemly, for a virgin to be alone with a man for so long."

Shakuntala gurgled laughter. "I'm serious!" insisted Rao. "People will say I married a slut. My reputation will be ruined."

She threw her arms around his neck, kissing him fiercely, sprawling them both to the floor.

"Gods above," gasped Rao. "I *am* marrying a slut!"

Shakuntala gurgled and gurgled. "Oh, Rao—I've missed you so *much*. No one ever made me laugh so!"

She kissed him again, and again, and again, before pulling her face away. Her liquid eyes were full of promise.

"We will be wed tomorrow," she decreed. "You will dance the greatest dance anyone ever saw."

He smiled ruefully. "I will not argue the point. I don't dare."

"You'd better not," she hissed. "I'm the empress. Can't even keep track, any longer, of my executioners. But there must be hundreds of the handy fellows."

Rao laughed, and hugged her tight. "No one ever made me laugh so," he whispered.

Seconds later, they were on their feet. Holding hands, they began moving toward the door beyond which Kungas and an empire's fortune lay waiting.

At the door, Rao paused. A strange look came upon him. Shakuntala had never seen that expression on Rao's face before. Hesitation, uncertainty, embarrassment, anxiety—for all the world, he seemed younger than she.

Shakuntala understood at once. "You are worried," she said, gently but firmly, "about our wedding night. All those years of self-discipline."

He nodded, mute. After a moment, softly: "I never—I never—"

"*Never?*" she asked archly. Cocking her head, squinting: "Even that time—I was fourteen, I remember—when I—"

"Enough!" he barked. Then, flushing a bit, Rao shrugged. "Almost," he muttered. "I tried—*so hard*. I fasted and meditated. But—perhaps not always. Perhaps."

He was still hesitant, uncertain, anxious. Shakuntala took his head between her hands and forced him to look at her squarely.

"Do not concern yourself, Rao. Tomorrow night you will be my husband, and you will perform your duty to perfection. Trust me."

He stared at her, as a disciple stares at a prophet.

"Trust me." Her voice was as liquid as her eyes. "I will see to it."

"I thought I might try this one," said Shakuntala, pointing to the illustration.

Irene's eyes widened. Almost bulged, in truth. "Are you *mad*? I wouldn't—"

She broke off, chuckling. "Of course, you're a dancer and an acrobat, trained by an assassin. I'm a broken-down old woman. Greek nobility, at that. I creak just rising from my reading chair."

Shakuntala smiled. "Not so old as all that, Irene. And not, I think, broken down at all."

Irene made a face. "Maybe so. But I'd still never try *that* one."

A moment later, Shakuntala was embracing her. "Thank you for loaning me the book, Irene. I'm sorry I took so long to return it. But I wanted to know it by heart."

Irene grinned. She didn't doubt the claim. The young empress' mind had been trained by the same man who shaped her body. Shakuntala probably *had* memorized every page.

"And thank you for everything else," the empress whispered. "I am forever in your debt."

As Irene ushered Shakuntala to the door, the empress snickered. "What's so funny?"

"You will be," predicted the empress. "Very soon."

They were at the door. Irene cocked her head quizzically.

Shakuntala's smile was very sweet. Like honey, used for bait.

"You know Kungas," she murmured. "Such a stubborn and dedicated man. But I convinced him I really wouldn't need a bodyguard tonight. I certainly won't need one after tomorrow, with Rao sharing my bed."

Irene was gaping when the empress slipped out the door. She was still gaping when Kungas slipped in.

He spotted the scented oils right away, resting on a shelf against the wall. "Don't think we'll need those," he mused. "Not tonight, for sure."

Then, catching sight of the book resting on the table, he ambled over and examined the open page.

"Not a chance," he pronounced. "Maybe you, Irene, slim as you are. But *me*?" He pointed to the illustration. "You think you could get a thick barbarian like me to—"

But Irene had reached him, by then, and he spoke no further words. Not for quite some time.

Irene liked surprises, but she got none that night. She had long known Kungas would be the best lover she ever had.

"By far," she whispered, hours later. Her leg slid over him, treasuring the moisture.

"I told you we wouldn't need oils," he whispered in reply.

They laughed, sharing that great joy also. But Irene, lifting her head and gazing down at Kungas, knew a greater one yet.

The mask was gone, without a trace. The open face that smiled up at her was simply that of a man in love. Her man.

Chapter 36
CHARAX
Autumn, 532 A.D.

"I don't understand what that monster is doing," snarled Coutzes. He ducked below the broken wall as another volley of arrows came sailing from the Malwa troops dug into a shattered row of buildings across the street. The arrows clattered harmlessly into another room of what had once been an artisan's shop. A leather worker, judging by the few tools and scraps of raw material which were still lying about.

Belisarius, his back comfortably propped against the same wall, raised a questioning eyebrow.

Coutzes jabbed his finger at the wall, pointing to the unseen enemy beyond. "What's the point of this, General? That *thing* is just throwing soldiers away. You watch. They'll fire one or two more volleys of arrows—none of which'll hit anything, except by blind luck—lob some grenades, and then charge across the street. We'll butcher 'em, they'll withdraw, and then they'll do it again. By the time we finally have to retreat to the next row, they'll be moving forward across hundreds of bodies as well as rubble."

The Thracian officer rubbed his face, smearing sweat and grime. "It's been like this for two weeks now. Our own casualties haven't really been that heavy. At this rate, it'll take them another month—at least!—to fight their way to the docks. And they'll have lost half their army—at least!—in the doing."

The scowl was back in full force. "I've heard of crude tactics, but *this*—?" For a moment, his youthful face was simply aggrieved. "I thought that *thing* was supposed to be superintelligent."

Belisarius smiled. The smile was crooked, but there was more of contempt in it than irony. "Link *is* superintelligent, Coutzes. But intelligence is always guided by the soul. Which Link has, whether it realizes it or not. Or, at least, it is the faithful servant of the new gods, and their souls."

Belisarius craned his head, staring up at the broken stones above him. "Those—" He blew out a sharp breath, like a dry spit. "Those *divine pigs* don't view people as human. Their soldiers are just tools. So many paving blocks on the road to human perfection. They look on a human life the same way you or I look on a blade. File the worn metal away, in order to get a sharp edge. And if the scrapings shriek with pain, who cares?"

Again, he blew out a breath; and, again, it was a spit. "As for the tactics, they make perfect sense—if you look at it Link's way. The truth is, the Malwa have already lost this army, and Link knows it. The monster knows we must have already destroyed all the supplies in Charax—or have them ready for destruction, at least."

"Which we have!" barked Coutzes.

Belisarius nodded. "So why bother with clever tactics? And they can't use the Ye-tai they have left as spearhead troops. Not any longer. After the casualties they've taken, they need those Ye-tai to maintain control of the regulars. If those poor bastards hadn't already been so beaten down—" Belisarius shook his head. "Most armies, by now, after what they've suffered, would have already mutinied."

He rubbed his hand against the rough wall behind his back. The gesture was accompanied by another shake of the head, as if Belisarius was contemplating the absurdity of trying to wear down stone with flesh.

"The truth is, Coutzes," he said softly, "what you're seeing is kind of a compliment. If I were an egotistical man, I'd be preening like a rooster."

Coutzes frowned. Belisarius' smile grew very crooked. "The one thing Link is bound and determined to do—the one thing it wants to salvage out of this catastrophe—is to obliterate *me*. Me, and the whole damned army that's caused Malwa more grief than all their other opponents put together."

Coutzes grinned from ear to ear. "You really think we've become that much of a pain in the ass to it?"

Belisarius snorted. "Pain in the *ass*? It'd be better to say—pain in the *belly*." He gave the young officer squatting next to him a look which was both serious and solemn. "Know this, Coutzes. Whether we survive or not, we have already gutted Malwa. Whatever happens, the invasion of Persia is over. *Finished.* Malwa can no longer even hope to launch another war of conquest. Not for years, at least. Link will try to salvage what it can of this army—which won't be much. But after the Nehar Malka, and Charax—"

He groped for an illustration. Aide provided it.

In not much more than a year, Belisarius, you have given the Malwa their own Stalingrad and Kursk. Link can only do, now, what Hitler did. Try to hold what it can, and retreat as little as possible. But it is the defender, from this day forward, not the aggressor.

Belisarius nodded. He did not attempt to provide his young subordinate with all the history which went behind Aide's statement, but he gave him the gist.

"Coutzes, there will be another great war against evil, in the future—or would have been, at least. Aide just reminded me of it."

He had Coutzes' undivided attention, now. The young Thracian knew of Aide. He had seen him. But, like all of Belisarius' officers, he thought of the crystal being as simply the Talisman of God. A pronouncement from Aide, so far as Coutzes was concerned, was as close to divine infallibility as any man would ever encounter.

Belisarius smiled, seeing that look of awe.

What are you grinning about? demanded Aide. The facets flashed. For an instant, Belisarius had an image of a crystalline rooster, prancing about with unrestrained self-glory. **I think "divine infallibility" fits me to perfection. Why don't *you* understand that obvious truth?**

Again, the facets flashed. Belisarius choked down a laugh. The crystalline rooster, for just a split second, had been staring at him with beady, accusing eyes. A barnyard fowl, demanding its just due. A combed and feathered deity, much aggrieved by agnostic insolence.

Belisarius waved his hand, as much to still Aide's humor as to illustrate his next words. "There came a time in that war, Coutzes, when the armies of wickedness were broken. Broken, not destroyed. But from that time forward, they could only retreat. They could only hold what they had, in the hopes that someday, in the future, they might be able to start their war of conquest anew."

Belisarius snarled, now. "Those foul beasts—they were called Nazis—were never given that chance. Their enemies, after breaking them, pressed on to their destruction." He jabbed a thumb over his shoulder, pointing to the inhuman monster lurking somewhere behind the wall. "Link knows that history as well as I do. And the *thing*, whatever else, is bound and determined to see that neither I—nor any of the soldiers of this magnificent army—are alive to participate in any future wars. Or else, it knows full well—"

He rolled his eyes, following the thumb. His next words were whispered. A promise, hissed: "I *will* be alive, monster. And I *will* give you Operation Bagration, and the destruction of Army Group Centre. And I *will* give you Sicily and D-Day, and the Falaise Pocket—except *this* time, beast, the pocket will be closed in time."

He turned his eyes back to Coutzes. Fury faded, replaced by wry humor. "As I said, this frenzied assault is quite a compliment. Feeds my pride no end, it does. Just think, Coutzes. Great gods of the future, convinced of their own perfection, have set themselves the single task of killing one pitiful, primitive, imperfect, preposterous, ridiculous, pathetic Thracian *goddam fucking son-of-a-bitch*."

Coutzes laughed. "Can't say I blame them!"

Another volley of arrows sailed overhead. Behind them came a volley of words—the sounds of Ye-tai bellowing commands. Coutzes popped his head over the wall. When he brought it down, he was frowning.

"I think—" He transferred the frown to Belisarius. "I want you out of here, General. They'll be starting the next assault any minute. A stray grenade—" He shook his head.

Belisarius did not argue the matter. He rose to a half-crouch and scuttled out of the room. In the roofless chamber beyond, Anastasius was waiting, along with the other cataphracts who were now serving as his additional bodyguards. Maurice had replaced

Valentinian with two of them, after Valentinian's capture. The cataphracts chosen had not taken offense at that relative estimation of their merits compared to Valentinian's. They had been rather pleased, actually, at the compliment. They had expected Maurice to choose twice that number.

Anastasius snorted, seeing the general scurry into the room. But he refrained from any further expression of displeasure.

Belisarius smiled. "It's important for a commanding officer to be seen on the front lines, Anastasius. You know that."

As the small body of Romans hurried out of the shattered ruins of an artisan's former workshop, heading south toward relative safety, Anastasius snorted again. But, again, he refrained from further comment. He had been through this dance with Belisarius so many times that he had long since given up hope of teaching new steps to his general.

One of the other cataphracts, new to the job, was not so philosophical. "For Christ's sake, Isaac," he whispered to his companion, "the general could lounge on the docks, for all the army cares. Be happier if he did, in fact."

Isaac shrugged. "Yeah, Priscus, that's what I think too. But maybe that's why he's Rome's best general—best ever, you ask me—and we're spear-chuckers."

Priscus' response, whatever it might have been, was buried beneath the sounds of grenades exploding a few dozen yards behind them. The Malwa were beginning a new assault. Seconds later, the shouts of charging men were blended with musket fire and more grenade explosions. And then, within half a minute, came the first sounds of steel meeting steel.

The cataphracts did not look back. Not once, in all the time it took them, guarding Belisarius, to clamber through the rubbled streets and shattered buildings which were all that days of Roman demolition and Malwa shelling had left of Charax's center district. Not until they finally reached the relatively undamaged harbor which made up the city's southern area did the cataphracts turn and look back to the north.

"Besides," said Isaac, renewing their conversation, "what are you complaining about, anyway?" He thrust his beard northward. "Would you rather be back there again? Fighting street to street?"

Priscus grimaced. Like Isaac, he had become Belisarius' bodyguard only a few days before. The initial pair of bodyguards whom

Maurice had selected to replace Valentinian had been replaced themselves, after the siege of Charax began. Maurice, determined to keep Belisarius alive, had made his final selection based on the most cold-blooded reasoning possible. Whichever soldiers among the bucellarii could demonstrate, in days of savage battle in the streets of Charax, that they were the most murderous, got the job.

Isaac and Priscus had been at the top of the list. They had earned that position in one of the most brutal tests ever devised by the human race. Neither of them had heard of Stalingrad, nor would they ever. But either of them, planted amongst the veterans of Chuikov's 62nd Army, would have felt quite at home. Language barriers be damned.

"Good point," muttered Priscus. He turned, along with Isaac, and plodded after Belisarius. The general was heading toward the heavy-walled warehouse where the Roman army had set up its headquarters. Priscus eyed the figure of his tall general, stooping into a small door. "At least he's got the good sense to leave before the blades get wet."

"So far," grunted Isaac. He tugged at one of the straps holding up his heavy cataphract gear. "Damn, I'm sick of walking around in this armor."

The cataphracts plodded on a few more steps. As they came to the door, Isaac repeated: "So far. But don't get your hopes up. Two weeks from now, three at the outside, the Malwa will have reached the harbor. You know what'll happen, when that day comes."

Priscus scowled. "Sallies, lance charges, the whole bit—with the general right in the middle of it. We'll wish Valentinian were here, then."

On that gloomy note, the two cataphracts stooped and forced their armored way through a door designed for midgets. The door led into what seemed to be a six-foot-long tunnel in the massive wall of the warehouse. The effort of that passage left them practically snarling.

Five minutes later, they were smiling like cherubs.

Chapter 37

As soon as Belisarius straightened after squeezing through the narrow passage, he saw Bouzes rushing toward him. Except for a well-lit area against the far wall, where Belisarius had set up his writing desk and map table, the interior of the cavernous warehouse was dark. Bouzes was in such a hurry that he tripped over some debris lying on the floor and wound up stumbling into Belisarius' arms.

"Easy, there, easy," chuckled Belisarius. He set Bouzes back up straight. "Things can't be that bad."

Bouzes muttered a quick apology. Then, pointing toward a door on the opposite wall: "Maurice says you've got to go up and see something. He told me to tell you as soon as you arrived."

Belisarius brow was creased, just slightly. "What's the problem?"

Bouzes shook his head. "Don't know. Maurice wouldn't tell me anything else. But he was very emphatic about it."

Belisarius strode toward the door. Behind him, he heard the heavy footsteps of his armored cataphracts following. The door, like the one he had just passed through, was low and narrow. Again, Belisarius had to stoop to pass through. Except for the huge doors designed for freight, the entire warehouse seemed to have been built by dwarves.

Once through the door, he clambered up a wooden staircase leading to the roof. As quickly as Belisarius was moving, the effort of negotiating the steep and narrow stairs was considerable, even for a man in his excellent condition and wearing only half-armor. He felt a moment's sympathy for his cataphract bodyguards. They'd be huffing by the time they made the same climb.

The staircase debouched into a small chamber. Again, Belisarius squeezed through a tiny door, and emerged into open air. Behind him, the northern wall of the warehouse reared up like a battlement. Ahead of him, the brick roof—braced underneath by heavy beams—formed a flat expanse stretching toward the sea. He could see the delta, glistening under a midday sun.

Belisarius had selected this warehouse for his headquarters because of its odd design. At one time, he suspected, the north wall of the building had been the outer wall of Charax. It was built like a fortification, at least—which might explain the tiny doors. When Charax expanded, and new walls were built, some enterprising merchant had simply built his warehouse against the six-foot-thick northern wall. The end result, so far as the Roman general was concerned, was as good a field headquarters as he could ask for. The massive north wall gave some protection from artillery while, at the same time, the flat roof provided him with a perfect vantage point from which to observe the delta.

He saw Maurice standing on the southern edge of the roof. There was no railing to keep someone from pitching over the side onto the docks thirty feet below, but Maurice seemed unconcerned. The chiliarch had apparently heard the squeaking of the door, for he was already looking at Belisarius when the general emerged onto the roof.

"Come here!" he hollered, holding up the telescope. "There's a new development I think you should consider."

Belisarius hurried over. As he made his way across the fifty-foot-wide expanse, he quickly scanned the entire area. From the roof, he could see all of southern Charax as well as the great delta which extended southward to the Persian Gulf itself, perhaps ten miles away. Charax had been built on the east bank of the largest tributary which formed the Tigris-Euphrates delta, on a spit extending south and west of the Mesopotamian mainland. The tributary could hardly be called a river. It was so broad that it was almost a small gulf in its own right. For all practical purposes, Charax was a port city which was surrounded by water from the west all the way around to its east-by-southeast quadrant.

His eyes scanned right, then left. He could see nothing that would cause Maurice such apparent concern. There were masses of Malwa troops on both banks of the tributary, but they had been there since the first few days of the siege. The Malwa had tried to position siege guns on those banks, where they could have fired into the harbor area, but had given up the effort after a week. The ground, as the reeds which covered the banks indicated, was much too soggy. The troops were there simply to keep the Romans from escaping while the main forces of the Malwa tried to hammer their way into the city from the north. They also kept the galleys patrolling the delta supplied with provisions.

He turned his eyes to the fore, looking for the galleys. Again, he could see nothing amiss. There had been upwards of twenty galleys stationed in Charax, when Belisarius broke into the city. Half of them had been on patrol, and all but three of the ones moored to the docks had managed to get free before Roman troops could seize them.

Since then, the Malwa had used the galleys to maintain a blockade. Belisarius' obvious escape route was to sail out on the cargo ships he had captured. But there was no way to get those ungainly vessels through a line of war galleys. The huge Malwa cargo ships might have been able to withstand ramming—some of them, at least—but the galleys were armed with rockets as well as rams. At close range, with no room to maneuver, rocket volleys would turn unarmored cargo ships into floating funeral pyres.

As it was, Belisarius' soldiers had been hard-pressed to extinguish the small conflagrations started on the moored ships by long-range rocket fire. Link was making no pretense of saving the cargo ships to evacuate the Malwa troops. Even though the vast majority of the rockets never came close to the docks, the galleys as well as the troops stationed on the banks had kept up a steady barrage since the beginning of the siege. Belisarius didn't want to think about the disciplinary measures which Link must be taking, to keep its troops driving forward into what, by now, even the dimwits among them must have realized was a suicide mission.

I'm sure that Link has promised the Ye-tai commanders that Malwa would save the Ye-tai, if the barbarians kept the regular troops under control.

Belisarius agreed with Aide's assessment. But, as he advanced toward Maurice, Belisarius could still see nothing in the delta to cause any concern. Outside of three galleys moored to a makeshift pier on the east bank, taking on supplies, the rest were on patrol. As usual, the Malwa kept five galleys close to the harbor, with the remainder spread out between one and two miles away.

When he came up to Maurice, the gray-haired chiliarch was studying the galleys themselves. His expression seemed one of grim satisfaction.

"They haven't seen it yet," he said. "Our elevation's better."

He handed Belisarius the telescope. Grim satisfaction was replaced by—

Before he even got the telescope up, in a motion so quick he almost gave himself a black eye, Belisarius knew. He only heard Maurice's next words dimly, through the rushing blood in his ears.

"Yeah, I thought you'd want to see it, lad. It's not often, after all, that a man gets to watch Venus rise from the waves."

Belisarius saw the glint before he spotted the masts. He had been looking for sails, until he realized there wouldn't be any. This close to their final destination, the Ethiopian warships would be advancing under oar.

But there was no doubt of what he was seeing. Belisarius was not a seaman, but he could tell the difference between a warship and a cargo vessel at a glance. The twelve vessels whose masts he could see, perhaps ten miles away, were obviously fighting craft. And he had enough experience, with perhaps a minute's study, to be able to distinguish the upperstructure of an Axumite warship from a Malwa galley.

"They're ours, all right," he muttered happily. "No doubt about it. But—" He brought the telescope back to the lead ship in the oncoming flotilla. There it was again. Something glinting.

He pulled the telescope away from his eye, frowning. Not worried, simply puzzled. "There's something odd—"

Maurice nodded. "You spotted it too? Something shining on and off, on the lead ship?" The chiliarch's eyes fixed on the horizon. "I saw it myself. First thing I spotted, in fact. Still haven't been able to figure out what it is. Might be a mirror, I suppose, if Antonina wanted to signal—"

Both men, simultaneously, realized the truth. And both, simultaneously, burst into laughter.

"Well, of course!" shouted Maurice gaily. "She's Venus, isn't she? Naturally she's got the biggest damn brass tits in the world!"

Belisarius said nothing coherent, until he stopped leaping about in a manner which was halfway between a drunken jig and a war dance. Then, before the astonished eyes of the cataphract bodyguards who had finally puffed their way onto the roof, the *strategos* of the Roman Empire and the commander of its finest army—normally as cool as ice in the face of the enemy—began taunting the distant Malwa troops like an eight-year-old boy in a schoolyard.

"That's my lady! That's my lady!" was the only one of those expressions which was not so gross, so obscene, so foul, so vile, and so vulgar, that Satan's minions would have fled in horror, taloned paws clasped over bat-ugly ears.

In the hours which followed, as Maurice and Vasudeva organized the escape from Charax, Belisarius paid no attention to the doings of his army.

There was no need for him to do so, of course. The plans for the escape had been made weeks before Charax was even seized. Ever since the Romans had taken the city, a large portion of the soldiers had been working like beavers to get ready for departure. The cargo ships were loaded with provisions. The city was mined for final destruction. All that remained to be done was drive out the horses, collect the civilians, and organize the fighting retreat back to the docks.

The horses were driven out within the first two hours. Released from their holding corrals near the docks, the panicked creatures were driven through broken streets toward the Malwa lines. It was a task which the Roman soldiers carried out with reluctance but, perhaps for that reason, as quickly as possible.

Most of the horses would die, they knew. Many would be killed by the Malwa themselves, either because they were mistaken for a cavalry charge or simply from being struck by stray missiles or grenades. Others would break their legs clambering through the rubble. Most of the horses who escaped the city, except for those captured by the Malwa, would probably die of starvation in the desert and swamps beyond. And even those horses which found themselves in the relative safety of Malwa captivity would, in all likelihood, be eaten by the Malwa troops as they themselves became desperate for food.

But the only alternative was to destroy them along with the city. There was absolutely no way to load them aboard the cargo ships. Transporting large numbers of horses by sea was a difficult enough task, under the best of circumstances. It would be impossible for an army making a hurried escape under enemy fire. Given the alternatives, the Romans would drive the horses out. Some would survive in the desert, after all, long enough to be captured by bedouin.

So, at least, Belisarius had explained the matter to his troops. And, so far as it went, the explanation was not dishonest. But the general's ultimate reason for the choice had not been humanitarian. When he needed to be, Belisarius could be as ruthless as any man alive. He knew full well that as soon as Link discovered that enemy warships were approaching Charax, it would understand— finally—the full extent of Belisarius' plan. At which point Link would order an all-out, frenzied assault on Charax, driving the Malwa troops forward as if they were beasts themselves. Stampeding herds of horses, meeting those incoming human herds, would create as much confusion as possible—confusion which would delay the Malwa advance, and give the escaping Romans that much greater a chance to save their own lives.

It took even less time to organize the evacuation of the civilians. The civilians were all women. There had been a handful of male Persian civilians when the Romans took the city. Within a day, after the women told their tales, they had been executed along with the Malwa soldiers with whom they had collaborated.

The female civilians had been warned days in advance, and now were being rounded up. But there was hardly any "rounding up" to do. Since the Romans had arrived and freed them from Malwa subjugation, none of Charax's women had strayed more than a few yards away from a Roman soldier at any time of the day or night. That was from their own choice, not coercion. They had been like half-drowned kittens, desperately clutching a log for survival.

As poor women thrust into such a wretched state have done throughout history, the survivors of Malwa Charax had become camp followers of the Roman army. Depending on their age, appearance, and temperament, they had become concubines, cooks, laundresses, nurses—more often than not, all of those combined. And if their current status was dismal, by abstract standards, it seemed like a virtual paradise to them.

The Roman soldiers, crude as they might be, were rarely brutal to their women. Belisarius' soldiers, at least. Other Roman armies might have been. But, between Belisarius' discipline—to which they had long been accustomed—and their own horror at Malwa bestiality, the soldiers had conducted themselves in a manner which might almost be called chivalrous. So long, of course, as the term "chivalrous" is understood to include: vulgarity; coarse humor; the unthinking assumption that the women would feed them, clean up after them and do the washing; and, needless to say, an instant readiness to copulate using any means short of outright rape.

In truth, the social position of most of the women was no worse than it had been before the Malwa invasion. More licentious, true. But there was this by way of compensation: the new men in their lives had proven themselves to be tough enough to give those women a real chance for survival. That is no small thing, in the vortex of a raging war. Belisarius, through his officers, had already told the women that they would be reunited with whatever families they might still have. But, not to his surprise, the majority had made clear that they would just as soon remain camp followers of his army—*wherever* it went.

The difficulty in evacuating the women, therefore, was not in collecting them. Those women who could move were gathered on the docks sooner than anyone else. The problem was that, even weeks after the liberation of Charax, many of the women could *not* move. At least a third of the women who had been enslaved in the military brothels were still too weak or sick to move under their own power. Their evacuation posed a major medical undertaking.

That evacuation took three hours, before all the litters were carried aboard the ships. In the end, only twelve women were left behind, in the medical ward set aside for the most badly abused slaves. All of them were unconscious, and so close to death that moving them seemed impossible.

The Roman officer in charge of evacuating that medical ward danced back and forth, fretful and indecisive. A nurse, who had herself been chained in one of the brothels, whispered to a Kushan soldier. He handed her his dagger. The nurse, cold-faced, ordered everyone out of the ward, using a tone which Empress Theodora would have approved. When she emerged, five minutes later, her face was calm, her manner relaxed. She had even taken the time to clean the dagger.

All that remained was the fighting retreat of the soldiers holding the front lines. Under any circumstances in the world, other than the one in which he found himself, Belisarius would have overseen that retreat personally. His bodyguards would have been driven half-insane, from the risks he would have taken. But today—

Maurice did not even bother to discuss it with Belisarius. He simply carried out the task himself. The work was not beyond his capability, after all. In truth, Maurice probably led that retreat as well as Belisarius could have. And there was an added advantage, at least to the soldiers who served as *Maurice's* bodyguards. The grizzled veteran had a proper understanding of the proper place of a proper commanding officer in the middle of a battle, thank you.

So, in one of history's little ironies, the military genius who led what was arguably, up to that day, the most daring and brilliant campaign of all time, played no role in its dramatic conclusion. Never even noticed it, in truth. Instead, his eye glued to a telescope, the general found himself undergoing a brand-new experience.

He knew, abstractly, of the anguish Antonina had always undergone whenever he went off to war. And he had chuckled, hearing the tales from Maurice and Irene afterward, of the way Antonina spent the day after his departure.

He was chuckling no longer. Belisarius, watching his wife wage a battle at sea—right under his eyes, but beyond his reach or control—finally understood what it meant. To stare at a horse.

Chapter 38

"Stay *down*, Antonina," grumbled Ousanas. The aqabe tsentsen looked to Matthew, and pointed at the woman forcing her head past his elbow. "Sit on her, if you have to."

Matthew flushed. Then, gingerly, advanced his great paws toward Antonina's shoulders.

Antonina gave him a quick glare. For a moment, Matthew retreated. But only for a moment. The inexorable clasp of unwanted protection returned.

"All right—all right!" snapped Antonina. She stepped back perhaps half an inch. Peevishly: "*Now* are you satisfied?"

"No!" came the immediate response. "I want you *down*, fool woman. Any minute now—"

A stretched-out shriek drew Ousanas' eyes back to the front. Through a narrow slit in the flagship's bow-shield, he could see the first volley of rockets heading their way from the line of Malwa galleys ahead.

"And *now* has come." He stepped back two paces, pushing Antonina behind him. With a little wave, he gestured Gersem forward. Wahsi's successor stepped up to the slit, where he could see well enough to guide the battle.

"Remember, Gersem," said Ousanas. "All that matters is to destroy the galleys. Whatever the cost. If need be—even if ours are destroyed—we can find a place on Belisarius' ships."

The new Dakuen commander nodded.

A moment later, the sound of the first rocket volley came hissing by overhead. As soon as the missiles went past the bow-shield, Ousanas and Antonina craned their heads to watch their flight.

"Way too long," muttered Ousanas. "But they've all been fitted with venturi. Let's hope the shields stand up."

He brought his eyes down to the short Roman woman standing next to him.

"I will not have you dead, when Belisarius comes aboard this ship," Ousanas said. "Not that, whatever else."

"We might all—"

Ousanas clapped his hands. An instant later, as helpless as a doll, Antonina was lowered onto the deck. Matthew and Leo each held an arm and a leg. Their grip on her was as delicate as possible, under the circumstances, but Antonina was not mollified. The entire process was accompanied by her own monologue.

"You're dismissed! Discharged, d'you hear?" was the only one of her spluttering phrases which was not so vituperative, so vindictive, so intemperate and so utterly foul-mouthed that Ousanas howled with laughter, clasping his hands over his belly.

Once her butt had been firmly planted on the deck, Antonina broke off her tirade and glared up at Ousanas. "You think this is funny?" she demanded.

Still laughing, Ousanas nodded. An instant later—even in her outrage, Antonina was stunned by the speed with which Ousanas could move, without, seemingly, any warning or effort—the aqabe tsentsen was sitting right next to her. He beamed down upon her from a height which was now only measured in inches instead of feet.

"Hysterically so," he pronounced. His next words were drowned under the sound of another rocket volley screaming overhead. Again, he and Antonina craned their necks, watching the rockets' trajectory.

"Can't see where they hit!" complained Antonina. Scowling: "Can't see anything, in this ridiculous position."

Ousanas' grin returned. "Which," he said with satisfaction, "is the whole point. You don't *need* to see where they hit. And if *you* can't see the rockets when they hit, we can hope *they* will return the favor."

Antonina's scowl, if anything, deepened. "That's the stupidest thing I ever heard! Those rockets'll go wherever they want to go.

You watch!" Deep, deep scowl. "Except we *won't* be able to watch because we can't see a damned thing so the rockets'll catch us by surprise and—"

The next volley of rockets caught them by surprise. The Malwa, apparently, had adjusted the angle of the rocket troughs perched in the bows of the oncoming galleys. The first signal of incoming fire which Antonina and Ousanas received was the sudden boom of rockets smashing into the bow-shield and caroming off to either side. They only caught glimpses of the missiles streaking past. Perhaps two seconds later, they heard the erupting warheads. Both of them knew, from the sound alone, that the rockets had exploded harmlessly in midair.

Antonina's displeasure vanished instantly. "Beautiful!" she cried. "Beautiful!"

She squirmed onto her knees, raising her head high enough to be able to see over the side of the ship. Ousanas made no objection. He even gave Matthew and Leo, squatting nearby, a reassuring little wave of the hand. The essence of the gesture was clear. *As long as the fool woman doesn't stick her head and her brass tits out where any Malwa can take a shot at her.*

Antonina's lips were pursed, now, with a faint worry. "One problem, though. I hadn't thought about it." She pointed forward. "We sure enough protect against bow shots. But the ricochets might hit one of the ships alongside. There isn't any shielding covering most of the ships."

Ousanas shrugged. "Won't matter, Antonina. Luck—good or bad—will happen as it will."

The bow shield bellied again under the impact of a new rocket volley. Again, the boom, almost like a drum; and, again, two missiles caromed by. And, again, exploded harmlessly over the waves.

Antonina, scanning right and left as she stared toward the stern of the flagship, was relieved by what she saw. The Ethiopian ship captains had already recognized the same danger and were responding. Charax's delta was several miles wide, giving plenty of sea room. The Axumite ships, advancing in a single line, were already spreading out.

Antonina watched several more rockets bounce off the shields on other ships and skitter past the entire formation. The angle of the shields, she realized, was so acute that only the worst possible luck could cause a rocket to carom sideways.

"The main thing," Ousanas continued—unlike Antonina, he had not bothered to watch the trajectories—"is that almost all the incoming rockets will be harmless. Once we get in ramming range, they'll stop firing."

He chuckled grimly. "Not even a fanatic Mahaveda priest will want to be in the bow of a ship plunging in for a ram."

Antonina turned back and hunkered lower. She studied the figure of Gersem in the bow. The new Dakuen commander, still peering intently through a slit in the shield, suddenly seemed very young.

Ousanas, apparently, could read minds. "Relax. I picked *him*, even though he's the most junior of the sub-officers, because he's also the best seaman."

"Says who?" demanded Antonina. "You know as much about boats as I do about—"

"Says all the *other* sub-officers," came the serene reply. Ousanas stretched out his arms, pointing to the Axumite ships ranging alongside them to both port and starboard.

"That's true on all of them. Existing commanders, of course, weren't replaced. But until the boarding starts, command of each of those ships is in the hands of the most capable captain. Rank be damned."

Mention of "boarding" focused Antonina's mind elsewhere. She turned and smiled sweetly at Matthew.

"I forgive you. Now, please bring me my gun."

It was Ousanas' turn to scowl. "What do you need that thing for?" he demanded. "*You* aren't going to be storming across any decks."

Antonina shook her head. "Certainly not!" Again, she smiled sweetly. "Whole idea's absurd. Unladylike."

Matthew returned with his mission accomplished. Antonina cradled the monstrous weapon, like a beloved child.

"But you never know," she said serenely. "Shit happens, in a battle."

Ousanas, plain to see, was not a happy man. But he made no further protest. What counter-argument could he advance? Antonina had just pronounced the oldest of all veteran wisdoms. "Shit happens," Matthew and Leo echoed, like a Greek chorus.

Antonina saw Gersem grow tense. Tense. Tense.

She held her breath. She couldn't see a blessed thing forward, but she knew the line of twelve Axumite ships had almost met the fifteen Malwa vessels charging toward them. By now, the enemy would be up to full ramming speed.

Held her breath. Held her breath.

"Relax," said Ousanas. He seemed as stolidly serene as a lump of granite. "O ye of little faith. Malwa galleys? In an open fight at sea—against *Axumites*?"

He raised his head, like a wolf baying at the moon. "Ha!"

That cry of derision blended into Gersem's sudden shouting command.

Within a minute, both the derision and the stolid serenity proved justified. And Antonina, once again, made a solemn vow not to meddle in the affairs of professionals.

Gersem timed the order perfectly. The Malwa galley driving straight upon them—bow against bow—was within yards of a collision. The Ethiopian warship, with experienced rowers and steersman, suddenly skittered aside. Then, at Gersem's new command, drove it forward in a quick lunge. And then—new command, *bellowed*—the rowers on the ship's starboard side lifted their oars straight up in a quick and coordinated motion. The maneuver was a perfectly executed *diekplous*, as the tactic was called by the Rhodians who were the Mediterranean's finest naval forces.

Disaster struck their Malwa opponent. The captain of that ship, as was true of all Malwa captains, was inexperienced in sea battle. Inexperienced, at least, against a real navy. As powerful as the Malwa Empire was, it rarely faced a challenge at sea from other kingdoms. The principal duty of the Malwa Empire's navy was to protect its merchant ships against pirates.

Arrogance and brute force are a splendid way to deal with pirates. They are poor methods, however, against one of the finest navies in the world.

The Malwa ship came driving in at full ramming speed. The Malwa captain, seeing that his opponent's vessel had no ram, was almost chortling with glee. He would split the enemy's prow in half, back away, and then finish them off with rockets. Once crippled, the enemy craft would no longer be able to hide behind that bizarre and infernally effective shield.

At the last possible moment, the Malwa captain ordered his rowers to slow the ship. No captain in his right mind will ram at full speed. The force of the collision might rupture his own bow. At the very least, his ram would be driven too deeply for extraction. Proper ramming tactics require: a full-speed lunge to get within ramming range as soon as possible; a sudden slowing of the ship with backthrust oars; then, in the last few feet, a simple collision. Ram splits hull, but is not wedged; back off, repeat if necessary.

Good tactics, classic tactics. But the Malwa captain never considered the possibility that his opponent would know those tactics just as well, have long since determined the proper counter, and have a captain, and rowers, and a steersman who were far superior to himself and his crew.

At Gersem's command, the Ethiopian ship sidled away from the ram. By the time the Malwa captain realized he was going to miss his strike, Gersem had ordered his ship into a forward lunge. The Malwa captain began screaming new commands to his confused rowers and steersman—

It was too late. The diekplous was done. The Malwa galley drifted inexorably forward. The Ethiopian ship, oars raised out of harm's way, drove down the side of the Malwa craft not more than two feet distant—starboard against starboard, practically scraping the hulls—smashing and shattering every Malwa oar it encountered. Which, given the Malwa crew's confusion and inexperience, was almost all of them.

The Malwa galley, as a vessel, was instantly crippled. Even worse was the damage to the crew. The oarbutts, flailing and splintering and hammering, killed only one man outright. But almost half of the Malwa galley's starboard rowers suffered broken bones, cracked skulls, and crushed ribs—and all of them were bruised and stunned. All order and discipline in the vessel collapsed, as the shouting commands of the officers were buried under screams and groans.

The port-side rowers gaped at the scene. And then, gaped wider at the sight of two five-inch cannon barrels approaching. Seconds later, many of those gaping mouths were swept out of existence entirely. Axumite marines were pouring over the side before the smoke cleared. Again, the murderous cry erupted: *Ta'akha Maryam! Ta'akha Maryam!*

The combat which followed lasted not more than five minutes. Six Malwa sailors escaped by diving over the side. One of them, a good swimmer in superb physical condition, would make it to the bank of the delta several miles away. The rest would drown, sharing the grim fate of their fellow crewmen.

In Charax's delta, Malwa would get no more mercy from Ethiopia than it had gotten from Rome in the city itself.

Antonina, huddling safely in the hull of her flagship, clasped the handcannon more tightly still. It was not fear which produced those whitened knuckles. Simply horror, at the sounds of unseen butchery not more than fifteen feet away. Cries of fury; cries of pain. Spears splitting flesh; sundering bone. Soft groans, and hissing agony, and death gurgling into silence.

All was silent, now, except the waves against the ships, and grunting exertion. Silent—except for the sodden noise of spears plunging, again and again, into corpses. Slaughter made certain, and certain, and certain. Once only, a low voice, filled with satisfaction: *Ta'akha Maryam.*

"I told you," said Ousanas serenely. The aqabe tsentsen, as had been true throughout the battle, had never so much as moved a hand. "O ye of little faith."

In the battle as a whole, Axum suffered the total loss of only one ship. It was a grievous loss, because the entire crew went with their vessel when the Malwa galley they were boarding suddenly erupted. What happened? No one would ever know. An accident, perhaps. Perhaps a fanatic priest.

Five other Axumite warships suffered major casualties. Numbers will tell, even against experience. Not every Axumite captain maneuvered as skillfully as Gersem. And, with twelve Axumite ships facing fifteen opponents, three Malwa galleys were left free to strike where they would.

Malwa's sea captains might have been arrogant and incautious, but they were by no means cowards. All three of those unharmed vessels rammed Axumite ships. Tried to, at least. One of the Malwa galleys was so badly bloodied by well-aimed cannon fire that it drew off—drifted off, rather; its captain and steersman slain, along with a third of the crew. The other two rammed, and then boarded.

But the final result, even there, was the same. The Malwa advantage in numbers was not enough—not even if they had been doubled—to offset the experience and ferocity of Axum's spearmen. The only difference was between a fight lost—badly lost—and an outright slaughter.

At Ousanas' command, the Axumite line reformed and advanced again toward Charax. The city's harbor was less than three miles away, now. Sharp-eyed Ethiopian lookouts reported that the Roman troop vessels were beginning to leave the docks.

There were only eight ships left in the Axumite fleet. In addition to the one destroyed outright, Ousanas had decided to abandon the two which had been rammed and one other which had been badly mauled. None of the three ships were in any danger of sinking, but they had been damaged enough to make them useless in combat. The sarwen on the three crippled vessels transferred quickly to other Ethiopian warships, filling out those crews which had suffered heavy casualties.

Eight ships, now, not twelve—but there were only five Malwa galleys left.

"Look at 'em," snorted Antonina, studying the enemy ships. "And they say women can't make up their minds!"

Ousanas grinned. "What you observe, Antonina, is a modern version of being caught in a myth. Between Scylla and Charybdis."

The commander of the Malwa inner squadron seemed to be torn by indecision. Or perhaps, as Ousanas said, he was simply caught between two monsters. At first, the five galleys headed toward the oncoming Ethiopians. Then, seeing the Roman ships casting loose from the docks, they headed back. The principal assignment of those galleys, after all, was to keep Belisarius and his men from escaping.

Then, seeing the first of the gigantic explosions which began to destroy what was left of Charax, the little Malwa fleet simply drifted aimlessly.

What to do? What to do? The harbor area was as yet untouched by either flame or gunpowder fury. The Malwa flotilla's commander knew that Belisarius would not set off the final round of explosions until he saw his way clear. With the rest of Charax a raging inferno—there had been naphtha mixed with the demolition charges—there was no possibility the oncoming Malwa army could reach the docks before the Roman ships were well into the delta. Where—

The Ethiopian warships were within a mile of the inner squadron. They would reach the Malwa galleys in less than ten minutes, long before the Roman troopships would be within effective rocket range.

Eight against five, now—and the flotilla commander had seen the carnage when the odds had favored Malwa.

Suddenly, from the eastern bank of the delta, signal rockets flared into the sky. Green, green, white. Within thirty seconds, all five Malwa galleys were pulling for the shore. Taking the only sensible course, when caught between monsters. *Get out of the way.*

"Will you look at them go?" chortled Antonina a few minutes later, watching the Malwa galleys scuttling eastward. "Jason and his Argonauts couldn't have made better speed."

Ousanas grinned. "Well, of course! What else can they do?"

He pointed straight ahead. The view was open, now. Already, the shields were being removed and the pole framework dismantled. The fleet of Roman troop vessels was completely clear of the harbor, which was beginning to burn fiercely. A rippling series of explosions shattered the docks themselves.

"To one side," Ousanas announced, "they have the famous general Belisarius, leading his fearsome men. To the other—*worse yet!*"

He began prancing about, lunging with his spear. "They face *me*! I was terrible, terrible—a demon!"

Antonina burst into laughter. "You spent the entire battle sitting on your ass! Fraud! Impostor!"

Ousanas shook his head. "That's because I understand the proper place of a commander in battle, woman." Scowling: "And what does that have to do with anything, anyway? It's the soul that matters, not the paltry flesh. Everybody knows that!"

He bared his teeth at the fleeing galleys. "The soul of Ousanas, that's what terrified them!" A majestic, condescending wave of the hand. "The sarwen helped, of course. A bit."

Antonina began to make a bantering rejoinder when something caught her eye.

Someone, rather. The nearest Roman troopship was less than two hundred yards away. A soldier was perched on the very tip of its bow. A tall man, he seemed to be. And he was waving wildly.

A moment later, Antonina was teetering on the very bow of her own ship, waving frantically, screaming incoherent phrases.

Jumping up and down, now. Ousanas barely managed to grab her before she fell over the side.

"Antonina! Be careful! In that cuirass, you'll drown in two minutes."

Antonina paid him no attention at all. She was weeping now, from sheer joy. Still waving her arms and screaming. And still jumping up and down. Small as she was, and for all his great strength, Ousanas had some difficulty in his newfound task.

"Marvelous," he growled. "Once again, I have to save a fool Roman woman from destruction."

Chapter 39

In the event, Ousanas wound up saving the fool Roman general. When the troopship was almost alongside Antonina's craft, Belisarius—he was leaping about himself, hollering his own ecstasy—slipped and fell over the side.

Antonina shrieked. Ousanas, by main force, hurled her back into Matthew's arms.

"Keep her here!" he bellowed. An instant later, Ousanas split the water in a clean dive.

He found Belisarius in less than fifteen seconds, floundering about, gulping for breath as he tried to unlace his armor. Fortunately, the general was an excellent swimmer and—more fortunately still—was not wearing full cataphract gear. Had he been, Belisarius would already have been dragged under. But the half-armor was heavy enough, and awkward to remove.

"Hold still," snarled Ousanas. He tucked his arm under Belisarius and began towing him to Antonina's ship. Belisarius instantly relaxed, using only his feet to help keep him afloat.

"Nice to see you again, Ousanas," he said cheerfully.

Ousanas snorted. "Tell me something, Belisarius." He paused for a breath. His powerful strokes had already brought them almost to the ship. "How did you Roman imbeciles manage to conquer half the world?"

Pause for a breath. They were alongside, now. Eager hands were lifting Belisarius out of the water. "Personally, I wouldn't let you out of the house to fetch water from a well. You'd fall in, for sure."

He got no answer. The Roman imbecile was already in the arms of Venus.

About ten minutes later, Belisarius and Antonina finally pried themselves apart. Belisarius winced.

"You have *got* to get rid of that cuirass," he muttered, rubbing his rib cage. He eyed the device respectfully. "It's even deadlier than it is obscene."

Antonina grinned up at him. "So take it off, then. You can do it. I know you can." The grin widened. "Seen you strip me naked, I have, faster than—"

"Hush, wife!" commanded Belisarius. He frowned with solemn, sober disapproval. The expression, alas, fell wide of its mark. Antonina's grin grew positively salacious.

"Oh sure, soldier, tell me the thought never crossed your mind. That's just a cudgel, stuck in your trousers, in case you're ambushed by footpads."

Belisarius burst out laughing. Antonina's eyes quickly studied the immediate area.

"Bit primitive," she mused, "but we could probably manage on one of the rowing benches, as long as you refrain from your usual acrobatics." She cast a cold eye on the small crowd surrounding them. "Have to get rid of the spectators, though. Tell you what. You're the general. You order 'em overboard and I'll shoot the laggards."

Her last remarks had not been made sotto voce. Rather the opposite. The small crowd grinned at her. Antonina tried to maintain the murderous gleam in her eye but, truth to tell, failed miserably. The giggles didn't help.

"Guess not." The sigh which followed would have provided the world with a new standard for melancholy. If she hadn't kept giggling.

Belisarius swept her back into his arms. Into her ear he whispered: "As it happens, love, I've arranged accommodations on the troopship. The captain's cabin, in point of fact. Reserved for our exclusive use."

"Let's get to it, then!" she hissed eagerly. "God, am I glad I married a general. Love a man who can plan ahead."

He sighed himself, now. There was genuine melancholy in the sound.

"Not quite yet," he murmured. "Tonight, love, tonight. But there's still work to be done."

Startled, she drew back her head and stared up at him. "It *is* done!" she protested.

Antonina swiveled her head, scanning the ships which seemed to fill the delta. "Isn't it? Didn't you get everyone off the docks?"

Belisarius smiled. "Oh, *that's* done. To perfection. Best planned and executed operation I've ever seen, if I say so myself." For a moment, he seemed a bit embarrassed. "I'll have to remember to compliment Maurice," he mumbled.

He drove past that awkward subject. "But there's something left, yet. Something else." His smile changed, became quite cold and ruthless. "Call it dessert, if you will."

Antonina was still staring at him in confusion. Belisarius turned his head. When he spotted Ousanas, he motioned him over with a little nod.

"Are you in charge?" he asked.

Ousanas grinned, as hugely as ever. "Is not King Eon a genius? Didn't I always say, when I was his dawazz, that the boy would go far? Make wise decisions—especially with regard to posts and positions?"

Belisarius chuckled. "Did you notice anything odd, in those last moments before our escape?"

Ousanas spoke without hesitation. "The signal rockets. Those galleys didn't flee. They were *summoned* to the shore. I did not understand that. I had expected them to launch a final desperate attack."

Belisarius' smile was no longer cold. It was purely feral. "Yes. That *is* interesting."

He said nothing further. But it only took Ousanas four seconds to understand. The aqabe tsentsen swiveled his head, staring at the far-distant piers where the five Malwa galleys were now moored.

"It is well known," he murmured, "that wounded animals make easy prey." He turned back to Belisarius. Predator grin met carnivore smile. "Ask any hunter, Roman. The best way to hunt is from a blind."

"Interesting you should mention that," purred Belisarius. "I was just thinking the same thing myself."

Chapter 40

THE GREAT COUNTRY
Autumn, 532 A.D.

On the day of the wedding, Kungas took command of all military forces in Deogiri. Rao, being the groom, naturally did not object. Neither did the various envoys and military commanders from the many kingdoms now allied with Shakuntala. They were intimidated by the Kushan, first of all. But even if they hadn't been, they would have been more than happy to let him take the responsibility.

More than happy. The truth was, the envoys were delighted. Now that they had had enough time to absorb the new reality, and get over their initial shock and outrage at Shakuntala's unexpected decision to marry Rao, the envoys were quite pleased by the whole situation. Well-nigh ecstatic, in fact.

All of the kingdoms which they represented had been petrified by Malwa. Their decision to seek the dynastic marriage with Andhra had been driven by sheer necessity, nothing more. They had approached the project with all the enthusiasm with which a man decides to amputate a limb in order to save his life.

Shakuntala had spurned their offers. Since the decision had been hers, she could hardly cast the blame on *them*. If they hadn't been diplomats, they would have been grinning ear to ear. They had the benefits of an alliance with resurgent Andhra—*without* the shackles of a dynastic marriage. If things turned out badly, they could always jettison Shakuntala in an instant. It wasn't as if *their* crown prince was married to the crazy woman, after all.

So let the rude, crude, lewd and uncouth Kushan barbarian take the responsibility. A low profile suited them just fine.

The forces now under Kungas' command were huge and motley. Deogiri was as crowded, that day, as any city in teeming Bengal. Under different circumstances, Kungas might have been driven half-mad by the chaos. But, probably not, given the man's unshakably phlegmatic disposition.

And *certainly* not, under the circumstances which actually prevailed.

His opponent, Lord Venandakatra, commander of the forces besieging Deogiri, was not called the Vile One by accident. A different man might have been called Venandakatra the Cruel, or Venandakatra the Terrible; or, simply, the Beast. But all of those cognomens carry a certain connotation of unbridled force and fury. They are the names given to a man who is feared as well as hated.

A vile man, on the other hand, is simply despised. A figure of contempt, when all is said and done.

On that day—*that* day—the Vile One was as thoroughly cowed as any commander of an army could be. And everybody knew it.

Venandakatra's own soldiers knew it. Throughout the day-long festivities in Deogiri, the Vile One never emerged once from his pavilion. His soldiers, from his top commanders down to the newest recruit, were as familiar as any Indian with what had now become a staple of the storyteller's trade. The tale of how a great Malwa lord's lust for a new concubine slave had been frustrated by a champion. Unrequited lust, no less, to make the story sweeter.

Today, that beautiful girl—once a slave and now an empress—would give herself to the man who had rescued her from Venandakatra. Right in front of the Vile One, dancing her wedding in his face. Taunting him with the virgin body that would never be his. Not now, not ever.

The Vile One, in his pavilion, gnashed his teeth with rage. Rage, seasoned with heavy doses of shame and humiliation. His soldiers, who despised the man not much less than his enemies, found it difficult not to laugh. They managed that task, of course. None of them were so foolish as to even smile—not with Venandakatra's spies and mahamimamsa prowling the camps and fieldworks. But they were about as likely to launch an assault on Deogiri, that day, as so many giggling mice would attack a lion's den in order to assuage Lord Rat's wounded vanity.

Kungas spent a pleasant day rubbing salt into the wound. He rotated all the various troops under his command across the northern battlements facing Venandakatra's pavilion and the bulk of his forces. Allowing Malwa's soldiery, if not the pavilion-enclosed Vile One himself, to see the full panoply of forces which were now arrayed against them.

By popular acclaim, the four hundred spearmen of the Dakuen sarwe were rotated through no less than three times. Partly, that was due to the exotic and splendid appearance of the Ethiopians. Black men from a far-off and fabled land—blacker than any Dravidian—sporting savage-looking spears and jaunty ostrich-feather headdresses. Mostly, however, it was due to the crowd's glee at the sight of four hundred bare asses, at Ezana's lead and command, hanging over the battlements in Malwa's face.

Better was still to come. By mid-afternoon, the wedding ceremony itself was finished and the bride and groom began to dance.

Shakuntala danced first. By custom, the husband should have done so. But the empress had decreed otherwise. Shakuntala was a wonderful dancer, in her own right, but she was not Rao's equal. No one was. So, she went first. Not because she was ashamed of her own skill, but simply because she wanted the people watching—and the world which would learn from their telling, in the years to come—to remember Rao in all his glory.

Her dance, in truth, was glorious itself. Shakuntala did not dance in the center square of the city, where the wedding had taken place. She did so on the top battlements of the northern wall, on a platform erected the day before, after hurriedly changing her costume.

When she appeared on the platform, the crowd gasped. Shakuntala had shed her elaborate imperial costume in favor of a dancer's garb. Her pantaloons, for all that they were tastefully dyed, bordered on scandal.

Yet, the crowd was pleased. At first, as she began her steps, they assumed that Shakuntala was simply taunting her enemy. Prancing, in all her youth and beauty, before the creature who had once dreamed of possessing her.

Which, of course, she was. Dancing, by its nature, is a sensuous act. That is as true for an elderly man or a portly matron, creaking and waddling their way through sober paces, as it is for anyone. But there is nothing quite as sensuous, dancing, as a young woman as agile as she is beautiful.

Shakuntala was both, and she took full advantage. It was well for Venandakatra that he never saw that dance. The Vile One would have ground his teeth to powder.

But, as Shakuntala's dance went on, and transmuted, the crowd realized the truth. Taunting her enemy was a trivial thing. Amusing, but soon discarded.

The Empress Shakuntala was not dancing for the Vile One. She was not, even, dancing for Andhra. She was dancing for her husband, now. The sensuousness of that dance, the sheer sexuality of it, was not a taunt. It was a promise, and a pledge, and, most of all, nothing but her own desire.

They had wondered, the great crowd. Now, they knew the truth. Watching the bare quicksilver feet of their empress, flashing in the wine of her beloved's heart, they knew. Statecraft, political calculation—even duty and obligation—were gone, as if they had never existed.

Andhra had married the Great Country, not because its own past required the doing, but because that was the future it had chosen freely. The future that it *desired*. When she finished—in defiance of all custom and tradition—the crowd burst into riotous applause. The applause went on for half an hour.

It was Rao's turn, now, and the crowd fell silent. His reputation as a dancer was known to all Marathas. But most of them had never seen it with their own eyes.

They saw him now, and never forgot. The tale would be passed on for generations.

He began, as a husband. And if his dance was not as purely sensual as Shakuntala's had been, no one who saw it doubted his own heart.

The dance went on, and on. And, as it went, slowly transformed a man's desire for a woman—the life she would give him, the children she would give him—into a people's desire for a future.

It was Majarashtra's dance, now. The Great Country was pledging its own troth. Love was there, along with desire. But there was also courage, and faith, and hope, and trust, and determination.

Majarashtra danced to its yet-unborn children, as much as it danced for its bride. It was a husband's dance, not a lover's. Every step, every gesture, every movement, carried the promise of fidelity.

Then, the dance changed again. The crowd grew utterly still.

This was the great dance. The terrible dance. The long-forbidden but never-forgotten dance. The dance of creation. The dance of destruction. The wheeling, whirling, dervish dance of time.

There was nothing of hatred in the dance. No longer. Love, yes, always. But even love receded, taking its honored place. This was the ultimate dance, which spoke the ultimate truth.

That truth, danced for all to see, held the crowd spellbound. Silent, but not abashed. No, not in the least. Every step, every gesture, every movement, carried the great promise. The crowd, understanding the promise, swelled with strength.

Empires are mighty. Time is mightier still. Tyrants come, tyrants go. Despots tread the stage, declaiming their glory. And then Time shows them the exit. People, alone, endure and endure. Theirs, alone, is the final power. No army can stand against it; no battlements hold it at bay.

It was over. The dance was done. A husband, taking his bride by the hand, led her into the chamber of Time. The people, watching them go, saw their own future approaching.

Once in the chamber, Rao's surety vanished. There was nothing left, now, of the superb dancer who had paced his certain steps. Stiff as a board, creaking his way to the bed, his eyes unfocused, Rao seemed like a man in a daze.

Shakuntala smiled and smiled. Smiling, she removed his clothes. Smiling, removed her own.

"Look at me, husband," she commanded.

Rao's eyes went to her. His breath stilled. He had never seen her nude. His mind groped, trying to wrap itself around such beauty. His body, rebelling against discipline, had no difficulty at all.

Shakuntala, still smiling, pressed herself against him, kissing, touching, stroking. His mind—locked tight by years of self-denial—was like a sheet of ice. His body, now in full and wild revolt, felt like pure magma.

"You made a pledge to my father, once," Shakuntala whispered. "Do you remember?"

He nodded, like a statue.

Shakuntala's smile became a grin. She moved away, undulating, and spread herself across the bed. Rao's eyes were locked onto the sight. But his mind, still, could not encompass the seeing.

"You have been neglectful in your duty, Rao," Shakuntala murmured, lying on the bed. " 'Teach her everything you know.' That was my father's command."

She curled, coiled, flexed.

"I never taught you *that*," Rao choked.

Arched, stretched. Liquid, smiling. Moisture, laughing.

"You taught me how to read," she countered. "I borrowed a book." Coiled, again; and arched; and stretched. Promise, open.

" 'Hold back *nothing*,' " she said. "That is your duty."

Denial shattered; self-discipline vanished with the wind. Rao moved, like a panther to his mate.

In the corridors beyond the chamber, servant women waited. Older women, in the main; Marathas, all. When they heard Shakuntala's wordless voice, announcing her defloration, they grinned. In another virgin, there might have been some pain in that cry. But for their fierce empress, there had been nothing beyond ecstasy and eager desire.

The thing was done. The pledge fulfilled. The promise kept.

The women scurried through the halls, spreading the word. But their efforts were quite needless. Shakuntala had never been a bashful girl. Now, becoming a woman, she fairly screamed her triumph.

The young men heard, waiting in the streets below. They had mounted their horses before the servants reached the end of the first corridor. By the time Majarashtra's women emerged onto the streets to tell the news, Majarashtra's sons and nephews had already left. By the time the dancing resumed, and the revelry began, they were carrying the message out of the gates and pounding it, on flying horseborne feet, in every direction.

The land called Majarashtra had been created, millions of years earlier, when the earth's magma boiled to the surface. The Deccan Traps, geologists of a later age would call it; solemnly explaining, to solemn students, that it had been perhaps the greatest—and most violent—volcanic episode in the planet's history.

Now, while Deogiri danced its glee, the Great Country began its new eruption. Dancing, with swift and spreading steps, the new time for Malwa. The time of death, and terror, and desperate struggle.

Malwa's soldiers already detested service in Majarashtra. From that day forward, they would speak of it in hushed and dreading tones. Much like soldiers of a later army, watching evil spill its intestines, would speak of the Russian Front.

Belisarius had planned, and schemed, and maneuvered, and acted, guided by Aide's vision of the Peninsular War.

He already had his Peninsular War. Now, he got the Pripet Marshes, and the maquis, and the Warsaw Ghetto, and the mountains cupping Dien Bien Phu, and the streets of Budapest, and every other place in the history of the species where empires, full of their short-memoried arrogance, learned, again, the dance of Time.

Time, of course, contains all things. Among them is farce.

Shakuntala's eyes were very wide. The young woman's face, slack with surprise.

"I thought it would—I don't know. Take longer."

Looking down on that loving, confused face from a distance of inches, Rao flushed deep embarrassment.

"I can't believe it," he muttered. "I haven't done that since I was fourteen."

Awkwardly, he groped for words. "Well," he fumbled, "well. Well. It *should* have, actually. Much longer." He took a breath. *How to explain?* Halting words followed, speaking of self-discipline too suddenly vanished, excessive eagerness, a dream come true without sufficient emotional preparation, and—and—

When Shakuntala finally understood—which didn't take long, in truth; she was inexperienced but very intelligent; though it seemed like ages to Rao—she burst into laughter.

"So!" she cried.

He had trained her to wrestle, also. In an instant, she squirmed out from under him and had him flat on his back. Then, straddling him, she began her chastisement.

"*So!*" Playfully, she punched his chest. "The truth is out!"

Punch. "Champion—*ha!* Hero—*ha!*" Punch. "I have been defrauded! Cheated!"

Rao was laughing himself, now. The laughs grew louder and louder, as he heard his wife bestow upon him his new cognomens of ridicule and ignominy. The Pant of Majarashtra. The Gust of the Great Country—*no!* The *Puff* of the Great Country.

Laughter drove out shame, and brought passion to fill the void. Soon enough—very soon—the empress ceased her complaints. And, by the end of a long night, allowed—regally magnanimous, for all the sweat—that her husband was still her champion.

Chapter 41

THE STRAIT OF HORMUZ
Autumn, 532 A.D.

A monster fled ruin and disaster. Licking its wounds, trailing blood, dragging its maimed limbs, the beast clawed back toward its lair. Silent, for all its agony; its cold mind preoccupied with plans for revenge. Revenge, and an eventual return to predation.

A different monster would have screamed, from fury and frustration as much as pain and fear. But that was not this monster's way. Not even when the hunter who had maimed it sprang, again, from ambush.

Though, for a moment, there might have been a gleam of hatred, somewhere deep inside those ancient eyes.

Chapter 42

Belisarius started to speak. Then, closed his mouth.

"Good, good," murmured Ousanas. The aqabe tsentsen glanced slyly at Antonina.

She returned the look with a sniff. "*My* husband is an experienced general," she proclaimed. "*My* husband is calm and cool on the eve of battle."

Ousanas chuckled. "So it seems. Though, for a moment there, I would have sworn he was about to tell experienced sea captains how to maneuver a fleet."

Belisarius never took his eyes off the approaching flotilla of Malwa vessels. But his crooked smile did make an appearance.

"What nonsense," he said firmly. "The idea's absurd." He turned his head, speaking to the man standing just behind him. "Isn't it, Maurice?"

Maurice scowled. "Of course it is. You'd spend ten minutes, before you got into it, telling Gersem which way the wind's blowing. After spending half an hour explaining what sails are for."

"It's the general's curse," muttered Belisarius. "Surly subordinates."

"After spending two hours describing what wind is in the first place," continued Maurice. "And three hours—" He stuck out a stubby finger, pointing to the sea around them. "Oh, Gersem—look! That stuff's called *water*."

Ousanas and Antonina burst out laughing. Belisarius, for all his ferocious frown, was hard-pressed not to join them.

After a moment, however, the amusement faded. They *were* hunting a monster, after all. And they were no longer lurking in ambush, hidden in a blind.

Behind him, Belisarius heard Maurice sigh. "All right, all right," the chiliarch muttered. "Fair's fair. You were right again, general. But I still don't know how you figured it out."

"I didn't 'figure it out,' exactly. It was a guess, that's all. But we had nothing to lose, except wasting a few days here in the Strait while the rest of the cargo ships carried the troops to Adulis."

Belisarius pointed north, sweeping his finger in a little arc. They were well into the Strait of Hormuz, now. The Persian mainland was a dim presence looming beyond the bow of the huge cargo vessel.

"That's about the worst terrain I can think of, to try to march an army through, without a reliable supply route. Any size army, much less that horde Link's got."

Maurice snorted. "Not much of a horde now! Not after we got done with them."

Belisarius shook his head. "Don't fool yourself, Maurice. We inflicted terrible casualties on them, true. And God knows how many died in the final destruction of the city. But I'm quite sure two thirds of the Malwa army is still intact." He grimaced, slightly. "Well—*alive*, anyway. 'Intact' is putting it too strongly."

He paused, studying the oncoming Malwa vessels. There were six ships in that little flotilla. The five galleys which had avoided the Ethiopians in the delta were escorting a cargo ship. That vessel, though it was larger than the galleys, was far smaller than the huge ship Belisarius was standing upon.

The general interrupted his own discourse. Leaning back from the rail, he shouted a question toward Gersem. The Axumite commander was perched in the very bow of the ship, bestowing his own intense scrutiny on the enemy.

"Three hundred tons, Belisarius!" came the reply. "Probably the largest ship they had left."

Belisarius chuckled, seeing Gersem's scowl. The Malwa vessel had been used as a supply ship on the Euphrates. The Ethiopian, a seaman, was half-outraged at the idea of using such a craft for a river barge. And he was already disgruntled, having been forced to captain this great, ugly, clumsy, ungainly Malwa vessel—instead of one of the Ethiopian warships which formed the rest of his fleet.

Belisarius returned to the subject. "Link has to try to save as many of those soldiers as it can, Maurice. It can save a few of them—they'll be Ye-tai, to a man—by using what's left of the supply ships on the river. But the only way to salvage the main forces is to use the supply fleet at Bharakuccha, waiting for the westbound monsoon. Thirty ships, according to the report Antonina got from Irene. Irene wrote that report just before she left Suppara, not many days ago. The ships were already loading provisions."

Mention of Irene's report brought a moment's silence, as the four people standing at the rail joined in a heartfelt smile of relief, delight, and bemusement. Relief, that they knew Irene was still alive to write reports. Delight, at the report itself. And bemusement, at the workings of fate.

Irene had written that report more out of sentiment than anything else. The odds of getting it into Antonina's hands were well-nigh astronomical. But—why not? There were no secrets in the report, after all, to keep from Malwa. And the captain of the Ethiopian smuggling ship had sworn—scoffing—that he could get the message through the Malwa blockade and back to Axum. Whether it would ever reach Antonina, of course, he could not promise.

In the event, that smuggler's ship had encountered the Ethiopian flotilla waiting at the Strait to ambush Link. The message had found its way into Antonina's hands the day before.

"I'd like to have been at that wedding," mused Belisarius. "Just to finally see Rao dance, right before me."

He closed his eyes, for a moment. He *had* seen Rao dance, but only in a vision. In another time, in another future, Belisarius had spent thirty years in Rao's company. He admired the Maratha chieftain—imperial consort, now—perhaps more than any other man he had ever known. And so, for a moment, he savored Rao's joy at being—finally, in *this* turn of the wheel—united with his soul's treasure.

Antonina spent that moment savoring another's joy. Irene was her best friend. She had been able to discern a subtle message contained within the depiction of political and military developments. Kungas had figured a bit too prominently in those sober sentences. *Quite* a bit too prominently, measured in sheer number of words. And why in the world would Irene, glowingly, take the trouble to describe an illiterate's progress at his books?

Uncertain, not knowing the man herself, Antonina had raised her suspicions with Belisarius. Her husband, once he realized what she was hinting at, had immediately burst into laughter.

"Of course!" he'd exclaimed. "It's a match made in heaven." Then, seeing her doubting face: "Trust me, love. If there's a man in the world who wouldn't be intimidated by Irene, it's Kungas. As for her—?" Shrugging, laughing. "You know how much she loves a challenge!"

The moment passed, soon enough. Within an hour, they would be in battle again.

"So what would Link do, Maurice? Would it send subordinates to organize the supply effort, while it led the march back to India?" Belisarius shook his head. "I didn't think that likely. No, I was almost sure Link would want to get to India itself, as fast as possible. Why else hold back the surviving galleys, at the last minute, in the battle of the delta? One of them, certainly; perhaps two. That would have been enough to send subordinates with a message."

He pointed at the cargo ship nestled among the Malwa galleys. They were less than two miles away. He was smiling, not like a man, but like a wolf smiles, seeing a fat and crippled caribou.

"*That*, my friends, is not a subordinate's ship. *That* is the best Link could do, replacing Great Lady Holi's luxury barge in Kausambi."

The smile vanished completely. Nothing was left, beyond pure ferocity.

"I own that monster, now. *Finally.*"

Belisarius' quiet, seething rage brought hidden, half-conscious thoughts to the surface. For the first time, Aide realized Belisarius' full intentions. Sooner, perhaps, than Belisarius did himself.

No! he cried. **You must not! It will kill you!**

Belisarius started. There had been sheer panic in that crystalline voice.

What is wrong, Aide? Forcefully: *We're not going to have this argument again. I've led charges in battle, often enough.*

That was different! You were fighting men, not a cyborg. Men who wanted to live, as much as you. Life means nothing to Link—not even its own!

Long minutes followed, while Belisarius waged a fierce argument with Aide. His companions, from experience, understood the meaning of his silence and his unfocused eyes. But, as the minutes passed, they grew concerned—none more so than Antonina. Not since they first encountered Aide, and he transported Belisarius into a vision of future horror, had she seen her husband spend so much time in that peculiar trance.

When he finally emerged, his face was bleak. Bleak, but bitterly determined.

Belisarius pointed to the Malwa cargo ship in which, if he was correct, Link was waiting. The ship was not more than a mile distant, now. Already, kshatriyas were erecting rocket troughs on the deck.

"There is something you should know. Aide just explained it to me. There is a reason the new gods choose women as the vessels for Link. Great Lady Holi, today. If she dies, Link will be transferred into the person—the body, I should say—of her niece, Sati. She is probably still in Kausambi. If Sati dies, there will be another girl, in that same line. Somewhere in Kausambi also, in all likelihood."

He paused, groping for a way to translate Aide's concepts. The effort was hopeless. Words like "genetics" and "mitochondrial DNA" would mean nothing to his companions. He barely understood them himself.

He waved his hand. "Never mind the specifics. Link is part machine, part human. The machine part, the core of it, is somewhere in India. Probably in Kausambi also. Its consciousness is passed, upon her death, from one woman to her successor. The new Link, once it's—'activated,' let's call it—has all the memories of the old one, up till the time she last—" Again, he groped for words. "Communicated with the machine."

He paused. Maurice, eagerly, filled the void. "You know what that means?" he demanded. The chiliarch gripped the rail fiercely, glaring at the enemy ship. "What it means," he hissed, "is that if we kill that old bitch, the Malwa will be thrown into complete confusion. The new Link—what's her name? Sati?—won't know what's happened since Holi left. That's been a year and a half, now! It'll take her months—*months*—to get things reorganized."

He turned from the rail, eager—*eager*. "God, General, that's *perfect!* We *need* that time, ourselves. Sure, we won this battle.

But our troops are exhausted, too. We need to refit, and hook back up with Agathius and the Persians, and send another mission to Majarashtra, and—"

He stumbled to a halt. Maurice, finally, saw the other side of the thing.

Antonina had understood at once. Her face was pale.

"You *can't* board that ship! Link will commit suicide! It has no reason not to. It's not human, it's just a—a *vessel*. A tool." She almost gasped. "It'll *want* to! The last thing it can afford is to be captured."

All of them, now, understood the implication. *So why not take its enemy with it?*

"It'll have that ship rigged," muttered Maurice. "Doing it right now, probably. Ready to blow it up once you're aboard."

Antonina ignored him. She was pale, pale. She knew that expression on Belisarius' face. Knew it all the better because it was so rare.

"*I don't give a damn,*" he snarled. "I've been fighting that monster for four years. I'm tired of tactics and strategy. *I'm just going to kill it.*"

Protest began to erupt, until a new voice spoke.

"Of course we will!" boomed Ousanas. "Nothing to it!"

All eyes fixed upon him. The aqabe tsentsen grinned. "Under other circumstances, of course, the deed would be insane. Foolish, suicidal!" He shrugged. "But you forget—you have *me!*" He began prancing around, lunging with his spear. "Terrible! A demon!"

Antonina was not amused, this time. She began to snarl a response, until she suddenly realized—

Ousanas was not prancing any longer. He was simply smiling, as serene as an icon.

"No, Antonina," he said softly, "I am not joking with you now. It is a simple fact"—again, he shrugged—"that I am the best hunter I know."

He pointed his finger at Link's ship. Not more than half a mile away, now. "Think clearly and logically. The monster cannot possibly have enough gunpowder to blow up the entire ship. It would only have brought defensive weapons. Rockets, grenades. It will set them to destroy its own cabin, after the boarding party arrives. That will take time."

He hefted his huge spear, as lightly as if were a mere twig. "Underneath, I think. Somewhere in the hold."

He turned to Belisarius. "You are determined, I imagine, to lead the boarding party yourself."

Belisarius' only answer was a snarl. Ousanas nodded. "*Do it, Roman*. Take your best men. I will see to the rest."

The argument still raged, but the issue was settled. Between them, Belisarius and Ousanas beat down all protest. Not even Anastasius—not even when ordered by Maurice—was prepared to stop the general. He remembered Valentinian, unyielding, on a mountainside in Persia. And knew that the champion's own general, this day, would do no less.

By then, the Ethiopian warships were already engaging the Malwa escort galleys. The battle was not quite as swift as that in the delta. Not quite. The Malwa had seen the diekplous, and tried to avoid it. But, while their caution prolonged the outcome, it did not change it. It simply made it the more certain. In less than ten minutes, the five galleys had been boarded and their crews slaughtered. The Ethiopians lost only one of their craft to ramming. Even then, they were able to rescue the entire crew before the ship finally foundered.

Belisarius, however, observed none of it. He had been engaged, throughout, in a new argument. Which he lost, just as surely and inevitably as he had won the first.

"*All right!*" he growled, glaring at his wife. Then, heaving a great sigh: "But you stay behind, Antonina—d'you hear? I won't have you in the front line!"

Her stubborn look faded, replaced by an insouciant smile. "Well, of course! I had no intention of *leading* the charge." A very delicate snort. "The whole idea's ridiculous. Unladylike."

Chapter 43

The monster waited. Patiently, with the sureness of eternal life. Not its own—that was meaningless—but that of its masters.

Everything was finished, now, except revenge. The deck of the ship was a carrion-eater's paradise. Firing from the height of their own huge craft, with those powerful bows, the cataphracts had swept all life away. The kshatriyas at the rocket troughs, and their Ye-tai guards, were nothing but ripped meat.

No loss. The rocket volleys, in the short time they lasted, had been futile. The enormous vessel upon which the monster's great enemy came had simply shrugged off the missiles. There had not been many to shrug off, in any event. Most of the rockets had been taken into the hold. They would soon be put to better use.

The monster waited, satisfied. Next to it, squatting by the throne, an assassin held the gong which would give the signal to the priests waiting below. The creature, like the priests and the special guards, was a devotee of the monster's cult. The assassin, when the monster gave the order, would do his duty without fail.

The monster waited. Cold, cold. But, perhaps, somewhere in those depths, glowed an ember of hot glee.

The monster had been fighting its great enemy—its tormentor— for four years. Today, finally, it was going to kill it.

The monster idled away the time in memory. It remembered the trickery at Gwalior, and the cunning which crushed Nika. It remembered an army broken at Anatha, and another destroyed at the Nehar Malka. It remembered the catastrophe at Charax.

Come to me, Belisarius. Come to me.

Chapter 44

Silently, Ousanas crept through the hold, watching for the guards. *Listening* for the guards, more precisely. The hold was as dark as a rain forest on a moonless night.

Ousanas had waited for the sun to go down before he entered the hatch leading into the hold from the ship's bow. The horizon was still aglow with sunset colors, but none of that faint illumination reached into the ship's interior.

There had been guards waiting by the entrance, of course. Two, hidden among the grain-carrying amphorae lashed against the hull. Excellent' assassins, both of them. Ousanas had been impressed. Before the feet of the Ye-tai corpse even touched the deck of the hold the assassins had been there, knives flashing. The blades had penetrated the gaps in the corpse's Roman armor with sure precision.

Excellent assassins. They had realized the truth with their first stabs, from feel alone. They were already withdrawing the wet blades by the time Ousanas dropped the rope holding the corpse upright and leapt through the hatch. But that was too late. Much too late. Ousanas crushed the first assassin's skull with a straight thrust of his spearbutt's iron ferrule. The blade did for the other.

He left the spear with them, still plunged into an assassin's chest. It would be knifework from here on. The hold was cramped, full of amphorae and sacks of provisions. No room there for Ousanas' huge spear.

He waited for a few minutes, crouched in the darkness, listening. There should have been a third guard somewhere nearby, to support the two at the entrance if need be.

Nothing. Ousanas was a bit surprised, but only a bit. The finest military mind in the world had predicted as much.

Ousanas smiled. It was a cold smile but, in the darkness, there was no one to see that murderous expression. Link's assassins were the ultimate elite in Malwa's military forces. And therefore—just as Belisarius had estimated—suffered from the inevitable syndrome of all Praetorian Guards. Deadly, yes. But, also—arrogant; too sure of themselves; scornful of their opponents. Well-trained, yes—but training is not the same thing as combat experience. Those assassins had not fought a real opponent in years. As Praetorian Guards have done throughout history, they had slipped from being killers to murderers.

Ousanas started moving again. Slowly, very slowly. He was in no hurry. Belisarius would wait until Ousanas gave the signal. The Roman general and his companions were perched on the stern, far from the cabin amidships. If the explosive charges went off, they should be able to escape unharmed. Even wearing armor, they could stay afloat long enough for the Axumite warships surrounding Link's vessel to rescue them.

For Ousanas himself, of course, things would be worse. Fatal, probably. The once and former hunter, now lieutenant to the King of Kings, cared not in the least. He had become a philosophical man, over the years. But he had always been a killer. He had walked alongside death's shadow since he was a boy.

Ousanas had his own scores to settle. He had admired King Kaleb, for all that he never spoke the words. Eon's father had possessed none of his son's quick wit. Still, he had been a good king. And Ousanas had been very fond of Tarabai and Zaia, and many of the people crushed in the stones of the Ta'akha Maryam.

Your turn, Malwa.

Black death crept through the hold. Two more murderers died by a killer's blade.

"I'll go first, General," stated Anastasius. The giant's heavy jaws were tight, as if he were expecting an argument.

Belisarius smiled. "By all means! I'm bold, but I'm not crazy. Link's guards are about the size of small hippos."

Anastasius sneered. "So am I." He hefted his mace. Huge muscles flexed under armor. "But *I* haven't spent the last few years wallowing in the lap of luxury."

"You will now," came Antonina's cheerful rejoinder. "Of course, given your philosophical bent, I'm sure you're planning to give it all away."

Anastasius grinned. When the Roman army seized Charax, they had also seized the Malwa paychests—not to mention the small mountain of gold, silver and jewelry which that huge army's officers had collected. The riches had been left behind in Charax when Link's army marched out of the city. Needless to say, it had *not* been left behind when the Romans sailed out.

Every soldier in Belisarius' army was now a wealthy man. Not measured by the standards of Roman senators, of course. But by the standards of Thracian, Greek and Syrian commoners—not to mention Kushan war prisoners—they were filthy, stinking, slobbering rich. Belisarius was a bit concerned about it, in fact. He would lose some of those veterans, now. But he wasn't too concerned. Most of the veterans would stay, eager to share in the booty from future campaigns. And for every man who left, seeking a comfortable retirement, there would be ten men stepping forward to take his place. Other Roman armies might have difficulty finding recruits. Once the news spread, Belisarius' army would be turning them away.

But that was a problem for the future. For now—

There came a sound, from below their feet. A faint, clapping noise, resounding through the hull. Like a firecracker, perhaps.

"That's it!" bellowed Anastasius. A moment later, the huge cataphract was charging toward the cabin. Right behind him came Leo and Isaac, Priscus and Matthew. Belisarius and Antonina brought up the rear.

Your turn, monster.

When Ousanas finally reached his goal, he waited in the darkness only long enough to make sure he had a correct count of the opposition.

The area of the hold amidships, directly under Link's cabin, had been hastily cleared of amphorae and grain sacks. In the small open area created—perhaps ten feet square—two priests and an assassin were crouching. The area was lit by two small lamps. One of the priests was holding a cluster of fuses in his hands. The other, a striker. The assassin's head was cocked, waiting for the signal to come from his master in the cabin above.

For a moment, Ousanas admired Malwa ingenuity. He, like Belisarius, had thought they would disassemble the rockets and jury-rig explosive charges under the cabin. Link's minions had chosen pristine simplicity, instead. True, there were grenades attached to the wooden underdeck. The fuses had been cut so short they were almost flush. But the rockets had simply been erected, like so many small trees, pointing directly upward. As soon as the fuses were lit, the cabin above would be riddled by two dozen missiles. The backblast from the rockets would ignite the grenades.

There was no reason to wait. Silently, slowly, Ousanas pulled the pin of his grenade. Then, with a quick and powerful flip of the wrist, he tossed the explosive device against the far wall of the hold. The grenade had been disassembled, its charge removed, and then reassembled. But the impact fuse made a very satisfactory noise in the confines of the hold.

Startled, the Malwa looked to the sound. The assassin realized the truth almost immediately. But "almost," facing a hunter like Ousanas, was not quick enough. The assassin's heart was ruptured by a Roman blade before he had his own dagger more than half-raised. He did manage to gash the African's leg before he died. Ousanas was quite impressed.

The priests never managed more than a gasp. Ousanas did not take the time to withdraw the blade from the assassin's back. If Belisarius had been there, watching, he would have seen an old suspicion confirmed. Ousanas *was* stronger than Anastasius. The aqabe tsentsen simply seized the priests' necks, one in each hand, and crushed the bones along with the windpipes.

Before he even lowered the bodies to the deck, Ousanas could hear the thundering footsteps of the cataphracts charging the cabin. Then, the door splintering, as Anastasius went through it like a hurricane. Then—

The hunter was grinning now. As always, in darkness and gloom, those gleaming teeth seemed like a beacon.

Good-bye, monster.

Anastasius was off balance when the first guard swung his tulwar. For that reason, he was unable to deflect the huge blade properly. Instead, his shield broke in half.

The guard gaped. That blow should have flattened his opponent, if nothing else. The guard was still gaping when Anastasius' mace crushed his skull.

Another guard swung a tulwar. Anastasius side-stepped the blow. Not as nimbly as Valentinian would have done, of course, but far more quickly than the guard would have ever imagined a man of Anastasius' size could move.

Anastasius might have slain that guard, easily, with another stroke of the mace. But he wanted to create some fighting room in the confines of the cabin. He could see four more guards crowding behind. So, instead, he dropped his mace and seized the guard in a half-nelson. Then, rolling his hip, he flung the man into his oncoming fellows.

Quickly, Anastasius lunged aside, pressing himself against the wall of the cabin. He would retrieve his mace later. For now, he simply needed to let his companions pass.

Leo came next, through the shattered door, roaring like an ogre. Truth be told, Leo was almost as dimwitted as the nickname "Ox" implied. So, as always in battle, he eschewed complicated tactics. And why not? He'd never needed them before.

He didn't need them this time, either. By the time Isaac and Priscus and Matthew forced their own immense and murderous bodies into the cabin, Leo had already killed one guard and disabled another.

The rest died within half a minute. The battle, for all its fury—eleven huge men hacking and hammering each other in a room the size of a small salon—was as one-sided as any Belisarius had ever seen.

He was not surprised. Watching from the doorway, Antonina peeking around his arm, Belisarius witnessed one of the few battles which went exactly according to plan.

He had known it would. Anastasius was the only Roman who matched the size of Link's special guards. But the others matched them in strength, if not in sheer bulk. And they, unlike the guards, were *not* a pampered "elite." They were the real thing. Swords and maces, wielded on battlefields and the cruel streets of Charax, went through the tulwars like fangs through soft flesh.

Silence, except for the ringing gong held in an assassin's hands. Then, *silence*, as Matthew's sword decapitated the gong holder.

Belisarius stepped into the room, staring at Link.

The monster was dying, now. With its inhuman intelligence, Link had already assessed the new reality. There would be no rockets coming through the floor, killing its great enemy. No grenades, to obliterate what might be left.

Link had been prepared for that possibility. So it had taken its last, pitiful revenge.

A jeweled cup slid out of the monster's hand. The body of an old woman—the monster's sheath—was already slumping in the ornate, bejeweled chair. An old woman's head lolled to the side.

It was a quick-acting poison. But there was still a gleam in those wizened eyes. A small gleam of triumph, perhaps. If nothing else, the monster's great enemy would not take its life.

Antonina shoved Belisarius aside. She sprang forward, raising her ugly and ungainly and detested handcannon.

Trusted weapon, now.

"Fuck you!" she screamed. Left hammer; rear trigger; fire. The first shot blew the monster's heart through its spine, spinning Antonina half-around. She spun back in an instant.

"Fuck you!" Right hammer; front trigger; fire. The second shot splattered the monster's brains against the far wall.

Antonina landed on her butt, driven down by the cuirass.

Her ass hurt. Her hands hurt. Her arms hurt. Her shoulders hurt. Her breasts hurt.

She raised her head, grinning up at her husband. "God, that feels great!"

Belisarius beamed proudly at his cataphracts. "That's my lady," he announced. "That's my lady!"

Epilogue
AN INTERRUPTION AND A CONCLUSION

The monster came to life. As the soul which had once inhabited a young woman's body was obliterated, the monster groped for consciousness.

The moment of confusion was brief.

Disaster was the first thought. *There has been a disaster.*

The monster examined its memory, with lightning speed. *Nothing. All was going well. What could have happened?*

There came an interruption.

"Are you all right, Lady Sati?"

A woman—plump, young, rather pretty—was staring at the monster, her face full of concern. "You seem—ill, perhaps. Your eyes—"

The monster's thoughts, as always, raced with inhuman speed. In an instant, she had the interruption categorized. One of Lady Sati's maids. Indira was her name. She had developed a certain closeness with her mistress.

That could be inconvenient. More interruptions might occur.

The monster swiveled its head. Yes. The assassins were at their post.

Kill her.

By the time the knives ceased their flashing work, the monster's thoughts had reached a preliminary conclusion.

Belisarius. No other explanation seems possible.

There was no anger in the thought. There was nothing in the thought.

A COMMAND AND A CHOICE

"Are you insane?" demanded Nanda Lal, the moment he strode into Venandakatra's pavilion. "Why have you not already begun the withdrawal?"

The Vile One clenched his jaws. Any other man but Nanda Lal—and the emperor, of course—would be caned for using that tone of voice to the Goptri of the Deccan. Caned, if he were lucky.

But—

Venandakatra controlled his rage. Barely. He thrust a finger at the ramparts of Deogiri. "I will have that city!" he screeched. "Whatever else, I will take it!"

Nanda Lal seized the Vile One by a shoulder and spun him around. Venandakatra was so astonished—*no one may touch me!*—that he stumbled, almost sprawling on the carpet. Then, he did sprawl. Nanda Lal's slap across the face did for that. Physical power, partly—the Malwa Empire's spymaster was a strong man, thick with muscle. But, mostly, Venandakatra's collapse was due to sheer, utter shock. No one had ever laid hands on Lord Venandakatra. He was the emperor's first cousin!

But, so was Nanda Lal. And the spymaster was in plain and simple fury.

"You idiot," hissed Nanda Lal. "You couldn't take Deogiri even when it was possible. *Today?*"

Angrily, the spymaster pointed through the open flap of the pavilion. Beyond lay the road to Bharakuccha. "I had to fight my way here, you imbecile! With a small army of Rajputs!"

He reached down, seized Venandakatra by his rich robes, and hauled him to his feet. There came another buffet; hard open palm across flabby cheek.

"If you move now—fool!—we can still extract your army with light casualties. By next week—the week after, for a certainty—half your soldiers will be dead by the time you reach Bharakuccha."

Contemptuously, Nanda Lal released his grip. Again, Venanda-katra collapsed to the carpet. His mouth was agape, his eyes unfo-cused.

Nanda Lal turned away, clasping his hands behind his back. "We can hope to hold Bharakuccha, and the line of the Narmada. The large towns in the north Deccan. That is all, for the moment. But we *must* hold Bharakuccha. If it is lost, our army in Mesopota-mia will starve."

His heavy jaws tightened. Nanda Lal opened his mouth, as if to speak further, but simply shook his head. The spymaster was not prepared to share his still-tentative analysis of the likely situation in Mesopotamia. His *fears* about Mesopotamia. Certainly not with Venandakatra.

"Do it," he commanded. He tapped the sash holding his own robes in place. An imperial scroll was thrust into that sash. "I have the full authority here to do anything I wish. That includes ordering your execution, Venandakatra."

He turned his head, glowering down at the sprawled man at his feet. "The scroll is not signed by the emperor alone, by the way. It also bears Great Lady Sati's signature."

Venandakatra's shock and outrage vanished instantly. His face, already pale, became ashen.

"Yes," grated Nanda Lal. "Great Lady *Sati*."

The spymaster looked to the northwest, through the open flap.

Quietly: "The siege of Deogiri is over, Venandakatra. By tomor-row morning, this army will be on the road to Bharakuccha. That is a given. The only choice you have is whether you will lead it. Or simply your head, stuck on a pike."

A DESIRE AND A DECISION

"Where do we stand with the new warships?" asked the King of Kings, striding into the room which served Axum as its war center.

Rukaiya looked up from her table in the center of the room. It was a large table, but little of its expanse was visible. Most of it was covered with scrolls and bound sheets of papyrus.

The queen pointed to the sheet in front of her. "I was just finishing a letter to John of Rhodes, thanking him for the last shipment of guns. We have enough now to outfit the first two vessels."

"Good, good," grunted Eon, coming up to the table. "I want to get them out to sea at once, so we can start ravaging the supply fleet as soon as it leaves Bharakuccha."

He leaned over and nuzzled his wife's hair. Smiling, she reached up and drew his head alongside her own. "There is more good news," she whispered.

Eon cocked his eyebrow. Rukaiya's smile widened.

"We'll call him Wahsi, of course, if it's a boy. But you really should start thinking about girls' names, too."

A QUESTION AND AN ANSWER

Kungas rose from the bed and padded to the window. Planting his hands on the sill, he stared out over Deogiri. The city was dark, except for the lamps glowing in one of the rooms of the nearby palace.

His lips twitched. "It's a good thing for him that he has an understanding wife."

Irene levered herself onto an elbow. "What? Is Dadaji working late again?"

Seeing the Kushan's nod, she chuckled. " 'Understanding' is hardly the word for it, Kungas. She'll be sitting there herself, you know that. As patient as the moon."

Kungas said nothing. Irene studied him, for a moment, reading the subtle signs in his face.

"What is it, Kungas?" she asked. "You've been preoccupied with something all night."

Kungas tapped the windowsill with his fingers. Irene stiffened, slightly. That was as close as the Kushan ever came to expressing nervous apprehension.

"What is it?" she demanded. "And don't tell any fables. You've got the jitters, I know you do. Something which involves me."

Kungas sighed. "There *are* disadvantages," he muttered, "to a smart woman." He turned away from the window and came back to the bed. Then, sitting on the edge, he gave Irene a level stare.

Abruptly: "I spoke to Kanishka and Kujulo today. About Peshawar, and my plans for the future."

She nodded approvingly. Kanishka and Kujulo were the key officers in the small army of Kushans serving Shakuntala. Irene had been pressing Kungas for weeks to raise the subject with them.

"And?" she asked, cocking her head.

"They have agreed to join me. They said, on balance, that they thought I would make a good king."

Again, he sighed. "Nonetheless, they were critical. Rather harshly so, in fact. They feel that I have neglected the first requirement of a successful dynasty."

He looked away. "They are quite correct, of course. So I promised them I would see to the matter immediately. If possible."

Irene stared at him, for a moment. Then she bolted upright, clutching the sheets to her chest.

"*What?*" she hissed. "You expect me—*me*, a Greek noblewoman accustomed to luxury and comfort—to go traipsing off with you into the wilds of Central Asia? Squat in some ruins in the middle of mountains and deserts, surrounded by barbarian hordes and God-knows-what other dangers?" Her eyes were very wide. "Be a queen for a bunch of Kushan mercenaries with delusions of grandeur? Spend the rest of my life in a desperate struggle to forge a kingdom out of nothing?"

Other than a slight tightening of his jaws, Kungas' face was a rigid mask. "I don't *expect*," he said softly. "I am simply asking. Hoping."

Irene flung her arms around his neck and dragged him down. Within a second, the huge, heavy bed was practically bouncing off the floor from her sheer energy. Quiver, shiver; quake and shake.

"Oh, Kungas!" she squealed. "We're going to have so much *fun!*"

A REMINDER AND A DISTINCTION

When he finished reading the letter from Emperor Skandagupta, Damodara turned his head and stared at the Tigris. For a moment, his gaze followed the river's course, north to Assyria—and Anatolia, and Constantinople beyond. Then, for a longer moment, the gaze came to rest on his army's camp. It was a well-built camp, solid, strong. Almost a permanent fort, after all the weeks of work.

"That's it, then," he said softly. "It's over."

He turned to the man at his side, folding the letter. "Prepare the army, Rana Sanga. We have been summoned back to India. The emperor urges great haste."

Sanga nodded. He began to turn away, but stopped. "If I may ask, Lord—what is to be our new assignment?"

Damodara sighed heavily. "Unrest is spreading all over India. The Deccan is in full revolt. Venandakatra has been driven back into Bharakuccha. He is confident that he can hold the city unaided, though he can't reconquer Majarashtra without assistance. That will end up being our task, no doubt. But first we must subdue Bihar and Bengal, while the emperor rebuilds the main army. He expects the Romans to attack our northwest provinces within a year. Two years, at the outside."

Sanga said nothing. But his face grew tight.

"It appears that you will be meeting Raghunath Rao again some day," mused Damodara. "After all these years. The bards and poets will be drooling."

Damodara studied Sanga closely. Then said, very softly: "The day may come, Rana Sanga—*may* come—when I will have to ask you to remember your oath."

Sanga's face, already tight, became as strained as a taut sheet. "I do not need to be reminded of honor, Lord Damodara," he grated harshly.

Damodara shook his head. "I did not say I would ask you to *honor* your oath, Sanga. Simply to remember it."

Sanga frowned. "What is the distinction?"

There was no answer. After a moment, shrugging angrily, Sanga stalked off.

Damodara remained behind, staring at the river. He found some comfort, perhaps, in the study of moving water.

A CONCERN AND AN EXPLANATION

"I am your obedient servant, Lord," said Narses, bowing his head.

As soon as Damodara left the tent, Narses' face broke into a grin. "We're on," he muttered, rubbing his hands.

Ajatasutra looked up from the chess board. "What are you so excited about?"

Narses stared at him. The grin faded, replaced by something which bordered on sadness.

"You have become like a son to me," said Narses abruptly.

Ajatasutra's face went blank. For a moment, no more. Then, a sly smile came. "That's not entirely reassuring, Narses. As I recall, the last time you adopted a spiritual offspring you tried to murder her."

Narses waved his hand. "Not right away," he countered. "Not for many years, in fact. Besides—"

The eunuch sat on the chair facing Ajatasutra. He stared down at the chess board. "Besides, the situation isn't comparable. *She* was an empress. You're just a poor adventurer."

Ajatasutra snorted. Narses glanced at the small chest in the corner of the tent. "Well—relatively speaking."

The assassin crossed his arms over his chest and leaned back in the chair. "Why don't you just come out with it, Narses? If you want to know my loyalties, ask."

The eunuch opened his mouth. Closed it. Ajatasutra laughed, quite gaily. "Gods above! I'd hate to live in your mind. You just can't do it, can you?"

Narses opened his mouth. Closed it.

Ajatasutra, still chuckling, shook his head. "Relax, old man. Like you said, I'm an adventurer. And I can't imagine anybody who'd provide me with more adventures than you."

Narses sighed. "Thank you," he whispered. His lips twisted wryly. "It means a great deal to me, Ajatasutra. Whether I'm capable of saying it or not."

Ajatasutra eyed the eunuch, for a moment. "I'm puzzled, though. Why the sudden concern?"

The assassin nodded toward the entrance of the tent. "I didn't catch any of your conversation with Damodara. But I did hear his last sentence. 'You do not have my permission to do anything, Narses.' That sounds pretty definite, to me."

Narses cackled. "What a novice! A babe in the woods!" He leaned forward. "You really must learn to parse a sentence properly, Ajatasutra. 'You do not have permission,' my boy, does not mean the same thing as: 'I forbid you.'"

Ajatasutra's eyes widened. Narses cackled again. "It's mate in six moves, by the way," the eunuch added.

A GREETING AND A GROUSE

There was not much left of Charax, when Belisarius and Antonina returned from Adulis a few weeks later. But the Persians had managed to salvage enough of the docks for their ship to be moored.

Emperor Khusrau was there to meet them, along with Baresmanas, Kurush and Agathius. The Persians were beaming happily. Agathius was not.

Politely, the Persians allowed Agathius to greet the general first. The Duke of Osrhoene limped forward, aiding his wooden leg and foot with a pair of crutches. "Fine mess you left me," he grumbled, the moment Belisarius came up to him.

Belisarius glanced around, frowning. "What did you expect? You knew I was going to wreck the place."

"Not *that*," snorted Agathius. "It's all the irate letters I've been getting from the empress. Theodora is demanding to know how I could have been so careless. Letting the Persians get their hands on gunpowder technology."

"Oh—*that*." Belisarius clapped Agathius on the shoulder. "You covered for me, I trust?"

Agathius shrugged. "Sure, why not? I still know how to bake bread, when I get cashiered in disgrace." Gloomily: "Assuming she lets me keep my head."

Belisarius turned to Antonina. "The two of you have never met, I believe. Antonina, meet one of my finest generals. Agathius, this is my wife. She is also, I might mention, Theodora's best friend."

Agathius extended his hand. "Well. It's certainly a pleasure to meet *you*."

A REGRET AND A CHEER

Much later that night, after Khusrau and his entourage left, Belisarius stretched lazily.

"There's something to be said for having Persians as allies," he announced. His admiring eyes roamed about the lavishly furnished pavilion which the Aryan emperor had provided for them.

Antonina grinned. "Cut it out, soldier. Since when have you given a damn about luxuries? You just like the idea of dehgans hammering away at somebody else, that's all."

Belisarius returned the grin with one of his own. "True, true," he admitted. "Fills me with pure glee, it does, thinking about the Malwa trying to retreat with those mean bastards climbing all over them."

After a moment, his amusement faded. Within a very short time, it was gone completely.

"It's not your fault, love," said Antonina gently.

Belisarius blew out his cheeks. "No. It isn't. And if I had to do it over again, I wouldn't hesitate for a minute. But—"

He sighed. "Most of them are just peasants, Antonina. Not more than twenty thousand will ever make it back to their families in India. Khusrau and Kurush will harry them mercilessly, all the way to the Indus valley." He rubbed his face. "And if Eon's new warships can keep the Malwa from landing supplies on the coast, there won't even be ten thousand survivors."

It's not your fault, said Aide.

Belisarius shook his head. "That's not the point, Aide. Antonina. I'm not concerned with fault. Malwa is to blame for the death of their soldiers, just as surely as they are for the crimes those soldiers committed while they were in Persia. No one else."

His hands curled into fists. "It's just—"

Belisarius turned his head, staring into the flame of a lamp. "It's just that there are times when I really wish I could have been a blacksmith."

Silence followed. A minute or so later, Maurice came into the pavilion. The chiliarch gazed on his general, still staring at the lamp.

"Indulging in the usual triumphal melancholy, are we?" he demanded.

Belisarius, not moving his eyes from the lamp, smiled crookedly. "Am I really that predictable?"

Maurice snorted. He advanced into the pavilion and placed a hand on Belisarius' shoulder.

"Well, cheer up, lad. I've got some good news. I'm expanding your bodyguard. You'll be leading a huge allied army on your next campaign. Got to have a more substantial bodyguard. Nothing else, the Persians will be miffed if you don't."

Belisarius scowled. "For the sake of Christ, Maurice. If you give me a Persian-style bodyguard I won't be able to see my hand in front of my face."

Maurice chuckled. "Oh, I wasn't thinking of anything that elaborate. Just going to add one more man, to give Anastasius, Isaac and Priscus a bit of a break. The new man's here, by the way, right outside the pavilion. I'd introduce you, except that it would be purely ridiculous. And I don't want to have to listen to him muttering about stupid formalities."

Belisarius was out of his chair and gone in an instant.

"See?" demanded Maurice. "Didn't I say I'd cheer him up?"

AN ACCUSATION AND A REPROOF

"He just let me go, General," said Valentinian. The cataphract hooked a thumb over his shoulder, in the direction of the Persian camp. A wild revelry seemed to be going on. "He let all the Roman prisoners go. He told me to tell you that was in exchange for the Rajput prisoners you left in the qanat."

Belisarius scratched his chin. "That I can understand. But why *you*? I offered him a fortune for your ransom."

Valentinian's narrow face creased into a grin. "If I survive long enough, General, I'll be asking you to remember that ransom. When you decide on a suitable retirement bonus."

Belisarius smiled, nodding. "That I will, Valentinian. You can be sure of it."

There was still a question in his eyes. Valentinian shrugged. "I really don't know, General. But he did say something strange, when I left."

Belisarius cocked his eyebrow. Again, Valentinian shrugged.

"Meant nothing to me. Kind of silly, I thought. But the last thing Damodara said, just as I was getting on the horse, was that he hoped you were a man with a proper respect for grammar."

Belisarius laughed, then. The laughter went on so long that Valentinian started muttering.

That sounded like "cryptic fucking clowns" to me, pronounced Aide.

Me too, replied Belisarius, still laughing. *But I'm sure we must be mistaken. Be terribly disrespectful of the high command!*

Certainly would! The facets flashed. The crystalline rooster reappeared, its beady eyes filled with accusation. **Speaking of which—**

The laughter went on and on. Maurice and Antonina emerged from the tent.

"We're in trouble, girl," announced Maurice. "Deep trouble. That drooling idiot's supposed to lead us all to final victory."

Antonina stiffened. "Watch your mouth! That's my husband you're talking about." She frowned. "Even if he is a fucking clown."